Footsteps in the sand, leading me on . . .

Looking up, I see the scaffold, the hooded figure with its head on the block, the hooded figure of the executioner, the sharp blade of the axe glinting in the burning sun.

The axe falls, the victim's severed head rolls on the wooded platform, the hood comes off—

"My head!" Raistlin whispered feverishly, twisting his thin hands together in anguish.

The executioner, laughing, removes his hood, revealing—

"My face!" Raistlin murmured, his fear spreading through his body like a malign growth, making him sweat and chill by turns. Clutching at his head, he tried to banish the evil visions that haunted his dreams continually, night after night, and lingered to disturb his waking hours as well, turning all he ate or drank to ashes in his mouth.

But they would not depart. Master of Past and Present!" Raistlin laughed hollowly—bitter, mocking laughter. "I am Master of nothing! All this power, and I am trapped! Trapped! Following in *his* footsteps, knowing that every second that passes has *passed before!* I see people I've never seen, yet I know them! I hear the echo of my own words before I speak them! This face! His hands pressed against his cheeks. This face! *His* face! Not mine! Not mine! Who am I? I am my own executioner!"

by Margaret Weis and Tracy Hickman

DRAGONLANCE CHRONICLES

Dragons of Autumn Twilight

Dragons of Winter Night

Dragons of Spring Dawning

DRAGONLANCE LEGENDS

Time of the Twins

War of the Twins

Test of the Twins

The Second Generation

Dragons of Summer Flame

THE WAR OF SOULS

Dragons of a Fallen Sun

Dragons of a Lost Star

April 2001

LEGENDS

VOLUME TWO

WAR OF THE TWINS

Margaret Weis & Tracy Hickman

Poetry By Michael Williams
Cover Art By Matt Stawicki
Interior Art By Valerie Valusek

DRAGONLANCE® LEGENDS
Volume Two
WAR OF THE TWINS

Cover art by Matt Stawicki
First Printing: May, 1986
Library of Congress Catalog Card Number: 00-190765

OPM 9 8 7 6 5 4

UK ISBN: 0-7869-2028-9
US ISBN: 0-7869-1805-5

620-T21805

U.S., CANADA,	EUROPEAN HEADQUARTERS
ASIA, PACIFIC, & LATIN AMERICA	Wizards of the Coast, Belgium
Wizards of the Coast, Inc.	T Hofveld 6d
P.O. Box 707	1702 Groot-Bijgaarden
Renton, WA 98057-0707	Belgium
+1-800-324-6496	+322 467 3360

Visit our web site at **www.wizards.com**

This book is dedicated to
you who are sharing our journeys through Krynn.
Thank you, reader, for walking this path with us.

—Margaret Weis and Tracy Hickman

The World of Krynn
The Continent of Ansalon

CIT...
LO...
NA...

DARGA...

PALANTHAS

SOLAM...

HIGH
CLERIST
TOWER

NORTHERN
ERGOTH

HYLO

SANCRIST

NEVERMIND

GWYNNED

SOLANTH...

THELGAARD

LEM...

GARNET

SOUTHERN
ERGOTH

WHITESTONE

CAERGOTH

CRISTYNE

ABANASINIA

SCHALLSEA

SOLACE

DALTIGOTH

XAK TSAROT

QUALINESTI

PAX THARKAS

TOWER
OF
HIGH
SORCERY

QUALINOST

ENSTAR

THORBARDIN

PLAINS OF
DUS...

SIRRION SEA

NOSTAR

TARSIS

ICE MOUNTAIN BAY

ICEWAL...
CASTLE

ICEWAL...

NORTH KEEP

NORDMAAR
KALAMAN
VALKINORD

WINSTON'S TOWER
KARTHAY

MITHAS

KOTHAS

GARGATH
KORNEN

BLOOD SEA OF ISTAR

GODSHOME

NERAKA

BLOODWATCH

SANCTION

BLOOD BAY

KHURI-KHAN
GOODLUND

ZAHAKAR
KENDERMORE

THE RUINS

BLODEN

TAKAR

SILVANESTI

SHALOST
SILVANOST

TOWERS OF ELI

ACIER

BOOK 1

The River Flows On . . .

The dark waters of time swirled about the archmage's black robes, carrying him and those with him forward through the years.

The sky rained fire, the mountain fell upon the city of Istar, plunging it down, down into the depths of the ground. The sea waters, taking mercy on the terrible destruction, rushed in to fill the void. The great Temple, where the Kingpriest was still waiting for the gods to grant him his demands, vanished from the face of the world. Even those sea elves who ventured into the newly-created Blood Sea of Istar looked in wonder at the place where the Temple had stood. There was nothing there now but a deep black pit. The sea water within was so dark and chill that even these elves, born and bred and living beneath the water, dared not swim near it.

But there were many on Ansalon who envied the inhabitants of Istar. For them at least, death had come swiftly.

For those who survived the immediate destruction on Ansalon, death came slowly, in hideous aspect—starvation, disease, murder . . .

War.

A hoarse, bellowing yell of fear and horror shattered Crysania's sleep. So sudden and awful was the yell and so deep her sleep that, for a moment, she could not even think what had wakened her. Terrified and confused, she stared around, trying to understand where she was, trying to discover what had frightened her so that she could scarcely breathe.

She was lying on a damp, hard floor. Her body shook convulsively from the chill that penetrated her bones; her teeth chattered from the cold. Holding her breath, she sought to hear something or see something. But the darkness around was thick and impenetrable, the silence was intense.

She let go her breath and tried to draw another, but the darkness seemed to be stealing it away. Panic gripped her. Desperately she tried to structure the darkness, to people it with shapes and forms. But none came to her mind. There was only the darkness and it had no dimension. It was eternal. . . .

Then she heard the yell again and recognized it as what had wakened her. And, though she came near gasping in

5

relief at the sound of another human voice, the fear she heard in that yell echoed in her soul.

Desperately, frantically trying to penetrate the darkness, she forced herself to think, to remember. . . .

There had been singing stones, a chanting voice—Raistlin's voice—and his arms around her. Then the sensation of stepping into water and being carried into a swift, vast darkness.

Raistlin! Reaching out a trembling hand, Crysania felt nothing near her but damp, chill stone. And then memory returned with horrifying impact. Caramon lunging at his brother with the flashing sword in his hand. . . . Her words as she cast a clerical spell to protect the mage. . . . The sound of a sword clanging on stone.

But that yell—it was Caramon's voice! What if he—

"Raistlin!" Crysania called fearfully, struggling to her feet. Her voice vanished, disappeared, swallowed up by the darkness. It was such a terrible feeling that she dared not speak again. Clasping her arms about her, shivering in the intense cold, Crysania's hand went involuntarily to the medallion of Paladine that hung around her neck. The god's blessing flowed through her.

"Light," she whispered and, holding the medallion fast, she prayed to the god to light the darkness.

Soft light welled from the medallion between her fingers, pushing back the black velvet that smothered her, letting her breathe. Lifting the chain over her head, Crysania held the medallion aloft. Shining it about her surroundings, she tried to remember the direction from which the yell had come.

She had quick impressions of shattered, blackened furniture, cobwebs, books lying scattered about the floor, bookshelves falling off walls. But these were almost as frightening as the darkness itself; it was the darkness that gave them birth. These objects had more right to this place than she.

And then the yell came again.

Her hand shaking, Crysania turned swiftly toward the sound. The light of the god parted the darkness, bringing two figures into shockingly stark relief. One, dressed in black robes, lay still and silent on the cold floor. Standing above that unmoving figure was a huge man. Dressed in blood-stained golden armor, an iron collar bolted around his neck, he stared into the darkness, his hands outstretched, his mouth open wide, his face white with terror.

The medallion slipped from Crysania's nerveless hand as she recognized the body lying huddled at the feet of the warrior.

"Raistlin!" she whispered.

Only as she felt the platinum chain slither through her fingers, only as the precious light around her wavered, did she think to catch the medallion as it fell.

She ran across the floor, her world reeling with the light that swung crazily from her hand. Dark shapes scurried from beneath her feet, but Crysania never noticed them. Filled with a fear more suffocating than the darkness, she knelt beside the mage.

He lay face down upon the floor, his hood cast over his head. Gently, Crysania lifted him, turning him over. Fearfully she pushed the hood back from his face and held the glowing medallion above him. Fear chilled her heart.

The mage's skin was ashen, his lips blue, his eyes closed and sunken into his hollow cheekbones.

"What have you done?" she cried to Caramon, looking up from where she knelt beside the mage's seemingly lifeless body. "What have you done?" she demanded, her voice breaking in her grief and her fury.

"Crysania?" Caramon whispered hoarsely.

The light from the medallion cast strange shadows over the form of the towering gladiator. His arms still outstretched, his hands grasping feebly at the air, he bent his head toward the sound of her voice. "Crysania?" he repeated again, with a sob. Taking a step toward her, he fell over his brother's legs and plunged headlong to the floor.

Almost instantly, he was up again, crouched on his hands and knees, his breath coming in quick gasps, his eyes still wide and staring. He reached out his hand.

"Crysania?" He lunged toward the sound of her voice. "Your light! Bring us your light! Quickly!"

"I have a light, Caramon! I—Blessed Paladine!" Crysania murmured, staring at him in the medallion's soft glow. "You are blind!"

Reaching out her hand, she took hold of his grasping, twitching fingers. At her touch, Caramon sobbed again in relief. His clinging hand closed over hers with crushing strength, and Crysania bit her lip with the pain. But she held onto him firmly with one hand, the medallion with the other.

Rising to her feet, she helped Caramon to his. The warrior's big body shook, and he clutched at her in desperate terror, his eyes still staring straight ahead, wild, unseeing. Crysania peered into the darkness, searching desperately for a chair, a couch . . . something.

And then she became aware, suddenly, that the darkness was looking back.

Hurriedly averting her eyes, keeping her gaze carefully within the light of her medallion, she guided Caramon to the only large piece of furniture she saw.

"Here, sit down," she instructed. "Lean up against this."

She settled Caramon on the floor, his back against an ornately carved wooden desk that, she thought, seemed vaguely familiar to her. The sight brought a rush of painful, familiar memories—she had seen it somewhere. But she was too worried and preoccupied to give it much thought.

"Caramon?" she asked shakily. "Is Raistlin d—Did you kill—" Her voice broke.

"Raistlin?" Caramon turned his sightless eyes toward the sound of her voice. The expression on his face grew alarmed. He tried to stand. "Raist! Where—"

"No. Sit back!" Crysania ordered in swift anger and fear. Her hand on his shoulder, she shoved him down.

Caramon's eyes closed, a wry smile twisted his face. For a moment, he looked very like his twin.

"No, I didn't kill him!" he said bitterly. "How could I? The last thing I heard was you cry out to Paladine, then everything went dark. My muscles wouldn't move, the sword fell from my hand. And then—"

But Crysania wasn't listening. Running back to where Raistlin lay a few feet from them, she knelt down beside the mage once again. Holding the medallion near his face, she reached her hand inside the black hood to feel for the lifebeat in his neck. Closing her eyes in relief, she breathed a silent prayer to Paladine.

"He's alive!" she whispered. "But then, what's wrong with him?"

"What *is* wrong with him?" Caramon asked, bitterness and fear still tinging his voice. "I can't see— "

Flushing almost guiltily, Crysania described the mage's condition.

Caramon shrugged. "Exhausted by the spell casting," he said, his voice expressionless. "And, remember, he was weak to begin with, at least so you told me. Sick from the nearness of the gods or some such thing." His voice sank. "I've seen him like that before. The first time he used the dragon orb, he could scarcely move afterward. I held him in my arms—"

He broke off, staring into the darkness, his face calm now, calm and grim, "There's nothing we can do for him," he said. "He has to rest."

After a short pause, Caramon asked quietly, "Lady Crysania, can you heal me?"

Crysania's skin burned. "I—I'm afraid not," she replied, distraught. "It—it must have been my spell that blinded you." Once more, in her memory, she saw the big warrior, the blood-stained sword in his hand, intent on killing his twin, intent on killing her—if she got in his way.

"I'm sorry," she said softly, feeling so tired and chilled she was almost sick. "But I was desperate and . . . and afraid. Don't worry, though," she added, "the spell is not permanent. It will wear off, in time."

Caramon sighed. "I understand," he said. "Is there a light in this room? You said you had one."

"Yes," she answered. "I have the medallion—"

"Look around. Tell me where we are. Describe it."

"But Raistlin—"

"He'll be all right!" Caramon snapped, his voice harsh and

commanding. "Come back here, near me. Do as I say! Our lives—his life—may depend on it! Tell me where we are!"

Looking into the darkness, Crysania felt her fear return. Reluctantly leaving the mage, she came back to sit beside Caramon.

"I—I don't know," she faltered, holding the glowing medallion high again. "I can't see much of anything beyond the medallion's light. But it seems to be some place I've been before, I just can't place it. There's furniture lying around, but it's all broken and charred, as though it had been in a fire. There are lots of books scattered about. There's a big wooden desk—you're leaning against it. It seems to be the only piece of furniture not broken. And it seems familiar to me," she added softly, puzzled. "It's beautiful, carved with all sorts of strange creatures."

Caramon felt beneath him with his hand. "Carpet," he said, "over stone."

"Yes, the floor is covered with carpet—or was. But it's torn now, and it looks like something's eaten it—"

She choked, seeing a dark shape suddenly skitter away from her light.

"What?" Caramon asked sharply.

"What's been eating the carpet apparently," Crysania replied with a nervous little laugh. "Rats." She tried to continue, "There's a fireplace, but it hasn't been used in years. It's all filled with cobwebs. In fact, the place is covered with cobwebs—"

But her voice gave out. Sudden images of spiders dropping from the ceiling and rats running past her feet made her shudder and gather her torn white robes around her. The bare and blackened fireplace reminded her of how cold she was.

Feeling her body tremble, Caramon smiled bleakly and reached out for her hand. Clasping it tightly, he said in a voice that was terrible in its calm, "Lady Crysania, if all we have to face are rats and spiders, we may count ourselves lucky."

She remembered the shout of sheer terror that had awakened her. Yet he hadn't been able to see! Swiftly, she glanced about. "What is it? You must have heard or sensed something, yet—"

"Sensed," Caramon repeated softly. "Yes, I *sensed* it. There are *things* in this place, Crysania. Horrible things. I can feel them watching us! I can feel their hatred. Wherever we are, we have intruded upon them. Can't you feel it, too?"

Crysania stared into the darkness. So it *had* been looking back at her. Now that Caramon spoke of it, she could sense something out there. Or, as Caramon said, some *things*!

The longer she looked and concentrated upon them, the more real they became. Although she could not see them, she knew they waited, just beyond the circle of light cast by the medallion. Their hatred was strong, as Caramon had said, and, what was worse, she felt their evil flow chillingly around her. It was like . . . like . . .

Crysania caught her breath.

"What?" Caramon cried, starting up.

"Sst," she hissed, gripping his hand tightly. "Nothing. It's just—I know where we are!" she said in hushed tones.

He did not answer but turned his sightless eyes toward her.

"The Tower of High Sorcery at Palanthas!" she whispered.

"Where Raistlin lives?" Caramon looked relieved.

"Yes . . . no," Crysania shrugged helplessly. "It's the same room I was in—his study—but it doesn't look the same. It looks like no one's lived here for maybe a hundred years or more and—Caramon! That's it! He said he was taking me to 'a place and time when there were no clerics!' That must be after the Cataclysm and before the war. Before—"

"Before he returned to claim this Tower as his own," Caramon said grimly. "And that means the curse is still upon the Tower, Lady Crysania. That means we are in the one place in Krynn where evil reigns supreme. The one place more feared than any other upon the face of the world. The one place where no mortal dare tread, guarded by the Shoikan Grove and the gods know what else! He has brought us here! We have materialized within its heart!"

Crysania suddenly saw pale faces appear outside the circle of light, as if summoned by Caramon's voice. Disembodied heads, staring at her with eyes long ago closed in dark and dismal death, they floated in the cold air, their mouths opening wide in anticipation of warm, living blood.

"Caramon, I can see them!" Crysania choked, shrinking close to the big man. "I can see their faces!"

"I felt their hands on me," Caramon said. Shivering convulsively, feeling her shivering as well, he put his arm about her, drawing her close to him. "They attacked me. Their touch froze my skin. That was when you heard me yell."

"But why didn't I see them before? What keeps them from attacking now?"

"You, Lady Crysania," Caramon said softly. "You are a cleric of Paladine. These are creatures spawned of evil, created by the curse. They do not have the power to harm you."

Crysania looked at the medallion in her hands. The light welled forth still, but—even as she stared at it—it seemed to dim. Guiltily, she remembered the elven cleric, Loralon. She remembered her refusal to accompany him. His words rang in her mind: *You will see only when you are blinded by the darkness. . . .*

"I am a cleric, true," she said softly, trying to keep the despair from her voice, "but my faith is . . . imperfect. These things sense my doubts, my weakness. Perhaps a cleric as strong as Elistan would have the power to fight them. I don't think I do." The glow dimmed further. "My light is failing, Caramon," she said, after a moment. Looking up, she could see the pallid faces eagerly drift nearer, and she shrank closer to him. "What can we do?"

"What *can* we do! I have no weapon! I can't see!" Caramon cried out in agony, clenching his fist.

"Hush!" Crysania ordered, grasping his arm, her eyes on the shimmering figures. "They seem to grow stronger when you talk like that! Perhaps they feed off fear. Those in the Shoikan Grove do, so Dalamar told me."

Caramon drew a deep breath. His body glistened with sweat, and he began to shake violently.

"We've got to try to wake up Raistlin," Crysania said.

"No good!" Caramon whispered through chattering teeth. "I know—"

"We have to try!" Crysania said firmly, though she shuddered at the thought of walking even a few feet under that terrible scrutiny.

"Be careful, move slowly," Caramon advised, letting her go.

Holding the medallion high, her eyes on the eyes of the darkness, Crysania crept over to Raistlin. She placed one hand on the mage's thin, black-robed shoulder. "Raistlin!" she said as loudly as she dared, shaking him. "Raistlin!"

There was no response. She might as well have tried to rouse a corpse. Thinking of that, she glanced out at the waiting figures. Would they kill *him*? she wondered. After all, he didn't exist in this time. The "master of past and present" had not yet returned to claim his property—this Tower.

Or had he?

Crysania called to the mage again and, as she did so, she kept her eyes on the undead, who were moving nearer as her light grew weaker.

"Fistandantilus!" she said to Raistlin.

"Yes!" Caramon cried, hearing her and understanding. "They recognize *that* name. What's happening? I feel a change...."

"They've stopped!" Crysania said breathlessly. "They're looking at him now."

"Get back!" Caramon ordered, rising to a half-crouch. "Keep away from him. Get that light away from him! Let them see him as he exists in *their* darkness!"

"No!" Crysania retorted angrily. "You're mad! Once the light's gone, they'll devour him—"

"It's our only chance!"

Lunging for Crysania blindly, Caramon caught her off guard. He grabbed her in his strong arms and yanked her away from Raistlin, hurling her to the floor. Then he fell across her smashing the breath from her body.

"Caramon!" She gasped for air. "They'll kill him! No—" Frantically, Crysania struggled against the big warrior, but he held her pinned beneath him.

The medallion was still clutched in her fingers. Its light glowed weaker and weaker. Twisting her body, she saw Raistlin, lying in darkness now, outside the circle of her light.

"Raistlin!" she screamed. "No! Let me up, Caramon! They're going to him...."

But Caramon held her all the more firmly, pressing her down against the cold floor. His face was anguished, yet grim and determined, his sightless eyes staring down at her. His flesh was cold against her own, his muscles tense and knotted.

She would cast another spell on him! The words were on her lips when a shrill cry of pain pierced the darkness.

"Paladine, help me!" Crysania prayed. . . .

Nothing happened.

Weakly, she tried one more time to escape Caramon, but it was hopeless and she knew it. And now, apparently, even her god had abandoned her. Crying out in frustration, cursing Caramon, she could only watch.

The pale, shimmering figures surrounded Raistlin now. She could see him only by the light of the horrid aura their decaying bodies cast. Her throat ached and a low moan escaped her lips as one of the ghastly creatures raised its cold hands and laid them upon his body.

Raistlin screamed. Beneath the black robes, his body jerked in spasms of agony.

Caramon, too, heard his brother's cry. Crysania could see it reflected in his deathly, pale face. "Let me up!" she pleaded. But, though cold sweat beaded his forehead, he shook his head resolutely, holding her hands tightly.

Raistlin screamed again. Caramon shuddered, and Crysania felt his muscles grow flaccid. Dropping the medallion, she freed her arms to strike at him with her clenched fists. But as she did so, the medallion's light vanished, plunging them both into complete darkness. Caramon's body was suddenly wrenched off hers. His hoarse, agonized scream mingled with the screams of his brother.

Dizzily, her heart racing in terror, Crysania struggled to sit up, her hand pawing the floor frantically for the medallion.

A face came near hers. She glanced up quickly from her search, thinking it was Caramon. . . .

It wasn't. A disembodied head floated near her.

"No!" she whispered, unable to move, feeling life drain from her hands, her body, her very heart. Fleshless hands grasped her arms, drawing her near; bloodless lips gaped, eager for warmth.

"Paladi—" Crysania tried to pray, but she felt her soul being sucked from her body by the creature's deadly touch.

Then she heard, dimly and far away, a weak voice chanting words of magic. Light exploded around her. The head so near her own vanished with a shriek the fleshless hands loosed their grasp. There was an acrid smell of sulfur.

"*Shirak.*" The explosive light was gone. A soft glow lit the room.

Crysania sat up. "Raistlin!" she whispered thankfully. Staggering to her hands and knees, she crawled forward across the blackened, blasted floor to reach the mage, who lay on his back, breathing heavily. One hand rested on the Staff of Magius. Light radiated from the crystal ball clutched in the golden dragon's claw atop the staff.

"Raistlin! Are you all right?"

Kneeling beside him, she looked into his thin, pale face as he opened his eyes. Wearily, he nodded. Then, reaching up, he drew her down to him. Embracing her, he stroked her soft, black hair. She could feel his heart beat. The strange warmth of his body drove away the chill.

"Don't be afraid!" he whispered soothingly, feeling her tremble. "They will not harm us. They have seen me and recognized me. They didn't hurt you?"

She could not speak but only shook her head. He sighed again. Crysania, her eyes closed, lay in his embrace, lost in comfort.

Then, as his hand went to her hair once more, she felt his body tense. Almost angrily, he grasped her shoulders and pushed her away from him.

"Tell me what happened," he ordered in a weak voice.

"I woke up here—" Crysania faltered. The horror of her experience and the memory of Raistlin's warm touch confused and unnerved her. Seeing his eyes grow cold and impatient, however, she made herself continue, keeping her voice steady. "I heard Caramon shout—"

Raistlin's eyes opened wide. "My brother?" he said,

startled. "So the spell brought him, too. I'm amazed I am still alive. Where is he?" Lifting his head weakly, he saw his brother, lying unconscious on the floor. "What's the matter with him?"

"I—I cast a spell. He's blind," Crysania said, flushing. "I didn't mean to, it was when he was trying to ki-kill you—in Istar, right before the Cataclysm—"

"You blinded him! Paladine . . . blinded *him*!" Raistlin laughed. The sound reverberated off the cold stones, and Crysania cringed, feeling a chill of horror. But the laughter caught in Raistlin's throat. The mage began to choke and gag, gasping for breath.

Crysania watched, helpless, until the spasm passed and Raistlin lay quietly once more. "Go on," he whispered irritably.

"I heard him yell, but I couldn't see in the darkness. The medallion gave me light, though, and I found him and I—I knew he was blind. I found you, too. You were unconscious. We couldn't wake you. Caramon told me to describe where we were and then I saw"—she shuddered—"I saw those . . . those horrible—"

"Continue," Raistlin said.

Crysania drew a deep breath, "Then the light from the medallion began to fail—"

Raistlin nodded.

"—and those . . . things came toward us. I called out to you, using the name Fistandantilus. That made them pause. Then"—Crysania's voice lost its fear and was edged with anger—"your brother grabbed me and threw me down on the floor, shouting something about 'let them see him as he exists in their own darkness!' When Paladine's light no longer touched you, those creature—" She shuddered and covered her face with her hands, still hearing Raistlin's terrible scream echoing in her mind.

"My brother said that?" Raistlin asked softly after a moment.

Crysania moved her hands to look at him, puzzled at his tone of mingled admiration and astonishment. "Yes," she said coldly after a moment. "Why?"

"He saved our lives," Raistlin remarked, his voice once more caustic. "The great dolt actually had a good idea. Perhaps you should leave him blind—it aids his thinking."

Raistlin tried to laugh, but it turned to a cough that nearly choked him instead. Crysania started toward him to help him, but he halted her with a fierce look, even as his body twisted in pain. Rolling to his side, he retched.

He fell back weakly, his lips stained with blood, his hands twitching. His breathing was shallow and too fast. Occasionally a coughing spasm wrenched his body.

Crysania stared at him helplessly.

"You told me once that the gods could not heal this malady. But you're dying, Raistlin! Isn't there *something* I can do?" she asked softly, not daring to touch him.

He nodded, but for a minute could neither speak nor move. Finally, with an obvious effort, he lifted a trembling hand from the chill floor and motioned Crysania near. She bent over him. Reaching up, he touched her cheek, drawing her face close to his. His breath was warm against her skin.

"Water!" He gasped inaudibly. She could understand him only by reading the movements of his blood-caked lips. "A potion . . . will help. . . ." Feebly, his hand moved to a pocket in his robes. "And . . . and warmth, fire! I . . . have not . . . the strength. . . ."

Crysania nodded, to show she understood.

"Caramon?" His lips formed the words.

"Those—those things attacked him," she said, glancing over at the big warrior's motionless body. "I'm not sure if he's still alive. . . ."

"We need him! You . . . must . . . heal him!" He could not continue but lay panting for air, his eyes closed.

Crysania swallowed, shivering. "Are—are you sure?" she asked hesitantly. "He tried to murder you—"

Raistlin smiled, then shook his head. The black hood rustled gently at the motion. Opening his eyes, he looked up at Crysania and she could see deep within their brown depths. The flame within the mage burned low, giving the eyes a soft warmth much different from the raging fire she had seen before.

"Crysania . . ." he breathed, "I . . . am going . . . to lose consciousness. . . . You . . . will . . . be alone . . . in this place of darkness. . . . My brother . . . can help. . . . Warmth . . ." His eyes closed, but his grasp on Crysania's hand tightened, as though endeavoring to use her lifeforce to cling to reality. With a violent struggle, he opened his eyes again to look directly into hers. "Don't leave this room!" he mouthed. His eyes rolled back in his head.

You will be alone! Crysania glanced around fearfully, feeling suffocated with terror. Water! Warmth! How could she manage? She couldn't! Not in this chamber of evil!

"Raistlin!" she begged, grasping his frail hand in both her hands and resting her cheek against it. "Raistlin, please don't leave me!" she whispered, cringing at the touch of his cold flesh. "I can't do what you ask! I haven't the power! I can't create water out of dust—"

Raistlin's eyes opened. They were nearly as dark as the room in which he lay. Moving his hand, the hand she held, he traced a line from her eyes down her cheek. Then the hand went limp, his head lolled to one side.

Crysania raised her own hand to her skin in confusion, wondering what he meant by such a strange gesture? It had not been a caress. He was trying to tell her something, that much had been apparent by his insistent gaze. But what? Her skin burned at his touch . . . bringing back memories. . . .

And then she knew.

I can't create water out of dust. . . .

"My tears!" she murmured.

CHAPTER 2

Sitting alone in the chill chamber, kneeling beside Raistlin's still body, seeing Caramon lying nearby, pale and lifeless, Crysania suddenly envied both of them fiercely. How easy it would be, she thought, to slip into unconsciousness and let the darkness take me! The evil of the place—which had seemingly fled at the sound of Raistlin's voice—was returning. She could feel it on her neck like a cold draft. Eyes stared at her from the shadows, eyes that were kept back, apparently, only by the light of the Staff of Magius, which still gleamed. Even unconscious, Raistlin's hand rested on it.

Crysania lay the archmage's other hand, the hand she held, gently across his chest. Then she sat back, her lips pressed tightly together, swallowing her tears.

"He's depending on me," she said to herself, talking to dispel the sounds of whispering she heard around her. "In his weakness, he is relying on my strength. All my life," she continued, wiping tears from her eyes and watching the water gleam on her fingers in the staff's light, "I have prided myself on my strength. Yet, until now, I never knew what true strength was." Her eyes went to Raistlin. "Now, I see it in him! I will not let him down!

"Warmth," she said, shivering so much that she could barely stand. "He needs warmth. We all do." She sighed helplessly. "Yet how am I to do that! If we were in Ice Wall Castle, my prayers alone would be enough to keep us warm. Paladine would aid us. But this chill is not the chill of ice or snow.

"It is deeper than that—freezing the spirit more than the blood. Here, in this place of evil, my faith might sustain me, but it will never warm us!"

Thinking of this and glancing around the room dimly seen by the light of the staff, Crysania saw the shadowy forms of tattered curtains hanging from the windows. Made of heavy velvet, they were large enough to cover all of them. Her spirits rose, but sank almost instantly as she realized they were far across the room. Barely visible within the writhing darkness, the windows were outside of the staff's circle of bright light.

"I'll have to walk over there," she said to herself, "in the shadows!" Her heart almost failed her, her strength ebbed. "I will ask Paladine's help." But, as she spoke, her gaze went to the medallion lying cold and dark on the floor.

Bending down to pick it up, she hesitated, fearing for a moment to touch it, remembering in sorrow how its light had died at the coming of the evil.

Once again, she thought of Loralon, the great elven cleric who had come to take her away before the Cataclysm. She had refused, choosing instead to risk her life, to hear the words of the Kingpriest—the words that called down the wrath of the gods. Was Paladine angry? Had he abandoned *her* in his anger, as many believed he had abandoned all of Krynn following the terrible destruction of Istar? Or was his divine guidance simply unable to penetrate the chill layers of evil that shrouded the accursed Tower of High Sorcery?

Confused and frightened, Crysania lifted the medallion. It did not glow. It did nothing. The metal felt cold in her hand. Standing in the center of the room, holding the medallion, her teeth chattering, she willed herself to walk to a window.

"If I don't," she muttered through stiff lips, "I'll die of the cold. We'll all die," she added, her gaze going back to the brothers. Raistlin wore his black velvet robes, but she remembered the icy feel of his hand in hers. Caramon was still dressed as he had been for the gladiator games in little more than golden armor and a loincloth.

Lifting her chin, Crysania cast a defiant glance at the unseen, whispering things that lurked around her, then she walked steadfastly out of the circle of magical light shed by Raistlin's staff.

Almost instantly, the darkness came alive! The whispers grew louder and, in horror, she realized she could understand the words!

> How loud your heart is calling, love,
> How close the darkness at your breast,
> How hectic are the rivers, love,
> Drawn through your dying wrist.

> And love, what heat your frail skin hides,
> As pure as salt, as sweet as death,
> And in the dark the red moon rides
> The foxfire of your breath.

There was a touch of chill fingers on her skin. Crysania started in terror and shrank back, only to see nothing there! Nearly sick with fear and the horror of the gruesome love song of the dead, she could not move for a long moment.

"No!" she said angrily. "I *will* go on! These creatures of evil shall not stop me! I am a cleric of Paladine! Even if my god has abandoned me, I will not abandon my faith!"

Raising her head, Crysania thrust out her hand as though she would actually part the darkness like a curtain. Then she continued to walk to the window. The hiss of whispers sounded around her, she heard eerie laughter, but nothing harmed her, nothing touched her. Finally, after a journey that seemed miles long, she reached the windows.

Clinging to the curtains, shaking, her legs weak, she drew

them aside and looked out, hoping to see the lights of the city of Palanthas to comfort her. There are other living beings out there, she said to herself, pressing her face against the glass. I'll see the lights—

But the prophecy had not yet been fulfilled. Raistlin—as master of the past and the present—had not yet returned with power to claim the Tower as would happen in the future. And so the Tower remained cloaked in impenetrable darkness, as though a perpetual black fog hung about it. If the lights of the beautiful city of Palanthas glowed, she could not see them.

With a bleak sigh, Crysania grasped hold of the cloth and yanked. The rotting fabric gave way almost instantly, nearly burying her in a shroud of velvet brocade as the curtains tumbled down around her. Thankfully, she wrapped the heavy material around her shoulders like a cloak, huddling gratefully in its warmth.

Clumsily tearing down another curtain, she dragged it back across the dark room, hearing it scrape against the floor as it collected broken pieces of furniture on its way.

The staff's magical light gleamed, guiding her through the darkness. Reaching it finally, she collapsed upon the floor, shaking with exhaustion and the reaction to her terror.

She hadn't realized until now how tired she was. She had not slept in nights, ever since the storm began in Istar. Now that she was warmer, the thought of wrapping up in the curtain and slipping into oblivion was irresistibly tempting.

"Stop it!" she ordered herself. Forcing herself to stand up, she dragged the curtain over to Caramon and knelt beside him. She covered him with the heavy fabric, pulling it up over his broad shoulders. His chest was still, he was barely breathing. Placing her cold hand on his neck, she felt for the lifebeat. It was slow and irregular. And then she saw marks upon his neck, dead white marks—as of fleshless lips.

The disembodied head floated in Crysania's memory. Shuddering, she banished it from her thoughts and, wrapped in the curtain, placed her hands upon Caramon's forehead.

"Paladine," she prayed softly, "if you have not turned from your cleric in anger, if you will only try to understand that what she does she does to honor *you*, if you can part this terrible darkness long enough to grant this one prayer—heal this man! If his destiny has *not* been fulfilled, if there is still something more he must do, grant him health. If not, then gather his soul gently to your arms, Paladine, that he may dwell eternally—"

Crysania could not go on. Her strength gave out. Weary, drained by terror and her own internal struggles, lost and alone in the vast darkness, she let her head sink into her hands and began to cry the bitter sobs of one who sees no hope.

And then she felt a hand touch hers. She started in terror, but this hand was strong and warm. "There now, Tika," said a deep, sleepy sounding voice. "It'll be all right. Don't cry."

Lifting her tear-stained face, Crysania saw Caramon's chest rise and fall with deep breaths. His face lost its deathly pallor, the white marks on his neck faded. Patting her hand soothingly, he smiled.

"It's jus' a bad dream, Tika," he mumbled. "Be all gone . . . by morning. . . ."

Gathering the curtain up around his neck, snuggling in its warmth, Caramon gave a great, gaping yawn and rolled over onto his side to drift into a deep, peaceful sleep.

Too tired and numb even to offer thanks, Crysania could only sit and watch the big man sleep for a moment. Then a sound caught her ear—the sound of water dripping! Turning, she saw—for the first time—a glass beaker resting on the edge of the desk. The beaker's long neck was broken and it lay upon its side, its mouth hanging over the edge. It had been empty a long time apparently, its contents spilled one hundred years before. But now it shone with a clear liquid that dripped upon the floor, gently, one drop at a time, each drop sparkling in the light of the staff.

Reaching out her hand, Crysania caught some of the drops in her palm, then lifted her hand hesitantly to her lips.

"Water!" she breathed.

The taste was faintly bitter, almost salty, but it seemed to her the most delicious water she had ever drunk. Forcing her aching body to move, she poured more water into her hand, gulping thirstily. Standing the beaker upright on the desk, she saw the water level rise again, replacing what she had taken.

Now she could thank Paladine with words that rose from the very depths of her being, so deep that she could not speak them. Her fear of the darkness and the creatures in it vanished. Her god had not abandoned her—he was with her still, even though—perhaps—she had disappointed him.

Her fears at ease, she took a final look at Caramon. Seeing him sleeping peacefully, the lines of pain smoothed from his face, she turned from him and walked over to where his brother lay huddled in his robes, his lips blue with cold.

Lying down beside the mage, knowing that the heat of their bodies would warm them both, Crysania wrapped the curtain over them and, resting her head on Raistlin's shoulder, she closed her eyes and let the darkness enfold her.

CHAPTER 3

"She called him 'Raistlin!'"

"But then—'Fistandantilus!'"

"How can we be certain? This is not right! He came not through the Grove, as was foretold. He came not with power! And these others? He was supposed to come alone!"

"Yet sense his magic! I dare not defy him. . . ."

"Not even for such rich reward?"

"The blood smell has driven you mad! If it is he, and he discovers you have feasted on his chosen, he will send you back to the everlasting darkness where you will dream always of warm blood and never taste it!"

"And if it is not, and we fail in our duties to guard this place, then She will come in her wrath and make that fate seem pleasant!"

Silence. Then,

"There is a way we can make certain. . . ."

"It is dangerous. He is weak, we might kill him."

"We must know! Better for him to die than for us to fail in our duty to Her Dark Majesty."

"Yes. . . . His death could be explained. His life . . . maybe not."

Cold, searing pain penetrated the layers of unconsciousness like slivers of ice piercing his brain. Raistlin struggled in their grasp, fighting through the fog of sickness and exhaustion to return for one brief moment to conscious awareness. Opening his eyes, fear nearly suffocated him as he saw two pallid heads floating above him, staring at him with eyes of vast darkness. Their hands were on his chest—it was the touch of those icy fingers that tore through his soul.

Looking into those eyes, the mage knew what they sought and sudden terror seized him. "No," he spoke without breath, "I will not live that again!"

"You will. We must know!" was all they said.

Anger at this outrage gripped Raistlin. Snarling a bitter curse, he tried to raise his arms from the floor to wrest the ghostly hands from their deadly grip. But it was useless. His muscles refused to respond, a finger twitched, nothing more.

Fury and pain and bitter frustration made him shriek, but it was a sound no one heard—not even himself. The hands tightened their grasp, the pain stabbed him, and he sank—not into darkness—but into remembrance.

There were no windows in the Learning Room where the seven apprentice magic-users worked that morning. No sunlight was admitted, nor was the light of the two moons—silver and red. As for the third moon, the black moon, its presence could be felt here as elsewhere on Krynn without being seen.

The room was lit by thick beeswax candles that stood in silver candleholders on the table. The candles could thus be easily picked up and carried about to suit the convenience of the apprentices as they went about their studies.

This was the only room in the great castle of Fistandantilus lit by candles. In all others, glass globes with continual light spells cast upon them hovered in the air, shedding magical radiance to lighten the gloom that was perpetual in this dark fortress. The globes were not used in the Learning Room, however, for one very good reason—if brought into this room, their light would instantly fail—a Dispel Magic spell was in constant effect here. Thus the need for candles and the need to keep out any influence that might be gleaned from the sun or the two light-shedding moons.

Six of the apprentices sat near each other at one table, some talking together, a few studying in silence. The seventh sat apart, at a table far across the room. Occasionally one of the six would raise his head and cast an uneasy glance at the one who sat apart, then lower his head quickly, for, no matter who looked or at what time, the seventh always seemed to be staring back at them.

The seventh found this amusing, and he indulged in a bitter smile. Raistlin had not found much to smile about during these months he had been living in the castle of Fistandantilus. It had not been an easy time for him. Oh, it had been simple enough to maintain the deception, keeping Fistandantilus from guessing his true identity, concealing his true powers, making it seem as if he were simply one of this group of fools working to gain the favor of the great wizard and thus become his apprentice.

Deception was life's blood to Raistlin. He even enjoyed his little games of oneupsmanship with the apprentices, always doing things just a little bit better, always keeping them nervous, offguard. He enjoyed his game with Fistandantilus, too. He could sense the archmage watching him. He knew what the great wizard was thinking—who *is* this apprentice? Where does he get the power that the archmage could feel burn within the young man but could not define.

Sometimes Raistlin thought he could detect Fistandantilus studying his face, as though thinking it looked familiar. . . .

No, Raistlin enjoyed the game. But it was totally unexpected that he come upon something he had *not* enjoyed. And that was to be forcibly reminded of the most unhappy time of his life—his old school days.

The Sly One—that had been his nickname among the apprentices at his old Master's school. Never liked, never trusted, feared even by his own Master, Raistlin spent a lonely, embittered youth. The only person who ever cared for him had been his twin brother, Caramon, and *his* love was so patronizing and smothering that Raistlin often found the hatred of his classmates easier to accept.

And now, even though he despised these idiots seeking to please a Master who would—in the end—only murder the one chosen, even though he enjoyed fooling them and taunting them, Raistlin still felt a pang sometimes, in the loneliness of the night, when he heard them together, laughing. . . .

Angrily, he reminded himself that this was all beneath his concern. He had a greater goal to achieve. He had to concentrate, conserve his strength. For today was the day, the day Fistandantilus would choose his apprentice.

You six will leave, Raistlin thought to himself. You will leave hating and despising me, and none of you will ever know that one of you owes me his life!

The door to the Learning Room opened with a creak, sending a jolt of alarm through the six black-robed figures sitting at the table. Raistlin, watching them with a twisted smile, saw the same sneering smile reflected on the wizened, gray face of the man who stood in the doorway.

The wizard's glittering gaze went to each of the six in turn, causing each to pale and lower his hooded head while hands toyed with spell components or clenched in nervousness.

Finally, Fistandantilus turned his black eyes to the seventh apprentice, who sat apart. Raistlin met his gaze without flinching, his twisted smile twisted further—into mockery. Fistandantilus's brows contracted. In swift anger, he slammed the door shut. The six apprentices started at the booming sound that shattered the silence.

The wizard walked to the front of the Learning Room, his steps slow and faltering. He leaned upon a staff and his old bones creaked as he lowered himself into a chair. The wizard's gaze went once more to the six apprentices seated before him and, as he looked at them—at their youthful, healthy bodies— one of Fistandantilus's withered hands raised to caress a pendant he wore on a long, heavy chain around his neck. It was an odd-looking pendant—a single, oval bloodstone set in plain silver.

Often the apprentices discussed this pendant among themselves, wondering what it did. It was the only ornamentation Fistandantilus ever wore, and all knew it must be highly valuable. Even the lowest level apprentice could sense the powerful spells of protection and warding laid upon it, guarding it from every form of magic. What did it do? they whispered, and their speculations ranged from drawing beings from the celestial planes to communicating with Her Dark Majesty herself.

One of their number, of course, could have told them. Raistlin knew what it did. But he kept his knowledge to himself.

Fistandantilus's gnarled and trembling hand closed over the bloodstone eagerly, as his hungry gaze went from one apprentice to the other. Raistlin could have sworn the wizard licked his lips, and the young mage felt a moment of sudden fear.

What if I fail? he asked himself, shuddering. He is powerful! The most powerful wizard who ever lived! Am I strong enough? What if—

"Begin the test," Fistandantilus said in a cracked voice, his gaze going to the first of the six.

Firmly, Raistlin banished his fears. This was what he had worked a lifetime to attain. If he failed, he would die. He had faced death before. In fact, it would be like meeting an old friend. . . .

One by one, the young mages rose from their places, opened their spellbooks, and recited their spells. If the Dispel Magic had not been laid upon the Learning Room, it would have been filled with wonderful sights. Fireballs would have exploded within its walls, incinerating all who were within range; phantom dragons would have breathed illusory fire; dread beings would have been dragged shrieking from other planes of existence. But, as it was, the room remained in candlelit calm, silent except for the chantings of the spellcasters and the rustling of the leaves of the spellbooks.

One by one, each mage completed his test, then resumed his seat. All performed remarkably well. This was not unexpected. Fistandantilus permitted only seven of the most skilled of the young male magic-users who had already passed the grueling Test at the Tower of High Sorcery to study further with him. Out of that number, he would choose one to be his assistant.

So they supposed.

The archmage's hand touched the bloodstone. His gaze went to Raistlin. "Your turn, mage," he said. There was a flicker in the old eyes. The wrinkles on the wizard's forehead deepened slightly, as though trying to recall the young man's face.

Slowly, Raistlin rose to his feet, still smiling the bitter, cynical smile, as if this were all beneath him. Then, with a nonchalant shrug, he slammed shut his spellbook. The other six apprentices exchanged grim glances at this. Fistandantilus frowned, but there was a spark in his dark eyes.

Glibly, sneeringly, Raistlin began to recite the complicated spell from memory. The other apprentices stirred at this show of skill, glaring at him with hatred and undisguised envy. Fistandantilus watched, his frown changing to a look of hunger so malevolent that it nearly broke Raistlin's concentration.

Forcing himself to keep his mind firmly on his work, the young mage completed the spell, and—suddenly—the Learning Room was lit by a brilliant flare of multicolored light, its silence shattered by the sound of an explosion!

Fistandantilus started, the grin wiped off his face. The other apprentices gasped.

"How did you break the Dispel Magic spell?" Fistandantilus demanded angrily. "What strange power is this?"

In answer, Raistlin opened his hands. In his palms he held a ball of blue and green flame, blazing with such radiance that no one could look at it directly. Then, with that same, sneering smile, he clapped his hands. The flame vanished.

The Learning Room was silent once more, only now it was the silence of fear as Fistandantilus rose to his feet. His rage shimmering around him like a halo of flame, he advanced upon the seventh apprentice.

Raistlin did not shrink from that anger. He remained standing calmly, coolly watching the wizard's approach.

"How did you—" Fistandantilus's voice grated. Then his gaze fell upon the young mage's slender hands. With a vicious snarl, the wizard reached out and grasped Raistlin's wrist.

Raistlin gasped in pain, the archmage's touch was cold as the grave. But he made himself smile still, though he knew his grin must look like a death's head.

"Flash powder!" Fistandantilus jerked Raistlin forward, holding his hand under the candlelight so that all could see. "A common sleight-of-hand trick, fit only for street illusionists!"

"Thus I earned my living," Raistlin said through teeth clenched against the pain. "I thought it suitable for use in such a collection of amateurs as you have gathered together, Great One."

Fistandantilus tightened his grip. Raistlin choked in agony, but he did not struggle or try to withdraw. Nor did he lower his gaze from that of his Master. Though his grip was painful, the wizard's face was interested, intrigued.

"So you consider yourself better than these?" Fistandantilus asked Raistlin in a soft, almost kindly voice, ignoring the angry mutterings of the apprentices.

Raistlin had to pause to gather the strength to speak through the haze of pain. "You know I am!"

Fistandantilus stared at him, his hand still grasping him by the wrist. Raistlin saw a sudden fear in the old man's eyes, a fear that was quickly quenched by that look of insatiable hunger. Fistandantilus loosed his hold on Raistlin's arm. The young mage could not repress a sigh of intense relief as he sank into his chair, rubbing his wrist. The mark of the archmage's hand could be seen upon it plainly—it had turned his skin icy white.

"Get out!" Fistandantilus snapped. The six mages rose, their black robes rustling about them. Raistlin rose, too. "You stay," the archmage said coldly.

Raistlin sat back down, still rubbing his injured wrist. Warmth and life were returning to it. As the other young mages filed out, Fistandantilus followed them to the door. Turning back, he faced his new apprentice.

"These others will soon be gone and we shall have the castle to ourselves. Meet me in the secret chambers far below when it is Darkwatch. I am conducting an experiment that will require your . . . assistance."

Raistlin watched in a kind of horrible fascination as the old wizard's hand went to the bloodstone, stroking it lovingly. For a moment, Raistlin could not answer. Then, he smiled sneeringly—only this time it was at himself, for his own fear.

"I will be there, Master," he said.

Raistlin lay upon the stone slab in the laboratory located far beneath the archmage's castle. Not even his thick black velvet robes could keep out the chill, and Raistlin shivered uncontrollably. But whether it was from the cold, fear, or excitement, he could not tell.

He could not see Fistandantilus, but he could hear him— the whisper of his robes, the soft thud of the staff upon the floor, the turning of a page in the spellbook. Lying upon the slab, feigning to be helpless under the wizard's influence, Raistlin tensed. The moment fast approached.

As if in answer, Fistandantilus appeared in his line of vision, leaning over the young mage with that look of eager hunger, the bloodstone pendant swinging from the chain around his neck.

"Yes," said the wizard, "you are skilled. More skilled and more powerful than any young apprentice I have met in these many, many years."

"What will you do to me?" Raistlin asked hoarsely. The note of desperation in his voice was not entirely forced. He *must* know how the pendant worked.

"How can that matter?" Fistandantilus questioned coolly, laying his hand upon the young mage's chest.

"My . . . object in coming to you was to learn," Raistlin said, gritting his teeth and trying not to writhe at the loathsome touch. "I would learn, even to the last!"

"Commendable," Fistandantilus nodded, his eyes gazing into the darkness, his thoughts abstracted. Probably going over the spell in his mind, Raistlin thought to himself. "I am going to enjoy inhabiting a body and a mind so thirsty for knowledge, as well as one that is innately skilled in the Art. Very well, I will explain. My last lesson, apprentice. Learn it well.

"You cannot know, young man, the horrors of growing old. How well I remember my first life and how well I remember the terrible feeling of anger and frustration I felt when I realized that I—the most powerful magic-user who had ever lived—was destined to be trapped in a weak and wretched body that was being consumed by age! My mind—my mind was sound! Indeed, I was stronger mentally than I had ever been in my life! But all this power, all this vast knowledge would be wasted—turned to dust! Devoured by worms!

"I wore the Red Robes then—

"You start. Are you surprised? Taking the Red Robes was a conscious, cold-blooded decision, made after seeing how best I could gain. In neutrality, one learns better, being able to draw from both ends of the spectrum and being beholden to neither. I went to Gilean, God of Neutrality, with my plea to be allowed to remain upon this plane and extend my knowledge. But, in this, the God of the Book could not help me. Humans were his creation, and it was because of my impatient human nature and the knowledge of the shortness of my life that I had pressed on with my studies. I was counseled to accept my fate."

Fistandantilus shrugged. "I see comprehension in your eyes, apprentice. In a way, I am sorry to destroy you. I think we could have developed a rare understanding. But, to make a long story short, I walked out into the darkness. Cursing the red moon, I asked that I be allowed to look upon the black. The Queen of Darkness heard my prayer and granted my request. Donning the Black Robes, I dedicated myself to her service and, in return, I was taken to her plane of existence. I have seen the future, I have lived the past. She gave me this pendant, so that I am able to choose a new body during my stay in this time. And, when I choose to cross the boundaries of time and enter the future, there is a body prepared and ready to accept my soul."

Raistlin could not repress a shudder at this. His lip curled in hatred. *His* was the body the wizard spoke of! Ready and waiting. . . .

But Fistandantilus did not notice. The wizard raised the bloodstone pendant, preparing to cast the spell.

Looking at the pendant as it glistened in the pale light cast by a globe in the center of the laboratory, Raistlin felt his heartbeat quicken. His hands clenched.

With an effort, his voice trembling with excitement that he hoped would be mistaken for terror, he whispered, "Tell me how it works! Tell me what will happen to me!"

Fistandantilus smiled, his hand slowly revolving the bloodstone above Raistlin's chest. "I will place this upon your breast, right over your heart. And, slowly, you will feel your lifeforce start to ebb from your body. The pain is, I believe, quite excruciating. But it will not last long, apprentice, if you do not struggle against it. Give in and you will quickly lose consciousness. From what I have observed, fighting only prolongs the agony."

"Are there no words to be spoken?" Raistlin asked, shivering.

"Of course," Fistandantilus replied coolly, his body bending down near Raistlin's, his eyes nearly on a level with the young mage's. Carefully, he placed the bloodstone on Raistlin's chest. "You are about to hear them. . . . They will be the last sounds you ever hear. . . ."

Raistlin felt his flesh crawl at the touch and for a moment could barely restrain himself from breaking away and fleeing. No, he told himself coldly, clenching his hands, digging his nails into the flesh so that the pain would distract his thoughts from fear, *I must hear the words!*

Quivering, he forced himself to lie there, but he could not refrain from closing his eyes, blotting out the sight of the evil, wizened face so near his own that he could smell the decaying breath. . . .

"That's right," said a soft voice, "relax. . . ." Fistandantilus began to chant.

Concentrating on the complex spell, the wizard closed his

own eyes, swaying back and forth as he pressed the blood-stone pendant into Raistlin's flesh. Fistandantilus did not notice, therefore, that his words were being repeated, murmured feverishly by the intended victim. By the time he realized something was wrong, he had ended the reciting of the spell and was standing, waiting, for the first infusion of new life to warm his ancient bones.

There was nothing.

Alarmed, Fistandantilus opened his eyes. He stared in astonishment at the black-robed young mage lying on the cold stone slab, and then the wizard made a strange, inarticulate sound and staggered backward in a sudden fear he could not hide.

"I see you recognize me at last," said Raistlin, sitting up. One hand rested upon the stone slab, but the other was in one of the secret pockets of his robes. "So much for the body waiting for you in the future."

Fistandantilus did not answer. His gaze darted to Raistlin's pocket, as though he would pierce through the fabric with his black eyes.

Quickly he regained his composure. "Did the great Par-Salian send you back here, little mage?" he asked derisively. But his gaze remained on the mage's pocket.

Raistlin shook his head as he slid off the stone slab. Keeping one hand in the pocket of his robes, he moved the other to draw back the black hood, allowing Fistandantilus to see his true face, not the illusion he had maintained for these past long months. "I came myself. I am Master of the Tower now."

"That's impossible," the wizard snarled.

Raistlin smiled, but there was no answering smile in his cold eyes, which kept Fistandantilus always in their mirrorlike gaze. "So you thought. But you made a mistake. You underestimated me. You wrenched part of my lifeforce from me during the Test, in return for protecting me from the drow. You forced me to live a life of constant pain in a shattered body, doomed me to dependence on my brother. You taught me to use the dragon orb and kept me alive when I would have died at the Great Library of Palanthas. During the War of the Lance, you helped me drive the Queen of Darkness back to the Abyss where she was no longer a threat to the world—or to you. Then, when you had gained enough strength in this time, you intended to return to the future and claim *my* body! *You* would have become *me*."

Raistlin saw Fistandantilus's eyes narrow, and the young mage tensed, his hand closing over the object he carried in his robes. But the wizard only said mildly, "That is all correct. What do you intend to do about it? Murder me?"

"No," said Raistlin softly, "*I* intend to become *you*!"

"Fool!" Fistandantilus laughed shrilly. Raising a withered hand, he held up the bloodstone pendant. "The only way you could do that is to use this on me! And it is protected against all forms of magic by charms the power of which you have no conception, little mage—"

His voice died away to a whisper, strangled in sudden fear and shock as Raistlin removed his hand from his robe. In his palm lay the bloodstone pendant.

"Protected from all forms of magic," said the young mage, his grin like that of a skull's, "but not protected against sleight-of-hand. Not protected against the skills of a common street illusionist. . . ."

Raistlin saw the wizard turn deathly pale. Fistandantilus's eyes went feverishly to the chain on his neck. Now that the illusion was revealed, he realized he held nothing in his hand.

A rending, cracking sound shattered the silence. The stone floor beneath Raistlin's feet heaved, sending the young mage stumbling to his knees. Rock blew apart as the foundation of the laboratory broke in half. Above the chaos rose Fistandantilus's voice, chanting a powerful spell of summoning.

Recognizing it, Raistlin responded, clutching the bloodstone in his hand as he cast a spell of shielding around his body to give himself time to work his magic. Crouched on the floor, he twisted around to see a figure burst through the foundation, its hideous shape and visage something seen only in insane dreams.

"Seize him, hold him!" Fistandantilus shrieked, pointing at Raistlin. The apparition surged across the crumbling floor toward the young mage and reached for him with its writhing coils.

Fear overwhelmed Raistlin as the creature from beyond worked its own horrible magic on him. The shielding spell crumbled beneath the onslaught. The apparition would devour his soul and feast upon his flesh.

Control! Long hours of study, long-practiced strength and rigorous self-discipline brought the words of the spell Raistlin needed to his mind. Within moments, it was complete. As the young mage began to chant the words of banishment, he felt the ecstasy of his magic flow through his body, delivering him from the fear.

The apparition hesitated.

Fistandantilus, furious, ordered it on.

Raistlin ordered it to halt.

The apparition glared at each, its coils twisting, its very appearance shifting and shimmering in the gusty winds of its creation. Both mages held it in check, watching the other intently, waiting for the eye blink, the lip twitch, the spasmodic jerk of a finger that would prove fatal.

Neither moved, neither seemed likely to move. Raistlin's endurance was greater, but Fistandantilus's magic came from ancient sources; he could call upon unseen powers to support him.

Finally, it was the apparition itself who could no longer endure. Caught between two equal, conflicting powers, tugged and pulled in opposite directions, its magical being could be held together no longer. With a brilliant flash, it exploded.

The force hurled both mages backward, slamming them into the walls. A horrible smell filled the chamber, and broken glass fell like rain. The walls of the laboratory were blackened and charred. Here and there, small fires burned with bright, multicolored flames, casting a lurid glow over the site of the destruction.

Raistlin staggered swiftly to his feet, wiping blood from a cut on his forehead. His enemy was not less quick, both knowing weakness meant death. The two mages faced each other in the flickering light.

"So, it comes to this!" Fistandantilus said in his cracked and ancient voice. "You could have gone on, living a life of ease. I would have spared you the debilities, the indignities of old age. Why rush to your own destruction!"

"You know," Raistlin said softly, breathing heavily, his strength nearly spent.

Fistandantilus nodded slowly, his eyes on Raistlin. "As I said," he murmured softly, "it is a pity this must happen. We could have done much together, you and I. Now—"

"Life for one. Death for the other," Raistlin said. Reaching out his hand, he carefully laid the bloodstone pendant upon the cold slab. Then he heard the words of chanting and raised his voice in an answering chant himself.

The battle lasted long. The two guardians of the Tower who watched the sight they had conjured up from the memories of the black-robed mage lying within their grasp, were lost in confusion. They had, up to this point, seen everything through Raistlin's vision. But so close now were the two magic-users that the Tower's guardians saw the battle through the eyes of *both* opponents.

Lightning crackled from fingertips, black-robed bodies twisted in pain, screams of agony and fury echoed amidst the crash of rock and timber.

Magical walls of fire thawed walls of ice, hot winds blew with the force of hurricanes. Storms of flame swept the hallways, apparitions sprang from the Abyss at the behest of their masters, elementals shook the very foundations of the castle. The great dark fortress of Fistandantilus began to crack, stones tumbling from the battlements.

And then, with a fearful shriek of rage and pain, one of the black-robed mages collapsed, blood flowing from his mouth.

Which was which? Who had fallen? The guardians sought frantically to tell, but it was impossible.

The other mage, nearly spent, rested a moment, then managed to drag himself across the floor. His trembling hand reached up to the top of the stone slab, groped about, then found and grasped the bloodstone pendant. With his last strength, the black-robed mage gripped the pendant and crawled back to kneel beside the still-living body of his victim.

The mage on the floor could not speak, but his eyes, as they gazed into the eyes of his murderer, cast a curse of such hideous aspect that the two guardians of the Tower felt even the chill of their tormented existence grow warm by comparison.

The black-robed mage holding the bloodstone hesitated. He was so close to his victim's mind that he could read the unspoken message of those eyes, and his soul shrank from what it saw. But then his lips tightened. Shaking his hooded head and giving a grim smile of triumph, he carefully and deliberately pressed the pendant down on the black-robed chest of his victim.

The body on the floor writhed in tormented agony, a shrill scream bubbled from his blood-frothed lips. Then, suddenly, the screams ceased. The mage's skin wrinkled and cracked like dry parchment, his eyes stared sightlessly into the darkness. He slowly withered away.

With a shuddering sigh, the other mage collapsed on top of the body of his victim, he himself weak, wounded, near death. But clutched in his hand was the bloodstone and flowing through his veins was new blood, giving him life that would—in time—fully restore him to health. In his mind was knowledge, memories of hundreds of years of power, spells, visions of wonders and terrors that spanned generations. But there, too, were memories of a twin brother, memories of a shattered body, of a prolonged, painful existence.

As two lives mingled within him, as hundreds of strange, conflicting memories surged through him, the mage reeled at the impact. Crouching beside the corpse of his rival, the black-robed mage who had been the victor stared at the bloodstone in his hand. Then he whispered in horror.

"Who am I?"

CHAPTER 4

The guardians slid away from Raistlin, staring at him with hollow eyes. Too weak to move, the mage stared back, his own eyes reflecting the darkness.

"I tell you this"—he spoke to them without a voice and was understood—"touch me again, and I will turn you to dust—as I did *him.*"

"Yes, Master," the voices whispered as their pale visages faded back into the shadows.

"What—" murmured Crysania sleepily. "Did you say something?" Realizing she had been sleeping with her head upon his shoulder, she flushed in confusion and embarrassment and hurriedly sat up. "Can-can I get you anything?" she asked.

"Hot water"—Raistlin lay back limply—"for . . . my potion."

Crysania glanced around, brushing her dark hair out of her eyes. Gray light seeped through the windows. Thin and wispy as a ghost, it brought no comfort. The Staff of Magius

40

cast its light still, keeping away the dark things of the night. But it shed no warmth. Crysania rubbed her aching neck. She was stiff and sore and she knew she must have been asleep for hours. The room was still freezing cold. Bleakly, she looked over at the cold and blackened firegrate.

"There's wood," she faltered, her gaze going to the broken furniture lying about, "but I-I have no tinder or flint. I can't—"

"Wake my brother!" snarled Raistlin, and immediately began to gasp for breath. He tried to say something further, but could do no more than gesture feebly. His eyes glittered with such anger and his face was twisted with such rage that Crysania stared at him in alarm, feeling a chill that was colder than the air around her.

Raistlin closed his eyes wearily and his hand went to his chest. "Please," he whispered in agony, "the pain . . ."

"Of course," Crysania said gently, overwhelmed with shame. What would it be like to live with such pain, day after day? Leaning forward, she drew the curtain from her own shoulders and tucked it carefully around Raistlin. The mage nodded thankfully but could not speak. Then, shivering, Crysania crossed the room to where Caramon lay.

Putting her hand out to touch his shoulder, she hesitated. What if he's still blind? she thought, or what if he can see and decides . . . decides to kill Raistlin?

But her hesitation lasted only a moment. Resolutely, she put her hand on his shoulder and shook him. If he does, she said to herself grimly, I will stop him. I did it once, I can do it again.

Even as she touched him, she was aware of the pale guardians, lurking in the darkness, watching her every move.

"Caramon," she called softly, "Caramon, wake up. Please! We need—"

"What?" Caramon sat up quickly, his hand going reflexively to his sword hilt—that wasn't there. His eyes focused on Crysania, and she saw with relief tinged with fear that he could see her. He stared at her blankly, however, without recognition, then looked quickly around his surroundings.

Then Crysania saw remembrance in the darkening of his

eyes, saw them fill with a haunted pain. She saw remembrance in the clenching of his jaw muscles and the cold gaze he turned upon her. She was about to say something—apologize, explain, rebuke—when his eyes grew suddenly tender as his face softened with concern.

"Lady Crysania," he said, sitting up and dragging the curtain from his body, "you're freezing! Here, put this around you."

Before she could say a word in protest, Caramon wrapped the curtain around her snugly. She noticed as he did so that he looked once at his twin. But his gaze passed quickly over Raistlin, as if he did not exist.

Crysania caught hold of his arm. "Caramon," she said, "he saved our lives. He cast a spell. Those things out there in the darkness leave us alone because he told them to!"

"Because they recognize one of their own!" Caramon said harshly, lowering his gaze and trying to withdraw his arm from her grasp. But Crysania held him fast, more with her eyes than her cold hand.

"You can kill him now," she said angrily. "Look, he's helpless, weak. Of course, if you do, we'll all die. But you were prepared to do that anyway, weren't you!"

"I can't kill him," Caramon said. His brown eyes were clear and cold, and Crysania—once again—saw a startling resemblance between the twins. "Let's face it, Revered Daughter, if I tried, you'd only blind me again."

Caramon brushed her hand from his arm.

"One of us, at least, should see clearly," he said.

Crysania felt herself flush in shame and anger, hearing Loralon's words echo in the warrior's sarcasm. Turning away from her, Caramon stood up quickly.

"I'll build a fire," he said in a cold, hard voice, "if those"—he waved a hand—"friends of my brother's out there will let me."

"I believe they will," Crysania said, speaking with equal coolness as she, too, rose to her feet. "They did not hinder me when . . . when I tore down the curtains." She could not help a quiver creeping into her voice at the memory of being trapped by those shadows of death.

Caramon glanced around at her and, for the first time, it occurred to Crysania what she must look like. Wrapped in a rotting black velvet curtain, her white robes torn and stained with blood, black with dust and ash from the floor. Involuntarily, her hand went to her hair—once so smooth, carefully braided and coiled. Now it hung about her face in straggling wisps. She could feel the dried tears upon her cheeks, the dirt, the blood. . . .

Self-consciously, she wiped her hand across her face and tried to pat back her hair. Then, realizing how futile and even stupid she must look, and angered still further by Caramon's pitying expression, she drew herself up with shabby dignity.

"So, I am no longer the marble maiden you first met," she said haughtily, "just as you are no longer the sodden drunk. It seems we have both learned a thing or two on our journey."

"I know I have," Caramon said gravely.

"Have you?" Crysania retorted. "I wonder! Did you learn—as I did—that the mages sent me back in time, knowing that I would not return?"

Caramon stared at her. She smiled grimly.

"No. You were unaware of that small fact, or so your brother said. The time device could be used by only one person—the person to whom it was given—you! The mages sent me back in time to die—because they feared me!"

Caramon frowned. He opened his mouth, closed it, then shook his head. "You could have left Istar with that elf who came for you"

"Would you have gone?" Crysania demanded. "Would you have given up your life in our time if you could help it? No! Am I so different?"

Caramon's frown deepened and he started to reply, but at that moment, Raistlin coughed. Glancing at the mage, Crysania sighed and said, "You better build the fire, or we'll all perish anyway." Turning her back on Caramon, who still stood regarding her silently, she walked over to his brother.

Looking at the frail mage, Crysania wondered if he had heard. She wondered if he were even still conscious.

He was conscious, but if Raistlin was at all aware of what

had passed between the other two, he appeared to be too weak to take any interest in it. Pouring some of the water into a cracked bowl, Crysania knelt down beside him. Tearing a piece from the cleanest portion of her robe, she wiped his face; it burned with fever even in the chill room.

Behind her, she heard Caramon gathering up bits of the broken wooden furniture and stacking it in the grate.

"I need something for tinder," the big man muttered to himself. "Ah, these books—"

At that, Raistlin's eyes flared open, his head moved and he tried feebly to rise.

"Don't, Caramon!" Crysania cried, alarmed. Caramon stopped, a book in his hand.

"Dangerous, my brother!" Raistlin gasped weakly. "Spellbooks! Don't touch them. . . ."

His voice failed, but the gaze of his glittering eyes was fixed on Caramon with a look of such apparent concern that even Caramon seemed taken aback. Mumbling something unintelligible, the big man dropped the book and began to search about the desk. Crysania saw Raistlin's eyes close in relief.

"Here's—Looks like . . . letters," Caramon said after a moment of shuffling through paper on the floor. "Would— would these be all right?" he asked gruffly.

Raistlin nodded wordlessly, and, within moments, Crysania heard the crackling of flame. Lacquer-finished, the wood of the broken furniture caught quickly, and soon the fire burned with a bright, cheering light. Glancing into the shadows, Crysania saw the pallid faces withdraw—but they did not leave.

"We must move Raistlin near the fire," she said, standing up, "and he said something about a potion—"

"Yes," Caramon answered tonelessly. Coming to stand beside Crysania, he stared down at his brother. Then he shrugged. "Let him magic himself over there if that's what he wants."

Crysania's eyes flashed in anger. She turned to Caramon, scathing words on her lips, but, at a weak gesture from Raistlin, she bit her lower lip and kept silent.

"You pick an inopportune time to grow up, my brother," the mage whispered.

"Maybe," said Caramon slowly, his face filled with unutterable sorrow. Shaking his head, he walked back over to stand by the fire. "Maybe it doesn't matter anymore."

Crysania, watching Raistlin's gaze follow his brother, was startled to see him smile a swift, secret smile and nod in satisfaction. Then, as he looked up at her, the smile vanished quickly. Lifting one arm, he motioned her to come near him.

"I can stand," he breathed, "with your help."

"Here, you'll need your staff," she said, extending her hand for it.

"Don't touch it!" Raistlin ordered, catching hold of her hand in his. "No," he repeated more gently, coughing until he could scarcely breathe. "Other hands . . . touch it . . . light fails. . . ."

Shivering involuntarily, Crysania cast a swift glance around the room. Raistlin, seeing her, and seeing the shimmering shapes hovering just outside the light of the staff, shook his head. "No, I do not believe they would attack us," he said softly as Crysania put her arms around him and helped him to rise. "They know who I am." His lip curled in a sneer at this, and he choked. "They know who I am," he repeated more firmly, "and they dare not cross me. But—" he coughed again, and leaned heavily upon Crysania, one arm around her shoulder, the other hand clutching his staff—"it will be safer to keep the light of the staff burning."

The mage staggered as he spoke and nearly fell. Crysania paused to let him catch his breath. Her own breath was coming more rapidly than normal, revealing the confused tangle of her emotions. Hearing the harsh rattle of Raistlin's labored breathing, she was consumed with pity for his weakness. Yet, she could feel the burning heat of the body pressed so near hers. There was the intoxicating scent of his spell components—rose petals, spice—and his black robes were soft to the touch, softer than the curtain around her shoulders. His gaze met hers as they stood there; for a moment, the mirrorlike surface of his eyes cracked and she saw warmth and passion. His arm around her tightened reflexively, drawing her closer without seeming to mean to do so.

Crysania flushed, wanting desperately to both run away and stay forever in that warm embrace. Quickly, she lowered her gaze, but it was too late. She felt Raistlin stiffen. Angrily, he withdrew his arm. Pushing her aside, he gripped his staff for support.

But he was still too weak. He staggered and started to fall. Crysania moved to help him, but suddenly a huge body interposed itself between her and the mage. Strong arms caught Raistlin up as if he were no more than a child. Caramon carried his brother to a frayed and blackened, heavily cushioned chair he had dragged near the fire.

For a few moments, Crysania could not move from where she stood, leaning against the desk. It was only when she realized that she was alone in the darkness, outside the light of both fire and staff, that she walked hurriedly over near the fire herself.

"Sit down, Lady Crysania," said Caramon, drawing up another chair and beating the dust and ash off with his hands as best he could.

"Thank you," she murmured, trying, for some reason, to avoid the big man's gaze. Sinking down into the chair, she huddled near the blaze, staring fixedly into the flames until she felt she had regained some of her composure.

When she was able to look around, she saw Raistlin lying back in his chair, his eyes closed, his breathing ragged. Caramon was heating water in a battered iron pot that he had dragged, from the looks of it, out of the ashes of the fireplace.

He stood before it, staring intently into the water. The firelight glistened on his golden armor, glowed on his smooth, tan skin. His muscles rippled as he flexed his great arms to keep warm.

He is truly a magnificently built man, Crysania thought, then shuddered. Once again, she could see him entering that room beneath the doomed Temple, the bloody sword in his hand, death in his eyes. . . .

"The water's ready," Caramon announced, and Crysania returned to the Tower with a start.

"Let me fix the potion," she said quickly, thankful for something to do.

Raistlin opened his eyes as she came near him. Looking into them, she saw only a reflection of herself, pale, wan, disheveled. Wordlessly, he held out a small, velvet pouch. As she took it, he gestured to his brother, then sank back, exhausted.

Taking the pouch, Crysania turned to find Caramon watching her, a look of mingled perplexity and sadness giving his face an unaccustomed gravity. But all he said was, "Put a few of the leaves in this cup, then fill it with the hot water."

"What is it?" Crysania asked curiously. Opening the pouch, her nose wrinkled at the strange, bitter scent of the herbs. Caramon poured the water into the cup she held.

"I don't know," he said, shrugging. "Raist always gathered the herbs and mixed them himself. Par-Salian gave the recipe to him after . . . after the Test, when he was so sick. I know"—he smiled at her—"it smells awful and must taste worse." His glance went almost fondly to his brother. "But it will help him." His voice grated harshly. Abruptly, he turned away.

Crysania carried the steaming potion to Raistlin, who clutched at it with trembling hands and eagerly brought the cup to his lips. Sipping at it, he breathed a sigh of relief and, once more, sank back among the cushions of the chair.

An awkward silence fell. Caramon was staring down at the fire once more. Raistlin, too, looked into the flames and drank his potion without comment. Crysania returned to her own chair to do what each of the others must be doing, she realized—trying to sort out thoughts, trying to make some sense of what had happened.

Hours ago, she had been standing in a doomed city, a city destined to die by the wrath of the gods. She had been on the verge of complete mental and physical collapse. She could admit this now, though she could not have then. How fondly she had imagined her soul to be girded round by the steel walls of her faith. Not steel, she saw now, with shame and regret. Not steel, but ice. The ice had melted in the harsh light of truth, leaving her exposed and vulnerable. If it had not been for Raistlin, she would have perished back there in Istar.

Raistlin . . . Her face flushed. This was something else she had never thought to contend with—love, passion. She had been betrothed to a young man, years ago, and she had been quite fond of him. But she had not loved him. She had, in fact, never really believed in love—the kind of love that existed in tales told to children. To be that wrapped up in another person seemed a handicap, a weakness to be avoided. She remembered something Tanis Half-Elven had said about his wife, Laurana—what was it? "When she is gone, it is like I'm missing my right arm. . . ."

What romantic twaddle, she had thought at the time. But now she asked herself, did she feel that way about Raistlin? Her thoughts went to the last day in Istar, the terrible storm, the flashing of the lightning, and how she had suddenly found herself in Raistlin's arms. Her heart contracted with the swift ache of desire as she felt, once again, his strong embrace. But there was also a sharp fear, a strange revulsion. Unwillingly, she remembered the feverish gleam in his eyes, his exultation in the storm—as if he himself had called it down.

It was like the strange smell of the spell components that clung to him—the pleasant smell of roses and spice, but— mingled with it—the cloying odor of decaying creatures, the acrid smell of sulfur. Even as her body longed for his touch, something in her soul shrank away in horror. . . .

Caramon's stomach rumbled loudly. The sound, in the deathly still chamber, was startling.

Looking up, her thoughts shattered, Crysania saw the big man blush deeply in embarrassment. Suddenly reminded of her own hunger—she couldn't remember the last time she had been able to choke down a mouthful of food—Crysania began to laugh.

Caramon looked at her dubiously, perhaps thinking her hysterical. At the puzzled look on the big man's face, Crysania only laughed harder. It felt good to laugh, in fact. The darkness in the room seemed pushed back, the shadows lifted from her soul. She laughed merrily and, finally, caught by the infectious nature of her mirth, Caramon began to laugh, too, though he still shook his head, his face red.

"Thus do the gods remind us we're human," Crysania said when she could speak, wiping the tears from her eyes. "Here we are, in the most horrible place imaginable, surrounded by creatures waiting eagerly to devour us whole, and all I can think of right now is how desperately hungry I am!"

"We need food," said Caramon soberly, suddenly serious. "And decent clothing, if we're going to be here long." He looked at his brother. "How long *are* we going to be here?"

"Not long," Raistlin replied. He had finished the potion, and his voice was already stronger. Some color had returned to his pale face. "I need time to rest, to recover my strength, and to complete my studies. This lady"—his glittering gaze went to Crysania, and she shivered at the sudden impersonal tone in his voice—"needs to commune with her god and renew her faith. Then, we will be ready to enter the Portal. At which time, my brother, you may go where you will."

Crysania felt Caramon's questioning glance, but she kept her face smooth and expressionless, though Raistlin's cool, casual mention of entering the dread Portal, of going into the Abyss and facing the Queen of Darkness froze her heart. She refused to meet Caramon's eyes, therefore, and stared into the fire.

The big man sighed, then he cleared his throat. "Will you send me home?" he asked his twin.

"If that is where you wish to go."

"Yes," Caramon said, his voice deep and stern. "I want to go back to Tika and to . . . talk to Tanis." His voice broke. "I'll have to . . . to explain, somehow, about Tas dying . . . back there in Istar. . . ."

"In the name of the gods, Caramon," Raistlin snapped, making an irritated motion with his slender hand, "I thought we had seen some glimmer of an adult lurking in that hulking body of yours! You will undoubtedly return to find Tasslehoff sitting in your kitchen, regaling Tika with one stupid story after another, having robbed you blind in the meantime!"

"What?" Caramon's face grew pale, his eyes widened.

"Listen to me, my brother!" Raistlin hissed, pointing a finger at Caramon. "The kender doomed himself when he disrupted

Par-Salian's spell. There is a very good reason for the prohibition against those of his race and the races of dwarves and gnomes traveling back in time. Since they were created by accident, through a quirk of fate and the god, Reorx's, carelessness, these races are not within the flow of time, as are humans, elves, and ogres—those races first created by the gods.

"Thus, the kender could have altered time, as he was quick to realize when I inadvertently let slip that fact. I could not allow that to happen! Had he stopped the Cataclysm, as he intended, who knows what might have occurred? Perhaps we might have returned to our own time to find the Queen of Darkness reigning supreme and unchallenged, since the Cataclysm was sent, in part, to prepare the world to face her coming and give it the strength to defy her—"

"So you murdered him!" Caramon interrupted hoarsely.

"I told him to get the device"—Raistlin bit the words—"I taught him how to use it, and I sent him home!"

Caramon blinked. "You did?" he asked suspiciously.

Raistlin sighed and laid his head back into the cushions of the chair. "I did, but I don't expect you to believe me, my brother." His hands plucked feebly at the black robes he wore. "Why should you, after all?"

"You know," said Crysania softly, "I seem to remember, in those last horrible moments before the earthquake struck, seeing Tasslehoff. He . . . he was with me . . . in the Sacred Chamber. . . ."

She saw Raistlin open his eyes a slit. His glittering gaze pierced her heart and startled her, distracting her thoughts for a moment.

"Go on," Caramon urged.

"I—I remember . . . he had the magical device. At least I think he did. He said something about it." Crysania put her hand to her forehead. "But I can't think what it was. It-it's all so dreadful and confused. But—I'm certain he said he had the device!"

Raistlin smiled slightly. "Surely, you will believe Lady Crysania, my brother?" He shrugged. "A cleric of Paladine will not lie."

"So Tasslehoff's home? Right now?" Caramon said, trying to assimilate this startling information. "And, when I go back, I'll find him—"

"—safe and sound and loaded down with most of your personal possessions," Raistlin finished wryly. "But, now, we must turn our attention to more pressing matters. You are right, my brother. We need food and warm clothing, and we are not likely to find either here. The time we have come forward to is about one hundred years after the Cataclysm. This Tower"—he waved his hand—"has been deserted all those years. It is now guarded by the creatures of darkness called forth by the curse of the magic-user whose body is still impaled upon the spikes of the gates below us. The Shoikan Grove has grown up around it, and there are none on Krynn who dare enter.

"None except myself, of course. No, no one can get inside. But the guardians will not prevent one of us—you, my brother, for example—from leaving. You will go into Palanthas and buy food and clothing. I could produce it with my magic, but I dare not expend any unnecessary energy between now and when I—that is Crysania and I—enter the Portal."

Caramon's eyes widened. His gaze went to the soot-blackened window, his thoughts to the horrifying stories of the Shoikan Grove beyond.

"I will give you a charm to guard you, my brother," Raistlin added in exasperation, seeing the frightened look on Caramon's face. "A charm will be necessary, in fact, but not to aid your way through the Grove. It is far more dangerous in here. The guardians obey me, but they hunger for your blood. Do not set foot outside this room without me. Remember that. You, too, Lady Crysania."

"Where is this . . . this Portal?" Caramon asked abruptly.

"In the laboratory, above us, at the top of the Tower," Raistlin replied. "The Portals were kept in the most secure place the wizards could devise because, as you can imagine, they are extremely dangerous!"

"It's like wizards to go tampering with what they should best leave alone," Caramon growled. "Why in the name of the gods did they create a gateway to the Abyss?"

Placing the tips of his fingers together, Raistlin stared into the fire, speaking to the flames as if they were the only ones with the power to understand him.

"In the hunger for knowledge, many things are created. Some are good, that benefit us all. A sword in your hands, Caramon, champions the cause of righteousness and truth and protects the innocent. But a sword in the hands of, say, our beloved sister, Kitiara, would split the heads of the innocent wide open if it suited her. Is this the fault of the sword's creator?"

"N—" Caramon began, but his twin ignored him.

"Long ago, during the Age of Dreams, when magic-users were respected and magic flourished upon Krynn, the five Towers of High Sorcery stood as beacons of light in the dark sea of ignorance that was this world. Here, great magics were worked, benefiting all. There were plans for greater still. Who knows but that now we might have been riding on the winds, soaring the skies like dragons. Maybe even leaving this wretched world and inhabiting other worlds, far away . . . far away. . . ."

His voice grew soft and quiet. Caramon and Crysania held very still, spellbound by his tone, caught up in the vision of his magic.

He sighed. "But that was not to be. In their desire to hasten their great works, the wizards decided they needed to communicate directly with each other, from one Tower to another, without the need for cumbersome teleportation spells. And so, the Portals were constructed."

"They succeeded?" Crysania's eyes shone with wonder.

"They succeeded!" Raistlin snorted. "Beyond their wildest dreams"—his voice dropped—"their worst nightmares. For the Portals could not only provide movement in one step between any of the far-flung Towers and fortresses of magic— but also into the realms of the gods, as an inept wizard of my own order discovered to his misfortune."

Raistlin shivered, suddenly, and drew his black robes more tightly around him, huddling close to the fire.

"Tempted by the Queen of Darkness, as only she can tempt mortal man when she chooses"—Raistlin's face grew pale—"he used the Portal to enter her realm and gain the prize she offered him nightly, in his dreams," Raistlin laughed, bitter, mocking laughter. "Fool! What happened to him, no one knows. But he never returned through the Portal. The Queen, however, did. And with her, came legions of dragons—"

"The first Dragon Wars!" Crysania gasped.

"Yes, brought upon us by one of my own kind with no discipline, no self-control. One who allowed himself to be seduced—" Breaking off, Raistlin stared broodingly into the fire.

"But, I never heard that!" Caramon protested. "According to the legends, the dragons came together—"

"Your history is limited to bedtime tales, my brother!" Raistlin said impatiently. "And just proves how little you know of dragons. They are independent creatures, proud, self-centered, and completely incapable of coming together to cook dinner, much less coordinate any sort of war effort. No, the Queen entered the world completely that time, not just the shadow she was during our war with her. She waged war upon the world, and it was only through Huma's great sacrifice that she was driven back."

Raistlin paused, hands to his lips, musing. "Some say that Huma did *not* use the Dragonlance to physically destroy her, as the legend goes. But, rather, the lance had some magical property allowing him to drive her back into the Portal and seal it shut. The fact that he *did* drive her back proves that—in this world—she is vulnerable." Raistlin stared fixedly into the flames. "Had there been someone—someone of *true* power at the Portal when she entered, someone capable of destroying her utterly instead of simply driving her back—then history might well have been rewritten."

No one spoke. Crysania stared into the flames, seeing, perhaps, the same glorious vision as the archmage. Caramon stared at his twin's face.

Raistlin's gaze suddenly left the flames, flashing into focus with a clear, cold intensity. "When I am stronger, tomorrow, I will ascend to the laboratory alone —his stern glance swept over both Caramon and Crysania—"and begin my preparations. You, lady, had best start communing with your god."

Crysania swallowed nervously. Shivering, she drew her chair nearer the fire. But suddenly Caramon was on his feet, standing before her. Reaching down, his strong hands gripped her arms, forcing her to look up into his eyes.

"This is madness, lady," he said, his voice soft and compassionate. "Let me take you from this dark place! You're frightened—you have reason to be afraid! Maybe not everything Par-Salian said about Raistlin was true. Maybe everything I thought about him wasn't true, either. Perhaps I've misjudged him. But I see this clearly, lady. You're frightened and I don't blame you! Let Raistlin do this thing alone! Let *him* challenge the gods—if that's what he wants! But you don't have to go with him! Come home! Let me take you back to our time, away from here."

Raistlin did not speak, but his thoughts echoed in Crysania's mind as clearly as if he had. *You heard the Kingpriest! You said yourself that you know his mistake! Paladine favors you. Even in this dark place, he grants your prayers. You are his chosen! You will succeed where the Kingpriest failed! Come with me, Crysania. This is our destiny!*

"I am frightened," Crysania said, gently disengaging Caramon's hands from her arms. "And I am truly touched by your concern. But this fear of mine is a weakness in me that I must combat. With Paladine's help, I will overcome it—before I enter the Portal with your brother."

"So be it," Caramon said heavily, turning away.

Raistlin smiled, a dark, secret smile that was not reflected in either his eyes or his voice.

"And now, Caramon," he said caustically, "if you are quite through meddling in matters you are completely incapable of comprehending, you had best prepare for your journey. It is midmorning, now. The markets—such as they are in these bleak times—are just opening." Reaching into a pocket in his black robes, Raistlin withdrew several coins and tossed them at his brother. "That should be sufficient for our needs."

Caramon caught the coins without thinking. Then he hesitated, staring at his brother with the same look Crysania had seen him wear in the Temple at Istar, and she remembered thinking, *what terrible hate . . . what terrible love!*

Finally, Caramon lowered his gaze, stuffing the money into his belt.

"Come here to me, Caramon," Raistlin said softly.

"Why?" he muttered, suddenly suspicious.

"Well, there is the matter of that iron collar around your neck. Would you walk the streets with the mark of slavery still? And then there is the charm." Raistlin spoke with infinite patience. Seeing Caramon hesitate still, he added, "I would not advise you leave this room without it. Still, that is your decision—"

Glancing over at the pallid faces, who were still watching intently from the shadows, Caramon came to stand before his brother, his arms crossed before his chest. "Now what?" he growled.

"Kneel down before me."

Caramon's eyes flashed with anger. A bitter oath burned on his lips, but, his eyes going furtively to Crysania, he choked back and swallowed his words.

Raistlin's pale face appeared saddened. He sighed. "I am exhausted, Caramon. I do not have the strength to rise. Please—"

His jaw clenched, Caramon slowly lowered himself, bending knee to floor so that he was level with his frail, black-robed twin.

Raistlin spoke a soft word. The iron collar split apart and fell from Caramon's neck, landing with a clatter on the floor.

"Come nearer," Raistlin said.

Swallowing, rubbing his neck, Caramon did as he was told. though he stared at his brother bitterly. "I'm doing this for Crysania," he said, his voice taut. "If it were just you and me, I'd let you rot in this foul place!"

Reaching out his hands, Raistlin placed them on either side of his twin's head with a gesture that was tender, almost caressing. "Would you, my brother?" the mage asked so softly it was no more than a breath. "Would you leave me? Back there, in Istar—would you truly have killed me?"

Caramon only stared at him, unable to answer. Then, Raistlin bent forward and kissed his brother on the forehead. Caramon flinched, as though he had been touched with a red-hot iron.

Raistlin released his grip.

Caramon stared at him in anguish. "I don't know!" he murmured brokenly. "The gods help me—I don't know!"

With a shuddering sob, he covered his face with his hands. His head sank into his brother's lap.

Raistlin stroked his brother's brown, curling hair. "There, now, Caramon," he said gently. "I have given you the charm. The things of darkness cannot harm you, not so long as I am here."

CHAPTER 5

aramon stood in the doorway to the study, peering out into the darkness of the corridor beyond—a darkness that was alive with whispers and eyes. Beside him was Raistlin, one hand on his twin's arm, the Staff of Magius in his other.

"All will be well, my brother," Raistlin said softly. "Trust me."

Caramon glanced at his twin out of the corner of his eye. Seeing his look, Raistlin smiled sardonically. "I will send one of these with you," the mage continued, motioning with his slender hand.

"I'd rather not!" Caramon muttered, scowling as the pair of disembodied eyes nearest him drew nearer still.

"Attend him," Raistlin commanded the eyes. "He is under my protection. You see me? You know who I am?"

The eyes lowered their gaze in reverence, then fixed their cold and ghastly stare upon Caramon. The big warrior shuddered and cast one final glance at Raistlin, only to see his brother's face turn grim and stern.

"The guardians will guide you safely through the Grove. You may have more to fear, however, once you leave it. Be wary, my brother. This city is not the beautiful, serene place it will become in two hundred years Now, refugees pack it, living in the gutters, the streets, wherever they can. Carts rumble over the cobblestones every morning, removing the bodies of those who died during the night. There are men out there who will murder you for your boots. Buy a sword, first thing, and carry it openly in your hand."

"I'll worry about the town," Caramon snapped. Turning abruptly, he walked off down the corridor, trying without much success to ignore the pale, glowing eyes that floated near his shoulder.

Raistlin watched until his brother and the guardian had passed beyond the staff's radius of magical light and were swallowed up by the noisome darkness. Waiting until even the echoes of his brother's heavy footfalls had faded, Raistlin turned and reentered the study.

Lady Crysania sat in her chair, trying without much success to comb her fingers through her tangled hair. Padding softly across the floor to stand near her, unseen, Raistlin reached into one of the pockets of his black robes and drew forth a handful of fine white sand. Coming up behind her, the mage raised his hand and let the sand drift down over the woman's dark hair.

"*Ast tasark simiralan krynawi,*" Raistlin whispered, and almost immediately Crysania's head drooped, her eyes closed, and she drifted into a deep, magical sleep. Moving to stand before her, Raistlin stared at her for long moments.

Though she had washed the stain of tears and blood from her face, the marks of her journey through darkness were still visible in the blue shadows beneath her long lashes, a cut upon her lip, and the pallor of her complexion. Reaching out his hand, Raistlin gently brushed back the hair that fell in dark tendrils across her eyes.

Crysania had cast aside the velvet curtain she had been using as a blanket as the room was warmed by the fire. Her white robes, torn and stained with blood, had come loose around her neck. Raistlin could see the soft curves of her breasts beneath the white cloth rising and falling with her deep, even breathing.

"Were I as other men, she would be mine," he said softly.

His hand lingered near her face, her dark, crisp hair curling around his fingers.

"But I am not as other men," Raistlin murmured. Letting her hair fall, he pulled the velvet curtain up around her shoulders and across her slumbering form. Crysania smiled from some sweet dream, perhaps, and nestled more snugly into the chair, resting her cheek upon her hand as she laid her head on the armrest.

Raistlin's hand brushed against the smooth skin of her face, recalling vivid memories. He began to tremble. He had but to reverse the sleep spell, take her in his arms, hold her as he held her when he cast the magic spell that brought them to this place. They would have an hour alone together before Caramon returned. . . .

"I am *not* as other men!" Raistlin snarled.

Abruptly walking away, his dour gaze encountered the staring, watchful eyes of the guardians.

"Watch over her while I am gone," he said to several half-seen, hovering spectres lurking in the dark shadows in the corner of the study. "You two," he ordered the two who been with him when he awakened, "accompany me."

"Yes, Master," the two murmured. As the staff's light fell upon them, the faint outlines of black robes could be seen.

Stepping out into the corridor, Raistlin carefully closed the door to the study behind him. He gripped the staff, spoke a soft word of command, and was instantly taken to the laboratory at the top of the Tower of High Sorcery.

He had not even drawn a breath when, materializing out of the darkness, he was attacked.

Shrieks and howls of outrage screamed around him. Dark shapes darted out of the air, daring the light of the staff as bonewhite fingers clutched for his throat and grasped his robes, rending the cloth. So swift and sudden was the attack and so awful the sense of hatred that Raistlin very nearly lost control.

But he was in command of himself quickly. Swinging the staff in a wide arc, shouting hoarse words of magic, he drove back the spectres.

"Talk to them!" he commanded the two guardians with him. "Tell them who I am!"

"Fistandantilus," he heard them say through a roaring in his ears, ". . . though his time has not yet come as was foretold . . . some magical experiment. . . ."

Weakened and dizzy, Raistlin staggered to a chair and slumped down into it. Bitterly cursing himself for not being prepared for such an onslaught and cursing the frail body that was, once again, failing him, he wiped blood from a jagged cut upon his face and fought to remain conscious.

This is *your* doing, my Queen. His thoughts came grimly through a haze of pain. You dare not fight me openly. I am too strong for you on this—my plane—of existence! You have your foothold in this world. Even now, the Temple has appeared in its perverted form in Neraka. You have wakened the evil dragons. They are stealing the eggs of the good dragons. But the door remains closed, the Foundation Stone has been blocked by self-sacrificing love. And that was your mistake. For now, by your entry into *our* plane, you have made it possible for us to enter *yours*! I cannot reach you yet . . . you cannot reach me. . . . But the time will come . . . the time will come. . . .

"Are you unwell, Master?" came a frightened voice near him. "I am sorry we could not prevent them from harming you, but you moved too swiftly! Please, forgive us. Let us help—"

"There is nothing you can do!" Raistlin snarled, coughing. He felt the pain in his chest ease. "Leave me a moment. . . . Let me rest. Drive these others out of here."

"Yes, Master."

Closing his eyes, waiting for the horrible dizziness and pain to pass, Raistlin sat for an hour in the darkness, going over his plans in his mind. He needed two weeks of unbroken rest and study to prepare himself. That time he would find here easily enough. Crysania was his—she would follow him willingly, eagerly in fact, calling down the power of Paladine to assist him in opening the Portal and fighting the dread Guardians beyond.

He had the knowledge of Fistandantilus, knowledge accumulated by the mage over the ages. He had his own knowledge, too, plus the strength of his younger body. By the time he was ready to enter, he would be at the height of his powers—the greatest archmage ever to have lived upon Krynn!

The thought comforted him and gave him renewed energy. The dizziness subsided finally, the pain eased. Rising to his feet, he cast a quick glance about the laboratory. He recognized it, of course. It looked exactly the same as when he had entered it in a past that was now two hundred years in the future. *Then* he had come with power—as foretold. The gates had opened, the evil guardians had greeted him reverently—not attacked him.

As he walked through the laboratory, the Staff of Magius shining to light his way, Raistlin glanced about curiously. He noticed odd, puzzling changes. Everything should have been *exactly* as it was when he would arrive two hundred years from now. But a beaker now standing intact had been broken when he found it. A spellbook now resting on the large stone table, he had discovered on the floor.

"Do the guardians disturb things?" he asked the two who remained with him. His robes rustled about his ankles as he made his way to the very back of the huge laboratory, back to the Door That Was Never Opened.

"Oh, no, Master," said one, shocked. "We are not permitted to touch anything."

Raistlin shrugged. Lots of things could happen in two hundred years to account for such occurrences. "Perhaps an earthquake," he said to himself, losing interest in the matter as he approached the shadows where the great Portal stood.

Raising the Staff of Magius, he shone its magical light ahead of him. The shadows fled the far corner of the laboratory, the corner where stood the Portal with its platinum carvings of the five dragon heads and its huge silver-steel door that no key upon Krynn could unlock.

Raistlin held the staff high . . . and gasped.

For long moments he could do nothing but stare, the breath wheezing in his lungs, his thoughts seething and burning. Then, his shrill scream of anger and rage and fury pierced the living fabric of the Tower's darkness.

So dreadful was the cry, echoing through the dark corridors of the Tower, that the evil guardians cowered back into their shadows, wondering if perhaps their dread Queen had burst in upon them.

Caramon heard the cry as he entered the door at the bottom of the Tower. Shivering with sudden terror, he dropped the packages he carried and, with trembling hands, lit the torch he had brought. Then, the naked blade of his new sword in his hand, the big warrior raced up the stairs two at a time.

Bursting into the study, he saw Lady Crysania looking around in sleepy fearfulness.

"I heard a scream—" she said, rubbing her eyes and rising to her feet.

"Are you all right?" Caramon gasped, trying to catch his breath.

"Why, yes," she said, looking startled, as she realized what he was thinking. "It wasn't me. I must have fallen asleep. It woke me—"

"Where's Raist?" Caramon demanded.

"Raistlin!" she repeated, alarmed, and started to push her way past Caramon when he caught hold of her.

"This is why you slept," he said grimly, brushing fine white sand from her hair. "Sleep spell."

Crysania blinked. "But why—"

"We'll find out."

"Warrior," said a cold voice almost in his ear.

Whirling, Caramon thrust Crysania behind him, raising his sword as a black-robed, spectral figure materialized out of the darkness. "You seek the wizard? He is above, in the laboratory. He is in need of assistance, and we have been commanded not to touch him."

"I'll go," Caramon said, "alone."

"I'm coming with you," Crysania said. "*I will* come with you," she repeated firmly, in response to Caramon's frown.

Caramon started to argue, then, remembering that she *was* a cleric of Paladine and had once before exerted her powers over these creatures of darkness, shrugged and gave in, though with little grace.

"What happened to him, if you were commanded not to touch him?" Caramon asked the spectre gruffly as he and Crysania followed it from the study out into the dark corridor. "Keep close to me," he muttered to Crysania, but the command was not necessary.

If the darkness had seemed alive before, it throbbed and pulsed and jittered and jabbered with life now as the guardians, upset by the scream, thronged the corridors. Though he was now warmly dressed, having purchased clothes at the marketplace, Caramon shivered convulsively with the chill that flowed from their undead bodies. Beside him, Crysania shook so she could barely walk.

"Let me hold the torch," she said through clenched teeth. Caramon handed her the torch, then encircled her with his right arm, drawing her near. She clasped her arm about him, both of them finding comfort in the touch of living flesh as they climbed the stairs after the spectre.

"What happened?" he asked again, but the spectre did not answer. It simply pointed up the spiral stairs.

Holding his sword in his left hand, his sword hand, Caramon and Crysania followed the spectre as it flowed up the stairs, the torchlight dancing and wavering.

After what seemed an endless climb, the two reached the top of the Tower of High Sorcery, both of them aching and frightened and chilled to the very heart.

"We must rest," Caramon said through lips so numb he was practically inaudible. Crysania leaned against him, her eyes closed, her breath coming in labored gasps. Caramon himself did not think he could have climbed another stair, and he was in superb physical condition.

"Where is Raist—Fistandantilus?" Crysania stammered after her breathing had returned somewhat to normal.

"Within." The spectre pointed again, this time to a closed door and, as it pointed, the door swung silently open.

Cold air flowed from the room in a dark wave, ruffling Caramon's hair and blowing aside Crysania's cloak. For a moment Caramon could not move. The sense of evil coming from within that chamber was overwhelming. But Crysania, her hand firmly clasped over the medallion of Paladine, began to walk forward.

Reaching out, Caramon drew her back. "Let me go first."

Crysania smiled at him wearily. "In any other case but this, warrior," she said, "I would grant you that privilege. But, here, the medallion I hold is as formidable a weapon as your sword."

"You have no need for any weapon," the spectre stated coldly. "The Master commanded us to see that you come to no harm. We will obey his request."

"What if he's dead?" Caramon asked harshly, feeling Crysania stiffen in fear beside him.

"If he had died," the spectre replied, its eyes gleaming, "your warm blood would already be upon our lips. Now enter."

Hesitantly, Crysania pressed close beside him, Caramon entered the laboratory. Crysania lifted the torch, holding it high, as both paused, looking around.

"There," Caramon whispered, the innate closeness that existed between the twins leading him to find the dark mass, barely visible on the floor at the back of the laboratory.

Her fears forgotten, Crysania hurried forward, Caramon following more slowly, his eyes warily scanning the darkness.

Raistlin lay on his side, his hood drawn over his face. The Staff of Magius lay some distance from him, its light gone out, as though Raistlin—in bitter anger—had hurled it from him. In its flight, it had, apparently, broken a beaker and knocked a spellbook to the floor.

Handing Caramon the torch, Crysania knelt beside the mage and felt for the lifebeat in his neck. It was weak and irregular, but he lived. She sighed in relief, then shook her head. "He's all right. But I don't understand. What happened to him?"

"He is not hurt physically," the spectre said, hovering near them. "He came to this part of the laboratory as though looking for something. And then he walked over here, muttering about a portal. Holding his staff high, he stood where he lies now, staring straight ahead. Then he screamed, hurled the staff from him, and fell to the floor, cursing in fury until he lost consciousness."

Puzzled, Caramon held the torch up. "I wonder what could have happened?" he murmured. "Why, there's nothing here! Nothing but a bare, blank wall!"

CHAPTER 6

How has he been?" Crysania asked softly as she entered the room. Drawing back the white hood from her head, she untied her cloak to allow Caramon to remove it from around her shoulders.

"Restless," the warrior replied with a glance toward a shadowed corner. "He has been impatient for your return."

Crysania sighed and bit her lip. "I wish I had better news," she murmured.

"I'm glad you don't," Caramon said grimly, folding Crysania's cloak over a chair. "Maybe he'll give up this insane idea and come home."

"I can't—" began Crysania, but she was interrupted.

"If you two are *quite* finished with whatever it is you are doing there in the darkness, perhaps you will come tell me what you discovered, lady."

Crysania flushed deeply. Casting an irritated glance at Caramon, she hurried across the room to where Raistlin lay on a pallet near the fire.

The mage's rage had been costly. Caramon had carried him

from the laboratory where they'd found him lying before the empty stone wall to the study. Crysania had made up a bed on the floor, then watched, helplessly, as Caramon ministered to his brother as gently as a mother to a sick child. But there was little even the big man could do for his frail twin. Raistlin lay unconscious for over a day, muttering strange words in his sleep. Once he wakened and cried out in terror, but he immediately sank back into whatever darkness he wandered.

Bereft of the light of the staff that even Caramon dared not touch and was forced to leave in the laboratory, he and Crysania sat huddled near Raistlin. They kept the fire burning brightly, but both were always conscious of the presence of the shadows of the guardians of the Tower, waiting, watching.

Finally, Raistlin awoke. With his first breath, he ordered Caramon to prepare his potion and, after drinking this, was able to send one of the guardians to fetch the staff. Then he beckoned to Crysania. "You must go to Astinus," he whispered.

"Astinus!" Crysania repeated in blank astonishment. "The historian? But why—I don't understand—"

Raistlin's eyes glittered, a spot of color burned into his pale cheek with feverish brilliance. "The Portal *is not here!*" he snarled, grinding his teeth in impotent fury. His hands clenched and almost immediately he began to cough. He glared at Crysania.

"Don't waste my time with fool questions! Just go!" he commanded in such terrible anger that she shrank away, startled. Raistlin fell back, gasping for breath.

Caramon glanced up at Crysania in concern. She walked to the desk, staring down unseeing at some of the tattered and blackened spellbooks that lay upon it.

"Now wait just a minute, lady," Caramon said softly, rising and coming to her. "You're not really considering going? Who is this Astinus anyway? And how do you plan to get through the Grove without a charm?"

"I have a charm," Crysania murmured, "given to me by your brother when—when we first met. As for Astinus, he is the keeper of the Great Library of Palanthas, the Chronicler of the History of Krynn."

"He may be that in our time, but he won't be there now!" Caramon said in exasperation. "Think, lady!"

"I am thinking," Crysania snapped, glancing at him in anger. "Astinus is known as the Ageless One. He was first to set foot upon Krynn, so the legends say, and he will be the last to leave it."

Caramon regarded her skeptically.

"He records all history as it passes. He knows everything that has happened in the past and is happening in the present. But"—Crysania glanced at Raistlin with a worried look—"he cannot see into the future. So I'm not certain what help he can be to us."

Caramon, still dubious and obviously not believing half of this wild tale, had argued long against her going. But Crysania only grew more determined, until, finally, even Caramon realized they had no choice. Raistlin grew worse instead of better. His skin burned with fever, he lapsed into periods of incoherence and, when he was himself, angrily demanded to know why Crysania hadn't been to see Astinus yet.

So she had braved the terrors of the Grove and the equally appalling terrors of the streets of Palanthas. Now she knelt beside the mage's bed, her heart aching as she watched him struggle to sit up—with his brother's help—his glittering gaze fixed eagerly upon her.

"Tell me everything!" he ordered hoarsely. "Exactly as it occurred. Leave out nothing."

Nodding wordlessly, still shaken by the terrifying walk through the Tower, Crysania tried to force herself to calm down and sort out her thoughts.

"I went to the Great Library and—and asked to see Astinus," she began, nervously smoothing the folds of the plain, white robe Caramon had brought her to replace the blood-stained gown she had worn. "The Aesthetics refused to admit me, but then I showed them the medallion of Paladine. That threw them into confusion, as you might well imagine." She smiled. "It has been a hundred years since any sign of the old gods has come, so, finally, one hurried off to report to Astinus.

"After waiting for some time, I was taken to his chamber

where he sits all day long and many times far into the night, recording the history of the world." Crysania paused, suddenly frightened at the intensity of Raistlin's gaze. It seemed he would snatch the words from her heart, if he could.

Looking away for a moment to compose herself, she continued, her own gaze now on the fire. "I entered the room, and he—he just sat there, writing, ignoring me. Then the Aesthetic who was with me announced my name, 'Crysania of the House of Tarinius,' as you told me to tell him. And then—"

She stopped, frowning slightly.

Raistlin stirred. "What?"

"Astinus looked up *then*," Crysania said in a puzzled tone, turning to face Raistlin. "He actually ceased writing and laid his pen down. And he said, '*You!*' in such a thundering voice that I was startled and the Aesthetic with me nearly fainted. But before I could say anything or ask what he meant or even how he knew me, he picked up his pen and—going to the words he had just written—crossed them out!"

"Crossed them out," Raistlin repeated thoughtfully, his eyes dark and abstracted. "Crossed them out," he murmured, sinking back down onto his pallet.

Seeing Raistlin absorbed in his thoughts, Crysania kept quiet until he looked up at her again.

"What did he do then?" the mage asked weakly.

"He wrote something down over the place where he had made the error, if that's what it was. Then he raised his gaze to mine again and I thought he was going to be angry. So did the Aesthetic, for I could feel him shaking. But Astinus was quite calm. He dismissed the Aesthetic and bade me sit down. Then he asked why I had come.

"I told him we were seeking the Portal. I added, as you instructed, that we had received information that led us to believe it was located in the Tower of High Sorcery at Palanthas, but that, upon investigation, we had discovered our information was wrong. The Portal was not there.

"He nodded, as if this did not surprise him. 'The Portal was moved when the Kingpriest attempted to take over the Tower. For safety's sake, of course. In time, it may return to the

Tower of High Sorcery at Palanthas, but it is not there now.'

" 'Where is it, then?' I asked.

"For long moments, he did not answer me. And then—" Here Crysania faltered and glanced over at Caramon fearfully, as if warning him to brace himself.

Seeing her look, Raistlin pushed himself up on the pallet. "Tell me!" he demanded harshly.

Crysania drew a deep breath. She would have looked away, but Raistlin caught hold of her wrist and, despite his weakness, held her so firmly, she found she could not break free of his deathlike grip.

"He—he said such information would cost you. Every man has his price, even he."

"Cost me!" Raistlin repeated inaudibly, his eyes burning.

Crysania tried unsuccessfully to free herself as his grasp tightened painfully.

"What *is* the cost?" Raistlin demanded.

"He said you would know!" Crysania gasped. "He said you had promised it to him, long ago."

Raistlin loosed her wrist. Crysania sank back away from him, rubbing her arm, avoiding Caramon's pitying gaze. Abruptly, the big man rose to his feet and stalked away. Ignoring him, ignoring Crysania, Raistlin sank back onto his frayed pillows, his face pale and drawn, his eyes suddenly dark and shadowed.

Crysania stood up and went to pour herself a glass of water. But her hand shook so she slopped most of it on the desk and was forced to set the pitcher down. Coming up behind her, Caramon poured the water and handed her the glass, a grave expression on his face.

Raising the glass to her lips, Crysania was suddenly aware of Caramon's gaze going to her wrist. Looking down, she saw the marks of Raistlin's hand upon her flesh. Setting the glass back down upon the desk, Crysania quickly drew her robe over her injured arm.

"He's doesn't mean to hurt me," she said softly in answer to Caramon's stern, unspoken glare. "His pain makes him impatient. What is our suffering, compared to his? Surely you of all people must understand that? He is so caught up in his greater vision that he doesn't know when he hurts others."

Turning away, she walked back to where Raistlin lay, staring unseeing into the fire.

"Oh, he knows all right," Caramon muttered to himself. "I'm just beginning to realize—he's known all along!"

Astinus of Palanthas, historian of Krynn, sat in his chamber, writing. The hour was late, very late, past Darkwatch, in fact. The Aesthetics had long ago closed and barred the doors to the Great Library. Few were admitted during the day, none at night. But bars and locks were nothing to the man who entered the Library and who now stood, a figure of darkness, before Astinus.

The historian did not glance up. "I was beginning to wonder where you were," he said, continuing to write.

"I have been unwell," the figure replied, its black robes rustling. As if reminded, the figure coughed softly.

"I trust you are feeling better?" Astinus still did not raise his head.

"I am returning to health slowly," the figure replied. "Many things tax my strength."

"Be seated, then," Astinus remarked, gesturing with the end of his quill pen to a chair, his gaze still upon his work.

The figure, a twisted smile on its face, padded over to the chair and sat down. There was silence within the chamber for many minutes, broken only by the scratching of Astinus's pen and the occasional cough of the black-robed intruder.

Finally, Astinus laid the pen down and lifted his gaze to meet that of his visitor. His visitor drew back the black hood from his face. Regarding him silently for long moments, Astinus nodded to himself.

"I do not know this face, Fistandantilus, but I know your eyes. There is something strange in them, however. I see the future in their depths. So you have become master of time, yet you do not return with power, as was foretold."

"My name is not Fistandantilus, Deathless One. It is Raistlin, and that is sufficient explanation for what has happened." Raistlin's smile vanished, his eyes narrowed. "But surely you knew that?" He gestured. "Surely the final battle between us is recorded—"

"I recorded the name as I recorded the battle," Astinus said coolly. "Would you care to see the entry . . . Fistandantilus?"

Raistlin frowned, his eyes glittered dangerously. But Astinus remained unperturbed. Leaning back in his chair, he studied the archmage calmly.

"Have you brought what I asked for?"

"I have," Raistlin replied bitterly. "Its making cost me days of pain and sapped my strength, else I would have come sooner."

And now, for the first time, a hint of emotion shone on Astinus's cold and ageless face. Eagerly, he leaned forward, his eyes shining as Raistlin slowly drew aside the folds of his black robes, revealing what seemed an empty, crystal globe hovering within his hollow chest cavity like a clear, crystalline heart.

Even Astinus could not repress a start at this sight, but it was apparently nothing more than an illusion, for, with a gesture, Raistlin sent the globe floating forward. With his other hand, he drew the black fabric back across his thin chest.

As the globe drifted near him, Astinus placed his hands upon it, caressing it lovingly. At his touch, the globe was filled with moonlight—silver, red, even the strange aura of the black moon was visible. Beneath the moons whirled vision after vision.

"You see time passing, even as we sit here," Raistlin said, his voice tinged with an unconscious pride. "And thus, Astinus, no longer will you have to rely on your unseen messengers from the planes beyond for your knowledge of what happens in the world around you. Your own eyes will be your messengers from this point forward."

"Yes! Yes!" Astinus breathed, the eyes that looked into the globe glimmering with tears, the hands that rested upon it shaking.

"And now my payment," Raistlin continued coldly. "Where is the Portal?"

Astinus looked up from the globe. "Can you not guess, Man

of the Future and the Past? You have read the histories. . . ."

Raistlin stared at Astinus without speaking, his face growing pale and chill until it might have been a deathmask.

"You are right. I *have* read the histories. So that is why Fistandantilus went to Zhaman," the archmage said finally.

Astinus nodded wordlessly.

"Zhaman, the magical fortress, located in the Plains of Dergoth . . . near Thorbardin—home of the mountain dwarves. And Zhaman is in land controlled by the mountain dwarves," Raistlin went on, his voice expressionless as though reading from a textbook. "And where, even now, their cousins, the hill dwarves, go—driven by the evil that has consumed the world since the Cataclysm to demand shelter within the ancient mountain home."

"The Portal is located—"

"—deep within the dungeons of Zhaman," Raistlin said bitterly. "Here, Fistandantilus fought the Great Dwarven War—"

"*Will fight* . . ." Astinus corrected.

"*Will fight,*" Raistlin murmured, "the war that will encompass his own doom!"

The mage fell silent. Then, abruptly, he rose to his feet and moved to Astinus's desk. Placing his hands upon the book, he turned it around to face him. Astinus observed him with cool, detached interest.

"You are right," Raistlin said, scanning the still-wet writing on the parchment. "I *am* from the future. I have read the *Chronicles*, as you penned them. Parts of them, at any rate. I remember reading this entry—one you *will* write there." He pointed to a blank space, then recited from memory. " 'As of this date, After Darkwatch falling 30, Fistandantilus brought me the Globe of Present Time Passing.' "

Astinus did not reply. Raistlin's hand began to shake. "You *will* write that?" he persisted, anger grating in his voice.

Astinus paused, then acquiesced with a slight shrug of his shoulders.

Raistlin sighed. "So I am doing nothing that *has not been done before!*" His hand clenched suddenly and, when he spoke again, his voice was tight with the effort it was taking to control himself.

"Lady Crysania came to you, several days ago. She said you were writing as she entered and that, after seeing her, you crossed something out. Show me what that was."

Astinus frowned.

"Show me!" Raistlin's voice cracked, it was almost a shriek.

Placing the globe to one side of the table, where it hovered near him, Astinus reluctantly removed his hands from its crystal surface. The light blinked out, the globe grew dark and empty. Reaching around behind him, the historian pulled out a great, leatherbound volume and, without hesitation, found the page requested.

He turned the book so that Raistlin could see.

The archmage read what had been written, then read the correction. When he stood up, his black robes whispering about him as he folded his hands within his sleeves, his face was deathly pale but calm.

"This alters time."

"This alters nothing," Astinus said coolly. "She came in his stead, that is all. An even exchange. Time flows on, undisturbed."

"And carries me with it?"

"Unless you have the power to change the course of rivers by tossing in a pebble," Astinus remarked wryly.

Raistlin looked at him and smiled, swiftly, briefly. Then he pointed at the globe. "Watch, Astinus," he whispered, "watch for the pebble! Farewell, Deathless One."

The room was empty, suddenly, except for Astinus. The historian sat silently, pondering. Then, turning the book back, he read once more what he had been writing when Crysania had entered.

On this date, Afterwatch rising 15, Denubis, a cleric of Paladine, arrived here, having been sent by the great archmage, Fistandantilus, to discover the whereabouts of the Portal. In return for my help, Fistandantilus will make what he has long promised me—the Globe of Present Time Passing. . . .

Denubis's name had been crossed out, Crysania's written in.

CHAPTER 7

"I'm dead," said Tasslehoff Burrfoot.

He waited expectantly a moment.

"I'm dead," he said again. "My, my. This must be the Afterlife."

Another moment passed.

"Well," said Tas, "one thing I can say for it—it certainly is *dark*."

Still nothing happened. Tas found his interest in being dead beginning to wane. He was, he discovered, lying on his back on something extremely hard and uncomfortable, cold and stony-feeling.

"Perhaps I'm laid out on a marble slab, like Huma's," he said, trying to drum up some enthusiasm. "Or a hero's crypt, like where we buried Sturm."

That thought entertained him a while, then, "Ouch!" He pressed his hand to his side, feeling a stabbing pain in his ribs and, at the same time, he noticed another pain in his head. He also came to realize that he was shivering, a sharp rock was poking him in the back, and he had a stiff neck.

"Well, I certainly didn't expect this," he snapped irritably. "I mean, by all accounts when you're dead, you're not supposed to feel anything." He said this quite loudly, in case someone was listening. "I said you're not supposed to feel anything!" he repeated pointedly when the pain did not go away.

"Drat!" muttered Tas. "Maybe it's some sort of mix-up. Maybe I'm dead and the word just hasn't gotten around my body yet. I certainly haven't gone all stiff, and I'm *sure* that's supposed to happen. So I'll just wait."

Squirming to get comfortable (first removing the rock from beneath his back), Tas folded his hands across his chest and stared up into the thick, impenetrable darkness. After a few minutes of this, he frowned.

"If this is being dead, it sure isn't all it's cracked up to be," he remarked sternly. "Now I'm not only dead, I'm bored, too. Well," he said after a few more moments of staring into the darkness, "I guess I can't do much about being dead, but I can do something about being bored. There's obviously been a mix-up. I'll just have to go talk to someone about this."

Sitting up, he started to swing his legs around to jump off the marble slab, only to discover that he was—apparently— lying on a stone floor. "How rude!" he commented indignantly. "Why not just dump me in someone's root cellar?"

Stumbling to his feet, he took a step forward and bumped into something hard and solid. "A rock," he said gloomily, running his hands over it. "Humpf! Flint dies and *he* gets a tree! *I* die and I get a rock. It's obvious someone's done something all wrong.

"Hey!—" he cried, groping around in the darkness. "Is anyone—Well, what do you know? I've still got my pouches! They let me bring everything with me, even the magical device. At least that was considerate. Still"—Tas's lips tightened with firm resolve—"someone better do something about this pain. I simply won't put up with it."

Investigating with his hands, since he couldn't see a thing, Tas ran his fingers curiously over the big rock. It seemed to be covered with carved images—runes, maybe? And *that* struck him as familiar. The shape of the huge rock, too, was odd.

"It isn't a rock after all! It's a table, seemingly," he said, puzzled. "A rock table carved with runes—" Then his memory returned. "I know!" he shouted triumphantly. "It's that big stone desk in the laboratory where I went to hunt for Raistlin and Caramon and Crysania, and found that they'd all gone and left me behind. I was standing there when the fiery mountain came down on top of me! In fact, that's the place where I died!"

He felt his neck. Yes, the iron collar was still there—the collar they had put on him when he was sold as a slave. Continuing to grope around in the darkness, Tas tripped over something. Reaching down, he cut himself on a something sharp.

"Caramon's sword!" he said, feeling the hilt. "I remember. I found it on the floor. And that means," said Tas with growing outrage, "that they didn't even *bury* me! They just left my body where it was! I'm in the basement of a ruined Temple." Brooding, he sucked his bleeding finger. A sudden thought occurred to him. "And I suppose they intend for me to *walk* to wherever it is I'm going in the Afterlife. They don't even provide transportation! This is really the last straw!"

He raised his voice to a shout. "Look!" he said, shaking his small fist. "I want to talk to whoever's in charge!"

But there was no sound.

"No light," Tas grumbled, falling over something else. "Stuck down in the bottom of a ruined temple—dead! Probably at the bottom of the Blood Sea of Istar. . . . Say," he said, pausing to think, "maybe I'll meet some sea elves, like Tanis told me about. But, no, I forgot"—he sighed—"I'm dead, and you can't, as far as I'm able to understand, meet people after you're dead. Unless you're an undead, like Lord Soth." The kender cheered up considerably. "I wonder how you get that job? I'll ask. Being a death knight must be *quite* exciting. But, first, I've got to find out where I'm supposed to be and why I'm not there!"

Picking himself up again, Tas managed to make his way to

what he figured was probably the front of the room beneath the Temple. He was thinking about the Blood Sea of Istar and wondering why there wasn't more water about when something else suddenly occurred to him.

"Oh, dear!" he muttered. "The Temple *didn't* go into the Blood Sea! It went to Neraka! I was in the Temple, in fact, when I defeated the Queen of Darkness."

Tas came to a doorway—he could tell by feeling the frame—and peered out into the darkness that was *so very* dark.

"Neraka, huh," he said, wondering if that was better or worse than being at the bottom of an ocean.

Cautiously, he took a step forward and felt something beneath his foot. Reaching down, his small hand closed over— "A torch! It must have been the one over the doorway. Now, somewhere in here, I've got a tinderbox—" Rummaging through several pouches, he came up with it at last.

"Strange," he said, glancing about the corridor as the torch flared to light. "It looks just like it did when I left it—all broken and crumbled after the earthquake. You'd think the Queen would have tidied up a bit by now. I don't remember it being in such a mess when I was in it in Neraka. I wonder which is the way out."

He looked back toward the stairs he had come down in his search for Crysania and Raistlin. Vivid memories of the walls cracking and columns falling came to his mind. "That's no good, that's for sure," he muttered, shaking his head. "Ouch, that hurts." He put his hand to his forehead. "But that was the only way out, I seem to recall." He sighed, feeling a bit low for a moment. But his kender cheerfulness soon surfaced. "There sure are a lot of cracks in the walls, though. Perhaps something's opened up."

Walking slowly, mindful of the pain in his head and his ribs, Tas stepped out into the corridor. He carefully checked out each wall without seeing anything promising until he reached the very end of the hall. Here he discovered a very large crack in the marble that, unlike the others, made an opening deeper than Tas's torchlight could illuminate.

No one but a kender could have squeezed into that crack, and, even for Tas, it was a tight fit, forcing him to rearrange all his pouches and slide through sideways.

"All I can say is—being dead is certainly a lot of bother!" he muttered, squeezing through the crack and ripping a hole in his blue leggings.

Matters didn't improve. One of his pouches got hung up on a rock, and he had to stop and tug at it until it was finally freed. Then the crack got so very narrow he wasn't at all certain he would make it. Taking off all his pouches, he held them and the torch over his head and, after holding his breath and tearing his shirt, he gave a final wiggle and managed to pop through. By this time, however, he was aching, hot, sweaty, and in a bad mood.

"I always wondered why people objected to dying," he said, wiping his face. "Now I know!"

Pausing to catch his breath and rearrange his pouches, the kender was immensely cheered to see light at the far end of the crack. Flashing his torch around, he discovered that the crack was getting wider, so—after a moment—he went on his way and soon reached the end—the source of the light.

Reaching the opening, Tas peered out, drew a deep breath and said, "Now *this* is more what I had in mind!"

The landscape was certainly like nothing he had ever seen before in his life. It was flat and barren, stretching on and on into a vast, empty sky that was lit with a strange glow, as if the sun had just set or a fire burned in the distance. But the whole sky was that strange color, even above him. And yet, for all the brightness, things around him were very dark. The land seemed to have been cut out of black paper and pasted down over the eerie-looking sky. And the sky itself was empty—no sun, no moons, no stars. Nothing.

Tas took a cautious step or two forward. The ground felt no different from any other ground, even though—as he walked on it—he noticed that it took on the same color as the sky. Looking up, he saw that, in the distance, it turned black again. After a few more steps, he stopped to look behind him at the ruins of the great Temple.

"Great Reorx's beard!" Tas gasped, nearly dropping his torch.

There was nothing behind him! Wherever it was he had come from was gone! The kender turned around in a complete circle. Nothing ahead of him, nothing behind him, nothing in any direction he looked.

Tasslehoff Burrfoot's heart sank right down to the bottom of his green shoes and stayed there, refusing to be comforted. This was, without a doubt, the most *boring* place he'd ever seen in his entire existence!

"This can't be the Afterlife," the kender said miserably. "This *can't* be right! There *must* be some mistake. Hey, wait a minute! I'm supposed to meet Flint here! Fizban said so and Fizban may have been a bit muddled about other things, but he didn't sound muddled about *that*!

"Let's see—how did that go? There was a big tree, a beautiful tree, and beneath it sat a grumbling, old dwarf, carving wood and—Hey! There's the tree! Now, where did that come from?"

The kender blinked in astonishment. Right ahead of him, where nothing had been just a moment before, he now saw a large tree.

"Not exactly my idea of a beautiful tree," Tas muttered, walking toward it, noticing—as he did so—that the ground had developed a curious habit of trying to slide out from under his feet. "But then, Fizban had odd taste and so, come to think of it, did Flint."

He drew nearer the tree, which was black—like everything else—and twisted and hunched over like a witch he'd seen once. It had no leaves on it. "That thing's been dead at least a hundred years!" Tas sniffed. "If Flint thinks *I'm* going to spend my Afterlife sitting under a dead tree with him, he's got another think coming. I—Hey, Flint!" The kender cried out, coming up to the tree and peering around. "Flint? Where are you? I—Oh, there you are," he said, seeing a short, bearded figure sitting on the ground on the other side of the tree. "Fizban told me I'd find you here. I'll bet you're surprised to see me! I—"

The kender came round the tree, then stopped short. "Say," he cried angrily, "you're not Flint! Who—Arack!"

Tas staggered backward as the dwarf who had been the Master of the Games in Istar suddenly turned his head and looked at him with such an evil grin on his twisted face that the kender felt his blood run cold—an unusual sensation; he couldn't remember ever experiencing it before. But before he had time to enjoy it, the dwarf leaped to his feet and, with a vicious snarl, rushed at the kender.

With a startled yelp, Tas swung his torch to keep Arack back, while with his other hand he fumbled for the small knife he wore in his belt. But, just as he pulled his knife out, Arack vanished. The tree vanished. Once again, Tas found himself standing smack in the center of nothing beneath that fire-lit sky.

"All right now," Tas said, a small quiver creeping into his voice, though he tried his best to hide it, "I don't think this is at all fun. It's miserable and horrible and, while Fizban didn't exactly promise the Afterlife would be one endless party, I'm *certain* he didn't have anything like this in mind!" The kender slowly turned around, keeping his knife drawn and his torch held out in front of him.

"I know I haven't been very religious," Tas added with a snuffle, looking out into the bleak landscape and trying to keep his feet on the weird ground, "but *I* thought I led a pretty good life. And I *did* defeat the Queen of Darkness. Of course, I had some help," he added, thinking that this might be a good time for honesty, "and I *am* a *personal* friend of Paladine and—"

"In the name of Her Dark Majesty," said a soft voice behind him, "what are *you* doing here?"

Tasslehoff sprang three feet into the air in alarm—a sure sign that the kender was completely unnerved—and whirled around. There—where there hadn't been anyone standing a moment before—stood a figure that reminded him very much of the cleric of Paladine, Elistan, only *this* figure wore black clerical robes instead of white and around its neck—instead of the medallion of Paladine—hung the medallion of the Five-Headed Dragon.

"Uh, pardon me, sir," stammered Tas, "but I'm not at all sure *what* I'm doing here. I'm not at all sure where *here* is, to be perfectly truthful, and—oh, by the way, my name's Tasslehoff Burrfoot." He extended his small hand politely. "What's yours?"

But the figure, ignoring the kender's hand, threw back its black cowl and took a step nearer. Tas was considerably startled to see long, iron-gray hair flow out from beneath the cowl, hair so long, in fact, that it would easily have touched the ground if it had not floated around the figure in a weird sort of way, as did the long, gray beard that suddenly seemed to sprout out of the skull-like face.

"S-say, that's quite . . . remarkable," Tas stuttered, his mouth dropping open. "How did you do that? And, I don't suppose you could tell me, but where did you say I was? You s-see—" The figure took another step nearer and, while Tas certainly wasn't afraid of him, or it, or whatever it was, the kender found that he didn't want it or him coming any closer for some reason. "I-I'm dead," Tas continued, trying to back up only to find that, for some unaccountable reason, something was blocking him, "and—by the way"—indignation got the better of fear—"are you in charge around here? Because I don't think this death business is being handled at all well! I hurt!" Tas said, glaring at the figure accusingly. "My head hurts and my ribs. And then I had to walk all this way, coming up out of the basement of the Temple—"

"The basement of the Temple!" The figure stopped now, only inches from Tasslehoff. Its gray hair floated as if stirred by a hot wind. Its eyes, Tas could see now, were the same red color as the sky, its face gray as ash.

"Yes!" Tas gulped. Besides everything else, the figure had a most horrible smell. "I—I was following Lady Crysania and she was following Raistlin and—"

"Raistlin!" The figure spoke the name in a voice that made Tas's hair literally stand up on his head. "Come with me!"

The figure's hand—a most peculiar-looking hand—closed over Tasslehoff's wrist. "Ow!" squeaked Tas, as pain shot through his arm. "You're hurting—"

But the figure paid no attention. Closing its eyes, as though lost in deep concentration, it gripped the kender tightly, and the ground around Tas suddenly began to shift and heave. The kender gasped in wonder as the landscape itself took on a rapid, fluid motion.

We're not moving, Tas realized in awe, the ground is!

"Uh," said Tas in a small voice, "where did you say I was?"

"You are in the Abyss," said the figure in a sepulchral tone.

"Oh, dear," Tas said sorrowfully, "I didn't think I was *that* bad." A tear trickled down his nose. "So this is the Abyss. I hope you don't mind me telling you that I'm frightfully disappointed in it. I always supposed the Abyss would be a fascinating place. But so far it isn't. Not in the least. It—it's awful boring and . . . ugly . . . and, I really don't mean to be rude, but there is a most peculiar smell." Sniffling, he wiped his nose on his sleeve, too unhappy even to reach for a pocket handkerchief. "Where did you say we were going?"

"You asked to see the person in charge," the figure said, and its skeletal hand closed over the medallion it wore around its neck.

The landscape changed. It was every city Tas had ever been in, it seemed, and yet none. It was familiar, yet he didn't recognize a thing. It was black, flat, and lifeless, yet teeming with life. He couldn't see or hear anything, yet all around him was sound and motion.

Tasslehoff stared at the figure beside him, at the shifting planes beyond and above and below him, and the kender was stricken dumb. For only the second time in his life (the first had been when he found Fizban alive when the old man was supposed to have been decently dead), Tas couldn't speak a word.

If every kender on the face of Krynn had been asked to name Places I'd Most Like To Visit, the plane of existence where the Queen of Darkness dwelled would have come in at least third on many lists.

But now, here was Tasslehoff Burrfoot, standing in the waiting room of the great and terrible Queen, standing in one of the most interesting places known to man or kender, and he had never felt unhappier in his life.

First, the room the gray-haired, black-robed cleric told him to stay in was completely empty. There weren't any tables with interesting little objects on them, there weren't any chairs (which was why he was standing). There weren't even any *walls*! In fact, the only way he knew he was in a room at all was that when the cleric told him to "stay in the waiting room," Tas suddenly *felt* he was in a room.

But, as far as he could see, he was standing in the middle of nothing. He wasn't even certain, at this point, which way was up or which way was down. Both looked alike—an eerie glowing, flame-like color.

He tried to comfort himself by telling himself over and over that he was going to meet the Dark Queen. He recalled stories Tanis told about meeting the Queen in the Temple at Neraka.

"I was surrounded by a great darkness," Tanis had said, and, even though it was months after the experience, his voice still trembled, "but it seemed more a darkness of my own mind than any actual physical presence. I couldn't breathe. Then the darkness lifted, and she spoke to me, though she said no word. I heard her in my mind. And I saw her in all her forms—the Five-Headed Dragon, the Dark Warrior, the Dark Temptress—for she was not completely in the world yet. She had not yet gained control."

Tas remembered Tanis shaking his head. "Still, her majesty and might were very great. She is, after all, a goddess—one of the creators of the world. Her dark eyes stared into my soul, and I couldn't help myself—I sank to my knees and worshipped her. . . ."

And now he, Tasslehoff Burrfoot, was going to meet the Queen as she was in her own plane of existence—strong and powerful. "Perhaps she'll appear as the Five-Headed Dragon." Tas said to cheer himself up. But even *that* wonderful prospect didn't help, though he had never seen a five-headed anything before, much less a dragon. It was as if all the spirit of adventure and curiosity were oozing out of the kender like blood dripping from a wound.

"I'll sing a bit," he said to himself, just to hear the sound of his own voice. "That generally raises my spirits."

He began to hum the first song that came into his head—a Hymn to the Dawn that Goldmoon had taught him.

> *Even the night must fail*
> *For light sleeps in the eyes*
> *And dark becomes dark on dark*
> *Until the darkness dies.*

> *Soon the eye resolves*
> *Complexities of night*
> *Into stillness, where the heart*
> *Falls into fabled light.*

Tas was just starting in on the second verse when he became aware, to his horror, that his song was echoing back to him—only the words were now twisted and terrible. . . .

> *Even the night must fail*
> *When light sleeps in the eyes,*
> *When dark becomes dark on dark*
> *And into darkness dies.*

> *Soon the eye dissolves,*
> *Perplexed by the teasing night,*
> *Into a stillness of the heart*
> *A fable of fallen light.*

"Stop it," cried Tas frantically into the eerie, burning silence that resounded with his song. "I didn't mean to say that! I—"

With startling suddenness, the black-robed cleric materialized in front of Tasslehoff, seeming to coalesce out of the bleak surroundings.

"Her Dark Majesty will see you now," the cleric said, and, before Tasslehoff could blink, he found himself in another place.

He knew it was another place, not because he had moved a step or even because this place was different from the last place, but that he *felt* he was someplace else. There was still the same weird glow, the same emptiness, except now he had the impression he wasn't alone.

The moment he realized this, he saw a black, smooth wooden chair appear—its back to him. Seated in it was a figure dressed in black, a hood pulled up over its head.

Thinking perhaps some mistake had been made and that the cleric had taken him to the wrong place, Tasslehoff—gripping his pouches nervously in his hand—walked cautiously around the chair to see the figure's face. Or perhaps the chair turned to around to see *his* face. The kender wasn't certain.

But, as the chair moved, the figure's face came into view.

Tasslehoff knew no mistake had been made.

It was not a Five-Headed Dragon he saw. It was not a huge warrior in black, burning armor. It was not even the Dark Temptress, who so haunted Raistlin's dreams. It was a woman dressed all in black, a tight-fitting hood pulled up over her hair, framing her face in a black oval. Her skin was white and smooth and ageless, her eyes large and dark. Her arms, encased in tight black cloth, rested on the arms of her chair, her white hands curved calmly around the ends of the armrests.

The expression on her face was not horrifying, nor terrifying, nor threatening, nor awe-inspiring; it was, in fact, not even an expression at all. Yet Tas was aware that she was scrutinizing him intensely, delving into his soul, studying parts of him that he wasn't even aware existed.

"I-I'm Tasslehoff Burrfoot, M-majesty," said the kender, reflexively stretching out his small hand. Too late, he realized his offense and started to withdraw his hand and bow, but then he felt the touch of five fingers in his palm. It was a brief touch, but Tas might have grabbed a handful of nettles. Five stinging branches of pain shot through his arm and bored into his heart, making him gasp.

But, as swiftly as they touched him, they were gone. He found himself standing very close to the lovely, pale woman, and so mild was the expression in her eyes that Tas might well

have doubted she was the cause of the pain, except that—
looking down at his palm—he saw a mark there, like a five-
pointed star.

Tell me your story.

Tas started. The woman's lips had not moved, but he heard
her speak. He realized, also, in sudden fright, that she probably knew more of his story than he did.

Sweating, clutching his pouches nervously, Tasslehoff
Burrfoot made history that day—at least as far as kender
storytelling was concerned. He told the entire story of his trip
to Istar in under five seconds. And every word was true.

"Par-Salian accidentally sent me back in time with my
friend Caramon. We were going to kill Fistandantilus only we
discovered it was Raistlin so we didn't. I was going to stop the
Cataclysm with a magical device, but Raistlin made me break
it. I followed a cleric named Lady Crysania down to a laboratory beneath the Temple of Istar to find Raistlin and make him
fix the device. The roof caved in and knocked me out. When I
woke up, they had all left me and the Cataclysm struck and
now I'm dead and I've been sent to the Abyss."

Tasslehoff drew a deep, quivering breath and mopped his
face with the end of his long topknot of hair. Then, realizing
his last comment had been less than complimentary, he hastened to add, "Not that I'm complaining, Your Majesty. I'm
certain whoever did this must have had quite a good reason.
After all, I did break a dragon orb, and I seem to recall once
someone said I took something that didn't belong to me, and
. . . and I wasn't as respectful of Flint as I should have been, I
guess, and once, for a joke, I hid Caramon's clothes while he
was taking a bath and he had to walk into Solace stark naked.
But"—Tas could not help a snuffle—"I always helped Fizban
find his hat!"

You are not dead, said the voice, *nor have you been sent here.
You are not, in fact, supposed to be here at all.*

At this startling revelation, Tasslehoff looked up directly
into the Queen's dark and shadowy eyes. "I'm not?" he
squeaked, feeling his voice go all queer. "Not dead?" Involuntarily, he put his hand to his head—which still ached. "So that

explains it! I just thought someone had botched things up—"

Kender are not allowed here, continued the voice.

"That doesn't surprise me," Tas said sadly, feeling much more himself since he wasn't dead. "There are quite a number of places on Krynn kender aren't allowed."

The voice might not have even heard him. *When you entered the laboratory of Fistandantilus, you were protected by the magical enchantment he had laid on the place. The rest of Istar was plunged far below the ground at the time the Cataclysm struck. But I was able to save the Temple of the Kingpriest. When I am ready, it will return to the world, as will I, myself.*

"But you won't win," said Tas before he thought. "I—I k-know," he stuttered as the dark-eyed gaze shot right through him. "I was th-there."

No, you were not there, for that has not happened yet. You see, kender, by disrupting Par-Salian's spell, you have made it possible to alter time. Fistandantilus—or Raistlin, as you know him—told you this. That was why he sent you to your death—or so he supposed. He did not want time altered: The Cataclysm was necessary to him so that he could bring this cleric of Paladine forward to a time when he will have the only true cleric in the land.

It seemed to Tasslehoff that he saw, for the first time, a flicker of dark amusement in the woman's shadowy eyes, and he shivered without understanding why.

How soon you will come to regret that decision, Fistandantilus, my ambitious friend. But it is too late. Poor, puny mortal. You have made a mistake—a costly mistake. You are locked in your own time loop. You rush forward to your own doom.

"I don't understand," cried Tas.

Yes, you do, said the voice calmly. *Your coming has shown me the future. You have given me the chance to change it. And, by destroying you, Fistandantilus has destroyed his only chance of breaking free. His body will perish again, as he perished long ago. Only this time, when his soul seeks another body to house it, I will stop him. Thus, the young mage, Raistlin, in the future, will take the Test in the Tower of High Sorcery, and he will die there. He will not live to thwart my plans. One by one, the others will die. For without Raistlin's help, Goldmoon will not find the blue crystal staff. Thus—the beginning of the end for the world.*

"No!" Tas whimpered, horror-stricken. "This—this can't be! I-I didn't mean to do this. I-I just wanted to-to go with Caramon on-on this adventure! He-he couldn't have made it alone. He *needed* me!"

The kender stared around frantically, seeking some escape. But, though there seemed everywhere to run, there was nowhere to hide. Dropping to his knees before the black-clothed woman, Tas stared up at her. "What have I done? What have I done?" he cried frantically.

You have done such that even Paladine might be tempted to turn his back upon you, kender.

"What will you do to me?" Tas sobbed wretchedly. "Where will I go?" He lifted a tear-streaked face. "I don't suppose you c-could send me back to Caramon? Or back to my own time?"

Your time no longer exists. As for sending you to Caramon, that is quite impossible, as you surely must understand. No, you will remain here, with me, so I may insure that nothing goes wrong.

"Here?" Tas gasped. "How long?"

The woman began to fade before his eyes, shimmering and finally vanishing into the nothingness around him. *Not long, I should imagine, kender. Not long at all. Or perhaps always. . . .*

"What do you—what does she mean?" Tas turned to face the gray-haired cleric, who had sprung up to fill the void left by Her Dark Majesty. "Not long or always?"

"Though not dead, you are—even now—dying. Your life-force is ebbing from you, as it must for any of the living who mistakenly venture down here and who have not the power to fight the evil that devours them from within. When you are dead, the gods will determine your fate."

"I see," said Tas, choking back a lump in his throat. He hung his head. "I deserve it, I suppose. Oh, Tanis, I'm sorry! I truly didn't mean to do it. . . ."

The cleric gripped his arm painfully. The surroundings changed, the ground shifted away beneath his feet. But Tasslehoff never noticed. His eyes filling with tears, he gave himself up to dark despair and hoped death would come quickly.

Chapter 8

ere you are," said the dark cleric.

"Where?" Tas asked listlessly, more out of force of habit than because he cared.

The cleric paused, then shrugged. "I suppose if there were a prison in the Abyss, you would be in it now."

Tas looked around. As usual, there was nothing there—simply a vast barren stretch of eerie emptiness. There were no walls, no cells, no barred windows, no doors, no locks, no jailer. And he knew, with deep certainty, that—this time—there was no escape.

"Am I supposed to just stand here until I drop?" Tas asked in a small voice. "I mean, couldn't I at least have a bed and a-a stool—oh!"

As he spoke, a bed materialized before his eyes, as did a three-legged, wooden stool. But even these familiar objects appeared so horrifying, sitting in the middle of nothing, that Tas could not bear to look at them long.

"Th-thank you," he stammered, walking over to sit down

upon the stool with a sigh. "What about food and water?"

He waited a moment, to see if these, too, would appear. But they didn't. The cleric shook his head, his gray hair forming a swirling cloud around him.

"No, the needs of your mortal body will be cared for while you are here. You will feel no hunger or thirst. I have even healed your wounds."

Tas suddenly noticed that his ribs had stopped hurting and the pain in his head was gone. The iron collar had vanished from around his neck.

"There is no need for your thanks," the cleric continued, seeing Tas open his mouth. "We do this so that you will not interrupt us in our work. And, so, farewell—"

The dark cleric raised his hands, obviously preparing to depart.

"Wait!" Tas cried, leaping up from his stool and clutching at the dark, flowing robes. "Won't I see you again? Don't leave me alone!" But he might as well have tried to grab smoke. The flowing robes slipped through his fingers, and the dark cleric disappeared.

"When you are dead, we will return your body to lands above and see that your soul speeds on its way . . . or stays here, as you may be judged. Until that time, we have no more need of contact with you."

"I'm alone!" Tas said, glancing around his bleak surroundings in despair. "Truly alone . . . alone until I die. . . . Which won't be long," he added sadly. Walking over, he sat down upon his stool. "I might as well die as fast as possible and get it over with. At least I'll probably go someplace different—I hope." He looked up into the empty vastness.

"Fizban," Tas said softly, "you probably can't hear me from clear down here. And I don't suppose there's anything you could do for me anyway, but I *did* want to tell you, before I die, that I didn't *mean* to cause all this trouble, disrupting Par-Salian's spell and going back in time when I wasn't supposed to go and all that."

Heaving a sigh, Tas pressed his small hands together, his lower lip quivering. "Maybe that doesn't count for much . . .

and I suppose that—if I must be honest—part of me went along with Caramon just because"—he swallowed the tears that were beginning to trickle down his nose—"just because it sounded like so much fun! But, truly, part of me went with him because he had no business going back into the past alone! He was fuddled because of the dwarf spirits, you see. And I promised Tika I'd look after him. Oh, Fizban! If there were just some way out of this mess, I'd try my best to straighten everything out. Honestly—"

"Hullothere."

"What?" Tas nearly fell off his stool. Whirling around, half thinking he might see Fizban, he saw, instead, only a short figure—shorter even than himself—dressed in brown britches, a gray tunic, and a brown leather apron.

"Isaidhullothere," repeated the voice, rather irritably.

"Oh, he-hello," Tas stammered, staring at the figure. It certainly didn't *look* like a dark cleric, at least Tas had never heard of any that wore brown leather aprons. But, he supposed, there could always be exceptions especially considering the fact that brown leather aprons are such useful things. Still, this person bore a strong resemblance to someone he knew, if only he could remember. . . .

"Gnosh!" Tas exclaimed suddenly, snapping his fingers. "You're a gnome! Uh, pardon me for asking such a personal question"—the kender flushed in embarrassment—"but are you—uh—dead?"

"Areyou?" the gnome asked, eyeing the kender suspiciously.

"No," said Tas, rather indignantly.

"WellI'mnoteither!" snapped the gnome.

"Uh, could you slow down a bit?" Tas suggested. "I know your people talk rapidly, but it makes it hard for us to understand, sometimes—"

"I said I'm not either!" the gnome shouted loudly.

"Thank you," Tas said politely. "And I'm not hard of hearing. You can talk in a normal tone of voice—er, talk *slowly* in a normal tone of voice," the kender hurried to add, seeing the gnome draw in a breath.

"What's . . . your . . . name?" the gnome asked, speaking at a snail's pace.

"Tasslehoff . . . Burrfoot." The kender extended a small hand, which the gnome took and shook heartily. "What's . . . yours? I mean—what's yours? Oh, no! I didn't mean—"

But it was too late. The gnome was off.

"Gnimshmarigongalesefrahootsputhturandotsamanella—"

"The short form!" Tas cried when the gnome stopped for breath.

"Oh." The gnome appeared downcast. "Gnimsh."

"Thank you. Nice meeting you—uh—Gnimsh," Tas said, sighing in relief. He had completely forgotten that every gnome's name provides the unwary listener with a complete account of the gnome's family's life history, beginning with his earliest known (or imagined) ancestor.

"Nice meeting you, Burrfoot," the gnome said, and they shook hands again.

"Will you be seated?" Tas said, sitting down on the bed and gesturing politely toward the stool. But Gnimsh gave the stool a scathing glance and sat down in a chair that materialized right beneath him. Tas gasped at the sight. It was truly a remarkable chair—it had a footrest that went up and down and rockers on the bottom that let the chair rock back and forth and it even tilted completely backward, letting the person sitting in it lie down if so inclined.

Unfortunately, as Gnimsh sat down, the chair tilted too far backward, flipping the gnome out on his head. Grumbling, he climbed back in it and pressed a lever. This time, the footrest flew up, striking him in the nose. At the same time, the back came forward and, before long, Tas had to help rescue Gnimsh from the chair, which appeared to be eating him.

"Drat," said the gnome and, with a wave of his hand, he sent the chair back to wherever it had come from, and sat down, disconsolately, on Tasslehoff's stool.

Having visited gnomes and seen their inventions before, Tasslehoff mumbled what was proper. "Quite interesting . . . truly an advanced design in chairs. . . ."

"No, it isn't," Gnimsh snapped, much to Tas's amazement. "It's a rotten design. Belonged to my wife's first cousin. I should have known better than to think of it. But"—he sighed—"sometimes I get homesick."

"I know," Tas said, swallowing a sudden lump in his throat. "If-if you don't mind my asking, what are you doing here, if you're—uh—not dead?"

"Will you tell me what *you're* doing here?" Gnimsh countered.

"Of course," said Tas, then he had a sudden thought. Glancing around warily, he leaned forward. "No one *minds*, do they?" he asked in a whisper. "That we're talking, I mean? Maybe we're not supposed to—"

"Oh, *they* don't care," Gnimsh said scornfully. "As long as we leave them alone, we're free to go around anywhere. Of course," he added, "anywhere looks about the same as here, so there's not much point."

"I see," Tas said with interest. "How do you travel?"

"With your mind. Haven't you figured that out yet? No, probably not." The gnome snorted. "Kender were never noted for their brains."

"Gnomes and kender *are* related," Tas pointed out in miffed tones.

"So I've heard," Gnimsh replied skeptically, obviously not believing any of it.

Tasslehoff decided, in the interests of maintaining peace, to change the subject. "So, if I want to go somewhere, I just think of that place and I'm there?"

"Within limits, of course," Gnimsh said. "You can't, for example, enter any of the holy precincts where the dark clerics go—"

"Oh." Tas sighed, that having been right up at the top of his list of tourist attractions. Then he cheered up again. "You made that chair come out of nothing and, come to think of it, *I* made this bed and this stool. If I think of something, will it just appear?"

"Try it," Gnimsh suggested.

Tas thought of something.

Gnimsh snorted as a hatrack appeared at the end of the bed. "Now *that's* handy."

"I was just practicing," Tas said in hurt tones.

"You better watch it," the gnome said, seeing Tas's face light up. "Sometimes things appear, but not quite the way you expected."

"Yeah." Tas suddenly remembered the tree and the dwarf. He shivered. "I guess you're right. Well, at least we have each other. Someone to talk to. You can't imagine how *boring* it was." The kender settled back on the bed, first imagining—with caution—a pillow. "Well, go ahead. Tell me your story."

"You start." Gnimsh glanced at Tas out of the corner of his eye.

"No, you're my guest."

"I insist."

"*I* insist."

"You. After all, I've been here longer."

"How do you know?"

"I just do. . . . Go on."

"But—" Tas suddenly saw this was getting nowhere, and though they apparently had all eternity, he didn't plan on spending it arguing with a gnome. Besides, there was no real reason why he *shouldn't* tell his story. He enjoyed telling stories, anyway. So, leaning back comfortably, he told his tale. Gnimsh listened with interest, though he did rather irritate Tas by constantly interrupting and telling him to "get on with it," just at the most exciting parts.

Finally, Tas came to his conclusion. "And so here I am. Now yours," he said, glad to pause for breath.

"Well," Gnimsh said hesitantly, looking around darkly as though afraid someone might be listening, "it all began years and years ago with my family's Life Quest. You do know"—he glared at Tas—"what a Life Quest is?"

"Sure," said Tas glibly. "My friend Gnosh had a Life Quest. Only his was dragon orbs. Each gnome has assigned to him a particular project that he must complete successfully or never get into the Afterlife." Tas had a sudden thought. "That's not why you're here, is it?"

"No." The gnome shook his wispy-haired head. "My family's Life Quest was developing an invention that could take us from one dimensional plane of existence to another. And"—Gnimsh heaved a sigh—"mine worked."

"It worked?" Tas said, sitting up in astonishment.

"Perfectly," Gnimsh answered with increasing despondency.

Tasslehoff was stunned. He'd never before heard of such a thing—a gnomish invention that worked . . . and perfectly, too!

Gnimsh glanced at him. "Oh, I know what you're thinking," he said. "I'm a failure. You don't know the half of it. You see—*all* of my inventions work. Every one."

Gnimsh put his head in his hands.

"How—how does that make you a failure?" Tas asked, confused.

Gnimsh raised his head, staring at him. "Well, what good is inventing something if it works? Where's the challenge? The need for creativity? For forward thinking? What would become of progress? You know," he said with deepening gloom, "that if I hadn't come here, they were getting ready to exile me. They said I was a distinct threat to society. I set scientific exploration back a hundred years."

Gnimsh's head drooped. "That's why I don't mind being here. Like you, I deserve it. It's where I'm likely to wind up anyway."

"Where is your device?" Tas asked in sudden excitement.

"Oh, *they* took it away, of course," Gnimsh answered, waving his hand.

"Well!"—the kender thought—"can't you imagine one? You imagined up that chair?"

"And you saw what *it* did!" Gnimsh replied. "Likely I'd end up with my father's invention. It took him to another plane of existence, all right. The Committee on Exploding Devices is studying it now, in fact, or at least they were when I got stuck here. What are you trying to do? Find a way out of the Abyss?"

"I have to," Tas said resolutely. "The Queen of Darkness will win the war, otherwise, and it will all be my fault. Plus,

I've got some friends who are in terrible danger. Well, one of them isn't exactly a friend, but he *is* an interesting person and, while he *did* try to kill me by making me break the magical device, I'm certain it was nothing personal. He had a good reason. . . ."

Tas stopped.

"That's it!" he said, springing up off the bed. "That's it!" he cried in such excitement that a whole forest of hatracks appeared around the bed, much to the gnome's alarm.

Gnimsh slid off his stool, eyeing Tas warily. "What's it?" he demanded, bumping into a hatrack.

"Look!" Tas said, fumbling with his pouches. He opened one, then another. "Here it is!" he said, holding a pouch open to show Gnimsh. But, just as the gnome was peering into it, Tas suddenly slammed it shut. "Wait!"

"What?" Gnimsh asked, startled.

"Are *they* watching?" Tas asked breathlessly. "Will they know?"

"Know what?"

"Just—will they know?"

"No, I don't suppose so," Gnimsh answered hesitantly. "I can't say for sure, since I don't know what it is they're not supposed to know. But I do know that they're all pretty busy, right now, from what I can tell. Waking up evil dragons and that sort of thing. Takes a lot of work."

"Good," Tas said grimly, sitting on the bed. "Now, look at this." He opened his pouch and dumped out the contents. "What does that remind you of?"

"The year my mother invented the device designed to wash dishes," the gnome said. "The kitchen was knee-deep in broken crockery. We had to—"

"No!" Tas snapped irritably. "Look, hold this piece next to this one and—"

"My dimensional traveling device!" Gnimsh gasped. "You're right! It *did* look something like this. Mine didn't have all these gewgaw jewels, but. . . . No, look. You've got it all wrong. I think that goes here, not there. Yes. See? And then this chain hooks on here and wraps around like oo. No, that's not quite the way. It must go . . . Wait, I see. This has to fit in there first." Sitting down on the bed, Gnimsh picked up one of the jewels and stuck it into place. "Now, I need another one of these red gizmos." He began sorting through the jewels. "What did you do to this thing, anyway?" he muttered. "Put it into a meat grinder?"

But the gnome, absorbed in his task, completely ignored Tas's answer. The kender, meanwhile, took advantage of the opportunity to tell his story again. Perching on the stool, Tas talked blissfully and without interruption while, totally forgetting the kender's existence, Gnimsh began to arrange the myriad jewels and little gold and silver things and chains, stacking them into neat piles.

All the while Tas was talking, though, he was watching Gnimsh, hope filling his heart. Of course, he thought with a pang, he *had* prayed to Fizban, and there was every possibility that, if Gnimsh got this device working, it might whisk them onto a moon or turn them both into chickens or something. But, Tas decided, he'd just have to take that chance. After all, he'd promised he'd try to straighten things out, and though finding a failed gnome wasn't quite what he'd had in mind, it was better than sitting around, waiting to die.

Gnimsh, meanwhile, had imagined up a piece of slate and a bit of chalk and was sketching diagrams, muttering, "Slide jewel A into golden gizmo B—"

wretched place, my brother," Raistlin remarked softly as he slowly and stiffly dismounted from his horse.

"We've stayed in worse," Caramon commented, helping Lady Crysania from her mount. "It's warm and dry inside, which makes it one hundred times better than out here. Besides," he added gruffly, glancing at his brother, who had collapsed against the side of his horse, coughing and shivering, "we none of us can ride farther without rest. I'll see to the horses. You two go on in."

Crysania, huddled in her sodden cloak, stood in the foot-deep mud and stared dully at the inn. It was, as Raistlin said, a wretched place.

What the name might have been, no one knew, for no sign hung above the door. The only thing, in fact, that marked it as an inn at all was a crudely lettered slate stuck in the broken front window that read, "WayFarrers WelCum". The stone building itself was old and sturdily constructed. But the roof was falling in, though attempts had been made, here and there, to patch it with thatch. One window was broken. An old felt hat covered it, supposedly to keep out the rain. The yard was nothing but mud and a few bedraggled weeds.

Raistlin had gone ahead. Now he stood in the open doorway, looking back at Crysania. Light glowed from inside, and the smell of wood smoke promised a fire. As Raistlin's face hardened into an expression of impatience, a gust of wind blew back the hood of Crysania's cloak, driving the slashing rain into her face. With a sigh, she slogged through the mud to reach the front door.

"Welcome, master. Welcome, missus."

Crysania started at the voice that came from beside her— she had not seen anyone when she entered. Turning, she saw an ill-favored man huddling in the shadows behind the door, just as it slammed shut.

"A raw day, master," the man said, rubbing his hands together in a servile manner. That, a grease-stained apron, and a torn rag thrown over his arm marked him as the innkeeper. Glancing around the filthy, shabby inn, Crysania thought it appropriate enough. The man drew nearer to them, still rubbing his hands, until he was so close to Crysania that she could smell the foul odor of his beery breath. Covering her face with her cloak, she drew away from him. He seemed to grin at this, a drunken grin that might have appeared foolish had it not been for the cunning expression in his squinty eyes.

Looking at him, Crysania felt for a moment that she would almost prefer to go back out into the storm. But Raistlin, with only a sharp, penetrating glance at the innkeeper, said coldly, "A table near the fire."

"Aye, master, aye. A table near the fire, aye. Good on such a wicked day as this be. Come, master, missus, this way." Bobbing and bowing in a fawning manner that was, once again, belied by the look in his eyes, the man shuffled sideways across the floor, never taking his gaze from them, herding them toward a dirty table.

"A wizard be ye, master?" asked the innkeeper, reaching out a hand to touch Raistlin's black robes but withdrawing it immediately at the mage's piercing glance. "One of the Black 'uns too. It's been a long while since we've seen the like, that it has," he continued. Raistlin did not answer. Overcome by another fit of coughing, he leaned heavily upon his staff. Crysania helped him to a chair near the fire. Sinking down into it, he huddled gratefully toward the warmth.

"Hot water," ordered Crysania, untying her wet cloak.

"What be the matter with 'im?" the innkeeper asked suspiciously, drawing back. "Not the burning fever, is it? Cause if it is, ye can go back out—"

"No," Crysania snapped, throwing off her cloak. "His illness is his own, of no harm to others." Leaning down near the mage, she glanced back up at the innkeeper. "I asked for hot water," she said peremptorily.

"Aye." His lip curled. He no longer rubbed his hands but shoved them beneath the greasy apron before he shuffled off.

Her disgust lost in her concern for Raistlin, Crysania forgot the innkeeper as she tried to make the mage more comfortable. She unfastened his traveling cloak and helped him remove it then spread it to dry before the fire. Searching the inn's common room, she discovered several shabby chair cushions and, trying to ignore the dirt that covered them, brought them back to arrange around Raistlin so that he could lean back and breathe more easily.

Kneeling beside him to help remove his wet boots, she felt a hand touch her hair.

"Thank you," Raistlin whispered, as she looked up.

Crysania flushed with pleasure. His brown eyes seemed warmer than the fire, and his hand brushed back the wet hair from her face with a gentle touch. She could not speak or move but remained, kneeling at his side, held fast by his gaze.

"Be you his woman?"

The innkeeper's harsh voice, coming from behind her, made Crysania start. She had neither seen him approach nor heard his shuffling step. Rising to her feet, unable to look at Raistlin, she turned abruptly to face the fire, saying nothing.

"She is a lady of one of the royal houses of Palanthas," said a deep voice from the doorway. "And I'll thank you to speak of her with respect, innkeep."

"Aye, master, aye," muttered the innkeeper, seemingly daunted by Caramon's massive girth as the big man came inside, bringing in a gust of wind and rain with him. "I'm sure I intended no disrespect and I hopes none was taken."

Crysania did not answer. Half-turning, she said in a muffled voice, "Here, bring that water to the table."

As Caramon shut the door and came over to join them, Raistlin drew forth the pouch that contained the herbal concoction for his potion. Tossing it onto the table, he directed Crysania, with a gesture, to prepare his drink. Then he sank back among the cushions, his breath wheezing, gazing into the flames. Conscious of Caramon's troubled gaze upon her, Crysania kept her gaze on the potion she was preparing.

"The horses are fed and watered. We've ridden them easy enough, so they'll be able to go on after an hour's rest. I want to reach Solanthus before nightfall," Caramon said after a moment's uncomfortable silence. He spread his cloak before the fire. The steam rose from it in clouds. "Have you ordered food?" he asked Crysania abruptly.

"No, just the—the hot water," she murmured, handing Raistlin his drink.

"Innkeep, wine for the lady and the mage, water for me, and whatever you have to eat," Caramon said, sitting down near the fire on the opposite side of the table from his brother. After weeks of traveling this barren land toward the Plains of Dergoth, they had all learned that one ate what was on hand at these roadside inns, if—indeed—there was anything at all.

"This is only the beginning of the fall storms," Caramon said quietly to his brother as the innkeeper slouched out of the room again. "They will get worse the farther south we travel. Are you resolved on this course of action? It could be the death of you."

"What do you mean by that?" Raistlin's voice cracked. Starting up, he sloshed some of the hot potion from the cup.

"Nothing, Raistlin," Caramon said, taken aback by his brother's piercing stare. "Just—just . . . your cough. It's always worse in the damp."

Staring sharply at his twin, and seeing that, apparently,

Caramon meant no more than he had said, Raistlin leaned back into the cushions once more. "Yes, I am resolved upon this course of action. So should you be too, my brother. For it is the only way you will ever see your precious home again."

"A lot of good it will do me if you die on the way," Caramon growled.

Crysania looked at Caramon in shock, but Raistlin only smiled bitterly. "Your concern touches me, brother. But do not fear for my health. My strength will be sufficient to get there and cast the final spell, if I do not tax myself overly in the meantime."

"It seems you have someone who will take care you do not do that," Caramon replied gravely, his gaze on Crysania.

She flushed again and would have made some remark, but the innkeeper returned. Standing beside them, a kettle of some steaming substance in one hand and a cracked pitcher in the other, he regarded them warily.

"Pardon my asking, masters," he whined, "but I'll see the color of yer money first. Times being what they are—"

"Here," said Caramon, taking a coin from his purse and tossing it upon the table. "Will that suit?"

"Aye, masters, aye." The innkeeper's eyes shone nearly as brightly as the silver piece. Setting down the kettle and pitcher, slopping stew onto the table, he grabbed the coin greedily, watching the mage all the while as though fearful he might make it disappear.

Thrusting the coin into his pocket, the innkeeper shuffled behind the slovenly bar and returned with three bowls, three horn spoons, and three mugs. These he also slapped down on the table, then stood back, his hands once more rubbing together. Crysania picked up the bowls and, staring at them in disgust, immediately began to wash them in the remaining hot water.

"Will there be anything else, masters, missus?" the innkeeper asked in such fawning tones that Caramon grimaced.

"Do you have bread and cheese?"

"Yes, master."

"Wrap some up then, in a basket."

"Ye'll be . . . traveling on, will ye?" the innkeeper asked.

Placing the bowls back upon the table, Crysania looked up, aware of a subtle change in the man's voice. She glanced at Caramon to see if he noticed, but the big man was stirring the stew, sniffing at it hungrily. Raistlin, seeming not to have heard, stared fixedly into the fire, his hands clasping the empty mug limply.

"We're certainly not spending the night here," Caramon said, ladling stew into the bowls.

"Ye'll find no better lodgings in—Where did you say you was headed?" the innkeeper asked.

"It's no concern of yours," Crysania replied coldly. Taking a full bowl of stew, she brought it to Raistlin. But the mage, after one look at the thick, grease-covered substance, waved it away. Hungry as she was, Crysania could only choke down a few mouthfuls of the mixture. Shoving the bowl aside, she wrapped herself in her still-damp cloak and curled up in her chair, closing her eyes and trying not to think that in an hour she'd be back on her horse, riding through the bleak, storm-ridden land once again.

Raistlin had already fallen asleep. The only sounds made were by Caramon, eating the stew with the appetite of an old campaigner, and by the innkeeper, returning to the kitchen to fix the basket as ordered.

Within an hour, Caramon brought the horses round from the stable—three riding horses and one pack horse, heavily laden, its burden covered with a blanket and secured with strong ropes. Helping his brother and Lady Crysania to mount, and seeing them both settled wearily into their saddles, Caramon mounted his own gigantic steed. The innkeeper stood out in the rain, bareheaded, holding the basket. He handed it up to Caramon, grinning and bobbing as the rain soaked through his clothes.

With curt thanks, and tossing another coin that landed in the mud at the innkeeper's feet, Caramon grabbed the reins of the pack horse and started off. Crysania and Raistlin followed, heavily muffled in their cloaks against the downpour.

The innkeeper, apparently oblivious to the rain, picked up the coin and stood watching them ride away. Two figures emerged from the confines of the stables, joining him.

Tossing the coin in the air, the innkeeper glanced at them. "Tell 'im—they travel the Solanthus road."

They fell easy victims to the ambush.

Riding in the failing light of the dismal day, beneath thick trees whose branches dripped water monotonously and whose fallen leaves obscured even the sound of their own horses' footfalls, each was lost in his or her own gloomy thoughts. None heard the galloping of hooves or the ring of bright steel until it was too late.

Before they knew what was happening, dark shapes dropped out of the trees like huge, terrifying birds, smothering them with their black-cloaked wings. It was all done quietly, skillfully.

One clambered up behind Raistlin, knocking the mage unconscious before he could turn. Another dropped from a branch beside Crysania, clasping his hand over her mouth and holding the point of his dagger to her throat. But it took three of them to drag Caramon from his horse and wrestle the big man to the ground, and, when the struggle was finally over, one of the robbers did not get to his feet. Nor would he, ever again, it seemed. He lay quite still in the mud, his head facing the wrong direction.

"Neck's broke," reported one of the robbers to a figure who came up—after all was over—to survey the handiwork.

"Neat job of it, too," the robber commented coolly, eyeing Caramon, who was being held in the grip of four men, his big arms bound with bowstrings. A deep cut on his head bled freely, the rainwater washing the blood down his face. Shaking his head, trying to clear it, Caramon continued to struggle.

The leader, noticing the bulging muscles that strained the strong, wet bowstrings until several of his guards looked at them apprehensively, shook his head in admiration.

Caramon, finally clearing the fuzziness from his head and shaking the blood and rainwater from his eyes, glanced around. At least twenty or thirty heavily armed men stood around them. Looking up at their leader, Caramon breathed a muttered oath. This man was easily the biggest human Caramon had ever seen!

His thoughts went instantly back to Raag and the gladiator arena in Istar. "Part ogre," he said to himself, spitting out a tooth that had been knocked loose in the fight. Remembering vividly the huge ogre who had helped Arack train the gladiators for the Games, Caramon saw that, though obviously human, this man had a yellow, ogre-ish cast to his skin and the same, flat-nosed face. He was larger than most humans, too— towering head and shoulders over the tall Caramon—with arms like tree trunks. But he walked with an odd gait, Caramon noticed, and he wore a long cloak that dragged the ground, hiding his feet.

Having been taught in the arena to size up an enemy and search out every weakness, Caramon watched the man closely. When the wind blew aside the thick fur cloak that covered him, Caramon saw in astonishment that the man had only one leg. The other was a steel pegleg.

Noticing Caramon's glance at his pegleg, the half-ogre grinned broadly and took a step nearer the big man. Reaching out a huge hand, the robber patted Caramon tenderly on the cheek.

"I admire a man who puts up a good fight," he said in a soft voice. Then, with startling swiftness, he doubled his hand into a fist, drew back his arm, and slugged Caramon in the jaw. The force of the blow knocked the big warrior backward, nearly causing those who held him to fall over, too. "But you'll pay for the death of my man."

Gathering his long, fur cloak around him, the half-ogre stumped over to where Crysania stood, held securely in the arms of one of the robbers. Her captor still had his hand over her mouth, and, though her face was pale, her eyes were dark and filled with anger.

"Isn't this nice," the half-ogre said softly. "A present, and it's not even Yule." His laughter boomed through the trees. Reaching out, he caught hold of her cloak and ripped it from her neck. His gaze flicked rapidly over her curving figure, well revealed as the rain soaked instantly through her white robes. His smile widened and his eyes glinted. He reached out a huge hand.

Crysania shrank away from him, but the half-ogre grabbed hold of her easily, laughing.

"Why, what's this bauble you wear, sweet one?" he asked, his gaze going to the medallion of Paladine she wore around her slender neck. "I find it . . . unbecoming. Pure platinum, it is!" He whistled. "Best let me keep it for you, dear. I fear that, in the pleasures of our passion, it might get lost—"

Caramon had recovered enough by now to see the half-ogre grasp the medallion in his hand. There was a glint of grim amusement in Crysania's eyes, though she shuddered visibly at the man's touch. A flash of pure, white light crackled through the driving rain. The half-ogre clutched at his hand. Drawing it back with a snarl of pain, he released Crysania.

There was a muttering among the men standing watching. The man holding Crysania suddenly loosened his grip and she jerked free, glaring at him angrily and pulling her cloak back around her.

The half-ogre raised his hand, his face twisted in rage. Caramon feared he would strike Crysania, when, at that moment, one of the man yelled out.

"The wizard, he's comin' to!"

The half-ogre's eyes were still on Crysania, but he lowered his hand. Then, he smiled. "Well, witch, you have won the first round, it seems." He glanced back at Caramon. "I enjoy contests—both in fighting and in love. This promises to be a night of amusement, all around."

Giving a gesture, he ordered the man who had been holding Crysania to take her in hand again, and the man did, though Caramon noticed it was with extreme reluctance. The half-ogre walked over to where Raistlin lay upon the ground, groaning in pain.

"Of all of them, the wizard's the most dangerous. Bind his hands behind his back and gag him," ordered the robber in a grating voice. "If he so much as croaks, cut out his tongue.

That'll end his spellcasting days for good."

"Why don't we just kill him now?" one of the men growled.

"Go ahead, Brack," said the half-ogre pleasantly, turning swiftly to regard the man who had spoken. "Take your knife and slit his throat."

"Not with *my* hands," the man muttered, backing up a step.

"No? You'd rather *I* was the one cursed for murdering a Black Robe?" the leader continued, still in the same, pleasant tone. "You'd enjoy seeing *my* sword hand wither and drop off?"

"I—I didn't mean that, of course, Steeltoe. I—I wasn't thinking, that's all."

"Then start thinking. He can't harm us now. Look at him," Steeltoe gestured to Raistlin. The mage lay on his back, his hands bound in front of him. His jaws had been forced open and a gag tied around his mouth. However, his eyes gleamed from the shadows of his hood in a baleful rage, and his hands clenched in such impotent fury that more than one of the strong men standing about wondered uneasily if such measures were adequate.

Perhaps feeling something of this himself, Steeltoe limped over to where Raistlin lay staring up at him with bitter hatred. As he stopped near the mage, a smile creased the half-ogre's yellowish face, and he suddenly slammed the steel toe of his pegleg against the side of Raistlin's head. The mage went limp. Crysania cried out in alarm, but her captor held her fast. Even Caramon was amazed to feel swift, sharp pain contract his heart as he saw his brother's form lying huddled in the mud.

"That should keep him quiet for a while. When we reach camp, we'll blindfold him and take him for a walk up on the Rock. If he slips and falls over the cliff, well, that's the way of things, isn't it, men? His blood won't be on our hands."

There was some scattered laughter, but Caramon saw more than a few glance uneasily at each other, shaking their heads.

Steeltoe turned away from Raistlin to examine with gleaming eyes the heavily laden pack horse. "We've made a rich haul this day, men," he said in satisfaction. Stumping back around, he came to where Crysania stood, pinned in the arms of her somewhat nervous captor.

"A rich haul, indeed," he murmured. One huge hand grasped Crysania's chin roughly. Bending down, he pressed his lips against hers in a brutal kiss. Trapped in the arms of her captor, Crysania could do nothing. She did not struggle; perhaps some inner sense told her this was precisely what the man wanted. She stood straight, her body rigid. But Caramon saw her hands clench and, when Steeltoe released her, she could not help but avert her face, her dark hair falling across her cheek.

"You know my policy, men," Steeltoe said, fondling her hair coarsely, "share the spoils among us—after I've taken my cut, of course."

There was more laughter at this and, here and there, some scattered cheering. Caramon had no doubt of the man's meaning and he guessed, from the few comments he heard, that this wouldn't be the first time "spoils" had been "shared."

But there were some young faces who frowned, glancing at each other in disquiet, shaking their heads. And there were even a few muttered comments, such as, "I'll have nought to do with a witch!" and "I'd sooner bed the wizard!"

Witch! There was that term again. Vague memories stirred in Caramon's mind—memories of the days when he and Raistlin had traveled with Flint, the dwarven metalsmith; days before the return of the true gods. Caramon shivered, suddenly remembering with vivid clarity the time they had come into a town that was going to burn an old woman at the stake for witchcraft. He recalled how his brother and Sturm, the ever noble knight, had risked their lives to save the old crone, who turned out to be nothing more than a second-rate illusionist.

But Caramon had forgotten, until now, how the people of this time viewed any type of magical powers, and Crysania's clerical powers—in these days when there were no true clerics—would be even more suspect. He shuddered, then forced himself to think with cold logic. Burning was a harsh death, but it was a far quicker one than—

"Bring the witch to me." Steeltoe limped across the trail to where one of his men held his horse. Mounting, he gestured. "Then follow with the others."

Crysania's captor dragged her forward. Reaching down, Steeltoe grabbed her under the arms and lifted her onto the horse, seating her in front of him. Grasping the reins in his hands, his thick arms wrapped around her, completely engulfing her. Crysania sat staring straight ahead, her face cold and impassive.

Does she know? Caramon wondered, watching helplessly as Steeltoe rode past him, the man's yellowish face twisted into a leer. She's always been sheltered, protected from things like this. Perhaps she doesn't realize what dreadful acts these men are capable of committing.

And then Crysania glanced back at Caramon. Her face was calm and pale, but there was a look of such horror in her eyes, horror and pleading, that he hung his head, his heart aching.

She knows. . . . The gods help her. She knows. . . .

Someone shoved Caramon from behind. Several men grabbed him and flung him, headfirst, over the saddle of his horse. Hanging upside down, his strong arms bound with the bowstrings that were cutting into his flesh, Caramon saw the men lift his brother's limp body and throw it over his own horse's saddle. Then the bandits mounted up and led their captives deeper into the forest.

The rain streamed down on Caramon's bare head as the horse plodded through the mud, jouncing him roughly. The pommel of the saddle jabbed him in the side; the blood rushing to his head made him dizzy. But all he could see in his mind as they rode were those dark, terror-filled eyes, pleading with him for help.

And Caramon knew, with sick certainty, that no help would come.

Chapter 10

Raistlin walked across a burning desert. A line of footsteps stretched before him in the sand, and he was walking in these footsteps. On and on the footsteps led him, up and down dunes of brilliant white, blazing in the sun. He was hot and tired and terribly thirsty. His head hurt, his chest ached, and he wanted to lie down and rest. In the distance was a water hole, cooled by shady trees. But, try as he might, he could not reach it. The footsteps did not go that way, and he could not move his feet any other direction.

On and on he plodded, his black robes hanging heavily about him. And then, nearly spent, he looked up and gasped in terror. The footsteps led to a scaffold! A black-hooded figure knelt with its head upon the block. And, though he could not see the face, he knew with terrible certainty that it was he himself who knelt there, about to die. The executioner stood above him, a bloody axe in his hand. The executioner, too, wore a black hood that covered his face. He raised the axe and held it poised above Raistlin's neck. And as the axe fell, Raistlin saw in his last moments a glimpse of his executioner's face. . . .

"Raist!" whispered a voice.

The mage shook his aching head. With the voice came the comforting realization that he had been dreaming. He struggled to wake up, fighting off the nightmare.

"Raist!" hissed the voice, more urgently.

A sense of real danger, not dreamed danger, roused the mage further. Waking fully, he lay still for a moment, keeping his eyes closed until he was more completely aware of what was going on.

He lay on wet ground, his hands bound in front of him, his mouth gagged. There was throbbing pain in his head and Caramon's voice in his ears.

Around him, he could hear sounds of voices and laughter, he could smell the smoke of cooking fires. But none of the voices seemed very near, except his brother's. And then everything came back to him. He remembered the attack, he remembered a man with a steel leg. . . . Cautiously, Raistlin opened his eyes.

Caramon lay near him in the mud, stretched out on his stomach, his arms bound tightly with bowstrings. There was a familiar glint in his twin's brown eyes, a glint that brought back a rush of memories of old days, times long past—fighting together, combining steel and magic.

And, despite the pain and the darkness around them, Raistlin felt a sense of exhilaration he had not experienced in a long time.

Brought together by danger, the bond between the two was strong now, letting them communicate with both word and thought. Seeing his brother fully cognizant of their plight, Caramon wriggled as close as he dared, his voice barely a breath.

"Is there any way you can free your hands? Do you still carry the silver dagger?"

Raistlin nodded once, briefly. At the beginning of time, magic-users were prohibited by the gods from carrying any type of weapon or wearing any sort of armor. The reason being, ostensibly, that they needed to devote time to study that could not be spent achieving proficiency in the art of weaponry. But, after the magic-users had helped Huma defeat the Queen of Darkness by creating the magical dragon orbs, the gods granted them the right to carry daggers upon their persons—in memory of Huma's lance.

Bound to his wrist by a cunning leather thong that would allow the weapon to slip down into his hand when needed, the silver dagger was Raistlin's last means of defense, to be used only when all his spells were cast . . . or at a time like this.

"Are you strong enough to use your magic?" Caramon whispered.

Raistlin closed his eyes wearily for a moment. Yes, he was strong enough. But—this meant a further weakening, this meant more time would be needed to regain strength to face the Guardians of the Portal. Still, if he didn't live that long . . .

Of course, he *must* live! he thought bitterly. Fistandantilus had lived! He was doing nothing more than following footsteps through the sand.

Angrily, Raistlin banished the thought. Opening his eyes, he nodded. *I am strong enough*, he told his brother mentally, and Caramon sighed in relief.

"Raist," the big man whispered, his face suddenly grave and serious, "you . . . you can guess what . . . what they plan for Crysania."

Raistlin had a sudden vision of that hulking, ogre-ish human's rough hands upon Crysania, and he felt a startling sensation—rage and anger such as he had rarely experienced gripped him. His heart contracted painfully and, for a moment, he was blinded by a blood-dimmed haze.

Seeing Caramon regarding him with astonishment, Raistlin realized that his emotions must be apparent on his face. He scowled, and Caramon continued hurriedly. "I have a plan."

Raistlin nodded irritably, already aware of what his brother had in mind.

Caramon whispered, "If I fail—"

—*I'll kill her first, then myself*, Raistlin finished. But, of course, there would be no need. He was safe . . . protected. . . .

Then, hearing men approaching, the mage closed his eyes,

thankfully feigning unconsciousness again. It gave him time to sort his tangled emotions and force himself to regain control. The silver dagger was cold against his arm. He flexed the muscles that would release the thong. And, all the while, he pondered that strange reaction he'd felt about a woman he cared nothing for . . . except her usefulness to him as a cleric, of course.

Two men jerked Caramon to his feet and shoved him forward. Caramon was thankful to notice that, beyond a quick glance to make certain the mage was still unconscious, neither man paid any attention to his twin. Stumbling along over the uneven ground, gritting his teeth against the pain from cramped, chilled leg muscles, Caramon found himself thinking about that odd expression on his brother's face when he mentioned Lady Crysania. Caramon would have called it the outraged expression of a lover, if seen on the face of any other man. But his brother? Was Raistlin capable of such an emotion? Caramon had decided in Istar that Raistlin wasn't, that he had been completely consumed by evil.

But now, his twin seemed different, much more like the old Raistlin, the brother he had fought side by side with so many times before, their lives in each other's keeping. What Raistlin had told Caramon about Tas made sense. So he hadn't killed the kender after all. And, though sometimes irritable, Raistlin was always unfailingly gentle with Crysania. Perhaps—

One of the guards jabbed him painfully in the ribs, recalling Caramon to the desperateness of their situation. Perhaps! He snorted. Perhaps it would all end here and now. Perhaps the only thing he would buy with his life would be swift death for the other two.

Walking through the camp, thinking over all he had seen and heard since the ambush, Caramon mentally reviewed his plan.

The bandit's camp was more like a small town than a thieves' hideout. They lived in crudely built log huts, keeping their animals sheltered in a large cave. They had obviously been here some time, and apparently feared no law—giving mute testimony to the strength and leadership capabilities of the half-ogre, Steeltoe.

But Caramon, having had more than a few run-ins with thieves in his day, saw that many of these men were not loutish ruffians. He had seen several glance at Crysania and shake their heads in obvious distaste for what was to come. Though dressed in little more than rags, several carried fine weapons—steel swords of the kind passed down from father to son, and they handled them with the care given a family heirloom, not booty. And, though he could not be certain in the failing light of the stormy day, Caramon thought he had noted on many of the swords the Rose and the Kingfisher— the ancient symbol of the Solamnic Knights.

The men were clean-shaven, without the long mustaches that marked such knights, but Caramon could detect in their stern, young faces traces of his friend, the knight, Sturm Brightblade. And, reminded of Sturm, Caramon was reminded, too, of what he knew of the history of the knighthood following the Cataclysm.

Blamed by most of their neighbors for bringing about the dreadful calamity, the knights had been driven from their homes by angry mobs. Many had been murdered, their families killed before their eyes. Those who survived went into hiding, roaming the land on their own or joining outlaw bands—like this one.

Glancing at the men as they stood about the camp cleaning their weapons and talking in low voices, Caramon saw the mark of evil deeds upon many faces, but he also saw looks of resignation and hopelessness. He had known hard times himself. He knew what it could drive a man to do.

All this gave him hope that his plan might succeed.

A bonfire blazed in the center of the encampment, not far from where he and Raistlin had been dumped on the ground. Glancing behind, he saw his brother still feigning unconsciousness. But he also saw, knowing what to look for, that the mage had managed to twist his body around into a position where he could both see and hear clearly.

As Caramon stepped forward into the fire's light, most of

the men stopped what they were doing and followed, forming a half-circle around him. Sitting in a large wooden chair near the blaze was Steeltoe, a flagon in his hand. Standing near him, laughing and joking, were several men Caramon recognized at once as typical toadies, fawning over their leader. And he was not surprised to see, at the edge of the crowd, the grinning, ill-favored face of their innkeeper.

Sitting in a chair beside Steeltoe was Crysania. Her cloak had been taken from her. Her dress was ripped open at the bodice—he could imagine by whose hands. And, Caramon saw with growing anger, there was a purplish blotch on her cheek. One corner of her mouth was swollen.

But she held herself with rigid dignity, staring straight ahead and trying to ignore the crude jokes and frightful tales being bandied back and forth. Caramon smiled grimly in admiration. Remembering the panic-stricken state of near madness to which she had been reduced during the last days of Istar, and thinking of her previous soft and sheltered life, he was pleased, if amazed, to see her reacting to this dangerous situation with a coolness Tika might have envied.

Tika. . . . Caramon scowled. He had not meant to think of Tika—especially not in connection with Lady Crysania! Forcing his thoughts to the present, he coldly averted his eyes from the woman to his enemy, concentrating on him.

Seeing Caramon, Steeltoe turned from his conversation and gestured broadly for the warrior to approach.

"Time to die, warrior," Steeltoe said to him, still in the same pleasant tone of voice. He glanced over lazily at Crysania. "I'm certain, lady, you won't mind if our tryst is postponed a few moments while I take care of this matter. Just think of this as a little before-bed entertainment, my dear." He stroked Crysania's cheek with his hand. When she moved away from him, her dark eyes flashing in anger, he changed his caress to a slap, hitting her across the face.

Crysania did not cry out. Raising her head, she stared back at her tormentor with grim pride.

Knowing that he could not let himself be distracted by concern for her, Caramon kept his gaze on the leader, studying him calmly. This man rules by fear and brute force, he thought to himself. Of those who follow, many do so reluctantly. They're all afraid of him; he's probably the only law in this godforsaken land. But he's obviously kept them well fed and alive when they would otherwise have perished. So they're loyal, but just how far will their loyalty go?

Keeping his voice evenly modulated, Caramon drew himself up, regarding the half-ogre with a look of disdain. "Is this how you show your bravery? Beating up women?" Caramon sneered. "Untie me and give me my sword, and we'll see what kind of man you really are!"

Steeltoe regarded him with interest and, Caramon saw uneasily, a look of intelligence on his brutish face.

"I had thought to have something more original out of you, warrior," Steeltoe said with a sigh that was part show and part not as he rose to his feet. "Perhaps you will not be such a challenge to me as I first thought. Still, I have nothing better to do this evening. *Early* in the evening, that is," he amended, with a leer and a rakish bow to Crysania, who ignored him.

The half-ogre threw aside the great fur cloak he wore and, turning, commanded one of his men to bring him his sword. The toadies scattered to do his bidding, while the other men moved to surround a cleared space to one side of the bonfire—obviously this was a sport that had been enjoyed before. During the confusion, Caramon managed to catch Crysania's eye.

Inclining his head, he glanced meaningfully toward where Raistlin lay. Crysania understood his meaning at once. Looking over at the mage, she smiled sadly and nodded. Her hand closed about the medallion of Paladine and her swollen lips moved.

Caramon's guards shoved him into the circle, and he lost sight of her. "It'll take more than prayers to Paladine to get us out of this one, lady," he muttered, wondering with a certain amount of amusement, if his brother was, at that moment, praying to the Queen of Darkness for help as well.

Well, he had no one to pray to, nothing to help him but his own muscle and bone and sinew.

They cut the bindings on his arms. Caramon flinched at the pain of blood returning to his limbs, but he flexed his stiff muscles, rubbing them to help the circulation and to warm himself. Then he stripped off his soaking-wet shirt and his breeches to fight naked. Clothes gave the enemy a chance for a hand-hold, so his old instructor, Arack the dwarf, had taught him in the Games Arena in Istar.

At the sight of Caramon's magnificent physique, there was a murmur of admiration from the men standing around the circle. The rain streamed down over his tan, well-muscled body, the fire gleamed on his strong chest and shoulders, glinting off his numerous battle scars. Someone handed Caramon a sword, and the warrior swung it with practiced ease and obvious skill. Even Steeltoe, entering the ring of men, seemed a bit disconcerted at the sight of the former gladiator.

But if Steeltoe was—momentarily—startled at the appearance of his opponent, Caramon was no less taken aback at the appearance of Steeltoe. Half-ogre and half-human, the man had inherited the best traits of both races. He had the girth and muscle of the ogres, but he was quick on his feet and agile, while, in his eyes, was the dangerous intelligence of a human. He, too, fought almost naked, wearing nothing but a leather loincloth. But what made Caramon's breath whistle between his teeth was the weapon the half-ogre carried—easily the most wonderful sword the warrior had ever seen in his life.

A gigantic blade, it was designed for use as a two-handed weapon. Indeed, Caramon thought, eyeing it expertly, there were few men he knew who could even have lifted it, much less wielded it. But, not only did Steeltoe heft it with ease, he used it with one hand! And he used it well, that much Caramon could tell from the half-ogre's practiced, well-timed swings. The steel blade caught the fire's light as he slashed the air. It hummed as it sliced through the darkness, leaving a blazing trail of light behind it.

As his opponent limped into the ring, his steel pegleg gleaming, Caramon saw with despair that he faced not the brutish, stupid opponent he had expected, but a skilled swordsman, an intelligent man, who had overcome his handicap to fight with a mastery two-legged men might well envy.

Not only had Steeltoe overcome his handicap, Caramon discovered after their first pass, but the half-ogre made use of it in a most deadly fashion.

The two stalked each other, feinting, each watching for any weakness in the opponent's defense. Then, suddenly, balancing himself easily on his good leg, Steeltoe used his steel leg as another weapon. Whirling around, he struck Caramon with the steel leg with such force that it sent the big man crashing to the ground. His sword flew from his hands.

Quickly regaining his balance, Steeltoe advanced with his huge sword, obviously intending to end the battle and get on to other amusements. But, though caught off guard, Caramon had seen this type of move in the arena. Lying on the ground, gasping for breath, feigning having had the wind knocked out of him, Caramon waited until his enemy closed on him. Then, reaching out, he grabbed hold of Steeltoe's good leg and jerked it out from beneath him.

The men standing around cheered and applauded. As the sound brought back vivid memories of the arena at Istar, Caramon felt his blood race. Worries about black-robed brothers and white-robed clerics vanished. So did thoughts of home. His self-doubts disappeared. The thrill of fighting, the intoxicating drug of danger, coursed through his veins, filling him with an ecstasy much like his twin felt using his magic.

Scrambling to his feet, seeing his enemy do the same, Caramon made a sudden, desperate lunge for his sword, which lay several feet from him. But Steeltoe was quicker. Reaching Caramon's sword first, he kicked it, sending it flying.

Even as he kept an eye on his opponent, Caramon glanced about for another weapon and saw the bonfire, blazing at the far end of the ring.

But Steeltoe saw Caramon's glance. Instantly guessing his objective, the half-ogre moved to block him.

Caramon made a run for it. The half-ogre's slashing blade sliced through the skin on his abdomen, leaving a glistening trail of blood behind. With a leaping dive, Caramon rolled near the logs, grabbed one by the end, and was on his feet as

Steeltoe drove his blade into the ground where the big man's head had been only seconds before.

The sword arced through the air again. Caramon heard it humming and barely was able to parry the blow with the log in time. Chips and sparks flew as the sword bit into the wood, Caramon having grabbed a log that was burning at one end. The force of Steeltoe's blow was tremendous, making Caramon's hands ring and the sharp edges of the log dig painfully into his flesh. But he held fast, using his great strength to drive the half-ogre backward as Steeltoe fought to recover his balance.

The half-ogre held firm, finally shoving his pegleg into the ground and pushing Caramon back. The two men slowly took up their positions again, circling each other. Then the air was filled with the flashing light of steel and flaming cinders.

How long they fought, Caramon had no idea. Time drowned in a haze of stinging pain and fear and exhaustion. His breath came in ragged gasps. His lungs burned like the end of the log, his hands were raw and bleeding. But still he gained no advantage. He had never in his life faced such an opponent. Steeltoe, too, who had entered the fight with a sneer of confidence, now faced his enemy with grim determination. Around them, the men stood silently now, enthralled by the deadly contest.

The only sounds at all, in fact, were the crackling of the fire, the heavy breathing of the opponents, or perhaps the splash of a body as one went down into the mud, or the grunt of pain when a blow told.

The circle of men and the firelight began to blur in Caramon's eyes. To his aching arms, the log felt heavier than a whole tree, now. Breathing was agony. His opponent was as exhausted as he, Caramon knew, from the fact that Steeltoe had neglected to follow up an advantageous blow, being forced to simply stand and catch his breath. The half-ogre had an ugly purple welt running along his side where Caramon's log had caught him. Everyone in the circle had heard the snapping of his ribs and seen the yellowish face contort in pain.

But he came back with a swipe of his sword that sent Caramon staggering backward, flailing away with the log in a frantic attempt to parry the stroke. Now the two stalked each other, neither hearing nor caring about anything else but the enemy across from him. Both knew that the next mistake would be fatal.

And then Steeltoe slipped in the mud. It was just a small slip, sending him down on his good knee, balancing on his pegleg. At the beginning of the battle, he would have been up in seconds. But his strength was giving out and it took a moment longer to struggle up again.

That second was what Caramon had been waiting for. Lurching forward, using the last bit of strength in his own body, Caramon lifted the log and drove it down as hard as he could on the knee to which the pegleg was attached. As a hammer strikes a nail, Caramon's blow drove the pegleg deep into the sodden ground.

Snarling in fury and pain, the half-ogre turned and twisted, trying desperately to drag his leg free, all the while attempting to keep Caramon back with slashing blows of his sword. Such was his tremendous strength that he almost succeeded. Even now, seeing his opponent trapped, Caramon had to fight the temptation to let his hurting body rest, to let his opponent go.

But there could be only one end to this contest. Both men had known that from the beginning. Staggering forward, grimly swinging his log, Caramon caught the half-ogre's blade and sent it flying from his hands. Seeing death in Caramon's eyes, Steeltoe still fought defiantly to free himself. Even at the last moment, as the log in the big man's hands whistled through the air, the half-ogre's huge hands made a clutching grasp for Caramon's arms—

The log smashed into the half-ogre's head with a wet, sodden thud and the crunch of bone, flinging the half-ogre backward. The body twitched, then was still. Steeltoe lay in the mud, his steel pegleg still pinning him to the ground, the rain washing away the blood and brains that oozed from the cracks in his skull.

Stumbling in weariness and pain, Caramon sank to his knees, leaning on the blood- and rain-soaked log, trying to catch his breath. There was a roaring in his ears—the angry shouts of men surging forward to kill him. He didn't care. It didn't matter. Let them come. . . .

But no one attacked.

Confused by this, Caramon raised his blurred gaze to a black-robed figure kneeling down beside him. He felt his brother's slender arm encircle him protectively, and he saw flickering darts of lightning flash warningly from the mage's fingers. Closing his eyes, Caramon leaned his head against his brother's frail chest and drew a deep, shuddering breath.

Then he felt cool hands touch his skin and he heard a soft voice murmur a prayer to Paladine. Caramon's eyes flared open. He shoved the startled Crysania away, but it was too late. Her healing influence spread through his body. He could hear the men gathered around him gasp as the bleeding wounds vanished, the bruises disappeared, and the color returned to his deathly pale face. Even the archmage's pyrotechnics had not created the outburst of alarm and shocked cries the healing did.

"Witchcraft! She healed him! Burn the witch!"

"Burn them both, witch and wizard!"

"They hold the warrior in thrall. We'll take them and free his soul!"

Glancing at his brother, he saw—from the grim expression on Raistlin's face—that the mage, too, was reliving old memories and understood the danger.

"Wait!" Caramon gasped, rising to his feet as the crowd of muttering men drew near. Only the fear of Raistlin's magic kept the men from rushing them, he knew, and—hearing his brother's sudden racking cough—Caramon feared Raistlin's strength might soon give out.

Catching hold of the confused Crysania, Caramon thrust her protectively behind him as he confronted the crowd of frightened, angry men.

"Touch this woman, and you will die as your leader died," he shouted, his voice loud and clear above the driving rain.

"Why should we let a witch live?" snarled one, and there were mutters of agreement.

"Because she's *my* witch!" Caramon said sternly, casting a defiant gaze around. Behind him, he heard Crysania draw in a sharp breath, but Raistlin gave her a warning glance and, if she had been going to speak, she sensibly kept quiet. "She does not hold me in thrall but obeys my commands and those of the wizard. She will do you no harm, I swear."

There were murmurs among the men, but their eyes, as they looked at Caramon, were no longer threatening. Admiration there had been—now he could see grudging respect and a willingness to listen.

"Let us be on our way," Raistlin began in his soft voice, "and we—"

"Wait!" rasped Caramon. Gripping his brother's arm, he drew him near and whispered. "I've got an idea. Watch over Crysania!"

Nodding, Raistlin moved to stand near Crysania, who stood quietly, her eyes on the now silent group of bandits. Caramon walked over to where the body of the half-ogre lay in the reddening mud. Leaning down, he wrested the great sword from Steeltoe's deathgrip and raised it high over his head. The big warrior was a magnificent sight, the firelight reflecting off his bronze skin, the muscles rippling in his arms as he stood in triumph above the body of his slain enemy.

"I have destroyed your leader. Now I claim the right to take his place!" Caramon shouted, his voice echoing among the trees. "I ask only one thing—that you leave this life of butchery and rape and robbery. We travel south—"

That got an unexpected reaction. "South! They travel south!" several voices cried and there was scattered cheering. Caramon stared at them, taken aback, not understanding. Raistlin, coming forward, clutched at him.

"What are you doing?" the mage demanded, his face pale.

Caramon shrugged, looking about in puzzled amazement at the enthusiasm he had created. "It just seemed a good idea to have an armed escort, Raistlin," he said. "The lands south of here are, by all accounts, wilder than those we have ridden through. I figured we could take a few of these men with us, that's all. I don't understand—"

A young man of noble bearing, who more than any of the others, recalled Sturm to Caramon's mind, stepped forward. Motioning the others to quiet down, he asked, "You're going south? Do you, perchance, seek the fabled wealth of the dwarves in Thorbardin?"

Raistlin scowled. "*Now* do you understand?" he snarled. Choking, he was shaken by a fit of coughing that left him weak and gasping. Had it not been for Crysania hurrying to support him, he might have fallen.

"I understand you need rest," Caramon replied grimly. "We all do. And unless we come up with some sort of armed escort, we'll never have a peaceful night's sleep. What do the dwarves in Thorbardin have to do with anything? What's going on?"

Raistlin stared at the ground, his face hidden by the shadows of his hood. Finally, sighing, he said coldly, "Tell them yes, we go south. We're going to attack the dwarves."

Caramon's eyes opened wide. "Attack Thorbardin?"

"I'll explain later," Raistlin snarled softly. "Do as I tell you."

Caramon hesitated.

Shrugging his thin shoulders, Raistlin smiled unpleasantly. "It is your only way home, my brother! And maybe our only way out of here alive."

Caramon glanced around. The men had begun to mutter again during this brief exchange, obviously suspicious of their intentions. Realizing he had to make a decision quickly or lose them for good—and maybe even face another attack—he turned back, vying for time to try to think things through further.

"We go south," he said, "it is true. But for our own reasons. What is this you say of wealth in Thorbardin?"

"It is said that the dwarves have stored great wealth in the kingdom beneath the mountain," the young man answered readily. Others around him nodded.

"Wealth they stole from humans," added one.

"Aye! Not just money," cried out a third, "but grain and

cattle and sheep. They'll eat like kings this winter, while our bellies go empty!"

"We have talked before of going south to take our share," the young man continued, "but Steeltoe said things were well enough here. There are some, though, who were having second thoughts."

Caramon pondered, wishing he knew more of history. He had heard of the Great Dwarfgate Wars, of course. His old dwarf friend, Flint, talked of little else. Flint was a hill dwarf. He had filled Caramon's head with tales of the cruelty of the mountain dwarves of Thorbardin, saying much the same things these men said. But to hear Flint tell it, the wealth the mountain dwarves stole had been taken from their cousins, the hill dwarves.

If this were true, then Caramon might well be justified in making this decision. He could, of course, do as his brother commanded. But something inside Caramon had snapped in Istar. Even though he was beginning to think he had misjudged his brother, he knew him well enough to continue to distrust him. Never again would he obey Raistlin blindly.

But then he sensed Raistlin's glittering eyes upon him, and he heard his brother's voice echo in his mind.

Your only way back home!

Caramon clenched his fist in swift anger, but Raistlin had him, he knew. "We go south to Thorbardin," he said harshly, his troubled gaze on the sword in his hand. Then he raised his head to look at the men around him. "Will you come with us?"

There was a moment's hesitation. Several of the men came forward to talk to the young nobleman, who was now apparently their spokesman. He listened, nodded, then faced Caramon once more.

"We would follow *you* without hesitation, great warrior," said the young man, "but what have you to do with this black-robed wizard? Who is *he*, that we should follow him?"

"My name is Raistlin," the mage replied. "This man is my bodyguard."

There was no response, only dubious frowns and doubtful looks.

"I am his bodyguard, that is true," Caramon said quietly, "but the mage's real name is Fistandantilus."

At this, there were sharp intakes of breath among the men. The frowns changed to looks of respect, even fear and awe.

"My name is Garic," the young man said, bowing to the archmage with the old-fashioned courtesy of the Knights of Solamnia. "We have heard of you, Great One. And though your deeds are dark as your robes, we live in a time of dark deeds, it seems. We will follow you and the great warrior you bring with you."

Stepping forward, Garic laid his sword at Caramon's feet. Others followed suit, some eagerly, others more warily. A few slunk off into the shadows. Knowing them for the cowardly ruffians they were, Caramon let them go.

He was left with about thirty men; a few of the same noble bearing as Garic, but most of them were ragged, dirty thieves and scoundrels.

"My army," Caramon said to himself with a grim smile that night as he spread his blanket in Steeltoe's hut the half-ogre had built for his own personal use. Outside the door, he could hear Garic talking to the other man Caramon had decided looked trustworthy enough to stand watch.

Bone-weary, Caramon had assumed he'd fall asleep quickly. But he found himself lying awake in the darkness, thinking, making plans.

Like most young soldiers, Caramon had often dreamed of becoming an officer. Now, unexpectedly, here was his chance. It wasn't much of a command, maybe, but it was a start. For the first time since they'd arrived in this god-forsaken time, he felt a glimmer of pleasure.

Plans tumbled over and over in his mind. Training, the best routes south, provisioning, supplies . . . These were new and different problems for the former mercenary soldier. Even in the War of the Lance, he had generally followed Tanis's lead. His brother knew nothing of these matters; Raistlin had informed Caramon coldly that he was on his own in this. Caramon found this challenging and—oddly—refreshing. These were flesh-and-blood problems, driving the dark and shadowy problems with his brother from his mind.

Thinking of his twin, Caramon glanced over to where Raistlin lay huddled near a fire that blazed in a huge stone fireplace. Despite the heat, he was wrapped in his cloak and as many blankets as Crysania had been able to find. Caramon could hear his brother's breath rattle in his lungs, occasionally he coughed in his sleep.

Crysania slept on the other side of the fire. Although exhausted, her sleep was troubled and broken. More than once she cried out and sat up suddenly, pale and trembling. Caramon sighed. He would have liked to comfort her—to take her in his arms and soothe her to sleep. For the first time, in fact, he realized how *much* he would like to do this. Perhaps it had been telling the men she was his. Perhaps it was seeing the half-ogre's hands on her, feeling the same sense of outrage he had seen reflected on his brother's face.

Whatever the reason, Caramon caught himself watching her that night in a much different way than he had watched her before, thinking thoughts that, even now, made his skin burn and his pulse quicken.

Closing his eyes, he willed images of Tika, his wife, to come to his mind. But he had banished these memories for so long that they were unsatisfying. Tika was a hazy, misty picture and she was far away. Crysania was flesh and blood and she was here! He was very much aware of her soft, even breathing. . . .

Damn! Women! Irritably, Caramon flopped over on his stomach, determined to sweep all thoughts of females beneath the rug of his other problems. It worked. Weariness finally stole over him.

As he drifted into sleep, one thing remained to trouble him, hovering in the back of his mind. It was not logistics, or red-haired warrior women, or even lovely, white-robed clerics.

It was nothing more than a look—the strange look he had seen Raistlin give him when Caramon had said the name "Fistandantilus."

It had not been a look of anger or irritation, as Caramon might have expected. The last thing Caramon saw before sleep erased the memory was Raistlin's look of stark, abject terror.

BOOK 2

The Army Of Fistandantilus

As the band of men under Caramon's command traveled south toward the great dwarven kingdom of Thorbardin, their fame grew—and so did their numbers. The fabled "wealth beneath the mountain" had long been legend among the wretched, half-starved people of Solamnia. That summer, they had seen most of their crops wither and die in the fields. Dread diseases stalked the land, more feared and deadly than even the savage bands of goblins and ogres who had been driven from their ancient lands by hunger.

Though it was autumn still, the chill of coming winter was in the night air. Faced with nothing but the bleak prospect of watching their children perish through starvation or cold or the illnesses that the clerics of these new gods could not cure, the men and women of Solamnia believed they had nothing to lose. Abandoning their homes, they packed up their families and their meager possessions to join the army and travel south.

From having to worry about feeding thirty men, Caramon suddenly found himself responsible for several hundred, plus women and children as well. And more came to the camp daily. Some were knights, trained with sword and spear; their nobility apparent even through their rags. Others were farmers, who held the swords Caramon put in their hands as they might have held their hoes. But there was a kind of grim nobility about them, too. After years of helplessly facing Famine and Want, it was an exhilarating thought to be preparing to face an enemy that could be killed and conquered.

Without quite realizing how it happened, Caramon found himself general of what was now being called the "Army of Fistandantilus."

At first, he had all he could manage to do in acquiring food for the vast numbers of men and their families. But memories of the lean days of mercenary life returned to him. Discovering those who were skilled hunters, he sent them ranging far afield in search of game. The women smoked the meat or dried it, so that what was not immediately used could be stored.

Many of those who came brought what grain and fruit they had managed to harvest. This Caramon pooled, ordering the grain pounded into flour or maize, baking it into the rock-hard but life-sustaining trail bread a traveling army could live on for months. Even the children had their tasks—snaring or shooting small game, fishing, hauling water, chopping wood.

Then he had to undertake the training of his raw recruits—drilling them in the use of spear and bow, of sword and shield.

Finally, he had to find those spears and bows, swords and shields.

And, as the army moved relentlessly south, word of their coming spread. . . .

CHAPTER I

ax Tharkas—a monument to peace. Now it had become a symbol of war.

The history of the great stone fortress of Pax Tharkas has its roots in an unlikely legend—the story of a lost race of dwarves known as the Kal-thax.

As humans cherish steel—the forging of bright weapons, the glitter of bright coin; as elves cherish their woodlands— the bringing forth and nurturing of life; so the dwarves cherish stone—the shaping of the bones of the world.

Before the Age of Dreams was the Age of Twilight when the history of the world is shrouded in the mists of its dawning. There dwelt in the great halls of Thorbardin a race of dwarves whose stonework was so perfect and so remarkable that the god Reorx, Forger of the World, looked upon it and marveled. Knowing in his wisdom that once such perfection had been attained by mortals there was nothing left in life to strive for, Reorx took up the entire Kal-thax race and brought them to live with him near heaven's forge.

Few examples remain of the ancient craftwork of the

Kal-thax. These are kept within the dwarven kingdom of Thorbardin and are valued above all other things. After the time of the Kal-thax, it was the lifelong ambition of each dwarf to gain such perfection in his stonework that he, too, might be taken up to live with Reorx.

As time went by, however, this worthy goal became perverted and twisted into an obsession. Thinking and dreaming of nothing but stone, the lives of the dwarves became as inflexible and unchanging as the medium of their craft. They burrowed deep into their ancient halls beneath the mountain, shunning the outside world. And the outside world shunned them.

Time passed and brought the tragic wars between elves and men. This ended with the signing of the Swordsheath Scroll and the voluntary exile of Kith-Kanan and his followers from the ancient elven homeland of Silvanesti. By the terms of the Swordsheath Scroll, the Qualinesti elves (meaning "freed nation") were given the lands west of Thorbardin for the establishment of their new homeland.

This was agreeable to both humans and elves. Unfortunately, no one bothered to consult the dwarves. Seeing this influx of elves as a threat to their way of life beneath the mountain, the dwarves attacked. Kith-Kanan found, to his sorrow, that he had walked away from one war only to find himself embroiled in another.

After many long years, the wise elven king managed to convince the stubborn dwarves that the elves had no interest in their stone. They wanted only the living beauty of their wilderness. Though this love for something changeable and wild was totally incomprehensible to the dwarves, they at last came to accept the idea. The elves were no longer seen as a threat. The races could, at last, become friends.

To honor this agreement, Pax Tharkas was built. Guarding the mountain pass between Qualinesti and Thorbardin, the fortress was dedicated as a monument to differences—a symbol of unity and diversity.

In those times, before the Cataclysm, elves and dwarves had together manned the battlements of this mighty fortress.

But now, dwarves alone kept watch from its two tall towers. For the evil time brought division once again to the races.

Retreating into their forested homeland of Qualinesti, nursing the wounds that drove them to seek solitude, the elves left Pax Tharkas. Safe inside their woodlands, they closed their borders to all. Trespassers—whether human or goblin, dwarf or ogre—were killed instantly and without question.

Duncan, King of Thorbardin, thought of this as he watched the sun drop down behind the mountains, falling from the sky into Qualinesti. He had a sudden, playful vision of the elves attacking the sun itself for daring to enter their land, and he snorted derisively. Well, they have good reason to be paranoid, he said to himself. They have good reason to shut out the world. What did the world do for them?

Entered their lands, raped their women, murdered their children, burned their homes, stole their food. And was it goblins or ogres, spawn of evil? No! Duncan growled savagely into his beard. It was those they had trusted, those they had welcomed as friends—humans.

And now it's our turn, Duncan thought, pacing the battlements, an eye on the sunset that had bathed the sky in blood. It's our turn to shut our doors and tell the world good riddance! Go to the Abyss in your own way and let us go to it in ours!

Lost in his thoughts, Duncan only gradually became aware that another person had joined him in his pacing; iron-shod steps keeping time with his. The new dwarf was head and shoulders taller than his king and, with his long legs, could have taken two steps for his king's one. But he had, out of respect, slowed his pace to match his monarch's.

Duncan frowned uncomfortably. At any other time, he would have welcomed this person's company. Now it came to him as a sign of ill omen. It threw a shadow over his thoughts, as the sinking sun caused the chill shadow of the mountain peaks to lengthen and stretch out their fingers toward Pax Tharkas.

"They'll guard our western border well," Duncan said by way of opening the conversation, his gaze on the borders of Qualinesti.

"Aye, Thane," the other dwarf answered, and Duncan cast a sharp glance at him from beneath his thick, gray eyebrows. Though the taller dwarf had spoken in agreement with his king, there was a reserve, a coolness in the dwarf's voice indicative of his disapproval.

Snorting in irritation, Duncan whirled abruptly in his pacing, heading the other direction, and had the amused satisfaction of having caught his fellow dwarf off guard. But the taller dwarf, instead of stumbling to turn around and catch up with his king, simply stopped and stood staring sadly out over the battlements of Pax Tharkas into the now shadowy elven lands beyond.

Irritably, Duncan first considered simply continuing on without his companion, then he came to a halt, giving the tall dwarf time to catch up. The tall dwarf made no move, however, so finally with an exasperated expression, Duncan turned and stomped back.

"By Reorx's beard, Kharas," he growled, "what is it?"

"I think you should meet with Fireforge," Kharas said slowly, his eyes on the sky that was now deepening to purple. Far above, a single, bright star sparkled in the darkness.

"I have nothing to say to him," Duncan said shortly.

"The Thane is wise," Kharas spoke the ritual words with a bow, but he accompanied it with a heavy sigh, clasping his hands behind his back.

Duncan exploded. "What you mean to say is 'The Thane's a stupid ass!'" The king poked Kharas in the arm. "Isn't that nearer the mark?"

Kharas turned his head, smiling, stroking the silken tresses of his long, curling beard that shone in the light of the torches being lit upon the walls. He started to reply, but the air was suddenly filled with noise—the ringing of boots, the stamping of feet and calling of voices, the clash of axes against steel: the changing of the watch. Captains shouted commands, men left their positions, others took them over. Kharas, observing this in silence, used it as a meaningful backing for his statement when he finally did speak.

"I think you should listen to what he has to say to you,

Thane Duncan," Kharas said simply. "There is talk that you are goading our cousins into war—"

"Me!" Duncan roared in a rage. "Me goading them into war! *They're* the ones who're on the march, swarming down out of their hills like rats! It was they who left the mountain. *We* never asked them to abandon their ancestral home! But no, in their stiff-necked pride they—" He sputtered on, relating a long history of wrongs, both justified and imagined. Kharas allowed him to talk, waiting patiently until Duncan had blown off most of his anger.

Then the tall dwarf said patiently, "It will cost you nothing to listen, Thane, and might buy us great gains in the long run. Other eyes than those of our cousins are watching, you may be certain."

Duncan growled, but he kept silent, thinking. Contrary to what he had accused Kharas of thinking, King Duncan was *not* a stupid dwarf. Nor did Kharas consider him such: Quite the contrary. One of seven thanes ruling the seven clans of the dwarven kingdom, Duncan had managed to ally the other thanedoms under his leadership, giving the dwarves of Thorbardin a king for the first time in centuries. Even the Dewar acknowledged Duncan their leader, albeit reluctantly.

The Dewar, or so-called dark dwarves, dwelt far beneath the ground, in dimly lit, foul-smelling caves that even the mountain dwarves of Thorbardin, who lived most of their lives below ground, hesitated to enter. Long ago, a trace of insanity had shown up in this particular clan, causing them to be shunned by the others. Now, after centuries of inbreeding forced upon them by isolation, the insanity was more pronounced, while those judged sane were an embittered, dour lot.

But they had their uses as well. Quick to anger, ferocious killers who took pleasure in killing, they were a valued part of the Thane's army. Duncan treated them well for that reason and because, at heart, he was a kind and just dwarf. But he was smart enough not to turn his back on them.

Likewise, Duncan was smart enough to consider the wisdom of Kharas's words. "Other eyes will be watching."

That was true enough. He cast a glance back to the west, this time a wary one. The elves wanted no trouble, of that he felt certain. Nevertheless, if they thought the dwarves likely to provoke war, they would act swiftly to protect their homeland. Turning, he looked to the north. Rumor had it that the warlike Plainsmen of Abanasinia were considering an alliance with the hill dwarves, whom they had allowed to camp upon their lands. In fact, for all Duncan knew, this alliance could have already been made. At least if he talked to this hill dwarf, Fireforge, he might find out.

Then, too, there were darker rumors still . . . rumors of an army marching from the shattered lands of Solamnia, an army led by a powerful, black-robed wizard. . . .

"Very well!" King Duncan snarled with no good grace. "You have won again, Kharas. Tell the hill dwarf I will meet him in the Hall of Thanes at the next watch. See if you can dredge up representatives from the other thanes. We'll do this above board, since that's what you recommend."

Smiling, Kharas bowed, his long beard nearly sweeping the tops of his boots. With a surly nod, Duncan turned and stomped below, his boots ringing out the measure of his displeasure. The other dwarves along the battlements bowed as their king passed but almost immediately turned back to their watch. Dwarves are an independent lot, loyal to their clans first and anyone else second. Though all respected Duncan, he was not revered and he knew it. Maintaining his position was a daily struggle.

Conversation, briefly interrupted by the passage of the king, renewed almost immediately. These dwarves knew war was coming, were eager for it, in fact. Hearing their deep voices, listening to their talk of battles and fighting, Kharas gave another sigh.

Turning in the opposite direction, he started off in search of the delegation of hill dwarves, his heart nearly as heavy as the gigantic war hammer he carried—a hammer few other dwarves could even lift. Kharas, too, saw war coming. He felt as he had felt once when, as a young child, he had traveled to the city of Tarsis and stood on the beach, watching in wonder as the waves crashed upon the shore. That war was coming seemed as inevitable and unstoppable as the waves themselves. But he was determined to do what he could to try to prevent it.

Kharas made no secret of his hatred of war, he was strong in his arguments for peace. Many among the dwarves found this odd, for Kharas was the acknowledged hero of his race. As a young dwarf in the days before the Cataclysm, he had been among those who fought the legions of goblins and ogres in the Great Goblin Wars fomented by the Kingpriest of Istar.

That was a time when there was still trust among races. Allies of the Knights, the dwarves had gone to their aid when the goblins invaded Solamnia. The dwarves and knights fought side by side, and young Kharas had been deeply impressed by the knightly Code and the Measure. The Knights, in turn, had been impressed by the young dwarf's fighting skill.

Taller and stronger than any others of his race, Kharas wielded a huge hammer that he had made himself—legend said it was with the god, Reorx's, help—and there were countless times he held the field alone until his men could rally behind him to drive off the invaders.

For his valor, the Knights awarded him the name "Kharas," which means "knight" in their language. There was no higher honor they could bestow upon an outsider.

When Kharas returned home, he found his fame had spread.

He could have been the military leader of the dwarves; indeed, he might have been king himself, but he had no such ambitions. He had been one of Duncan's strongest supporters, and many believed Duncan owed his rise to power in his clan to Kharas. But, if so, that fact had not poisoned their relationship. The older dwarf and the younger hero became close friends—Duncan's rock-hard practicality keeping Kharas's idealism well-grounded.

And then came the Cataclysm. In those first, terrible years following the shattering of the land, Kharas's courage shone as an example to his beleaguered people. His had been the speech that led the thanes to join together and name Duncan king. The Dewar trusted Kharas, when they trusted no other. Because of this unification, the dwarves had survived and even managed to thrive.

Now, Kharas was in his prime. He had been married once, but his beloved wife perished during the Cataclysm, and dwarves, when they wed, wed for life. There would be no sons bearing his name, for which Kharas, contemplating the bleak future he foresaw ahead for the world, was almost thankful.

"Reghar Fireforge, of the hill dwarves, and party."

The herald pronounced the name, stamping the butt end of his ceremonial spear upon the hard, granite floor. The hill dwarves entered, walking proudly up to the throne where Duncan sat in what was now called the Hall of Thanes in the fortress of Pax Tharkas. Behind him, in shorter chairs that had been hastily dragged in for the occasion, sat the six representatives of the other clans to act as witnesses for their thanes. They were witnesses only, there to report back to their thanes what had been said and done. Since it was war time, all authority rested with Duncan. (At least as much of it as he could claim.)

The witnesses were, in fact, nothing more than captains of their respective divisions. Though supposedly a single unit made up collectively of all the dwarves from each clan, the army was, nonetheless, merely a collection of clans gathered together. Each clan provided its own units with its own leaders; each clan lived separate and apart from the others. Fights among the clans were not uncommon—there were blood feuds that went back for generations. Duncan had tried his best to keep a tight lid on these boiling cauldrons, but—every now and then—the pressure built too high and the lid blew off.

Now, however, facing a common foe, the clans were united. Even the Dewar representative, a dirty-faced, ragged captain named Argat who wore his beard braided in knots in a barbaric fashion and who amused himself during the proceedings by skillfully tossing a knife into the air and catching it as it descended, listened to the proceedings with less than his usual air of sneering contempt.

There was, in addition, the captain of a squadron of gully dwarves. Known as the Highgug, he was there by Duncan's courtesy only. The word "gug" meaning "private" in gully dwarf language, this dwarf was therefore nothing more than a "high private," a rank considered laughable in the rest of the army. It was an outstanding honor among gully dwarves, however, and the Highgug was held in awe by most of his troops. Duncan, always politic, was unfailingly polite to the Highgug and had, therefore, won his undying loyalty. Although there were many who thought this might have been more of a hindrance than a help, Duncan replied that you never knew when such things could come in handy.

And so the Highgug was here as well, though few saw him. He had been given a chair in an obscure corner and told to sit still and keep quiet, instructions he followed to the letter. In fact, they had to return to remove him two days later.

"Dwarves is dwarves," was an old saying common to the populace of the rest of Krynn when referring to the differences between the hill dwarves and the mountain dwarves.

But there *were* differences—vast differences, to the dwarvish mind, though these might not have been readily apparent to any outside observer. Oddly enough, and neither the elves nor the dwarves would admit it, the hill dwarves had left the ancient kingdom of Thorbardin for many of the same reasons that the Qualinesti elves left the traditional homeland of Silvanesti.

The dwarves of Thorbardin lived rigid, highly structured lives. Everyone knew his or her place within his or her own clan. Marriage between clans was unheard of; loyalty to the clan being the binding force of every dwarf's life. Contact with the outside world was shunned—the very worst punishment that could be inflicted upon a dwarf was exile; even execution was considered more merciful. The dwarf's idea of an idyllic life was to be born, grow up, and die without ever sticking one's nose outside the gates of Thorbardin.

Unfortunately, this was—or at least had been in the past—

a dream only. Constantly called to war to defend their holdings, the dwarves were forced to mix with the outside world. And—if there were no wars—there were always those who sought the dwarven skill in building and who were willing to pay vast sums to acquire it. The beautiful city of Palanthas had been lovingly constructed by a veritable army of dwarves, as had many of the other cities in Krynn. Thus a race of well-traveled, free-spirited, independent dwarves came about. They talked of intermarriage between the clans, they spoke matter-of-factly about trade with humans and elves. They actually expressed a desire to live in the open air. And—most heinous of all—they expressed the belief that other things in life might hold more importance than the crafting of stone.

This, of course, was seen by the more rigid dwarves as a direct threat to dwarvish society itself, so, inevitably, the split occurred. The independent dwarves left their home beneath the mountain in Thorbardin. The parting did not occur peacefully. There were harsh words on both sides. Blood feuds started then that would last for hundreds of years. Those who left took to the hills where, if life wasn't all they had hoped for, at least it was free—they could marry whom they chose, come and go as they chose, earn their own money. The dwarves left behind simply closed ranks and became even more rigid, if that were possible.

The two dwarves facing each other now were thinking of this, as they sized each other up. They were also thinking, perhaps, that this was a historic moment—the first time both sides had met in centuries.

Reghar Fireforge was the elder of the two, a top-ranking member of the strongest clan of hill dwarves. Though nearing his two-hundredth Day of Life Gift, the old dwarf was hale and hearty still. He came of a long-lived clan. The same could not be said of his sons, however. Their mother had died of a weak heart and the same malady seemed to run in the family. Reghar had lived to bury his eldest son and, already, he could see some of the same symptoms of an early death in his next oldest—a young man of seventy-five, just recently married.

Dressed in furs and animal skins, looking as barbaric (if cleaner) than the Dewar, Reghar stood with his feet wide apart, staring at Duncan, his rock-hard eyes glittering from beneath brows so thick many wondered how the old dwarf could see at all. His hair was iron gray, so was his beard, and he wore it plaited and combed and tucked into his belt in hill-dwarf fashion. Flanked by an escort of hill dwarves—all dressed much the same—the old dwarf was an impressive sight.

King Duncan returned Reghar's gaze without faltering—this staring-down contest was an ancient dwarvish practice and, if the parties were particularly stubborn, had been known to result in both dwarves keeling over from exhaustion unless interrupted by some neutral third party. Duncan, as he regarded Reghar grimly, began to stroke his own curled and silky beard that flowed freely over his broad stomach. It was a sign of contempt, and Reghar, noticing it without admitting that he noticed it, flushed in anger.

The six clan members sat stoically in their chairs, prepared for a long sitting. Reghar's escort spread their feet and fixed their eyes on nothing. The Dewar continued to toss his knife in the air—much to everyone's annoyance. The Highgug sat in his corner, forgotten except for the redolent odor of gully dwarf that pervaded the chill room. It seemed likely, from the look of things, that Pax Tharkas would crumble with age around their heads before anyone spoke. Finally, with a sigh, Kharas stepped in between Reghar and Duncan. Their line of vision broken, each party could drop his gaze without losing dignity.

Bowing to his king, Kharas turned and bowed to Reghar with profound respect. Then he retreated. Both sides were now free to talk on an equal basis, though each side privately had its own ideas about how equal that might be.

"I have granted you audience," Duncan stated, starting matters off with formal politeness that, among dwarves, never lasted long, "Reghar Fireforge, in order to hear what brings our kinsmen on a journey to a realm they chose to leave long ago."

"A good day it was for us when we shook the dust of the moldy old tomb from our feet," Reghar growled, "to live in the open like honest men instead of skulking beneath the rock like lizards."

Reghar patted his plaited beard, Duncan stroked his. Both stared at each other. Reghar's escort wagged their heads, thinking their chieftain had come off better in the first verbal contest.

"Then why is it that the honest men have returned to the moldy old tomb, except that they come as grave robbers?" Duncan snapped, leaning back with an air of self-satisfaction.

There was a murmur of appreciation from the six mountain dwarves, who clearly thought their thane had scored a point.

Reghar flushed. "Is the man who takes back what was stolen from him first a thief?" he demanded.

"I fail to understand the point of that question," Duncan said smoothly, "since you have nothing of value anyone would want to steal. It is said even the kender avoid your land."

There was appreciative laughter from the mountain dwarves, while the hill dwarves literally shook with rage— that being a mortal insult. Kharas sighed.

"I'll tell you about stealing!" Reghar snarled, his beard quivering with anger. "Contracts—that's what you've stolen! Underbidding us, working at a loss to take the bread from our mouths! And there've been raids into our lands—stealing our grain and cattle! We've heard the stories of the wealth you've amassed and we've come to claim what is rightfully ours! No more, no less!"

"Lies!" roared Duncan, leaping to his feet in a fury. "All lies! What wealth lies below the mountain we've worked for, with honest sweat! And here you come back, like spendthrift children, whining that your bellies are empty after wasting the days carousing when you should have been working!" He made an insulting gesture. "You even look like beggars!"

"Beggars, is it?" Reghar roared in his turn, his face turning a deep shade of purple. "No, by Reorx's beard! If I was starving and you handed me a crust of bread, I'd spit on your shoes! Deny that you're fortifying this place, practically on our borders! Deny that you've roused the elves against us, causing them to cut off their trade! Beggars! No! By Reorx's beard and his forge and his hammer, we'll come back, but it'll be as conquerors! We'll have what is rightfully ours and teach you a lesson to boot!"

"You'll come, you sniveling cowards"—Duncan sneered— "hiding behind the skirts of a black-robed wizard and the bright shields of human warriors, greedy for spoils! They'll stab you in the back and then rob your corpses!"

"Who should know better about robbing corpses!" Reghar shouted. "You've been robbing ours for years!"

The six clan members sprang out of their chairs, and Reghar's escort jumped forward. The Dewar's high-pitched laughter rose above the thundering shouts and threats. The Highgug crouched in his corner, his mouth wide open.

The war might have started then and there had not Kharas run between the two sides, his tall figure towering over everyone. Pushing and shoving, he forced both sides to back off. Still, even after the two were separated, there was the shout of derision, the occasional insult hurled. But—at a stern glance from Kharas—these soon ceased and all fell into a sullen, surly silence.

Kharas spoke, his deep voice gruff and filled with sadness. "Long ago, I prayed the god to grant me the strength to fight injustice and evil in the world. Reorx answered my prayer by granting me leave to use his forge, and there, on the forge of the god himself, I made this hammer. It has shone in battle since fighting the evil things of this world and protecting my homeland, the homeland of my people. Now, you, my king, would ask of me that I go to war against my kinsmen? And you, my kinsmen, would threaten to bring war to our land? Is this where your words are leading you—that I should use this hammer against my own blood?"

Neither side spoke. Both glowered at each other from beneath tangled brows, both seemed almost half-ashamed. Kharas's heartfelt speech touched many. Only two heard it unmoved. Both were old men, both had long ago lost any illusions about the world, both knew this rift had grown too wide to be bridged by words. But the gesture had to be made.

"Here is my offer, Duncan, King of Thorbardin," Reghar said, breathing heavily. "Withdraw your men from this fortress. Give Pax Tharkas and the lands that surround it to us and our human allies. Give us one-half of the treasure beneath the mountain—the half that is rightfully ours—and allow those of us who might choose to do so to return to the safety of the mountain if the evil grows in this land. Persuade the elves to lift their trade barriers, and split all contracts for masonry work fifty-fifty.

"In return, we will farm the land around Thorbardin and trade our crops to you for less than it's costing you to grow them underground. We'll help protect your borders and the mountain itself, if need arises."

Kharas gave his lord a pleading look, begging him to consider—or at least negotiate. But Duncan was beyond reasoning, it seemed.

"Get out!" he snarled. "Return to your black-robed wizard! Return to your human friends! Let us see if your wizard is powerful enough to blow down the walls of this fortress, or uproot the stones of our mountain. Let us see how long your human friends remain friends when the winter winds swirl about the campfires and their blood drips on the snow!"

Reghar gave Duncan a final look, filled with such enmity and hatred it might well have been a blow. Then, turning on his heel, he motioned to his followers. They stalked out of the Hall of Thanes and out of Pax Tharkas.

Word spread quickly. By the time the hill dwarves were ready to leave, the battlements were lined with mountain dwarves, shouting and hooting derisively. Reghar and his party rode off, their faces stern and grim, never once looking back.

Kharas, meanwhile, stood in the Hall of Thanes, alone with his king (and the forgotten Highgug). The six witnesses had all returned to their clans, spreading the news. Kegs of ale and the potent drink known as dwarf spirits were broached that night in celebration. Already, the sounds of singing and raucous laughter could be heard echoing through the great stone monument to peace.

"What would it have hurt to negotiate, Thane?" Kharas asked, his voice heavy with sorrow.

Duncan, his sudden anger apparently vanished, looked at the taller dwarf and shook his head, his graying beard brushing against his robes of state. He was well within his rights to refuse to answer such an impertinent question. Indeed, no one but Kharas would have had the courage to question Duncan's decision at all.

"Kharas," Duncan said, putting his hand on his friend's arm affectionately, "tell me—is there treasure beneath the mountain? Have we robbed our kinsmen? Do we raid their lands, or the lands of the humans, for that matter? Are their accusations just?"

"No," Kharas answered, his eyes meeting those of his sovereign steadily.

Duncan sighed. "You have seen the harvest. You know that what little money remains in the treasury we will spend to lay in what we can for this winter."

"Tell them this!" Kharas said earnestly. "Tell them the truth! They are not monsters! They are our kinsmen, they will understand—"

Duncan smiled sadly, wearily. "No, they are not monsters. But, what is worse, they have become like children." He shrugged. "Oh, we could tell them the truth—show them even. But they would not believe us. They would not believe their own eyes. Why? Because they *want* to believe otherwise!"

Kharas frowned, but Duncan continued patiently. "They want to believe, my friend. More than that, they *have* to believe. It is their only hope for survival. They have nothing, nothing except that hope. And so they are willing to fight for it. I understand them." The old king's eyes dimmed for a moment, and Kharas—staring at him in amazement—realized then that his anger had been all feigned, all show.

"Now they can return to their wives and their hungry children and they can say, 'We will fight the usurpers! When we win, you will have full bellies again.' And that will help them forget their hunger, for a while."

Kharas's face twisted in anguish. "But to go this far! Surely, we can share what little—"

"My friend," Duncan said softly, "by Reorx's Hammer, I swear this—if I agree to their terms, we would all perish. Our race would cease to exist."

Kharas stared at him. "As bad as that?" he asked.

Duncan nodded. "Aye, as bad as that. Few only know this—the leaders of the clans, and now you. And I swear you to secrecy. The harvest was disastrous. Our coffers are nearly empty, and now we must hoard what we can to pay for this war. Even for our own people, we will be forced to ration food this winter. With what we have, we calculate that we can make it—barely. Add hundreds of more mouths—" He shook his head.

Kharas stood pondering, then he lifted his head, his dark eyes flashing. "If that is true, then so be it!" he said sternly. "Better we all starve to death, than die fighting each other!"

"Noble words, my friend," Duncan answered. The beating of drums thrummed through the room and deep voices raised in stirring war chants, older than the rocks of Pax Tharkas, older—perhaps—than the bones of the world itself. "You can't eat noble words, though, Kharas. You can't drink them or wrap them around your feet or burn them in your firepit or give them to children crying in hunger."

"What about the children who will cry when their father leaves, never to return?" Kharas asked sternly.

Duncan raised an eyebrow. "They will cry for a month," he said simply, "then they will eat his share of the food. And wouldn't he want it that way?"

With that, he turned and left the Hall of Thanes, heading for the battlements once more.

As Duncan counseled Kharas in the Hall of Thanes, Reghar Fireforge and his party were guiding their short-statured, shaggy hill ponies out of the fortress of Pax Tharkas, the hoots and laughter of their kinsmen ringing in their ears.

Reghar did not speak a word for long hours, until they were well out of sight of the huge double towers of the fortress. Then, when they came to a crossing in the road, the old dwarf reined in his horse.

Turning to the youngest member of the party, he said in a grim, emotionless voice, "Continue north, Darren Ironfist." The old dwarf drew forth a battered, leather pouch. Reaching inside, he pulled out his last gold piece. For a long moment he stood staring at it, then he pressed it into the hands of the dwarf. "Here. Buy passage across the New Sea. Find this Fistandantilus and tell him . . . tell him—"

Reghar paused, realizing the enormity of his action. But, he had no choice. This had been decided before he left. Scowling, he snarled, "Tell him that, when he gets here, he'll have an army waiting to fight for him."

CHAPTER 2

The night was cold and dark over the lands of Solamnia. The stars above gleamed with a sparkling, brittle light. The constellations of the Platinum Dragon, Paladine, and Takhisis, Queen of Darkness, circled each other endlessly around Gilean's Scales of Balance. It would be two hundred years or more before these same constellations vanished from the skies, as the gods and men waged war over Krynn.

For now, each was content with watching the other.

If either god had happened to glance down, he or she would, perhaps, have been amused to see what appeared to be mankind's feeble attempts to imitate their celestial glory. On the plains of Solamnia, outside the mountain fortress city of Garnet, campfires dotted the flat grasslands, lighting the night below as the stars lit the night above.

The Army of Fistandantilus.

The flames of the campfires were reflected in shield and breastplate, danced off sword blades and flashed on spear tip. The fires shone on faces bright with hope and new-found pride, they burned in the dark eyes of the camp followers and leaped up to light the merry play of the children.

Around the campfires stood or sat groups of men, talking and laughing, eating and drinking, working over their equipment. The night air was filled with jests and oaths and tall tales. Here and there were groans of pain, as men rubbed shoulders and arms that ached from unaccustomed exercise. Hands calloused from swinging hoes were blistered from wielding spears. But these were accepted with good-natured shrugs. They could watch their children play around the campfires and know that they had eaten, if not well, at least adequately that night. They could face their wives with pride. For the first time in years, these men had a goal, a purpose in their lives.

There were some who knew this goal might well be death, but those who knew this recognized and understood it and made the choice to remain anyway.

"After all," said Garic to himself as his replacement came to relieve him of his guard duty, "death comes to all. Better a man meet it in the blazing sunlight, his sword flashing in his hand, than to have it come creeping up on him in the night unawares, or clutch at him with foul, diseased hands."

The young man, now that he was off duty, returned to his campfire and retrieved a thick cloak from his bedroll. Hastily gulping down a bowl of rabbit stew, he then walked among the campfires.

Headed for the outskirts of the camp, he walked with purpose, ignoring many invitations to join friends around their fires. These he waved off genially and continued on his way. Few thought anything of this. A great many fled the lights of the fires at night. The shadows were warm with soft sighs and murmurs and sweet laughter.

Garic *did* have an appointment in the shadows, but it was not with a lover, though several young women in camp would have been more than happy to share the night with the handsome young nobleman. Coming to a large boulder, far from camp and far from other company, Garic wrapped his cloak about him, sat down, and waited.

He did not wait long.

"Garic?" said a hesitant voice.

"Michael!" Garic cried warmly, rising to his feet. The two men clasped hands and then, overcome, embraced each other warmly.

"I couldn't believe my eyes when I saw you ride into camp today, cousin," Garic continued, gripping the other young man's hand as though afraid to let him go, afraid he might disappear into the darkness.

"Nor I you," said Michael, holding fast to his kinsmen and trying to rid his throat of a huskiness it seemed to have developed. Coughing, he sat down on the boulder and Garic joined him. Both remained silent for a few moments as they cleared their throats and pretended to be stern and soldierly.

"I thought it was a ghost," Michael said with a hollow attempt at a laugh. "We heard you were dead. . . ." His voice died and he coughed again. "Confounded damp weather," he muttered, "gets in a man's windpipes."

"I escaped," Garic said quietly. "But my father, my mother, and my sister were not so lucky."

"Anne?" Michael murmured, pain in his voice.

"She died quickly," Garic said quietly, "as did my mother. My father saw to that, before the mob butchered him. It made them mad. They mutilated his body—"

Garic choked. Michael gripped his arm in sympathy. "A noble man, your father. He died as a true Knight, defending his home. A better death than some face," he added grimly, causing Garic to look at him with a sharp, penetrating glance. "But, what is your story? How did you get away from the mob? Where have you been this last year?"

"I did not get away from them," Garic said bitterly. "I arrived when it was all over. Where I had been did not matter"—the young man flushed—"but I should have been with them, to die with them!"

"No, your father would not have wanted that." Michael shook his head. "You live. You will carry on the name."

Garic frowned, his eyes glinted darkly. "Perhaps. Though I have not lain with a woman since—" He shook his head. "At any rate, I could only do for them what I could. I set fire to the castle—"

Michael gasped, but Garic continued, unhearing.

"—so that the mobs should not take it over. My family's ashes remain there, among the blackened stones of the hall my great-great-grandfather built. Then I rode aimlessly, for a time, not much caring what happened to me. Finally, I met up with a group of other men, many like myself—driven from their homes for various reasons.

"They asked no questions. They cared nothing about me except that I could wield a sword with skill. I joined them and we lived off our wits."

"Bandits?" Michael asked, trying to keep a startled tone from his voice and failing, apparently, for Garic cast him a dark glance.

"Yes, bandits," the young man answered coldly. "Does that shock you? That a Knight of Solamnia should so forget the Code and the Measure that he joins with bandits? I'll ask you this, Michael—where were the Code and the Measure when they murdered my father, your uncle? Where are they anywhere in this wretched land?"

"Nowhere, perhaps," Michael returned steadily, "except in our hearts."

Garic was silent. Then he began to weep, harsh sobs that tore at his body. His cousin put his arms around him, holding him close. Garic gave a shuddering sigh, wiping his eyes with the back of his hand.

"I have not cried once since I found them," he said in a muffled voice. "And you are right, cousin. Living with robbers, I had sunk into a pit from which I might not have escaped, but for the general—"

"This Caramon?"

Garic nodded. "We ambushed him and his party one night. And that opened my eyes. Before, I had always robbed people without much thought or, sometimes, I even enjoyed it— telling myself it was dogs like these who had murdered my father. But in this party there was a woman and the magic-user. The wizard was ill. I hit him, and he crumpled at my touch like a broken doll. And the woman—I knew what they would do to her and the thought sickened me. But, I was afraid of the leader—Steeltoe, they called him. He was a beast! Half-ogre.

"But the general challenged him. I saw true nobility that night—a man willing to give his life to protect those weaker than himself. And he won." Garic grew calmer. As he talked, his eyes shone with admiration. "I saw, then, what my life had become. When Caramon asked if we would come with him, I agreed, as did most of the others. But it wouldn't have mattered about them—I would have gone with him anywhere."

"And now you're part of his personal guard?" Michael said, smiling.

Garic nodded, flushing with pleasure. "I—I told him I was no better than the others—a bandit, a thief. But he just looked at me, as though he could see inside my soul, and smiled and said every man had to walk through a dark, starless night and, when he faced the morning, he'd be better for it."

"Strange," Michael said. "I wonder what he meant?"

"I think I understand," Garic said. His glance went to the far edge of the camp where Caramon's huge tent stood, smoke from the fires curling around the fluttering, silken flag that was a black streak against the stars. "Sometimes, I wonder if he isn't walking through his own 'dark night.' I've seen a look on his face, sometimes—" Garic shook his head. "You know," he said abruptly, "he and the wizard are twin brothers."

Michael's eyes opened wide. Garic confirmed it with a nod. "It is a strange relationship. There's no love lost between them."

"One of the Black Robes?" Michael said, snorting. "I should think not! I wonder the mage even travels with us. From what I have heard, these wizards can ride the night winds and summon forces from the graves to do their battles."

"This one could do that, I've no doubt," Garic replied, giving a smaller tent next to the general's a dark glance. "Though I have seen him do his magic only once—back at the bandit camp—I know he is powerful. One look from his eyes, and my stomach shrivels inside of me, my blood turns to water. But, as I said, he was not well when we first met up with them. Night after night, when he still slept in his brother's tent, I heard him cough until I did not think he could draw breath again. How can a man live with such pain, I asked myself more than once."

"But he seemed fine when I saw him today."

"His health has improved greatly. He does nothing to tax it, however. Just spends all day in his tent, studying the spell-books he carries with him in those great, huge chests. But he's walking his 'dark night,' too," Garic added. "A gloom hangs about him, and it's been growing the farther south we travel. He is haunted by terrible dreams. I've heard him cry out in his sleep. Horrible cries—they'd wake the dead."

Michael shuddered, then, sighing, looked over at Caramon's tent. "I had grave misgivings about joining an army led, they say, by one of the Black Robes. And of all the wizards who have ever lived, this Fistandantilus is rumored to be the most powerful. I had not fully committed myself to join when I rode in today. I thought I would look things over, find out if it's true they go south to help the oppressed people of Abanasinia in their fight against mountain dwarves."

Sighing again, he made a gesture as if to stroke long mustaches, but his hand stopped. He was clean-shaven, having removed the ages-old symbol of the Knights—the symbol that led, these days, to death.

"Though my father still lives, Garic," Michael continued, "I think he might well trade his life for your father's death. We were given a choice by the lord of Vingaard Keep—we could stay in the city and die or leave and live. Father would have died. I, too, if we'd had only ourselves to think of. But we could not afford the luxury of honor. A bitter day it was when we packed what we could on a mean cart and left the Hall. I saw them settled in a wretched cottage in Throytl. They'll be all right, for the winter at least. Mother is strong and does the work of a man. My little brothers are good hunters. . . ."

"Your father?" Garic asked gently when Michael stopped talking.

"His heart broke that day," Michael said simply. "He sits

staring out the window, his sword on his lap. He has not spoken one word to anyone since the day we left the family hall."

Michael suddenly clenched his fist. "Why am I lying to you, Garic? I don't give a damn about oppressed people in Abanasinia! I came to find the treasure! The treasure beneath the mountain! And glory! Glory to bring back the light in his eyes! If we win, the Knights can lift their heads once more!"

He, too, gazed at the small tent next to the large one—the small tent that had the sign of a wizard's residence hung upon it, the small tent that everyone in the camp avoided, if possible. "But, to find this glory, led by the man called the Dark One. The Knights of old would not have done so. Paladine—"

"Paladine has forgotten us," Garic said bitterly. "We are left on our own. I know nothing of black-robed wizards, I care little about that one. I stay here and I follow because of one man—the general. If he leads me to my fortune, well and good. If not"—Garic sighed deeply—"then he has at least led me to find peace within myself. I could wish the same for him," he said, beneath his breath. Then, rising, he shook off his gloomy thoughts.

Michael rose, too.

"I must return to camp and get some sleep. It is early waking tomorrow," Garic said. "We're preparing to march within the week, so I hear. Well, cousin, will you stay?"

Michael looked at Garic. He looked at Caramon's tent, its bright-colored flag with the nine-pointed star fluttering in the chill air. He looked at the wizard's tent. Then, he nodded. Garic grinned widely. The two clasped hands and walked back to the campfires, arms around each other's shoulders.

"Tell me this, though," Michael said in a hushed voice as they walked, "is it true this Caramon keeps a witch?"

CHAPTER 3

here are you going?" Caramon demanded harshly. Stepping into his tent, his eyes blinked rapidly to try to get accustomed to the shadowy darkness after the chill glare of the autumn sun.

"I'm moving out," Crysania said, carefully folding her white clerical robes and placing them in the chest that had been stored beneath her cot. Now it sat open on the floor beside her.

"We've been through this," Caramon growled in a low voice. Glancing behind him at the guards outside the tent entrance, he carefully lowered the tent flap.

Caramon's tent was his pride and joy. Having originally belonged to a wealthy Knight of Solamnia, it had been brought to Caramon as a gift by two young, stern-faced men, who—though they claimed to have "found" it—handled it with such skilled hands and loving care that it was obvious they had no more "found" it than they had found their own arms or legs.

Made of some fabric none in this day and age could

identify, it was so cunningly woven that not a breath of wind penetrated even the seams. Rainwater rolled right off it; Raistlin said it had been treated with some sort of oil. It was large enough for Caramon's cot, several large chests containing maps, the money, and jewels they brought from the Tower of High Sorcery, clothes and armor, plus a cot for Crysania, as well as a chest for her clothing. Still, it did not seem crowded when Caramon received visitors.

Raistlin slept and studied in a smaller tent made of the same fabric and construction that was pitched near his brother's. Though Caramon had offered to share the larger tent, the mage had insisted upon privacy. Knowing his twin's need for solitude and quiet, and not particularly enjoying being around his brother anyway, Caramon had not argued. Crysania, however, had openly rebelled when told she must remain in Caramon's tent.

In vain, Caramon argued that it was safer for her there. Stories about her "witchcraft," the strange medallion of a reviled god she wore, and her healing of the big warrior had spread quickly through the camp and were eagerly whispered to all newcomers. The cleric never left her tent but that dark glances followed her. Women grabbed their babies to their breasts when she came near. Small children ran from her in fear that was half mocking and half real.

"I am well aware of your arguments," Crysania remarked, continuing to fold her clothes and pack them away without looking up at the big man. "And I don't concede them. Oh"— she stopped him as he drew a breath to speak—"I've heard your stories of witch-burning. More than once! I do not doubt their validity, but that was in a day and age far removed from this one."

"Whose tent are you moving to, then?" Caramon asked, his face flushing. "My brother's?"

Crysania ceased folding the clothes, holding them for long moments over her arm, staring straight ahead. Her face did not change color. It grew, if possible, a shade more pale. Her lips pressed tightly together. When she answered, her voice was cold and calm as a winter's day. "There is another small tent, similar to his. I will live in that one. You may post a guard, if you think it necessary."

"Crysania, I'm sorry," Caramon said, moving toward her. She still did not look at him. Reaching out his hands, he took hold of her arms, gently, and turned her around, forcing her to face him. "I . . . I didn't mean that. Please forgive me. And, yes, I think it *is* necessary to post a guard! But there is no one I trust, Crysania, unless it is myself. And, even then—" His breathing quickened, the hands on her arms tightened almost imperceptibly.

"I love you, Crysania," he said softly. "You're not like any other woman I've ever known! I didn't mean to. I don't know how it happened. I—I didn't even really much *like* you when I first met you. I thought you were cold and uncaring, wrapped up in that religion of yours. But when I saw you in the clutches of that half-ogre, I saw your courage, and when I thought about what—what they might do to you—"

He felt her shudder involuntarily; she still had dreams about that night. She tried to speak, but Caramon took advantage of her reaction to hurry on.

"I've seen you with my brother. It reminds me of the way I was, in the old days"—his voice grew wistful—"you care for him so tenderly, so patiently."

Crysania did not break free of his grasp. She simply stood there, looking up at him with clear, gray eyes, holding the folded white robe close against her chest. "This, too, is a reason, Caramon," she said sadly. "I have sensed your growing"—now she flushed, slightly—"affection for me and, while I know you too well to believe you would ever force attentions on me that I would consider unwelcome, I do not feel comfortable sleeping in the same tent alone with you."

"Crysania!" Caramon began, his face anguished, his hands trembling as they held her.

"What you feel for me isn't love, Caramon," Crysania said softly. "You are lonely, you miss your wife. It is *her* you love. I know, I've seen the tenderness in your eyes when you talk about Tika."

His face darkened at the sound of Tika's name.

"What would you know of love?" Caramon asked abruptly, releasing his grasp and looking away. "I love Tika, sure. I've loved lots of women. Tika's loved her share of men, too, I'll wager." He drew in an angry breath. That wasn't true, and he knew it. But it eased his own guilt, guilt he'd been wrestling with for months. "Tika's human!" he continued surlily. "*She's* flesh and blood—not some pillar of ice!"

"What do *I* know of love?" Crysania repeated, her calm slipping, her gray eyes darkening in anger. "I'll tell you what I know of love. I—"

"Don't say it!" Caramon cried in a low voice, completely losing control of himself and grabbing her in his arms. "Don't say you love Raistlin! He doesn't deserve your love! He's using you, just like he used me! And he'll throw you away when he's finished!"

"Let go of me!" Crysania demanded, her cheeks stained pink, her eyes a deep gray.

"Can't you see!" Caramon cried, almost shaking her in his frustration. "Are you blind?"

"Pardon me," said a soft voice, "if I am interrupting. But there is urgent news."

At the sound of that soft voice, Crysania's face went white, then scarlet. Caramon, too, started at the sound, his hands loosening their hold. Crysania drew back from him and, in her haste, stumbled over the chest and fell to her knees. Her face well hidden by her long, black, flowing hair, she remained kneeling beside the chest, pretending to rearrange her things with hands that shook.

Scowling, his own face flushed an ugly red, Caramon turned to face his twin.

Raistlin coolly regarded his brother with his mirrorlike eyes. There was no expression on his face, as there had been no expression in his voice when he spoke upon first entering. But Caramon had seen, for a split second, the eyes crack. The glimpse of the dark and burning jealousy inside appalled him, hitting him an almost physical blow. But the look was gone instantly, leaving Caramon to doubt if he had truly seen it. Only the tight, knotted feeling in the pit of his stomach and the sudden bitter taste in his mouth made him believe it had been there.

"What news?" he growled, clearing his throat.

"Messengers have arrived from the south," Raistlin said.

"Yes?" Caramon prompted, as his brother paused.

Casting off his hood, Raistlin stepped forward, his gaze holding his brother's gaze, binding them together, making the resemblance between them strong. For an instant, the mage's mask dropped.

"The dwarves of Thorbardin are preparing for war!" Raistlin hissed, his slender hand clenching into a fist. He spoke with such intense passion that Caramon blinked at him in astonishment and Crysania raised her head to regard him with concern.

Confused and uncomfortable, Caramon broke free of his brother's feverish stare and turned away, pretending to shuffle some maps on the map table. The warrior shrugged. "I don't know what else you expected," he said coolly. "It was your idea, after all. Talking of hidden wealth. We've made no secret of the fact that's where we're headed. In fact, it's practically become our recruiting slogan! 'Join up with Fistandantilus and raid the mountain!'"

Caramon tossed this off thoughtlessly, but its effect was startling. Raistlin went livid. He seemed to try to speak, but no intelligible sounds came from his lips, only a blood-stained froth. His sunken eyes flared, as the moon on an ice-bound lake. His fist still clenched, he took a step toward his brother.

Crysania sprang to her feet. Caramon—truly alarmed—took a step backward, his hand closing over the hilt of his sword. But, slowly and with a visible effort, Raistlin regained control. With a vicious snarl, he turned and walked from the tent, his intense anger still so apparent, however, that the guards shivered as he passed them.

Caramon remained standing, lost in confusion and fear, unable to comprehend why his brother had reacted as he did. Crysania, too, stared after Raistlin in perplexity until the sound of shouting voices outside the tent roused both of them from their thoughts. Shaking his head, Caramon walked over to the entrance. Once there, he half-turned but did not look at Crysania as he spoke.

"If we are truly preparing for war," he said coldly, "I can't take time to worry about you. As I have stated before, you won't be safe in a tent by yourself. So you'll continue to sleep here. I'll leave you alone, you may be certain of that. You have my word of honor."

With this, he stepped outside the tent and began conferring with his guards.

Flushing in shame, yet so angry she could not speak, Crysania remained in the tent for a moment to regain her composure. Then she, too, walked from the tent. One glance at the guards' faces and she realized at once that, despite the fact that she and Caramon had kept their voices low, part of their conversation had been overheard.

Ignoring the curious, amused glances, she looked around quickly and saw the flutter of black robes disappearing into the forest. Returning to the tent, she caught up her cloak and, tossing it hurriedly around her shoulders, headed off in the same direction.

Caramon saw Crysania enter the woods near the edge of camp. Though he had not seen Raistlin, he had a pretty good idea of why Crysania was headed in that direction. He started to call to her. Though he did not know of any real danger lurking in the scraggly forest of pine trees that stood at the base of the Garnet Mountains, in these unsettled times, it was best not to take chances.

As her name was on his lips, however, he saw two of his men exchange knowing looks. Caramon had a sudden vivid picture of himself calling after the cleric like some love-sick youth, and his mouth snapped shut. Besides, here was Garic coming up, followed by a weary-looking dwarf and a tall, dark-skinned young man decked out in the furs and feathers of a barbarian.

The messengers, Caramon realized. He would have to meet with them. But—His gaze went once more to the forest. Crysania had vanished. A premonition of danger seized Caramon. It was so strong that he almost crashed through the trees after her, then and there. Every warrior's instinct called to him. He could put no name to his fear, but it was there, it was real.

Yet, he could not rush off, leaving these emissaries, while he went chasing after a girl. His men would never respect him again. He could send a guard, but that would make him look almost as foolish. There was no help for it. Let Paladine look after her, if that was what she wanted. Gritting his teeth, Caramon turned to greet the messengers and lead them into his tent.

Once there, once he had made them comfortable and had exchanged formal and meaningless pleasantries, once food had been brought and drinks poured, he excused himself and slipped out the back. . . .

Footsteps in the sand, leading me on. . . .

Looking up, I see the scaffold, the hooded figure with its head on the block, the hooded figure of the executioner, the sharp blade of the axe glinting in the burning sun.

The axe falls, the victim's severed head rolls on the wooden platform, the hood comes off—

"My head!" Raistlin whispered feverishly, twisting his thin hands together in anguish.

The executioner, laughing, removes his hood, revealing—

"My face!" Raistlin murmured, his fear spreading through his body like a malign growth, making him sweat and chill by turns. Clutching at his head, he tried to banish the evil visions that haunted his dreams continually, night after night, and lingered to disturb his waking hours as well, turning all he ate or drank to ashes in his mouth.

But they would not depart. "Master of Past and Present!" Raistlin laughed hollowly—bitter, mocking laughter. "I am Master of nothing! All this power, and I am trapped! Trapped! Following in *his* footsteps, knowing that every second that passes has *passed before*! I see people I've never seen, yet I know them! I hear the echo of my own words before I speak them! This face!" His hands pressed against his cheeks. "This face! *His* face! Not mine! Not mine! Who am I? I am my own executioner!"

His voice rose to a shriek. In a frenzy, not realizing what he was doing, Raistlin began to claw at his skin with his nails as though his face were a mask, and he could tear it from his bones.

"Stop! Raistlin, what are you doing? Stop, please!"

He could barely hear the voice. Firm but gentle hands grasped his wrists, and he fought them, struggling. But then the madness passed. The dark and frightful waters in which he had been drowning receded, leaving him calm and drained. Once more, he could see and feel and hear. His face stung. Looking down, he saw blood on his nails.

"Raistlin!" It was Crysania's voice. Lifting his gaze, he saw her standing before him, holding his hands away from his face, her eyes wide and filled with concern.

"I'm all right," Raistlin said coldly. "Leave me alone!" But, even as he spoke, he sighed and lowered his head again, shuddering as the horror of the dream washed over him. Pulling a clean cloth from a pocket, he began to dab at the wounds on his face.

"No, you're not," Crysania murmured, taking the cloth from his shaking hand and gently touching the bleeding gouges. "Please, let me do this," she said, as he snarled something unintelligible. "I know you won't let me heal you, but there is a clear stream near. Come, drink some water, rest and let me wash these "

Sharp, bitter words were on Raistlin's lips. He raised a hand to thrust her away. But then he realized that he didn't want her to leave. The darkness of the dream receded when she was with him. The touch of warm, human flesh was comforting after the cold fingers of death.

And so, he nodded with a weary sigh.

Her face pale with anguish and concern, Crysania put her arm around him to support his faltering steps, and Raistlin allowed himself to be led through the forest, acutely conscious of the warmth and the motion of her body next to his.

Reaching the bank of the stream, the archmage sat down upon a large, flat rock, warmed by the autumn sun. Crysania dipped her cloth in the water and, kneeling next to him, cleaned the wounds on his face. Dying leaves fell around them, muffling sound, falling into the stream to be whisked away by the water.

Raistlin did not speak. His gaze followed the path of the leaves, watching as each clung to the branch with its last, feeble strength, watching as the ruthless wind tore it from its hold, watching as it swirled in the air to fall into the water, watching as it was carried off into oblivion by the swift-running stream. Looking past the leaves into the water, he saw the reflection of his face wavering there. He saw two long, bloody marks down each cheek, he saw his eyes—no longer mirrorlike, but dark and haunted. He saw fear, and he sneered at himself derisively.

"Tell me," said Crysania hesitantly, pausing in her ministrations and placing her hand over his, "tell me what's wrong. I don't understand. You've been brooding ever since we left the Tower. Has it something to do with the Portal being gone? With what Astinus told you back in Palanthas?"

Raistlin did not answer. He did not even look at her. The sun was warm on his black robes, her touch was warmer than the sun. But, somewhere, some part of his mind was coldly balancing, calculating—tell her? What will I gain? More than if I kept silent?

Yes . . . draw her nearer, enfold her, wrap her up, accustom her to the darkness. . . .

"I know," he said finally, speaking as if reluctantly, yet—for some reason—still not looking at her as he spoke, but staring into the water, "that the Portal is in a place near Thorbardin, in the magical fortress called Zhaman. This I discovered from Astinus.

"Legend tells us that Fistandantilus undertook what some call the Dwarfgate Wars so that he could claim the mountain kingdom of Thorbardin for his own. Astinus relates much the same thing in his *Chronicles*"—Raistlin's voice grew bitter—"*much* the same thing! But, read between the lines, read closely, as I *should* have read but, in my arrogance, did not, and you will read the truth!"

His hands clenched. Crysania sat before him, the damp,

blood-stained cloth held fast, forgotten as she listened, enthralled.

"Fistandantilus came here to do *the very same thing I came here to do!*" Raistlin's words hissed with a strange, foreboding passion. "He cared nothing for Thorbardin! It was all a sham, a ruse! He wanted one thing—and that was to reach the Portal! The dwarves stood in his way, as they stand in mine. They controlled the fortress then, they controlled the land for miles around it. The only way he could reach it was to start a war so that he could get close enough to gain access to it! And, so, history repeats itself.

"For I must do what he did. . . . I *am* doing what he did!"

His expression bitter, he stared silently into the water.

"From what I have read of Astinus's *Chronicles*," Crysania began, speaking hesitantly, "the war was bound to come anyway. There has long been bad blood between the hill dwarves and their cousins. You can't blame yourself—"

Raistlin snarled impatiently. "I don't give a damn about the dwarves! They can sink into the Sirrion, for all I care." Now he looked at her, coldly, steadily. "You say you have read Astinus's works on this. If so, think! What caused the end of the Dwarfgate Wars?"

Crysania's eyes grew unfocused as she sought back in her mind, trying to recall. Then her face paled. "The explosion," she said softly. "The explosion that destroyed the Plains of Dergoth. Thousands died and so did—"

"*So did Fistandantilus!*" Raistlin said with grim emphasis.

For long moments, Crysania could only stare at him. Then the full realization of what he meant sank in. "Oh, but surely not!" she cried, dropping the blood-stained cloth and clutching Raistlin's hands with her own. "You're not the same person! The circumstances are different. They must be! You've made a mistake!"

Raistlin shook his head, smiling cynically. Gently disengaging his hand from hers, he reached out and touched her chin, raising her head so that she looked directly into his eyes. "No, the circumstances are *not* different. I have *not* made a mistake. I am caught in time, rushing forward to my own doom."

"How do you know? How can you be certain?"

"I know because—one other perished with Fistandantilus that day."

"Who?" Crysania asked, but even before he told her she felt a dark mantle of fear settle upon her shoulders, falling around her with a rustle as soft as the dying leaves.

"An old friend of yours," Raistlin's smile twisted. "Denubis!"

"Denubis!" she repeated soundlessly.

"Yes," Raistlin replied, unconsciously letting his fingers trace along her firm jaw, cup her chin in his hand. "That much I learned from Astinus. If you will recall, your cleric friend was already drawn to Fistandantilus, even though he refused to admit it to himself. He had his doubts about the church, much the same as yours. I can only assume that during those final, horrifying days in Istar, Fistandantilus persuaded him to come—"

"You didn't persuade *me*," Crysania interrupted firmly. "I chose to come! It was my decision!"

"Of course," Raistlin said smoothly, letting go of her. He hadn't realized what he was doing, caressing her soft skin. Now, unbidden, he felt his blood stir. He found his gaze going to her curving lips, her white neck. He had a sudden vivid image of her in his brother's arms. He remembered the wild surge of jealousy he had felt.

This must not happen! he reprimanded himself. It will interfere with my plans. . . . He started to rise, but Crysania caught hold of his hand with both of hers and rested her cheek in his palm.

"No," she said softly, her gray eyes looking up at him, shining in the bright sunlight that filtered through the leaves, holding him with her steadfast gaze, "we will alter time, you and I! You are more powerful than Fistandantilus. I am stronger in my faith than Denubis! I heard the Kingpriest's demands of the gods. I know his mistake! Paladine will answer my prayers as he has in the past. Together, we will change the ending . . . you and I. . . ."

Caught up in the passion of her words, Crysania's eyes

deepened to blue, her skin, cool on Raistlin's hand, flushed a delicate pink. Beneath his fingers, he could feel the lifeblood pulse in her neck. He felt her tenderness, her softness, her smoothness . . . and suddenly he was down on his knees beside her. She was in his arms. His mouth sought her lips, his lips touched her eyes, her neck. His fingers tangled in her hair. Her fragrance filled his nostrils, and the sweet ache of desire filled his body.

She yielded to his fire, as she had yielded to his magic, kissing him eagerly. Raistlin sank down into the soft carpet of dying leaves. Lying back, he drew Crysania down with him, holding her in his arms. The sunlight in the blue autumn sky was brilliant, blinding him. The sun itself beat upon his black robes with a unbearable heat, almost as unbearable as the pain inside his body.

Crysania's skin was cool to his feverish touch, her lips like sweet water to a man dying of thirst. He gave himself up to the light, shutting his eyes against it. And then, the shadow of a face appeared in his mind: a goddess—dark-haired, dark-eyed, exultant, victorious, laughing. . . .

"No!" Raistlin cried. "No!" he shrieked in half-strangled tones as he hurled Crysania from him. Trembling and dizzy, he staggered to his feet.

His eyes burned in the sunlight. The heat upon his robes was stifling, and he felt himself gasping for air. Drawing his black hood over his head, he stood, shaking, trying to regain his composure, his control.

"Raistlin!" Crysania cried, clinging to his hand. Her voice was warm with passion. Her touch worsened the pain, even as it promised to ease it. His resolve began to crumble, the pain tore at him. . . .

Furiously, Raistlin snatched his hand free. Then, his face grim, he reached out and grasped the fragile white cloth of her robes. With a jerk, he ripped it from her shoulders, while, with the other hand, he shoved her half-naked body down into the leaves.

"Is this what you want?" he asked, his voice taut with anger. "If so, wait here for my brother. He's bound to be along soon!" He paused, struggling for breath.

Lying on the leaves, seeing her nakedness reflected starkly in those mirrorlike eyes, Crysania clutched the torn cloth to her breast and stared at him wordlessly.

"Is *this* what we have come here to attain?" Raistlin continued relentlessly. "I thought your aim was higher, Revered Daughter! You boast of Paladine, you boast of your powers. Did you think that this might be the answer to your prayers? That I would fall victim to your charms?"

That shot told! He saw her flinch, her gaze waver. Closing her eyes, she rolled over, sobbing in agony, clasping her torn robe to her body. Her black hair fell across her bare shoulders, the skin of her back was white and soft and smooth. . . .

Turning abruptly, Raistlin walked away. He walked rapidly and, as he walked, he felt calm return to him. The ache of passion subsided, leaving him once more able to think clearly.

His eyes caught a glimpse of movement, a flash of armor. His smile curled into a sneer. As he had predicted, there went Caramon, setting out in search of her. Well, they were welcome to each other. What did it matter to him?

Reaching his tent, Raistlin entered its cool, dark confines. The sneer still curled his lips but, recalling his weakness, recalling how close he'd come to failure, recalling—against his will—her soft, warm lips, it faded. Shaking, he collapsed into a chair and let his head sink into his hands.

But the smile was back, half an hour later, when Caramon burst into his tent. The big man's face was flushed, his eyes dilated, his hand on the hilt of his sword.

"I should kill you, you damned bastard!" he said in a choked voice.

"What for this time, my brother?" Raistlin asked in irritation, continuing to read the spellbook he was studying. "Have I murdered another of your pet kender?"

"You know damn well what for!" Caramon snarled with an oath. Lurching forward, he grabbed the spellbook and slammed it shut. His fingers burned as he touched its night-blue binding, but he didn't even feel the pain. "I found Lady

Crysania in the woods, her clothes ripped off, crying her heart out! Those marks on your face—"

"Were made by my hands. Did she tell you what happened?" Raistlin interrupted.

"Yes, but—"

"Did she tell you that *she* offered herself to *me*?"

"I don't believe—"

"And that *I* turned her down," Raistlin continued coldly, his eyes meeting his brother's unwaveringly.

"You arrogant son of a—"

"And even now, she probably sits weeping in her tent, thanking the gods that I love her enough to cherish her virtue." Raistlin gave a bitter, mocking laugh that pierced Caramon like a poisoned dagger.

"I don't believe you!" Caramon said softly. Grabbing hold of his brother's robes, he yanked Raistlin from his chair. "I don't believe her! She'd say anything to protect your miserable—"

"Remove your hands, brother!" Raistlin said in a flat, soft whisper.

"I'll see you in the Abyss!"

"I said remove your hands!" There was a flash of blue light, a crackle and sizzling sound, and Caramon screamed in pain, loosening his hold as a jarring, paralyzing shock surged through his body.

"I warned you," Raistlin straightened his robes and resumed his seat.

"By the gods, I *will* kill you this time!" Caramon said through clenched teeth, drawing his sword with a trembling hand.

"Then do so," Raistlin snapped, looking up from the spellbook he had reopened, "and get it over with. This constant threatening becomes boring!"

There was an odd gleam in the mage's eyes, an almost eager gleam—a gleam of invitation.

"Try it!" he whispered, staring at his brother. "Try to kill me! You will *never* get home again. . . ."

"That doesn't matter!" Lost in blood-lust, overwhelmed by

jealousy and hatred, Caramon took a step toward his brother, who sat, waiting, that strange, eager look upon his thin face.

"Try it!" Raistlin ordered again.

Caramon raised his sword.

"General Caramon!" Alarmed voices shouted outside; there was the sound of running footsteps. With an oath, Caramon checked his swing and hesitated, half-blinded by tears of rage, staring grimly at his brother.

"General! Where are you?" The voices sounded closer, and there were the answering voices of his guard, directing them to Raistlin's tent.

"Here!" Caramon finally shouted. Turning from his brother, he thrust the sword back into its scabbard and yanked open the tent flap. "What is it?"

"General, I—Sir, your hands! They're burned. How—?"

"Never mind. What's the matter?"

"The witch, sir. She's gone!"

"Gone?" Caramon repeated in alarm. Casting his brother a vicious glance, the big man hurried out of the tent. Raistlin heard his booming voice demanding explanations, the men giving them.

Raistlin did not listen. He closed his eyes with a sigh. Caramon had not been allowed to kill him.

Ahead of him, stretched out before him in a straight, narrow line, the footsteps led inexorably on.

CHAPTER 4

aramon had once complimented her on her riding skill. Until leaving Palanthas with Tanis Half-Elven to ride south to seek the magical Forest of Wayreft, Crysania had never been nearer a horse than seated inside one of her father's elegant carriages. Women of Palanthas did not ride, not even for pleasure, as did the other Solamnic women.

But that had been in her other life.

Her other life. Crysania smiled grimly to herself as she leaned over her mount's neck and dug her heels into its flanks, urging it forward at a trot. How far away it seemed; long ago and distant.

She checked a sigh, ducking her head to avoid some low-hanging branches. She did not look behind her. Pursuit would not be very swift in coming, she hoped. There were the messengers—Caramon would have to deal with them first—and he dared not send any of his guards out without him. Not after the witch!

Suddenly, Crysania laughed. If anyone ever looked like a

witch, I do! She had not bothered to change her torn robes. When Caramon had found her in the woods, he had fastened them together with clasps from his cloak. The robes had ceased, long ago, to be snowy white; from travel and wear and being washed in streams, they had dulled to a dove-colored gray. Now, torn and mud-spattered, they fluttered around her like bedraggled feathers. Her cloak whipped out behind her as she rode. Her black hair was a tangled mass. She could scarcely see through it.

She rode out of the woods. Ahead of her stretched the grasslands, and she reined in the horse for a moment to study the land lying ahead of her. The animal, used to plodding along with the ranks of the slow-moving army, was excited by this unaccustomed exercise. It shook its head and danced sideways a few steps, looking longingly at the smooth expanse of grass, begging for a run. Crysania patted its neck.

"Come on, boy," she urged, giving it free rein.

Nostrils flaring, the horse laid back its ears and sprang forward, galloping across the open grasslands, thrilling in its newfound freedom. Clinging to the creature's neck, Crysania gave herself up to the pleasure of *her* newfound freedom. The warm afternoon sun was a pleasant contrast to the sharp, biting wind in her face. The rhythm of the animal's gallop, the excitement of the ride, and the faint edge of fear she always felt on horseback numbed her mind, easing the ache in her heart.

As she rode, her plans crystallized in her mind, becoming clearer and sharper. Ahead of her, the land darkened with the shadows of a pine forest; above her, to her right, the snow-capped peaks of the Garnet Mountains glistened in the bright sunshine. Giving the reins a sharp jerk to remind the animal that she was in control, Crysania slowed the horse's mad gallop and guided it toward the distant woods.

Crysania had been gone from camp almost an hour before Caramon managed to get matters organized enough to set off in pursuit. As Crysania had foreseen, he had to explain the emergency to the messengers and make certain they were not offended before he could leave. This involved some time, because the Plainsman spoke very little Common and no dwarven, and, while the dwarf spoke Common fairly well (one reason he had been chosen as messenger), he couldn't understand Caramon's strange accent and was constantly forcing the big man to repeat himself.

Caramon had begun trying to explain who Crysania was and what her relationship was to him, but that proved impossible for either the dwarf or the Plainsman to comprehend. Finally, Caramon gave up and told them, bluntly, what they were bound to hear in camp anyway—that she was his woman and she had run off.

The Plainsman nodded in understanding. The women of his tribe, being notably wild, occasionally took it into their heads to do the same thing. He suggested that when Caramon caught her, he have all her hair cut off—the sign of a disobedient wife. The dwarf was somewhat astonished—a dwarven woman would as soon think of running away from home and husband as she would of shaving her chin whiskers. But, he reminded himself dourly, he was among humans and what could you expect?

Both bid Caramon a quick and successful journey and settled down to enjoy the camp's stock of ale. Heaving a sigh of relief, Caramon hurried out of his tent to find that Garic had saddled a horse and was holding it ready for him.

"We picked up her trail, General," the young man said, pointing. "She rode north, following a small animal trail into the woods. She's on a fast horse—" Garic shook his head a moment in admiration. "She stole one of the best, I'll say that for her, sir. But, I wouldn't think she'd get far."

Caramon mounted. "Thank you, Garic," he began, then stopped as he saw another horse being led up. "What's this?" he growled. "I said I was going alone—"

"I am coming, too, my brother," spoke a voice from the shadows.

Caramon looked around. The archmage came out of his tent, dressed in his black traveling cloak and boots. Caramon scowled, but Garic was already respectfully helping Raistlin to mount the thin, nervous black horse the archmage favored. Caramon dared not say anything in front of the men—and his brother knew it. He saw the amused glint in Raistlin's eyes as he raised his head, the sunlight hitting their mirrored surface.

"Let's be off, then," Caramon muttered, trying to conceal his anger. "Garic, you're in command while I'm gone. I don't expect it will be long. Make certain that our guests are fed and get those farmers back out there on the field. I want to see them spearing those straw dummies when I return, not each other!"

"Yes, sir," Garic said gravely, giving Caramon the Knight's salute.

A vivid memory of Sturm Brightblade came to Caramon's mind, and with it days of his youth; days when he and his brother had traveled with their friends—Tanis, Flint the dwarven metalsmith, Sturm. . . . Shaking his head, he tried to banish the memories as he guided his horse out of camp.

But they returned to him more forcefully when he reached the trail into the woods and caught a glimpse of his brother riding next to him, the mage keeping his horse just a little behind the warrior's, as usual. Though he did not particularly like riding, Raistlin rode well, as he did all things well if he set his mind to it. He did not speak nor even look at his brother, keeping his hood cast over his head, lost in his own thoughts. This was not unusual—the twins had sometimes traveled for days with little verbal communication.

But there was a bond between them, nonetheless, a bond of blood and bone and soul. Caramon felt himself slipping into the old, easy comradeship. His anger began to melt away—it had been partly at himself, anyhow.

Half-turning, he spoke over his shoulder.

"I—I'm sorry . . . about . . . back there, Raist," he said gruffly as they rode deeper into the forest, following Crysania's clearly marked trail. "What you said was true—she did tell me that . . . that she—" Caramon floundered, blushing. He twisted around in the saddle. "That she—Damn it, Raist! Why did you have to be so rough with her?"

Raistlin lifted his hooded head, his face now visible to his brother. "I had to be rough," he said in his soft voice. "I had to make her see the chasm yawning at her feet, a chasm that, if we fell into it, would destroy us all!"

Caramon stared at his twin in wonder. "You're not human!"

To his astonishment, Raistlin sighed. The mage's harsh, glittering eyes softened a moment. "I am more human than you realize, my brother," he said in a wistful tone that went straight to Caramon's heart.

"Then love her, man!" Caramon said, dropping back to ride beside his brother. "Forget this nonsense about chasms and pits or whatever! You may be a powerful wizard and she may be a holy cleric, but, underneath those robes, you're both flesh and blood! Take her in your arms and . . . and. . . ."

Caramon was so carried away that he checked his horse, stopping in the middle of the trail, his face lit with his passion and enthusiasm. Raistlin brought his horse to a stop, too. Leaning forward, he laid his hand on his brother's arm, his burning fingers searing Caramon's skin. His expression was hard, his eyes once again brittle and cold as glass.

"Listen to me, Caramon, and try to understand," Raistlin said in an expressionless tone that made his twin shudder. "I am incapable of love. Haven't you realized that, yet? Oh, yes, you are right—beneath these robes I am flesh and blood, more's the pity. Like any other man, I am capable of lust. That's all it is . . . lust."

He shrugged. "It would probably matter little to me if I gave in to it, perhaps weaken me some temporarily, nothing more. It would certainly not affect my magic. But"—his gaze went through Caramon like a sliver of ice—"it would destroy Crysania when she found out. And she *would* find out!"

"You black-hearted bastard!" Caramon said through clenched teeth.

Raistlin raised an eyebrow. "Am I?" he asked simply. "If I were, wouldn't I just take my pleasure as I found it? I am capable of understanding and controlling myself—unlike others."

Caramon blinked. Spurring his horse, he proceeded down the trail again, lost in confusion. Somehow, his brother had managed, once again, to turn everything upside down. Suddenly he, Caramon, felt consumed with guilt—a prey to animal instincts he wasn't man enough to control, while his brother—by admitting he was incapable of love—appeared noble and self-sacrificing. Caramon shook his head.

The two followed Crysania's trail deeper into the woods. It was easy going, she had kept to the path, never veering, never bothering, even, to cover her tracks.

"Women!" Caramon muttered after a time. "If she was going to have a sulking fit, why didn't she just do it the easy way and walk! Why did she have to take a blasted horseback ride halfway into the countryside?"

"You do not understand her, my brother," Raistlin said, his gaze on the trail. "Such is not her intent. She has a purpose in this ride, believe me."

"Bah!" Caramon snorted. "This from the expert on women! I've been married! I know! She's ridden off in a huff, knowing we'll come after her. We'll find her somewhere along here, her horse ridden into the ground, probably lame. She'll be cold and haughty. We'll apologize and . . . and I'll let her have her damn tent if she wants it and—see there! What'd I tell you?" Bringing his horse to a halt, he gestured across the flat grasslands. "There's a trail a blind gully dwarf could follow! Come on."

Raistlin did not answer, but there was a thoughtful look on his thin face as he galloped after his brother. The two followed Crysania's trail across the grasslands. They found where she entered the woods again, came to a stream and crossed it. But there, on the bank of the stream Caramon brought his horse to a halt.

"What the—" He looked left and right, guiding his animal around in a circle. Raistlin stopped, sighing, and leaned over the pommel of his saddle.

"I told you," he said grimly. "She has a purpose. She is clever, my brother. Clever enough to know your mind and how it works . . . when it *does* work!"

Caramon glowered at his twin but said nothing.

Crysania's trail had disappeared.

As Raistlin said, Crysania had a purpose. She was clever and intelligent, she guessed what Caramon would think and she purposefully misled him. Though certainly not skilled in woodslore herself, for months now, she had been with those who were. Often lonely—few spoke to the "witch"—and often left to her own devices by Caramon, who had problems of command to deal with, and Raistlin, who was wrapped up in his studies, Crysania had little to do but ride by herself, listening to the stories of those about her and learning from them.

Thus it had been a simple thing to.double back on her own trail, riding her horse down the center of the stream, leaving no tracks to follow. Coming to a rocky part of the shore where, again, her horse would leave no tracks, she left the stream. Entering the woods, she avoided the main trail, searching instead for one of the many, smaller animal trails that led to the stream. Once on it, she covered her tracks as best she could. Although she did it crudely, she was fairly certain Caramon would not give her credit enough even for that, so she had no fear he would follow her.

If Crysania had known Raistlin rode with his brother, she might have had misgivings, for the mage seemed to know her mind better than she did herself. But she didn't, so she continued ahead at a leisurely pace—to rest the horse and to give herself time to go over her plans.

In her saddlebags, she carried a map, stolen from Caramon's tent. On the map was marked a small village nestled in the mountains. It was so small it didn't even have a name—at least not one marked on the map. But this village was her destination. Here she planned to accomplish a two-fold purpose: she would alter time and she would prove—to Caramon and his brother and herself—that she was more than a piece of useless, even dangerous, baggage. She would prove her own worth.

Here, in this village, Crysania intended to bring back the worship of the ancient gods.

This was not a new thought for her. It was something she had often considered attempting but had not for a variety of reasons. The first was that both Caramon and Raistlin had absolutely forbidden her to use any clerical powers while in camp. Both feared for her life, having seen witch-burnings themselves in their younger days. (Raistlin had, in fact, nearly been a victim himself, until rescued by Sturm and Caramon.)

Crysania herself had enough common sense to know that none of the men or their families traveling with the army would listen to her, all of them firmly believing that she *was* a witch. The thought had crossed her mind that if she could get to people who knew nothing of her, tell them her story, give them the message that the gods had *not* abandoned man, but that man had abandoned the gods, then they would follow her as they would follow Goldmoon two hundred years later.

But it was not until she had been stung by Raistlin's harsh words that she had gathered the courage to act. Even now, leading the horse at a walk through the quiet forest in the twilight, she could still hear his voice and see his flashing eyes as he reprimanded her.

I deserved it, she admitted to herself. I had abandoned my faith. I was using my "charms" to try to bring him to me, instead of my example to bring him to Paladine. Sighing, she absently brushed her fingers through her tangled hair. If it had not been for *his* strength of will, I would have fallen.

Her admiration for the young archmage, already strong, deepened—as Raistlin had foreseen. She determined to restore his faith in her and prove herself worthy, once more, of his trust and regard. For, she feared, blushing, he must have a very low opinion of her now. By returning to camp with a corps of followers, of true believers, she planned not only to show him that he was wrong—that time could be altered by bringing clerics into a world where, before, there were none—but also she hoped to extend her teachings throughout the army itself.

Thinking of this, making her plans, Crysania felt more at peace with herself than she had in the months since they'd come to this time period. For once she was doing something on her own. She wasn't trailing along behind Raistlin or being ordered about by Caramon. Her spirits rose. By her calculations, she should reach the village just before dark.

The trail she was on had been steadily climbing up the side of the mountain. Now it topped a rise and then dipped down, descending into a small valley. Crysania halted the horse. There, nestled in the valley, she could at last see the village that was her destination.

Something struck her as odd about the village, but she was not yet a seasoned enough traveler to have learned to trust her instincts about such things. Knowing only that she wanted to reach the village before darkness fell, and eager to put her plan into immediate action, Crysania mounted her horse once more and rode down the trail, her hand closing over the medallion of Paladine she wore around her neck.

"Well, what do we do now?" Caramon asked, sitting astride his horse and looking both up and down the stream.

"*You're* the expert on women," Raistlin retorted.

"All right, I made a mistake," Caramon grumbled. "That doesn't help us. It'll be dark soon, and then we'll never find her trail. I haven't heard you come up with any helpful suggestions," he grumbled, glancing at his brother balefully. "Can't you magic up something?"

"I would have 'magicked up' brains for you long ago, if I could have," Raistlin snapped peevishly. "What would you like me to do—make her appear out thin air or look for her in my crystal ball? No, I won't waste my strength. Besides it's not necessary. Have you a map, or did you manage to think that far ahead?"

"I have a map," Caramon said grimly, drawing it out of his belt and handing it to his brother.

"You might as well water the horses and let them rest," Raistlin said, sliding off his. Caramon dismounted as well and led the horses to the stream while Raistlin studied the map.

By the time Caramon had tethered the horses to a bush and returned to his brother, the sun was setting. Raistlin held the map nearly up to his nose trying to read it in the dusk.

Caramon heard him cough and saw him hunch down into his traveling cloak.

"You shouldn't be out in the night air," Caramon said gruffly.

Coughing again, Raistlin gave him a bitter glance. "I'll be all right."

Shrugging, Caramon peered over his brother's shoulder at the map. Raistlin pointed a slender finger at a small spot, halfway up the mountainside.

"There," he said.

"Why? What would she go to some out-of-the-way place like that for?" Caramon asked, frowning, puzzled. "That doesn't make any sense."

"Because you have still not seen her purpose!" Raistlin returned. Thoughtfully, he rolled up the map, his eyes staring into the fading light. A dark line appeared between his brows.

"Well?" Caramon prompted skeptically. "What is this great purpose you keep mentioning? What's the matter?"

"She has placed herself in grave danger," Raistlin said suddenly, his cool voice tinged with anger. Caramon stared at him in alarm.

"What? How do you know? Do you see—"

"Of course I can't see, you great idiot!" Raistlin snarled over his shoulder as he walked rapidly to his horse. "I think! I use my brain! She is going to this village to establish the old religion. She is going there to tell them of the true gods!"

"Name of the Abyss!" Caramon swore, his eyes wide. "You're right, Raist," he said, after a moment's thought. "I've heard her talk about trying that, now I think of it. I never believed she was serious, though."

Then, seeing his brother untying his horse and preparing to mount, he hurried forward and laid his hand on his brother's bridle. "Just a minute, Raist! There's nothing we can do now. We'll have to wait until morning." He gestured into the mountains. "You know as well as I do that we don't dare ride those wretched trails after dark. We'd be taking a chance on the horses stumbling into a hole and breaking a leg. To say nothing of what *lives* in these god-forsaken woods."

"I have my staff for light," Raistlin said, motioning to the Staff of Magius, snug in its leather carrier on the side of saddle. He started to pull himself up, but a fit of coughing forced him to pause, clinging to the saddle, gasping for breath.

Caramon waited until the spasm eased. "Look, Raist," he said in milder tones, "I'm just as worried about her as you are—but I think you're overreacting. Let's be sensible. It's not as if she were riding into a den of goblins! That magical light'll draw to us whatever's lurking out there in the night like moths to a candleflame. The horses are winded. You're in no shape to go on, much less fight if we have to. We'll make camp here for the night. You get some rest, and we'll start fresh in the morning."

Raistlin paused, his hands on his saddle, staring at his brother. It seemed as if he might argue, then a coughing fit seized him. His hands slipped to his side, he laid his forehead against the horse's flank as if too exhausted to move.

"You are right, my brother," he said, when he could speak.

Startled at this unusual display of weakness, Caramon almost went to help his twin, but checked himself in time—a show of concern would only bring a bitter rebuke. Acting as if nothing were at all amiss, he began untying his brother's bedroll, chatting along, not really thinking about what he was saying.

"I'll spread this out, and you rest. We can probably risk a small fire, and you can heat up that potion of yours to help your cough. I've got some meat here and a few vegetables Garic threw together for me." Caramon prattled on, not even realizing what he was saying. "I'll fix up a stew. It'll be just like the old days.

"By the gods!" He paused a moment, grinning. "Even though we never knew where our next steel piece was coming from, we still ate well in those days! Do you remember? There was a spice you had. You'd toss it in the pot. What was it?" He gazed off into the distance, as though he could part the mists of time with his eyes. "Do you remember the one I'm talking about? You use it in your spellcasting. But it made damn good stews, too! The name . . . it was like ours—marjere, marjorie?

Hah!"—Caramon laughed—"I'll never forget the time that old master of yours caught us cooking with his spell components! I thought he'd turn himself inside out!"

Sighing, Caramon went back to work, tugging at the knots. "You know, Raist," he said softly, after a moment, "I've eaten wondrous food in wondrous places since then—palaces and elf woods and all. But nothing could quite match that. I'd like to try it again, to see if it was like I remember it. It'd be like old times—"

There was a soft rustle of cloth. Caramon stopped, aware that his brother had turned his black hooded head and was regarding him intently. Swallowing, Caramon kept his eyes fixedly on the knots he was trying to untie. He hadn't meant to make himself vulnerable and now he waited grimly for Raistlin's rebuke, the sarcastic gibe.

There was another soft rustle of cloth, and then Caramon felt something soft pressed into his hand—a tiny bag.

"Marjoram," Raistlin said in a soft whisper. "The name of the spice is marjoram. . . ."

CHAPTER 5

It wasn't until Crysania rode into the outskirts of the village itself that she realized something was wrong.

Caramon, of course, would have noticed it when he first looked down at the village from the top of the hill. He would have detected the absence of smoke from the cooking fires. He would have noted the unnatural silence—no sounds of mothers calling for children or the plodding thuds of cattle coming in from the fields or neighbors exchanging cheerful greetings after a long day's work. He would have seen that no smoke rose from the smithy's forge, wondered uneasily at the absence of candlelight glowing from the windows. Glancing up, he would have seen with alarm the large number of carrion birds in the sky, circling. . . .

All this Caramon or Tanis Half-Elven or Raistlin or any of them would have noted and, if forced to go on, he would have approached the village with hand on sword or a defensive magic spell on the lips.

But it was only after Crysania cantered into the village

and, staring around, wondered where everyone was, that she experienced her first glimmerings of uneasiness. She became aware of the birds, then, as their harsh cries and calls of irritation at her presence intruded on her thoughts. Slowly, they flapped away, in the gathering darkness, or perched sullenly on trees, melting into the shadows.

Dismounting in front of a building whose swinging sign proclaimed it an inn, Crysania tied the horse to a post and approached the front door. If it was an inn, it was a small one, but well-built and neat with ruffled curtains in the windows and a general air of cheery welcome about it that seemed, somehow, sinister in the eerie silence. No light came from the window. Darkness was rapidly swallowing the little town. Crysania, pushing open the door, could barely see inside.

"Hello?" she called hesitantly. At the sound of her voice, the birds outside squawked raucously, making her shiver. "Is anyone here? I'd like a room—"

But her voice died. She knew, without doubt that this place was empty, deserted. Perhaps everyone had left to join the army? She had known of entire villages to do so. But, looking around, she realized that that wasn't true in this case. There would have been nothing left here except furniture; the people would have taken their possessions with them.

Here, the table was set for dinner....

Stepping farther inside as her eyes adjusted to the dimness, she could see glasses still filled with wine, the bottles sitting open in the center of the table. There was no food. Some of the dishes had been knocked off and lay broken on the floor, next to some gnawed-on bones. Two dogs and a cat skulking about, looking half-starved, gave her an idea of how that had happened.

A staircase ran up to the second floor. Crysania thought about going up it, but her courage failed her. She would look around the town first. Surely someone was here, someone who could tell her what was going on.

Picking up a lamp, she lit it from the tinder box in her pack, then went back out into the street, now almost totally dark. What had happened? Where was everyone? It did not look as if the town had been attacked. There were no signs of fighting—no broken furniture, no blood, no weapons lying about. No bodies.

Her uneasiness grew as she walked outside the door of the inn. Her horse whinnied at the sight of her. Crysania suppressed a wild desire to leap up on it and ride away as fast as she could. The animal was tired; it could go no farther without rest. It needed food. Thinking of that, Crysania untied it and led it around to the stable behind the inn. It was empty. Not unusual—horses were a luxury these days. But it was filled with straw and there was water, so at least the inn was prepared to receive travelers. Placing her lamp on a stand, Crysania unsaddled her exhausted animal and rubbed it down, crudely and clumsily she knew, having never done it before.

But the horse seemed satisfied enough and, when she left, was munching oats it found in a trough.

Taking her lamp, Crysania returned to the empty, silent streets. She peered into dark houses, looked into darkened shop windows. Nothing. No one. Then, walking along, she heard a noise. Her heart stopped beating for an instant, the lamplight wavered in her shaking hand. She stopped, listening, telling herself it was a bird or an animal.

No, there it was again. And again. It was an odd sound, a kind of swishing, then a plop. Then a swish again, followed by a plop. Certainly there was nothing sinister or threatening about it. But still Crysania stood there, in the center of the street, unwilling to move toward the noise to investigate.

"What nonsense!" she told herself sternly. Angry at herself, disappointed at the failure—apparently—of her plans, and determined to discover what was going on, Crysania boldly walked forward. But her hand, she noted nervously, seemed of its own accord to reach for the medallion of her god.

The sound grew louder. The row of houses and small shops came to an end. Turning a corner, walking softly, she suddenly realized she should have doused her lamplight. But the thought came too late. At the sight of the light, the figure that had been making the odd sound turned abruptly, flung up his arm to shield his eyes, and stared at her.

"Who are you?" the man's voice called. "What do you want?" He did not sound frightened, only desperately tired, as if her presence were an additional, great burden.

But instead of answering, Crysania walked closer. For now she had figured out what the sound was. He had been shoveling! He held the shovel in his hand. He had no light. He had obviously been working so hard he was not even aware that night had fallen.

Raising her lamp to let the light shine on both of them, Crysania studied the man curiously. He was young, younger than she—probably about twenty or twenty-one. He was human, with a pale, serious face, and he was dressed in robes that, save for some strange, unrecognizable symbol upon them, she would have taken for clerical garb. As she drew nearer, Crysania saw the young man stagger. If his shovel had not been in the ground, he would have fallen. Instead, he leaned upon it, as if exhausted past all endurance.

Her own fears forgotten, Crysania hurried forward to help him. But, to her amazement, he stopped her with a motion of his hand.

"Keep away!" he shouted.

"What?" Crysania asked, startled.

"Keep away!" he repeated more urgently. But the shovel would support him no longer. He fell to his knees, clutching his stomach as if in pain.

"I'll do no such thing," Crysania said firmly, recognizing that the young man was ill or injured. Hurrying forward, she started to put her arm around him to help him up when her gaze fell upon what he had been doing.

She halted, staring in horror.

He had been filling in a grave—a mass grave.

Looking down into a huge pit, she saw bodies—men, women, children. There was not a mark upon them, no sign of blood. Yet they were all dead; the entire town, she realized numbly.

And then, turning, she saw the young man's face, she saw sweat pouring from it, she saw the glazed, feverish eyes. And then she knew.

"I tried to warn you," he said wearily, choking. "The burning fever."

"Come along," said Crysania, her voice trembling with grief. Turning her back firmly on the ghastly sight behind her, she put her arms around the young man. He struggled weakly.

"No! Don't!" he begged. "You'll catch it! Die . . . within hours. . . ."

"You are sick. You need rest," she said. Ignoring his protests, she led him away.

"But the grave," he whispered, his horrified gaze going to the dark sky where the carrion birds circled. "We can't leave the bodies—"

"Their souls are with Paladine," Crysania said, fighting back her own nausea at the thought of the gruesome feasting that would soon commence. Already she could hear the cackles of triumph. "Only their shells still lie there. They understand that the living come first."

Sighing, too weak to argue, the young man bowed his head and put his arm around Crysania's neck. He was, she noted, unbelievably thin—she scarcely felt his weight at all as he leaned against her. She wondered how long it had been since he'd eaten a good meal.

Walking slowly, they left the gravesite. "My house, there," he said, gesturing feebly to a small cabin on the edge of the village.

Crysania nodded. "Tell me what happened," she said, to keep his thoughts and her own from the sound of flapping birds' wings behind them.

"There's not much to tell," he said, shivering with chills. "It strikes quickly, without warning. Yesterday, the children were playing in the yards. Last night, they were dying in their mothers' arms. Tables were laid for dinner that no one was able to eat. This morning, those who were still able to move dug that grave, their own grave, as we all knew then. . . ."

His voice failed, a shudder of pain gripping him.

"It will be all right now," Crysania said. "We'll get you in bed. Cool water and sleep. I'll pray. . . ."

"Prayers!" The young man laughed bitterly. "I am their cleric!" He waved a hand back at the grave. "You see what good prayers have done!"

"Hush, save your strength," Crysania said as they arrived at the small house. Helping him lie down upon the bed, she shut the door and, seeing a fire laid, lit it with the flame from her lamp. Soon it was blazing. She lit candles and then returned to her patient. His feverish eyes had been following her every move.

Drawing a chair up next to the bed, she poured water into a bowl, dipped a cloth into it, then sat down beside him, to lay the cool cloth across his burning forehead.

"I am a cleric, too," she told him, lightly touching the medallion she wore around her neck, "and I am going to pray to my god to heal you."

Setting the bowl of water on a small table beside the bed, Crysania reached out to the young man and placed her hands upon his shoulders. Then she began to pray. "Paladine—"

"What?" he interrupted, clutching at her with a hot hand. "What are you doing?"

"I am going to heal you," Crysania said, smiling at him with gentle patience. "I am a cleric of Paladine."

"Paladine!" The young man grimaced in pain, then—catching his breath—looked up at her in disbelief. "That's who I thought you said. How can you be one of *his* clerics? They vanished, so it's told, right before the Cataclysm."

"It's a long story," Crysania replied, drawing the sheets over the young man's shivering body, "and one I will tell you later. But, for now, believe that I am truly a cleric of this great god and that he will heal you!"

"No!" the young man cried, his hand wrapping around hers so tightly it hurt. "I am a cleric, too, a cleric of the Seeker gods. I tried to heal my people"—his voice cracked—"but there . . . there was nothing I could do. They died!" His eyes closed in agony. "I prayed! The gods . . . didn't answer."

"That's because these gods you pray to are false gods," Crysania said earnestly, reaching out to smooth back the young man's sweat-soaked hair. Opening his eyes, he regarded her intently. He was handsome, Crysania saw, in a serious, scholarly fashion. His eyes were blue, his hair golden.

"Water," he murmured through parched lips. She helped him sit up. Thirstily, he drank from the bowl, then she eased him back down on the bed. Staring at her still, he shook his head, then shut his eyes wearily.

"You know of Paladine, of the ancient gods?" Crysania asked softly.

The young man's eyes opened, there was a gleam of light in them. "Yes," he said bitterly. "I know of them. I know they smashed the land. I know they brought storms and pestilence upon us. I know evil things have been unleashed in this land. And then they left. In our hour of need, they abandoned us!"

Now it was Crysania's turn to stare. She had expected denial, disbelief, or even total ignorance of the gods. She knew she could handle that. But this bitter anger? This was not the confrontation she had been prepared to face. Expecting superstitious mobs, she had found instead a mass grave and a dying young cleric.

"The gods did *not* abandon us," she said, her voice quivering in her earnestness. "They are here, waiting only for the sound of a prayer. The evil that came to Krynn man brought upon himself, through his own pride and willful ignorance."

The story of Goldmoon healing the dying Elistan and thereby converting him to the ancient faith came vividly to Crysania filling her with exultation. She would heal this young cleric, convert him. . . .

"I am going to help you," she said. "Then there will be time to talk, time for you to understand."

Kneeling down beside the bed once more, she clasped the medallion she wore around her neck and again began, "Paladine—"

A hand grabbed her roughly, hurting her, breaking her hold on the medallion. Startled, she looked up. It was the young cleric. Half-sitting up, weak, shivering with fever, he still stared at her with a gaze that was intense but calm.

"No," he said steadily, "*you* must understand. You don't need to convince me. I believe you!" He looked up into the shadows above him with a grim and bitter smile. "Yes, Paladine is with you. I can sense his great presence. Perhaps my eyes have been opened the nearer I approach death."

"This is wonderful!" Crysania cried ecstatically. "I can—"

"Wait!" The cleric gasped for breath, still holding her hand. "Listen! *Because* I believe I refuse . . . to let you heal me."

"What?" Crysania stared at him, uncomprehending. Then, "You're sick, delirious," she said firmly. "You don't know what you're saying."

"I do," he replied. "Look at me. Am I rational? Yes?"

Crysania, studying him, had to nod her head.

"Yes, you must admit it. I am . . . not delirious. I am fully conscious, comprehending."

"Then, why—?"

"Because," he said softly, each breath coming from him with obvious pain, "if Paladine is here—and I believe he is, now—then why is he . . . letting this happen! Why did he let my people die? Why does he permit this suffering? Why did he cause it? Answer me!" He clutched at her angrily. "Answer me!"

Her own questions! Raistlin's questions! Crysania felt her mind stumbling in confused darkness. How could she answer him, when she was searching so desperately for these answers herself?

Through numb lips, she repeated Elistan's words: "We must have faith. The ways of the gods cannot be known to us, we cannot see—"

Lying back down, the young man shook his head wearily and Crysania herself fell silent, feeling helpless in the face of such violent, intense anger. I'll heal him anyway, she determined. He is sick and weak in mind and body. He cannot be expected to understand. . . .

Then she sighed. No. In other circumstances, Paladine might have allowed it. The god will not grant my prayers, Crysania knew in despair. In his divine wisdom, he will gather the young man to himself and then all will be made clear.

But it could not be so now.

Suddenly, Crysania realized bleakly that time could not be altered, at least not this way, not by her. Goldmoon would restore man's faith in the ancient gods in a time when terrible anger such as this had died, when man would be ready to listen and to accept and believe. Not before.

Her failure overwhelmed her. Still kneeling by the bed, she bowed her head in her hands and asked to be forgiven for not being willing to accept or understand.

Feeling a hand touch her hair, she looked up. The young man was smiling wanly at her.

"I'm sorry," he said gently, his fever-parched lips twitching. "Sorry . . . to disappoint you."

"I understand," Crysania said quietly, "and I will respect your wishes."

"Thank you," he replied. He was silent. For long moments, the only sound that could be heard was his labored breathing. Crysania started to stand up, but she felt his hot hand close over hers. "Do one thing for me," he whispered.

"Anything," she said, forcing herself to smile, though she could barely see him through her tears.

"Stay with me tonight . . . while I die. . . ."

CHAPTER 6

Climbing the stairs leading up to the scaffold. Head bowed. Hands tied behind my back. I struggle to free myself, even as I mount the stairs, though I know it is useless—I have spent days, weeks, struggling to free myself, to no avail.

The black robes trip me. I stumble. Someone catches me, keeps me from falling, but drags me forward, nonetheless. I have reached the top. The block, stained dark with blood, is before me. Frantically now I seek to free my hands! If only I can loosen them! I can use my magic! Escape! Escape!

"There is no escape!" laughs my executioner, and I know it is myself speaking! My laughter! My voice! "Kneel, pathetic wizard! Place your head upon the cold and bloody pillow!"

No! I shriek with terror and rage and fight desperately, but hands grab me from behind. Viciously, they force me to my knees. My shrinking flesh touches the chill and slimy block! Still I wrench and twist and scream and still they force me down.

A black hood is drawn over my head . . . but I can hear the executioner coming closer, I can hear his black robes rustling around his *ankles, I can hear the blade being lifted . . . lifted. . . .*

"Raist! Raistlin! Wake up!"

Raistlin's eyes opened. Staring upward, dazed and wild with terror, he had no idea for a moment where he was or who had wakened him.

"Raistlin, what is it?" the voice repeated.

Strong hands held him firmly, a familiar voice, warm with concern, blotting out the whistling scream of the executioner's falling axe blade. . . .

"Caramon!" Raistlin cried, clutching at his brother. "Help me! Stop them! Don't let them murder me! Stop them! Stop them!"

"Shhhh, I won't let them do anything to you, Raist," Caramon murmured, holding his brother close, stroking the soft brown hair. "Shhh, you're all right. I'm here . . . I'm here."

Laying his head on Caramon's chest, hearing his twin's steady, slow heartbeat, Raistlin gave a deep, shuddering sigh. Then he closed his eyes against the darkness and sobbed like a child.

"Ironic, isn't it?" Raistlin muttered bitterly some time later, as his brother stirred up the fire and set an iron pot filled with water on it to boil. "The most powerful mage who has ever lived, and I am reduced to a squalling babe by a dream!"

"So you're human," Caramon grunted, bending over the pot, watching it closely with the rapt attention all pay to the business of forcing water to boil more quickly. He shrugged. "You said it yourself."

"Yes . . . human!" Raistlin repeated savagely, huddled, shivering, in his black robes and traveling cloak.

Caramon glanced at him uneasily at this, remembering what Par-Salian and the other mages had told him at the Conclave held in the Tower of High Sorcery. *Your brother intends to challenge the gods! He seeks to become a god himself!*

But even as Caramon looked at his brother, Raistlin drew his knees up close to his body, rested his hands upon his knees, and laid his head down upon them wearily. Feeling a strange choking sensation in his throat, vividly remembering the warm and wonderful feeling he had experienced when his brother had reached out to him for comfort, Caramon turned his attention back to the water.

Raistlin's head snapped up, suddenly.

"What was that?" he asked at the same time Caramon, hearing the sound as well, rose to his feet.

"I dunno," Caramon said softly, listening. Padding soft-footed, the big man moved with surprising swiftness to his bedroll, grasped his sword, and drew it from its scabbard.

Acting in the same moment, Raistlin's hand closed over the Staff of Magius that lay beside him. Twisting to his feet like a cat, he doused the fire, upending the kettle over it. Darkness descended on them with a soft, hissing sound as the coals sputtered and died.

Giving their eyes time to become accustomed to the sudden change, both the brothers stood still, concentrating on their hearing.

The stream near which they were camped burbled and lapped among the rocks, branches creaked and leaves rattled as a sharp breeze sprang up, slicing through the autumn night. But what they had heard was neither wind in the trees nor water.

"There it is," said Raistlin in a whisper as his brother came to stand beside him. "In the woods, across the stream."

It was a scrabbling sound, like someone trying unsuccessfully to creep through unfamiliar territory. It lasted a few moments, then stopped, then began again. Either some *one* unfamiliar with the territory or some *thing*—clumsy, heavy-booted.

"Goblins!" hissed Caramon.

Gripping his sword, he and his brother exchanged glances. The years of darkness, of estrangement between them, the jealousy, hatred—everything vanished within that instant. Reacting to the shared danger, they were one, as they had been in their mother's womb.

Moving cautiously, Caramon set foot in the stream. The red moon, Lunitari, glimmered through the trees. But it was new tonight. Looking like the wick of a pinched-out candle, it gave little light. Fearing to turn his foot upon a stone, Caramon tested each step carefully before he put his weight upon it. Raistlin followed, holding his darkened staff in one hand, resting his other lightly upon his brother's shoulder for balance.

They crossed the stream as silently as the wind whispering across the water and reached the opposite bank. They could still hear the noise. It was made by something living, though, there was no doubt. Even when the wind died, they could hear the rustling sound.

"Rear guard. Raiding party!" Caramon mouthed, half-turning so that his brother could hear.

Raistlin nodded. Goblin raiding parties customarily sent scouts to keep watch upon the trail when they rode in to loot a village. Since it was a boring job and meant that the goblins elected had no share in the killing or the spoils, it generally fell to those lowest in rank—the least skilled, most expendable members of the party.

Raistlin's hand closed suddenly over Caramon's arm, halting him momentarily.

"Crysania!" the mage whispered. "The village! We must know where the raiding party is!"

Caramon scowled. "I'll take it alive!" He indicated this with a gesture of his huge hand wrapping itself around an imaginary goblin neck.

Raistlin smiled grimly in understanding. "And I will question it," he hissed, making a gesture of his own.

Together, the twins crept up the trail, taking care to keep in the shadows so that even the faintest glimmer of moonlight should not be reflected from buckle or sword. They could still hear the sound. Though it ceased sometimes, it always started again. It remained in the same location. Whoever or whatever it was appeared to have no idea of their approach. They drew toward it, keeping to the edges of the trail until they were—as well as they could judge—practically opposite it.

The sound, they could tell now, was in the woods, about twenty feet off the trail. Glancing swiftly around, Raistlin's sharp eyes spotted a thin trail. Barely visible in the pale light of moon and stars, it branched off from the main one—an animal trail, probably leading down to the stream. A good place for scouts to lie hidden, giving them quick access to the main trail if they decided to attack, an easy escape route if the opposition proved too formidable.

"Wait here!" Caramon signed.

A rustle of his black hood was Raistlin's response. Reaching out to hold aside a low, overhanging branch, Caramon entered the forest, moving slowly and stealthily about two feet away from the faint animal trail that led into it.

Raistlin stood beside a tree, his slender fingers reaching into one of his many, secret pockets, hastily rolling a pinch of sulfur up in a tiny ball of bat guano. The words to the spell were in his mind. He repeated them to himself. Even as he did this, however, he was acutely conscious of the sound of his brother's movements.

Though Caramon was trying to be quiet, Raistlin could hear the creak of the big man's leather armor, the metal buckles' jingle, the crack of a twig beneath his feet as he moved away from his waiting twin. Fortunately, their quarry was continuing to make so much noise that the warrior would probably proceed unheard. . . .

A horrible shriek rang through the night, followed by a frightful yelling and thrashing sound, as if a hundred men were crashing through the wilderness.

Raistlin started.

Then a voice shouted, "Raist! Help! Aiiihh!"

More thrashing, the sound of tree limbs snapping, a thumping sound. . . .

Gathering his robes around him, Raistlin ran swiftly onto the animal trail, the time for concealment and secrecy past. He could hear his brother yelling, still. The sound was muffled, but clear, not choked or as if he were in pain.

Racing through the woods, the archmage ignored the branches that slapped his face and the brambles that caught at his robes. Breaking suddenly and unexpectedly into a clearing, he stopped, crouching, beside a tree. Ahead of him, he could see movement—a gigantic black shadow that seemed to be hovering in the air, floating above the ground. Grappling with the shadowy creature, yelling and cursing horribly, was—by the sound—Caramon!

"*Ast kiranann Soth-aran/Suh kali Jalaran.*" Raistlin chanted the words and tossed the small ball of sulfur high above him, into the leaves of the trees. An instantaneous burst of light in the branches was accompanied by a low, booming explosion. The treetops burst into flame, illuminating the scene below.

Raistlin darted forward, the words of a spell on his lips, magical fire crackling from his fingertips.

He stopped, staring in astonishment.

Before him, hanging upside down by one leg from a rope suspended over a tree branch, was Caramon. Suspended next to him, scrabbling frantically in fear of the flames, was a rabbit.

Raistlin stared, transfixed, at his brother. Shouting for help, Caramon turned slowly in the wind while flaming leaves fell all about him.

"Raist!" He was still yelling. "Get me—Oh—"

Caramon's next revolution brought him within sight of his astounded twin. Flushing, the blood rushing to his head, Caramon gave a sheepish grin. "Wolf snare," he said.

The forest was ablaze with brilliant orange light. The fire flickered on the big man's sword, which lay on the ground where he'd dropped it. It sparkled on Caramon's shining armor as he revolved slowly around again. It gleamed in the frantic, panic-stricken eyes of the rabbit.

Raistlin snickered.

Now it was Caramon's turn to stare in hurt astonishment at his brother. Revolving back around to face him, Caramon twisted his head, trying to see Raistlin right side up. He gave a pitiful, pleading look.

"C'mon, Raist! Get me down!"

Raistlin began to laugh silently, his shoulders heaving.

"Damn it, Raist! This isn't funny!" Caramon blustered, waving his arms. This gesture, of course, caused the snared warrior to stop revolving and begin to swing from side to side. The rabbit, on the other end of the snare, started swinging, too, pawing even more frantically at the air. Soon, the two of them were spinning in opposite directions, circling each other, entangling the ropes that held them.

"Get me down!" Caramon roared. The rabbit squealed in terror.

This was too much. Memories of their youth returned vividly to the archmage, driving away the darkness and horror that had clutched at his soul for what seemed like years unending. Once again he was young, hopeful, filled with dreams. Once again, he was with his brother, the brother who was closer to him than any other person had ever been, would ever be. His bumbling, thick-headed, beloved brother. . . . Raistlin doubled over. Gasping for air, the mage collapsed upon the grass and laughed wildly, tears running down his cheeks.

Caramon glared at him—but this baleful look from a man being held upside down by his foot simply increased his twin's mirth. Raistlin laughed until he thought he might have hurt something inside him. The laughter felt good. For a time, it banished the darkness. Lying on the damp ground of the glade illuminated by the light of the flaming trees, Raistlin laughed harder, feeling the merriment sparkle through his body like fine wine. And then Caramon joined in, his booming bellow echoing through the forest.

Only the falling of blazing bits of tree striking the ground near him recalled Raistlin to himself. Wiping his streaming eyes, so weak from laughter he could barely stand, the mage staggered to his feet. With a flick of his hand, he brought forth the little silver dagger he wore concealed upon his wrist.

Reaching up, stretching his full height, the mage cut the rope wrapped around his brother's ankle. Caramon plunged to the ground with a curse and thudding crash.

Still chuckling to himself, the mage walked over and cut the cord that some hunter had tied around the rabbit's hind leg, catching hold of the animal in his arms. The creature was half-mad with terror, but Raistlin gently stroked its head and murmured soft words. Gradually, the animal grew calm, seeming almost to be in a trance.

"Well, we took him alive," Raistlin said, his lips twitching.

He held up the rabbit. "I don't think we'll get much information out of him, however."

So red in the face he gave the impression of having tumbled into a vat of paint, Caramon sat up and began to rub a bruised shoulder.

"Very funny," he muttered, glancing up at the animal with a shamefaced grin. The flames in the treetops were dying, though the air was filled with smoke and, here and there, the grass was burning. Fortunately, it had been a damp, rainy autumn, so these small fires died quickly.

"Nice spell," Caramon commented, looking up into the glowing remains of the surrounding treetops as, swearing and groaning, he hauled himself to his feet.

"I've always liked it," Raistlin replied wryly. "Fizban taught it to me. You remember?" Looking up into the smoldering trees, he smiled. "I think that old man would have appreciated this."

Cradling the rabbit in his arms, absently petting the soft, silken ears, Raistlin walked from the smoke-filled woods. Lulled by the mage's caressing fingers and hypnotic words, the rabbit's eyes closed. Caramon retrieved his sword from the brush where he'd dropped it and followed, limping slightly.

"Damn snare cut off my circulation." He shook his foot to try to get the blood going.

Heavy clouds had rolled in, blotting out the stars and snuffing Lunitari's flame completely. As the flames in the trees died, the woods were plunged into darkness so thick that neither brother could see the trail ahead.

"I suppose there is no need for secrecy now," Raistlin murmured. "*Shirak.*" The crystal on the top of the Staff of Magius began to glow with a bright, magical brilliance.

The twins returned to their camp in silence, a companionable, comfortable silence, a silence they had not shared in years. The only sounds in the night were the restless stirring of their horses, the creak and jingle of Caramon's armor, and the soft rustle of the mage's black robes as he walked. Behind them, once, they heard a crash—the falling of a charred branch.

Reaching camp, Caramon ruefully stirred at the remains of

their fire, then glanced up at the rabbit in Raistlin's arms.

"I don't suppose you'd consider that breakfast."

"I do not eat goblin flesh," Raistlin answered with a smile, placing the creature down on the trail. At the touch of the cold ground beneath its paws, the rabbit started, its eyes flared open. Staring around for an instant to get its bearings, it suddenly bolted for the shelter of the woods.

Caramon heaved a sigh, then, chuckling to himself, sat down heavily upon the ground near his bedroll. Removing his boot, he rubbed his bruised ankle.

"*Dulak*," Raistlin whispered and the staff went dark. He laid it beside his bedroll, then laid down, drawing the blankets up around him.

With the return of darkness, the dream was there. Waiting.

Raistlin shuddered, his body suddenly convulsed with chills. Sweat covered his brow. He could not, dared not close his eyes! Yet, he was so tired . . . so exhausted. How many nights had it been since he'd slept? . . .

"Caramon," he said softly.

"Yeah," Caramon answered from the darkness.

"Caramon," Raistlin said after a moment's pause, "do . . . do you remember how, when we were children, I'd have those . . . those horrible dreams? . . ." His voice failed him for a moment. He coughed.

There was no sound from his twin.

Raistlin cleared his throat, then whispered, "And you'd guard my sleep, my brother. You kept them away. . . ."

"I remember," came a muffled, husky voice.

"Caramon," Raistlin began, but he could not finish. The pain and weariness were too much. The darkness seemed to close in, the dream crept from its hiding place.

And then there was the jingle of armor. A big, hulking shadow appeared beside him. Leather creaking, Caramon sat down beside his brother, resting his broad back against a tree trunk and laying his naked sword across his knees.

"Go to sleep, Raist," Caramon said gently. The mage felt a rough, clumsy hand pat him on the shoulder. "I'll stay up and keep watch. . . ."

Wrapping himself in his blankets, Raistlin closed his eyes. Sleep, sweet and restful, stole upon him. The last thing he remembered was a fleeting fancy of the dream approaching, reaching out its bony hands to grasp him, only to be driven back by the light from Caramon's sword.

CHAPTER 7

Caramon's horse shifted restlessly beneath him as the big man leaned forward in the saddle, staring down into the valley at the village. Frowning darkly, he glanced at his brother. Raistlin's face was hidden behind his black hood. A steady rain had started about dawn and now dripped dull and monotonously around them. Heavy gray clouds sagged above them, seemingly upheld by the dark, towering trees. Other than the drip of water from the leaves, there was no sound at all.

Raistlin shook his head. Then, speaking gently to his horse, he rode forward. Caramon followed, hurrying to catch up, and there was the sound of steel sliding from a scabbard.

"You will not need your sword, my brother," Raistlin said without turning.

The horses' hooves clopped through the mud of the road, their sound thudding too loudly in the thick, rain-soaked air. Despite Raistlin's words, Caramon kept his hand upon the hilt of his sword until they rode into the outskirts of the small village. Dismounting, he handed the reins of his horse to his brother, then, cautiously, approached the same small inn Crysania had first seen.

Peering inside, he saw the table set for dinner, the broken crockery. A dog came dashing up to him hopefully, licking his hand and whimpering. Cats slunk beneath the chairs, vanishing into the shadows with a guilty, furtive air. Absently patting the dog, Caramon was about to walk inside when Raistlin called.

"I heard a horse. Over there."

Sword drawn, Caramon walked around the corner of the building. After a few moments, he returned, his weapon sheathed, his brow furrowed.

"It's hers," he reported. "Unsaddled, fed, and watered."

Nodding his hooded head as though he had expected this information, Raistlin pulled his cloak more tightly about him.

Caramon glanced uneasily about the village. Water dripped from the eaves, the door to the inn swung on rusty hinges, making a shrill squeaking sound. No light came from any of the houses, no sounds of children's laughter or women calling to each other or men complaining about the weather as they went to their work. "What is it, Raist?"

"Plague," said Raistlin.

Caramon choked and instantly covered his mouth and nose with his cloak. From within the shadows of the cowl, Raistlin's mouth twisted in an ironic smile.

"Do not fear, my brother," he said, dismounting from his horse. Taking the reins, Caramon tied both animals to a post, then came to stand beside his twin. "We have a true cleric with us, have you forgotten?"

"Then where is she?" Caramon growled in a muffled voice, still keeping his face covered.

The mage's head turned, staring down the rows of silent, empty houses. "There, I should guess," he remarked finally. Caramon followed his gaze and saw a single light flickering in the window of a small house at the other end of the village.

"I'd rather be walking into a camp of ogres," Caramon muttered as he and his brother slogged through the muddy, deserted streets. His voice was gruff with a fear he could not hide. He could face with equanimity the prospect of dying with six inches of cold steel in his gut. But the thought of dying helplessly, wasted by something that could not be fought, that floated unseen upon the air, filled the big man with horror.

Raistlin did not reply. His face remained hidden. What his thoughts might have been, his brother could not guess. The two reached the end of the row of houses, the rain spattering all around them with thudding plops. They were nearing the light when Caramon happened to glance to his left.

"Name of the gods!" he whispered as he stopped abruptly and grasped his brother by the arm.

He pointed to the mass grave.

Neither spoke. With croaks of anger at their approach, the carrion birds rose into the air, black wings flapping. Caramon gagged. His face pale, he turned hurriedly away. Raistlin continued to stare at the sight a moment, his thin lips tightening into a straight line.

"Come, my brother," he said coldly, walking toward the small house again.

Glancing in at the window, hand on the hilt of his sword, Caramon sighed and, nodding his head, gave his brother a sign. Raistlin pushed gently upon the door, and it opened at his touch.

A young man lay upon a rumpled bed. His eyes were closed, his hands folded across his chest. There was a look of peace upon the still, ashen face, though the closed eyes were sunken into gaunt cheekbones and the lips were blue with the chill of death. A cleric dressed in robes that might once have been white knelt on the floor beside him, her head bowed on her folded hands. Caramon started to say something, but Raistlin checked him with a hand on his arm, shaking his hooded head, unwilling to interrupt her.

Silently, the twins stood together in the doorway, the rain dripping around them.

Crysania was with her god. Intent upon her prayers, she was unaware of the twins' entrance until, finally, the jingle and creak of Caramon's armor brought her back to reality.

Lifting her head, her dark, tousled hair falling about her shoulders, she regarded them without surprise.

Her face, though pale with weariness and sorrow, was composed. Though she had not prayed to Paladine to send them, she knew the god answered prayers of the heart as well as those spoken openly. Bowing her head once more, giving thanks, she sighed, then rose to her feet and turned to face them.

Her eyes met Raistlin's eyes, the light of the failing fire causing them to gleam even in the depths of his hood. When she spoke, her voice seemed to her to blend with the sound of the falling raindrops.

"I failed," she said.

Raistlin appeared undisturbed. He glanced at the body of the young man. "He would not believe?"

"Oh, he believed." She, too, looked down at the body. "He refused to let me heal him. His anger was . . . very great." Reaching down, she drew the sheet up over the still form. "Paladine has taken him. Now he understands, I am certain."

"He does," Raistlin remarked. "Do you?"

Crysania's head bowed, her dark hair fell around her face. She stood so still for so long that Caramon, *not* understanding, cleared his throat and shifted uneasily.

"Uh, Raist—" he began softly.

"Shh!" Raistlin whispered.

Crysania raised her head. She had not even heard Caramon. Her eyes were a deep gray now, so dark they seemed to reflect the archmage's black robes. "I understand," she said in a firm voice. "For the first time, I understand and I see what I must do. In Istar, I saw belief in the gods lost. Paladine granted my prayer and showed me the Kingpriest's fatal weakness— pride. The god gave me to know how I might avoid that mistake. He gave me to know that, if I asked, he would answer.

"But Paladine also showed me, in Istar, how weak I was. When I left the wretched city and came here with you, I was little more than a frightened child, clinging to you in the terrible night. Now, I have regained my strength. The vision of this tragic sight has burned into my soul."

As Crysania spoke, she drew nearer Raistlin. His eyes held hers in an unblinking gaze. She saw herself in their flat surface. The medallion of Paladine she wore around her neck shone with a cold, white light. Her voice grew fervent, her hands clasped together tightly.

"That sight will be before my eyes," she said softly, coming to stand before the archmage, "as I walk with you through the Portal, armed with my faith, strong in my belief that together you and I will banish darkness from the world forever!"

Reaching out, Raistlin took hold of her hands. They were numb with cold. He enclosed them in his own slender hands, warming them with his burning touch.

"We have no need to alter time!" Crysania said. "Fistandantilus was an evil man. What he did, he did for his own personal glory. But we care, you and I. *That* alone will be sufficient to change the ending. I know—my god has spoken to me!"

Slowly, smiling his thin-lipped smile, Raistlin brought Crysania's hands to his mouth and kissed them, never taking his eyes from her.

Crysania felt her cheeks flush, then caught her breath. With a choked, half-strangled sound, Caramon turned abruptly and walked out the door.

Standing in the oppressive silence, the rain beating down upon his head, Caramon heard a voice thudding at his brain with the same monotonous, dull tone as the drops spattering about him.

He seeks to become a god. He seeks to become a god!

Sick and afraid, Caramon shook his head in anguish. His interest in the army, his fascination with being a "general," his attraction to Crysania, and all the other, thousand worries had driven from his mind the real reason he had come back. Now—with Crysania's words—it returned to him, hitting him like a wave of chill sea water.

Yet all he could think of was Raistlin as he was last night. How long had it been since he'd heard his brother laugh like that? How long had it been since they'd shared that warmth, that closeness? Vividly, he remembered watching Raistlin's face as he guarded his twin's sleep. He saw the harsh lines of cunning smooth, the bitter creases around the mouth fade. The archmage looked almost young again, and Caramon remembered their childhood and young manhood together— those days that had been the happiest of his life.

But then came, unbidden, a hideous memory, as though his soul were taking a perverse delight in torturing and confusing him. He saw himself once more in that dark cell in Istar, seeing clearly, for the first time, his brother's vast capability for evil. He remembered his firm determination that his brother must die. He thought of Tasslehoff. . . .

But Raistlin had explained all that! He had explained things at Istar. Once again, Caramon felt himself foundering.

What if Par-Salian is wrong, what if they are all wrong? What if Raist and Crysania *could* save the world from horror and suffering like this?

"I'm just a jealous, bumbling fool," Caramon mumbled, wiping the rainwater from his face with a trembling hand. "Maybe those old wizards are all like me, all jealous of him."

The darkness deepened about him, the clouds above grew denser, changing from gray to black. The rain beat down more heavily.

Raistlin came out the door, Crysania with him, her hand on his arm. She was wrapped in her thick cloak, her grayish-white hood drawn up over her head. Caramon cleared his throat.

"I'll go bring him out and put him with the others," he said gruffly, starting for the door. "Then I'll fill in the grave—"

"No, my brother," Raistlin said. "No. This sight will not be hidden in the ground." He cast back his hood, letting the rain wash over his face as he lifted his gaze to the clouds. "This sight will flare in the eyes of the gods! The smoke of their destruction will rise to heaven! The sound will resound in their ears!"

Caramon, startled at this unusual outburst, turned to look at his twin. Raistlin's thin face was nearly as gaunt and pale as the corpse's inside the small house, his voice tense with anger.

"Come with me," he said, abruptly breaking free of Crysania's hold and striding toward the center of the small village. Crysania followed, holding her hood to keep the slashing wind and rain from blowing it off. Caramon came after, more slowly.

Stopping in the middle of the muddy, rain-soaked street, Raistlin turned to face Crysania and his brother as they came up to him.

"Get the horses, Caramon—ours and Crysania's. Lead them to those woods outside of town"—the mage pointed—"blindfold them, then return to me."

Caramon stared at him.

"Do it!" Raistlin commanded, his voice rasping.

Caramon did as he was told, leading the horses away.

"Now, stand there," Raistlin continued when his twin returned. "Do not move from that spot. Do not come close to me, my brother, no matter what happens." His gaze went to Crysania, who was standing near him, then back to his brother. "You understand, Caramon."

Caramon nodded wordlessly and, reaching out, gently took Crysania's hand.

"What is it?" she asked, holding back.

"His magic," Caramon replied.

He fell silent as Raistlin cast a sharp, imperious glance at him. Alarmed by the strange, fiercely eager expression on Raistlin's face, Crysania suddenly drew nearer Caramon, shivering. The big man, his eyes on his frail twin, put his arm around her. Standing together in the pounding rain, almost not daring to breathe lest they disturb him, they watched the archmage.

Raistlin's eyes closed. Lifting his face to the heavens, he raised his arms, palms outward, toward the lowering skies. His lips moved, but—for a moment—they could not hear him. Then, though he did not seem to raise his voice, each could begin to make out words—the spidery language of magic. He repeated the same words over and over, his soft voice rising and falling in a chant. The words never changed, but the way he spoke them, the inflection of each, varied every time he repeated the phrase.

A hush settled over the valley. Even the sound of the falling rain died in Caramon's ears. All he could hear was the soft chanting, the strange and eerie music of his brother's voice. Crysania pressed closer still, her dark eyes wide, and Caramon patted her reassuringly.

As the chanting continued, a feeling of awe crept over Caramon. He had the distinct impression that he was being drawn irresistibly toward Raistlin, that everything in the world was being drawn toward the archmage, though—in looking fearfully around—Caramon saw that he hadn't moved from the spot. But, turning back to stare at his brother, the feeling returned even more forcibly.

Raistlin stood in the center of the world, his hands outstretched, and all sound, all light, even the air itself, seemed to rush eagerly into his grasp. The ground beneath Caramon's feet began to pulse in waves that flowed toward the archmage.

Raistlin lifted his hands higher, his voice rising ever so slightly. He paused, then he spoke each word in the chant slowly, firmly. The winds rose, the ground heaved. Caramon had the wild impression that the world was rushing in upon his brother, and he braced his feet, fearful that he, too, would be sucked into Raistlin's dark vortex.

Raistlin's fingers stabbed toward the gray, boiling heavens. The energy that he had drawn from ground and air surged through him. Silver lightning flashed from his fingers, striking the clouds. Brilliant, jagged light forked down in answer, touching the small house where the body of the young cleric lay. With a shattering explosion, a ball of blue-white flame engulfed the building.

Again Raistlin spoke and again the silver lightning shot from his fingers. Again another streak of light answered, striking the mage! This time it was Raistlin who was engulfed in red-green flame.

Crysania screamed. Struggling in Caramon's grasp, she sought to free herself. But, remembering his brother's words, Caramon held her fast, preventing her from rushing to Raistlin's side.

"Look!" he whispered hoarsely, gripping her tightly. "The flames do not touch him!"

Standing amidst the blaze, Raistlin lifted his thin arms higher, and the black robes blew around him as though he were in the center of a violent wind storm. He spoke again. Fiery fingers of flame spread out from him, lighting the darkness, ran through the wet grass, dancing on top of the water as though it were covered with oil. Raistlin stood in the center, the hub of a vast, spoked wheel of flame.

Crysania could not move. Awe and terror such as she had never before experienced paralyzed her. She held onto Caramon, but he offered her no comfort. The two clung together like frightened children as the flames surged around them. Traveling through the streets, the fire reached the buildings and ignited them with one bursting explosion after another.

Purple, red, blue, and green, the magical fire blazed upward, lighting the heavens, taking the place of the cloud-shrouded sun. The carrion birds wheeled in fear as the tree they had occupied became a living torch.

Raistlin spoke again, one last time. With a burst of pure, white light, fire leaped down from the heavens, consuming the bodies in the mass grave.

Wind from the flames gusted about Crysania, blowing the hood from her head. The heat was intense, beating upon her face. The smoke choked her, she could not breathe. Sparks showered around her, flames flickered at her feet until it seemed that she, too, must end up part of the conflagration. But nothing touched her. She and Caramon stood safely in the midst of the blaze. And then Crysania became aware of Raistlin's gaze upon her.

From the fiery inferno in which he stood, the mage beckoned.

Crysania gasped, shrinking back against Caramon.

Raistlin beckoned again, his black robes flowing about his body, rippling with the wind of the fire storm he had created. Standing within the center of the flames, he held out his hands to Crysania.

"No!" Caramon cried, holding fast to her. But Crysania,

never taking her eyes from Raistlin, gently loosened the big man's grip and walked forward.

"Come to me, Revered Daughter!" Raistlin's soft voice touched her through the chaos and she knew she was hearing it in her heart. "Come to me through the flame. Come taste the power of the gods. . . ."

The heat of the blazing fire that enveloped the archmage burned and scorched her soul. It seemed her skin must blacken and shrivel. She heard her hair crackling. Her breath was sucked from her lungs, searing them painfully. But the fire's light entranced her, the flames danced, luring her forward, even as Raistlin's soft voice urged her toward him.

"No!" Behind her, she could hear Caramon cry out, but he was nothing to her, less than the sound of her own heart beating. She reached the curtain of flame. Raistlin extended his hand, but, for an instant, she faltered, hesitating.

His hand burned! She saw it withering, the flesh black and charred.

"Come to me, Crysania. . . ." whispered his voice.

Reaching out her hand, trembling, she thrust it into the flame. For an instant, there was searing, heart-stopping pain. She cried out in horror and anguish, then Raistlin's hand closed over hers, drawing her through the blazing curtain. Involuntarily, she closed her eyes.

Cool wind soothed her. She could breathe sweet air. The only heat she felt was the warm, familiar heat from the mage's body. Opening her eyes, she saw that she stood close to him. Raising her head, she gazed up into his face . . . and felt a swift, sharp ache in her heart.

Raistlin's thin face glistened with sweat, his eyes reflected the pure, white flame of the burning bodies, his breath came fast and shallow. He seemed lost, unaware of his surroundings. And there was a look of ecstasy on his face, a look of exultation, of triumph.

"I understand," Crysania said to herself, holding onto his hands. "I understand. This is why he cannot love me. He has only one love in this life and that is his magic. To this love he will give everything, for this love he will risk everything!"

The thought was painful, but it was a pleasant kind of melancholy pain.

"Once again," she said to herself, her eyes dimming with tears, "he is my example. Too long have I let myself be preoccupied with petty thoughts of this world, of myself. He is right. Now I taste the power of the gods. I must be worthy—of them and of him!"

Raistlin closed his eyes. Crysania holding onto him, felt the magic drain from him as though his life's blood were flowing from a wound. His arms fell to his sides. The ball of flame that had enveloped them flickered and died.

With a sigh that was little more than a whisper, Raistlin sank to his knees upon the scorched ground. The rain resumed. Crysania could hear it hiss as it struck the charred remains of the still-smoldering village. Steam rose into the air, flitting among the skeletons of the buildings, drifting down the street like ghosts of the former inhabitants.

Kneeling beside the archmage, Crysania smoothed back his brown hair with her hand. Raistlin opened his eyes, looking at her without recognition. And in them she saw deep, undying sorrow—the look of one who has been permitted to enter a realm of deadly, perilous beauty and who now finds himself, once more, cast down into the gray, rain-swept world.

The mage slumped forward, his head bowed, his arms hanging limply. Crysania looked up at Caramon as the big man hurried over.

"Are you all right?" he asked her.

"I'm all right," she whispered. "How is he?"

Together, they helped Raistlin rise to his feet. He seemed completely unaware of their very existence. Tottering with exhaustion, he sagged against his brother.

"He'll be fine. This always happens." Caramon's voice died, then he muttered, "Always happens! What I am saying? I've never seen anything like that in my life! Name of the gods"—he stared at his twin in awe—"I've never seen power like that! I didn't know! I didn't know. . . ."

Supported by Caramon's strong arm, Raistlin leaned against his twin. He began to cough, gasping for air, choking until he could barely stand. Caramon held onto him tightly. Fog and smoke swirled about their feet, the rain splashed down around them. Here and there came the crash of burning wood, the hiss of water upon flame. When the coughing fit passed, Raistlin raised his head, life and recognition returning to his eyes.

"Crysania," he said softly, "I asked you to do that because you must have implicit faith in me and in my power. If we succeed in our quest, Revered Daughter, then we will enter the Portal and we will walk with our eyes open into the Abyss—a place of horror unimaginable."

Crysania began to shiver uncontrollably as she stood before him, held mesmerized by his glittering eyes.

"You must be strong, Revered Daughter," he continued intently. "And that is the reason I brought you on this journey. I have gone through my own trials. You had to go through yours. In Istar, you faced the trials of wind and water. You came through the trial of darkness within the Tower, and now you have withstood the trial by fire. But one more trial awaits you, Crysania! One more, and you must prepare for it, as must we all."

His eyes closed wearily, he staggered. Caramon, his face grim and suddenly haggard, caught hold of his twin and, lifting him, carried him to the waiting horses.

Crysania hurried after them, her concerned gaze on Raistlin. Despite his weakness, there was a look of sublime peace and exultation on his face.

"What's wrong?" she asked.

"He sleeps," Caramon said, his voice deep and gruff, concealing some emotion she could not guess at.

Reaching the horses, Crysania stopped a moment, turning to look behind her.

Smoke rose from the charred ruins of the village. The skeletons of the buildings had collapsed into heaps of pure white ash, the trees were nothing but branched smoke drifting up to the heavens. Even as she watched, the rain beat down upon the ash, changing it to mud, washing it away. The fog blew to shreds, the smoke was swept away on the winds of the storm.

The village was gone as though it had never been.

Shivering, Crysania clutched her cloak about her and turned to Caramon, who was placing Raistlin into his saddle, shaking him, forcing him to wake up enough to ride.

"Caramon," Crysania said as the warrior came over to help her. "What did Raistlin mean—'another trial.' I saw the look on your face when he said it. You know, don't you? You understand?"

Caramon did not answer immediately. Next to them, Raistlin swayed groggily in his saddle. finally, his head bowed, the mage lapsed once more into sleep. After assisting Crysania, Caramon walked over to his own horse and mounted. Then, reaching over, he took the reins from the limp hands of his slumbering brother. They rode back up the mountain, through the rain, Caramon never once looking behind at the village.

In silence, he guided the horses up the trail. Next to him, Raistlin slumped over his mount's neck. Caramon steadied his brother with a firm, gentle hand.

"Caramon?" Crysania asked softly as they reached the summit of the mountain.

The warrior turned to look at Crysania. Then, with a sigh, his gaze went to the south, where, far from them, lay Thorbardin. The storm clouds massed thick and dark upon the distant horizon.

"It is an old legend that, before he faced the Queen of Darkness, Huma was tested by the gods. He went through the trial of wind, the trial of fire, the trial of water. And his last test," Caramon said quietly, "was the trial of blood."

Song of Huma
(Reprise)

Through cinders and blood, the harvest of dragons,
Traveled Huma, cradled by dreams of the Silver Dragon,
The Stag perpetual, a signal before him.
At last the eventual harbor, a temple so far to the east
That it lay where the east was ending.
There Paladine appeared
In a pool of stars and glory, announcing
That of all choices, one most terrible had fallen to Huma.
For Paladine knew that the heart is a nest of yearnings,
That we can travel forever toward the light, becoming
What we can never be.

BOOK 3

Footsteps In The Sand . . .

The Army of Fistandantilus surged southward, reaching Caergoth just as the last of the leaves were blowing from the tree limbs and the chill hand of winter was getting a firm grip upon the land.

The banks of New Sea brought the army to a halt. But Caramon, knowing he was going to have to cross it, had long had his preparations underway. Turning over command of the main part of the army to his brother and the most trusted of his subordinates, Caramon led a group of his best-trained men to the shores of New Sea. Also with him were all the blacksmiths, woodwrights, and carpenters who had joined the army.

Caramon made his command post in the city of Caergoth. He had heard of the famous port city all his life—his former life. Three hundred years after the Cataclysm would find it a bustling, thriving harbor town. But now, one hundred years after the fiery mountain had struck Krynn, Caergoth was a town in confusion. Once a small farming community in the middle of the Solamnic Plain, Caergoth was still struggling with the sudden appearance of a sea at its doorstep.

Looking down from his quarters where the roads in town ended—suddenly—in a precarious drop down steep cliffs to the beaches below, Caramon thought—incongruously—of Tarsis. The Cataclysm had robbed that town of its sea, leaving its boats stranded upon the sands like dying sea birds, while here, in Caergoth, New Sea lapped on what was once plowed ground.

Caramon thought with longing of those stranded ships in Tarsis. Here, in Caergoth, there were a few boats but not nearly enough for his needs. He sent his men ranging up and down the coast for hundreds of miles, with orders to either purchase or commandeer sea-going vessels of any type, their crews with them, if possible. These they sailed to Caergoth, where the smiths and the craftsmen re-outfitted them to carry as great a load as possible for the short journey across the

Straits of Schallsea to Abanasinia.

Daily, Caramon received reports on the build-up of the dwarven armies—how Pax Tharkas was being fortified; how the dwarves had imported slave labor (gully dwarves) to work the mines and the steel forges day and night, turning out weapons and armor; how these were being carted to Thorbardin and taken inside the mountain.

He also received reports from the emissaries of the hill dwarves and the Plainsmen. He heard about the great gathering of the tribes in Abanasinia, putting aside blood feuds to fight together for survival. He heard about the preparations of the hill dwarves, who were also forging weapons, using the same gully-dwarf slave labor as their cousins, the mountain dwarves.

He had even made discreet advances to the elves in Qualinesti. This gave Caramon an eerie feeling, for the man to whom he sent his message was none other than Solostaran, Speaker of the Suns, who had—just weeks ago—died in Caramon's own time. Raistlin had sneered at hearing of this attempt to draw the elves into the war, knowing full well what their answer would be. The archmage had, however, not been without a secret hope, nurtured in the dark hours of the night, that *this time* it might prove different. . . .

It didn't.

Caramon's men never even had a chance to speak to Solostaran. Before they could dismount from their horses, arrows zinged through the air, thudding into the ground, forming a deadly ring around each of them. Looking into the aspen woods, they could see literally hundreds of archers, each with an arrow nocked and ready. No words were spoken. The messengers left, carrying an elven arrow to Caramon in answer.

The war itself, in fact, was beginning to give Caramon an eerie feeling. Piecing together what he had heard Raistlin and Crysania discussing, it suddenly occurred to Caramon that everything he was doing had all been done before. The thought was almost as nightmarish to him as to his brother, though for vastly different reasons.

"I feel as though that iron ring I wore round my neck in Istar had been bolted back on," Caramon muttered to himself one night as he sat in the inn at Caergoth that he had taken over for his command post. "I'm a slave again, same as I was then. Only this time it's worse, because—even when I was a slave—at least I had freedom to choose whether I was going to draw breath or not that day. I mean, if I'd wanted to die, I could have fallen on my sword and died! But now I'm not even given that choice, apparently."

It was a strange and horrifying concept for Caramon, one he dwelt on and mulled over many nights, one he knew he didn't understand. He would like to have talked it over with his brother, but Raistlin was back at the inland camp with the army and even if they had been together, Caramon was certain his twin would have refused to discuss it.

Raistlin, during this time, had been gaining in strength almost daily. Following the use of his magical spells that consumed the dead village in a blazing funeral pyre, the archmage had laid almost dead to the world for two days. Upon waking from his feverish sleep, he had announced that he was hungry. Within the next few days, he ate more solid food than he had been able to tolerate in months. The cough vanished. He rapidly regained strength and added flesh to his bones.

But he was still tormented by nightmares that not even the strongest of sleeping potions could banish.

Day and night, Raistlin pondered his problem. If only he could learn Fistandantilus's fatal mistake, he might be able to correct it!

Wild schemes came to mind. The archmage even toyed with the idea of traveling forward to his own time to research, but abandoned the idea almost immediately. If consuming a village in flame had plunged him into exhaustion for two days, the time-travel spell would prove even more wearing. And, though only a day or two might pass in the present while he recuperated, eons would flit by in the past. Finally, if he did make it back, he wouldn't have the strength needed to battle the Dark Queen.

And then, just when he had almost given up in despair, the answer came to him. . . .

CHAPTER
I

Raistlin lifted the tent flap and walked out. The guard on duty started and shuffled uncomfortably. The appearance of the archmage was always unnerving, even to those of his own personal guard. No one ever heard him coming. He always seemed to materialize out of the air. The first indication of his presence was the touch of burning fingers upon a bare arm, or soft, whispered words, or the rustle of black robes.

The wizard's tent was regarded with wonder and awe though no one had ever seen anything strange emanating from it. Many, of course, watched—especially the children, who secretly hoped to see a horrible monster break free of the archmage's control and go thundering through the camp, devouring everyone in sight until *they* were able to tame it with a bit of gingerbread.

But nothing of the kind ever happened. The archmage carefully nurtured and conserved his strength. Tonight would be different, Raistlin reflected with a sigh and scowl. But it couldn't be helped.

"Guard," he murmured.

"M-my lord?" the guard stammered in some confusion. The archmage rarely spoke to anyone, let alone a mere guard.

"Where is Lady Crysania?"

The guard could not suppress a curl of his lip as he answered that the "witch" was, he believed, in General Caramon's tent, having retired for the evening.

"Shall I send someone for her, my lord?" he asked Raistlin with such obvious reluctance that the mage could not help but smile, though it was hidden in the shadows of his black hood.

"No," Raistlin replied, nodding as if pleased at this information. "And my brother, have you word of him? When is his return expected?"

"General Caramon sent word that he arrives tomorrow, my lord," the guard continued in a mystified tone, certain that the mage knew this already. "We are to await his arrival here and let the supply train catch up with us at the same time. The first wagons rolled in this afternoon, my lord." A sudden thought struck the guard. "If—if you're thinking of changing these orders, my lord, I should call the Captain of the Watch—"

"No, no, nothing of the sort," Raistlin replied soothingly. "I merely wanted to make certain that I would not be disturbed this night—for anything or by anyone. Is that clear, uh—what is your name?"

"M-michael, lordship," the guard answered. "Certainly, my lord. If such are your orders, I will carry them out."

"Good," Raistlin said. The archmage was silent for a moment, staring out into the night which was cold but bright with the light from Lunitari and the stars. Solinari, waning, was nothing but a silver scratch across the sky. More important, to Raistlin's eyes, was the moon he alone could see. Nuitari, the Black Moon, was full and round, a hole of darkness amid the stars.

Raistlin took a step nearer the guard. Casting his hood back slightly from his face, he let the light of the red moon strike his eyes. The guard, startled, involuntarily stepped backward, but his strict training as a Knight of Solamnia made him catch himself.

Raistlin felt the man's body stiffen. He saw the reaction and smiled again. Raising a slender hand, he laid it upon the guard's armored chest.

"No one is to enter my tent for *any* reason," the archmage repeated in the soft, sibilant whisper he knew how to use so effectively. "No matter what happens! No one—Lady Crysania, my brother, you yourself . . . no one!"

"I—I understand, my lord," Michael stammered.

"You may hear or see strange things this night," Raistlin continued, his eyes holding the guard's in their entrancing gaze. "Ignore them. Any who enters this tent does so at the risk of his own life . . . *and mine!*"

"Y-yes, lord!" Michael said, swallowing. A trickle of sweat rolled down his face, though the night air was exceedingly cool for autumn.

"You are—or were—a Knight of Solamnia?" Raistlin asked abruptly.

Michael seemed uncomfortable, his gaze wavered. His mouth opened, but Raistlin shook his head. "Never mind. You do not have to tell me. Though you have shaved your mustaches, I can tell it by your face. I knew a Knight once, you see. Therefore, swear to me, by the Code and the Measure, that you will do as I ask."

"I swear, by the Code and . . . the Measure . . ." Michael whispered.

The mage nodded, apparently satisfied, and turned to reenter his tent. Michael, free of those eyes in which he saw only himself reflected, returned to his post, shivering beneath his heavy, woolen cloak. At the last moment, however, Raistlin paused, his robes rustling softly around him.

"Sir Knight," he whispered.

Michael turned.

"If anyone enters this tent," the mage said in a gentle, pleasant voice, "and disturbs my spellcasting and—if I survive—I will expect to find nothing but your corpse upon the ground. That is the only excuse I will accept for failure."

"Yes, my lord," Michael said, more firmly, though he kept his voice low. "*Est Sularas oth Mithas.* My Honor is My Life."

"Yes." Raistlin shrugged. "So it generally ends."

The archmage entered his tent, leaving Michael to stand in the darkness, waiting for the new-gods-knew-what to happen in the tent behind him. He wished his cousin, Garic, were here to share this strange and forbidding duty. But Garic was with Caramon. Michael hunched his shoulders deeper into his cloak and looked longingly out into the camp. There were bonfires, warm spiced wine, good fellowship, the sounds of laughter. Here, all was wrapped in thick, red-tinged, starlit darkness. The only sound Michael could hear was the sound of his armor jingling as he began to shake uncontrollably.

Crossing the tent floor, Raistlin came to a large, wooden chest that sat upon the floor beside his bed. Carved with magical runes, the chest was the only one of Raistlin's possessions—beside the Staff of Magius—that the mage allowed no one but himself to touch. Not that any sought to try. Not after the report of one of the guards, who had mistakenly attempted to lift it.

Raistlin had not said a word, he simply watched as the guard dropped it with a gasp.

The chest was bitterly cold to the touch, the guard reported in a shaken voice to his friends around the fire that night. Not only that, but he was overcome by a feeling of horror so great it was a wonder he didn't go mad.

Since that time, only Raistlin himself moved it, though how, no one could say. It was always present in his tent, yet no one could ever recall seeing it on any of the pack horses.

Lifting the lid of the chest, Raistlin calmly studied the contents—the nightblue-bound spellbooks, the jars and bottles and pouches of spell components, his own black-bound spellbooks, an assortment of scrolls, and several black robes folded at the bottom. There were no magical rings or pendants, such as might have been found in the possession of lesser mages. These Raistlin scorned as being fit only for weaklings.

His gaze passed quickly over all the items, including one slim, well-worn book that might have made the casual observer pause and stare, wondering that such a mundane item was kept with objects of arcane value. The title—written in flamboyant letters to attract the attention of the buyer—was *Sleight-of-Hand Techniques Designed to Amaze and Delight!* Below that was written *Astound Your Friends! Trick the Gullible!* There might have been more but the rest had been worn away long ago by young, eager, loving hands.

Passing over this book that, even now, brought a thin smile of remembrance to the mage's lips, Raistlin reached down among his robes, uncovered a small box, and drew it forth. This, too, was guarded by runes carved upon its surface. Muttering magical words to nullify their effects, the mage opened the box reverently. There was only one thing inside—an ornate, silver stand. Carefully, Raistlin removed the stand and, rising to his feet, carried it to the table he had placed in the center of the tent.

Settling himself into a chair, the mage put his hand into one of the secret pockets of his robes and pulled forth a small crystal object. Swirling with colors, it resembled at first glance nothing more sinister than a child's marble. Yet, looking at the object closely, one saw that the colors trapped within were alive. They could be seen constantly moving and shifting, as though seeking escape.

Raistlin placed the marble upon the stand. It looked ludicrous perched there, much too small. And then, suddenly, as always, it was perfectly right. The marble had grown, the stand had shrunk ... perhaps Raistlin himself had shrunk, for now the mage felt himself to be the one that appeared ludicrous.

It was a common feeling and he was accustomed to it, knowing that the dragon orb—for such was the shimmering, swirling-colored crystal globe—sought always to put its user at a disadvantage. But, long ago (no—in time to come!), Raistlin had mastered the dragon orb. He had learned to control the essence of dragonkind that inhabited it.

Relaxing his body, Raistlin closed his eyes and gave himself up to his magic. Reaching out, he placed his fingers upon the cold crystal of the dragon orb and spoke the ancient words.

"Ast bilak moiparalan/Suh akvlar tantangusar."

The chill of the orb began to spread through his fingers, causing his very bones to ache. Gritting his teeth, Raistlin repeated the words.

"Ast bilak moiparalan/Suh akvlar tantangusar."

The swirling colors within the orb ceased their lazy meandering and began to spin madly. Raistlin stared within the dazzling vortex, fighting the dizziness that assailed him, keeping his hands placed firmly upon the orb.

Slowly, he whispered the words again.

The colors ceased to swirl and a light glowed in the center. Raistlin blinked, then frowned. The light should have been neither black nor white, all colors yet none, symbolizing the mixture of good and evil and neutrality that bound the essence of the dragons within the orb. Such it had always been, ever since the first time he had looked within the orb and fought for its control.

But the light he saw now, though much the same as he had seen before, seemed ringed round by dark shadows. He stared at it closely, coldly, banishing any fanciful flights of imagination. His frown deepened. There *were* shadows hovering about the edges . . . shadows of . . . wings!

Out of the light came two hands. Raistlin caught hold of them—and gasped.

The hands pulled him with such strength that, totally unprepared, Raistlin nearly lost control. It was only when he felt himself being drawn into the orb by the hands within the shadowy light that he exerted his own force of will and yanked the hands back toward him.

"What is the meaning of this?" Raistlin demanded sternly. "Why do you challenge me? Long ago, I became your master."

She calls. . . . She calls and we must obey!

"Who calls who is more important than I?" Raistlin asked with a sneer, though his blood suddenly ran colder than the touch of the orb.

Our Queen! We hear her voice, moving in our dreams, disturbing our sleep. Come, master, we will take you! Come, quickly!

The Queen! Raistlin shuddered involuntarily, unable to stop himself. The hands, sensing him weakening, began to draw him in once more. Angrily, Raistlin tightened his grip on them and paused to try to sort his thoughts that swirled as madly as the colors within the orb.

The Queen! Of course, he should have foreseen this. She had entered the world—partially—and now she moved among the evil dragons. Banished from Krynn long ago by the sacrifice of the Solamnic Knight, Huma, the dragons, both good and evil, slept in deep and secret places.

Leaving the good dragons to sleep on undisturbed, the Dark Queen, Takhisis, the Five-Headed Dragon, was awaking the evil dragons, rallying them to her cause as she fought to gain control of the world.

The dragon orb, though composed of the essences of all dragons—good, evil, and neutral—would, of course, react strongly to the Queen's commands, especially as—for the present—its evil side was predominant, enhanced by the nature of its master.

Are those shadows I see the wings of dragons, or shadows of my own soul? Raistlin wondered, staring into the orb.

He did not have leisure for reflection, however. All of these thoughts flitted through his mind so rapidly that between the drawing of one breath and the releasing of it, the archmage saw his grave danger. Let him lose control for an instant, and Takhisis would claim him.

"No, my Queen," he murmured, keeping a tight grip upon the hands within the orb. "No, it will not be so easy as this."

To the orb he spoke softly but firmly, "I am your master still. I was the one who rescued you from Silvanesti and Lorac, the mad elven king. I was the one who carried you safely from the Blood Sea of Istar. I am Rai—" He hesitated, swallowed the suddenly bitter taste in his mouth, then said through clenched teeth, "I am . . . Fistandantilus—Master of Past and of Present—and I command you to obey me!"

The orb's light dimmed. Raistlin felt the hands holding his own tremble and start to slip away. Anger and fear shot through him, but he suppressed these emotions instantly and kept his clasp firmly upon the hands. The trembling ceased, the hands relaxed.

We obey, master.

Raistlin dared not breathe a sigh of relief.

"Very well," he said, keeping his voice stern, a parent speaking to a chastened child (but what a dangerous child! he thought). Coldly, he continued, "I must contact my apprentice in the Tower of High Sorcery in Palanthas. Heed my command. Carry my voice through the ethers of time. Bring my words to Dalamar."

Speak the words, master. He shall hear them as he hears the beating of his own heart, and so shall you hear his response.

Raistlin nodded. . . .

CHAPTER 2

alamar shut the spellbook, clenching his fist in frustration. He was certain he was doing everything right, pronouncing the words with the proper inflection, repeating the chant the prescribed number of times. The components were those called for. He had seen Raistlin cast this spell a hundred times. Yet, he could not do it.

Putting his head wearily in his hands, he closed his eyes and brought memories of his *Shalafi* to mind, hearing Raistlin's soft voice, trying to remember the exact tone and rhythm, trying to think of anything he might be doing wrong.

It didn't help. Everything seemed the same! Well, thought Dalamar with a tired sigh, I must simply wait until he returns.

Standing up, the dark elf spoke a word of magic and the continual light spell he had cast upon a crystal globe standing on the desk of Raistlin's library winked out. No fire burned in the grate. The late spring night in Palanthas was warm and fine. Dalamar had even dared open the window a crack.

Raistlin's health at the best of times was fragile. He abhorred fresh air, preferring to sit in his study wrapped in warmth and the smells of roses and spice and decay. Ordinarily, Dalamar did not mind. But there were times, particularly in the spring, when his elven soul longed for the woodland home he had left forever.

Standing by the window, smelling the perfume of renewed life that not even the horrors of the Shoikan Grove could keep from reaching the Tower, Dalamar let himself think, just for a moment, of Silvanesti.

A dark elf—one who is cast from the light. Such was Dalamar to his people. When they'd caught him wearing the Black Robes that no elf could even look upon without flinching, practicing arcane arts forbidden to one of his low rank and station, the elven lords had bound Dalamar hand and foot, gagged his mouth, and blindfolded his eyes. Then he had been thrown in a cart and driven to the borders of his land.

Deprived of his sight, Dalamar's last memories of Silvanesti were the smells of aspen trees, blooming flowers, rich loam. It had been spring then, too, he recalled.

Would he go back if he could? Would he give up this to return? Did he feel any sorrow, regret? Without conscious volition, Dalamar's hand went to his breast. Beneath the black robes, he could feel the wounds in his chest. Though it had been a week since Raistlin's hand had touched him, burning five holes into his flesh, the wounds had not healed. Nor would they ever heal, Dalamar knew with bitter certainty.

Always, the rest of his life, he would feel their pain. Whenever he stood naked, he would see them, festering scabs that no skin would cover. Such was the penalty he had paid for his treachery against his *Shalafi*.

As he had told the great Par-Salian, Head of the Order, master of the Tower of High Sorcery in Wayreth—and Dalamar's master, too, of a sort, since the dark elf mage had, in reality, been a spy for the Order of Mages who feared and distrusted Raistlin as they had feared no mortal in their history—"It was no more than I deserved."

Would he leave this dangerous place? Go back home, go back to Silvanesti?

Dalamar stared out the window with a grim, twisted smile,

reminiscent of Raistlin, the *Shalafi*. Almost unwillingly, Dalamar's gaze went from the peaceful, starlit night sky back indoors, to the rows and rows of nightblue-bound spellbooks that lined the walls of the library. In his memory, he saw the wonderful, awful, beautiful, dreadful sights he had been privileged to witness as Raistlin's apprentice. He felt the stirrings of power within his soul, a pleasure that outweighed the pain.

No, he would never return. Never leave. . . .

Dalamar's musings were cut short by the sound of a silver bell. It rang only once, with a sweet, low sound. But to those living (and dead) within the Tower, it had the effect of a shattering gong splitting the air. Someone was attempting to enter! Someone had won through the perilous Shoikan Grove and was at the gates of the Tower itself!

His mind having already conjured up memories of Par-Salian, Dalamar had sudden unwelcome visions of the powerful, white-robed wizard standing on his doorstep. He could also hear in his mind what he had told the Council only nights earlier—"If any of you came and tried to enter the Tower while he was gone, I would kill you."

On the words of a spell, Dalamar disappeared from the library to reappear, within the drawing of a breath, at the Tower entrance.

But it was not a conclave of flashing-eyed wizards he faced. It was a figure dressed in blue dragonscale armor, wearing the hideous, horned mask of a Dragon Highlord. In its gloved hand, the figure held a black jewel—a nightjewel, Dalamar saw—and behind the figure he could sense, though he could not see, the presence of a being of awesome power—a death knight.

The Dragon Highlord was using the jewel to hold at bay several of the Tower's Guardians; their pale visages could be seen in the dark light of the nightjewel, thirsting for her living blood. Though Dalamar could not see the Highlord's face beneath the helm, he could feel the heat of her anger.

"Lord Kitiara," Dalamar said gravely, bowing. "Forgive this rude welcome. If you had but let us know you were coming—"

Yanking off the helm, Kitiara glared at Dalamar with cold, brown eyes that reminded the apprentice forcibly of her kinship to the *Shalafi*.

"—you would have had an even more interesting reception planned for me, no doubt!" she snarled with an angry toss of her dark, curly hair. "I come and go where I please, especially to pay a visit to my brother!" Her voice literally shook with rage. "I made my way through those god-cursed trees of yours out there, then I'm attacked at his front door!" Her hand drew her sword. She took a step forward. "By the gods, I should teach you a lesson, elven slime—"

"I repeat my apologies," Dalamar said calmly, but there was a glint in his slanted eyes that made Kit hesitate in her reckless act.

Like most warriors, Kitiara tended to regard magic-users as weaklings who spent time reading books that could be put to better use wielding cold steel. Oh, they could produce some flashy results, no doubt, but when put to the test, she would much rather rely on her sword and her skill than weird words and bat dung.

Thus she pictured Raistlin, her half-brother, in her mind, and this was how she pictured his apprentice—with the added mark against Dalamar that he was only an elf—a race noted for its weakness.

But Kitiara was, in another respect, different from most warriors—the main reason she had outlived all who opposed her. She was skilled at assessing her opponents. One look at Dalamar's cool eyes and composed stature—in the face of her anger—and Kitiara wondered if she might not have encountered a foe worthy of her.

She didn't understand him, not yet—not by any means. But she saw and recognized the danger in this man and, even as she made a note to be wary of it and to use it, if possible, she found herself attracted to it. The fact that it went with such handsome features (he didn't look at all elvish, now that she thought of it) and such a strong, muscular body (whose frame admirably filled out the black robes), made it suddenly occur to her that she might accomplish more by being friendly than intimidating. Certainly, she thought, her eyes lingering on the elf's chest, where the black robes had parted slightly and she could see bronze skin beneath, it might be much more entertaining.

Thrusting her sword back in its sheath, Kitiara continued her step forward, only now the light that had flashed on the blade flashed in her eyes.

"Forgive me, Dalamar—that's your name, isn't it?" Her scowl melted into the crooked, charming smile that had won so many. "That damned Grove unnerves me. You are right. I should have notified my brother I was coming, but I acted on impulse." She stood close to Dalamar now, very close. Looking up into his face, hidden as it was by the shadows of his hood, she added, "I . . . often act on impulse."

With a gesture, Dalamar dismissed the Guardians. Then the young elf regarded the woman before him with a smile of charm that rivaled her own.

Seeing his smile, Kitiara held out her gloved hand. "Forgiven?"

Dalamar's smile deepened, but he only said, "Remove your glove, lord."

Kitiara started and, for an instant, the brown eyes dilated dangerously. But Dalamar continued to smile at her. Shrugging, Kitiara jerked one by one at the fingers of the leather glove, baring her hand.

"There," she said, her voice tinged with scorn, "you see that I hold no concealed weapon."

"Oh, I already knew that," Dalamar replied, now taking the hand in his own. His eyes still on hers, the dark elf drew her hand up to his lips and kissed it lingeringly. "Would you have had me deny myself this pleasure?"

His lips were warm, his hands strong, and Kitiara felt the blood surge through her body at his touch. But she saw in his eyes that he knew her game and she saw, too, that it was one he played himself. Her respect rose, as did her guard. Truly a foe worthy of her attention—her undivided attention.

Slipping her hand from his grasp, Kitiara put it behind her back with a playful female gesture that contrasted oddly with her armor and her manlike, warrior stance. It was a gesture designed to attract and confuse, and she saw from the elf's slightly flushed features that it had succeeded.

"Perhaps I have concealed weapons beneath my armor you should search for sometime," she said with a mocking grin.

"On the contrary," Dalamar returned, folding his hands in his black robes, "your weapons seem to me to be in plain sight. Were I to search you, lord, I would seek out that which the armor guards and which, though many men have penetrated, none has yet touched." The elven eyes laughed.

Kitiara caught her breath. Tantalized by his words, remembering still the feel of those warm lips upon her skin, she took another step forward, tilting her face to the man's.

Coolly, without seeming aware of his action, Dalamar made a graceful move to one side, slightly turning away from Kitiara. Expecting to be caught up in the man's arms, Kit was, instead, thrown off balance. Awkwardly, she stumbled.

Recovering her balance with feline skill, she whirled to face him, her face flushed with embarrassment and fury. Kitiara had killed men for less than mocking her like this. But she was disconcerted to see that he was, apparently, totally unaware of what he had done. Or was he? His face was carefully devoid of all expression. He was talking about her brother. No, he had done that on purpose. He would pay. . . .

Kit knew her opponent now, conceded his skill. Characteristically, she did not waste time berating herself for her mistake. She had left herself open, she had taken a wound. Now, she was prepared.

"—I deeply regret that the *Shalafi* is not here," Dalamar was saying. "I am certain that your brother will be sorry to learn he has missed you."

"Not here?" Kit demanded, her attention caught instantly. "Why, where is he? Where would he go?"

"I am certain he told you," Dalamar said with feigned surprise. "He has gone back to the past to seek the wisdom of Fistandantilus and from thence to discover the Portal through which he will—"

"You mean—he went anyway! Without the cleric?" Suddenly Kit remembered that no one was supposed to have known that she had sent Lord Soth to kill Crysania in order to stop her brother's insane notion of challenging the Dark Queen. Biting her lip, she glanced behind her at the death knight.

Dalamar followed her gaze, smiling, seeing every thought beneath that lovely, curling hair. "Oh, you knew about the attack on Lady Crysania?" he asked innocently.

Kit scowled. "You know damn well I knew about the attack! And so does my brother. He's not an idiot, if he is a fool."

She spun around on her heel. "You told me the woman was dead!"

"She was," intoned Lord Soth, the death knight, materializing out of the shadows to stand before her, his orange eyes flaring in their invisible sockets. "No human could survive my assault." The orange eyes turned their undying gaze to the dark elf. "And your master could not have saved her."

"No," Dalamar agreed, "but *her* master could and did. Paladine cast a counter-spell upon his cleric, drawing her soul to him, though he left the shell of her body behind. The *Shalafi's* twin, your half-brother, Caramon, lord"—Dalamar bowed to the infuriated Kitiara—"took the woman to the Tower of High Sorcery where the mages sent her back to the only cleric powerful enough to save her—the Kingpriest of Istar."

"Imbeciles!" Kitiara snarled, her face going livid. "They sent her back to him! That's just what Raistlin wanted!"

"They knew that," Dalamar said softly. "I told them—"

"*You* told them?" Kitiara gasped.

"There are matters I should explain to you," Dalamar said. "This may take some time. At least let us be comfortable. Will you come to my chambers?"

He extended his arm. Kitiara hesitated, then laid her hand upon his forearm. Catching hold of her around her waist, he pulled her close to his body. Startled, Kitiara tried to pull away, but she didn't try very hard. Dalamar held her with a grip both strong and firm.

"In order for the spell to transport us," he said coolly, "you need to stand as close to me as possible."

"I'm quite capable of walking," Kit returned. "I have little use for magic!"

But, even as she spoke, her eyes looked into his, her body pressed against his hard, well-muscled body with sensuous abandon.

"Very well," Dalamar shrugged and suddenly vanished.

Looking around, startled, Kit heard his voice. "Up the spiral staircase, lord. After the five hundred and thirty-ninth step, turn left."

"And so you see," Dalamar said, "I have as great a stake in this as do you. I have been sent, by the Conclave of all three Orders—the Black, the White, and the Red—to stop this appalling thing from happening."

The two relaxed in the dark elf's private, sumptuously appointed quarters within the Tower. The remains of an elegant repast had been whisked away by a graceful gesture of the elf's hand. Now, they sat before a fire that had been lit more for the sake of its light than its warmth on this spring night. The dancing flames seemed more conducive to conversation. . . .

"Then why *didn't* you stop him?" Kit demanded angrily, setting her golden goblet down with a sharp clinking sound. "What's so difficult about that?" Making a gesture with her hand, she added words to suit her action. "A knife in the back. Quick, simple." Giving Dalamar a look of scorn, she sneered. "Or are you above that, you mages?"

"Not above it," Dalamar said, regarding Kitiara intently. "There are subtler means we of the Black Robes generally use to rid ourselves of our enemies. But not against *him*, lord. Not your brother."

Dalamar shivered slightly and drank his wine with undue haste.

"Bah!" Kitiara snorted.

"No, listen to me and understand, Kitiara," Dalamar said softly. "You do not know your brother. You do not know him and, what is worse, *you do not fear him*! That will lead to your doom."

"Fear him? That skinny, hacking wretch? You're not serious—" Kitiara began, laughing. But her laughter died. She leaned forward. "You *are* serious. I can see it in your eyes!"

Dalamar smiled grimly. "I fear him as I fear nothing in this world—including death." Reaching up, the dark elf grasped the seam of his black robes and ripped it open, revealing the wounds on his chest.

Kitiara, mystified, looked at the wounds, then looked up at the dark elf's pale face. "What weapon made those? I don't recog—"

"His hand," Dalamar said without emotion. "The mark of his five fingers. This was his message to Par-Salian and the Conclave when he commanded me to give them his regards."

Kit had seen many terrible sights—men disemboweled before her eyes, heads hacked off, torture sessions in the dungeons beneath the mountains known as the Lords of Doom. But, seeing those oozing sores and seeing, in her mind, her brother's slender fingers burning into the dark elf's flesh, she could not repress a shudder.

Sinking back in her chair, Kit went over carefully in her mind everything Dalamar had told her, and she began to think that, perhaps, she *had* underestimated Raistlin. Her face grave, she sipped her wine.

"And so he plans to enter the Portal," she said to Dalamar slowly, trying to readjust her thinking along these new and startling lines. "He will enter the Portal with the cleric. He will find himself in the Abyss. Then what? Surely he knows he cannot fight the Dark Queen on her own plane!"

"Of course he knows," Dalamar said. "He is strong, but—there—she is stronger. And so he intends to lure her out, to force her to enter this world. Here, he believes, he can destroy her."

"Mad!" Kitiara whispered with barely enough breath to say the word. "He is mad!" She hastily set her wine goblet down, seeing the liquid slopping over her shaking hand. "He has seen her in this plane when she was but a shadow, when she was blocked from entering completely. He cannot imagine what she would be like—!"

Rising to her feet, Kit nervously crossed the soft carpet with its muted images of trees and flowers so beloved of the elves. Feeling suddenly chilled, she stood before the fire. Dalamar came to stand beside her, his black robes rustling. Even as Kit spoke, absorbed in her own thoughts and fears, she was conscious of the elf's warm body near hers.

"What do your mages think will happen?" she asked abruptly. "Who will win, if he succeeds in this insane plan? Does he have a chance?"

Dalamar shrugged and, moving a step nearer, put his hands on Kitiara's slender neck. His fingers softly caressed her smooth skin. The sensation was delicious. Kitiara closed her eyes, drawing a deep, shivering breath.

"The mages do not know," Dalamar said softly, bending down to kiss Kitiara just below her ear. Stretching like a cat, she arched her body back against his.

"Here he would be in his element," Dalamar continued, "the Queen would be weakened. But she certainly would not be easily defeated. Some think the magical battle between the two could well destroy the world."

Lifting her hand, Kitiara ran it through the elf's thick, silken hair, drawing his eager lips to her throat. "But . . . does he have a chance?" she persisted in a husky whisper.

Dalamar paused, then drew back away from her. His hands still on her shoulders, he turned Kitiara around to face him. Looking into her eyes, he saw what she was thinking. "Of course. There's always a chance."

"And what is it you will do, if he succeeds in entering the Portal?" Kitiara's hands rested lightly on Dalamar's chest, where her half-brother had left his terrible mark. Her eyes, looking into the elf's, were luminous with passion that almost, but not quite, hid her calculating mind.

"I am to stop him from returning to this world," Dalamar said. "I am to block the Portal so that he cannot come through." His hand traced her crooked, curving lips.

"What will be your reward for so dangerous an assignment?" She pressed closer, biting playfully at his fingertips.

"I will be Master of the Tower, then," he answered. "And the next head of the Order of Black Robes. Why?"

"I could help you," Kitiara said with a sigh, moving her fingers over Dalamar's chest and up over his shoulders, kneading her hands into his flesh like a cat's paws. Almost convulsively, Dalamar's hands tightened around her, drawing her nearer still.

"I could help," Kitiara repeated in a fierce whisper. "You cannot fight him alone."

"Ah, my dear"—Dalamar regarded her with a wry, sardonic smile—"who would you help—me or him?"

"Now that," said Kitiara, slipping her hands beneath the tear in the fabric of the dark elf's black robes, "would depend entirely upon who's winning!"

Dalamar's smile broadened, his lips brushed her chin. He whispered into her ear, "Just so we understand each, lord."

"Oh, we understand each other," Kitiara said, sighing with pleasure. "And now, enough of my brother. There is something I would ask. Something I have long been curious about. What do magic-users wear beneath their robes, dark elf?"

"Very little," Dalamar murmured. "And what do warrior women wear beneath their armor?"

"Nothing."

Kitiara was gone.

Dalamar lay, half-awake and half-asleep, in his bed. Upon his pillow, he could still smell the fragrance of her hair—perfume and steel—a strange, intoxicating mixture not unlike Kitiara herself.

The dark elf stretched luxuriously, grinning. She would betray him, he had no doubt about that. And she knew he would destroy her in a second, if necessary, to succeed in his purpose. Neither found the knowledge bitter. Indeed, it added an odd spice to their lovemaking.

Closing his eyes, letting sleep drift over him, Dalamar heard, through his open window, the sound of dragonwings spreading for flight. He imagined her, seated upon her blue dragon, the dragonhelm glinting in the moonlight. . . .

Dalamar!

The dark elf started and sat up. He was wide awake. Fear coursed through his body. Trembling at the sound of that familiar voice, he glanced about the room.

"*Shalafi?*" He spoke hesitantly. There was no one there. Dalamar put his hand to his head. "A dream," he muttered.

Dalamar!

The voice again, this time unmistakable. Dalamar looked around helplessly, his fear increasing. It was completely unlike Raistlin to play games. The archmage had cast the time-travel spell. He had journeyed back in time. He had been gone a week and was not expected to return for many more. Yet Dalamar knew that voice as he knew the sound of his own heartbeat!

"*Shalafi*, I hear you," Dalamar said, trying to keep his tone firm. "Yet I cannot see you. Where—"

I am, as you surmise, back in time, apprentice. I speak to you through the dragon orb. I have an assignment for you. Listen to me carefully and follow my instructions exactly. Act at once. No time must be lost. Every second is precious. . . .

Closing his eyes that he might concentrate, Dalamar heard the voice clearly, yet he also heard sounds of laughter floating in through the open window. A festival of some sort, designed to honor spring, was beginning. Outside the gates of Old City, bonfires burned, young people exchanged flowers in the light and kisses in the dark. The air was sweet with rejoicing and love and the smell of spring blooming roses.

But then Raistlin began speaking and Dalamar heeded none of these. He forgot Kitiara. He forgot love. He forgot springtime. Listening, questioning, understanding, his entire body tingled with the voice of his *Shalafi*.

Chapter 3

Bertrem padded softly through the halls of the Great Library of Palanthas. His Aesthetics' robes whispered about his ankles, their rustle keeping time to the tune Bertrem hummed as he went along. He had been watching the spring festival from the windows of the Great Library and now, as he returned to his work among the thousands and thousands of books and scrolls housed within the Library, the melody of one of the songs lingered in his head.

"Ta-tum, ta-tum," Bertrem sang in a thin, off-key voice, pitched low so as not to disturb the echoes of the vast, vaulted halls of the Great Library.

The echoes were all that could be disturbed by Bertrem's singing, the Library itself being closed and locked for the night. Most of the other Aesthetics—members of the order whose lives were spent in study and maintenance of the Great Library's collection of knowledge gathered from the beginning of Krynn's time—were either sleeping or absorbed in their own works.

"Ta-tum, ta-tum. My lover's eyes are the eyes of the doe. Ta-tum, ta-tum. And I am the hunter, closing in . . ." Bertrem even indulged in an impromptu dance step.

"Ta-tum, ta-tum. I lift my bow and draw my arrow—" Bertrem skipped around a corner. "I loose the shaft. It flies to my lover's heart and—Ho, there! Who are you?"

Bertrem's own heart leaped into his throat, very nearly strangling the Aesthetic as he was suddenly confronted with a tall, black-robed and hooded figure standing in the center of the dimly lit marble hall.

The figure did not answer. It simply stared at him in silence.

Gathering his wits and his courage and his robes about him, Bertrem glared at the intruder.

"What business have you here? The Library's closed! Yes, even to those of the Black Robes." The Aesthetic frowned and waved a pudgy hand. "Be gone. Return in the morning, and use the front door, like everyone else."

"Ah, but I am not everyone else," said the figure, and Bertrem started, for he detected an elvish accent though the words were Solamnic. "As for doors, they are for those without the power to pass through walls. I have that power, as I have the power to do other things, many not so pleasant."

Bertrem shuddered. This smooth, cool elven voice did not make idle threats.

"You are a dark elf," Bertrem said accusingly, his brain scrambling about, trying to think what to do. Should he raise the alarm? Yell for help?

"Yes." The figure removed his black hood so that the magical light imprisoned in the globes hanging from the ceiling—a gift from the magic-users to Astinus given during the Age of Dreams—fell upon his elven features. "My name is Dalamar. I serve—

"Raistlin Majere!" Bertrem gasped. He glanced about uneasily, expecting the black-robed archmage to leap out at him any moment.

Dalamar smiled. The elven features were delicate, handsome. But there was a cold, single-minded purposefulness about them that chilled Bertrem. All thoughts of calling for help vanished from the Aesthetic's mind.

"Wha-what do you want?" he stammered.

"It is what my master wants," Dalamar corrected. "Do not be frightened. I am here seeking knowledge, nothing more. If you aid me, I will be gone as swiftly and silently as I have come."

If I don't aid him. . . . Bertrem shivered from head to toe. "I will do what I can, magus," the Aesthetic faltered, "but you should really talk to. . . ."

"Me," came a voice out of the shadows.

Bertrem nearly fainted in relief.

"Astinus!" he babbled, pointing at Dalamar, "this . . . he . . . I didn't let him . . . appeared . . . Raistlin Majere . . ."

"Yes, Bertrem," Astinus said soothingly. Coming forward, he patted the Aesthetic on the arm. "I know everything that has transpired." Dalamar had not moved, nor even indicated that he was aware of Astinus's presence. "Return to your studies, Bertrem," Astinus continued, his deep baritone echoing through the quiet hallways. "I will handle this matter."

"Yes, Master!" Bertrem backed thankfully down the hall, his robes fluttering about him, his gaze on the dark elf, who had still neither moved nor spoken. Reaching the corner, Bertrem vanished around it precipitously, and Astinus could hear, by the sounds of his flapping sandals, that he was running down the hallway.

The head of the Great Library of Palanthas smiled, but only inwardly. To the eyes of the dark elf watching him, the man's calm, ageless face reflected no more emotion than the marble walls about them.

"Come this way, young mage," Astinus said, turning abruptly and starting off down the hall with a quick, strong stride that belied his middle-aged appearance.

Caught by surprise, Dalamar hesitated, then—seeing he was being left behind—hurried to catch up.

"How do you know what I seek?" the dark elf demanded.

"I am a chronicler of history," Astinus replied imperturbably "Even as we speak and walk, events transpire around us and I am aware of them. I hear every word spoken, I see every deed committed, no matter how mundane, how good, how evil. Thus I have watched throughout history. As I was the first, so shall I be the last. Now, this way."

Astinus made a sharp turn to his left. As he did so, he lifted a glowing globe of light from its stand and carried it with him in his hand. By the light, Dalamar could see long rows of books standing on wooden shelves. He could tell by their smooth leather binding that they were old. But they were in excellent condition. The Aesthetics kept them dusted and, when necessary, rebound those particularly worn.

"Here is what you want"—Astinus gestured—"the Dwarfgate Wars"

Dalamar stared. "All these?" He gazed down a seemingly endless row of books, a feeling of despair slowly creeping over him.

"Yes," Astinus replied coldly, "and the next row of books as well."

"I—I . . ." Dalamar was completely at a loss. Surely Raistlin had not guessed the enormity of this task. Surely he couldn't expect him to devour the contents of these hundreds of volumes within the specified time limit. Dalamar had never felt so powerless and helpless before in his life. Flushing angrily, he sensed Astinus's icelike gaze upon him.

"Perhaps I can help," the historian said placidly. Reaching up, without even reading the spine, Astinus removed one volume from the shelf. Opening it, he flipped quickly through the thin, brittle pages, his eyes scanning the row after row of neat precisely written, black-inked letters.

"Ah, here it is." Drawing an ivory marker from a pocket of his robes, Astinus laid it across a page in the book, shut it carefully, then handed the book to Dalamar. "Take this with you. Give him the information he seeks. And tell him this—'The wind blows. The footsteps in the sand will be erased, but only after he has trod them.' "

The historian bowed gravely to the dark elf, then walked past him, down the row of books to reach the corridor again. Once there, he stopped and turned to face Dalamar, who was standing, staring, clutching the book Astinus had thrust into his hands.

"Oh, young mage. You needn't come back here again. The book will return of its own accord when you are finished. I cannot have you frightening the Aesthetics. Poor Bertrem will have undoubtedly taken to his bed. Give your *Shalafi* my greetings."

Astinus bowed again and disappeared into the shadows.

Dalamar remained standing, pondering, listening to the historian's slow, firm step fade down the hallway. Shrugging, the dark elf spoke a word of magic and returned to the Tower of High Sorcery.

"What Astinus gave me is his own commentary on the Dwarfgate Wars, *Shalafi*. It is drawn from the ancient texts he wrote—"

Astinus would know what I need. Proceed.

"Yes, *Shalafi*. This begins the marked passage—

'And the great archmage, Fistandantilus, used the dragon orb to call forward in time to his apprentice, instructing him to go the Great Library at Palanthas and read in the books of history there to see if the result of his great undertaking would prove successful.' " Dalamar's voice faltered as he read this and eventually died completely as he re-read this amazing statement.

Continue! came his *Shalafi's* voice, and though it resounded more in his mind than his ears, Dalamar did not miss the note of bitter anger. Hurriedly tearing his gaze from the paragraph, written hundreds of years previously, yet accurately reflecting the mission he had just undertaken, Dalamar continued.

"'It is important here to note this: the *Chronicles* as they existed *at that point in time* indicate—'

"That part is underscored, *Shalafi*," Dalamar interrupted himself.

What part?

" '—at that point in time' is underscored."

Raistlin did not reply, and Dalamar, momentarily losing his place, found it and hastened on.

"—'indicated' that the undertaking would have been successful. Fistandantilus, along with the cleric, Denubis, should have been able, from all indications that the great archmage saw, to safely enter the Portal. What might have happened in the Abyss, of course, is unknown, since the actual historical events transpired differently.

" 'Thus, believing firmly that his ultimate goal of entering the Portal and challenging the Queen of Darkness was within his reach, Fistandantilus pursued the Dwarfgate Wars with renewed vigor. Pax Tharkas fell to the armies of the hill dwarves and the Plainsmen. (See *Chronicles* Volume 126, Book 6, pages 589-700.) Led by Fistandantilus's great general, Pheragas—the former slave from Northern Ergoth whom the wizard had purchased and trained as a gladiator in the Games at Istar—the Army of Fistandantilus drove back the forces of King Duncan, forcing the dwarves to retreat to the mountain fastness of Thorbardin.

" 'Little did Fistandantilus care for this war. It simply served to further his own ends. Finding the Portal beneath the towering mountain fortress known as Zhaman, he established his headquarters there and began the final preparations that would give him the power to enter the forbidden gates, leaving his general to fight the war.

" 'What happened at this point is beyond even me to relate with accuracy, since the magical forces at work here were so powerful it obscured my vision.

" 'General Pheregas was killed fighting the Dewar, the dark dwarves of Thorbardin. At his death, the Army of Fistandantilus crumbled. The mountain dwarves swarmed out of Thorbardin toward the fortress of Zhaman.

" 'During the fighting, aware that the battle was lost and that they had little time, Fistandantilus and Denubis hastened to the Portal. Here the great wizard began to cast his spell.

" 'At the same instant, a gnome, being held prisoner by the dwarves of Thorbardin, activated a time-traveling device he had constructed in an effort to escape his confinement. Contrary to every recorded instance in the history of Krynn, this gnomish device actually worked. It worked quite well, in fact.

" 'I can only speculate from this point on, but it seems probable that the gnome's device interacted somehow with the delicate and powerful magical spells being woven by Fistandantilus. The result we know all too clearly.

" 'A blast occurred of such magnitude that the Plains of Dergoth were utterly destroyed. Both armies were almost completely wiped out. The towering mountain fortress of Zhaman shattered and fell in upon itself, creating the hill now called Skullcap.

" 'The unfortunate Denubis died in the blast. Fistandantilus should have died as well, but his magic was so great that he was able to cling to some portion of life, though his spirit was forced to exist upon another plane until it found the body of a young magic-user named Raistlin Majere. . . .' "

Enough!

"Yes, *Shalafi*," Dalamar murmured.

And then Raistlin's voice was gone.

Dalamar, sitting in the study, knew he was alone. Shivering violently, he was completely overawed and amazed by what he had just read. Seeking to make some meaning of it, the dark elf sat in the chair behind the desk— Raistlin's desk—lost in thought until night's shadows withdrew and gray dawn lit the sky.

A tremor of excitement made Raistlin's thin body quiver. His thoughts were confused, he would need a period of cool study and reflection to make absolutely certain of what he had discovered. One phrase shone with dazzling brilliance in his mind—*the undertaking would have been successful!*

The undertaking would have been successful!

Raistlin sucked in his breath with a gasp, realizing at that point only that he had ceased breathing. His hands upon the dragon orb's cold surface shook. Exultation swept over him. He laughed the strange, rare laughter of his, for the footsteps he saw in his dream led to a scaffold no longer, but to a door of platinum, decorated with the symbols of the Five-Headed Dragon. At *his* command, it would open. He had simply to find and destroy this gnome—

Raistlin felt a sharp tug on his hands.

"Stop!" he ordered, cursing himself for losing control.

But the orb did not obey his command. Too late, Raistlin realized he was being drawn inside. . . .

The hands had undergone a change, he saw as they pulled him closer and closer. They had been unrecognizable before—neither human nor elven, young nor old. But now they were the hands of a female, soft, supple, with smooth white skin and the grip of death.

Sweating, fighting down the hot surge of panic that threatened to destroy him, Raistlin summoned all his strength—both physical and mental—and fought the will behind the hands.

Closer they drew him, nearer and nearer. He could see the face now—a woman's face, beautiful, dark-eyed; speaking words of seduction that his body reacted to with passion even as his soul recoiled in loathing.

Nearer and nearer. . . .

Desperately, Raistlin struggled to pull away, to break the grip that seemed so gentle yet was stronger than the bonds of his life force. Deep he delved into his soul, searching the hidden parts—but for what, he little knew. Some part of him, somewhere, existed that would save him. . . .

An image of a lovely, white-robed cleric wearing the medallion of Paladine emerged. She shone in the darkness and, for a moment, the hands' grasp loosened—but only for a moment. Raistlin heard a woman's sultry laughter. The vision shattered.

"My brother!" Raistlin called through parched lips, and an image of Caramon came forward. Dressed in golden armor, his sword flashing in his hands, he stood in front of his twin, guarding him. But the warrior had not taken a step before he was cut down—from behind.

Nearer and nearer. . . .

Raistlin's head slumped forward, he was rapidly losing strength and consciousness. And then, unbidden, from the innermost recesses of his soul, came a lone figure. It was not robed in white, it carried no gleaming sword. It was small and grubby and its face was streaked with tears.

In its hand, it held only a dead . . . very dead . . . rat.

Caramon arrived back in camp just as the first rays of dawn were spreading through the sky. He had ridden all night and was stiff, tired, and unbelievably hungry.

Fond thoughts of his breakfast and his bed had been comforting him for the last hour, and his face broke into a grin as the camp came into sight. He was about to put the spurs to his weary horse when, looking ahead into the camp itself, the big man reined in his horse and brought his escort to a halt with an upraised hand.

"What's going on?" he asked in alarm, all thoughts of food vanishing.

Garic, riding up beside him, shook his head, mystified.

Where there should have been lines of smoke rising from morning cooking fires and the disgruntled snorts of men being roused from a night's sleep, the camp resembled a beehive after a bear's feast. No cooking fires were lit, people ran about in apparent aimlessness or stood clustered together in groups that buzzed with excitement.

Then someone caught sight of Caramon and let out a yell. The crowd came together and surged forward. Instantly, Garic shouted and, within moments, he and his men had galloped up to form a protective shield of armor-clad bodies around their general.

It was the first time Caramon had seen such a display of loyalty and affection from his men and, for a moment, he was so overcome he could not speak. Then, gruffly clearing his throat, he ordered them aside.

"It's not a mutiny," he growled, riding forward as his men reluctantly parted to let him pass. "Look! No one's armed. Half of 'em are women and children. But—" he grinned at them—"thanks for the thought."

His gaze went particularly to the young knight, Garic, who flushed with pleasure even as he kept his hand on his sword hilt.

By this time, the outer fringes of the crowd had reached Caramon. Hands grasped his bridle, startling his horse, who—thinking this was battle—pricked its ears dangerously, ready to lash out with its hooves as it had been trained.

"Stand back!" Caramon roared, barely holding the animal in check. "Stand back! Have you all gone mad? You look like just what you are—a bunch of farmers! Stand back, I say! Did your chickens all get loose? What's the meaning of this? Where are my officers?"

"Here, sir," came a voice of one of the captains. Red-faced, embarrassed, and angry, the man shoved his way through the crowd. Chagrined at the reprimand from their commander, the men calmed down and the shouting died to a few mutterings as a group of guards, arriving with the captain, began to try to break up the mob.

"Begging the general's pardon for all this, sir," the captain said as Caramon dismounted and patted his horse's neck soothingly. The animal stood still under Caramon's touch, though its eyes rolled and its ears still twitched.

The captain was an older man, not a Knight but a mercenary of thirty years' experience. His face was seamed with scars, he was missing part of his left hand from a slashing sword blow, and he walked with a pronounced limp. This morning, the scarred face was flushed with shame as he faced his young general's stern gaze.

"The scouts sent word of yer comin', sir, but afore I could get to you, this pack o' wild dogs"—he glowered at the retreating men—"lit out for you like you was a bitch in heat. Beggin' the general's pardon," he muttered again, "and meanin' no disrespect."

Caramon kept his face carefully composed. "What's happened?" he asked, leading his tired horse into camp at a walk. The captain did not answer right away but cast a significant glance at Caramon's escort.

Caramon understood. "Go on ahead, men," he said, waving his hand. "Garic, see to my quarters."

When he and the captain were alone—or as alone as possible in the crowded camp where everyone was staring at them in eager curiosity—Caramon turned to question the man with a glance.

The old mercenary said just two words: "The wizard."

Reaching Raistlin's tent, Caramon saw with a sinking heart the ring of armed guards surrounding it, keeping back onlookers. There were audible sighs of relief at the sight of Caramon, and many remarks of "General's here now. He'll take care of things," much nodding of heads, and some scattered applause.

Encouraged by a few oaths from the captain, the crowd opened up an aisle for Caramon to walk through. The armed guards stepped aside as he passed, then quickly closed ranks again. Pushing and shoving, the crowd peered over the guards, straining to see. The captain having refused to tell him what was going on, Caramon would not have been surprised to find anything from a dragon sitting atop his brother's tent to the whole thing surrounded by green and purple flame.

Instead, he saw one young man standing guard and Lady Crysania pacing in front of the closed tent flap.

Caramon stared at the young man curiously, thinking he recognized him.

"Garic's cousin," he said hesitantly, trying to remember the name. "Michael, isn't it?"

"Yes, general," the young Knight said. Drawing himself up straight, he attempted a salute. But it was a feeble attempt. The young man's face was pale and haggard, his eyes red-rimmed. He was clearly about to drop from exhaustion, but he held his spear before him, grimly barring the way into the tent.

Hearing Caramon's voice, Crysania looked up.

"Thank Paladine!" she said fervently.

One look at her pale face and sunken gray eyes, and Caramon shivered in the bright morning sunlight.

"Get rid of them!" he ordered the captain, who immediately began to issue orders to his men. Soon, with much swearing and grumbling, the crowd started to break up, most figuring the excitement was over now anyway.

"Caramon, listen to me!" Crysania laid her hand on his arm. "This—"

But Caramon shrugged off Crysania's hand. Ignoring her attempts to speak, he started to push past Michael. The young knight raised his spear, blocking his path.

"Out of my way!" Caramon ordered, startled.

"I am sorry, sir," Michael said in firm tones, though his lips trembled, "but Fistandantilus told me *no one* was to pass."

"You see," said Crysania in exasperation as Caramon fell back a pace, staring at Michael in perplexed anger. "I tried to tell you, if you'd only listened! It's been like this all night, and I *know* something dreadful's happened inside! But Raistlin made him take an oath—by the Code and the Rules or some such thing—"

"Measure," Caramon muttered, shaking his head. "The Code and the Measure." He frowned, thinking of Sturm. "A code no knight will break on pain of death."

"But this is insane!" Crysania cried. Her voice broke. She covered her face with her hand a moment. Caramon put his arm around her hesitantly, fearing a reprimand, but she leaned against him gratefully.

"Oh, Caramon, I've been so frightened!" she murmured. "It was awful. I woke out of a sound sleep, hearing Raistlin screaming my name. I ran over here—There were flashes of light inside his tent. He was shrieking incoherent words, then I heard him call your name . . . and then he began to moan in despair. I tried to get in but . . ." She made a weak gesture toward Michael, who stood staring straight ahead. "And then his voice began to . . . to fade! It was awful, as though he were being sucked away somehow!"

"Then what happened?"

Crysania paused. Then, hesitantly, "He . . . he said something else. I could barely hear it. The lights went out. There was a sharp crack and . . . everything was still, horribly still!" She closed her eyes, shuddering.

"What did he say? Could you understand?"

"That's the strange part." Crysania raised her head, looking at him in confusion. "It sounded like . . . Bupu."

"Bupu!" Caramon repeated in astonishment. "Are you sure?"

She nodded.

"Why would he call out the name of a gully dwarf?" Caramon demanded.

"I haven't any idea." Crysania sighed wearily, brushing her hair back out of her eyes. "I've wondered the same thing. Except—wasn't that the gully dwarf who told Par-Salian how kind Raistlin had been to her?"

Caramon shook his head. He would worry about gully dwarves later. Now, his immediate problem was Michael. Vivid memories of Sturm came back to him. How many times had he seen that look on the knight's face? An oath by the Code and the Measure—

Damn Raistlin!

Michael would stand at his post now until he dropped and then, when he awoke to find he had failed, he'd kill himself. There had to be some way around this—around him! Caramon glanced at Crysania. She could use her clerical powers to spellbind the young man. . . .

Caramon shook his head. That would have the entire camp ready to burn her at the stake! Damn Raistlin! Damn clerics! Damn the Knights of Solamnia and damn their Code and their Measure!

Heaving a sigh, he walked up to Michael. The young man raised his spear threateningly, but Caramon only lifted his hands high, to show they were empty.

He cleared his throat, knowing what he wanted to say, yet uncertain how to begin. And then as he thought about Sturm, suddenly he could see the Knight's face once again, so clearly that he marveled. But it was not as he had seen it in life—stern, noble, cold. And then Caramon knew—he was seeing Sturm's face in death! Marks of terrible suffering and pain had smoothed away the harsh lines of pride and inflexibility. There was compassion and understanding in the dark, haunted eyes and—it seemed to Caramon—that the Knight smiled on him sadly.

For a moment, Caramon was so startled by this vision that he could say nothing, only stare. But the image vanished, leaving in its place only the face of a young Knight, grim, frightened, exhausted—determined. . . .

"Michael," Caramon said, keeping his hands raised, "I had a friend once, a Knight of Solamnia. He—he's dead now. He died in a war far from here when—But that doesn't matter. Stur—my friend was like you. He believed in the Code and . . . and the Measure. He was ready to give his life for them. But, at the end, he found out there was something more important than the Code and the Measure, something that the Code and the Measure had forgotten."

Michael's face hardened stubbornly. He gripped his spear tighter.

"Life itself," Caramon said softly.

He saw a flicker in the Knight's red-rimmed eyes, a flicker that was drowned by a shimmer of tears. Angrily, Michael blinked them away, the look of firm resolution returning, though—it seemed to Caramon—it was now mingled with a look of desperation.

Caramon caught hold of that desperation, driving his words home as if they were the point of a sword seeking his enemy's heart. "*Life*, Michael. That's all there is. That's all we have. Not just our lives, but the lives of everyone on this world. It's what the Code and the Measure were designed to protect, but somewhere along the line that got all twisted around and the Code and the Measure became more important than life."

Slowly, still keeping his hands raised, he took a step toward the young man.

"I'm not asking you to leave your post for any treacherous reason. And you and I both know you're not leaving it from cowardice." Caramon shook his head. "The gods know what you must have seen and heard tonight. I'm asking you to leave it out of compassion. My brother's inside there, maybe dying, maybe dead. When he made you swear that oath, he couldn't have foreseen this happening. I must go to him. Let me pass, Michael. There is nothing dishonorable in that."

Michael stood stiffly, his eyes straight ahead. And then, his face crumpled. His shoulders slumped, and the spear fell from his nerveless hand. Reaching out, Caramon caught the young man in his big arms and held him close. A shuddering sob tore through the young man's body. Caramon patted his shoulder awkwardly.

"Here, one of you"—he looked around—"find Garic— Ah, there you are," he said in relief as the young Knight came running over. "Take your cousin back to the fire. Get some hot food inside him, then see that he sleeps. You there—" he motioned to another guard—"take over here."

As Garic led his cousin away, Crysania started to enter the tent, but Caramon stopped her. "Better let me go first, lady," he said.

Expecting an argument, he was surprised to see her meekly step aside. Caramon had his hand on the tent flap when he felt her hand upon his arm.

Startled, he turned.

"You are as wise as Elistan, Caramon," she said, regarding him intently. "I could have said those words to the young man. Why didn't I?"

Caramon flushed. "I—I just understood him, that's all," he muttered.

"I didn't *want* to understand him." Crysania, her face pale, bit her lip. "I just wanted him to obey me."

"Look, lady," Caramon said grimly, "you can do your soul-searching later. Right now, I need your help!"

"Yes, of course." The firm, self-confident look returned to Crysania's face. Without hesitation, she followed Caramon into Raistlin's tent.

Mindful of the guard outside, and any other curious eyes, Caramon shut the tent flap quickly. It was dark and still inside; so dark that at first neither could make out anything in the shadows. Standing near the entrance, waiting until their eyes grew accustomed to the dimness, Crysania clutched at Caramon suddenly.

"I can hear him breathing!" she said in relief.

Caramon nodded and moved forward slowly. The brightening day was driving night from the tent, and he could see more clearly with each step he took.

"There," he said. He hurriedly kicked aside a camp stool that blocked his way. "Raist!" he called softly as he knelt down.

The archmage was lying on the floor. His face was ashen, his thin lips blue. His breathing was shallow and irregular, but he was breathing. Lifting his twin carefully, Caramon carried him to his bed. In the dim light, he could see a faint smile on Raistlin's lips, as though he were lost in a pleasant dream.

"I think he's just sleeping now," Caramon said in a mystified voice to Crysania, who was covering Raistlin with a blanket. "But something's happened. That's obvious." He looked around the tent in the brightening light. "I wonder—Name of the gods!"

Crysania looked up, glancing over her shoulder.

The poles of the tent were scorched and blackened, the material itself was charred and, in some places, appeared to have melted. It looked as though it had been swept by fire, yet incongruously, it remained standing and did not appear to have been seriously damaged. It was the object on the table, however, that had brought the exclamation from Caramon.

"The dragon orb!" he whispered in awe.

Made by the mages of all three Robes long ago, filled with the essence of good, evil, and neutral dragons, powerful enough to span the banks of time, the crystal orb still stood upon the table, resting on the silver stand Raistlin had made for it.

Once it had been an object of magical, enchanting light.

Now it was a thing of darkness, lifeless, a crack running down its center. Now—"It's broken," Caramon said in a quiet voice.

The Army of Fistandantilus sailed across the Straits of Schallsea in a ramshackle fleet made up of many fishing boats, row boats, crude rafts, and gaudily decorated pleasure boats. Though the distance was not great, it took over a week to get the people, the animals, and the supplies transported.

By the time Caramon was ready to make the crossing, the army had grown to such an extent that there were not enough boats to ferry everyone across at once. Many craft had to make several trips back and forth. The largest boats were used to carry livestock. Converted into floating barns, they had stalls for the horses and the scrawny cattle and pens for the pigs.

Things went smoothly, for the most part, though Caramon got only about three hours of sleep each night, so busy was he with the problems that everyone was sure only he could solve—everything from seasick cattle to a chest-load of swords that was accidentally dropped overboard and had to be retrieved. Then, just when the end was in sight and nearly everyone was across, a storm came up. Whipping the seas to froth, it wrecked two boats that slipped from their moorings and prevented anyone from crossing for two days. But, eventually, everyone made it in relatively good shape, with only a few cases of seasickness, one child tumbling overboard (rescued), and a horse that broke its leg kicking down its stall in a panic (killed and butchered).

Upon landing on the shores of Abanasinia, the army was met by the chief of the Plainsmen—the tribes of barbarians inhabiting the northern plains of Abanasinia who were eager to gain the fabled gold of Thorbardin—and also by representatives from the hill dwarves. When he met with the representative of the hill dwarves, Caramon experienced a profound shock that unnerved him for days.

"Reghar Fireforge and party," announced Garic from the entrance to the tent. Standing aside, the knight allowed a group of three dwarves to enter.

That name ringing in his ears, Caramon stared at the first dwarf in disbelief. Raistlin's thin fingers closed painfully over his arm.

"Not a word!" breathed the archmage.

"But he—he looks . . . and the name!" Caramon stammered in a low voice.

"Of course," Raistlin said matter-of-factly, "this is Flint's grandfather."

Flint's grandfather! Flint Fireforge—his old friend. The old dwarf who had died in Tanis's arms at Godshome, the old dwarf—so gruff and irascible, yet so tender-hearted, the dwarf who had seemed ancient to Caramon. He had not even been born yet! This was his grandfather.

Suddenly the full scope of where he was and what he was doing struck Caramon a physical blow. Before this, he might have been adventuring in his own time. He knew then that he hadn't really been taking any of this seriously. Even Raistlin "sending" him home had seemed as simple as the archmage putting him on a boat and bidding him farewell. Talk of "altering" time he'd put out of his mind. It confused him, seeming to go round in a closed, endless circle.

Carmon feld hot, then cold. Flint hadn't been born yet.

Tanis didn't exist, Tika didn't exist. *He, himself, didn't exist!* No! It was too implausible! It couldn't be!

The tent tilted before Caramon's eyes. He was more than half afraid he might be sick. Fortunately, Raistlin saw the pallor of his brother's face. Knowing intuitively what his twin's brain was trying to assimilate, the mage rose to his feet and, moving gracefully in front of his momentarily befuddled brother, spoke suitable words of welcome to the dwarves. But, as Raistlin did so, he shot a dark, penetrating glance at Caramon, reminding him sternly of his duty.

Pulling himself together, Caramon was able to thrust the disturbing and confusing thoughts from his mind, telling himself he would deal with them later in peace and quiet. He'd been doing that a lot lately. Unfortunately, the peace and quiet time never seemed to come about . . . .

Getting to his feet, Caramon was even able to shake hands calmly with the sturdy, gray-bearded dwarf.

"Little did I ever think," Reghar said bluntly, sitting down in the chair offered him and accepting a mug of ale, which he quaffed at one gulp, "that I'd be making deals with humans and wizards, especially against my own flesh and blood." He scowled into the empty mug. Caramon, with a gesture, had the lad who attended him refill it.

Reghar, still with the same scowl, waited for the foam to settle. Then, sighing, he raised it to Caramon, who had returned to his chair. "*Durth Zamish och Durth Tabor.* Strange times makes strange brothers."

"You can say that again," Caramon muttered with a glance at Raistlin. The general lifted his glass of water and drank it. Raistlin—out of politeness—moistened his lips from a glass of wine, then set it down.

"We will meet in the morning to discuss our plans," Caramon said. "The chief of the Plainsmen will be here then, too." Reghar's scowl deepened, and Caramon sighed inwardly, foreseeing trouble. But he continued in a hearty, cheerful tone. "Let's dine together tonight, to seal our alliance."

At this, Reghar rose to his feet. "I may have to fight with the barbarians," he growled. "But, by Reorx's beard, I don't have to eat with them—or you either!"

Caramon stood up again. Dressed in his best ceremonial armor (more gifts from the knights), he was an imposing sight. The dwarf squinted up at the warrior.

"You're a big one, ain't you?" he said. Snorting, he shook his head dubiously. "I mistrust there's more muscle in your head than brain."

Caramon could not help smiling, though his heart ached. It sounded so much like Flint talking!

But Raistlin did not smile.

"My brother has an excellent mind for military matters," the mage said coldly and unexpectedly. "When we left Palanthas, there were but three of us. It is due to General Caramon's skill and quick thinking that we are able to bring this mighty army to your shores. I think you would find it well to accept his leadership."

Reghar snorted again, peering at Raistlin keenly from beneath his bushy gray, overhanging eyebrows. His heavy armor clanging and rattling about him, the dwarf turned and started to stump out of the tent, then he paused.

"Three of you, from Palanthas? And now—this?" His piercing, dark-eyed gaze went to Caramon, his hand made a sweeping gesture, encompassing the tent, the knights in the shining armor who stood guard outdoors, the hundreds of men he had seen working together to unload supplies from the ships, other men practicing their fighting techniques, the row after row of cooking fires . . . .

Overwhelmed and astounded by his brother's unaccustomed praise, Caramon couldn't answer. But he managed to nod.

The dwarf snorted again, but there was a glint of grudging admiration in his eyes as he clanked and rattled his way out of the tent.

Reghar suddenly poked his head back inside. "I'll be at yer dinner," he snarled ungraciously, then stomped off.

"I, too, must be leaving, my brother," Raistlin said absently as he rose to his feet and walked toward the tent entrance. His hands folded in his black robes, he was lost in thought when he felt a touch on his arm. Irritated at the disturbance, he glanced at his brother.

"Well?"

"I—I just want to say . . . thank you." Caramon swallowed, then continued huskily. "For what you said. You—you never said . . . anything like that about me . . . before."

Raistlin smiled. There was no light in his eyes from that thin-lipped smile, but Caramon was too flushed and pleased to notice.

"It is only the simple truth, my brother," Raistlin replied, shrugging. "And it helped accomplish our objective, since we need these dwarves as our allies. I have often told you that you have hidden resources if you would only take the time and trouble to develop them. We *are* twins after all," the mage added sardonically. "I did not think we could be so unlike as you had convinced yourself."

The mage started to leave again but once more felt his brother's hand on his arm. Checking an impatient sigh, Raistlin turned.

"I wanted to kill you back in Istar, Raistlin—" Caramon paused, licking his lips—"and . . . and I think I had cause. At least, from what I knew then. Now, I'm not so certain." He sighed, looking down at his feet, then raising his flushed face. "I—I'd like to think that you did this—that you put the mages in a position where they had to send me back in time—to help me learn this lesson. That may not be the reason," Caramon hastened to add, seeing his brother's lips compress and the cold eyes grow colder, "and I'm sure it isn't—at least all of it. You are doing this for yourself, I know that. But—I think, somewhere, some part of you cares, just a little. Some part of you saw I was in trouble and you wanted to help."

Raistlin regarded his brother with amusement. Then he shrugged again. "Very well, Caramon. If this romantic notion of yours will help you fight better, if it will help you plan your strategies better, if it will aid your thinking, and—above all—if it will let me get out of this tent and back to my work, then—by all means—cradle it to your breast! It matters little to me."

Withdrawing his arm from his brother's grasp, the mage

stalked to the entrance to the tent. Here he hesitated. Half-turning his hooded head, he spoke in a low voice, his words exasperated, yet tinged with a certain sadness.

"You never did understand me, Caramon."

Then he left, his black robes rustling around his ankles as he walked.

The banquet that evening was held outdoors. Its beginnings were less than propitious.

The food was set on long tables of wood, hastily constructed from the rafts that had been used to cross the straits. Reghar arrived with a large escort, about forty dwarves. Darknight, Chief of the Plainsmen, who—with his grim face and tall, proud stance, reminded Caramon forcibly of Riverwind—brought with him forty warriors. In turn, Caramon chose forty of his men whom he knew (or at least hoped) could be trusted and could hold their liquor.

Caramon had figured that, when the groups filed in, the dwarves would sit by themselves, the Plainsmen by themselves, and so forth. No amount of talking would get them to mingle. Sure enough, after each group had arrived, all stood staring at each other in grim silence; the dwarves gathered around their leader, the Plainsmen around theirs, while Caramon's men looked on uncertainly.

Caramon came to stand before them. He had dressed with care, wearing his golden armor and helmet from the gladiatorial games, plus some new armor he'd had made to match. With his bronze skin, his matchless physique, his strong, handsome face, he was a commanding presence and even the dour dwarves exchanged looks of reluctant approval.

Caramon raised his hands.

"Greetings to my guests!" he called in his loud, booming baritone. "Welcome. This is a dinner of fellowship, to mark alliance and newfound friendship among our races—"

At this there were muttered, scoffing words and snorts of derision. One of the dwarves even spat upon the ground, causing several Plainsmen to grip their bows and take a step forward—this being considered a dreadful insult among

Plainspeople. Their chief stopped them, and, coolly ignoring the interruption, Caramon continued.

"We are going to be fighting together, perhaps dying together. Therefore, let us start our meeting this first night by sitting together and sharing bread and drink like brothers. I know that you are reluctant to be parted from your kinsmen and friends, but I want you to make new friends. And so, to help us get acquainted, I have decided we should play a little game."

At this, the dwarves' eyes opened wide, beards wagged, and low mutterings rumbled through the air like thunder. No grown dwarf ever played games! (Certain recreational activities such as "Stone Strike" and "Hammer Throw" were considered sports.) Darknight and his men brightened, however; the Plainsmen lived for games and contests, these being considered almost as much fun as making war on neighboring tribes.

Waving his arm, Caramon gestured to a new, huge, cone-shaped tent that stood behind the tables and had been the object of many curious, suspicious stares from dwarves and Plainsmen alike. Standing over twenty feet tall, it was topped by Caramon's banner. The silken flag with the nine-pointed star fluttered in the evening wind, illuminated by the great bonfire burning nearby.

As all stared at the tent, Caramon reached out and, with a yank of his strong hand, pulled on a rope. Instantly, the canvas sides of the tent fell to the ground and, at a signal from Caramon, were dragged away by several grinning young boys.

"What nonsense is this?" Reghar growled, fingering his axe.

A single heavy post stood in a sea of black, oozing mud. The post's shaft had been planed smooth and gleamed in the firelight. Near the top of the post was a round platform made of solid wood, except for several irregularly shaped holes that had been cut into it.

But it was not the sight of the pole or the platform or the mud that brought forth sudden exclamations of wonder and excitement from dwarves and humans alike. It was the sight of what was embedded in the wood at the very top of the post. Shining in the firelight, their crossed handles flashing, were a sword and a battle-axe. But these were not the crude iron weapons many carried. These were of the finest wrought steel, their exquisite workmanship apparent to those who stood twenty feet below, staring up at them.

"Reorx's beard!" Reghar drew a deep, quivering breath. "Yon axe is worth the price of our village! I'd trade fifty years of my life for a weapon such as that!"

Darknight, staring at the sword, blinked his eyes rapidly as swift tears of longing caused the weapon to blur in his vision.

Caramon smiled. "These weapons are yours!" he announced.

Darknight and Reghar both stared at him, their faces registering blank astonishment.

"If—" Caramon continued, "you can get them down!"

A vast hubbub of voices broke out among both dwarves and men. Immediately, everyone broke into a run for the pit, forcing Caramon to shout over the turmoil.

"Reghar and Darknight—each of you may choose nine warriors to help you! The first to gain the prizes wins them for his own!"

Darknight needed no urging. Without bothering to get help, he leaped into the mud and began to wade toward the post. But with each step, he sank farther and farther, the mud growing deeper and deeper as he neared his objective. By the time he reached the post, he had sunk past his knees in the sticky substance.

Reghar—more cautious—took time to observe his opponent. Calling on nine of his stoutest men to help, the dwarven leader and his men stepped into the mud. The entire contingent promptly vanished, their heavy armor causing them to sink almost immediately. Their fellows helped drag them out. Last to emerge was Reghar.

Swearing an oath to every god he could think of, the dwarf wrung mud out of his beard, then, scowling, proceeded to strip off his armor. Holding his axe high over his head, he waded back into the mud, not even waiting for his escort.

Darknight had reached the pole. Right at the base, the mud wasn't so deep—there was firm ground below it. Grasping the pole with his arms, the chieftain dragged himself up out of the mud and wrapped his legs around it. He moved up about three feet, grinning broadly at his tribesmen who cheered him on. Then, suddenly, he began to slide back down. Gritting his teeth, he strove desperately to hang on, but it was useless. At last, the great chieftain slid slowly down to the base, amid howls of dwarven derision. Sitting in the mud, he glared grimly at the pole. It had been greased with animal fat.

More swimming that walking, Reghar at last reached the base of the pole. He was waist-deep in mud by that time, but the dwarf's great strength kept him going.

"Stand aside," he growled to the frustrated Plainsman. "Use your brains! If we can't go up, we'll bring the prize down to us!"

A grin of triumph on his mud-splattered, bearded face, Reghar drew back his axe and aimed a mighty blow at the pole.

Grinning to himself, Caramon winced in anticipation.

There was a tremendous ringing sound. The dwarf's axe rebounded off the pole as if it had struck the side of a mountain—the pole had been hewn from the thick trunk of an ironwood tree. As the reverberating axe flew from the dwarf's stinging hands, the force of the blow sent Reghar sprawling on his back in the mud. Now it was the Plainsmen's turn to laugh—none louder than their mud-covered chief.

Glaring at each other, dwarf and human tensed. The laughter died, replaced by angry mutterings. Caramon held his breath. Then Reghar's eyes went to the notched axe that was slowly sinking into the ooze. He glanced up at the beautiful axe, its steel flashing in the firelight, and—with a growl, turned to face his men.

Reghar's escort, now stripped of their armor, had waded out to him by now. Shouting and gesturing, Reghar motioned them to line up at the base of the slick pole. Then the dwarves began to form a pyramid. Three stood at the bottom, two climbed upon their backs, then another. The bottom row sank into mud past their waists but, eventually finding the firm ground at the bottom, stood fast.

Darknight watched for a moment in grim silence, then he called to nine of his warriors. Within moments, the humans were forming their own pyramid. Being shorter, the dwarves were forced to make their pyramid smaller at the base and extend it up by single dwarves to reach the top. Reghar himself made the final ascent. Teetering on the pinnacle as the dwarves swayed and groaned beneath him, his arms strained to reach the platform—but he wasn't tall enough.

Darknight, climbing over the backs of his own men, easily reached the underside of the platform. Then, laughing at the scowl on Reghar's mud-covered face, the chieftain tried to pull himself through one of the odd-shaped openings.

He couldn't fit.

Squeezing, swearing, holding his breath was no help. The human could not force even his wiry-framed body through the small hole. At that moment, Reghar made a leap for the platform. . . .

And missed.

The dwarf sailed through the air, landing with a splat in the mud below, while the force of his jump caused the entire dwarven pyramid to topple, sending dwarves everywhere.

This time, though, the humans didn't laugh. Staring down at Reghar, Darknight suddenly jumped down into the mud himself. Landing next to the dwarf, he grabbed hold of him and dragged him to the surface of the ooze.

Both were, by this time, almost indistinguishable, covered head to foot with the black goop. They stood, staring at each other.

"You know," said Reghar, wiping mud from his eyes, "that I'm the only one who can fit through that hole."

"And you know," said Darknight through clenched teeth, "that I'm the only who can get you up there."

The dwarf grabbed the Plainsman's hand. The two moved quickly over to the human pyramid. Darknight climbed first, providing the last link to the top. Everyone cheered as Reghar climbed up onto the human's shoulders and easily squirmed through the hole.

Scrambling up onto the platform, the dwarf grasped the hilt of the sword and the handle of the axe and raised them triumphantly over his head. The crowd fell silent. Once again, human and dwarf eyed each other suspiciously.

This is it! Caramon thought. How much of Flint did I see in you, Reghar? How much of Riverwind in you, Darknight? So much depends on this!

Reghar looked down through the hole at the stern face of the Plainsman. "This axe, which must have been forged by Reorx himself, I owe to you, Plainsman. I will be honored to fight by your side. And, if you're going to fight with me, you need a decent weapon!"

Amid cheers from the entire camp, he handed the great, gleaming sword down through the hole to Darknight.

CHAPTER 5

The banquet lasted well into the night. The field rang with laughter and shouts and good-natured oaths sworn in dwarven and tribal tongues as well as Solamnic and Common.

It was easy for Raistlin to slip away. In the excitement, no one missed the silent, cynical archmage.

Walking back to his tent, which Caramon had refurbished for him, Raistlin kept to the shadows. In his black robes, he was nothing more than a glimpse of movement seen from the corner of the eye.

He avoided Crysania's tent. She was standing in the entryway, watching the fun with a wistful expression on her face. She dared not join them, knowing that the presence of the "witch" would harm Caramon immensely.

How ironic, thought Raistlin, that a black-robed wizard is tolerated in this time, while a cleric of Paladine is scorned and reviled.

Treading softly in his leather boots across the field where the army camped, barely even leaving footprints in the damp grass, Raistlin found a grim sort of amusement in this. Glancing up at the constellations in the sky, he regarded both the Platinum Dragon and the Five-Headed Dragon opposite with a slight sneer.

The knowledge that Fistandantilus might have succeeded if it had not been for the unforeseen intervention of some wretched gnome had brought dark joy to Raistlin's being. By all his calculations, the gnome was the key factor. The gnome had altered time, apparently, though just how he had done that was unclear. Still, Raistlin figured that all he had to do was to get to the mountain fortress of Zhaman, then, from there, it would be simple indeed to make his way into Thorbardin, discover this gnome, and render him harmless.

Time—which had been altered previously—would return to its proper flow. Where Fistandantilus had failed, *he* would succeed.

Therefore, even as Fistandantilus had done before him, Raistlin now gave the war effort his undivided interest and attention to make certain that he would be able to reach Zhaman. He and Caramon spent long hours poring over old maps, studying the fortifications, comparing what they remembered from their journeys in these lands in a time yet to come and trying to guess what changes might have occurred.

The key to winning the battle was the taking of Pax Tharkas.

And that, Caramon had said more than once with a heavy sigh, seemed well-nigh impossible.

"Duncan's bound to have it heavily manned," Caramon argued, his finger resting on the spot on the map that marked the great fort. "You remember what it's like, Raist. You remember how it's built, between those two sky-high mountain peaks! Those blasted dwarves can hold out there for years! Close the gates, drop the rocks from that mechanism, and we're stuck. It took silver dragons to lift those rocks, as I recall," the big man added gloomily.

"Go around it," Raistlin suggested.

Caramon shook his head. "Where?" His finger moved west. "Qualinesti on one side. The elves'd cut us to meat and hang us up to dry." He moved east. "This way's either sea or mountain. We don't have boats enough to go by sea and, look"—he moved his finger down—"if we land here, to the south, in that desert, we're stuck right in the middle—both flanks exposed—Pax Tharkas to the north, Thorbardin to the south."

The big man paced the room, pausing occasionally to glare at the map in irritation.

Raistlin yawned, then stood up, resting his hand lightly on Caramon's arm. "Remember this, my brother," he said softly, "Pax Tharkas *did* fall!"

Caramon's face darkened. "Yeah," he muttered, angry at being reminded of the fact that this was all just some vast game he seemed to be playing. "I don't suppose you remember how?"

"No." Raistlin shook his head. "But it will fall. . . ."

He paused, then repeated quietly, "It *will* fall!"

Out of the forest, wary of the lights of lodge and campfire and even moon and stars, crept three dark, squat figures. They hesitated on the outskirts of the camp, as though uncertain of their destination. Finally, one pointed, muttering something. The other two nodded and, now moving rapidly, they hurried through the darkness.

Quickly they moved, but not quietly. No dwarf could ever move quietly, and these seemed noisier than usual. They creaked and rattled and stepped on every brittle twig, muttering curses as they blundered along.

Raistlin, awaiting them in the darkness of his tent, heard them coming from far off and shook his head. But he had reckoned on this in his plans, thus he had arranged this meeting when the noise and hilarity of the banquet would provide suitable cover.

"Enter," he said wryly as the clumping and stomping of ironshod feet halted just outside the tent flap.

There was a pause, accompanied by heavy breathing and a muttered exclamation, no one wanting to be the first to touch the tent. This was answered by a snarling oath. The tent flap was yanked open with a violence that nearly tore the strong fabric and a dwarf entered, apparently the leader, for he advanced with a bold swagger while the other two, who came after him, were nervous and cringing.

The lead dwarf advanced toward the table in the center of the tent, moving swiftly though it was pitch dark. After years of living underground, the Dewar had developed excellent night vision. Some, it was rumored, even had the gift of elvensight that allowed them to see the glow of living beings in the darkness.

But, good though the dwarf's eyes were, he could make out nothing at all about the black-robed figure that sat facing him across the desk. It was as though, looking into deepest night, he saw something darker—like a vast chasm suddenly yawning at his feet. This Dewar was strong and fearless, reckless even; his father had died a raving lunatic. But the dark dwarf found he could not repress a slight shiver that started at the back of his neck and tingled down the length of his spine.

He sat down. "You two," he said in dwarven to those with him, "watch the entrance."

They nodded and retreated quickly, only too glad to leave the vicinity of the black-robed figure and crouch beside the opening, peering out into the shadows. A sudden flare of light made them start up in alarm, however. Their leader raised his arm with a vicious oath, shielding his eyes.

"No light . . . no light!" he cried in crude Common. Then his tongue clove to the roof of his mouth and for a moment all he could make were garbled noises. For the light came, not from torch or candle, but from a flame that burned in the palm of the mage's cupped hand.

All dwarves are, by nature, suspicious and distrustful of magic. Uneducated, given to superstition, the Dewar were terrified of it and thus even this simple trick that nearly any street illusionist could perform caused the dwarf to suck in his breath in fear.

"I see those I deal with," Raistlin said in a soft, whispering voice. "Do not fear, this light will not be detected from outside or, if it is, anyone passing will assume I am studying."

Slowly, the Dewar lowered his arm, blinking his eyes painfully in the brightness of the light. His two associates seated themselves again, even nearer the entrance this time. This Dewar leader was the same one who had attended Duncan's council meeting. Though his face was stamped with the half-mad, half-calculating cruelty that marked most of his race, there was a glimmer of rational intelligence in his dark eyes that made him particularly dangerous.

These eyes were now assessing the mage across from him, even as the mage assessed him. The Dewar was impressed. He had about as much use for humans as most dwarves. A human magic-user was doubly suspect. But the Dewar was a shrewd judge of character, and he saw in the mage's thin lips, gaunt face, and cold eyes a ruthless desire for power that he could both trust and understand.

"You . . . Fistandantilus?" the Dewar growled roughly.

"I am." The mage closed his hand and the flame vanished, leaving them once more in the darkness—for which the dwarf, at least, was relieved. "And I speak dwarven, so we may converse in your language. I would prefer that, in fact, so that there can be no chance of misunderstanding."

"Well and good." The Dewar leaned forward. "I am Argat, thane of my clan. I receive your message. We are interested. But we must know more."

"Meaning 'what's in it for us?'" Raistlin said in a mocking voice. Extending his slender hand, he pointed to a corner of his tent.

Looking in the direction indicated, Argat saw nothing. Then an object in one corner of the tent began to glow, softly at first, then with increasing brilliance. Argat once again sucked in his breath, but this time in wonder and disbelief rather than fear.

Suddenly, he cast Raistlin a sharp, suspicious glance.

"By all means, go examine it for yourself," Raistlin said with a shrug. "You may take it with you tonight, in fact . . . if we come to terms."

But Argat was already out of his chair, stumbling over to the corner of the tent. Falling to his knees, he plunged his hands into the coffer of steel coins that shone with a bright, magical gleam. For long moments, he could do nothing but stare at the wealth with glittering eyes, letting the coins run through his fingers. Then, with a shuddering sigh, he stood up and came back to his seat.

"You have plan?"

Raistlin nodded. The magical glow of the coins faded, but there was still a faint glimmer that continually drew the dwarf's gaze.

"Spies tell us," said Raistlin, "that Duncan plans to meet our army on the plains in front of Pax Tharkas, intending to defeat us there or, if unable to do so, at least inflict heavy casualties. If we are winning, he will withdraw his forces back into the fortress, close the gates and operate the mechanism that drops thousands of tons of rocks down to block those gates.

"With the stores of food and weapons he has cached there, he can wait until we either give up and retreat or until his own reinforcements arrive from Thorbardin to pen us up in the valley. Am I correct?"

Argat ran his fingers through his black beard. Drawing out his knife, he flipped it into the air and caught it deftly. Glancing at the mage, he stopped suddenly, spreading his hands wide.

"I sorry. A nervous habit," he said, grinning wickedly. "I hope I not alarm you. If it make you uneasy, I can—"

"If it makes me uneasy, I can deal with it," Raistlin observed mildly. "Go ahead." He gestured. "Try it."

Shrugging, but feeling uncomfortable under the gaze of those strange eyes that he could sense but could not see within the shadows of the black hood, Argat tossed the knife into the air—

A slender, white hand snaked out of the darkness, snatched the knife by the hilt, and deftly plunged the sharp blade into the table between them.

Argat's eyes glinted. "Magic," he growled.

"Skill," said Raistlin coldly. "Now, are we going to continue this discussion or play games that I excelled at in my childhood?"

"Your information accurate," muttered Argat, sheathing his knife. "That Duncan's plan."

"Good. *My* plan is quite simple. Duncan will be inside the fortress itself. He will not take the field. He will give the command to shut the gates."

Raistlin sank back into his chair, the tips of his long fingers came together. "When that command comes, the gates will not shut."

"That easy?" Argat sneered.

"That easy." Raistlin spread his hands. "Those who would shut them die. All you must do is hold the gates open for minutes only, until we have time to storm them. Pax Tharkas will fall. Your people lay down their arms and offer to join up with us.

"Easy, but for one flaw," Argat said, eyeing Raistlin shrewdly. "Our homes, families, in Thorbardin. What become of them if we turn traitor?"

"Nothing," Raistlin said. Reaching into a pouch at his side, the mage pulled forth a rolled scroll tied with black ribbon. "You will have this delivered to Duncan." Handing it to Argat, he motioned. "Read it."

Frowning, still regarding Raistlin with suspicion, the dwarf took the roll, untied it, and—carrying it over near the chest of coins—read it by their faint, magical glow.

He looked up at Raistlin, astonished. "This . . . this in language of my people!"

Raistlin nodded, somewhat impatiently. "Of course, what did you expect? Duncan would not believe it otherwise."

"But"—Argat gaped—"that language is secret, known only to the Dewar and a few others, such as Duncan, king—"

"Read!" Raistlin gestured irritably. "I haven't got all night."

Muttering an oath to Reorx, the dwarf read the scroll. It took him long moments, though the words were few. Stroking his thick, tangled beard, he pondered. Then, rising, he rolled the scroll back up and held it in his hand, tapping it slowly in his palm.

"You're right. This solve everything." He sat back down, his dark eyes, fixed on the mage, narrowing. "But I want something else give to Duncan. Not just scroll. Something . . . impressive."

"What does your kind consider 'impressive'?" Raistlin asked his lip curling. "A few dozen hacked-up bodies—"

Argat grinned. "The head of your general."

There was a long silence. Not a rustle, not a whisper of cloth betrayed Raistlin's thoughts. He even seemed to stop breathing. The silence lasted until it seemed to Argat to become a living entity itself, so powerful was it.

The dwarf shivered, then scowled. No, he would stick to this demand. Duncan would be forced to proclaim him a hero, like that bastard Kharas.

"Agreed." Raistlin's voice was level, without tone or emotion. But, as he spoke, he leaned over the table. Sensing the archmage gliding closer, Argat pulled back. He could see the glittering eyes now, and their deep, black chilling depths pierced him to the very core of his being.

"Agreed," the mage repeated. "See that you keep your part of the bargain."

Gulping, Argat gave a sickly smile. "You not called the Dark One without reason, are you, my friend?" he said, attempting a laugh as he rose to his feet, thrusting the scroll in his belt.

Raistlin did not answer, indicating he had heard only by a rustle of his hood. Shrugging, Argat turned and motioned to his companions, making a commanding gesture at the chest in the corner. Hurrying over, the two shut it and locked it with a key Raistlin drew out of the folds of his robes and silently handed to them. Though dwarves are accustomed to carrying heavy burdens with ease, the two grunted slightly as they lifted the chest. Argat's eyes shone with pleasure.

The two dwarves preceded their leader from the tent. Bearing their burden between them, they hurried off to the safe shadows of the forest. Argat watched them, then turned back to face the mage, who was, once more, a pool of blackness within blackness.

"Do not worry, friend. We not fail you."

"No, friend," said Raistlin softly. "You won't."

Argat started, not liking the mage's tone.

"You see, Argat, that money has been cursed. If you double-cross me, you and anyone else who has touched that money will see the skin of your hands turn black and begin to rot away. And when your hands are a bleeding mass of stinking flesh, the skin of your arms and your legs will blacken. And, slowly, as you watch helplessly, the curse will spread over your entire body. When you can no longer stand on your decaying feet, you will drop over dead."

Argat made a strangled, inarticulate sound. "You—you're lying!" he managed to snarl.

Raistlin said nothing. He might very well have disappeared from the tent for all Argat knew. The dwarf couldn't see the mage or even sense his presence. What he did hear were shouts of laughter from the lodge as the door burst open. Light streamed out, dwarves and men staggered out into the night air.

Cursing under his breath, Argat hurried off.

But, as he ran, he wiped his hands frantically upon his trousers.

CHAPTER 6

awn. Krynn's sun crept up from behind the mountains slowly, almost as if it knew what ghastly sights it would shed its light upon this day. But time could not be stopped. Finally appearing over the mountains peaks, the sun was greeted with cheers and the clashing of sword against shield by those who were, perhaps, looking upon dawn for the last time in their lives.

Among those who cheered was Duncan, King of the Mountain Dwarves. Standing atop the battlements of the great fortress of Pax Tharkas, surrounded by his generals, Duncan heard the deep, hoarse voices of his men swelling up around him and he smiled with satisfaction. This would be a glorious day.

Only one dwarf was not cheering. Duncan didn't even have to look at him to be aware of the silence that thundered in his heart as loudly as the cheers thundered in his ears.

Standing apart from the others was Kharas, hero of the dwarves. Tall, splendid in his shining armor, his great hammer clasped in his large hands, he stood staring at the sunrise and, if anyone had looked, they would have seen tears trickling down his face.

But no one looked. Everyone's gaze carefully avoided Kharas. Not because he wept, though tears are considered a childish weakness by dwarves. No, it was not because Kharas wept that everyone keep their eyes averted from him. It was because, when his tears fell, they trickled unimpeded, down a bare face.

Kharas had shaved his beard.

Even as Duncan's eyes swept the plains before Pax Tharkas, even as his mind took in the disposition of the enemy, spreading out upon the barren plains, their spear tips glittering in the light of the sun, the Thane could still feel the boundless shock that had overwhelmed his soul that morning when he had seen Kharas take his place upon the battlements, bare-faced. In his hands, the dwarf held the long, curling tresses of his luxurious beard and, as they watched in horror, Kharas hurled them out over the battlements.

A beard is a dwarf's birthright, his pride, his family's pride. In deep grief, a dwarf will go through the mourning time without combing his beard, but there is only one thing that will cause a dwarf to shave his beard. And that is shame. It is the mark of disgrace—the punishment for murder, the punishment for stealing, the punishment for cowardice, the punishment for desertion.

"Why?" was all that the stunned Duncan could think of to ask.

Staring out over the mountains, Kharas answered in a voice that split and cracked like rock. "I fight this battle because you order me to fight, Thane. I pledged you my loyalty and I am honor-bound to obey that pledge. But, as I fight, I want all to know that I find no honor in killing my kinsmen, nor even humans who have, more than once, fought at my side. Let all know, Kharas goes forward this day in shame."

"A fine figure you will look to those you lead!" Duncan responded bitterly.

But Kharas shut his mouth and would say no more.

"Thane!" Several men called at once, diverting Duncan's

attention back to the plains. But he, too, had seen the four figures, tiny as toys from this distance, detach themselves from the army and ride toward Pax Tharkas. Three of the figures carried fluttering flags. The fourth carried only a staff from which beamed a clear, bright light that could be seen in the growing daylight, even at this distance.

Two of the standards Duncan recognized, of course. The banner of the hill dwarves, with its all-too-familiar symbol of anvil and hammer, was repeated in different colors on Duncan's own banner. The banner of the Plainsmen he had never seen before, but he knew it at once. It suited them—the symbol of the wind sweeping over prairie grass. The third banner, he presumed, must belong to this upstart general who had ridden out of nowhere.

"Humpf!" Duncan snorted, eyeing the banner with its symbol of the nine-pointed star with scorn. "From all we've heard, he should be carrying a banner with the sign of the Thieves' Guild upon it, coupled with a mooing cow!"

The generals laughed.

"Or dead roses," suggested one. "I hear many renegade Knights of Solamnia ride among his thieves and farmers."

The four figures galloped across the plain, their standards fluttering behind, their horses' hooves puffing up clouds of dust.

"The fourth one, in black robes, would be the wizard, Fistandantilus?" Duncan asked gruffly, his heavy brows nearly obliterating his eyes in a frown. Dwarves have no talent for magic and therefore despise and distrust it above all things.

"Yes, Thane," responded a general.

"Of all of them, I fear him the most," Duncan muttered in dark tones.

"Bah!" An old general stroked his long beard complacently. "You need not fear this wizard. Our spies tell us his health is poor. He uses his magic rarely, if at all, spending most of his time skulking in his tent. Besides, it would take an army of wizards as powerful as he to take this fortress by magic."

"I suppose you're right," Duncan said, reaching up to stroke his own beard. Catching a glimpse of Kharas out of the corner of his eye, he halted his hand, suddenly uncomfortable, and abruptly clasped his hands behind his back. "Still, keep your eyes on him" He raised his voice. "You sharpshooters—a bag of gold to the one whose arrow lodges in the wizard's ribs!"

There was a resounding cheer that hushed immediately as the four came to a halt before the fortress. The leader, the general, raised his hand palm outward in the ancient gesture of parley. Striding across the battlements and clambering up onto a block of stone that had been placed there for this very purpose, Duncan placed his hands on his hips, spread his legs, and stared down grimly.

"We would talk!" General Caramon shouted from below. His voice boomed and echoed among the walls of the steep mountains that flanked the fortress.

"All has been said!" Duncan returned, the dwarf's voice sounding nearly as powerful, though he was about one-fourth the size of the big human.

"We give you one last chance! Restore to your kinsmen what you know to be rightfully theirs! Return to these humans what you have taken from them. Share your vast wealth. After all, the dead cannot spend it!"

"No, but you living would find a way, wouldn't you?" Duncan boomed back, sneering. "What we have, we earned by honest toil, working in our homes beneath the mountains, not roaming the land in the company of savage barbarians. Here is our answer!"

Duncan raised his hand. Sharpshooters, ready and waiting, drew back the strings of their bows. Duncan's hand fell, and a hundred arrows whizzed through the air. The dwarves on the battlements began to laugh, hoping to see the four turn their horses and ride madly for their lives.

But the laughter died on their lips. The figures did not move as the arrows arced toward them. The black-robed wizard raised his hand. Simultaneously, the tip of each arrow burst into flame, the shaft became smoke and, within moments, all dwindled away to nothing in the bright morning air.

"And there is our answer!" The general's stern, cold voice drifted upwards. Turning his horse, he galloped back to his armies, flanked by the black-robed wizard, the hill dwarf, and the Plainsman.

Hearing his men muttering among themselves and seeing them cast dour, dubious looks at each other, Duncan firmly squelched his own momentary doubt and turned to face them, his beard quivering with rage.

"What is this?" he demanded angrily. "Are you frightened by the tricks of some street illusionist? What am I leading, an army of men—or of children?"

Seeing heads lower and faces flush in embarrassment, Duncan climbed down from his vantage point. Striding across to the other side of the battlements, he looked down into the vast courtyard of the mighty fortress that was formed, not by man-made walls, but by the natural walls of the mountains themselves. Caves lined the sides. Ordinarily, smoke and the sounds of metal being mined and forged into steel would have poured forth from their gaping mouths. But the mines were shut down today, as were the forges.

This morning, the courtyard teemed with dwarves. Dressed in their heavy armor, they bore shields and axes and hammers, favored weapons of the infantry. All heads raised when Duncan appeared and the cheering that had momentarily died began again.

"It is war!" Duncan shouted above the noise, raising his hands.

The cheering increased, then stopped. After a moment's silence, the deep dwarven voices raised in song.

> *Under the hills the heart of the axe*
> *Arises from cinders the still core of the fire,*
> *Heated and hammered the handle an afterthought,*
> *For the hills are forging the first breath of war.*
> *The soldier's heart sires and brothers*
> *The battlefield.*
> *Come back in glory*
> *Or on your shield.*

Out of the mountains in the midst of the air,
The axes are dreaming dreaming of rock,
Of metal alive through the ages of ore,
Stone on metal metal on stone.
The soldier's heart contains and dreams
The battlefield.
Come back in glory
Or on your shield.

Red of iron imagined from the vein,
Green of brass green of copper
Sparked in the fire the forge of the world,
Consuming in its dream as it dives into bone.
The soldier's heart lies down, completes
The battlefield.
Come back in glory
Or on your shield.

His blood stirred by the song, Duncan felt his doubts vanish as the arrows had vanished in the still air. His generals were already descending from the battlements, hurrying to take up their positions. Only one remained, Argat, general of the Dewar. Kharas remained, too. Duncan looked over at Kharas now, and opened his mouth to speak.

But the hero of the dwarves simply regarded his king with a dark, haunted gaze, then, bowing toward his thane, turned and followed after the others to take his place as one of the leaders of the infantry.

Duncan glared at him angrily. "May Reorx send his beard up in flames!" he muttered as he started to follow. He would be present when the great gates swung open and his army marched out into the plains. "Who does he think he is? My own sons would not act so to me! This must not go on. After the battle, he will be put in his place."

Grumbling to himself, Duncan was nearly to the stairs leading downward when he felt a hand upon his arm. Looking up, he saw Argat.

"I ask you, King," said the dwarf in his crude language, "to think again. Our plan is good one. Abandon worthless hunk of rock. Let them have it." He gestured toward the armies out in the plains. "They not fortify it. When we retreat back to Thorbardin, they chase after us into the plains. Then we retake Pax Tharkas and—*bam*"—the dark dwarf clapped his hands shut—"we have them! Caught between Pax Tharkas on north and Thorbardin on south."

Duncan stared coldly at the Dewar. Argat had presented this strategy at the War Council, and Duncan had wondered at the time how he had come up with it. The Dewar generally took little interest in military matters, caring about only one thing—their share of the spoils. Was it Kharas, trying once again to get out of fighting?

Duncan angrily shook off the Dewar's arm. "Pax Tharkas will never fall!" he said. "Your strategy is the strategy of the coward. I will give up nothing to these rabble, not one copper piece, not one pebble of ground! I'd sooner die here!"

Stomping away, Duncan clattered down the stairs, his beard bristling in his wrath.

Watching him go, Argat's lip twisted in a sneer. "Perhaps you would die upon this wretched rock, Duncan King. But not Argat." Turning to two Dewar who had been standing in the shadows of a recessed corner, the dark dwarf nodded his head twice. The dwarves nodded in return, then quickly hurried away.

Standing upon the battlements, Argat watched as the sun climbed higher in the sky. Preoccupied, he began to absent-mindedly rub his hands upon his leather armor as though trying to clean them.

The Highgug was not certain, but he had the feeling something was wrong.

Though not terribly perceptive, and understanding little of the complex tactics and strategies of warfare, it occurred to the Highgug nevertheless that dwarves returning victorious from the field of battle did not come staggering into the fortress covered with blood and fall down dead at his feet.

One or two, he might have considered the fortunes of war,

but the number of dwarves doing this sort of thing seemed to be increasing at a truly alarming rate. The Highgug decided to see if he could find out what was going on.

He took two steps forward, then, hearing the most dreadful commotion behind him, came to a sudden halt. Heaving a heavy sigh, the Highgug turned around. He had forgotten his company.

"No, no, no!" the Highgug shouted angrily, waving his arms in the air. "How many time I tell you?—Stay Here! Stay Here! King tell Highgug—'You gugs Stay Here.' That mean Stay Here! You got that?"

The Highgug fixed his company with a stern eye, causing those still on their feet and able to meet the gaze of that eye (the other was missing) to tremble in shame. Those gully dwarves in the company who had stumbled over their pikes, those who had dropped their pikes, those who had, in the confusion, accidentally stabbed a neighbor with a pike, those who were lying prone on the ground, and those who had gotten turned around completely and were now stalwartly facing the rear, heard their commander's voice and quailed.

"Look, gulphfunger slimers," snarled the Highgug, breathing noisily, "I go find out what go on. It not seem right, everyone coming back into fort like this. No singing—only bleeding. This not the way king tell Highgug things work out. So I Go. You Stay Here. Got that? Repeat."

"I Go," echoed his troops obediently. "You Stay Here."

The Highgug tore at his beard. "No! *I* Go! *You*—Oh, never mind!" Stalking off in a rage, he heard behind him—once again—the clattering of falling pikes hitting the ground.

Perhaps fortunately, the Highgug did not have far to go. Otherwise, when he returned, he would have found about half of his command dead, skewered on the ends of their own pikes. As it was, he was able to discover what he needed to know and return to his troops before they had inadvertently killed more than half a dozen or so.

The Highgug had taken only about twenty steps when he rounded a corner and very nearly ran into Duncan, his king. Duncan did not notice him, his back being turned. The king was engrossed in a conversation with Kharas and several commanding officers. Taking a hasty step backwards, the Highgug looked and listened anxiously.

Unlike many of the dwarves who had returned from the field of battle, whose heavy plate mail was so dented it looked like they had tumbled down a rocky mountainside, Kharas's armor was dented only here and there. The hero's hands and arms were bloodied to the elbows, but it was the enemy's blood, not his own that he wore. Few there were who could withstand the mighty swings of the hammer he carried. Countless were the dead that fell by Kharas's hand, though many wondered, in their last moments, why the tall dwarf sobbed bitterly as he dealt the killing blow.

Kharas was not crying now, however. His tears were gone, completely dry. He was arguing with his king.

"We are beaten on the field, Thane," he said sternly. "General Ironhand was right to order the retreat. If you would hold Pax Tharkas, we must fall back and shut the gates as we had planned. Remember, this was not a moment that was unforeseen, Thane."

"But a moment of shame, nonetheless," Duncan growled with a bitter oath. "Beaten by a pack of thieves and farmers!"

"That pack of thieves and farmers has been well-trained, Thane," Kharas said solemnly, the generals nodding grudging agreement to his words. "The Plainsmen glory in battle and our own kinsmen fight with the courage with which they are born. And then comes sweeping down from the hills the Knights of Solamnia on their horses."

"You must give the command, Thane!" one of the generals said. "Or prepare to die where we stand."

"Close the god-cursed gates, then!" Duncan shouted in a rage. "But do not drop the mechanism. Not until the last possible moment. There may be no need. It will cost them dearly to try to breach the gates, and I want to be able to get out again without having to clear away tons of rock."

"Close the gates, close the gates!" rang out many voices.

Everyone in the courtyard, the living, the wounded, even the dying, turned their heads to see the massive gates swing shut. The Highgug was among these, staring in awe. He had heard of these great gates—how they moved silently on gigantic, oiled hinges that worked so smoothly only two dwarves on each side were needed to pull them shut. The Highgug was somewhat disappointed to hear that the mechanism was not going to be operated. The sight of tons of rock tumbling down to block the gates was one he was sorry to miss.

Still, this should be quite entertaining. . . .

The Highgug caught his breath at the next sight, very nearly strangling himself. Looking at the gate, he could see beyond it, and what he saw was paralyzing.

A vast army was racing toward him. And it was not *his* army!

Which meant it must be the enemy, he decided after a moment's deep thought, there being—as far as he knew—only two sides to this conflict—his and theirs.

The noonday sun shone brightly upon the armor of the Knights of Solamnia, it flashed upon their shields and glittered upon their drawn swords. Farther behind them came the infantry at a run. The Army of Fistandantilus was dashing for the fortress, hoping to reach it before the gates could be closed and blocked. Those few mountain dwarves brave enough to stand in their way were cut down by flashing steel and trampling hoof.

The enemy was getting closer and closer. The Highgug swallowed nervously. He didn't know much about military maneuvers, but it did seem to him that this would be an excellent time for the gates to shut. It seemed that the generals thought so too, for they were now all running in that direction, yelling and screaming.

"In the name of Reorx, what's taking them—" Duncan began.

Suddenly, Kharas's face grew pale.

"Duncan," he said quietly, "we have been betrayed. You must leave at once."

"Wh-what?" Duncan stammered in bewilderment. Standing on his toes, he tried in vain to see over the crowd milling about in the courtyard. "Betrayed! How—"

"The Dewar, my Thane," Kharas said, able, with his unusual height, to see what was transpiring. "They have murdered the gate wardens, apparently, and are now fighting to keep the gates open."

"Slay them!" Duncan's mouth frothed in his anger, saliva dribbled down his beard. "Slay every one of them!" The dwarven king drew his own sword and leaped forward. "I'll personally—"

"No, Thane!" Kharas caught hold of him, dragging him back. "It is too late! Come, we must get to the griffons! You must go back to Thorbardin, my king!"

But Duncan was beyond all reason. He fought Kharas viciously. Finally, the younger dwarf, with a grim face, doubled his great fist and punched his king squarely on the jaw. Duncan stumbled backward, reeling from the blow but not down.

"I'll have your head for this!" the king swore, grasping feebly for his sword hilt. One more blow from Kharas finished the job, however. Duncan sprawled onto the ground and lay there quietly.

With a grieving face, Kharas bent down, lifted his king, plate-mail armor and all, and—with a grunt—heaved the stout dwarf over his shoulder. Calling for some of those still able to stand and fight to cover him, Kharas hurried off toward where the griffons waited, the comatose king hanging, arms dangling, over his shoulder.

The Highgug stared at the approaching army in horrified fascination. Over and over echoed in his mind Duncan's last command to him—"You Stay Here."

Turning around, running back to his troop, that was exactly what the Highgug intended to do.

Although gully dwarves have a well-deserved reputation for being the most cowardly race living upon Krynn, they can—when driven into a corner—fight with a ferocity that generally amazes an enemy.

Most armies, however, use gully dwarves only in support positions, keeping them as far to the rear as possible since it is almost even odds that a regiment of gully dwarves will inflict as much damage to its own side as it will ever succeed in doing to an enemy.

Thus Duncan had posted the only detachment of gully dwarves currently residing in Pax Tharkas—they were former mine workers—in the center of the courtyard and told them to stay there, figuring this would be the best way to keep them out of mischief. He had given them pikes, in the unlikely event that the enemy would crash through the gates with a cavalry charge.

But that was what was happening. Seeing the Army of Fistandantilus closing in upon them, knowing that they were trapped and defeated, all the dwarves in Pax Tharkas were thrown into confusion.

A few kept their heads. The sharpshooters on the battlements were raining arrows into the advancing foe, slowing them somewhat. Several commanders were gathering their regiments, preparing to fight as they retreated to the mountains. But most were just fleeing, running for their lives to the safety of the surrounding hills.

And soon only one group stood in the path of the approaching army—the gully dwarves.

"This is it," the Highgug called hastily to his men as he came huffing and puffing back. His face was white beneath the dirt, but he was calm and composed. He had been told to Stay Here and, by Reorx's beard, he was going to Stay Here.

However, seeing that most of his men were starting to edge away, their eyes wide at the sight of the thundering horses which could now be seen approaching the open gates, the Highgug decided this called for a little morale boost.

Having drilled them for just such an occasion, the Highgug had also taught his troops a war chant and was quite proud of it. Unfortunately, they'd never yet got it right.

"Now," he shouted, "what you give me?"

"Death!" his men all shouted cheerfully with one voice.

The Highgug cringed. "No, no, no!" he yelled in exasperation, stomping on the ground. His men looked at each other, chagrined.

"I tell you, gulphbludders—it's—"

"Undying loyalty!" cried one suddenly in triumph.

The others scowled at him, muttering "brown nose." One jealous neighbor even poked him in the back with a pike. Fortunately, it was the butt end (he was holding it upside down) or serious damage might have been incurred.

"That's it," said the Highgug, trying not to notice that the sound of hoofbeats was getting louder and louder behind him. "Now, we try again. What you give me?"

"Un-undy . . . dying loy . . . loy . . . alty." This was rather straggled-sounding, many stumbling over the difficult words. It certainly seemed to lack the ring (or the enthusiasm) of the first.

A hand shot up in the back.

"Well, what is it, Gug Snug?" snarled the Highgug.

"Us got to give . . . undying . . . loyal . . . ty when dead?"

The Highgug glared at him with his one good eye.

"No, you phungerwhoop," he snapped, gritting his teeth. "Death or undying loyalty. Whichever come first."

The gully dwarves grinned, immensely cheered by this.

The Highgug, shaking his head and muttering, turned around to face the enemy. "Set pikes!" he shouted.

That was a mistake and he knew it as soon as he said it, hearing the vast turmoil and confusion and swearing (and a few groans of pain) behind him.

But, by that time, it didn't matter. . . .

The sun set in a blood-red haze, sinking down into the silent forests of Qualinesti.

All was quiet in Pax Tharkas, the mighty, impregnable fortress having fallen shortly after midday. The afternoon had been spent in skirmishes with pockets of dwarves, who were retreating, fighting, back into the mountains. Many had escaped, the charge of the knights having been effectively held up by a small group of pikesmen, who had stood their ground when the gates were breached, stubbornly refusing to budge.

Kharas, carrying the unconscious king in his arms, flew by

griffon back to Thorbardin, accompanied by those of Duncan's officers still alive.

The remainder of the army of the mountain dwarves, at home in the caves and rocks of the snow-covered passes, were making their way back to Thorbardin. The Dewar who had betrayed their kinsmen were drinking Duncan's captured ale and boasting of their deeds, while most of Caramon's army regarded them with disgust.

Tonight, as the sun set, the courtyard was filled with dwarves and humans celebrating their victory, and by officers trying in vain to stem the tide of drunkenness that was threatening to wash everyone under. Shouting, bullying, and smashing a few heads together, they managed to drag off enough to post the watch and form burial squads.

Crysania had passed her trial by blood. Though she had been kept well away from the battle by a watchful Caramon, she had—once they entered the fort—managed to elude him. Now, cloaked and hooded, she moved among the wounded, surreptitiously healing those she could without drawing unwanted attention to herself. And, in later years, those who survived would tell stories to their grandchildren, claiming that they had seen a white-robed figure bearing a shining light around her neck, who laid her gentle hands upon them and took away their pain.

Caramon was, meanwhile, meeting with officers in a room in Pax Tharkas, planning their strategy, though the big man was so exhausted he could barely think straight.

Thus, few saw the single, black-robed figure entering the open gates of Pax Tharkas. It rode upon a restive black horse that shied at the smell of blood. Pausing, the figure spoke a few words to his mount, seeming to soothe the animal. Those that did see the figure paused for a moment in terror, many having the fevered (or drunken) impression that it was Death in person, come to collect the unburied.

Then someone muttered, "the wizard," and they turned away, laughing shakily or breathing a sigh of relief.

His eyes obscured by the depths of his black hood, yet intently observing all around him, Raistlin rode forward until he came to the most remarkable sight on the entire field of battle—the bodies of a hundred or more gully dwarves, lying (for the most part) in even rows, rank upon rank. Most still held their pikes (many upside down) clutched tightly in their dead hands. There were also lying among them, though, a few horses that had been injured (generally accidentally) by the wild stabs and slashings of the desperate gully dwarves. More than one animal, when hauled off, was noted to have teeth marks sunk into its forelegs. At the end, the gully dwarves had dropped the useless pikes to fight as they knew best—with tooth and nail.

"This wasn't in the histories," Raistlin murmured to himself, staring down at the wretched little bodies, his brow furrowed. His eyes flashed. "Perhaps," he breathed, "this means time has already been altered?"

For long moments he sat there, pondering. Then suddenly he understood.

None saw Raistlin's face, hidden as it was by his hood, or they would have noted a swift, sudden spasm of sorrow and anger pass across it.

"No," he said to himself bitterly, "the pitiful sacrifice of these poor creatures was left out of the histories not because it did not happen. It was left out simply because—"

He paused, staring grimly down at the small broken bodies. "No one cared. . . ."

CHAPTER
7

"I must see the general!"

The voice pierced through the soft, warm cloud of sleep that wrapped Caramon like the down-filled comforter on the bed—the first real bed he'd slept in for months.

"Go 'way," mumbled Caramon and heard Garic say the same thing, or close enough. . . .

"Impossible. The general is sleeping. He's not to be disturbed."

"I must see him. It's urgent!"

"He hasn't slept in almost forty-eight hours—"

"I know! But—"

The voices dropped. Good, Caramon thought, now I can go back to sleep. But he found, unfortunately, that the lowered voices only made him more wakeful. Something was wrong, he knew it. With a groan, he rolled over, dragging the pillow on top his head. Every muscle in his body ached; he had been on horseback almost eighteen hours without rest. Surely Garic could handle it. . . .

The door to his room opened softly.

Caramon squeezed his eyes shut, burrowing farther down into the feather bed. It occurred to him as he did so that, a couple of hundred years from now, Verminaard, the evil Dragon Highlord, would sleep in this very same bed. Had someone wakened him like this, that morning the Heroes had freed the slaves of Pax Tharkas? . . .

"General," said Garic's soft voice. "Caramon."

There was a muttered oath from the pillow.

Perhaps, when I leave, I'll put a frog in the bed, Caramon thought viciously. It would be nice and stiff in two hundred years. . . .

"General," Garic persisted, "I'm sorry to wake you, sir, but you're needed in the courtyard at once."

"What for?" growled Caramon, throwing off the blankets and sitting up, wincing at the soreness in his thighs and back. Rubbing his eyes, he glared at Garic.

"The army, sir. It's leaving."

Caramon stared at him. "What? You're crazy."

"No, s-sir," said a young soldier, who had crept in after Garic and now stood behind him, his eyes wide with awe at being in the presence of his commanding officer—despite the fact that the officer was naked and only half-awake. "They— they're gathering in the courtyard, n-now, sir. . . . The dwarves and the Plainsmen and . . . and some of ours."

"Not the Knights," Garic added quickly.

"Well . . . well . . ." Caramon stammered, then waved his hand. "Tell them to disperse, damn it! This is nonsense." He swore. "Name of the gods, three-fourths of them were dead drunk last night!"

"They're sober enough this morning, sir. And I think you should come," Garic said softly. "Your brother is leading them."

"What's the meaning of this?" Caramon demanded, his breath puffing white in the chill air. It was the coldest morning of the fall. A thin coat of frost covered the stones of Pax Tharkas, mercifully obliterating the red stains of battle.

Wrapped in a thick cloak, dressed only in leather breeches and boots that he had hastily thrown on, Caramon glanced about the courtyard. It was crowded with dwarves and men, all standing quietly, grimly, in ranks, waiting for the order to march.

Caramon's stern gaze fixed itself on Reghar Fireforge, then shifted to Darknight, chief of the Plainsmen.

"We went over this yesterday," Caramon said. His voice taut with barely contained anger, he came to stand in front of Reghar. "It'll take another two days for our supply wagons to catch up. There's not enough food left here for the march, you told me that yourself last night. And you won't find so much as a rabbit on the Plains of Dergoth—"

"*We* don't mind missing a few meals," grunted Reghar, the emphasis on the "we" leaving no doubt as to his meaning. Caramon's love of his dinner was well-known.

This did nothing to improve the general's humor. Caramon's face flushed. "What about weapons, you long-bearded fool?" he snapped. "What about fresh water, shelter, food for the horses?"

"We won't be in the Plains that long," Reghar returned, his eyes flashing. "The mountain dwarves, Reorx curse their stone hearts, are in confusion. We must strike now, before they can get their forces back together."

"We went over this last night!" Caramon shouted in exasperation. "This was just a *part* of their force we faced here. Duncan's got another whole damn army waiting for you beneath the mountain!"

"Perhaps. Perhaps not," Reghar snarled surlily, staring southward and folding his arms in front of him. "At any rate, we've changed our minds. We're marching today—with or without you."

Caramon glanced at Darknight, who had remained silent throughout this conversation. The chief of the Plainsmen only nodded, once. His men, standing behind him, were stern and quiet, though—here and there—Caramon saw a few green-tinged faces and knew that many had not fully recovered from last night's celebration.

Finally, Caramon's gaze shifted to a black-robed figure seated on a black horse. Though the figure's eyes were shadowed by his black hood, Caramon had felt their intense, amused gaze ever since he walked out of the door of the gigantic fortress.

Turning abruptly away from the dwarf, Caramon stalked over to Raistlin. He was not surprised to find Lady Crysania on her horse, muffled in a thick cloak. As he drew nearer, he noticed that the bottom of the cleric's cloak was stained dark with blood. Her face, barely visible above a scarf she had wound around her neck and chin, was pale but composed. He wondered briefly where she had been and what she had been doing during the long night. His thoughts were centered, however, on his twin.

"This is your doing," he said in a low voice, approaching Raistlin and laying his hand upon the horse's neck.

Raistlin nodded complacently, leaning forward over the pommel of the saddle to talk to his brother. Caramon could see his face, cold and white as the frost on the pavement beneath their feet.

"What's the idea?" Caramon demanded, still in the same low voice, "What's this all about? You know we can't march without supplies!"

"You're playing this much too safely, my brother," said Raistlin. He shrugged and added, "The supply trains will catch up with us. As for weapons, the men have picked up extra ones here after the battle. Reghar is right—we must strike quickly, before Duncan can get organized."

"You should have discussed this with me!" Caramon growled, clenching his fist. "*I* am in command!"

Raistlin looked away, shifting slightly in his saddle. Caramon, standing near him, felt his brother's body shiver beneath the black robes. "There wasn't time," the archmage said after a moment. "I had a dream last night, my brother. *She* came to me—my Queen ... Takhisis.... It is imperative that I reach Zhaman as soon as possible."

Caramon gazed at his brother in silent, sudden understanding. "They mean nothing to you!" he said softly, gesturing to the men and dwarves standing, waiting behind him. "You're interested in one thing only, reaching your precious Portal!" His bitter gaze shifted to Crysania, who regarded him calmly, though her gray eyes were dark and shadowed from a sleepless, horror-filled night spent among the wounded and dying. "You, too? You support him in this?"

"The trial of blood, Caramon," she said softly. "It must be stopped—forever. I have seen the ultimate evil mankind can inflict upon itself."

"I wonder!" Caramon muttered, glancing at his twin.

Reaching up with his slender hands, Raistlin slowly drew back the folds of his hood, leaving his eyes visible. Caramon recoiled, seeing himself reflected in the flat surface, seeing his face—haggard, unshaven, his hair uncombed, fluttering raggedly in the wind. And then, as Raistlin stared at him, holding him in an intense gaze as a snake charms a bird, words came into Caramon's mind.

You know me well my brother. The blood that flows in our veins speaks louder than words sometimes. Yes, you are right. I care nothing for this war. I have fought it for one purpose only, and that is to reach the Portal. These fools will carry me that far. Beyond that, what does it matter to me whether we win or lose?

I have allowed you to play general, Caramon, since you seemed to enjoy your little game. You are, in fact, surprisingly good at it. You have served my purpose adequately. You will serve me still. You will lead the army to Zhaman. When Lady Crysania and I are safely there, I will send you home. Remember this, my brother—the battle on the Plains of Dergoth was lost! You cannot change that!

"I don't believe you!" Caramon said thickly, staring at Raistlin with wild eyes. "You wouldn't ride to your own death! You must know something! You—"

Caramon choked, half-strangled. Raistlin drew nearer to him, seeming to suck the words out of his throat.

My counsel is my own to keep! What I know or do not know does not concern you, so do not tax your brain with fruitless speculation.

"I'll tell them," Caramon said forcing the words out through clenched teeth. "I'll tell them the truth!"

Tell them what? That you have seen the future? That they are doomed? Seeing the struggle in Caramon's anguish-filled face, Raistlin smiled. *I think not, my brother. And now, if you ever want to return to your home again, I suggest you go upstairs, put on your armor, and lead your army.*

The archmage lifted his hands and pulled his hood down low over his eyes again. Caramon drew in his breath with a gasp, as though someone had dashed cold water in his face. For a moment, he could only stand staring at his twin, shivering with a rage that nearly overpowered him.

All he could think of, at that moment, was Raistlin . . . laughing with him by the tree . . . Raistlin holding the rabbit . . . That camaraderie between them had been real. He would swear it! And yet, this, too, was real. Real and cold and sharp as the blade of a knife shining in the clear light of morning.

And, slowly, the light from that knife blade began to penetrate the clouds of confusion in Caramon's mind, severing another of the ties that bound him to his brother.

The knife moved slowly. There were many ties to cut.

The first gave in the blood-soaked arena at Istar, Caramon realized. And he felt another part as he stared at his brother in the frost-rimed courtyard of Pax Tharkas.

"It seems I have no choice," he said, tears of anger and pain blurring the image of his brother in his sight.

"None," Raistlin replied. Grasping the reins, he made ready to ride off. "There are things I must attend to. Lady Crysania will ride with you, of course, in the vanguard. Do not wait for me. I will ride behind for a time."

And so I'm dismissed, Caramon said to himself. Watching his brother ride away, he felt no anger anymore, just a dull, gnawing ache. An amputated limb left behind such phantom pain, so he had heard once. . . .

Turning on his heel, feeling more than hearing the heavy silence that had settled over the courtyard, the general walked alone to his quarters and slowly began to put on his armor.

When Caramon returned, dressed in his familiar golden armor, his cape fluttering in the wind, the dwarves and

Plainsmen and the men of his own army raised their voices in a resounding cheer.

Not only did they truly admire and respect the big man, but all credited him with the brilliant strategy that had brought them victory the day before. General Caramon was lucky, it was said, blessed by some god. After all, wasn't it luck that had kept the dwarves from closing the gates?

Most had felt uncomfortable when it was rumored they might be riding off without him. There had been many dark glances cast at the black-robed wizard, but who dared voice disapproval?

The cheers were immensely comforting to Caramon and, for a moment, he could say nothing. Then, finding his voice, he gruffly issued orders as he made ready to ride.

With a gesture, Caramon called one of the young Knights forward.

"Michael, I'm leaving you here in Pax Tharkas, in command," he said, pulling on a pair of gloves. The young Knight flushed with pleasure at this unexpected honor, even as he glanced behind at the hole his leaving made in the ranks.

"Sir, I'm only a low-ranking—Surely, someone more qualified—"

Smiling at him sadly, Caramon shook his head. "I know your qualifications, Michael. Remember? You were ready to die to fulfill a command, and you found the compassion to disobey. It won't be easy, but do the best you can. The women and children will stay here, of course. And I'll send back any wounded. When the supply trains arrive, see that they're sent on as quickly as possible." He shook his head. "Not that it is likely to be soon enough," he muttered. Sighing, he added, "You can probably hold out the winter here, if you have to. No matter what happens to us. . . ."

Seeing the Knights glance at each other, their faces puzzled and worried, Caramon abruptly bit off his words. No, his bitter foreknowledge must not be allowed to show. Feigning cheerfulness, therefore, he clapped Michael upon the shoulder, added something brave and inane, then mounted his horse amidst wild yelling.

The yells increased as the standard-bearer raised the army's standard. Caramon's banner with its nine-pointed star gleamed brightly in the sun. His Knights formed ranks behind him. Crysania came up to ride with them, the Knights parting, with their usual chivalry, to let her take her place. Though the Knights had no more use for the witch than anyone else in camp, she was a woman, after all, and the Code required them to protect and defend her with their lives.

"Open the gates!" Caramon shouted.

Pushed by eager hands, the gates swung open. Casting a final glance around to see that all was in readiness, Caramon's eyes suddenly encountered those of his twin.

Raistlin sat upon his black horse within the shadows of the great gates. He did not move nor speak. He simply sat, watching, waiting.

For as long as it took to draw a shared, simultaneous breath, the twins regarded each other intently, then Caramon turned his face away.

Reaching over, he grabbed his standard from his bearer. Holding it high over his head, he cried out one word, "Thorbardin!" The morning sun, just rising above the peaks, burned golden on Caramon's armor. It sparkled golden on the threads of the banner's star, glittered golden on the spear tips of the long ranks behind him.

"Thorbardin!" he cried once again and, spurring his horse, he galloped out of the gates.

"Thorbardin!" His cry was echoed by thunderous yells and the clashing of sword against shield. The dwarves began their familiar, eerie, deep-throated chant, "Stone and metal, metal and stone, stone and metal, metal and stone," stomping their iron-shod feet to it in stirring rhythm as they marched out of the fort in rigid lines.

They were followed by the Plainsmen, who moved in less orderly fashion. Wrapped in their fur cloaks against the chill, they walked in leisurely fashion, sharpening weapons, tying feathers in their hair, or painting strange symbols on their faces. Soon, growing tired of the rigid order, they would drift off the road to travel in their accustomed hunting packs. After the barbarians came Caramon's troop of farmers and thieves, more than a few of them staggering from the after-effects of last night's victory party. And finally, bringing up the rear, were their new allies, the Dewar.

Argat tried to catch Raistlin's eye as he and his men trooped out, but the wizard sat wrapped in black upon his black horse, his face hidden in darkness. The only flesh and blood part of him visible were the slender, white hands, holding the horse's reins.

Raistlin's eyes were not on the Dewar, nor on the army marching past him. They were on the gleaming golden figure riding at the army's head. And it would have taken a sharper eye than the Dewar's to note that the wizard's hands gripped the reins with an unnatural tightness or that the black robes shivered, for just a moment, as if with a soft sigh.

The Dewar marched out, and the courtyard was empty except for the camp followers. The women wiped away their tears and, chatting among themselves, returned to their tasks. The children clambered up onto the walls to cheer the army as long as it was in sight. The gates to Pax Tharkas swung shut at last, sliding smoothly and silently upon their oiled hinges.

Standing on the battlements alone, Michael watched the great army surge southward, their spear tips shining in the morning sun, their warm breath sending up puffs of mist, the chanting of the dwarves echoing through the mountains.

Behind them rode a single, solitary figure, cloaked in black. Looking at the figure, Michael felt cheered. It seemed a good omen. Death now rode behind the army, instead of in front.

The sun shone upon the opening of the gates of Pax Tharkas; it set upon the closing of the gates of the great mountain fastness of Thorbardin. As the water-controlled mechanism that operated the gates groaned and wheezed, part of the mountain itself appeared to slide into place upon command. When shut and sealed, in fact, the gates were impossible to tell from the face of the rock of the mountain itself, so cunning was the craftsmanship of the dwarves who had spent years constructing them.

The shutting of the gates meant war. News of the marching

of the Army of Fistandantilus had been reported, carried by spies upon the swift wings of griffons. Now the mountain fastness was alive with activity. Sparks flew in the weapons makers' shops. Armorers fell asleep, hammers in their hands. The taverns doubled their business overnight as everyone came to boast of the great deeds they would accomplish on the field of battle.

Only one part of the huge kingdom beneath the ground was quiet, and it was to this place that the hero of the dwarves turned his heavy footsteps two days after Caramon's army had left Pax Tharkas.

Entering the great Hall of Audience of the King of the Mountain Dwarves, Kharas heard his boots ring hollowly in the bowl-shaped chamber that was carved of the stone of the mountain itself. The chamber was empty now, save for several dwarves seated at the front on a stone dais.

Kharas passed the long rows of stone benches where, last night, thousands of dwarves had roared approval as their king declared war upon their kinsmen.

Today was a War Meeting of the Council of Thanes. As such, it did not require the presence of the citizenry, so Kharas was somewhat startled to find himself invited. The hero was in disgrace—everyone knew it. There was speculation, even, that Duncan might have Kharas exiled.

Kharas noted, as he drew near, that Duncan was regarding him with an unfriendly eye, but this may have had something to do with the fact that the king's eye and left cheekbone above his beard were undeniably black and swollen—a result of the blow Kharas had inflicted.

"Oh, get up, Kharas," Duncan snapped as the tall, beardless dwarf bowed low before him.

"Not until you have forgiven me, Thane," Kharas said, retaining his position.

"Forgiven you for what—knocking some sense into a foolish old dwarf?" Duncan smiled wryly. "No, you're not forgiven for that. You are thanked." The king rubbed his jaw. " 'Duty is painful,' goes the proverb. Now I understand. But enough of that."

Seeing Kharas straighten, Duncan held out a scroll of parchment. "I asked you here for another reason. Read this."

Puzzled, Kharas examined the scroll. It was tied with black ribbon but was not sealed. Glancing at the other thanes, who were all assembled, each in his own stone chair sitting somewhat lower than the king's, Kharas's gaze went to one chair in particular—a vacant chair, the chair of Argat, Thane of the Dewar. Frowning, Kharas unrolled the scroll and read aloud, stumbling over the crude language of the Dewar.

Duncan, of the Dwarves of Thorbardin, King.

Greetings from those you now call traitor.

This scroll is deliver to you from us who know that you will punish Dewar under the mountain for what we did at Pax Tharkas. If this scroll is deliver to you at all, it mean that we succeed in keeping the gates open.

You scorn our plan in Council. Perhaps now you see wisdom. The enemy is led by the wizard now. Wizard is friend of ours. He make army march for the Plains of Dergoth. We march with them, friend with them. When the hour to come, those you call traitor will strike. We will attack the enemy from within and drive them under your axe-blades.

If you to have doubt of our loyalty, hold our people hostage beneath the mountain until such time we return. We promise great gift we deliver to you as proof loyalty.

Argat, of the Dewar, Thane

Kharas read the scroll through twice, and his frown did not ease. If anything, it grew darker.

"Well?" demanded Duncan.

"I have nothing to do with traitors," Kharas said, rolling up the scroll and handing it back in disgust.

"But if they are sincere," Duncan pursued, "this could give us a great victory!"

Kharas raised his eyes to meet those of his king, who sat on the dais above him. "If, at this moment, Thane, I could talk to our enemy's general, this Caramon Majere, who—by all accounts—is a fair and honorable man, I would tell him exactly what peril threatens him, even if it meant that we ourselves would go down in defeat."

The other thanes snorted or grumbled.

"You should have been a Knight of Solamnia!" one muttered, a statement not intended as a compliment.

Duncan cast them all a stern glance, and they fell into a sulking silence.

"Kharas," Duncan said patiently, "we know how you feel about honor, and we applaud you for that. But honor will not feed the children of those who may die in this battle, nor will it keep our kinsmen from picking clean our bones if we ourselves fall. No," Duncan continued, his voice growing stern and deep, "there is a time for honor and a time when one must do what he must." Once again, he rubbed his jaw. "You yourself showed me that."

Kharas's face grew grim. Absent-mindedly raising a hand to stroke the flowing beard that was no longer there, he dropped his hand uncomfortably and, flushing, stared down at his feet.

"Our scouts have verified this report," Duncan continued. "The army has marched."

Kharas looked up, scowling. "I don't believe it!" he said. "I didn't believe it when I heard it! They have left Pax Tharkas? Before their supply wagons got through? It must be true then, the wizard must be in charge. No general would make that mistake—"

"They will be on the Plains within the next two days. Their objective is, according to our spies, the fortress of Zhaman, where they plan to set up headquarters. We have a small garrison there that will make a token defense and then retreat, hopefully drawing them out into the open."

"Zhaman," Kharas muttered, scratching his jaw since he could no longer tug at his beard. Abruptly, he took a step forward, his face now eager. "Thane, if I can present a plan that will end this war with a minimum of bloodshed, will you listen to it and allow me to try?"

"I'll listen," said Duncan dubiously, his face setting into rigid lines.

"Give me a hand-picked squadron of men, Thane, and I will undertake to kill this wizard, this Fistandantilus. When he is dead, I will show this scroll to his general and to our kinsmen. They will see that they have been betrayed. They will see the might of our army lined up against them. They must surely surrender!"

"And what are we to do with them if they *do* surrender?" Duncan snapped irritably, though he was going over the plan in his mind even as he spoke. The other thanes had ceased muttering into their beards and were looking at each other, heavy brows knotting over their eyes.

"Give them Pax Tharkas, Thane," Kharas said, his eagerness growing. "Those who want to live there, of course. Our kinsmen will, undoubtedly, return to their homes. We could make a few concessions to them—very few," he added hastily, seeing Duncan's face darken. "That would be arranged with the surrender terms. But there would be shelter and protection for the humans and our kinsmen during the winter—they could work in the mines. . . ."

"The plan has possibilities," Duncan muttered thoughtfully. "Once you're in the desert, you could hide in the Mounds—"

He fell silent, pondering. Then he slowly shook his head. "But it is a dangerous course, Kharas. And all may be for nought. Even if you succeed in killing the Dark One—and I remind you that he is said to be a wizard of great power— there is every possibility you will be killed before you can talk to this General Majere. Rumor has it he is the wizard's twin brother!"

Kharas smiled wearily, his hand still on his smooth-shaven jaw. "That is a risk I will take gladly, Thane, if means that no more of my kinsmen will die at my hands."

Duncan glared at him, then, rubbing his swollen jaw, he heaved a sigh. "Very well," he said. "You have our leave. Choose your men with care. When will you go?"

"Tonight, Thane, with your permission."

"The gates of the mountain will open to you, then they will close. Whether they open again to admit you victorious or to disgorge the armed might of the mountain dwarves will be dependent upon you, Kharas. May Reorx's flame shine on your hammer."

Bowing, Kharas turned and walked from the hall, his step swifter and more vigorous than it had been when he arrived.

"There goes one we can ill afford to lose," said one of the thanes, his eyes on the retreating figure of the tall, beardless dwarf.

"He was lost to us from the beginning," Duncan snapped harshly. But his face was haggard and lined with grief as he muttered, "Now, we must plan for war."

CHAPTER 8

"No water again," Caramon said quietly.

Reghar scowled. Though the general's voice was carefully expressionless, the dwarf knew that he was being held accountable. Realizing that he was, in large part, to blame, didn't help matters. The only feeling more wretched and unbearable than guilt is the feeling of well-deserved guilt.

"There'll be another water hole within half a day's march," Reghar growled, his face setting into granite. "They were all over the place in the old days, like pock marks."

The dwarf waved an arm. Caramon glanced around. As far as the eye could see there was nothing—not tree, not bird, not even scrubby bushes. Nothing but endless miles of sand, dotted here and there with strange, domed mounds. Far off in the distance, the dark shadows of the mountains of Thorbardin hovered before his eyes like the lingering remembrance of a bad dream.

The Army of Fistandantilus was losing before the battle even started.

After days of forced marching, they had finally come out of the mountain pass from Pax Tharkas and were now upon the Plains of Dergoth. Their supplies had not caught up with them and, because of the rapid pace at which they were moving, it looked as if it might be more than a week before the lumbering wagons found them.

Raistlin pressed the need for haste upon the commanders of the armies and, though Caramon opposed his brother openly, Reghar supported the archmage and managed to sway the Plainsmen to their side as well. Once again, Caramon had little choice but to go along. And so the army rose before dawn, marched with only a brief rest at midday, and continued until twilight when they stopped to make camp while there was still light enough to see.

It did not seem like an army of victors. Gone were the comradeship, the jokes, the laughter, the games of evening. Gone was the singing by day; even the dwarves ceased their stirring chant, preferring to keep their breath for breathing as they marched mile after weary mile. At night, the men slumped down practically where they stood, ate their meager rations, and then fell immediately into exhausted sleep until kicked and prodded by the sergeants to begin another day.

Spirits were low. There were grumblings and complaints, especially as the food dwindled. This had not been a problem in the mountains. Game had been plentiful. But once on the Plains, as Caramon had foretold, the only living things they saw were each other. They lived on hard-baked, unleavened bread and strips of dried meat rationed out twice per day— morning and night. And Caramon knew that if the supply wagons didn't catch up with them soon, even this small amount would be cut in half.

But the general had other concerns besides food, both of which were more critical. One was a lack of fresh water. Though Reghar had told him confidently that there were water holes in the Plains, the first two they discovered were dry. Then—and only then—had the old dwarf dourly admitted that the last time he'd set eyes on these Plains was in the days before the Cataclysm. Caramon's other problem was the rapidly deteriorating relationships between the allies.

Always threadbare at best, the alliance was now splitting apart at the seams. The humans from the north blamed their current problems on the dwarves and the Plainsmen since they had supported the wizard.

The Plainsmen, for their part, had never been in the mountains before. They discovered that fighting and living in mountainous terrain was cold and snowy and, as the chief put it crudely to Caramon, "it is either too *up* or too *down*."

Now, seeing the gigantic mountains of Thorbardin looming on the southern horizon, the Plainsmen were beginning to think that all the gold and steel in the world wasn't as beautiful as the golden, *flat* grasslands of their home. More than once Caramon saw their dark eyes turn northward, and he knew that one morning he would awaken and find they had gone.

The dwarves, for their part, viewed the humans as cowardly weaklings who ran crying home to mama the minute things got a little tough. Thus they treated the lack of food and water as a petty annoyance. The dwarf who even dared *hint* he was thirsty was immediately set upon by his fellows.

Caramon thought of this and he thought of his numerous other problems as he stood in the middle of the desert that evening, kicking at the sand with the toe of his boot.

Then, raising his eyes, Caramon's gaze rested on Reghar. Thinking Caramon was not watching him, the old dwarf lost his rocky sternness—his shoulders slumped, and he sighed wearily. His resemblance to Flint was painful in its intensity. Ashamed of his anger, knowing it was directed more at himself than anyone else, Caramon did what he could to make amends.

"Don't worry. We've enough water to last the night. Surely we'll come on a water hole tomorrow, don't you think?" he said, patting Reghar clumsily on the back. The old dwarf glanced up at Caramon, startled and instantly suspicious, fearing he might be the butt of some joke.

But, seeing Caramon's tired face smiling at him cheerfully, Reghar relaxed. "Aye," the dwarf said with a grudging smile in return. "Tomorrow for sure."

Turning from the dry water hole, the two made their way back to camp.

Night came early to the Plains of Dergoth. The sun dropped behind the mountains rapidly, as though sick of the sight of the vast, barren desert wasteland. Few campfires glowed; most of the men were too tired to bother lighting them, and there wasn't any food to cook anyway. Huddling together in their separate groups, the hill dwarves, the northerners, and the Plainsmen regarded each other suspiciously. Everyone, of course, shunned the Dewar.

Caramon, glancing up, saw his own tent, sitting apart from them all, as though he had simply written them off.

An old Krynnish legend told of a man who had once committed a deed so heinous that the gods themselves gathered to inflict his punishment. When they announced that, henceforth, the man was to have the ability to see into the future, the man laughed, thinking he had outwitted the gods. The man had, however, died a tortured death—something Caramon had never been able to understand.

But now he understood, and his soul ached. Truly, no greater punishment could be inflicted upon any mortal. For, by seeing into the future and knowing what the outcome will be, man's greatest gift—hope—is taken away.

Up until now, Caramon had hoped. He had believed Raistlin would come up with a plan. He had believed his brother wouldn't let this happen. Raistlin *couldn't* let this happen. But now, knowing that Raistlin truly didn't care what became of these men and dwarves and the families they had left behind, Caramon's hope died. They were doomed. There was nothing he could do to prevent what had happened before from happening again.

Knowing this and knowing the pain that this must inevitably cost him, Caramon began to unconsciously distance himself from those he had come to care about. He began to think about home.

Home! Almost forgotten, even purposefully shoved to the back of his mind, memories of his home now flooded over him with such vivid clarity—once he let them—that sometimes, in the long, lonely evenings, he stared into a fire he could not see for his tears.

It was the one thought that kept Caramon going. As he led his army closer and closer to their defeat, each step led him closer to Tika, closer to home. . . .

"Look out there!" Reghar grabbed hold of him, shaking him from his reverie. Caramon blinked and looked up just before he stumbled into one of the strange mounds that dotted the Plains.

"What are these confounded contrivances anyway?" Caramon grumbled, glaring at it. "Some type of animal dwelling? I've heard tell of squirrels without tails who live in homes like these upon the great flatlands of Estwilde." He eyed the structure that was nearly three feet tall and just as wide, and shook his head. "But I'd hate to meet up with the squirrel who built this!"

"Bah! Squirrel indeed!" Reghar scoffed. "Dwarves built these! Can't you tell? Look at the workmanship." He ran his hand lovingly over the smooth-sided dome. "Since when did Nature do such a perfect job?"

Caramon snorted. "Dwarves! But—why? What for? Not even dwarves love work so much that they do it for their health! Why waste time building mounds in a desert?"

"Observation posts," Reghar said succinctly.

"Observation?" Caramon grinned. "What do they observe? Snakes?"

"The land, the sky, armies—like ours." Reghar stamped his foot, raising a cloud of dust. "Hear that?"

"Hear what?"

"That." Reghar stamped again. "Hollow."

Caramon's brow cleared. "Tunnels!" His eyes opened wide. Looking around the desert at mound after mound rising up out of the flatlands, he whistled softly.

"Miles of 'em!" Reghar said, nodding his head. "Built so long ago that they were old to my great-grandfather. Of course"—the dwarf sighed—"most of them haven't been used in that long either. Legend had it that there were once fortresses between here and Pax Tharkas, connecting up with the Kharolis Mountains. A dwarf could walk from Pax Tharkas to Thorbardin without ever once seeing the sun, if the old tales be true.

"The fortresses are gone now. And many of the tunnels, in all likelihood. The Cataclysm wrecked most of 'em. Still," Reghar continued cheerfully, as he and Caramon resumed walking, "I wouldn't be surprised if Duncan hadn't a few spies down there, skulking about like rats."

"Above or below, they'll see us coming from a long way off," Caramon muttered, his gaze scanning the flat, empty land.

"Aye," Reghar said stoutly, "and much good it will do them."

Caramon did not answer, and the two kept going, the big man returning alone to his tent and the dwarf returning to the encampment of his people.

In one of the mounds, not far from Caramon's tent, eyes *were* watching the army, watching its every move. But those eyes weren't interested in the army itself. They were interested in three people, three people only. . . .

"Not long now," Kharas said. He was peering out through slits so cunningly carved into the rock that they allowed those in the mound to look out but prevented anyone looking at the outside of the mound from seeing in. "How far do you make the distance?"

This to a dwarf of ancient, scruffy appearance, who glanced out the slits once in a bored fashion, then glanced down the length of the tunnel. "Two hundred, fifty-three steps. Bring you smack up in the center," he said without hesitation.

Kharas looked back out onto the Plains to where the general's large tent sat apart from the campfires of his men. It seemed marvelous to Kharas that the old dwarf could judge the distance so accurately. The hero might have expressed doubts, had it been anyone but Smasher. But the elderly thief who had been brought out of retirement expressly for this mission had too great a reputation for performing remarkable feats—a reputation that almost equaled Kharas's own.

"The sun is setting," Kharas reported, rather unnecessarily since the lengthening shadows could be seen slanting against the rock walls of the tunnel behind him. "The general returns. He is entering his tent." Kharas frowned. "By Reorx's beard, I hope he doesn't decide to change his habits tonight."

"He won't," Smasher said. Crouched comfortably in a corner, he spoke with the calm certainty of one who had (in former days) earned a living by watching the comings and—more particularly—the goings of his fellows. "First two things you learn when yer breakin' house—everyone has a routine and no one likes change. Weather's fine, there've been no startlements, nothin' out there 'cept sand an' more sand. No, he won't change."

Kharas frowned, not liking this reminder of the dwarf's lawless past. Well aware of his own limitations, Kharas had chosen Smasher for this mission because they needed someone skilled in stealth, skilled in moving swiftly and silently, skilled in attacking by night, and escaping into the darkness.

But Kharas, who had been admired by the Knights of Solamnia for his honor, suffered pangs of conscience nonetheless. He soothed his soul by reminding himself that Smasher had, long ago, paid for his misdeeds and had even performed several services for his king that made him, if not a completely reputable character, at least a minor hero.

Besides, Kharas said to himself, think of the lives we will save.

Even as he thought this, he breathed a sigh of relief. "You are right, Smasher. Here comes the wizard from his tent and here comes the witch from hers."

Grasping the handle of his hammer strapped securely to his belt with one hand, Kharas used the other hand to shift a shortsword he had tucked into his belt into a slightly more comfortable position. Finally, he reached into a pouch, drew out a piece of rolled parchment, and with a thoughtful, solemn expression on his beardless face, tucked it into a safe pocket in his leather armor.

Turning to the four dwarves who stood behind him, he said, "Remember, do not harm the woman or the general any more than is necessary to subdue them. But—the wizard must die, and he must die quickly, for he is the most dangerous."

Smasher grinned and settled back more comfortably. He would not be going along. Too old. That would have insulted him once, but he was of an age now where it came as a compliment. Besides, his knees creaked alarmingly.

"Let them settle in," the old thief advised. "Let them start their evening meal, relax. Then"—drawing his hand across his throat, he chortled—"two hundred and fifty-three steps. . . ."

Standing guard duty outside the general's tent, Garic listened to the silence within. It was more disturbing and seemed to echo louder than the most violent quarrel.

Glancing inside through the tent flap opening, he saw the three sitting together as they did every night, quiet, muttering only occasionally, each one apparently wrapped in his or her own concerns.

The wizard was deeply involved in his studies. Rumor had it that he was planning some great, powerful spells that would blow the gates of Thorbardin wide open. As for the witch, who knew what she was thinking? Garic was thankful, at least, that Caramon was keeping an eye on her.

There had been some weird rumors about the witch among the men. Rumors of miracles performed at Pax Tharkas, of the dead returning to life at her touch, of limbs growing back onto bloody stumps. Garic discounted these, of course. Still, there was something about her these days that made the young man wonder if his first impressions had been correct.

Garic shifted restlessly in the cold wind that swept over the desert. Of the three in the tent, he worried most about his general. Over the past months, the young knight had come to revere and idolize Caramon. Observing him closely, trying to be as much like him as possible, Garic noticed Caramon's obvious depression and unhappiness which the big man thought he was doing quite well at hiding. For Garic, Caramon had taken the place of the family he had lost, and now the young

Knight brooded over Caramon's sorrow as he would have brooded about an older brother.

"It's those blasted dark dwarves," Garic muttered out loud, stomping his feet to keep them from going numb. "I don't trust 'em, that's for certain. I'd send them packing, and I'll bet the general would, too, if it weren't for his bro—"

Garic stopped, holding his breath, listening.

Nothing. But he could have sworn. . . .

Hand on the hilt of his sword, the young Knight stared out into the desert. Though hot by day, it was a cold and forbidding place at night. Off in the distance, he saw the campfires. Here and there, he could see the shadows of men passing by.

Then he heard it again. A sound behind him. Directly behind him. The sound of heavy, iron-shod boots. . . .

"What was that?" Caramon asked, lifting his head.

"The wind," Crysania muttered, glancing at the tent and shivering, watching as the fabric rippled and breathed like a living thing. "It blows incessantly in this horrid place."

Caramon half-rose, hand on his sword hilt. "It wasn't the wind."

Raistlin glanced up at his brother. "Oh, sit down!" he snarled softly in irritation, "and finish your dinner so that we can end this. I must return to my studies."

The archmage was going over a particularly difficult spell chant in his mind. He had been wrestling with it for days, trying to discover the correct voice inflection and pronunciation needed to unlock the secrets of the words. So far, they had eluded his grasp and made little sense.

Shoving his still-full plate aside, Raistlin started to stand—

—when the world literally gave way beneath his feet.

As though he were on the deck of a ship sliding down a steep wave, the sandy ground canted away from under foot. Staring down in amazement, the archmage saw a vast hole opening up before him. One of the poles that held up the tent slipped and toppled into it, causing the tent to sag. A lantern hanging from the supports swung wildly, shadows pitching and leaping around like demons.

Instinctively, Raistlin caught hold of the table and managed to save himself from falling into the rapidly widening hole. But, even as he did so, he saw figures crawling up through the hole—squat, bearded figures. For an instant, the wildly dancing light flashed off steel blades, shone in dark, grim eyes. Then the figures were plunged in shadows.

"Caramon!" Raistlin shouted, but he could tell by the sounds behind him—a vicious oath and the rattle of a steel sword sliding from its scabbard—that Caramon was well aware of the danger.

Raistlin heard, too, a strong, feminine voice calling on the name of Paladine, and saw the glimmering outline of pure, white light, but he had no time to worry about Crysania. A huge dwarven warhammer, seemingly wielded by the darkness itself, flashed in the lantern light, aiming right at the mage's head.

Speaking the first spell that came to his mind, Raistlin saw with satisfaction an invisible force pluck the hammer from the dwarf's hand. By his command, the magical force carried the hammer through the darkness to drop it with a thud in the corner of the tent.

At first numbed by the unexpectedness of the attack, Raistlin's mind was now active and working. Once the initial shock had passed, the mage saw this as simply another irritating interruption to his studies. Planning to end it quickly, the archmage turned his attention to his enemy, who stood before him, regarding him with eyes that were unafraid.

Feeling no fear himself, calm in the knowledge that nothing could kill him since he was protected by time, Raistlin called upon his magic in cool, unhurried fashion.

He felt it coiling and gathering within his body, felt the ecstasy course through him with a sensual pleasure. This would be a pleasant diversion from his studies, he decided. An interesting exercise ... Stretching out his hands, he began to pronounce the words that would send bolts of blue lightning sizzling through his enemy's writhing body. Then he was interrupted.

With the suddenness of a thunder clap, two figures

appeared before him, leaping out of the darkness at him as though they had dropped from a star.

Tumbling at the mage's feet, one of the figures stared up at him in wild excitement.

"Oh, look! It's Raistlin! We made it, Gnimsh! We made it! Hey, Raistlin! Bet you're surprised to see me, huh? And, oh, have I got the most wonderful story to tell you! You see, I was dead. Well, I wasn't actually, but—"

"Tasslchoff!" Raistlin gasped.

Thoughts sizzled in Raistlin's mind as the lightning might have sizzled from his fingertips.

The first—a kender! Time could be altered!

The second—Time *can* be altered. . . .

The third—I can die!

The shock of these thoughts jolted through Raistlin's body, burning away the coolness and calmness so necessary to the magic-user for casting his complex spells.

As both the unlooked-for solution to his problem and the frightful realization of what it might cost him penetrated his brain, Raistlin lost control. The words of the spell slipped from his mind. But his enemy still advanced.

Reacting instinctively, his hand shaking, Raistlin jerked his wrist, bringing into his palm the small silver dagger he carried with him.

But it was too late . . . and too little.

CHAPTER 9

Kharas's concentration was completely centered on the man he had vowed to kill. Reacting with the trained single-mindedness of the military mindset, he paid no attention to the startling appearance of the two apparitions, thinking them, perhaps, nothing more than beings conjured up by the archmage.

Kharas saw, at the same time, the wizard's glittering eyes go blank. He saw Raistlin's mouth—opened to recite deadly words—hang flaccid and loose, and the dwarf knew that for a few seconds at least, his enemy was at his mercy.

Lunging forward, Kharas drove his shortsword through the black, flowing robes and had the satisfaction of feeling it hit home.

Closing with the stricken mage, he drove the blade deeper and deeper into the human's slender body. The man's strange, burning heat enveloped him like a blazing inferno. A hatred and an anger so intense struck Kharas a physical blow, knocking him backward and slamming him into the ground.

But the wizard was wounded—mortally. That much

Kharas knew. Staring up from where he lay, looking into those searing, baleful eyes, Kharas saw them burn with fury, but he saw them fill with pain as well. And he saw—by the leaping, swaying light of the lantern—the hilt of his shortsword sticking out of the mage's gut. He saw the wizard's slender hands curl around it, he heard him scream in terrible agony. He knew he had no reason to fear. The wizard could harm him no longer.

Stumbling to his feet, Kharas reached out his hand and jerked the sword free. Crying out in bitter anguish, his hands deluged in his own blood, the wizard pitched forward onto the ground and lay still.

Kharas had time to look around then. His men were fighting a pitched battle with the general who, hearing his brother scream, was livid with fear and anger. The witch was nowhere to be seen, the eerie white light that had shone from her was gone, lost in the darkness.

Hearing a strangled sound from his left, Kharas turned to see the two apparitions the archmage had summoned staring down in stunned horror at the wizard's body. Getting a good look at them, Kharas was startled to see that these demons conjured from the nether planes were nothing more sinister than a kender in bright blue leggings and a balding gnome in a leather apron.

Kharas didn't have time to ponder this phenomenon. He had accomplished what he came for, at least he had almost. He knew he could never talk to the general, not now. His main concern was getting his men out safely. Running across the tent, Kharas picked up his warhammer and, yelling to his men in dwarven to get out of his way, flung it straight at Caramon.

The hammer struck the man a glancing blow on the head, knocking him out but not killing him. Caramon dropped like a felled ox and, suddenly, the tent was deathly silent.

It had all taken just a few short minutes.

Glancing through the tent flap, Kharas saw the young Knight who stood guard lying senseless upon the ground. There was no sign that anyone sitting around those far-off fires had heard or seen anything unusual.

Reaching up, the dwarf stopped the lantern from swinging and looked around. The wizard lay in a pool of his own blood. The general lay near him, his hand reaching out for his brother as though that had been his last thought before he lost consciousness. In a corner lay the witch, on her back, her eyes closed.

Seeing blood on her robes, Kharas glared sternly at his men. One of them shook his head.

"I'm sorry, Kharas," the dwarf said, looking down at her and shivering. "But—the light from her was so bright! It split my head open. All I could think of was to stop it. I—I wouldn't have been able to, but then the wizard screamed and she cried out, and her light wavered. I hit her, then, but not very hard. She's not hurt badly."

"All right." Kharas nodded. "Let's go." Retrieving his hammer, the dwarf looked down at the general lying at his feet. "I'm sorry," he said, fishing out the little bit of parchment and tucking it into the man's outstretched hand. "Maybe, sometime, I can explain it to you." Rising, he looked around. "Everyone all right? Then let's get out of here."

His men hurried to the tunnel entrance.

"What about these two?" one asked, stopping by the kender and the gnome.

"Take them," Kharas said sharply. "We can't leave them here, they'll raise the alarm."

For the first time, the kender seemed to come to life.

"No!" he cried, looking at Kharas with pleading, horrified eyes. "You can't take us! We just got here! We've found Caramon and now we can go home! No, please!"

"Take them!" Kharas ordered sternly.

"No!" the kender wailed, struggling in his captor's arms. "No, please, you don't understand. We were in the Abyss and we escaped—"

"Gag him," Kharas growled, peering down into the tunnel beneath the tent to see that all was well. Motioning for them to hurry, he knelt beside the hole in the ground.

His men descended into the tunnel, dragging the gagged kender, who was still putting up such a fight—kicking with his legs and clawing at them—that they were finally forced to stop and truss him up like a chicken before they could haul him away. They had nothing to worry about with their other captive, however. The poor gnome was so horrified that he had lapsed into a state of shock. Staring around helplessly, his mouth gaping wide open, he quietly did whatever he was told.

Kharas was the last to leave. Before jumping down into the tunnel, he took a final glance about the tent

The lantern hung quite still now, shedding its soft, glowing light upon a scene from a nightmare. Tables were smashed, chairs were overturned, food was scattered everywhere. A thin trail of blood ran from beneath the body of the black-robed magic-user. Forming a pool at the lip of the hole, the blood began to drip, slowly, down into the tunnel.

Leaping into the hole, Kharas ran a safe distance down the tunnel, then stopped. Grabbing up the end of a length of rope lying on the tunnel floor, he gave the rope a sharp yank. The opposite end of the rope was tied to one of the support beams right beneath the general's tent. The jerk on the rope brought the beam tumbling down. There was a low rumble. Then, in the distance, he could see stone falling, and his vision was obscured by a thick cloud of dust.

The tunnel now safely blocked behind him, Kharas turned and hurried after his men.

"General—"

Caramon was on his feet, his big hands reaching out for the throat of his enemy, a snarl contorting his face.

Startled, Garic stumbled backward.

"General!" he cried. "Caramon! It's me!"

Sudden, stabbing pain and the sound of Garic's familiar voice penetrated Caramon's brain. With a moan, he clasped his head in his hands and staggered. Garic caught him as he fell, lowering him safely into a chair.

"My brother?" Caramon said thickly.

"Caramon—I—" Garic swallowed.

"My brother!" Caramon rasped, clenching his fist.

"We took him to his tent," Garic replied softly. "The wound is—"

"What? The wound is what?" Caramon snarled impatiently, raising his head and staring at Garic with blood-shot, pain-filled eyes.

Garic opened his mouth, closed it, then shook his head. "M-my father told me about wounds like it," he mumbled. "Men lingering for days in dreadful agony...."

"You mean it's a belly wound," Caramon said.

Garic nodded and then covered his face with his hand. Caramon, looking at him closely, saw that the young man was deathly white. Sighing, closing his eyes, Caramon braced himself for the dizziness and nausea he knew would assail him when he stood up again. Then, grimly, he rose to his feet. The darkness whirled and heaved around him. He made himself stand steadily and, when it had settled, opened his eyes.

"How are you?" he asked Garic, looking intently at the young Knight.

"I'm all right," Garic answered, and his face flushed with shame. "Th-they took me ... from behind."

"Yeah." Caramon saw the matted blood in the young man's hair. "It happens. Don't worry about it." The big warrior smiled without mirth. "They took me from the front."

Garic nodded again, but it was obvious from the expression on his face that this defeat preyed on his mind.

He'll go over it, Caramon thought wearily. We all have to face it sooner or later.

"I'll see my brother now," he said, starting out of the tent with uneven steps. Then he stopped. "Lady Crysania?"

"Asleep. Knife wound glanced off her ... uh ... ribs. I—We dressed it ... as well as we could. We had to ... rip open her robes." Garic's flush deepened. "And we gave her some brandy to drink...."

"Does she know about Raist—Fistandantilus?"

"The wizard forbade it."

Caramon raised his eyebrows, then frowned. Glancing around at the wrecked tent, he saw the trail of blood on the trampled dirt floor. Drawing a deep breath, he opened the tent flap and walked unsteadily outside, Garic following.

"The army?"

"They know. The word spread." Garic spread his hands helplessly. "There was so much to do. We tried to go after the dwarves—"

"Bah!" Caramon snorted, wincing as pain shot through his head. "They would have collapsed the tunnel."

"Yes. We tried digging, but you might as well dig up the whole damn desert," Garic said bitterly.

"What about the army?" Caramon persisted, pausing outside Raistlin's tent. Inside, he could hear a low moaning sound.

"The men are upset," Garic said with a sigh. "Talking, confused. I don't know."

Caramon understood. He glanced into the darkness of his brother's tent. "I'll go in alone. Thank you for all you've done, Garic," he added gently. "Now, go get some rest before you pass out. I'm going to need you later on, and you'll be no help to me sick."

"Yes, sir," Garic said. He started to stagger off, then stopped, turning back. Reaching beneath the breastplate of his armor, he withdrew a blood-soaked bit of parchment. "We— we found this . . . in your hand, sir. The handwriting's dwarven. . . ."

Caramon looked at it, opened it, read it, then rolled it back up without comment, tucking it into his belt.

Guards surrounded the tents now. Gesturing to one, Caramon waited until he saw Garic being helped to his bed. Then, bracing himself, he stepped into Raistlin's tent.

A candle burned on a table, near a spellbook that had been left open—the archmage had obviously been expecting to return to his studies soon after dinner. A middle-aged, battle-scarred dwarf—Caramon recognized him as one of Reghar's staff—crouched in the shadows near the bed. A guard beside the entrance saluted when Caramon entered.

"Wait outside," Caramon ordered, and the guard left.

"He won't let us touch 'im," the dwarf said laconically, nodding toward Raistlin. "Wound's gotta be dressed. Won't help much, of course. But it might hold some of 'im inside for a bit."

"I'll tend to him," Caramon said harshly.

Hands on his knees, the dwarf shoved himself up. Hesitating, he cleared his throat as if wondering whether or not to speak. Decision made, he squinted up at Caramon with shrewd, bright eyes.

"Reghar said I was to tell you. If you want me to do it . . . you know—end it quick, I've done it afore. Sort of a knack I've got. I'm a butcher by trade, you see—"

"Get out."

The dwarf shrugged. "As you say. Up to you. If it was my brother, though—"

"Get out!" Caramon repeated softly. He did not look at the dwarf as he left, nor even hear the sounds of his heavy boots. All his senses were concentrated on his twin.

Raistlin lay on his bed, still dressed, his hands clenched over the horrible wound. Stained black with blood, the mage's robes and flesh were gummed together in a ghastly mass. And he was in agony. Rolling involuntarily back and forth upon the bed, every breath the mage exhaled was a low, incoherent moan of pain. Every breath he drew in was bubbling torture.

But to Caramon, the most awful sight of all was his brother's glittering eyes, staring at him, aware of him, as he moved nearer the bed. Raistlin was conscious.

Kneeling down beside his brother's bed, Caramon laid a hand upon his twin's feverish head. "Why didn't you let them send for Crysania?" he asked softly.

Raistlin grimaced. Gritting his teeth, he forced the words out through blood-stained lips. "Paladine . . . will . . . not . . . heal . . . me!" The last was a gasp, ending in a strangled scream.

Caramon stared at him, confused. "But—you're dying! You *can't* die! You said—"

Raistlin's eyes rolled, his head tossed. Blood trickled from his mouth. "Time . . . altered. . . . All . . . changed!"

"But—"

"Leave me! Let me die!" Raistlin shrieked in anger and pain, his body writhing.

Caramon shuddered. He tried to look upon his brother with pity, but the face, gaunt and twisted in suffering, was not a face he knew.

The mask of wisdom and intelligence had been stripped away, revealing the splintered lines of pride, ambition, avarice, and unfeeling cruelty beneath. It was as if Caramon, seeing a face he had known always, were seeing his twin for the first time.

Perhaps, Caramon thought, Dalamar saw this face in the Tower of High Sorcery as Raistlin burned holes in his flesh with his bare hands. Perhaps Fistandantilus, too, saw the face as he died. . . .

Repulsed, his very soul shaken with horror, Caramon tore his gaze from that hideous, skull-like visage and, hardening his own expression, reached out his hand. "At least let me dress the wound."

Raistlin shook his head vehemently. A blood-covered hand wrenched itself free from holding his very life inside him to clutch at Caramon's arm. "No! End it! I have failed. The gods are laughing. I can't . . . bear . . ."

Caramon stared at him. Suddenly, irrationally, anger took hold of the big man—anger that rose from years of sarcastic gibes and thankless servitude. Anger that had seen friends die because of this man. Anger that had seen himself nearly destroyed. Anger that had seen love devoured, love denied. Reaching out his hand, Caramon grasped hold of the black robes and jerked his brother's head up off the pillow.

"No, by the gods," Caramon shouted with a voice that literally shook with rage. "No, you will not die! Do you hear me?" His eyes narrowed. "You will not die, *my brother*! All your life, you have lived only for yourself. Now, even in your death, you seek the easy way out—for you! You'd leave me trapped here without a second's thought. You'd leave Crysania! No, brother! You *will* live, damn you! You'll live to send me back home. What you do with yourself after that is your concern."

Raistlin looked at Caramon and, despite his pain, a gruesome parody of a smile touched his lips. It almost seemed he might have laughed, but a bubble of blood burst in his mouth instead. Caramon loosened his hold of his brother's robes, almost but not quite, hurling him backward. Raistlin collapsed back upon the pillow. His burning eyes devoured Caramon. At that moment the only life in them was bitter hatred and rage.

"I'm going to tell Crysania," Caramon said grimly, rising to his feet, ignoring Raistlin's glare of fury. "At least she must have the chance to try to heal you. Yes, if looks could kill, I know I'd be dead right now. But, listen to me, Raistlin or Fistandantilus or whoever you are—if it is Paladine's will that you die before you can commit greater harm in this world, then so be it. I'll accept that fate and so will Crysania. But if it is his will that you live, we'll accept that, too—and so will you!"

Raistlin, his strength nearly spent, kept hold of his bloody clasp around Caramon's arm, clutching at him with fingers already seeming to stiffen in death.

Firmly, his lips pressed together, Caramon detached his brother's hand. Rising to his feet, he left his brother's bedside hearing, behind him, a ragged moan of agonized torment. Caramon hesitated, that moan going straight to his heart. Then he thought of Tika, he thought of home. . . .

Caramon kept walking. Stepping outside into the night, heading quickly for Crysania's tent, the big warrior glanced to one side and saw the dwarf, standing nonchalantly in the shadows, whittling a piece of wood with a sharp knife.

Reaching into his armor, Caramon withdrew the piece of parchment. He had no need to reread it. The words were few and simple.

The wizard has betrayed you and the army. Send a messenger to Thorbardin to learn the truth.

Caramon tossed the parchment upon the ground.

What a cruel joke!
What a cruel and twisted joke!

Through the hideous torment of his pain, Raistlin could hear the laughter of the gods. To offer him salvation with one hand and snatch it away with the other! How they must revel in his defeat!

Raistlin's tortured body twisted in spasms and so did his soul, writhing in impotent rage, burning with the knowledge that he had failed.

Weak and puny human! he heard the voices of the gods shout. Thus do we remind you of your mortality!

He would not face Paladine's triumph. To see the god sneering at him, glorying in his downfall—no! Better to die swiftly, let his soul seek what dark refuge it could find. But that bastard brother of his, that other half of him, the half he envied and despised, the half he should have been—by rights. To deny him this . . . this last blessed solace. . . .

Pain convulsed his body. "Caramon!" Raistlin cried alone into the darkness. "Caramon, I need you! Caramon, don't leave me!" He sobbed, clutching his stomach, curling up in a tight ball. "Don't leave me . . . to face this . . . alone!"

And then his mind lost the thread of its consciousness. Visions came to the mage as his life spilled out from between his fingers. Dark dragon wings, a broken dragon orb . . . Tasslehoff . . . a gnome . . .

My salvation . . .

My death . . .

Bright, white light, pure and cold and sharp as a sword, pierced the mage's mind. Cringing, he tried to escape, tried to submerge himself in warm and soothing darkness. He could hear himself begging with Caramon to kill him and end the pain, end the bright and stabbing light.

Raistlin heard himself say those words, but he had no knowledge of himself speaking. He knew he spoke only because, in the reflection of the bright, pure light, he saw his brother turn away from him.

The light shone more brightly and it became a face of light, a beautiful, calm, pure face with dark, cool, gray eyes. Cold hands touched his burning skin.

"Let me heal you."

The light hurt, worse than the pain of steel. Screaming, twisting, Raistlin tried to escape, but the hands held him firmly.

"Let me heal you."

"Get . . . away! . . ."

"Let me heal you!"

Weariness, a vast weariness, came over Raistlin. He was tired of fighting—fighting the pain, fighting the ridicule, fighting the torment he'd lived with all his life.

Very well. Let the god laugh. He's earned it, after all, Raistlin thought bitterly. Let him refuse to heal me. And then I'll rest in the darkness. . . . the soothing darkness. . . .

Shutting his eyes, shutting them tightly against the light, Raistlin waited for the laughter—

—and saw, suddenly, the face of the god.

Caramon stood outside in the shadows of his brother's tent, his aching head in his hands. Raistlin's tortured pleas for death cut through him. Finally, he could stand it no longer. The cleric had obviously failed. Grasping the hilt of his sword, Caramon entered the tent and walked toward the bed.

At that moment, Raistlin's cries ceased.

Lady Crysania slumped forward over his body, her head falling onto the mage's chest.

He's dead! Caramon thought. Raistlin's dead.

Staring at his brother's face, he did not feel grief. Instead, he felt a kind of horror stealing over him at the sight, thinking, What a grotesque mask for death to wear!

Raistlin's face was rigid as a corpse's, his mouth gaped open, no sound came from it. The skin was livid. The sightless eyes, fixed in the sunken cheeks, stared straight before him.

Taking a step nearer, so numb he was unable to feel grief or sorrow or relief, Caramon looked closer at that strange expression on the dead man's face and then realized, with a riveting shock, that Raistlin was *not* dead! The wide, fixed eyes stared at this world sightlessly, but that was only because they were seeing another.

A whimpering cry shook the mage's body, more dreadful

to hear than his screams of agony. His head moved slightly, his lips parted, his throat worked but made no sound.

And then Raistlin's eyes closed. His head lolled to one side, the writhing muscles relaxed. The look of pain faded, leaving his face drawn, pallid. He drew a deep breath, let it out with a sigh, drew another. . . .

Jolted by what he had seen, uncertain whether he should feel thankful or only more deeply grieved to know his brother lived, Caramon watched life return to his twin's torn and bleeding body.

Slowly shaking off the paralyzed feeling that comes sometimes to one awakened suddenly from a deep sleep, Caramon knelt beside Crysania and, grasping her gently, helped her stand. She stared at him, blinking, without recognition. Then her gaze shifted immediately to Raistlin. A smile crossed her face. Closing her eyes, she murmured a prayer of thankfulness. Then, pressing her hand to her side, she sagged against Caramon. There was fresh blood visible on her white robes.

"You should heal yourself," Caramon said, helping her from the tent, his strong arm supporting her faltering footsteps.

She looked up at him and, though weak, her face was beautiful in its calm triumph.

"Perhaps tomorrow," she answered softly. "This night, a greater victory is mine. Don't you see? This is the answer to my prayers."

Looking at her peaceful, serene beauty, Caramon felt tears come to his eyes.

"So this is your answer?" he asked gruffly, glancing out over the camp. The fires had burned down to heaps of ash and coal. Out of the corner of his eye, Caramon saw someone go running off, and he knew that the news would be quickly spread that the wizard and the witch, between them, had somehow managed to restore the dead to life.

Caramon felt bile rise in his mouth. He could picture the talk, the excitement, the questions, the speculations, the dark looks and shaking heads, and his soul shrank from it. He wanted only to go to bed and sleep and forget everything.

But Crysania was talking. "This is your answer, too, Caramon," she said fervently. "This is the sign from the gods we have both sought." Stopping, she turned to face him, looking up at him earnestly. "Are you still as blind as you were in the Tower? Don't you yet believe? We placed the matter in Paladine's hands and the god has spoken. Raistlin was meant to live. He was meant to do this great deed. Together, he and I and you, if you will join us, will fight and overcome evil as I have fought and overcome death this night!"

Caramon stared at her. Then his head bowed, his shoulders slumped. I don't want to fight evil, he thought wearily. I just want to go home. Is that too much to ask?

Lifting his hand, he began to rub his throbbing temple. And then he stopped, seeing in the slowly brightening light of dawn the marks of his brother's bloody fingers still upon his arm. "I'm posting a guard inside your tent," he said harshly. "Get some sleep. . . ."

He turned away.

"Caramon," Crysania called.

"What?" He stopped with a sigh.

"You will feel better in the morning. I will pray for you tonight. Good night, my friend. Remember to thank Paladine for his grace in granting your brother his life."

"Yeah, sure," Caramon mumbled. Feeling uncomfortable, his headache growing worse, and knowing that he was soon going to be violently sick, he left Crysania and stumbled back to his tent.

Here, by himself, in the darkness, he was sick, retching in a corner until he no longer had anything left to bring up. Then, falling down upon his bed, he gave himself up at last to pain and to exhaustion.

But as the darkness closed mercifully over him, he remembered Crysania's words—"thank Paladine for your brother's life."

The memory of Raistlin's stricken face floated before Caramon, and the prayer stuck in his throat.

Donkey (A) follows Carrot (B) turning Main Shaft (C) which activates cogs and pulleys; Top cog (D) winds rope (E) which lifts or lowers cage (F).

Problem: In certain positions, cage squashes donkey.

apping lightly on the guest stone that stood outside Duncan's dwelling, Kharas waited nervously for the answer. It came soon. The door opened, and there stood his king.

"Enter and welcome, Kharas," Duncan said, reaching out and pulling the dwarf.

Flushing in embarrassment, Kharas stepped inside his king's dwelling place. Smiling at him kindly, to put him at ease, Duncan led the way through his house to his private study.

Built far underground, in the heart of the mountain kingdom, Duncan's home was a complex maze of rooms and tunnels filled with the heavy, dark, solid wood furniture that dwarves admire. Though larger and roomier than most homes in Thorbardin, in all other respects Duncan's dwelling was almost exactly like the dwelling of every other dwarf. It would have been considered the height of bad taste had it been otherwise. Just because Duncan was king didn't give him the right to put on airs. So, though he kept a staff of servants, he answered his own door and served his guests with his own hands. A widower, he lived in the house with his two sons, who were still unmarried, both being young (only eighty or so).

The study Kharas entered was obviously Duncan's favorite room. Battle-axes and shields decorated the walls, along with a fine assortment of captured hobgoblin swords with their curved blades, a minotaur trident won by some distant ancestor, and, of course, hammers and chisels and stone-working tools.

Duncan made his guest comfortable with true dwarvish hospitality, offering him the best chair, pouring out the ale, and stirring up the fire. Kharas had been here before, of course; many times, in fact. But now he felt uncomfortable and ill at ease, as though he had entered the house of a stranger. Perhaps it was because Duncan, though he treated his friend with his usual courtesy, occasionally regarded the beardless dwarf with an odd, penetrating gaze.

Noticing this unusual look in Duncan's eyes, Kharas found it impossible to relax and sat fidgeting in his chair, nervously wiping the foam from his mouth with the back of his hand while waiting for the formalities to end.

They did, quickly. Pouring himself a mug of ale, Duncan drained it at a sitting. Then, placing the mug on the table by his arm, he stroked his beard, staring at Kharas with a dark, somber expression.

"Kharas," he said finally, "you told us the wizard was dead."

"Yes, Thane," Kharas replied, startled. "It was a mortal blow I struck him. No man could have survived—"

"He did," Duncan replied shortly.

Kharas scowled. "Are you accusing me—"

Now it was Duncan who flushed. "No, my friend! Far be it. I am certain that, whatever may have happened, you truly believed you killed him." Duncan sighed heavily. "But our scouts report seeing him in camp. He was wounded, apparently. At least, he could no longer ride. The army moved on to Zhaman, however, carrying the wizard with them in a cart."

"Thane!" Kharas protested, his face flushing in anger. "I swear to you! His blood washed over my hands! I yanked the sword from his body. By Reorx!" The dwarf shuddered. "I saw the death look in his eyes!"

"I don't doubt you, son!" Duncan said earnestly, reaching out to pat the young hero's shoulder. "I never heard of anyone surviving a wound such as you described—except in the old days, of course, when clerics still walked the land."

Like all other true clerics, dwarven clerics had also vanished right before the Cataclysm. Unlike other races on Krynn, the dwarves, however, never abandoned their belief in their ancient god, Reorx, the Forger of the World. Although the dwarves were upset with Reorx for causing the Cataclysm, their belief in their god was too deeply ingrained and too much a part of their culture simply to toss out after one minor infraction on the god's part. Still, they were angered enough to no longer worship him openly.

"Have you any idea how this might have happened?" Duncan asked, frowning.

"No, Thane," Kharas said heavily. "But I did wonder why we hadn't received a reply from General Caramon." He pondered. "Has anyone questioned those two prisoners we brought back? They might know something."

"A kender and a gnome?" Duncan snorted. "Bah! What could either of those two possibly know? Besides, there is no need to question them. I am not particularly interested in the wizard anyway. In fact, the reason I called you here to tell you this news, Kharas, was to insist that now you forget this talk of peace and concentrate on the war."

"There is more to those two than beards, Thane," Kharas muttered, quoting an old expression. It was obvious he hadn't heard a word. "I think you should—"

"I know what you think," Duncan said grimly. "Apparitions, conjured up by the wizard. And I tell you that's ridiculous! What self-respecting wizard would ever conjure up a kender? No, they're servants or something, most likely. It was dark and confused in there. You said so yourself."

"I'm not sure," Kharas replied, his voice soft. "If you had

seen the mage's face when he looked at them! It was the face of one who walks the plains and suddenly sees a coffer of gold and jewels lying in the sand at his feet. Give me leave, Thane," Kharas said eagerly. "Let me bring them before you. Talk to them, that's all I ask!"

Duncan heaved a vast sigh, glaring at Kharas gloomily.

"Very well," he snapped. "I don't suppose it can hurt. But"—Duncan studied Kharas shrewdly—"if this proves to be nothing, will you promise me to give up this wild notion and concentrate on the business of war? It will be a hard fight, son," Duncan added more gently, seeing the look of true grief on his young hero's beardless face. "We need you, Kharas."

"Aye, Thane," Kharas said steadily. "I'll agree. If this proves to be nothing."

With a gruff nod, Duncan yelled for his guards and stumped out of the house, followed more slowly by a thoughtful Kharas.

Traversing the vast underground dwarven kingdom, winding down streets here and up streets there, crossing the Urkhan Sea by boat, they eventually came to the first level of the dungeons. Here were held prisoners who had committed minor crimes and infractions—debtors, a young dwarf who had spoken disrespectfully to an elder, poachers, and several drunks, sleeping off overnight revels. Here, too, were held the kender and the gnome.

At least, they had been—last night.

"It all comes," said Tasslehoff Burrfoot as the dwarven guard prodded him along, "of not having a map."

"I thought you said you'd been here before," Gnimsh grumbled peevishly.

"Not *before*," Tas corrected. "*After*. Or maybe *later* would be a better word. About two hundred years later, as near as I can figure. It's quite a fascinating story, actually. I came here with some friends of mine. Let's see . . . that was right after Goldmoon and Riverwind were married and before we went to Tarsis. Or was it after we went to Tarsis?" Tas pondered. "No, it couldn't have been, because Tarsis was where the building fell on me and—"

"I'veheardthatstory!" Gnimsh snapped.

"What?" Tas blinked.

"I've ... heard ... it!" Gnimsh shouted loudly. His thin, gnomish voice echoed in the underground chamber, causing several passersby to glare at him sternly. Their faces grim, the dwarven guards hurried their recaptured prisoners along.

"Oh," Tas said, crestfallen. Then the kender cheered up. "But the king hasn't and we're being taken to see him. He'll probably be quite interested. . . ."

"You said we weren't supposed to say anything about coming from the future," Gnimsh said in a loud whisper, his long leather apron flapping about his feet. "We're supposed to act like we belong here, remember?"

"That was when I thought everything would go right," Tas said with a sigh. "And everything was going right. The device worked, we escaped from the Abyss—"

"They let us escape—" Gnimsh pointed out.

"Well, whatever," Tas said, irritated at the reminder. "Anyway, we *got out*, which is all that counts. And the magical device worked, just like you said"—Gnimsh smiled happily and nodded—"and we found Caramon. Just like you said— the device was cali-cala-whatever to return to him—"

"Calibrated," Gnimsh interrupted.

"—but then"—Tas chewed nervously on the end of his top-knot of hair—"everything went all wrong, somehow. Raistlin stabbed, maybe dead. The dwarves hauling us off without ever giving me a chance to tell them they were making a serious mistake."

The kender trudged along, pondering deeply. Finally, he shook his head. "I've thought it over, Gnimsh. I know it's a desperate act and one I wouldn't ordinarily resort to, but I don't think we have any choice. The situation has gotten completely out of hand." Tas heaved a solemn sigh. "I think we should tell the truth."

Gnimsh appeared extremely alarmed at this drastic action, so alarmed, in fact, that he tripped over his apron and fell flat on the ground. The guards, neither of whom spoke Common, hauled him to his feet and dragged the gnome the rest of way, coming at last to a halt before a great, wooden door. Here other guards, eyeing the kender and the gnome with disgust, shoved on the doors, slowly pushing them open.

"Oh, I've been here!" Tas said suddenly. "Now I know where we are."

"*That's* a big help," Gnimsh muttered.

"The Hall of Audience," Tas continued. "The last time we were here, Tanis got sick. He's an elf, you know. Well, half an elf, anyway, and he hated living underground." The kender sighed again. "I wish Tanis was here now. He'd know what to do. I wish *someone* wise was here now."

The guards shoved them inside the great hall. "At least," Tas said to Gnimsh softly, "we're not alone. At least we've got each other."

"Tasslehoff Burrfoot," said the kender, bowing before the king of the dwarves, then bowing again to each of the thanes seated in the stone seats behind and on a lower level than Duncan's throne. "And this is—"

The gnome pushed forward eagerly. "Gnimshmari—"

"Gnimsh!" Tas said loudly, stepping on the gnome's foot as Gnimsh paused for breath. "Let me do the talking!" the kender scolded in an audible whisper.

Scowling, Gnimsh lapsed into hurt silence as Tas looked around the hall brightly.

"Gee, you're not planning a lot in the way of renovation the next two hundred years, are you? It's going to look just about the same. Except I seem to remember that crack there— no, over there. Yes, that one. It's going to get quite a bit bigger in the future. You might want to—"

"Where do you come from, kender?" Duncan growled.

"Solace," said Tas, remembering he was telling the truth. "Oh, don't worry if you've never heard of it. It doesn't exist yet. They hadn't heard of it in Istar, either, but that didn't matter so much because no one cared about anything in Istar that wasn't there. In Istar, I mean. Solace is north of Haven, which isn't there either but will be sooner than Solace, if you take my meaning."

Duncan, leaning forward, glowered at Tas alarmingly from beneath his thick eyebrows. "You're lying."

"I am not!" Tas said indignantly. "We came here using a magical device that I had borrowed—sort of—from a friend. It worked fine when I had it, but then I accidentally broke it. Well, actually that wasn't my fault. But that's another story. At any rate, I survived the Cataclysm and ended up in the Abyss. *Not* a nice place. Anyway, I met Gnimsh in the Abyss and he fixed it. The device, I mean, not the Abyss. He's really a wonderful fellow," Tas continued confidentially, patting Gnimsh on the shoulder. "He's a gnome, all right, but his inventions work."

"So—you *are* from the Abyss!" Kharas said sternly. "You admit it! Apparitions from the Realms of Darkness! The black-robed wizard conjured you, and you came at his bidding."

This startling accusation actually rendered the kender speechless.

"Wh-wh"—Tas sputtered for a moment incoherently, then found his voice—"I've never been so insulted! Except perhaps when the guard in Istar referred to me as a—a cut-cutpur—well, never mind. To say nothing of the fact that if Raistlin was going to conjure up anything, I certainly don't think it would be us. Which reminds me!" Tas glared back sternly at Kharas. "Why did you go and kill him like that? I mean, maybe he *wasn't* what you might call a really nice person. And maybe he *did* try to kill me by making me break the magical device and then leaving me behind in Istar for the gods to drop a fiery mountain on. But"—Tas sighed wistfully—"he was certainly one of the most *interesting* people I've ever known."

"Your wizard isn't dead, as you well know, apparition!" Duncan growled.

"Look, I'm not an appari—Not dead?" Tas's face lit up. "Truly? Even after you stabbed him like that and all the blood and everything and—Oh! I know how! Crysania! Of course! Lady Crysania!"

"Ah, the witch!" Kharas said softly, almost to himself as the thanes began to mutter among themselves.

"Well, she is kind of cold and impersonal sometimes," Tas said, shocked, "but I certainly don't think that gives you any right to call her names! She's a cleric of Paladine, after all."

"Cleric!" The thanes began to laugh.

"There's your answer," Duncan said to Kharas, ignoring the kender. "Witchcraft."

"You are right, of course, Thane," Kharas said, frowning, "but—"

"Look," Tas begged, "if you'd just let me go! I keep trying to tell you dwarves. This is all a dreadful mistake! I've got to get to Caramon!"

That caused a reaction. The thanes immediately hushed.

"You know General Caramon?" Kharas asked dubiously.

"General?" Tas repeated. "Wow! Won't Tanis be surprised to hear that? General Caramon! Tika would laugh. . . . Uh, of course I know Cara—General Caramon," Tas continued hurriedly, seeing Duncan's eyebrows coming together again. "He's my best friend. And if you'll only listen to what I'm trying to tell you, Gnimsh and I came here with the magical device to find Caramon and take him home. He doesn't want to be here, I'm sure. You see, Gnimsh fixed the device so that it will take more than one person—"

"Take him home where?" Duncan growled. "The Abyss? Perhaps the wizard conjured him up, too!"

"No!" Tas snapped, beginning to lose patience. "Take him home to Solace, of course. And Raistlin, too, if he wants to go. I can't imagine what they're doing here, in fact. Raistlin couldn't stand Thorbardin the last time we were here, which will be in about two hundred years. He spent the whole time coughing and complaining about the damp. Flint said—Flint Fireforge, that is, an old friend of mine—"

"Fireforge!" Duncan actually jumped up from his throne, glaring at the kender. "You're a friend of Fireforge?"

"Well, you needn't get so worked up," Tas said, somewhat startled. "Flint had his faults, of course—always grumbling and accusing people of stealing things when I was *truly* intending to put that bracelet right back where I found it, but that doesn't mean you—"

"Fireforge," Duncan said grimly, "is the leader of our enemies. Or didn't you know that?"

"No," said Tas with interest, "I didn't. Oh, but I'm sure it couldn't be the same Fireforge," he added after some thought. "Flint won't be born for at least another fifty years. Maybe it's his father. Raistlin says—"

"Raistlin? Who is this Raistlin?" Duncan demanded.

Tasslehoff fixed the dwarf with a stern eye. "You're not paying attention. Raistlin is the wizard. The one you killed— Er, the one you didn't kill. The one you thought you killed but didn't."

"His name isn't Raistlin. It's Fistandantilus!" Duncan snorted. Then, his face grim, the dwarven king resumed his seat. "So," he said, looking at the kender from beneath his bushy eyebrows, "you're planning to take this wizard who was healed by a cleric when there are no clerics in this world and a general you claim is your best friend back to a place that doesn't exist to meet our enemy who hasn't been born yet using a device, built by a gnome, which actually works?"

"Right!" cried Tas triumphantly. "You see there! Look what you can learn when you just listen!"

Gnimsh nodded emphatically.

"Guards! Take them away!" Duncan snarled. Spinning around on his heel, he looked at Kharas coldly. "You gave me your word. I'll expect to see you in the War Council room in ten minutes."

"But, Thane! If he truly knows General Caramon—"

"Enough!" Duncan was in a rage. "War is coming, Kharas. All your honor and all your noble yammering about slaying kinsmen can't stop it! And you will be out there on the field of battle or you can take your face that shames us all and hide it in the dungeons along with the rest of the traitors to our people—the Dewar! Which will it be?"

"I serve you, of course, Thane," Kharas said, his face rigid. "I have pledged my life."

"See you remember that!" Duncan snapped. "And to keep your thoughts from wandering, I am ordering that you be confined to your quarters except to attend the War Council meetings and that, further, these two"—he waved at Tas and Gnimsh—"are to be imprisoned and their whereabouts kept secret until after the war has ended. Death come upon the head of any who defy this command."

The thanes glanced at each other, nodding approvingly, though one muttered that it was too late. The guards grabbed hold of Gnimsh and Tas, the kender still protesting volubly as they led him away.

"I was telling the truth," he wailed. "You've got to believe me! I know it sounds funny, but, you see, I—I'm not quite used to—uh—telling the truth! But give me a while. I'm sure I'll get the hang of it someday. . . ."

Tasslehoff wouldn't have believed it was possible to go down so far beneath the surface of the world as the guards were taking them if his own feet hadn't walked it. He remembered once Flint telling him once that Reorx lived down here, forging the world with his great hammer.

"A nice, cheerful sort of person *he* must be," Tas grumbled, shivering in the cold until his teeth chattered. "At least if Reorx was forging the world, you'd think it'd be warmer."

"Trustdwarves," muttered Gnimsh.

"What?" It seemed to the kender that he'd spent the last half of his life beginning every sentence he spoke to the gnome with "what?"

"I said trust dwarves!" Gnimsh returned loudly. "Instead of building their homes in active volcanoes, which, though slightly unstable, provide an excellent source of heat, they build theirs in old dead mountains." He shook his wispy-haired head. "Hard to believe we're cousins."

Tas didn't answer, being preoccupied with other matters—like how do we get out of this one, where do we go if we do get out, and when are they likely to serve dinner? There seeming to be no immediate answers to any of these (including dinner), the kender lapsed into a gloomy silence.

Oh, there was one rather exciting moment—when they were lowered down a narrow rocky tunnel that had been bored straight down into the mountain. The device they used to lower people down this tunnel was called a "lift" by the gnomes, according to Gnimsh. ("Isn't 'lift' an inappropriate name for it when it's going *down*?" Tas pointed out, but the gnome ignored him.)

Since no immediate solution to his problems appeared forthcoming, Tas decided not to waste his time in this interesting place moping about. He therefore enjoyed the journey in the lift thoroughly, though it was rather uncomfortable in spots when the rickety, wooden device—operated by muscular dwarves pulling on huge lengths of rope—bumped against the side of the rocky tunnel as it was being lowered, jouncing the occupants about and inflicting numerous cuts and bruises on those inside.

This proved highly entertaining, especially as the dwarven guards accompanying Tas and Gnimsh shook their fists, swearing roundly in dwarven at the operators up above them.

As for the gnome, Gnimsh was plunged into a state of excitement impossible to believe. Whipping out a stub of charcoal and borrowing one of Tas's handkerchiefs, he plopped himself down on the floor of the lift and immediately began to draw plans for a New Improved Lift.

"Pulleyscablessteam," he yammered to himself happily, busily sketching what looked to Tas like a giant lobster trap on wheels. "Updownupdown. Whatfloor? Steptotherear. Capacity:thirtytwo. Stuck? Alarms! Bellswhistleshorns."

When they eventually reached ground level, Tas tried to watch carefully to see where they were going (so that they could leave, even if he didn't have a map), but Gnimsh was hanging onto him, pointing to his sketch and explaining it to him in detail.

"Yes, Gnimsh. Isn't that interesting?" Tas said, only half-listening to the gnome as his heart sank even lower than where they were standing. "Soothing music by a piper in the corner? Yes, Gnimsh, that's a great idea."

Gazing around as their guards prodded them forward, Tas sighed. Not only did this place look as boring as the Abyss, it had the added disadvantage of smelling even worse. Row after row of large, crude prison cells lined the rocky walls. Lit by torches that smoked in the foul, thin air, the cells were filled to capacity with dwarves.

Tas gazed at them in growing confusion as they walked down the narrow aisle between cell blocks. These dwarves didn't look like criminals. There were males, females, even children crammed inside the cells. Crouched on filthy blankets, huddled on battered stools, they stared glumly out from behind the bars.

"Hey!" Tas said, tugging at the sleeve of a guard. The kender spoke some dwarven, having picked it up from Flint. "What is all this?" he asked, waving his hand. "Why are all these people in here?" (At least that's what he hoped he said. There was every possibility he might have inadvertently asked the way to the nearest alehouse.)

But the guard, glowering at him, only said, "Dewar."

CHAPTER II

"Dewar?" Tas repeated blankly.

The guard, however, refused to elaborate but prodded Tas on ahead with a vicious shove. Tas stumbled, then kept walking, glancing about, trying to figure out what was going on. Gnimsh, meanwhile, apparently seized by another fit of inspiration, was going on about "hydraulics."

Tas pondered. Dewar, he thought, trying to remember where he'd heard that word. Suddenly, he came up with the answer.

"The dark dwarves!" he said. "Of course! I remember! They fought for the Dragon Highlord. But, they didn't live down here the last time—or I suppose it will be the next time—we were here. Or will come here. Drat, what a muddle. Surely they don't live in prison cells, though. Hey"—Tas tapped the dwarf again—"what did they do! I mean, to get thrown in jail?"

"Traitors!" the dwarf snapped. Reaching a cell at the far end of the aisle, he drew out a key, inserted it into the lock, and swung the door open.

Peering inside, Tas saw about twenty or thirty Dewar crowded into the cell. Some lay lethargically on the floor, others sat against the wall, sleeping. One group, crouched together off in a corner, were talking in low voices when the guard arrived. They quit immediately as soon as the cell door opened. There were no women or children in this cell, only males; and they regarded Tas, the gnome, and the guard with dark, hate-filled eyes.

Tas grabbed Gnimsh just as the gnome—still yammering about people getting stuck between floors—was just about to walk absentmindedly into the cell.

"Well, well," Tas said to the dwarven guard as he dragged Gnimsh back to stand beside him, "this tour was quite—er—entertaining. Now, if you'll just take us back to our cells, which were, I must say, *very nice* cells—so light and airy and roomy—I think I can safely promise that my partner and I won't be taking any more unauthorized excursions into your city, though it *is* an extremely interesting place and I'd like to see more of it. I—"

But the dwarf, with a rough shove of his hand, pushed the kender into the cell, sending him sprawling.

"I wish you'd make up your mind," Gnimsh snapped irritably, stumbling inside after Tas. "Are we going in or out?"

"I guess we're in," Tas said ruefully, sitting up and looking doubtfully at the Dewar, who were staring back in silence. The guards' heavy boots could be heard stumping back up the corridor, accompanied by shouted obscenities and threats from the surrounding cells.

"Hello," Tas said, smiling in friendly fashion, but *not* offering to shake hands. "I'm Tasslehoff Burrfoot and this is my friend, Gnimsh, and it looks like we're going to be cellmates, doesn't it now? So, what's your names? Er, now, I say, that isn't very nice. . . ."

Tas drew himself up, glaring sternly at one of the Dewar, who had risen to his feet and was approaching them.

A tall dwarf, his face was nearly invisible beneath a thick matting of tangled hair and beard. He grinned suddenly. There was a flash of steel and a large knife appeared in his hand. Shuffling forward, he advanced upon the kender, who retreated as far as possible into a corner, dragging Gnimsh with him.

"Whoarethesepeople?" Gnimsh squeaked in alarm, having finally taken note of their dismal surroundings.

Before Tas could answer, the Dewar had the kender by the neck and was holding the knife to his throat.

This is it! Tas thought with regret. I'm dead this time for sure. Flint will get a chuckle out of this one!

But the dark dwarf's knife inched right past Tas's face. Reaching his shoulder, the dark dwarf expertly cut through the straps of Tas's pouches, sending them and their contents tumbling to the floor.

Instantly, chaos broke out in the cell as the Dewar leaped for them. The dwarf with the knife grabbed as many as he could, slashing and hacking at his fellows, trying to drive them back. Everything vanished within seconds.

Clutching the kender's belongings, the Dewar immediately sat down and began rummaging through them. The dark dwarf with the knife had managed to make the richest haul. Clutching his booty to his chest, he returned to a place against the back of the cell, where he and his friends immediately began to shake the contents of the pouches onto the floor.

Gasping in relief, Tas sank down to the cold, stone floor. But it was a worried sigh of relief, nonetheless, for Tas figured that when the pouches had lost their appeal, the Dewar would get the bright idea of searching *them* next.

"And we'll certainly be a lot easier to search if we're corpses," he muttered to himself. That led, however, to a sudden thought.

"Gnimsh!" he whispered urgently. "The magical device! Where is it?"

Gnimsh, blinking, patted one pocket in his leather apron and shook his head. Patting another, he pulled out a T-square and a bit of charcoal. He examined these carefully for a moment then, seeing that neither was the magical device, stuffed them back into his pockets. Tas was seriously considering throttling him when, with a triumphant smile, the gnome reached into his boot and pulled out the magical device.

During their last incarceration, Gnimsh had managed to make the device collapse again. Now it had resumed the size and shape of a rather ordinary, nondescript pendant instead of the intricate and beautiful sceptre that it resembled when fully extended.

"Keep it hidden!" Tas warned. Glancing at the Dewar, he saw that they were absorbed in fighting over what they'd found in his pouches. "Gnimsh," he whispered, "this thing worked to get us out of the Abyss and you said it was cali-calo-caliwhatever'd to go straight to Caramon, since he was the one Par-Salian gave it to. Now, I really don't want it to take us anywhere in *time* again, but do you think it would work for, say, just a short hop? If Caramon is general of that army, he can't be far from here."

"That's a great idea!" Gnimsh's eyes began to shine. "Just a minute, let me think. . . ."

But they were too late. Tas felt a touch on his shoulder. His heart leaping into his throat, the kender whirled around with what he hoped was the Grim Expression of a Hardened Killer on his face. Apparently it was for the Dewar who had touched him stumbled back in terror hurriedly flinging his hands up for protection.

Noting that this was a youngish-appearing dwarf with a halfway sane look in his eye, Tasslehoff sighed and relaxed, while the Dewar, seeing that the kender wasn't going to eat him alive, quit shaking and looked at him hopefully.

"What is it?" Tas asked in dwarven. "What do you want?"

"Come. You come." The Dewar made a beckoning gesture. Then, seeing Tas frown, he pointed, then beckoned again, hedging back farther into the cell.

Tas rose cautiously to his feet. "Stay here, Gnimsh," he said. But the gnome wasn't listening. Muttering happily to himself, Gnimsh was occupied with twisting and turning little somethings on the device.

Curious, Tas crept after the Dewar. Maybe this fellow had discovered the way out. Maybe he'd been digging a tunnel . . . .

The Dewar, still motioning, led the kender to the center of the cell. Here, he stopped and pointed. "Help?" he said hopefully.

Tas, looking down, didn't see a tunnel. What he saw was a Dewar lying on a blanket. The dwarf's face was covered with sweat, his hair and beard were soaking wet. His eyes were closed and his body jerked and twitched spasmodically. At the sight, Tas began to shiver. He glanced around the cell. Then, his gaze coming back to the young Dewar, he regretfully shook his head.

"No," Tas said gently, "I'm sorry. There's . . . nothing I can do. I—I'm sorry." He shrugged helplessly.

The Dewar seemed to understand, for he sank back down beside the sick dwarf, his head bowed disconsolately.

Tas crept back to where Gnimsh was sitting, feeling all numb inside. Slumping down into the corner, he stared into the dark cell, seeing and hearing what he should have seen and heard right away—the wild, incoherent ramblings, cries of pain, cries for water and, here and there, the awful silence of those who lay very, very still.

"Gnimsh," Tas said quietly, "these dwarves are sick. Really sick. I've seen it before in days to come. These dwarves have the plague."

Gnimsh's eyes widened. He almost dropped the magical device.

"Gnimsh," said Tas, trying to speak calmly, "we've got to get out of here fast! The way I see it, the only choices we have down here are dying by knifepoint—which, while undoubtedly interesting, does have its drawbacks, or dying rather slowly and boringly of the plague."

"I think it will work," Gnimsh said, dubiously eyeing the magical device. "Of course, it might take us right back to the Abyss—"

"Not really a *bad* place," Tas said, slowly rising to his feet and helping Gnimsh to his. "Takes a bit getting used to, and I don't suppose *they'd* be wildly happy to see us again, but I think it's definitely worth a try."

"Very well, just let me make an adjustment—"

"Do not touch it!"

The familiar voice came from the shadows and was so stern and commanding that Gnimsh froze in his tracks, his hand clutching the device.

"Raistlin!" cried Tas, staring about wildly. "Raistlin! We're here! We're here!"

"I know where you are," the archmage said coldly, materializing out of the smoky air to stand before them in the cell.

His sudden appearance brought gasps and screams and cries from the Dewar. The one in the corner with the knife snaked to his feet and lunged forward.

"Raistlin, look ou—" Tas shrieked.

Raistlin turned. He did not speak. He did not raise his hand. He simply stared at the dark dwarf. The Dewar's face went ashen. Dropping the knife from nerveless fingers, he shrank back and attempted to hide himself in the shadows. Before turning back to the kender, Raistlin cast a glance around the cell. Silence fell instantly. Even those who were delirious hushed.

Satisfied, Raistlin turned back to Tas.

"—out," Tas finished lamely. Then the kender's face brightened. He clapped his hands. "Oh, Raistlin! It's so good to see you! You're looking really well, too. Especially for having a— er—sword stuck in your—uh—Well, never mind that. And you came to rescue us, didn't you? That's splendid! I—"

"Enough driveling!" Raistlin said coolly. Reaching out a hand, he grabbed Tas and jerked him close. "Now, tell me— where did you come from?"

Tas faltered, staring up into Raistlin's eyes. "I—I'm not sure you're going to believe this. No one else does. But it's the truth, I swear it!"

"Just tell me!" Raistlin snarled, his hand deftly twisting Tasslehoff's collar.

"Right!" Tas gulped and squirmed. "Uh, remember—it helps if you let me breathe occasionally. Now, let's see. I tried to stop the Cataclysm and the device broke. I—I'm sure you didn't mean to," Tas stammered, "but you—uh—seem to have given me the wrong instructions. . . ."

·"I did. Mean to, that is," Raistlin said grimly. "Go on."

"I'd like to, but it's . . . hard to talk without air. . . ."

Raistlin loosened his hold on the kender slightly. Tas drew a deep breath. "Good! Where was I? Oh, yes. I followed Lady Crysania down, down, down into the very bottom part of the Temple in Istar, when it was falling apart, you know? And I saw her go into this room and I knew she must be going to see you, because she said your name, and I was hoping you'd fix the device—"

"Be quick!"

"R-right." Speeding up as much as possible, Tas became nearly incomprehensible. "And then there was a thud behind me and it was Caramon, only he didn't see me, and everything went dark, and when I woke up, you were gone, and I looked up in time to see the gods throw the fiery mountain—" Tas drew a breath. "Now *that* was something. Would you like to hear about—No? Well, some other time.

"I—I guess I must have gone back to sleep again, because I woke up and everything was quiet. I thought I must be dead only I wasn't. I was in the Abyss, where the Temple went after the Cataclysm."

"The Abyss!" Raistlin breathed. His hand trembled.

"*Not* a nice place," Tas said solemnly. "Despite what I said earlier. I met the Queen—" The kender shivered. "I—I don't think I want to talk about that now, if you don't mind." He held out a trembling hand. "But there's her mark, those five little white spots . . . anyway, she said I had to stay down there forever, be-because now she could change history and win the war. And I didn't mean to"— Tas stared pleadingly at Raistlin—"I just wanted to help Caramon. But then, while I was down in the Abyss, I found Gnimsh—"

"The gnome," Raistlin said softly, his eyes on Gnimsh, who was staring at the magic-user in amazement, not daring to move.

"Yes." Tas twisted his head to smile at his friend. "He'd built a time-traveling device that worked—actually worked, think of that! And, whoosh! Here we are!"

"You escaped the Abyss?" Raistlin turned his mirrorlike gaze on the kender.

Tas squirmed uncomfortably. Those last few moments haunted his dreams at night, and kender rarely dreamed. "Uh, sure," he said, smiling up at the archmage in what he hoped was a disarming manner.

It was apparently wasted, however. Raistlin, preoccupied, was regarding the gnome with an expression that suddenly made Tas go cold all over.

"You said the device broke?" Raistlin said softly.

"Yes," Tas swallowed. Feeling Raistlin's hold on him slacken, seeing the mage lost in thought, Tas wriggled slightly, endeavoring to free himself from the mage's grasp. To his surprise, Raistlin let him go, releasing his grip so suddenly that Tas nearly tumbled over backward.

"The device was broken," Raistlin murmured. Suddenly, he stared at Tas intently. "Then—who fixed it?" The archmage's voice was little more than a whisper.

Edging away from Raistlin, Tas hedged. "I—I hope the mages won't be angry. Gnimsh didn't actually *fix* it. You'll tell Par-Salian, won't you, Raistlin? I wouldn't want to get into trouble—well, any *more* trouble with him than I'm in already. We didn't do anything to the device, not really. Gnimsh just— uh—sort of put it back together—the way it was, so that it worked "

"He reassembled it?" Raistlin persisted, that same, strange expression in his eyes.

"Y-yes." With a weak grin, Tas scrambled back to poke Gnimsh in the ribs just as the gnome was about to speak. "Re . . . assembled. That's the word, all right. Reassembled."

"But, Tas—" Gnimsh began loudly. "Don't you remember what happened? I—"

"Just shut up!" Tas whispered. "And let me do the talking. We're in a lot of trouble here! Mages don't like having their devices messed with, even if you did make it better! I'm sure I can make Par-Salian understand that, when I see him. He'll undoubtedly be pleased that you fixed it. After all, it must have been rather bothersome for them, what with the device only transporting one person at a time and all that. I'm sure Par-Salian will see it that way, but I'd rather be the one to tell him—if you take my meaning. Raistlin's kind of . . . well, jumpy about things like that. I don't think he'd understand and, believe me"—with a glance at the mage and a gulp—"this isn't the time to try to explain."

Gnimsh, glancing dubiously at Raistlin, shivered and crowded closer to Tas.

"He's looking at me like he's going to turn me inside out!" the gnome muttered nervously.

"That's how he looks at everyone," Tas whispered back. "You'll get used to it."

No one spoke. In the crowded cell, one of the sick dwarves moaned and cried out in delirium. Tas glanced over at them uneasily, then looked at Raistlin. The magic-user was once again staring at the gnome, that strange, grim, preoccupied look on his pale face.

"Uh, that's really all I can tell you now, Raistlin," Tas said loudly, with another nervous glance at the sick dwarves. "Could we go now? Will you swoosh us out of here the way you used to in Istar? That was great fun and—"

"Give me the device," Raistlin said, holding out his hand.

For some reason—perhaps it was that look in the mage's eye, or perhaps it was the cold dampness of the underground dungeons—Tas began to shiver. Gnimsh, holding the device in his hand, looked at Tas questioningly.

"Uh, would you mind if we just sort of kept it awhile?" Tas began. "I won't lose it—"

"Give me the device." Raistlin's voice was soft.

Tas swallowed again. There was a funny taste in his mouth. "You—you better give it to him, Gnimsh."

The gnome, blinking in a befuddled manner and obviously trying to figure out what was going on, only stared at Tas questioningly.

"It—it'll be all right," Tas said, trying to smile, though his face had suddenly gone all stiff. "Raist-Raistlin's a friend of mine, you see. He'll keep it safe. . . ."

Shrugging, Gnimsh turned and, taking a few shuffling

steps forward, held out the device in his palm. The pendant looked plain and uninteresting in the dim torchlight. Stretching forth his hand, Raistlin slowly and carefully took hold of the device. He studied it closely, then slipped it into one of the secret pockets in his black robes.

"Come to me, Tas," Raistlin said in a gentle voice, beckoning to him.

Gnimsh was still standing in front of Raistlin, staring disconsolately at the pocket into which the device had disappeared. Catching hold of the gnome by the strings of his leather apron, Tas dragged Gnimsh back away from the mage. Then, clasping Gnimsh by the hand, Tas looked up.

"We're ready, Raistlin," he said brightly. "Whoosh away! Gee, won't Caramon be surprised—"

"I said—come here, Tas," Raistlin repeated in that soft, expressionless voice. His eyes were on the gnome.

"Oh, Raistlin, you're not going to leave him here, are you?" Tas wailed. Dropping Gnimsh's hand, he took a step forward. "Because, if you are, I'd just as soon stay. I mean, he'll never get out of this by himself. And he's got this wonderful idea for a mechanical lift—"

Raistlin's hand snaked out, caught hold of Tas by the arm, and yanked him over to stand beside him. "No, I'm not going to leave him here, Tas."

"You see? He's going to whoosh us back to Caramon. The magic's great fun," Tas began, twisting around to face Gnimsh and trying to grin, though the mage's strong fingers were hurting him most dreadfully. But at the sight of Gnimsh's face, Tas's grin vanished. He started to go back to his friend, but Raistlin held him fast.

The gnome was standing all by himself, looking thoroughly confused and pathetic, still clutching Tas's handkerchief in his hand.

Tas squirmed. "Oh, Gnimsh, please. It'll be all right. I told you, Raistlin's my fri—"

Raising one hand, holding Tas by the collar with the other, the archmage pointed a finger at the gnome. Raistlin's soft voice began to chant, "*Ast kiranann kair—*"

Horror broke over Tas. He had heard those words of magic before. . . .

"No!" he shrieked in anguish. Whirling, he looked up into Raistlin's eyes. "No!" he screamed again, hurling himself bodily at the mage, beating at him with his small hands.

"—*Gardurm Soth-arn/Suh kali Jalaran!*" Raistlin finished calmly.

Tas, his hands still grasping Raistlin's black robes, heard the air begin to crackle and sizzle. Turning with an incoherent cry, the kender watched bolts of flame shoot from the mage's fingers straight into the gnome. The magical lightning struck Gnimsh in the chest. The terrible energy lifted the gnome's small body and flung it backward, slamming it into the stone wall behind.

Gnimsh crumpled to the floor without so much as a cry. Smoke rose from his leather apron. There was the sweet, sickening smell of burning flesh. The hand holding the kender's handkerchief twitched, and then was still.

Tas couldn't move. His hands still entangled in Raistlin's robes, he stood, staring.

"Come along, Tas," Raistlin said.

Turning, Tas looked up at Raistlin. "No," he whispered, trembling, trying to free himself from Raistlin's strong grip. Then he cried out in agony. "You murdered him! Why? He was my friend!"

"My reasons are my own," Raistlin said, holding onto the writhing kender firmly. "Now you are coming with me."

"No, I'm not!" Tas cried, struggling frantically. "You're not interesting or exciting—you're evil—like the Abyss! You're horrible and ugly, and I won't go anywhere with you! Ever! Let me go! Let me go!"

Blinded by tears, kicking and screaming and flailing out with his clenched fists, Tas struck at Raistlin in a frenzy.

Coming out of their terror, the Dewar in the cell began shouting in panic, arousing the attention of dwarves in the other cells. Shrieking and yelling, other Dewar crowded close against the bars, trying to see what was going on.

Pandemonium broke out. Above the cries and shouts could

be heard the deep voices of the guards, yelling something in dwarven.

His face cold and grim, Raistlin laid a hand on Tasslehoff's forehead and spoke swift, soft words. The kender's body relaxed instantly. Catching him before he fell to the floor, Raistlin spoke again, and the two of them disappeared, leaving the stunned Dewar to stand, gaping, staring at the vacant space on the floor and the body of the dead gnome, lying huddled in the corner.

An hour later Kharas, having escaped his own confinement with ease, made his way to the cellblock where the Dewar clans were being held captive.

Grimly, Kharas stalked down the aisles.

"What's going on?" he asked a guard. "It seems awfully quiet."

"Ah, some sort of riot a while back," the guard muttered. "We never could figure out what the matter was."

Kharas glanced around sharply. The Dewar stared back at him not with hatred but with suspicion, even fear.

Growing more worried as he went along, sensing that something frightful had occurred, the dwarf quickened his pace. Reaching the last cell, he looked inside.

At the sight of Kharas, those Dewar who could move leaped to their feet and backed into the farthest corner possible. There they huddled together, muttering and pointing at the front corner of the cell.

Looking over, Kharas frowned. The body of the gnome lay limply on the floor.

Casting a furious glance at the stunned guard, Kharas turned his gaze upon the Dewar.

"Who did this?" he demanded. "And where's the kender?"

To Kharas's amazement, the Dewar—instead of sullenly denying the crime—immediately surged forward, all of them babbling at once. With an angry, slashing hand motion, Kharas silenced them. "You, there"—he pointed at one of the Dewar, who was still holding onto Tas's pouches—"where did you get that pouch? What happened? Who did this?

Where is the kender?"

As the Dewar shambled forward, Kharas looked into the dark dwarf's eyes. And he saw, to his horror, that any sanity the dark dwarf might once have possessed was now completely gone.

"I saw 'im," the Dewar said, grinning. "I saw 'im. In 'is black robes and all. He come for the gnome. An' 'e come for the kender. An' 'e's comin' fer us nex'!"

The dark dwarf laughed horribly. "Us nex'!" he repeated.

"Who?" Kharas asked sternly. "Saw who? Who came for the kender?"

"Why, hisself!" whispered the Dewar, turning to gaze upon the gnome with wild, staring eyes. "Death . . ."

CHAPTER 12

o one had set foot inside the magical fortress of Zhaman for centuries. The dwarves viewed it with suspicion and distrust for several reasons. One, it had belonged to wizards. Two, its stonework was not dwarven, nor was it even natural. The fortress had been raised—so legend told—up out of the ground by magic, and it was magic that still held it together.

"*Has* to be magic," Reghar grumbled to Caramon, giving the tall thin spires of the fortress a scathing glance. "Otherwise, it would have toppled over long ago."

The hill dwarves, refusing to a dwarf to stick so much as the tip of their beards inside the fortress, set up camp outside, on the plains. The Plainsmen did likewise. Not so much from fear of the magical building—though they looked at it askance and whispered about it in their own language—but from the fact that they felt uneasy in any building.

The humans, scoffing at these superstitions, entered the ancient fortress, laughing loudly about spooks and haunts. They stayed one night. The next morning found them setting up camp in the open, muttering about fresh air and sleeping better beneath the stars.

"What went on here?" Caramon asked his brother uneasily as they walked through the fortress on their arrival. "You said it wasn't a Tower of High Sorcery, yet it's obviously magical. Wizards built it. And"—the big man shivered—"there's a strange feeling about it—not eerie, like the Towers. But a feeling of . . . of— " He floundered.

"Of violence," Raistlin murmured, his darting, penetrating gaze encompassing all the objects around him, "of violence and of death, my brother. For this was a place of experimentation. The mages built this fortress far away from civilized lands for one reason—and that was that they knew the magic conjured here might well escape their control. And so it did— often. But here, too, emerged great things—magics that helped the world."

"Why was it abandoned?" Lady Crysania asked, drawing her fur cloak around her shoulders more tightly. The air that flowed through the narrow stone hallways was chill and smelled of dust and stone.

Raistlin was silent for long moments, frowning. Slowly, quietly, they made their way through the twisting halls. Lady Crysania's soft leather boots made no sound as she walked, Caramon's heavy booted footsteps echoed through the empty chambers, Raistlin's rustling robes whispered through the corridors, the Staff of Magius upon which he leaned thumping softly on the floor. As quiet as they were, they could almost have been the ghosts of themselves, moving through the hallways. When Raistlin spoke, his voice made both Caramon and Crysania start.

"Though there have always been the three Robes—good, neutral, and evil—among the magic-users, we have, unfortunately, not always maintained the balance," Raistlin said. "As people turned against us, the White Robes withdrew into their Towers, advocating peace. The Black Robes, however, sought—at first—to strike back. They took over this fortress and used it in experiments to create armies." He paused. "Experiments that were not successful at that time, but which led to the creation of draconians in our own age.

"With this failure, the mages realized the hopelessness of their situation. They abandoned Zhaman, joining with their fellows in what became known as the Lost Battles."

"You seem to know your way around here," Caramon observed.

Raistlin glanced sharply at his brother, but Caramon's face was smooth, guileless—though there was, perhaps, a strange, shadowed look in his brown eyes.

"Do you not yet understand, my brother?" Raistlin said harshly, coming to a stop in a drafty, dark corridor. "I have never been here, yet I have walked these halls. The room I sleep in I have slept in many nights before, though I have yet to spend a night in this fortress. I am a stranger here, yet I know the location of every room, from those rooms of meditation and study at the top to the banquet halls on the first level."

Caramon stopped, too. Slowly he looked around him, staring up at the dusty ceiling, gazing down the empty hallways where sunlight filtered through carved windows to lie in square tiles upon the stone floors. His gaze finally came back to meet that of his twin.

"Then, Fistandantilus," he said, his voice heavy, "you know that this is also going to be your tomb."

For an instant, Caramon saw a tiny crack in the glass of Raistlin's eyes, he saw—not anger—but amusement, triumph. Then the bright mirrors returned. Caramon saw only himself reflected there, standing in a patch of weak, winter sunlight.

Crysania moved next to Raistlin. She put her hands over his arm as he leaned upon his staff and regarded Caramon with cold, gray eyes. "The gods are with us," she said. "They were not with Fistandantilus. Your brother is strong in his art, I am strong in my faith. We will not fail!"

Still looking at Caramon, still keeping his twin's reflection in the glistening orbs of his eyes, Raistlin smiled. "Yes," he whispered, and there was a slight hiss to his words, "truly, the gods are with us!"

Upon the first level of the great, magical fortress of Zhaman were huge, stone-carved halls that had—in past days—been places of meeting and celebration. There were also, on the first level, rooms that had once been filled with books, designed for quiet study and meditation. At the back end were kitchens and storage rooms, long unused and covered by the dust of years.

On the upper levels were large bedrooms filled with quaint, old-fashioned furniture, the beds covered with linens preserved through the years by the dryness of the desert air. Caramon, Lady Crysania, and the officers of Caramon's staff slept in these rooms. If they did not sleep soundly, if they woke up sometimes during the night thinking they had heard voices chanting strange words or glimpsing wisps of ghostly figures fluttering through the moonlit darkness, no one mentioned these in the daylight.

But after a few nights, these things were forgotten, swallowed up in larger worries about supplies, fights breaking out between humans and dwarves, reports from spies that the dwarves of Thorbardin were massing a huge, well-armed force.

There was also in Zhaman, on the first level, a corridor that appeared to be a mistake. Anyone venturing into it discovered that it wandered off from a short hallway and ended abruptly in a blank wall. It looked for all the world as if the builder had thrown down his tools in disgust, calling it quits.

But the corridor was not a mistake. When the proper hands were laid upon that blank wall, when the proper words were spoken, when the proper runes were traced in the dust of the wall itself, then a door appeared, leading to a great staircase cut from the granite foundation of Zhaman.

Down, down the staircase, down into darkness, down—it seemed—into the very core of the world, the proper person could descend. Down into the dungeons of Zhaman. . . .

"One more time." The voice was soft, patient, and it dove and twisted at Tasslehoff like a snake. Writhing around him, it sank its curved teeth into his flesh, sucking out his life.

"We will go over it again. Tell me about the Abyss," said the voice. "Everything you remember. How you entered.

What the landscape is like. Who and what you saw. The Queen herself, how she looked, her words. . . ."

"I'm trying, Raistlin, truly!" Tasslehoff whimpered. "But . . . we've gone over it and over it these last couple of days. I can't think of anything else! And, my head's hot and my feet and my hands are cold and . . . the room's spinning 'round and 'round. If—if you'd make it stop spinning, Raistlin, I think I might be able to recall . . ."

Feeling Raistlin's hand on his chest, Tas shrank down into the bed. "No!" he moaned, trying desperately to wriggle away. "I'll be good, Raistlin! I'll remember. Don't hurt me, not like poor Gnimsh!"

But the archmage's hand only rested lightly on the kender's chest for an instant, then went to his forehead. Tas's skin burned, but the touch of that hand burned worse.

"Lie still," Raistlin commanded. Then, lifting Tas up by the arms, Raistlin stared intently into the kender's sunken eyes.

Finally, Raistlin dropped Tas back down into the bed and, muttering a bitter curse, rose to his feet.

Lying upon a sweat-soaked pillow, Tas saw the black-robed figure hover over him an instant, then, with a flutter and swirl of robes, it turned and stalked out of the room. Tas tried to lift his head to see where Raistlin was going, but the effort was too much. He fell back limply.

Why am I so weak? he wondered. What's wrong? I want to sleep. Maybe I'll quit hurting then. Tas closed his eyes. But they flew open again as if he had wires attached to his hair. No, I can't sleep! he thought fearfully. There are things out there in the darkness, horrible things, just waiting for me to sleep! I've seen them, they're out there! They're going to leap out and—

As if from a great distance, he heard Raistlin's voice, talking to someone. Peering around, trying desperately to keep sleep away from him, Tas decided to concentrate on Raistlin. Maybe I'll find out something, he thought drearily. Maybe I'll find out what's the matter with me.

Looking over, he saw the black-robed figure talking to a squat, dark figure. Sure enough, they were discussing him. Tas tried to listen, but his mind kept doing strange things—going off to play somewhere without inviting his body along. So Tas couldn't be certain if he was hearing what he was hearing or dreaming it.

"Give him some more of the potion. That should keep him quiet," a voice that sounded like Raistlin's said to the short, dark figure. "There's little chance anyone will hear him down here, but I can't risk it."

The short, dark figure said something. Tas closed his eyes and let the cool waters of a blue, blue lake—Crystalmir Lake—lap over his burning skin. Maybe his mind had decided to take his body along after all.

"When I am gone," Raistlin's voice came up out of the water, "lock the door after me and extinguish the light. My brother has grown suspicious of late. Should he discover the magical door, he will undoubtedly come down here. He must find nothing. All these cells should appear empty."

The figure muttered, and the door squeaked on its hinges.

The water of Crystalmir suddenly began to boil around Tas. Tentacles snaked up out of it, grasping for him. His eyes flew open. "Raistlin!" he begged. "Don't leave me. Help me!"

But the door banged shut. The short, dark figure shuffled over to Tas's bedside. Staring at it with a kind of dreamlike horror, Tas saw that it was a dwarf. He smiled.

"Flint?" he murmured through parched, cracked lips. "No! Arack!" He tried to run, but the tentacles in the water were reaching out for his feet.

"Raistlin!" he screamed, frantically trying to scramble backward. But his feet wouldn't move. Something grabbed hold of him! The tentacles! Tas fought, shrieking in panic.

"Shut up, you bastard. Drink this." The tentacles gripped him by the topknot and shoved a cup to his lips. "Drink, or I'll pull your hair out by the roots!"

Choking, staring at the figure wildly, Tas took a sip. The liquid was bitter but cool and soothing. He was thirsty, so thirsty! Sobbing, Tas grabbed the cup away from the dwarf and gulped it down. Then he lay back on his pillow. Within moments, the tentacles slipped away, the pain in his limbs left him, and the clear, sweet waters of Crystalmir closed over his head.

Crysania came out of a dream with the distinct impression that someone had called her name. Though she could not remember hearing a sound, the feeling was so strong and intense that she was immediately wide awake, sitting up in bed, before she was truly aware of what it was that had awakened her. Had it been a part of the dream? No. The impression remained and grew stronger.

Someone was in the room with her! She glanced about swiftly. Solinari's light, coming through a small corner at the far end of the room, did little to illuminate it. She could see nothing, but she heard movement. Crysania opened her mouth to call the guard. . . .

And felt a hand upon her lips. Then Raistlin materialized out of night's darkness, sitting on her bed.

"Forgive me for frightening you, Revered Daughter," he said in a soft whisper, barely above a breath. "I need your help and I do not wish to attract the attention of the guards." Slowly, he removed his hand.

"I wasn't frightened," Crysania protested. He smiled, and she flushed. He was so near her that he could feel her trembling. "You just . . . startled me, that's all. I was dreaming. You seemed a part of the dream."

"To be sure," Raistlin replied quietly. "The Portal is here, and thus we are very near the gods."

It isn't the nearness of the gods that is making me tremble, Crysania thought with a quivering sigh, feeling the burning warmth of the body beside hers, smelling his mysterious, intoxicating fragrance. Angrily, she moved away from him, firmly suppressing her desires and longings. *He* is above such things. Would she show herself weaker?

She returned to the subject abruptly. "You said you needed my help. Why?" Sudden fear gripped her. Reaching out impulsively, she grasped his hand. "You are well, aren't you? Your wound—?"

A swift spasm of pain crossed Raistlin's face, then his

expression grew bitter and hard. "No, I am well," he said curtly.

"Thanks be to Paladine," Crysania said, smiling, letting her hand linger in his.

Raistlin's eyes grew narrow. "The god has no thanks of mine!" he muttered. The hand holding hers clenched, hurting her.

Crysania shivered. It seemed for an instant as if the burning heat of the mage's body so near hers was drawing out her own, leaving her chilled. She tried to remove her hand from his, but Raistlin, brought out of his bitter reverie by her movement, turned to look at her.

"Forgive me, Revered Daughter," he said, releasing her. "The pain was unendurable. I prayed for death. It was denied me."

"You know the reason," Crysania said, her fear lost in her compassion. Her hand hesitated a moment, then dropped to the coverlet near his trembling hand, yet not touching him.

"Yes, and I accept it. Still, I cannot forgive him. But that is between your god and myself," Raistlin said reprovingly.

Crysania bit her lip. "I accept my rebuke. It was deserved." She was silent a moment. Raistlin, too, was not inclined to speak, the lines in his face deepening.

"You told Caramon that the gods were with us. So, then, you have communed with my god . . . with Paladine?" Crysania ventured to ask hesitantly.

"Of course," Raistlin smiled his twisted smile. "Does that surprise you?"

Crysania sighed. Her head drooped, the dark hair falling around her shoulders. The faint moonlight in the room made her black hair glimmer with a soft, blue radiance, made her skin gleam purest white. Her perfume filled the room, filled the night. She felt a touch upon her hair. Lifting her head, she saw Raistlin's eyes burn with a passion that came from a source deep within, a source that had nothing to do with magic. Crysania caught her breath, but at that moment Raistlin stood up and walked away.

Crysania sighed. "So, you have communed with both the gods, then?" she asked wistfully.

Raistlin half-turned. "I have communed with all three," he replied of offhandedly.

"Three?" She was startled. "Gilean?"

"Who is Astinus but Gilean's mouthpiece?" Raistlin said scornfully. "If, indeed, he is not Gilean himself, as some have speculated. But, this must be nothing new to you—"

"I have never talked to the Dark Queen," Crysania said.

"Haven't you?" Raistlin asked with a penetrating look that shook the cleric to the core of her soul. "Does she not know of your heart's desire? Hasn't she offered it to you?"

Looking into his eyes, aware of his nearness, feeling desire sweep over her, Crysania could not reply. Then, as he continued to watch her, she swallowed and shook her head. "If she has," she answered in almost inaudible tones, "she has given it with one hand and denied it to me with the other."

Crysania heard the black robes rustle as if the mage had started. His face, visible in the moonlight, was, for an instant, worried and thoughtful. Then it smoothed.

"I did not come here to discuss theology," Raistlin said with a slight sneer. "I have another, more immediate worry."

"Of course." Crysania flushed, nervously brushing her tangled hair out of her face. "Once again, I apologize. You needed me, you said—"

"Tasslehoff is here."

"Tasslehoff?" Crysania repeated in blank amazement.

"Yes, and he is very ill. Near death, in fact. I need your healing skills."

"But, I don't understand. Why—How did he come to be here?" Crysania stammered, bewildered. "You said he had returned to our own time."

"So I believed," Raistlin replied gravely. "But, apparently, I was mistaken. The magical device brought him here, to this time. He has been wandering the world in the manner of kender, enjoying himself thoroughly. Eventually, hearing of the war, he arrived here to share in the adventure. Unfortunately, he has, in his wanderings, contracted the plague."

"This is terrible! Of course I'll come." Catching up her fur cloak from the end of her bed, she wrapped it around her shoulders, noticing, as she did so, that Raistlin turned away from her. Staring out the window, into the silver moonlight, she saw the muscles of his jaw tighten, as if with some inner struggle.

"I am ready," Crysania said in smooth, businesslike tones, fastening her cloak. Raistlin turned back and extended his hand to her. Crysania looked at him, puzzled.

"We must travel the pathways of the night," he said quietly. "As I told you, I do not want to alert the guards."

"But why not?" she said. "What difference—"

"What will I tell my brother?"

Crysania paused. "I see. . . ."

"You understand my dilemma?" Raistlin asked, regarding her intently. "If I tell him, it will be a worry to him, at a time he can ill afford to add burdens to those he already carries. Tas has broken the magical device. That will upset Caramon, too, even though he is aware I plan to send him home. But—I should tell him the kender is here."

"Caramon *has* looked worried and unhappy these past few days," Crysania said thoughtfully, concern in her voice.

"The war is not going well," Raistlin informed her bluntly. "The army is crumbling around him. The Plainsmen talk every day of leaving. They may be gone now, for all we know. The dwarves under Fireforge are an untrustworthy lot, pressuring Caramon into striking before he is ready. The supply wagons have vanished, no one knows what has become of them. His own army is restless, upset. On top of all this, to have a kender roaming about, chattering aimlessly, distracting him . . ."

Raistlin sighed. "Still, I cannot—in honor—keep this from him."

Crysania's lips tightened. "No, Raistlin. I do not think it would be wise to tell him." Seeing Raistlin look dubious, she continued earnestly. "There is nothing Caramon can do. If the kender is truly ill, as you suspect, I can heal him, but he will be weak for several days. It would only be an added worry to your brother. Caramon plans to march in a few days' time. We will tend the kender, then have him completely recovered, ready to meet his friend on the field if such is his desire."

The archmage sighed again, in reluctance and doubt. Then, he shrugged. "Very well, Revered Daughter," he said. "I will be guided by you in this. Your words are wise. We will not tell Caramon that the kender has returned."

He moved close to her; and Crysania, looking up at him caught a strange smile upon his face, a smile that—for just this once—was reflected in his glittering eyes. Startled, upset without quite knowing why, she drew back, but he put his arm around her, enveloping her in the soft folds of his black sleeves, holding her close.

Closing her eyes, she forgot that smile. Nestling close, wrapped in his warmth, she listened to his rapid heartbeat . . . .

Murmuring the words of magic, he transformed them both into nothingness. Their shadows seemed to hover for an instant in the moonlight, then these, too, vanished with a whisper.

"You are keeping him here? In the dungeons?" Crysania asked, shivering in the chill, dank air.

"*Shirak.* "Raistlin caused the crystal atop the Staff of Magius to fill the room with soft light. "He lies over there," the mage said, pointing.

A crude bed stood up against one wall. Giving Raistlin a reproachful glance, Crysania hurried to the bedside. As the cleric knelt beside the kender and laid her hand on his feverish forehead, Tas cried out. His eyes flared open, but he stared at her unseeing. Raistlin, following more slowly, gestured to a dark dwarf who was crouched in a corner. "Leave us," the mage motioned, then came to stand by the bedside. Behind him, he heard the door to the cell close.

"How can you keep him locked up in the darkness like this?" Crysania demanded.

"Have you ever treated plague victims before, Lady Crysania?" Raistlin asked in an odd tone.

Startled, she looked up at him, then flushed and averted her eyes.

Smiling bitterly, Raistlin answered his own question. "No, of course not. The plague never came to Palanthas. It never struck the beautiful, the wealthy. . . ." He made no effort to hide his contempt, and Crysania felt her skin burn as though she were the one with the fever.

"Well, it came to us," Raistlin continued. "It swept through the poorer sections of Haven. Of course, there were no healers. Nor were there even many who would stay to care for those who were afflicted. Even their own family members fled them. Poor, pathetic souls. I did what I could, tending them with the herb skill I had acquired. If I could not cure them, at least I could ease their pain. My Master disapproved." Raistlin spoke in an undertone, and Crysania realized that he had forgotten her presence. "So did Caramon—fearing for my health, he said. Bah!" Raistlin laughed without mirth. "He feared for himself. The thought of the plague frightens him more than an army of goblins. But how could I turn my back on them? They had no one . . . no one. Wretched, dying . . . dying alone."

Staring at him dumbly, Crysania felt tears sting her eyes. Raistlin did not see her. In his mind, he was back in those stinking little hovels that huddled on the outskirts of town as though they had run there to hide. He saw himself moving among the sick in his red robes, forcing the bitter medicine down their throats, holding the dying in his arms, easing their last moments. He worked among the sick grimly, asking for no thanks, expecting none. His face—the last human face many would see—expressed neither compassion nor caring. Yet the dying found comfort. Here was one who understood, here was one who lived with pain daily, here was one who had looked upon death and was not afraid. . . .

Raistlin tended the plague victims. He did what he felt he had to do at the risk of his own life, but why? For a reason he had yet to understand. A reason, perhaps, forgotten. . . .

"At any rate"—Raistlin returned to the present—"I discovered that light hurt their eyes. Those who recovered were occasionally stricken blind by—"

A terrified shriek from the kender interrupted him.

Tasslehoff was staring at him wildly. "Please, Raistlin! I'm trying to remember! Don't take me back to the Dark Queen—"

"Hush, Tas," Crysania said softly, gripping the kender with both hands as Tas seemed to be trying, literally, to climb into the wall behind him. "Calm down, Tas. It is Lady Crysania. Do you know me? I'm going to help you."

Tas transferred his wide-eyed, feverish gaze to the cleric, regarding her blankly for a moment. Then, with a sob, he clutched at her. "Don't let him take me back to the Abyss, Crysania! Don't let him take you! It's horrible, horrible. We'll all die, die like poor Gnimsh. The Dark Queen told me!"

"He's raving," Crysania murmured, trying to disengage Tas's clinging hands and force him to lie back down. "What strange delusions. Is this common with plague victims?"

"Yes," Raistlin replied. Regarding Tas intently, the mage knelt by the bedside. "Sometimes it's best to humor them. It may calm him. Tasslehoff—"

Raistlin laid his hand upon the kender's chest. Instantly, Tas collapsed back onto the bed, shrinking away from the mage, shivering and staring at him in horror. "I'll be good, Raistlin." He whimpered. "Don't hurt me, not like poor Gnimsh. Lightning, lightning!"

"Tas," said Raistlin firmly, with a hint of anger and exasperation in his voice that caused Crysania to glance over at him reprovingly.

But, seeing only a look of cool concern on his face, she supposed she must have mistaken his tone. Closing her eyes, she touched the medallion of Paladine she wore around her neck and began to murmur a healing prayer.

"I'm not going to hurt you, Tas. Shhh, lie still." Seeing Crysania lost in her communion with her god, Raistlin hissed, "Tell me, Tas. Tell me what the Dark Queen said."

The kender's face lost its bright, feverish flush as Crysania's soft words flowed over him, sweeter and cooler than the waters of his delirious imaginings. The diminishing fever left Tas's face a ghastly, ashen color. A faint glimmering of sense returned to his eyes. But he never took his gaze from Raistlin.

"She told me . . . before we left. . . ." Tas choked.

"Left?" Raistlin leaned forward. "I thought you said you escaped!"

Tas blanched, licking his dry, cracked lips. He tried to tear his gaze away from the mage, but Raistlin's eyes, glittering in the light of the staff, held the kender fast, draining the truth from him. Tas swallowed. His throat hurt.

"Water," he pleaded.

"When you've told me!" Raistlin snarled with a glance at Crysania, who was still kneeling, her head in her hands, praying to Paladine.

Tas gulped painfully. "I . . . I thought we were . . . escaping. We used th-the device and began . . . to rise. I saw . . . the Abyss, the plane, flat, empty, fall away beneath m-my feet. And"—Tas shuddered—"it wasn't empty anymore! There . . . there were shadows and—" He tossed his head, moaning. "Oh, Raistlin, don't make me remember! Don't make me go back there!"

"Hush!" Raistlin whispered, covering Tas's mouth with his hand. Crysania glanced up in concern, only to see Raistlin tenderly stroking the kender's cheek. Seeing Tas's terrified expression and pale face, Crysania frowned and shook her head.

"He is better," she said. "He will not die. But dark shadows hover around him, preventing Paladine's healing light from restoring him fully. They are the shadows of these feverish ramblings. Can you make anything from them?" Her feathery brows came together. "Whatever it is seems very real to him. It must have been something dreadful to have unnerved a kender like this."

"Perhaps, lady, if you left, he would feel more comfortable talking to me," Raistlin suggested mildly. "We are such old friends."

"True," Crysania smiled, starting to rise to her feet. To her amazement, Tas grabbed her hands.

"Don't leave me with him, lady!" He gasped. "He killed Gnimsh! Poor Gnimsh. I saw him di-die!" Tas began to weep. "Burning lightning . . ."

"There, there, Tas," Crysania said soothingly, gently but

firmly forcing the kender to lie back down. "No one's going to hurt you. Whoever killed this—uh—Gnimsh can't harm you now. You're with your friends. Isn't he, Raistlin?"

"My magic is powerful," Raistlin said softly. "Remember that, Tasslehoff. Remember the power of my magic."

"Yes, Raistlin," Tas replied, lying quite still, pinned by the mage's fixed and staring gaze.

"I think it would be wise if you remained behind to talk to him," Crysania said in an undertone. "These dark fears will prey on him and hinder the healing process. I will return to my room on my own, with Paladine's help."

"So we agree not to tell Caramon?" Raistlin glanced at Crysania out of the corner of his eye.

"Yes," Crysania said firmly. "This would only worry him unnecessarily." She looked back at her patient. "I will return in the morning, Tasslehoff. Talk to Raistlin. Unburden your soul. Then sleep." Laying her cool hand upon Tas's sweat-covered forehead, she added, "May Paladine be with you."

"Caramon?" Tas said hopefully. "Did you say Caramon? Is he here?"

"Yes, and when you've slept and eaten and rested, I'll take you to him."

"Couldn't I see him now!" Tas cried eagerly, then he cast a fearful sideways glance at Raistlin. "If—if it wouldn't be too much trouble, that is. . . ."

"He's very busy," Raistlin said coldly. "He is a general now, Tasslehoff. He has armies to command, a war to fight. He has no time for kenders."

"No, I—I suppose not," Tas said with a small sigh, lying back on his pillow, his eyes still on Raistlin.

With a final, soft pat on his head, Crysania stood up. Holding the medallion of Paladine in her hand, she whispered a prayer and was gone, vanishing into the night.

"And now, Tasslehoff," Raistlin said in a soft voice that made Tas tremble, "we are alone." With his strong hands, the mage pulled the blankets up over the kender's body and straightened the pillow beneath his head. "There, are you comfortable?"

Tas couldn't speak. He could only stare at the archmage in growing horror.

Raistlin sat down on the bed beside him. Putting one slender hand upon Tas's forehead, he idly caressed the kender's skin and smoothed back his damp hair.

"Do you remember Dalamar, my apprentice, Tas?" Raistlin asked conversationally. "You saw him, I believe at the Tower of High Sorcery, am I correct?" Raistlin's fingers were light as the feet of spiders upon Tas's face. "Do you recall, at one point, Dalamar tore open his black robes, exhibiting five wounds upon his chest? Yes, I see you recall that. It was his punishment, Tas. Punishment for hiding things from me." Raistlin's fingers stopped crawling about the kender's skin and remained in one place, exerting a slight pressure on Tas's forehead.

Tas shivered, biting his tongue to keep from crying out. "I—I remember, Raistlin."

"An interesting experience, don't you think?" Raistlin said offhandedly. "I can burn through your flesh with a touch, as I might burn through, say"—he shrugged—"butter with a hot knife. Kender are fond of interesting experiences, I believe."

"Not—not quite *that* interesting," Tas whispered miserably. "I'll tell you, Raistlin! I'll tell you everything that—that happened." He closed his eyes a moment, then began to talk, his entire body quivering with the remembered terror. "We—we seemed not to rise up out of the Abyss so much as . . . as the Abyss dropped away beneath us! And then, like I said, I saw it wasn't empty. I could see shadows and I thought . . . I thought they were valleys and mountains . . . ."

Tas's eyes flared open. He stared at the mage in awe. "It wasn't! Those shadows were *her* eyes, Raistlin! And the hills and valleys were *her* nose and mouth. We were rising up out of her face! She looked at me with eyes that were bright and gleamed with fire, and she opened her mouth and I—I thought she was going to swallow us! But we only rose higher and higher and she fell away beneath us, swirling, and then she looked at me and she said . . . she said. . . ."

"What did she say?" Raistlin demanded. "The message

was to me! It must have been! *That* was why she sent you! What did the Queen say?"

Tas's voice grew hushed. "She said, 'Come home . . .' "

Thehe effect of his
words upon Raistlin startled Tasslehoff just about as much as
anything had ever startled him in his entire life. Tas had seen
Raistlin angry before. He had seen him pleased, he had seen
him commit murder, he had seen the mage's face when
Kharas, the dwarven hero, drove his sword blade into the
mage's flesh.

But he had never seen an expression on it like this.

Raistlin's face went ashen, so white Tas thought for a wild
moment that the mage had died, perhaps been struck dead on
the spot. The mirrorlike eyes seemed to shatter; Tas saw himself reflected in tiny, splintered shards of the mage's vision.
Then he saw the eyes lose all recognition, go completely
blank, staring ahead sightlessly.

The hand that rested upon Tas's head began to tremble violently. And, as the kender watched in astonishment, he saw
Raistlin seem to shrivel up before him. His face aged percep-
tively. When he rose to his feet, still staring unseeing around
him, the mage's entire body shook.

"Raistlin?" Tas asked nervously, glad to have the mage's attention off him but bewildered by his strange appearance. The kender sat up weakly. The terrible dizziness had gone, along with the weird, unfamiliar feeling of fear. He felt almost like himself again.

"Raistlin . . . I didn't mean anything. Are *you* going to be sick now? You look awfully queer—"

But the archmage didn't answer. Staggering backward, Raistlin fell against the stone wall and just stood there, his breathing rapid and shallow. Covering his face with his hand, he fought desperately to regain control of himself, a fight with some unseen opponent that was yet as visible to Tas as if the mage had been fighting a spectre.

Then, with a low, hollow cry of rage and anguish, Raistlin lurched forward. Gripping the Staff of Magius, his black robes whipping around him, he fled through the open door.

Staring after Raistlin in astonishment, Tas saw him hurtle past the dark dwarf standing guard in the doorway. The dwarf took one look at the mage's cadaverous face as Raistlin ran blindly past him, and, with a wild shriek, whirled around and dashed off in the opposite direction.

So amazing was all this that it took Tas a few moments to realize he wasn't a prisoner anymore.

"You know," the kender said to himself, putting his hand on his forehead, "Crysania was right. I *do* feel better now that I've gotten that off my mind. It didn't do much for Raistlin, unfortunately, but then I don't care about that. Well, much." Tas sighed. "I'll never understand why he killed poor Gnimsh. Maybe I'll have a chance to ask him someday.

"But, now"—the kender glanced around—"the first thing to do is find Caramon and tell him I've got the magical device and we can go home. I never thought I'd say this," Tas said wistfully, swinging his feet to the floor, "but home sounds *awfully* nice right now!"

He was going to stand up, but his legs apparently preferred to be back in bed because Tas suddenly found himself sitting down again.

"This won't do!" Tas said, glaring at the offending parts of his body. "You're nowhere without me! Just remember that! I'm boss and when I say move—you'll move! Now, I'm going to stand up again," Tas warned his legs sternly. "And I expect some cooperation."

This speech had some effect. His legs behaved a bit better this time and the kender, though still somewhat wobbly, managed to make his way across the dark room toward the torch-lit corridor he could see beyond the door.

Reaching it, he peeped cautiously up and down the hall, but no one was in sight. Creeping out into corridor, he saw nothing but dark, closed-up cells like the one he'd been in— and a staircase at one end, leading up. Looking down the other end, he saw nothing but dark shadows.

"I wonder where I am?" Tas made his way down the corridor toward the staircase—that being, as far as he could tell, the only way up. "Oh, well!"—the kender reflected philosophically—"I don't suppose it matters. One *good* thing about having been in the Abyss is that every place else, no matter how dismal, looks congenial by comparison."

He had to stop a moment for a brief argument with his legs—they still seemed much inclined to return to bed—but this momentary weakness passed, and the kender reached the bottom of the staircase. Listening, he could hear voices.

"Drat," he muttered, coming to a halt and ducking back into the shadows. "Someone's up there. Guards, I suppose. Sounds like dwarves. Those whatcha'ma call-ems—Dewar." Tas stood, quietly, trying to make out what the deep voices were saying. "You'd think they could speak a civilized language," he snapped irritably. "One a fellow could understand. They sound excited, though."

Curiosity finally getting the better of him, Tas crept up the first flight of stone steps and peered around the corner. He ducked back quickly with a sigh. "Two of 'em. Both blocking the stair. And there's no way around them."

His pouches with his tools and weapons were gone, left behind in the mountain dungeon of Thorbardin. But he still had his knife. "Not that it will do much good against *those*." Tas reflected, envisioning once again the huge battle-axes he'd seen the dwarves holding.

He waited a few more moments, hoping the dwarves would leave. They certainly seemed worked up, but they also appeared rooted to the spot.

"I can't stay here all night or day, whichever it is," the kender grumbled. "Well, as dad said, 'always try talk before the lockpick.' The very *worst* they could do to me, I suppose— not counting killing me, of course—would be to lock me back up. And, if I'm any judge of locks, I could probably be out again in about half-an-hour." He began to climb the stairs. "Was it dad who said that," he pondered as he climbed, "or Uncle Trapspringer?"

Rounding the corner, he confronted two Dewar, who appeared considerably startled to see him. "Hello!" the kender said cheerfully. "My name is Tasslehoff Burrfoot." He extended a hand. "And your names are? Oh, you're not going to tell me. Well, that's all right. I probably couldn't pronounce them anyway. Say, I'm a prisoner and I'm looking for the fellow who was keeping me locked up in that cell back there. You probably know him—a black-robed magic-user. He was interrogating me, when something I said took him by surprise, I think, because he had a sort of a fit and ran out of the room. And he forgot to lock the door behind him. Did either of you see which way he—Well!" Tas blinked. "How rude."

This in response to the actions of the Dewar who, after regarding the kender with growing looks of alarm on their faces, shouted one word, turned, and bolted.

"*Antarax*," Tas repeated, looking after them, puzzled. "Let's see. That sounds like dwarven for ... for ... Oh, of course! Burning death. Ah—they think I've still got the plague! Mmmmm, that's handy. Or is it?"

The kender found himself alone in another long corridor, every bit as bleak and dismal as the one he'd just left. "I still don't know where I am, and no one seems inclined to tell me. The only way out is that staircase down there and those two are heading for it so I guess the best thing to do is just tag along. Caramon's bound to be around here somewhere."

But Tas's legs, which had already registered a protest

against walking, informed the kender in no uncertain terms that running was out of the question. He stumbled along as fast as possible after the dwarves, but they had dashed up the stairs and were out of sight by the time he had made it half-way down the corridor. Puffing along, feeling a bit dizzy but determined to find Caramon, Tas climbed the stairs after them. As he rounded a corner, he came to a sudden halt.

"Oops," he said, and hurriedly ducked into the shadows. Clapping a hand over mouth, he severely reprimanded himself. "Shut up, Burrfoot! It's the whole Dewar army."

It certainly seemed like it. The two he had been following had met up with about twenty other dwarves. Crouching in the shadows, Tas could hear them yelping excitedly, and he expected them to come tromping down after him any moment . . . . But nothing happened.

He waited, listening to the conversation, then, risking a peep, he saw that some of the dwarves present didn't look like Dewar. They were clean, their beards were brushed, and they were dressed in bright armor. Arid they didn't appear pleased. They glared grimly at one of the Dewar, as though they'd just as soon skin him as not.

"Mountain dwarves!" Tas muttered to himself in astonishment, recognizing the armor. "And, from what Raistlin said, *they're* the enemy. Which means they're supposed to be in their mountain, not in ours. Provided we're in a mountain, of course, which I'm beginning to think likely from the looks of it. But, I wonder—"

As one of the mountain dwarves began speaking, Tas brightened. "Finally, someone who knows how to talk!" The kender sighed in relief. Because of the mixture of races, the dwarf was speaking a crude version of Common and dwarven.

The gist of the conversation, as near as Tas could follow, was that the mountain dwarf didn't give a cracked stone about a crazed wizard or a wandering, plague-ridden kender.

"We came here to get the head of this General Caramon," the mountain dwarf growled. "You said that the wizard promised it would be arranged. If it is, we can dispense with the wizard. I'd just as soon not deal with a Black Robe anyway.

And now answer me this, Argat. Are your people ready to attack the army from within? Are you prepared to kill this general? Or was this just a trick? If so, you will find it will go hard with your people back in Thorbardin."

"It no trick!" Argat growled, his fist clenching. "We ready to move. The general is in the War Room. The wizard said he make sure him alone with just bodyguard. Our people get the hill dwarves to attack. When *you* keep your part bargain, when scouts give signal that great gates to Thorbardin are open—"

"The signal is sounding, even as we speak," the mountain dwarf snapped. "If we were above ground level, you could hear the trumpets. The army rides forth!"

"Then we go!" Argat said. Bowing, he added with a sneer, "If your lordship dares, come with us—we take General Caramon's head right now!"

"I will join you," the mountain dwarf said coldly, "if only to make certain you plot no further treachery."

What else the two said was lost on Tas, who leaned back against the wall. His legs had gone all prickly-feeling, and there was a buzzing noise in his ears.

"Caramon," he whispered, clutching at his head, trying to think. "They're going to kill him! And Raistlin's done this!" Tas shuddered. "Poor Caramon. His own twin. If he knew that, it would probably just kill him dead on the spot. The dwarves wouldn't need axes."

Suddenly, the kender's head snapped up. "Tasslehoff Burrfoot!" he said angrily. "What are you doing—standing around like a gully dwarf with one foot in the mud. You've got to save him! You promised Tika you'd take care of him, after all."

"Save him? How, you doorknob?" boomed a voice inside of him that sounded suspiciously like Flint's. "There must be twenty dwarves! And you armed with that rabbit-killer!"

"I'll think of something," Tas retorted. "So just keep sitting under your tree."

There was a snorting sound. Resolutely ignoring it, the kender stood up tall and straight, pulled out his little knife, and crept quietly—as only kender can—down the corridor.

CHAPTER 14

She had the dark, curly hair and the crooked smile that men would later find so charming in her daughter. She had the simple, guileless honesty that would characterize one of her sons and she had a gift—a rare and wonderful power—that she would pass on to the other.

She had magic in her blood, as did her son. But she was weak— weak-willed, weak-spirited. Thus she let the magic control her, and thus, finally, she died.

Neither the strong-souled Kitiara nor the physically strong Caramon was much affected by their mother's death. Kitiara hated her mother with bitter jealousy, while Caramon, though he cared about his mother, was far closer to his frail twin. Besides, his mother's weird ramblings and mystical trances made her a complete enigma to the young warrior.

But her death devastated Raistlin. The only one of her children who truly understood her, he pitied her for her weakness, even as he despised her for it. And he was furious at her for dying, furious at her for leaving him alone in this world, alone with the gift. He was angry and, deep within, he was filled with fear, for Raistlin saw in her his own doom.

Following the death of her father, his mother had gone into a grief-stricken trance from which she never emerged. Raistlin had been helpless. He could do nothing but watch her dwindle away. Refusing food, she drifted, lost, onto magical planes only she could see. And the mage—her son—was shaken to his very core.

He sat up with her on that last night. Holding her wasted hand in his, he watched as her sunken, feverish eyes stared at wonders conjured up by magic gone berserk.

That night, Raistlin vowed deep within his soul that no one and nothing would ever have the power to manipulate him like this—not his twin brother, not his sister, not the magic, not the gods. He and he alone would be the guiding force of his life.

He vowed this, swearing it with a bitter, binding oath. But he was a boy still—a boy left alone in darkness as he sat there with his mother the night she died. He watched her draw her last, shuddering breath. Holding her thin hand with its delicate fingers (so like his own!), he pleaded softly through his tears, "Mother, come home . . . . Come home!"

Now at Zhaman he heard these words again, challenging him, mocking him, daring him. They rang in his ears, reverberated in his brain with wild, discordant clangings. His head bursting with pain, he stumbled into a wall.

Raistlin had once seen Lord Ariakas torture a captured knight by locking the man inside a bell tower. The dark clerics rang the bells of praise to their Queen that night—all night. The next morning, the man had been found dead—a look of horror upon his face so profound and awful that even those steeped in cruelty were quick to dispose of the corpse.

Raistlin felt as if he were imprisoned within his own bell tower, his own words ringing his doom in his skull. Reeling, clutching his head, he tried desperately to blot out the sound.

"Come home . . . come home. . . ."

Dizzy and blinded by the pain, the mage sought to outrun it. He staggered about with no clear idea of where he was, searching only for escape. His numb feet lost their footing. Tripping over the hem of his black robe, he fell to his knees.

An object leaped from a pocket in his robes and rolled out onto the stone floor. Seeing it, Raistlin gasped in fear and anger. It was another mark of his failure—the dragon orb, cracked, darkened, useless. Frantically he grabbed for it, but it skittered like a marble across the flagstone, eluding his clawing grasp.

Desperate, he crawled after it and, finally, it rolled to a stop. With a snarl, Raistlin started to take hold of it, then halted. Lifting his head, his eyes opened wide. He saw where he was, and he shrank back, trembling.

Before him loomed the Great Portal.

It was exactly like the one in the Tower of High Sorcery in Palanthas. A huge oval door standing upon a raised dais, it was ornamented and guarded by the heads of five dragons. Their sinuous necks snaking up from the floor, the five heads faced inward, five mouths open, screaming silent tribute to their Queen.

In the Tower at Palanthas, the door to the Portal was closed. None could open it except from within the Abyss itself, coming the opposite direction—an egress from a place none ever left. This door, too, was closed, but there were two who could enter—a White-Robed Cleric of Infinite Goodness and a Black-Robed Archmage of Infinite Evil. It was an unlikely combination. Thus the great wizards hoped to seal forever this terrible entrance onto an immortal plane.

An ordinary mortal, looking into that Portal, could see nothing but stark, chill darkness.

But Raistlin was no longer ordinary. Drawing nearer and nearer his goddess, bending his energies and his studies toward this one object, the archmage was now in a state suspended between both worlds. Looking into the closed door, *he* could almost penetrate that darkness! It wavered in his vision. Wrenching his gaze from it, he turned his attention back to retrieving the dragon orb.

How did it escape me? he wondered angrily. He kept the orb in a bag hidden deep within a secret pocket of his robes.

But then he sneered at himself, for he knew the answer. Each dragon orb was endowed with a strong sense of self-preservation. The one at Istar had escaped the Cataclysm by tricking the elven king, Lorac, into stealing it and taking it into Silvanesti. When the orb could no longer use the insane Lorac, it had attached itself to Raistlin. It had sustained Raistlin's life when he was dying in Astinus's library. It had conspired with Fistandantilus to take the young man to the Queen of Darkness. Now, sensing the greatest danger of its existence, it was trying to flee him.

He would not allow it! Reaching out, his hand closed firmly over the dragon orb.

There was a shriek. . . .

The Portal opened.

Raistlin looked up. It had not opened to admit him. No, it had opened to warn him—to show him the penalty of failure.

Prostrate upon his knees, clutching the orb to his chest, Raistlin felt the presence and the majesty of Takhisis, Queen of Darkness rise up before him. Awe-stricken, he cowered, trembling, at the Dark Queen's feet.

This is your doom! Her words hissed in his mind. *Your mother's fate will be your own. Swallowed by your magic, you will be held forever spellbound without even the sweet consolation of death to end your suffering!*

Raistlin collapsed. He felt his body shrivel. Thus he had seen the withered body of Fistandantilus shrivel at the touch of the bloodstone.

His head resting on the stone floor as it rested upon the executioner's block of his nightmare, the mage was about to admit defeat. . . .

But there was a core of strength within Raistlin. Long ago, Par-Salian, head of the Order of White Robes, had been given a task by the gods. They needed a magic-user strong enough to help defeat the growing evil of the Queen of Darkness. Par-Salian had searched long and had at last chosen Raistlin. For he had seen within the young mage this inner core of strength. It had been a cold, shapeless mass of iron when Raistlin was young. But Par-Salian hoped that the white-hot fire of suffering, pain, war, and ambition would forge that mass into finest tempered steel.

Raistlin lifted his head from the cold stone.

The heat of the Queen's fury beat around him. Sweat poured from his body. He could not breathe as fire seared his lungs. She tormented him, mocked him with his own words, his own visions. She laughed at him, as so many had laughed at him before. And yet, even as his body shivered with a fear unlike any he had ever known, Raistlin's soul began to exult.

Puzzled, he tried to analyze it. He sought to regain control and, after an exertion that left him weak and shaking, he banished the ringing sounds of his mother's voice from his ears. He closed his eyes to his Queen's mocking smile.

Darkness enveloped him and he saw, in the cool, sweet darkness, his Queen's fear.

She was afraid . . . afraid of him!

Slowly, Raistlin rose to his feet. Hot winds blew from the Portal, billowing the black robes around him until he seemed enveloped in thunderclouds. He could look directly into the Portal now. His eyes narrowed. He regarded the dread door with a grim, twisted smile. Then, lifting his hand, Raistlin hurled the dragon orb into the Portal.

Hitting that invisible wall, the orb shattered. There was an almost imperceptible scream. Dark, shadowy wings fluttered around the mage's head, then, with a wail, the wings dissolved into smoke and were blown away.

Strength coursed through Raistlin's body, strength such as he had never known. The knowledge of his enemy's weakness affected him like an intoxicating liquor. He felt the magic flow from his mind into his heart and from there to his veins. The accumulated, combined power of centuries of learning was his—his and Fistandantilus's!

And then he heard it, the clear, clarion call of a trumpet, its music cold as the air from the snow-covered mountains of the dwarven homelands in the distance. Pure and crisp, the trumpet call echoed in his mind, driving out the distracting voices, calling him into darkness, giving him a power over death itself.

Raistlin paused. He hadn't intended to enter the Portal this soon. He would have like to have waited just a little longer. But now would do, if necessary. The kender's arrival meant time could be altered. The death of the gnome insured there would be no interference from the magical device—the interference that had proved the death of Fistandantilus.

The time had come.

Raistlin gave the Portal a last, lingering glance. Then, with a bow to his Queen, he turned and strode purposefully away up the corridor.

Crysania knelt in prayer in her room.

She had started to go back to bed after her return from the kender, but a strange feeling of foreboding filled her. There was a breathlessness in the air. A sense of waiting made her pause. Sleep would not come. She was alert, awake, more awake than she had ever been in her entire life.

The sky was filled with light—the cold fire of the stars burning in the darkness; the silver moon, Solinari, shining like a dagger. She could see every object in her room with an uncanny clarity, Each seemed alive, watching, waiting with her.

Transfixed, she stared at the stars, tracing the lines of the constellations—Gilean, the Book, the Scales of Balance; Takhisis, the Queen of Darkness, the Dragon of Many Colors and of None; Paladine, the Valiant Warrior, the Platinum Dragon. The moons—Solinari, God's Eye; Lunitari, Night Candle. Beyond them, ranged about the skies, the lesser gods, and among them, the planets.

And, somewhere, the Black Moon—the moon only his eyes could see.

Standing, staring into the night, Crysania's fingers grew cold as she rested them upon the chill stone. She realized she was shivering and she turned around, telling herself it was time to sleep. . . .

But there was still that tremulous intake of breath about the night. "Wait," it whispered. "Wait. . . ."

And then she heard the trumpet. Pure and crisp, its music

pierced her heart, crying a paean of victory that thrilled her blood.

At that moment, the door to her room opened.

She was not surprised to see him. It was as if she had been expecting his arrival, and she turned, calmly, to face him.

Raistlin stood silhouetted in the doorway, outlined against the light of torches blazing in the corridor and outlined as well by his own light which welled darkly from beneath his robes, an unholy light that came from within.

Drawn by some strange force, Crysania looked back into the heavens and saw, gleaming with that same dark light, Nuitari—the Black Moon.

For a moment, she closed her eyes, overwhelmed by the dizzying rush of blood, the beating of her heart. Then, feeling herself grow strong, she opened them again to find Raistlin standing before her.

She caught her breath. She had seen him in the ecstasy of his magic, she had seen him battling defeat and death. Now she saw him in the fullness of his strength, in the majesty of his dark power. Ancient wisdom and intelligence were etched into his face, a face that she barely recognized as his own.

"It is time, Crysania," he said, extending his hands.

She took hold of his hands. Her fingers were chilled, his touch burned them. "I am afraid," she whispered.

He drew her near.

"You have no need to be afraid," he said. "Your god is with you. I see that clearly. It is my goddess who is afraid, Crysania. I sense her fear! Together, you and I will cross the borders of time and enter the realm of death. Together, we will battle the Darkness. Together, we will bring Takhisis to her knees!"

His hands caught her close to his breast, his arms embraced her. His lips closed over hers, stealing her breath with his kiss.

Crysania closed her eyes and let the magical fire, the fire that consumed the bodies of the dead, consume her body, consume the cold, frightened, white-robed shell she had been hiding in all these years.

He drew back, tracing her mouth with his hand, raising her chin so that she could look into his eyes. And there, reflected in the mirror of his soul, she saw herself, glowing with a flaming aura of radiant, pure, white light. She saw herself beautiful, beloved, worshipped. She saw herself bringing truth and justice to the world, banishing forever sorrow and fear and despair.

"Blessed be to Paladine," Crysania whispered.

"Blessed be," Raistlin replied. "Once again, I give you a charm. As I protected you through Shoikan Grove, so you shall be guarded when we pass through the Portal."

She trembled. Drawing her near, holding her close one last time, he pressed his lips upon her forehead. Pain shot through her body and seared her heart. She flinched but did not cry out. He smiled at her.

"Come."

On the whispered words of a winged spell, they left the room to the night, just as the red rays of Lunitari spilled into the darkness—blood drawn from Solinari's glittering knife.

CHAPTER 15

The supply wagons?" Caramon asked in even, measured tones—the tones of one who already knows the answer.

"No word, sir," replied Garic, avoiding Caramon's steady gaze. "But . . . but we expect them—"

"They won't be coming. They've been ambushed. You know that." Caramon smiled wearily.

"At least we've found water," Garic said lamely, making a valiant effort to sound cheerful, which failed miserably. Keeping his gaze fixed on the map spread on the table before him, he nervously drew a small circle around a tiny green dot on the parchment.

Caramon snorted. "A hole that is emptied by midday. Oh, sure, it fills again at night, but my own sweat tastes better. Blasted stuff must be tainted by sea water."

"Still, it's drinkable. We're rationing, of course, and I've set guards around it. But it doesn't look like it's going to run dry."

"Oh, well. There won't be men enough left to drink it to worry about it after a while," Caramon said, running his hand through his curly hair with a sigh. It was hot in the room, hot and stuffy. Some overzealous servant had tossed wood onto the fire before Caramon, accustomed to living outdoors, could stop him. The big man had thrown open a window to let the fresh, crisp air inside, but the blaze roaring at his back was toasting him nicely nonetheless. "What's the desertion count today?"

Garic cleared his throat. "About—about one hundred, sir," he said reluctantly.

"Where'd they go? Pax Tharkas?"

"Yes, sir. So we believe."

"What else?" Caramon asked grimly, his eyes studying Garic's face. "You're keeping something back."

The young knight flushed. Garic had a passing wish, at this moment, that lying was not against every code of honor he held dear. As he would have given his life to spare this man pain, so he would almost have lied. He hesitated, then—looking at Caramon—he saw it wasn't necessary. The general knew already.

Caramon nodded slowly. "The Plainsmen?"

Garic looked down at the maps.

"All of them?"

"Yes, sir."

Caramon's eyes closed. Sighing softly, he picked up one of the small wooden figures that had been spread out on the map to represent the placement and disposition of his troops. Rolling it around in his fingers, he grew thoughtful. Then, suddenly, with a bitter curse, he turned and heaved the figurine into the fire. After a moment, he let his aching head sink into his hands.

"I don't suppose I blame Darknight. It won't be easy for him and his men, even now. The mountain dwarves undoubtedly hold the mountain passes behind us—that's what happened to the supply wagons. He'll have to fight his way home. May the gods go with him."

Caramon was silent a moment, then his fists clenched. "Damn my brother," he cursed. "Damn him!"

Garic shifted nervously. His gaze darted about the room, fearful that the black-robed figure might materialize from the shadows.

"Well," Caramon said, straightening and studying the maps once again, "this isn't getting us anywhere. Now, our only hope—as I see it—is to keep what's left of our army here in the plains. We've got to draw the dwarves out, force them to fight in the open so we can utilize our cavalry. We'll never win our way into the mountain," he added, a note of bitterness creeping into his voice, "but at least we can retreat with a hope of winning back to Pax Tharkas with our forces still intact. Once there, we can fortify it and—"

"General." One of the guards at the door entered the room, flushing at having to interrupt. "Begging your pardon, sir, but a messenger's arrived."

"Send him in."

A young man entered the room. Covered with dust, his cheeks red from the cold, he cast the blazing fire a longing glance but stepped forward first to deliver his message.

"No, go on, warm yourself," Caramon said, waving the man over to the fireplace. "I'm glad someone can appreciate it. I have a feeling your news is going to be foul to the taste anyway."

"Thank you, sir," the man said gratefully. Standing near the blaze, he spread his hands out to the warmth. "My news is this—the hill dwarves have gone."

"Gone?" Caramon repeated in blank astonishment, rising to his feet. "Gone where? Surely not back—"

"They march on Thorbardin." The messenger hesitated. "And, sir, the Knights went with them."

"That's insane!" Caramon's fist crashed down upon the table, sending the wooden markers flying through the air, the maps rolling off the edges. His face grew grim. "My brother."

"No, sir. It was apparently the Dewar. I was instructed to give you this." Drawing a scroll from his pouch, he handed it to Caramon, who quickly opened it.

General Caramon,

I have just learned from Dewar spies that the gates to the mountain will open when the trumpet sounds. We plan to steal a march on them. Rising at dawn, we will reach there by nightfall. I am sorry there wasn't time to inform you of this. Rest assured, you will receive what share of the spoils you are due, even if you arrive late. Reorx's light shine on your axes.

Reghar Fireforge.

Caramon's mind went back to the piece of blood-stained parchment he'd held in his hand not long ago. *The wizard has betrayed you. . . .*

"Dewar," Caramon scowled. "Dewar spies. Spies all right, but not for us! Traitors all right, but not to their own people!"

"A trap!" Garic said, rising to his feet as well.

"And we fell into it like a bunch of damn rabbits," Caramon muttered, thinking of another rabbit in a trap; seeing, in his mind's eyes, his brother setting it free. "Pax Tharkas falls. No great loss. It can always be retaken—especially if the defenders are dead. Our people deserting in droves, the Plainsmen leaving. And now the hill dwarves marching to Thorbardin, the Dewar marching with them. And, when the trumpet sounds—"

The clear, clarion call of a trumpet rang out. Caramon started. Was he hearing it or was it a dream, borne on the wings of a terrible vision? He could almost see it being played out before his eyes—the Dewar, slowly, imperceptibly spreading out among the hill dwarves, infiltrating their ranks. Hand creeping to axe, hammer . . .

Most of Reghar's people would never know what hit them, would never have a chance to strike.

Caramon could hear the shouts, the thudding of iron-shod boots, the clash of weapons, and the harsh, discordant cries of deep voices. It was real, so very real. . . .

Lost in his vision, Caramon only dimly became aware of the sudden pallor of Garic's face. Drawing his sword, the young Knight sprang toward the door with a shout that jolted Caramon back to reality. Whirling, he saw a black tide of dark dwarves surging outside the door. There was a flash of steel.

"Ambush!" Garic yelled.

"Fall back!" Caramon thundered. "Don't go out there! The Knights are gone—we're the only ones here! Stay inside the room. Bolt the door." Leaping after Garic, he grabbed the Knight and hurled him back. "You guards, retreat!" he yelled to the two who were still standing outside the door and who were now battling for their lives.

Caramon gripped the arm of one of the guards to drag him into the room, bringing his sword down upon the head of an attacking Dewar at the same time. The dwarf's helm shattered. Blood spattered over Caramon, but he paid no attention. Shoving the guard behind him, Caramon hurled himself bodily at the horde of dark dwarves packed into the corridor, his sword slashing a bloody swath through them.

"Fall back, you fool!" he shouted over his shoulder at the second guard, who hesitated only a moment, then did as ordered. Caramon's ferocious charge had the intended effect of catching the Dewar off-balance—they stumbled backward in momentary panic at the sight of his battle-rage. But, that was all the panic was—momentary. Already Caramon could see them starting to recover their wits and their courage.

"General! Look out!" shouted Garic, standing in the doorway, his sword still in hand. Turning, Caramon headed back for the safety of the map room. But his foot slipped on the blood-covered stones and the big man fell, wrenching his knee painfully.

With a wild howl, the Dewar leaped on him.

"Get inside! Bolt the door, you—" The rest of Caramon's words were lost as he disappeared beneath a seething mass of dwarves.

"Caramon!"

Sick at heart, cursing himself for hanging back, Garic jumped into the fray. A hammer blow crashed into his arm, and he heard the bone crunch. His left hand went oddly limp. Well, he thought, oblivious to the pain, at least it wasn't my sword arm. His blade swung, a dark dwarf fell headless. An axe blade whined, but its wielder missed his mark. The dwarf was cut down from behind by one of the guards at the door.

Though unable to stand, Caramon still fought. A kick from his uninjured leg sent two dwarves reeling backward to crash into their fellows. Twisting onto his side, the big man smashed the hilt of his sword through the face of another dwarf, splashing blood up to his elbows. Then, in the return stroke, he thrust the blade through the guts of another. Garic's charge spared his life for an instant, but it seemed it was an instant only.

"Caramon! Above you!" shrieked Garic, battling viciously.

Rolling onto his back, Caramon looked up to see Argat standing over him, his axe raised. Caramon lifted his sword, but at that moment four dark dwarves leaped on him, pinning him to the floor.

Almost weeping in rage, heedless of the weapons flashing around him, Garic tried desperately to save Caramon. But there were too many dwarves between him and his general. Already, the Dewar's axe blade was falling. . . .

The axe fell—but it fell from nerveless hands. Garic saw Argat's eyes open wide in profound astonishment. The dwarf's axe fell to the blood-slick stones with a ringing clatter as the dark dwarf himself toppled over on top of Caramon. Staring at Argat's corpse, Garic saw a small knife sticking out of the back of the dwarf's neck.

He looked up to see the dark dwarf's killer and gasped in astonishment.

Standing over the body of the dead traitor was, of all things, a kender.

Garic blinked, thinking perhaps the fear and pain had done something strange to his mind, causing him to see phantoms. But there wasn't time to try to figure out this astounding occurrence. The young Knight had finally managed to reach his general's side. Behind him, he could hear the guards shouting and driving back the Dewar who, seeing their leader fall, had suddenly lost a great deal of their enthusiasm for a fight that was supposed to have been an easy slaughter.

The four dwarves who were holding Caramon stumbled back hastily as the big man struggled out from beneath Argat's body. Reaching down, Garic jerked the dead dwarf up by the back of his armor and tossed the body to one side, then hauled Caramon to his feet. The big man staggered, groaning, as his crippled knee gave way under his weight.

"Help us!" Garic cried unnecessarily to the guards, who were already by his side. Half-dragging and half-carrying Caramon, they assisted the limping man into the map room.

Turning to follow, Garic cast a quick glance around the corridor. The dark dwarves were eyeing him uncertainly. He caught a glimpse of other dwarves behind them—mountain dwarves, his mind registered.

And there, seemingly rooted to the spot, was the strange kender who had come out of nowhere, apparently, to save Caramon's life. The kender's face ashen, there was a green look about his lips. Not knowing what else to do, Garic wrapped his good arm around the kender's waist and, lifting him off his feet, hauled him back into the map room. As soon as he was inside, the guards slammed and bolted the door.

Caramon's face was covered with blood and sweat, but he grinned at Garic. Then he assumed a stern look.

"You damn fool knight," he growled. "I gave you a direct order and you disobeyed! I ought to—"

But his voice broke off as the kender, wriggling in Garic's grasp, raised his head.

"Tas," whispered Caramon, stunned.

"Hello, Caramon," Tas said weakly. "I—I'm awfully glad to see you again. I've got lots to tell you and it's very important and I really should tell you now but I . . . I think . . . I'm going . . . to faint."

"And so that's it," Tas said softly, his eyes dim with tears as he looked into Caramon's pale, expressionless face. "He lied to me about how to work the magical device. When I tried, it came apart in my hands. I *did* get to see the fiery mountain fall," he added, "and that was *almost* worth all the trouble. It might have even been worth dying to see. I'm not sure, since I haven't died yet, although I thought for a while I had. It certainly *wouldn't* be worth it, though, if I had to spend the Afterlife in the Abyss, which is *not* a nice place. I can't imagine why he wants to go there."

Tas sighed. "But, anyway, I could forgive him for that"— the kender's voice hardened and his small jaw set firmly— "but not for what he did to poor Gnimsh and what he tried to do to you—"

Tasslehoff bit his tongue. He hadn't meant to say that.

Caramon looked at him. "Go on, Tas," he said. "Tried to do to me?"

"N-nothing," Tas stammered, giving Caramon a sickly smile. "Just my rambling. You know me."

"What *did* he try to do?" Caramon smiled bitterly. "I didn't suppose there was anything left he *could* do to me."

"Have you killed," Tas muttered.

"Ah, yes." Caramon's expression did not change. "Of course. So *that's* what the dwarf's message meant."

"He gave you to—to the Dewar," Tas said miserably. "They were going to take your head back to King Duncan. Raistlin sent away all the Knights in the castle, telling them you'd ordered them off to Thorbardin." Tas waved his hand at Garic and the two guards. "He told the Dewar you'd have only your bodyguards "

Caramon said nothing. He felt nothing—neither pain nor anger, nor surprise. He was empty. Then a great surge of longing for his home, for Tika, for his friends, for Tanis, Laurana, for Riverwind and Goldmoon, rushed in to fill up that vast emptiness.

As if reading his thoughts, Tas rested his small head on Caramon's shoulder. "Can we go back to our own time now?" he said, looking up at Caramon wistfully. "I'm awfully tired. Say, do you think I could stay with you and Tika for a while? Just until I'm better. I wouldn't be a bother—I promise. . . ."

His eyes dim with tears, Caramon put his arm around the kender and held him close. "As long as you want, Tas," he said. Smiling sadly, he stared into the flames. "I'll finish the house. It won't take more than a couple of months. Then we'll go visit Tanis and Laurana. I promised Tika we'd do that. I promised her a long time ago, but I never seemed to get there. Tika always wanted to see Palanthas, you know. And maybe all of us could go to Sturm's tomb. I never did get a chance to tell him good-bye."

"And we can visit Elistan, and—Oh!" Tas's face grew alarmed. "Crysania! Lady Crysania! I tried to tell her about Raistlin, but she doesn't believe me. We can't leave her!" He leaped to his feet, wringing his hands. "We can't let him take her to that horrible place!"

Caramon shook his head. "We'll try to talk to her again, Tas. I don't think she'll listen, but at least we can try." He heaved himself up painfully. "They'll be at the Portal now. Raistlin can't wait much longer. The fortress will fall to the mountain dwarves soon.

"Garic," he said, limping over to where the Knight sat. "How's it going?"

One of the other Knights had just finished setting Garic's broken arm. They were tying it up in a rude sling, binding it to his side so that it was immobile. The young man looked up at Caramon, gritting his teeth with the pain but managing a smile nonetheless.

"I'll be fine, sir," he said weakly. "Don't worry."

Smiling, Caramon drew up a chair next to him. "Feel like traveling?"

"Of course, sir."

"Good. Actually, I guess you don't have much choice. This place will be overrun soon. You've got to try to go out now." Caramon rubbed his chin. "Reghar told me there were tunnels running beneath the plains, tunnels that lead from Pax Tharkas to Thorbardin. My advice is to find these. That shouldn't be too difficult. Those mounds out there lead down to them. You should be able to use the tunnels to at least get out of here safely."

Garic did not answer. Glancing at the other two guards, he said quietly, "You say 'your advice,' sir. What about you? Aren't you coming with us?"

Caramon cleared his throat and started to answer, but he

couldn't talk. He stared down at his feet. This was a moment he had been dreading and, now that it was here, the speech he had carefully prepared blew out of his head like a leaf in the wind.

"No, Garic," he said finally, "I'm not." Seeing the Knight's eyes flash and guessing what he was thinking, the big man raised his hand. "No, I'm not going to do anything so foolish as to throw my life away on some noble, stupid cause—like rescuing my commanding officer!"

Garic flushed in embarrassment as Caramon grinned at him.

"No," the big man continued more somberly, "I'm not a Knight, thank the gods. I have enough sense to run when I'm beaten. And right now"—he couldn't help but sigh—"I'm beaten." He ran his hand through his hair. "I can't explain this so that you'll understand it. I'm not sure I understand, not fully. But—let's just say that the kender and I have a magical way home."

Garic glanced from one to the other. "Not your brother!" he said, frowning darkly.

"No," Caramon answered, "not my brother. Here, he and I part company. He has his own life to live and—I finally see—I have mine." He put his hand on Garic's shoulder. "Go to Pax Tharkas. You and Michael do what you can to help those who make it there safely survive the winter."

"But—"

"That's an order, Sir Knight," Caramon said harshly.

"Yes, sir." Garic averted his face, his hand brushing quickly across his eyes.

Caramon, his own face growing gentle, put his arm around the young man. "Paladine be with you, Garic," he said, clasping him close. He looked at the others. "May he be with all of you."

Garic looked up at him in astonishment, tears glistening on his cheeks. "Paladine?" he said bitterly. "The god who deserted us?"

"Don't lose your faith, Garic," Caramon admonished, rising to his feet with a pain-filled grimace. "Even if you can't believe in the god, put your trust in your heart. Listen to its voice above the Code and the Measure. And, someday, you'll understand."

"Yes, sir," Garic murmured. "And . . . may whatever gods you believe in be with you, too, sir."

"I guess they have been," Caramon said, smiling ruefully, "all my life. I've just been too damn thick-headed to listen. Now, you better be off."

One by one, he bade the other young Knights farewell, feigning to ignore their manful attempts to hide their tears. He was truly touched by their sorrow at parting—a sorrow he shared to such an extent that he could have broken down and wept like a child himself.

Cautiously, the Knights opened the door and peered out into the corridor. It was empty, except for the corpses. The Dewar were gone. But Caramon had no doubt this lull would last only long enough for them to regroup. Perhaps they were waiting until reinforcements arrived. Then they would attack the map room and finish off these humans.

Sword in hand, Garic led his Knights out into the blood-spattered corridor, planning to follow Tas's somewhat confused directions on how to reach the lower levels of the magical fortress. (Tas had offered to draw them a map, but Caramon said there wasn't time.)

When the Knights were gone, and the last echoes of their footfalls had died away, Tas and Caramon set off in the opposite direction. Before they went, Tas retrieved his knife from Argat's body.

"And you said once that a knife like this would be good only for killing vicious rabbits," Tas said proudly, wiping the blood from the blade before thrusting it into his belt.

"Don't mention rabbits," Caramon said in such an odd, tight voice that Tas looked at him and was startled to see his face go deathly pale.

CHAPTER
16

This was his moment. The moment he had been born to face. The moment for which he had endured the pain, the humiliation, the anguish of his life. The moment for which he had studied, fought, sacrificed . . . killed.

He savored it, letting the power flow over him and through him, letting it surround him, lift him. No other sounds, no other objects, nothing in this world existed for him this moment now save the Portal and the magic.

But even as he exulted in the moment, his mind was intent upon his work. His eyes studied the Portal, studied every detail intently—although it was not really necessary. He had seen it myriad times in dreams both sleeping and waking. The spells to open it were simple, nothing elaborate or complex. Each of the five dragon heads surrounding and guarding the Portal must be propitiated with the correct phrase. Each must be spoken to in the proper order. But, once that was done and the White-Robed Cleric had exhorted Paladine to intercede and hold the Portal open, they would enter. It would close behind them.

And he would face his greatest challenge.

The thought excited him. His rapidly beating heart sent blood surging through his veins, throbbing in his temples, pulsing in his throat. Looking at Crysania, he nodded. It was time.

The cleric, her own face flushed with heightened excitement, her eyes already shimmering with the luster of the ecstasy of her prayers, took her place directly inside the Portal, facing Raistlin. This move required that she place utter, complete, unwavering confidence in him. For one wrong syllable spoken, the wrong breath drawn at the wrong moment, the slightest slip of the tongue or hand gesture would be fatal to her, to himself.

Thus had the ancients—devising ways to guard this dread gate that they, because of their folly, could not shut—sought to protect it. For a wizard of the Black Robes—who had committed the heinous deeds they knew *must* be committed to arrive at this point, and a Cleric of Paladine—pure of faith and soul—to put implicit trust in each other was a ludicrous supposition.

Yet, it had happened once: bound by the false charm of the one and the loss of faith of the other, Fistandantilus and Denubis had reached this point. And it would happen again, it seemed, with two bound by something that the ancients, for all their wisdom, had not foreseen—a strange, unhallowed love.

Stepping into the Portal, looking at Raistlin for the last time upon this world, Crysania smiled at him. He smiled back, even as the words for the first spell were forming in his mind.

Crysania raised her arms. Her eyes stared beyond Raistlin now, stared into the brilliant, beautiful realms where dwelt her god. She had heard the last words of the Kingpriest, she knew the mistake he had made—a mistake of pride, demanding of the god in his arrogance what he should have requested in humility.

At that moment Crysania had come to understand why the gods had—in their righteous anger—inflicted destruction upon the world. And she had known in her heart that Paladine would answer *her* prayers, as he had not answered those of the Kingpriest. This was Raistlin's moment of greatness. It was also her own.

Like the holy Knight, Huma, she had been through her trials. Trials of fire, darkness, death, and blood. She was ready. She was prepared.

"Paladine, Platinum Dragon, your faithful servant comes before you and begs that you shed your blessing upon her. Her eyes are open to your light. At last, she understands what you have, in your wisdom, been trying to teach her. Hear her prayer, Radiant One. Be with her. Open this Portal so that she may enter and go forward bearing your torch. Walk with her as she strives to banish the darkness forever!"

Raistlin held his breath. All depended on this! Had he been right about her? Did she possess the strength, the wisdom, the faith? Was she truly Paladine's chosen? . . .

A pure and holy light began to glimmer from Crysania. Her dark hair shimmered, her white robes shone like sunlit clouds, her eyes gleamed like the silver moon. Her beauty at this moment was sublime.

"Thank you for granting my prayer, God of Light," Crysania murmured, bowing her head. Tears sparkled like stars upon her pale face. "I will be worthy of you!"

Watching her, enchanted by her beauty, Raistlin forgot his great goal. He could only stare at her, entranced. Even the thoughts of his magic—for a heartbeat—fled.

Then he exulted. Nothing! Nothing could stop him now . . .

"Oh, Caramon!" whispered Tasslehoff in awe.

"We're too late," Caramon said.

The two, having made their way through the dungeons to the very bottom level of the magical fortress, came to a sudden halt—their eyes on Crysania. Enveloped in a halo of silver light, she stood in the center of the Portal, her arms outstretched, her face lifted to the heavens. Her unearthly beauty pierced Caramon's heart.

"Too late? No!" Tas cried in anguish. "We can't be!"

"Look, Tas," Caramon said sadly. "Look at her eyes. She's blind. Blind! Just as blind as I was in the Tower of High Sorcery. She cannot see through the light. . . ."

"We've got to *try* to talk to her, Caramon!" Tas clutched at him frantically. "We can't let her go. It—it's my fault! I'm the one who told her about Bupu! She might not have come if it hadn't been for me! I'll talk to her!"

The kender leaped forward, waving his arms. But he was jerked back suddenly by Caramon, who caught hold of him by his tassel of hair. Tas yelped in pain and protest, and—at the sound—Raistlin turned.

The archmage stared over at his twin and the kender for an instant without seeming to recognize them. Then recognition dawned in his eyes. It was not pleasant.

"Hush, Tas," Caramon whispered. "It's not your fault. Now, stay put!" Caramon thrust the kender behind a thick, granite pillar. "Stay there," the big man ordered. "Keep the pendant safe—and yourself, too."

Tas's mouth opened to argue. Then he saw Caramon's face and, looking down the corridor, he saw Raistlin. Something came over the kender. He felt as he had in the Abyss— wretched and frightened. "Yes, Caramon," he said softly. "I'll stay here. I—I promise. . . ."

Leaning against the pillar, shivering, Tas could see in his mind poor Gnimsh lying crumpled on the cell floor.

Giving the kender a final, warning glance, Caramon turned and limped down the corridor toward where his brother stood.

Gripping the Staff of Magius in his hand, Raistlin watched him warily. "So you survived," he commented.

"Thanks to the gods, not you," Caramon replied.

"Thanks to *one* god, my dear brother," Raistlin said with a slight, twisted smile. "The Queen of Darkness. She sent the kender back here, and it was he, I presume, who altered time, allowing your life to be spared. Does it gall you, Caramon, to know you owe your life to the Dark Queen?"

"Does it gall you to know you owe her your soul?"

Raistlin's eyes flashed, their mirrorlike surface cracking for just an instant. Then, with a sardonic smile, he turned away. Facing the Portal, he lifted his right hand and held it palm out, his gaze upon the dragon's head at the lower right of the oval-shaped entrance.

"Black Dragon." His voice was soft, caressing. *"From darkness to darkness/My voice echoes in the emptiness."*

As Raistlin spoke these words, an aura of darkness began to form around Crysania, an aura of light as black as the night-jewel, as black as the light of the dark moon. . . .

Raistlin felt Caramon's hand close over his arm. Angrily, he tried to shake off his brother's grasp, but Caramon's grip was strong.

"Take us home, Raistlin. . . ."

Raistlin turned and stared, his anger forgotten in his astonishment. "What?" His voice cracked.

"Take us home," Caramon repeated steadily.

Raistlin laughed contemptuously.

"You are such a weak, sniveling fool, Caramon!" he snarled. Irritably he tried to shake off his twin's grip. He might as well have tried to shake off death. "Surely you must know by now what I have done! The kender must have told you about the gnome, You know I betrayed you. I would have left you for dead in this wretched place. And still you cling to me!"

"I'm clinging to you because the waters are closing over your head, Raistlin," Caramon said.

His gaze went down to his own, strong, sun-burned hand holding his brother's thin wrist, its bones as fragile as the bones of a bird, its skin white, almost transparent. Caramon fancied he could see the blood pulse in the blue veins.

"My hand upon your arm. That's all we have." Caramon paused and drew a deep breath. Then, his voice deep with sorrow, he continued, "Nothing can erase what you have done, Raist. It can never be the same between us. My eyes have been opened. I now see you for what you are."

"And yet you beg me to come with you!" Raistlin sneered.

"I could learn to live with the knowledge of what you are

and what you have done." Looking intently into his brother's eyes Caramon said softly, "But you have to live with yourself, Raistlin. And there are times in the night when that must be damn near unbearable."

Raistlin did not respond. His face was a mask, impenetrable, unreadable.

Caramon swallowed a huskiness in his throat. His grip on his twin's arm tightened. "Think of this, though. You *have* done good in your life, Raistlin—maybe better than most of us. Oh, I've helped people. It's easy to help someone when that help is appreciated. But you helped those who only threw it back in your face. You helped those who didn't deserve it. You helped even when you knew it was hopeless, thankless." Caramon's hand trembled. "There's still good you could do . . . to make up for the evil. Leave this. Come home."

Come home . . . come home. . . .

Raistlin closed his eyes, the ache in his heart almost unendurable. His left hand stirred, lifted. Its delicate fingers hovered near his brother's hand, touching it for an instant with a touch as soft as the feet of a spider. On the edges of reality, he could hear Crysania's soft voice, praying to Paladine. The lovely white light flickered upon his eyelids.

Come home. . . .

When Raistlin spoke next, his voice was soft as his touch.

"The dark crimes that stain my soul, brother, you cannot begin to imagine. If you knew, you would turn from me in horror and in loathing." He sighed, shivering slightly. "And, you are right. Sometimes, in the night, even I turn from myself."

Opening his eyes, Raistlin stared fixedly into his brother's. "But, know this, Caramon—I committed those crimes intentionally, willingly. Know this, too—there are darker crimes before me, and I will commit them, intentionally, willingly. . . ." His gaze went to Crysania, standing unseeing in the Portal, lost in her prayers, shimmering with beauty and power.

Caramon looked at her and his face grew grim.

Raistlin, watching, smiled. "Yes, my brother. She will enter the Abyss with me. She will go before me and fight my battles. She will face dark clerics, dark magic-users, spirits of the dead doomed to wander in that cursed land, plus the unbelievable torments that my Queen can devise. All these will wound her in body, devour her mind, and shred her soul. Finally, when she can endure no more, she will slump to the ground to lie at my feet . . . bleeding, wretched, dying.

"She will, with her last strength, hold out her hand to me for comfort. She will not ask me to save her. She is too strong for that. She will give her life for me willingly, gladly. All she will ask is that I stay with her as she dies."

Raistlin drew a deep breath, then shrugged. "But I will walk past her, Caramon. I will walk past her without a look, without a word. Why? Because I will need her no longer. I will continue forward toward my goal, and my strength will grow even as the blood flows from her pierced heart."

Half-turning, once again he raised his left hand, palm outward. Looking at the head of the dragon upon the top of the Portal, he softly said the second chant. *"White Dragon. From this world to the next/My voice cries with life."*

Caramon's gaze was on the Portal, on Crysania, his mind swamped by horror and revulsion. Still he held onto his brother. Still he thought to make one last plea. Then he felt the thin arm beneath his hand make a sharp, twisting motion. There was a flash, a swift movement, and the gleaming blade of a silver dagger pressed against the flesh of his throat, right where his life's blood pulsed in his neck.

"Let go of me, my brother," Raistlin said.

And though he did not strike with the dagger, it drew blood anyway; drew blood not from flesh but from soul. Quickly and cleanly, it sliced through the last spiritual tie between the twins. Caramon winced slightly at the swift, sharp pain in his heart.

But the pain did not endure. The tie was severed. Free at last, Caramon released his twin's arm without a word.

Turning, he started to limp back to where Tas waited, still hidden behind the pillar.

"One final hint of caution, my brother," Raistlin said coldly, returning the dagger to the thong he wore on his wrist.

Caramon did not respond, he neither stopped walking nor turned around.

"Be wary of that magical time device," Raistlin continued with a sneer. "Her Dark Majesty repaired it. It was she who sent the kender back. If you use it, you could find yourselves in a most unpleasant place!"

"Oh, but she didn't fix it!" Tas cried, popping out from behind the pillar. "Gnimsh did. Gnimsh fixed it! Gnimsh, my friend. The gnome that you murdered! I—"

"Use it then," Raistlin said coldly. "Take him and yourself out of here, Caramon. But remember I warned you."

Caramon caught hold of the angry kender. "Easy, Tas. That's enough. It doesn't matter now."

Turning around, Caramon faced his twin. Though the warrior's face was drawn with pain and weariness, his expression was one of peace and calm, one who knows himself at last. Stroking Tas's topknot of hair soothingly with his hand, he said, "Come on, Tas. Let's go home. Farewell, my brother."

Raistlin didn't hear. Facing the Portal, he was once again lost in his magic. But, out of the corner of his eye, even as he began the third chant, Raistlin saw his twin take the pendant from Tas and began the manipulations that would transfer its shape from pendant to the magical time-travel device.

Let them go. Good riddance! Raistlin thought. Finally, I am free of that great hulking idiot!

Looking back at the Portal, Raistlin smiled. A circle of cold light, like the harsh glare of the sun upon snow, surrounded Crysania. The archmage's behest to the White Dragon had been heard.

Raising his hand, facing the third dragon's head in the lower left part of the Portal, Raistlin recited its chant.

"Red Dragon. From darkness to darkness I shout/Beneath my feet all is made firm."

Red lines shot from Crysania's body through the white light, through the black aura. Red and burning as blood, they spanned the gap from Raistlin to the Portal—a bridge to beyond.

Raistlin raised his voice. Turning to the right, he called to the fourth dragon. *"Blue Dragon. Time that flows/Hold in your course."*

Blue streams of light flowed over Crysania, then began to swirl. As though floating in water, she leaned her head back, her arms extended, her robes drifting about her in the whirling flashes of light, her hair drifting black upon the currents of time.

Raistlin felt the Portal shiver. The magical field was starting to activate and respond to his commands! His soul quivered in a joy that Crysania shared. Her eyes glistened with rapturous tears, her lips parted in a sweet sigh. Her hands spread and, at her touch, the Portal opened!

Raistlin's breath caught in his throat. The surge of power and ecstasy that coursed through his body nearly choked him. He could see through the Portal now. He could see glimpses of the plane beyond, the plane forbidden to mortal men.

From somewhere, dimly heard, came his brother's voice activating the magical device—"Thy time is thy own, though across it you travel . . . Grasp firmly the beginning and the end . . . destiny be over your head. . . ."

Home. *Come home. . . .*

Raistlin began the fifth chant. *"Green Dragon. Because by fate even the gods are cast down/Weep ye all with me."*

Raistlin's voice cracked, faltered. Something was wrong ! The magic pulsing through his body slowed, turned sluggish. He stammered out the last few words, but each breath was an effort. His heart ceased to beat for an instant, then started again with a great leap that shook his frail frame.

Shocked and confused, Raistlin stared frantically at the Portal. Had the final spell worked? No! The light around Crysania was beginning to waver. The field was shifting!

Desperately, Raistlin cried the words of the last chant again. But his voice cracked, snapping back on him like a whip, stinging him. What was happening? He could feel the magic slither from his grasp. He was losing control. . . .

Come home. . . .

His Queen's voice laughing, mocking. His brother's voice

pleading, sorrowful. . . . And then, another voice—a shrill
kender voice—only half-heard, lost in his greater affairs. Now
it flashed through his brain with a blinding light.

Gnimsh fixed it. . . . The gnome, my friend . . .

As the dwarf's blade had penetrated Raistlin's shrinking
flesh, so now the remembered words of Astinus's *Chronicles*
stabbed his soul:

*At the same instant a gnome, being held prisoner by the dwarves
of Thorbardin, activated a time-traveling device. . . . The gnome's
device interacted somehow with the delicate and powerful magical
spells being woven by Fistandantilus. . . . A blast occurred of such
magnitude that the Plains of Dergoth were utterly destroyed. . . .*

Raistlin clenched his fists in anger. Killing the gnome had
been useless! The wretched creature had tampered with the
device *before* his death. History would repeat itself! Footsteps
in the sand. . . .

Looking into the Portal, Raistlin saw the executioner step
out from it. He saw his own hand lift his own black hood, he
saw the flash of the axe blade descending, his own hands
bringing it down upon his own neck!

The magical field began to shift violently. The dragon
heads surrounding the Portal shrieked in triumph. A spasm of
pain and terror twisted Crysania's face. Looking into her eyes,
Raistlin saw the same look he had seen in his mother's eyes as
they stared unseeing into a far-distant plane.

Come home. . . .

Within the Portal itself, the swirling lights began to whirl
madly. Spinning out of control, they rose up around the limp
body of the cleric as the magical flames had risen around her
in the plague town. Crysania cried out in pain. Her flesh
began to wither in the beautiful, deadly fire of uncontrolled
magic.

Half-blinded by the brilliance, tears ran from Raistlin's
eyes as he stared into the swirling vortex. And then he saw—
the Portal was closing.

Hurling his magical staff to the floor, Raistlin unleashed his
rage in a bitter, incoherent scream of fury.

Out of the Portal, in answer, came lilting, mocking laughter.

Come home. . . .

A feeling of calmness stole over Raistlin—the cold calm of despair. He had failed. But *She* would never see him grovel. If he must die, he would die within his magic. . . .

He lifted his head. He rose to his feet. Using all of his great powers—powers of the ancients, powers of his own, powers he had no idea he possessed, powers that rose from somewhere dark and hidden even from himself—Raistlin raised his arms and his voice screamed out once again. But this time it was not an incoherent shriek of frustrated helplessness. This time, his words were clear. This time he shouted words of command—words of command that had never been uttered upon this world before.

This time his words were heard and understood.

The field held. *He* held it! He could feel himself holding onto it. At his command, the Portal shivered and ceased to close.

Raistlin drew a deep, shuddering breath. Then, out of the corner of his eye, somewhere to his right, he saw a flash. The magical time-travel device had been activated!

The field jumped and surged wildly. As the device's magic grew and spread, its powerful vibrations caused the very rocks of the fortress to begin to sing. In a devastating wave, their songs surged around Raistlin. The dragons' shrieking answered in anger. The ageless voices of the rocks and the timeless voices of the dragons fought, flowed together, and finally combined in a discordant, mind-shattering cacophony.

The sound was deafening, ear-splitting. The force of the two powerful spells sundered the ground. The earth beneath Raistlin's feet shuddered. The singing rocks split wide open. The metallic dragons' heads cracked. . . .

The Portal itself began to crumble.

Raistlin fell to his knees. The magical field was tearing loose, splitting apart like the bones of the world itself. It was breaking, splintering and, because Raistlin still held onto it, it began to tear him apart as well.

Pain shot through his head. His body convulsed. He writhed in agony.

It was a terrible choice he faced. Let go, and he would fall, fall to his doom, fall into a nothingness to which the most abject darkness was preferable. And yet, if he held it, he knew he would be ripped apart, his body dismembered by the forces of magic he had generated and could no longer control.

His muscles ripped from his bones, sinews shredding, tendons snapping.

"Caramon!" Raistlin moaned, but Caramon and Tas had vanished. The magical device, repaired by the one gnome whose inventions worked, had, indeed, worked. They were gone. There was no help.

Raistlin had seconds to live, moments to act. Yet the pain was so excruciating that he could not think.

His joints were being wrested from their sockets, his eyes plucked from his face, his heart torn from his body, his brain sucked from his skull.

He could hear himself screaming and he knew it was his death cry. Still he fought on, as he had fought all his life.

I . . . will . . . control. . . .

The words came from his mouth, stained with his blood. . . .

I will control. . . .

Reaching out, his hand closed over the Staff of Magius.

I will!

And then he was hurtling forward into a blinding, swirling, crashing wave of many-colored lights—

Come home . . . come home. . . .

ACKNOWLEDGMENTS

There are many people whose interest in and work on the DRAGONLANCE books and modules have made the series the success it is today. We deeply appreciate their help and support.

Members of the DRAGONLANCE Design Team: Harold Johnson, Laura Hickman, Douglas Niles, Jeff Grubb, Michael Dobson, Michael Breault, Bruce Heard, Roger E. Moore.

Songs and Poems: Michael Williams

Original Cover Artwork: Larry Elmore

Interior Artwork: Valerie A. Valusek

Design: Ruth Hoyer

Maps: Steve Sullivan

Editor: Jean Blashfield Black

Valuable assistance and advice: Patrick L. Price, Dezra and Terry Phillips, John "Dalamar" Walker, Carolyn Vanderbilt, Bill Larson, Janet and Gary Pack

1987 DRAGONLANCE Calendar Artists: Clyde Caldwell, Larry Elmore, Keith Parkinson, Jeff Easley

And, finally, we want to thank all of you who have taken the time to write to us. We appreciate it very much.

—Margaret Weis and Tracy Hickman

Legends Trilogy

Margaret Weis & Tracy Hickman

Each volume available for the first time ever in hardcover!

TIME OF THE TWINS
Volume I

Caramon Majere vows to protect Crysania, a devout cleric, in her quest to save Raistlin from himself. But both are soon caught in the dark mage's deadly designs, and their one hope is a frivolous kender.

April 2004

WAR OF THE TWINS
Volume II

Catapulted through time by Raistlin's dark magics, Caramon and Crysania are forced to aid the mage in his quest to defeat the Queen of Darkness.

June 2004

TEST OF THE TWINS
Volume III

As Raistlin's plans come to fruition, Caramon comes face to face with his destiny. Old friends and strange allies come to aid him, but Caramon must take the final step alone.

November 2004

Follow Mina from the War of Souls into the chaos of post-war Krynn.

AMBER AND ASHES
The Dark Disciple, Volume I

Margaret Weis

With Paladine and Takhisis gone, the lesser gods vie for primacy over Krynn. Recruited to a new faith by a god of evil, Mina leads a religion of the dead, and kender and a holy monk are all that stand in the way of the dark stain spreading across Ansalon.

First in a new series from *New York Times* best-selling author Margaret Weis.

August 2004

The Elven Nations Trilogy is back in print in all-new editions!

FIRSTBORN
Volume One

Paul B. Thompson & Tonya C. Cook

In moments, the fate of two leaders is decided. Sithas, firstborn son of the elf monarch Sithel, is destined to inherit the crown and kingdom from his father. His twin brother Kith-Kanan, born just a few heartbeats later, must make his own destiny. Together—and apart—the princes will see their world torn asunder for the sake of power, freedom, and love.

New edition in October 2004

THE KINSLAYER WAR
Volume Two

Douglas Niles

Timeless and elegant, the elven realm seems unchanging. But when the dynamic human nation of Ergoth presses on the frontiers of the Silvanesti realm, the elves must awaken—and unite—to turn back the tide of human conquest. Prince Kith-Kanan, returned from exile, holds the key to victory.

New edition in November 2004

THE QUALINESTI
Volume Three

Paul B. Thompson & Tonya C. Cook

Wars done, the weary nations of Krynn turn to rebuilding their exhausted lands. In the mountains, a city devoted to peace, Pax Tharkas, is carved from living stone by elf and dwarf hands. In the new nation of Qualinesti, corruption seeks to undermine this new beginning. A new generation of elves and humans must band together if the noble experiment of Kith-Kanan is to be preserved.

New edition in December 2004

Long before the War of the Lance, other heroes made their mark upon Ansalon.

Revisit these classic tales, including the *New York Times* best-seller *The Legend of Huma*, in these brand new editions!

THE LEGEND OF HUMA
Heroes, Volume One
Richard A. Knaak
January 2004

STORMBLADE
Heroes, Volume Two
Nancy Varian Berberick
April 2004

WEASEL'S LUCK
Heroes, Volume Three
Michael Williams
May 2004

KAZ THE MINOTAUR
Heroes, Volume Four
Richard A. Knaak
July 2004

THE GATES OF THORBARDIN
Heroes, Volume Five
Dan Parkinson
August 2004

GALEN BENIGHTED
Heroes, Volume Six
Michael Williams
November 2004

Strife and warfare tear at the land of Ansalon

FLIGHT OF THE FALLEN
The Linsha Trilogy, Volume Two

Mary H. Herbert

As the Plains of Dust are torn asunder by invading barbarian forces, Rose Knight Linsha Majere is torn between two vows—her pledge to the Knighthood, and her pledge to guard the eggs of the dragon overlord Iyesta. To keep her honor, Linsha will have to make the ultimate sacrifice.

September 2004

CITY OF THE LOST
The Linsha Trilogy, Volume One

Available Now!

LORD OF THE ROSE
Rise of Solamnia, Volume One

Douglas Niles

In the wake of the War of Souls, the realms of Solamnia are wracked by strife and internecine warfare, and dire external threats lurk on its borders. A young lord, marked by courage and fateful flaws, emerges from the hinterlands. His vow: he will unite the fractious reaches of the ancient knighthood—or die in the attempt.

November 2004

The War of Souls is at an end,
but the tales of Krynn continue…

THE SEARCH FOR POWER:
DRAGONS FROM THE WAR OF SOULS
Edited by Margaret Weis

After the War of Souls, dragons are much harder to find, but they should still be avoided. They come in all hues and sizes and can be just as charming and mischievous as they are evil and deadly. The best-known **Dragonlance** authors spin tales of these greatest of beasts, in all their variety and splendor.

May 2004

PRISONER OF HAVEN
The Age of Mortals
Nancy Varian Berberick

Usha and Dezra Majere find that a visit to the city of Haven might make them permanent residents. The two must fight both the forces of the evil dragon overlord and one another in their attempts to free the city—and themselves.

June 2004

WIZARDS' CONCLAVE
The Age of Mortals
Douglas Niles

The gods have returned to the world of **Dragonlance**, but their power is far from secure. Dalamar the Dark, together with the Red Mistress, Jenna of Palanthas, must gather the forces of traditional magic for a momentous battle that will determine the future of sorcery in the world.

July 2004

THE LAKE OF DEATH
The Age of Mortals
Jean Rabe

Dhamon, a former Dark Knight cursed to roam in dragon form, prays that something left behind in the submerged city of Qualinost has the magical power to make him human again. But gaining such an elven relic could come at a terrible price: his honor, or the lives of his companions.

October 2004

The Minotaur Wars

Richard A. Knaak

A new trilogy featuring the minotaur race that continues the story from the *New York Times* best-selling War of Souls trilogy!

Now available in paperback!
NIGHT OF BLOOD
Volume One

As the War of Souls spreads, a terrible, bloody coup led by the ambitious General Hotak and his wife, the High Priestess Nephera, overtakes the minotaur empire. With legions of soldiers and the unearthly magic of the Forerunners at his command, the new emperor turns his sights towards Ansalon. But not all his enemies lie dead...

February 2004

New in hardcover!
TIDES OF BLOOD
Volume Two

Making a bold pact with the ogres, and with the assurances of the mysterious warrior-woman Mina sweetly ringing in his ears, the minotaur emperor Hotak decides to invade Ansalon. But betrayal comes from the least expected quarters, and an escaped slave called Faros, the last of the blood of the lawful emperor, stirs up a fresh, vengeance-driven rebellion.

April 2004

The Ergoth Trilogy

Paul B. Thompson & Tonya C. Cook

Explore the history of the ancient **Dragonlance®** world!

THE WIZARD'S FATE
Volume Two

The old Emperor is dead, sending shock
waves throughout the Ergoth Empire. Dark
forces gather as two brothers vie bitterly for the
throne. Key to the struggle for succession are
the rogue sorcerer Mandes and peasant general
Lord Tolandruth—sworn enemies of one
another—and the noble lady Tol loves, whose
first loyalty is to her husband, the Crown Prince.

February 2004

A HERO'S JUSTICE
Volume Three

The Ergoth Empire has been invaded on two
fronts, and the teeming horde streaming across
the plain is no human army. As the warriors
of Ergoth reel back, defeated and broken, the
cry goes up far and wide, "Where is Lord
Tolandruth?!" Banished by Emperor Ackal V, no
one had seen Tol in more than six years. To save
Ergoth, Egrin Raemel's son rides forth to find Tol
and forge an alliance between a kender queen,
an aging beauty, and a lost and brilliant general.

December 2004

A WARRIOR'S JOURNEY
Volume One
Available Now

TWO NEW WAYS TO OWN THE PATHS OF DARKNESS BY *NEW YORK TIMES* BEST-SELLING AUTHOR

R.A. SALVATORE

New in hardcover!
PATHS OF DARKNESS
COLLECTORS EDITION
A **Forgotten Realms**® Omnibus
February 2004

•

PATHS OF DARKNESS
GIFT SET
A new boxed set of all four titles in paperback
September 2004

Contains: *The Silent Blade, The Spine of the World,*
Servant of the Shard, Sea of Swords

Wulfgar the barbarian has returned from death to his companions:
Drizzt, Catti-brie, Regis, and Bruenor. Yet the road to freedom will
be long for him, and his path will lead through darkness before he
emerges into the light. And along the way he will find old enemies,
new allies, and someone to love.

THERE ARE A HUNDRED GODS LOOKING OVER FAERÛN, EACH WITH A THOUSAND SERVANTS OR MORE. SERVANTS WE CALL... THE PRIESTS

LADY OF POISON
Bruce R. Cordell

Evil has the Great Dale in its venomous grip. Monsters crawl from the shadows, disease and poison ravage the townsfolk, and dark cults gather in the night. Not all religions, after all, work for good.

July 2004

MISTRESS OF NIGHT
Dave Gross

Fighting a goddess of secrets can be a dangerous game. Werewolves stalk the moonlit night, goddesses clash in the heavens, and a lone priestess will sacrifice everything to stop them.

September 2004

QUEEN OF THE DEPTHS
Voronica Whitney-Robinson

Far below the waves, evil swims. The ocean goddess is a fickle mistress who toys with man and ship alike. How can she be trusted when the seas run red with blood?

May 2005

MAIDEN OF PAIN
Kameron M. Franklin

The book that **Forgotten Realms®** novel fans have been waiting for—the result of an exhaustive international talent search. The newest star in the skies of Faerûn tells a story of torture, sacrifice, and betrayal.

July 2005

ADVENTURES IN THE REALMS!

THE YELLOW SILK
The Rogues
Don Bassingthwaite

More than just the weather is cold and bitter in the wind-swept realm of Altumbel. When a stranger travels from the distant east to reclaim his family's greatest treasure, he finds just how cold and bitter a people can be.

February 2004

DAWN OF NIGHT
The Erevis Cale Trilogy, Book II
Paul S. Kemp

He's left Sembia far behind. He's made new friends. He's made new enemies. And now Erevis Cale himself is changing into something, and he's not sure exactly what it is.

June 2004

REALMS OF DRAGONS
The Year of Rogue Dragons
Edited by Philip Athans

All new stories by R.A. Salvatore, Richard Lee Byers, Ed Greenwood, Elaine Cunningham, and a host of **Forgotten Realms** stars breathe new life into the great wyrms of Faerûn.

December 2004

READERS CAN'T GET ENOUGH OF KATE MESSNER!

EYE OF THE STORM

A BANK STREET BEST CHILDREN'S BOOKS OF THE YEAR BOOK

AN INDIE NEXT LIST PICK

"A great addition to any collection." —*LMC*

"Plenty of action. . . . These heart-pounding scenes
will be a hit." —*School Library Journal*

"This fast-paced read will sweep readers along
to its powerful . . . conclusion." —*VOYA*

Wake Up Missing

AN INDIE NEXT LIST PICK

"Combines a fascinating concept with page-turning
suspense. . . . A wild roller-coaster ride through the
Florida swamps." —Margaret Peterson Haddix, author of
The Missing series and the Shadow Children series

"Loved it! Mystery, intrigue, danger, and creepy futuristic science
set in today's world? Yes, please!" —Lisa McMann, *New York
Times* bestselling author of *Wake* and *The Unwanteds*

"A winner." —Bruce Coville, author of The Unicorn
Chronicles and *My Teacher Is an Alien*

Sugar and Ice

The Brilliant Fall of Gianna Z.

EYE OF THE STORM

BOOKS BY KATE MESSNER

The Brilliant Fall of Gianna Z.
Sugar and Ice
Eye of the Storm
Wake Up Missing

EYE OF THE STORM

KATE MESSNER

WALKER BOOKS FOR YOUNG READERS
AN IMPRINT OF BLOOMSBURY
NEW YORK   LONDON   NEW DELHI   SYDNEY

First published in the United States of America in March 2012
by Walker Books for Young Readers, an imprint of Bloomsbury Publishing, Inc.
Paperback edition published in April 2014
www.bloomsbury.com

Bloomsbury is a registered trademark of Bloomsbury Publishing Plc

For information about permission to reproduce selections from this book, write to
Permissions, Walker BFYR, 1385 Broadway, New York, New York 10018
Bloomsbury books may be purchased for business or promotional use. For information on bulk purchases
please contact Macmillan Corporate and Premium Sales Department at specialmarkets@macmillan.com

"Geometry" from The Yellow House on the Corner, Carnegie Mellon University Press, Pittsburgh, PA.
© 1980 by Rita Dove. Reprinted by permission of the author.

The Library of Congress has cataloged the hardcover edition as follows:
Messner, Kate.
Eye of the storm / by Kate Messner. — 1st U.S. ed.
p.   cm.
Summary: Jaden's summer visit with her meteorologist father, who has just returned from spending four years
in Russia conducting weather experiments not permitted in the United States, fills her with apprehension and
fear as she discovers that living at her father's planned community, Placid Meadows, is anything but placid.
ISBN 978-0-8027-2313-0 (hardcover)
[1. Fathers and daughters—Fiction. 2. Storms—Fiction. 3. Weather—Fiction.
4. Climatology—Fiction. 5. Mystery and detective stories.] I. Title.
PZ7.M5615Ey 2012   [Fic]—dc22   2011006393

ISBN 978-0-8027-3435-8 (paperback)

Book design by Nicole Gastonguay
Typeset by Westchester Book Composition
Printed and bound in the U.S.A. by Thomson-Shore Inc., Dexter, Michigan
2 4 6 8 10 9 7 5 3

For my aunt, Maureen Lahue,
and for all librarians
fighting the good fight
for books and knowledge

Chapter 1

There are no words to describe this sound.

In the old days, they said tornadoes sounded like freight trains. I've seen video archives of survivors being interviewed, all out of breath. They describe an approaching rumble and then a roar. Wind pouring out of the sky. Buildings shaking. And finally, the train rumbling off, fading away as the storm lumbers on.

But that was then.

There are no words for the sound of what is happening now.

A thick, dark shadow is snaking down from the cloud that followed us from the airport. It's wider and stronger than anything those people in the video archives had ever seen. Bigger than anything they could have imagined.

It is headed straight for us.

"No worries, Jaden," Dad says, but both our DataSlates are wailing with high-pitched storm alerts. His eyes dart to the rearview mirror as he pulls the HV into a safety lot.

I've heard about these huge roadside shelters, but we don't have them at home in Vermont. The one time Mom and I got caught out with a storm coming, we just knocked on somebody's door. It goes without saying in New England: on storm days, you let anybody who needs help into your safe room.

But in this part of Oklahoma, there are fewer houses now, hardly any doors to knock on. This huge concrete structure is the first building we've seen for miles. It's almost full, but Dad maneuvers into one of the last spaces. "We'll be fine here."

"Good timing, I guess." My voice shakes, even though I try to pretend it's no big deal; Mom warned me the storms would be more frequent here, but I never thought I'd see one before we even got to Dad's house.

"That good timing's no accident." Dad leans back in his seat and picks up his DataSlate. The glow of the screen lights his face an eerie blue, even as the sky outside grows darker. "When StormSafe got the government contract to build these lots, we put one every fifteen miles on major roads so you'd never be more than a few minutes from safety."

"That's how much warning you get when a storm's coming?"

"Give or take."

They're like the Revolutionary War–era taverns I learned about in my online history course, spaced fifteen miles apart because that's how far a traveler could ride in a day. Here we are, 275 years later, driving hydrogen vehicles instead of horses, and we're back to needing shelter every fifteen miles.

Lightning flashes outside. I tug my backpack from the floor into my lap and run the strap between my fingers, over and over, so I can concentrate on that instead of the pounding in my chest. I can't freak out. Not on my first day with Dad in four years. He lives for storms like this.

A plastic chair tumbles, legs over arms over legs, past the entrance we came in.

"This is turning into a good one." Dad cranks the volume on his DataSlate so we can hear the regional news feed over the screaming wind. If they mention the storm, we'll know it's big. Normally, they send out the DataSlate alerts that replaced the old tornado sirens and leave it at that. Mom said when she was growing up, her town got on national news once when a tornado wiped out half a mobile home park. *National* news!

Now the news feeds only report the biggest of the big, the true monsters. It sounds like this could be one of them.

"The National Storm Center confirms a tornado warning for all of eastern Logan County," the voice on the DataSlate says. "NSC meteorologists say the system that developed this afternoon has spawned three separate tornadoes—the latest, a possible NF-6. Residents are advised to get to safe rooms immediately."

"NF-6?" I swallow hard. We have our share of storms back home—who doesn't?—but the worst I've seen was the NF-4 that ripped the roof off Mom's environmental science lab at the University of Vermont.

"Could be." Dad leans to see past me, out the shelter door. The tornado doesn't even have its funnel shape anymore; the thick, jerking rope has swelled into a churning blur of brown-black wind.

"It's rain-wrapped!" Dad shouts over the roaring. "Tough to see how big it's grown. But at least it's not a Niner!" That's weather-geek slang for an NF-9, the second highest rating on the new scale they developed a decade ago when it became clear the storms had outgrown the old Enhanced Fujita Scale that went from one to five. When I was a baby, EF-5 was the worst a tornado could be. The New Fujita Scale goes up to ten, though nobody's ever seen a ten touch down. What would they call it? A Tenner?

The lights flicker, and I grip the door handle.

"Relax, Jaden." Dad punches me lightly on the arm, and it sets something off inside me. All the swallowed-up storm jitters rise in my throat, and I want to scream. Instead, I swallow that, too, and my eyes fill with tears.

I've been on the ground all of two hours, and I'm not used to it here. None of it feels like home.

Not the desolate brown flatness of the land.

Not the stark concrete gray of the shelters.

And not the storms. Especially not storms like this.

Dad should know that.

Maybe he'd understand how I feel, understand *me*, if he hadn't spent the past four years in Russia, doing weather experiments that weren't allowed in the United States. Maybe he'd ask how I'm doing now that—

"Jaden, look!" He holds up his DataSlate and turns the radar screen my way. "This hook echo is incredible!"

He points to the blob on the screen. It's churning, growing, hungry enough to swallow half of Oklahoma. A curled-up green extension sticks out one side of the storm, like a witch's finger calling us in.

I know what he wants me to say. He wants me to *ooh* and *ahh* and talk about the rotation like we used to when I was little and I'd sit on his lap, and he'd laugh because I knew how to read a satellite map before I was five. He wants me to be WeatherGirl, the nickname he gave me before he left, before he and Mom split up, before the storms got this bad, before everything. He wants me to say how awesome it is, how fantastic and powerful. How amazing.

But it's not. It is terrifying and loud, pounding the concrete shelter we're hiding in with uprooted hackberry shrubs and tree trunks and God knows what else. I grab the door and hold on.

"Relax, Jaden. This is no big deal around here. You're safe. I designed this shelter model myself. StormSafe tested these things under conditions that were far more—"

He's trying to comfort me, but he is screaming, *screaming* over the storm he says is no big deal. So I scream back.

"Dad, *stop!*" I put my head down on the dashboard and press my hands into my eyes, but I still can't escape from the sound. Forget the passing freight train. This is like being *inside* the engine of the train, inside the throat of some ancient Greek monster that's roared down out of the sky. It's throwing recycling bins and branches, torn-off roof tiles so frantic and flapping they look like huge tortured birds, all flying past the entrance to the lot. I scream again, "Just stop! Stop!" And I don't know if I'm screaming at Dad or the storm or both. But neither responds.

Finally, I sit up and open my eyes. Dad is ignoring the weather outside, staring at me. He closes the radar image—the storm looks even bigger in the glimpse I catch before it's sucked into a folder on his screen—and pulls up his StormSafe corporate log-in page. He turns the slate away from me as if I'd be able to see or remember his stupid password in the middle of this and pokes at the onscreen keys. "Relax," he says. "It's weakening now."

I squeeze my eyes closed against the pounding, against the attack from the wind and debris, and I don't answer him. But as if by magic, the roar of that monster-from-the-sky fades back into something more like an old-fashioned freight train and then dissolves altogether.

I don't open my eyes.

I sit, listening to the train rumble off. I squeeze my eyes shut tighter and think.

This was not a storm. It was a monster.

This is not home.

And this is not the same father I used to have, the one who tucked me into bed, singing songs about the wind.

That father took me out for ice cream on a summer night four years ago. He ordered rainbow sprinkles on his cone, right along with me, and he told me why he had to go on another trip. Why he wasn't coming home anytime soon. Why he needed to open a new StormSafe headquarters in a country that would allow him to do his research. And he left.

This father who has come back to me . . . I open one eye a crack. His fingers fly over the DataSlate. His eyes focus on the scrolling columns of numbers, laser-intense. Fierce.

He feels like someone I don't even know.

Chapter 2

No matter how bad things get in Logan County, no matter how the clouds swirl, how the radar screens light up, I'll be safe in Placid Meadows.

Perfectly, one hundred percent safe.

That's what Dad promised Mom, how he convinced her to send me here, to the heart of the storm belt, for the summer. And his new, self-sufficient StormSafe community does sound impressive. Safety. Higher water and kilowatt allowances, thanks to Placid Meadows' private solar and wind energy reserves. Eye on Tomorrow Science Camp, the state-of-the-art program Dad's corporation runs for "the best and brightest young minds" in the world. Dad said it went without saying that I was one of them and sent me admissions papers, but I still wanted to take the official entrance exam. When I answered the last question on my DataSlate and pressed the SUBMIT button, the score that appeared on the screen put me in the top five percent of applicants. I couldn't argue that I didn't belong there.

Plus Mom had her own research project waiting in the shadow

of an active Costa Rican volcano. Not to be outdone by my father's adoration of storms, Mom's had her own love affair . . . with frogs. While Dad's been studying the effects of global warming on storm formation, she's been researching its impact on wildlife in sensitive ecosystems, particularly rain forest amphibians like the poison dart frog. Mom's wanted to take this trip for years but had nobody I could stay with until now.

"This must be WeatherGirl!" As we pull up to the Placid Meadows gate, a beanpole of a man leans down into the HV window.

Dad nods in my direction. "This is indeed my daughter Jaden, the infamous WeatherGirl." My stomach's still tangled from the storm, but I smile; nobody's called me that in four years, and even though I'm a total science geek, I'm surprised Dad still thinks about me that way. Surprised, and I guess a little pleased.

"Hi, Jaden. I'm Lou." He points to the shiny silver name tag on his navy blue uniform. There's a StormSafe emblem above his name. Does everybody here work for Dad? "Any update on the expansion, Dr. Meggs?"

"Unfortunately, no," Dad says. "Looks like Phase Two is going to be delayed a bit."

"What's Phase Two?" I ask.

"Phase One of Placid Meadows is full, and we have two dozen families waitlisted, so we're going to expand the development. *If* we can get the land we need."

Lou chuckles. "Those farmers getting you down?"

Dad isn't smiling anymore. "Honestly, why someone would be crazy enough to stay here to run a dying farm is beyond me. And why *anybody* would turn down an offer that's five times what the property is worth . . ." Dad shakes his head, then looks at the dashboard clock. "I'd better get Jaden home." He lifts two fingers from the steering wheel in a wave.

When he drives through the Placid Meadows gate, it's like driving from Kansas into the Land of Oz.

From the minute I stepped off the plane, Oklahoma has been a place of charcoal skies and yellow-gray clouds. It's like Florida when the hurricanes started getting bigger; no one lives here anymore unless they're too attached to family farms or they can't afford to leave. The oil wells were abandoned a decade ago when the international fossil fuels ban took effect. The sprawling cattle ranches are ghost towns. It's a state abandoned, except for a few farms, storm-torn mobile home parks, and corrections department energy farms, where convicted criminals ride generator-cycles outside in the daytime and sleep in StormSafe bunkers at night. It's a black-and-white world, with shades of brown.

But Placid Meadows blooms in full, all-of-a-sudden color.

A billowing garden of bright flowers divides the street. In the middle is a fat boulder with a bronze plaque affixed to it. WELCOME TO PLACID MEADOWS, A STORMSAFE COMMUNITY, it says in calm, loopy cursive. All around, the garden bursts with reds and pinks and fuchsias. Tall purples tip their heads, and spreading silver-blues creep along the curb.

"It's beautiful." I lower my window to breathe in all that brightness, and for the first time since I said good-bye to Mom at the airport in Burlington, I almost feel calm.

Dad pulls over and smiles, and his face relaxes into something I almost recognize from the Dad I had before. "Isn't it the most gorgeous garden you've ever seen?"

I nod, but this new glimpse of Dad is more interesting than the plants now. The DataSlate man from the car seems to have been sucked into a folder deep inside him. Now he looks like someone who might order rainbow sprinkles on an ice cream cone again someday. Between that and the flowers, I feel my heart lift. Maybe this summer will be all right.

"The flowers are so perfect." I lean out my window.

"Of course they are. Everything we plant is DNA-ture; it's the best." He puts the HV back in gear. "We better go. Mirielle's making an early dinner."

Mirielle. The stepmom I've only seen on my DataSlate videophone, and always with my new half sister, Remi, in her arms.

Dad pulls away from the garden, farther into the development.

The street is lined with StormSafe houses, concrete structures tinted mauve, slate blue, and sea green. They have windows, which surprises me a little; they must be made of glass that's engineered not to shatter under pressure. And there are bigger buildings, without windows.

"Are those houses, too?" I ask.

"Nope—that one's the community warehouse." Dad nods toward a big brick-colored structure as we pass. "DNA-ture delivers food orders once a week so we don't need to go out to the regional grocery store."

No wonder the farms Dad mentioned to Lou aren't doing so well.

Dad points out my window. "Here's the entertainment dome."

He slows down as we pass a building that looks like the big skating rink at home. The electronic sign outside has a schedule of showings. Movies. Sporting events. Ballet and theater streamed in live from the National Arts Center in New York. And something called Museum Night, with Natural History: Jurassic Period on Tuesday and American History 1900–2050 on Thursday.

"What's Museum Night?" I ask as Dad pulls away.

He smiles a little. "Do you remember when you were really small—I think you were three—when we took you to closing ceremonies for the American Museum of Natural History in New York City?"

"Kind of." I remember walking through a room with huge dinosaurs and another one with all kinds of rocks and gems. And Mom was crying. "Mostly, I remember Mom being sad."

Dad nods. "It broke her heart when the government decided most of the major museums needed to close so artifacts could be protected in underground bunkers until the storm crisis is resolved. But this place"—he looks in the rearview mirror—"is the museum of the future. It's all holograms, so it changes every night. What did it say for this week?"

"Jurassic and American History."

"Great shows; you should go," Dad says. "You walk a path through the dome, and you'll see dinosaurs approaching. The T-Rex looks like it's about to eat you for dinner." He chuckles. "They're just holograms, so they don't bite, but they're realistic. American History is fascinating, too. You meet history makers of the twentieth and twenty-first centuries—Martin Luther King, Steve Jobs, Al Gore—and former presidents, too. I think they have Barack Obama and Grace Farley in this show."

"Interesting," I say, and it is. But then I have another flash of memory from the museum's closing night—the feel of a cool, rough dinosaur tail under my hand when I ducked under the velvet rope to touch it, even though the signs said not to. It felt real, like it might come alive and roar any second. A hologram could never feel like that.

We turn a corner, and Dad slows down. "That's Risha Patel, the girl I told you about on our video-call last week."

The girl looks about my age. Her long black hair has a bright green streak along one side. She must have a BeatBud in her ear because she's bobbing her head back and forth to something fast and playing imaginary drums in the air, right above the handlebars of her bicycle as she rides along, hands-free.

Dad speeds up again, but I turn in my seat and stare.

She is riding a bike.

Nobody rides bikes anymore at home. The storms churn up so fast, there's not a kid in our neighborhood who's allowed to ride more than halfway down the block, so why bother? Amelia was the last of my friends to give hers up. She held out right through last summer and never cared how ridiculous she looked riding up and down the street, back and forth, alone. When we laughed, she told us that in her mind, she was going all over town, through the woods past the big tree house where our moms used to camp out when they were little, branches brushing her cheeks as she flew down the trails. But at the end of the summer, we got our StormSafe Mall and Teen Center, and even Amelia figured that was better than imaginary trails. The recycling crew picked up her bike at the beginning of October.

Was this girl imagining faraway places, too?

"Does she live right around here?" I ask Dad.

He shakes his head. "The Patels live on the other side of the development. Closer to the Eye on Tomorrow campus."

"Wow." I scan the horizon. The storm we just saw has already barreled off, but there are more clouds churning in the west. "She's far from home for a storm day."

Dad laughs. "I see it's going to take you a while to get used to being a StormSafe kid." He slows down and pulls into the driveway of an adobe-colored concrete box. "It's different here." He presses a button on the dashboard, and a dome-shaped mouth yawns open on one wall. He pulls the HV forward into what must be the Storm-Safe version of a garage. Three bicycles are lined up inside, one in my favorite color, electric blue.

"We ride bikes all over the place here. In fact," he says, nodding to the fleet along the wall, "it was supposed to be a surprise, but the blue one's yours. You'll love having that freedom again."

"But . . . how can that be safe? I know the *houses* are safer here, but if you're outside . . . I mean, the storms are even worse than at home, so—"

"How many times do I have to tell you?" Dad shakes his head, smiling. "While you are inside the gates of Placid Meadows, you are safe. Totally and completely safe."

He presses another button on the dashboard. The garage door rumbles again, and behind us, the mouth on this safe, safe house slides shut.

Chapter 3

When Dad opens the kitchen door, French disco music bursts out to meet us. Mirielle is twirling around the room barefoot in a long flowered skirt and lemon-yellow tank top. Remi is six months old now and swaddled in a big, every-colored scarf slung around Mirielle's neck like she is part of the outfit.

Mirielle presses a button to send the potatoes down for peeling and—"Oh!"—almost twirls into me on her way back for the carrots. "Jaden, you're here!" She leans in to kiss my cheek. I smell Remi's head—soap and baby. Mirielle turns to Dad. "Did you get caught in the storm? I hate when you have to go out there." She says it as if "out there" and "in here" are totally different planets.

"I know, love." Dad steps up to the biometric panel on the refrigerator. He presses a finger to the reflective glass and taps impatiently, waiting for it to identify him by his print. "We spent about ten minutes in a safety lot. No problem." For some reason, relief cools my face when the fridge sends Dad out a glass of iced tea. He still drinks it with lemon, and at this point, anything that hasn't changed is welcome.

"You want something to drink?" Dad asks.

"No thanks." I look past him and wonder where my room is.

Mirielle catches me peering into the living room. "Would you like to see the rest of the house?"

"Go ahead." Dad steps up and rests his finger on another biometric panel just outside a steel door on the wall opposite the kitchen appliances. "I'm going to check in with headquarters before dinner."

I stand by the door for a second and see a bank of computers inside before I realize Dad's office won't be part of my tour. Then I follow Mirielle out of the kitchen and up a spiral staircase to a sleeping loft. It's bigger than mine at home, but it has a bedspread of the same bright blue. I wonder if they did this on purpose, tried to make my room look like home so I wouldn't miss Mom so much.

But then Mirielle pulls open the little drawer on my nightstand, and what I see inside makes me miss Mom even more.

It's a book. The hardcover kind with pages you turn by catching the corner with your fingertip. We have this one at home, but I didn't bring any paper books; Dad says reading paper books is like driving on square, stone wheels. He's been reading exclusively on his DataSlate since before I was born.

This book is by Rita Dove, an American poet who loves math as much as she loves words. In the photograph on the book jacket, she's beautiful and maybe around Mom's age, but she must be in her nineties now. I sit down on the bed and flip through the pages to find my favorite, "Geometry." It's about what she feels like when she proves a mathematical theorem.

... the house expands:
the windows jerk free to hover near the ceiling,
the ceiling floats away with a sigh.

When I first read this poem, the ceiling part freaked me out a little. Then Mom told me it was written way back in 1980, before most people knew what it was like to have the roof blow off your house for real.

I run my hand over the raised letters on the book's cover. "Did my mom send this?"

Mirielle smiles and sits next to me. "She thought you might miss your books, so she had your great-aunt Linda pick up a copy at the antique shop and drop it off when your father wasn't home." Mirielle glances toward the door. "She suggested I tuck it away for you."

"Aunt Linda? Really?" Even though she's technically my great-aunt, I've always known her as Aunt Linda. I haven't seen her in years, though. She paints and gardens, and I'm not surprised she likes poetry, too. She took care of Dad when he was little, pretty much raised him. I put the book down next to me. "How close does she live?"

"About twenty miles. But she and your father don't really talk."

"How come? Won't I get to see her? It's been a long time."

Mirielle's pretty green eyes cloud over. "Your father thought Linda should move to Placid Meadows, but she'd have no part of it. He was furious, and so no . . . she doesn't drop in for dinner."

My disappointment must show on my face. Mirielle reaches out and touches my arm. "But she is your relative, too, no? Maybe we will have a visit one day while your father is at work." She stands up, tucks the book back in the nightstand, and gently closes the drawer. She smiles like we're sharing a secret, and I realize we are. We both know Dad wouldn't want paper books cluttering up his house.

Besides, it's poetry. Dad always says a world like ours needs science to save it, that pretty words never protected anybody from a storm.

Which reminds me. "How do I get to the safe room from here?"

"There is no one safe room," Mirielle says. "Everywhere is safe."

The ugly concrete designs make perfect sense now, and so does Dad's promise to Mom. The whole *house* must be a giant safe room.

"I will show you the living room instead, yes?"

On the way downstairs, we pass the bathroom, and I peek inside. It's enormous, and there's no liter-meter on the wall, like at home. Could the Placid Meadows water rations be so much higher that we don't even have to keep track? I add longer showers to the list of good things about living here for the summer.

"Here we are." Mirielle steps into the living room. One whole wall is an entertainment window. There are plush black chairs, an antique rocker, a leather sofa, and bookcases like ours at home. But no books. Here, the shelves are full of digital frames. Most are storm shots, black-gray blurs of tornadoes from Dad's research trips all over the world, but the two frames on the end have a slide-show of family photos.

I stand next to Mirielle and watch the images change.

Mirielle and Dad at their wedding in Russia two years ago. Eating cake.

Dancing.

Photos of Remi as a newborn.

Then pictures of me.

There are a bunch of photos taken in the first house Mom and Dad owned. I'm three years old, pushing a toy lawn mower in the yard. It's the old-fashioned kind that needed a person to steer it. There's me in a high chair with jam smeared all over my face.

Then I am four. Dressed for my first day of school. The tornadoes were spreading north then. I'd been so excited for school but so scared that a storm would sweep away the house while I was gone.

There are school photos for the next three years. I am five, then six, then seven. My backpack goes from purple, to pink, to red with blue stripes, to bright orange.

When the picture changes again, I am eight. The counter is torn up behind me—they must have been installing the SmartKitchen— and books are spread out on the table. That was the year before they built the StormSafe schools and shelters, and we all home-schooled with classes streamed to our computers. Mom created most of her own lessons, though, and I loved staying home. It was just before Dad left for Russia, too, the last year we were whole.

The frame flashes again, and suddenly, my face looks older— last year's school picture. Mom must have beamed it here.

"We need a new photograph of you," Mirielle says. "Your hair is longer now."

"Yeah, a little."

I step closer to the shelves to look at the other frame with family photos, the smaller one. One of the pictures looks like an old-fashioned portrait of my father.

"Is that Dad?"

Mirielle has been humming softly to Remi. "Hmm?" She stops and leans toward the frame. "Oh, no, that's your *grand-père*; these are your father's parents, Enam and Athena, when they were young. You have seen photos of them before, yes?"

I have, but never one that looks so real. There is something fierce in my grandmother's eyes. An intensity that looks like it should have burned out the camera's lens. "She reminds me a little of Dad," I say, and wonder how much Mirielle knows about the woman who would have been her mother-in-law.

I never met Grandma Athena. She died way before I was born, and it was Mom, not Dad, who told me about her. Like Dad, she had an amazing mind. She studied with a ferocity that made people afraid of her. She met Grandpa in graduate school, married him four months later, and had Dad right after they graduated. When the September 11th terrorist attacks happened in 2001 and the United States went to war with Afghanistan, Grandpa enlisted in the military and Grandma went to work for some secret government science program. It was all classified—like the scientists who developed the atomic bomb during World War II—so nobody knew exactly what she was doing.

When Dad was twelve, Grandpa was killed in Afghanistan, Grandma died in a car accident, and Dad had to go live with Aunt Linda, all within a few weeks. Mom says that's everything she knows; Dad never talked about it and still doesn't. I've always known not to ask.

Before today, I'd only seen one picture of Grandma Athena, faded on paper. It made her look old and brittle, too. But this photo feels alive, as if I might catch her blinking, and I have trouble looking away until Mirielle breaks the spell. "You must be hungry."

"Kind of." I follow her back to the kitchen. "Want me to hold the baby?"

Mirielle unsnuggles Remi from the scarf. She fusses for a minute but then gets a handful of my brown hair wrapped around her fist and curls up against me.

I turn back to the living room for one more look at Grandma Athena, but the picture has already changed.

Chapter 4

"Did you try the broccoli?" Dad raises his eyebrows at the perfectly formed trees piled on one side of my plate. "It's DNA-ture's bestselling vegetable for a reason, you know."

"I know." I've seen the pop-up ad on my DataSlate so many times I can quote it. *"DNA-ture: Vegetables Even Kids Will Love. Our foods have the undesirable qualities bioengineered right out of them."*

"It's true." Dad picks up a stalk from my plate. "No bitterness. No mushiness."

"Still the same old broccoli." I stand to take my plate to the auto-clean bin.

"Still the same old Jaden. Stubborn as usual." He frowns and pops the broccoli into his mouth.

I should have known better than to knock DNA-ture, the bio-botanicals company he runs along with StormSafe—but as I open my mouth to apologize, I see him smiling. "I'm going back to my office. There are still some storms around to deal with." I'm about to ask Dad how he'll "deal with" them when the doorbell rings.

"Would you answer that for me?" Mirielle asks, leaning down to pick up Remi.

The air-drumming girl with the green-streaked hair, Risha, is about to push the doorbell again when I answer. "Oh!" she says, jumping back a little. She brushes hair from her eyes, and two gold bangles, patterned with zeros and ones, clang together on her wrist. "You're here! Yay! I mean, hi!"

"Hi to you, too! I'm Jaden."

"I know." She bounces on the toes of her pink high tops. ". . . and my mom told me you're almost thirteen like me and you're going to Eye on Tomorrow, too. I'm Risha. Want to go for a bike ride?"

"What a good idea!" Mirielle joins us at the door. "Risha can show you around."

"Okay." The clouds are dark, but they're still a ways off, and Mirielle doesn't seem worried. "Let me get my bike."

I head for the garage, thinking how weird it feels to say that again.

My bike.

Riding a bicycle was something I thought was gone forever. Something future kids would hear about in stories from the old times, before the earth's average temperature grew so warm, before the atmosphere became so unstable, so friendly to huge storms. I thought bikes were gone, like hikes in the woods and picnics that aren't in the backyard. Somehow, Dad's company has found a way to give those things back to people.

"Come on!" Risha coasts by me, pedaling backward as fast as

she can, her sneakers a hot-pink blur. "We'll go by my house and then campus."

We ride around a corner, and Risha waves to two girls jogging on the sidewalk. "Hey, Tess! Ava!"

They wave back as we zip past them.

"Will they be at camp?" I ask, pumping harder to catch up with Risha.

"The Beekman twins? Of course." She lets out a snort that sounds more like a rhinoceros than a skinny girl with a delicate nose. "They moved into Placid Meadows a couple years ago, so they were in all my classes at school. Their father owns the British company that produced the first successful HV model. The storms in Britain have gotten bad, too, so he brought the family here and *paid* their way in."

Her tone of voice makes me glad I insisted on taking the test, even though Dad was ready to enroll me without it. "Is the camp mostly Placid Meadows kids?" I ask.

"It depends." Risha pedals up a small hill. "A few really high scorers moved here with their families, all expenses paid. Some guys who live around here like Alex and Tomas—I'll introduce you, but I have dibs on Tomas—come for free, too. My mom says it was part of the tax deal your dad's company got. They have to provide opportunities for local kids." She crests the top of the hill and starts coasting. I follow her down and over a bridge that crosses a little creek. Just on the other side, she squeezes her hand brakes and stops so abruptly I almost bump her rear tire.

"Here's my house," she says.

It looks like Dad's, right down to the gobble-up-your-car garage door, only this one is pale blue instead of adobe colored. "It's pretty," I say.

"Not really." She laughs. "But it's bigger than our apartment in New York, and safer. Plus it's close to school." She points to a concrete and steel building halfway down the block. It looks brand new. "And not far from the Entertainment Dome."

"Do you go there a lot?"

Risha shrugs. "Not really. Once you know when the T-Rex is going to pop out, it's not that exciting. And the American History show just makes me mad. Can you believe they spent so long arguing before the courts decided that people can marry whoever they want? Maybe if they'd worried more about carbon emissions back then and less about bossing everybody around, we'd still have real museums with real stuff in them, you know?"

Risha lets out a huff and starts pedaling straight ahead, but the clouds off to our left catch my attention. They're closer. And darker.

"Hey, Risha, do you want to head home?"

"Why? Don't you want to see the campus?" She keeps riding.

The wind whips up dirt from the empty lot, and it stings my cheeks. "Risha, shouldn't we go? It looks bad over there."

She hollers something over her shoulder but I can't hear what, and then she turns—an abrupt right down a driveway I would have missed—and stops. Looming ahead of us is a building twenty times the size of the houses. It's behind a fancy, locked wrought-iron gate.

"Whoa!" I pull my bike up next to her. "What's this?"

"Eye on Tomorrow." Risha leans on her handlebars and rests

her chin on her hands, grinning at the building. "Where the brightest minds of today prepare to lead us into the future. And that's just the reception building. You'll see the rest in the morning."

The reception building gleams, all steel and windows. There are another half dozen shining buildings behind it, built around a grassy quad. The largest has a huge white dome—five times the size of the Entertainment Dome—growing out of the center. Dad told me this place was impressive, but I thought he was exaggerating. This summer camp for schoolkids looks more high-tech than Mom's university.

It makes sense, though. StormSafe created Eye on Tomorrow four years ago as a model for the government's new Surge Ahead program to create leaders in math and science. The United States had been behind other countries in those areas when the storms intensified. Now, it's like everybody suddenly figured out science is important, so they're building facilities for gifted students around the country. Eye on Tomorrow was the first—and is apparently still the best.

"Were you here last summer?" I ask Risha.

She nods. "Once you test in, you get to come every summer. The idea is for campers to keep coming back and then work for StormSafe and its sister companies once they get out of school. Doesn't your dad tell you anything?" She looks at her watch. "Come on, it's almost eight o'clock, and I want to show you one more thing if you can keep a secret because my parents would kill me if they found out, and yours probably would, too. You can keep a secret, right?" She looks at me over her shoulder.

"Sure, I guess."

She leads the way down another hidden path through some brush. A branch tugs at my hair, and I have a pang of missing Amelia. She'd love this hike ride, with real trees and trails that aren't just in her imagination.

"Well, look who made it," a deep, older-than-us boy voice calls out, and again, I almost bump Risha's back tire because she stops so fast. In front of her, a chain-link fence rises up from the dusty ground to way over our heads. This must be the edge of Placid Meadows; the fence stretches out in both directions. The only opening is where the barrier is interrupted by a big old oak tree whose trunk and branches apparently ignored the fence and kept right on growing, twisting the wires and pulling open a gap that looks just big enough to squeeze through.

On the other side of the fence, two boys stand back a few steps, straddling bicycles of their own. Theirs are older and rusted, like they've been out in a storm or two.

"Sorry I'm late." Risha shrugs at the taller of the two boys. She jumps off her bike, climbs through the gap in the fence, and motions for me to come, too.

"We thought you stood us up."

"Never." She gestures toward me as I'm pulling a twig out of my hair. "This is my friend Jaden."

"Hey." The tall boy smiles one of those lazy, movie-star smiles with his eyes half closed. He must be the one she has dibs on.

"Jaden Meggs, meet Tomas Hazen and Alex Carillo."

"Hi." I nod to Tomas and wave past him to Alex, who's shorter, about my height, with dark skin like Risha's and black hair that curls around his ears.

"Hey." His brown eyes are asking questions, and he tips his head. "Meggs?"

"Jaden," I say. "I just moved in—"

"With your dad? *The* Stephen Meggs?" He looks at Risha and raises his eyebrows.

"Yes, her dad is Dr. Meggs, Alex. Get over it." Risha glares at him. "She's visiting for the summer because she qualified for Eye on Tomorrow." She turns to me. "*Somebody*'s a little touchy about DNAture because his parents don't believe in factory-made foods. They're part of the organic farming collective that still grows stuff in fields."

"Yeah, well, somebody else can't seem to take no for an answer when a piece of property's *not* for sale." Alex folds his arms in front of him.

"Well, maybe *somebody* shouldn't have accepted the camp scholarship if he thought Jaden's dad was so horrible. But I bet you'll be there tomorrow." Risha walks off toward the riverbank with Tomas.

I'm left here with Alex. "I don't know much about my dad's work," I squeak out.

"Sorry," Alex says, looking down. Risha's argument seems to have taken the wind out of him. "I'm kind of defensive about the farm." He scuffs his work boots in the dust. "You must know your dad wants to build more houses, right?"

I wish I didn't. But I remember his conversation with Lou about Phase Two. "I kind of heard about it. He's offered to buy your farm?"

"Yeah . . . about ten times." Alex puts down the kickstand, climbs off his bike, and stands looking out over the field. "Most everybody's selling. Mom keeps telling Dad we should take the money, but he won't. Every time your dad sends somebody with another offer, they fight. Selling this place would kill my dad. I know it would." He shrugs. "This is what we do."

"Well, it's not like you *have* to sell. He's just asking," I say. But I remember the frustration in my father's voice when he talked about the land. I bet he's been pushing hard.

"I know. And she's right, too." Alex nods reluctantly toward Risha, who's tossing stones into the river with Tomas. "What I said before was dumb. You're not your dad."

"I don't even know if my dad is my dad anymore." The words slip out before I can filter what I'm saying to this boy I just met. They hang in the air like dust, and Alex looks at me. I bend down to pluck a blade of grass and arrange it between my thumbs to make a whistle. Amelia used to do it all the time and finally taught me how. I lift my hands to my mouth and blow. It sounds like a crow.

"You have some impressive skills there," Alex says, smiling a little.

"Thanks." I try to do it again, but the grass slips from my hands and flutters back to the ground. "Unfortunately, it's not a very useful skill. Do you think they have grass-whistling at Eye on Tomorrow?"

Alex frowns. "Hmm . . . you could study how the force of your breath and the width of the grass affect the rate of vibration. . . ."

"I think I'll stick to meteorology."

"Yeah?" Alex says. "That's what I studied last summer. What's your focus going to be?"

"Honestly?" I haven't told anyone this yet, not even Dad. "What I've always wanted to do is work on storm dissipation. You know . . . the theory that you can actually stop a tornado from forming if you change the conditions in the storm so—"

"I know what storm dissipation is." Alex looks at me as if he's seeing me for the first time, as if we just arrived at the fence. "How'd you get interested in that?"

"I don't know." I lean against the fence next to him, watching Risha and Tomas trying to balance on a log at the edge of the river. They're laughing, and it makes me think of Mom's tree house in the woods from when she was young. She took me there once, on a day when that seemed safe. I climbed up and watched the sun peeking in and out of the leaves. I never wanted to leave. "My mom tells stories about when she was little, before it got like this. I always kind of wish I could have lived back then. Without the storms being part of everybody's lives."

A gust of wind whips the tree branches back and forth over our heads, and a few leaves fly past. One gets stuck in a diamond in the fence. I reach out for it, just as Alex does the same. But he pulls his hand back and looks up at the swirling gray sky. The dark wall cloud in the west is looming closer.

"Hey, Tomas!" he calls. "We gotta get going."

"But we just got here." Risha pouts for a second, but then she's smiling again. "See you in the morning, bright and early!"

"Too early." Tomas grins. "See ya."

Alex waves, and they get on their bikes and ride away.

"Risha, we should go, too. It's getting bad."

We climb back through the fence and head for our bikes. Risha looks back and sighs. "He is so cute."

For a second, Alex's dark eyes flash in my mind, but I know she's talking about Tomas. I climb on my bike and put up the kickstand. "He seems nice. Kind of quiet, huh?"

"He's usually more fun. His mom's been sick, having all these tests, and they just figured out it's pancreatic cancer."

"They can get her treatment, can't they?" Pancreatic cancer was one of the last kinds to be totally cured, but there've been treatment centers around for at least five years now.

"Yeah, but not here. Probably New York—Tomas's brother is in college there—but his dad's worried about the farm and where they'll stay and money and everything. They'll figure it out; it's just on his mind is all."

Wind shakes the trees, and suddenly the weather's on my mind. It's getting darker. "Risha, come on. We need to go."

She looks at me as if I've suggested she bring an umbrella out on a perfectly sunny day. She's not even on her bike yet. "We're fine, Jaden. It's not like it's coming *here*."

But then thunder rumbles, and I don't wait to find out. I start pedaling, and once we're back on the main road, I see the storm *is* closer—way closer. The sky has turned a gray-green color that makes my stomach churn. I don't know if Risha's following, and I don't look up. I remember the turns, back over the bridge, past Risha's house, and back to Dad and Mirielle's place.

I stop in the driveway, gasping for breath.

Risha skids up next to me. "Now what?"

I turn to her, ready to tell her how crazy she is, but over her shoulder, I see the wall cloud, the heart of the storm, moving away from us.

I can only stare.

"It's going the other way," I say finally.

"They always do." Risha tips her head and looks at me. "Let me get this right, Jay-girl. Your father runs the company that built this place. And he didn't bother to let you know you're safe from the tornadoes here?"

"Well, he did, but . . ." I remember his words in the car. His promise to Mom. To me.

Inside the gate, you are completely, one hundred percent safe.

"I figured it just had safer . . . safe rooms or something." I can't stop staring at the cloud that seemed to bounce off our neighborhood as if the chain-link fence extended all the way to the heavens. As if steel wires could keep out the weather.

Risha rolls her eyes. "It's not only the houses. It's *all* of Placid Meadows. That's the whole deal with a StormSafe community; technology keeps the entire property safe."

"How?"

"Well, I don't know exactly." Risha frowns a little. "I always assumed the storms got . . . like . . . zapped at the perimeter somehow. But whatever it is, it works. They *never* hit us. It's even in the contracts."

"In the contracts?" Since when did nature make contracts with anybody?

"When you buy a house. Right there with the number of bedrooms and deeded rights to the playground and whatever. That's why people are willing to pay so much to live in such ugly houses, I guess." She laughs a little and looks at her watch. "I'm going to head home. Grandma's making chicken tandoori." She rides off in the direction of the storm clouds that are barreling off toward someone else's home.

Not ours.

Never ours.

It's in the contract.

Chapter 5

"You won't need that," Dad says as I'm sliding my DataSlate into my backpack Monday morning. "Eye on Tomorrow supplies everything except the brainpower."

"Seriously?" Back home, nobody leaves the house without a DataSlate; how else would you get an alert when a storm's coming? But Dad reminds me.

"You're in Placid Meadows now. You don't need the storm alert." He smiles. "We don't allow DataSlates at camp anyway, until everyone's settled and understands the rules about keeping research confidential."

"Okay." I pull my DataSlate out of my backpack and run my finger around the cool, smooth edge.

"See you this afternoon." Dad goes to his office. A few notes of Mozart drift out before the door slides shut behind him.

I put my DataSlate back in my bag—I'll feel too weird without it—toss the whole thing over my shoulder on the way to the garage, and take off on my bike.

When I get to camp, the wrought-iron gate is wide open, and

Risha's inside, riding her bike around the drop-off driveway with some other kids. There's a boy with a brush cut pacing back and forth on the sidewalk. Maybe he's new, like me. Tess and Ava Beekman, those twins from Britain, are sitting on the grass talking with a couple of boys.

"Hey, Jaden!" Risha waves and almost swerves into a dented green pickup idling by the reception building.

I gasp, first because I think Risha's going to crash, and second, because somebody's driving a gas-powered vehicle. They've been illegal for ten years. How could somebody still be driving one around? Are the rules here that different?

"Easy, genius!" Alex climbs out of the truck, waves to the woman driving, and brushes dried grass from his faded jeans. "Don't run me over on the first day."

Risha doesn't let a second go by. "Where's Tomas?"

"He had to help his mom; I guess she's been feeling pretty crummy. He'll be here later." Alex turns to me and smiles. "You up for this?"

"Of course." But looking up at the tower beyond the reception building, the billowing white dome next to it, the sprawling campus, I wonder if I really am.

Alex turns to say hi to another boy getting dropped off, and Risha and I start toward the reception building. I lean close to her as we walk. "What's up with the truck?"

She makes a scared face. "Oh my gosh, you're not a spy with the International Climate Commission, are you?"

"No, but—"

Risha laughs. "I'm kidding. You didn't really think it was gas-powered, did you? Nobody's that dumb. A bunch of the farmers around here have rigged up old trucks to run on vegetable oil. Kind of messy, but it's cheaper than a new HV." She pulls open the door to the lobby.

"Welcome, welcome." The man waving us inside has a reddish-brown ponytail and a face full of freckles that run together in splotches over his nose. He looks young enough to be a camper, but his badge says VAN GARDNER, EYE ON TOMORROW STAFF.

He steps up to me and smiles. "First summer here?"

I nod.

"I'm Van, camp director." He shakes my hand, then turns to Alex. "Good to have you back, my man." He nods at Risha. "Planning more work in bio-botanicals?"

She shakes her head. "I'd rather be in the cloning lab this summer if I can. Tomas was telling me about it, and it sounds interesting."

While Risha talks with Van, I reach over my shoulder to get my DataSlate from my backpack. I want to see if Mom answered the message I sent after dinner last night. Reception in the jungle's probably too spotty for videophone to work, but she should at least have text messaging.

"They're going to take that," Alex says. "No outside technology in the beginning."

"Really?" I pretend to be surprised.

"Got a drive you can put your stuff on so you don't lose too much when they destroy it?"

"Destroy it?"

Alex raises his eyebrows. "Last kid who brought a DataSlate had to watch while they took it out back and ran over it with the Eye on Tomorrow field trip vehicle. They tried to run him over, too, but he was fast." A smile creeps onto his face.

"Very funny."

"I'm just messing with you. They *will* take it for now, though. You can get it at the end of the day."

Sure enough, Van steps up and holds out his hand. "Sorry, Alex speaks the truth."

I give it to him, and he points us toward the auditorium. "Let's head into orientation and get this show on the road."

I end up sitting between Alex and Risha, but all her attention turns toward Tomas when he arrives. "You're doing cloning again, right? Because that's what I'm requesting."

"So, Jaden," Alex says. "You and I kind of have the same area of interest."

"Yeah, I've always liked weather," is all I can think to say. My fingers are itching for the DataSlate Van took away. Even if I can't connect with Mom, having it makes me feel like she's not so far away.

"All right, campers! Good morning!" Van bounds down the wide steps to the podium at the front of the auditorium. "I'm going to help you get your bearings. These first few days, we'll walk through the facilities and review rules and regulations."

Van presses a button on the podium, and legs grow up from out of the floor in front of us, materializing from the shiny black shoes on up. I know it's only a holo-sim, but it still startles me. Within a few seconds, the figure has a torso, arms, a neck. And finally, a face.

My father's face.

And my father's voice.

"Good morning, Eye on Tomorrow campers."

Dad's American StormSafe employees opened Eye on Tomorrow four years ago, right after he left for Russia, but it doesn't surprise me that it's his face and voice greeting the campers. Even from overseas, Dad would have made sure his vision played out the way he wanted.

"We are so very glad that you're here," the holo-sim says.

It's just a computer-generated projection, but it makes my hands go cold, as if this picture made of light has Dad's real eyes and mind. Does it know I brought my DataSlate even though he said not to? That it was confiscated?

I look up, but the eyes on the holo-sim look like they're focused on something in the back of the auditorium. No one else seems fazed by Dad's appearance. Tomas is watching Risha doodle on her notebook, zeros and ones like those on her bracelets. I watch, too, for a second, until Dad's voice starts up again.

"As you know, Eye on Tomorrow is a special place. Here, you'll be provided with the most exclusive data sets, the most advanced technology, the most elite instructors . . ."

I glance over at Van and catch him mouthing the words that holo-Dad must deliver to every new summer crew.

"Along with that privilege comes responsibility. Here at Eye on Tomorrow, we expect campers to arrive on time each morning. Bring nothing but yourselves for now; we supply everything except the brainpower. And leave with nothing. No equipment, data files, or documents may be taken from the campus at the end of the day, and photography is prohibited, to protect the unique learning environment we've worked so hard to build."

"Now let's all keep an Eye on Tomorrow." The holo-sim winks. "And always do your best, because we'll have our eye on you." Then it vanishes from the top of Dad's head down to the last shiny black toe of his shoe, as if someone took an eraser to the air and rubbed him out, atom by atom.

Van steps forward. "Ready to take a walk?"

Alex taps my shoulder. "So are you requesting meteorology for a focus area? Some people work in teams."

Is he asking if I want to work with him? This is the same kid who didn't like my last name yesterday. "Haven't really thought about it yet."

"Well sure, there's no rush," he says, and looks down at his hands resting on the seat in front of us.

"You coming?" Risha calls from the door, and I realize we're holding up the line.

I leave Alex's not-quite-an-invitation alone for now and hurry to the door. When we step outside, sunlight burns my eyes, and warm, wet outdoor air wraps around me. Risha and Tomas have gone ahead, so I walk with Alex.

"This way." Van points us toward the next building over, the one with the white dome, a giant golf ball perched on top of a short, thick column of glass. "Might as well start with the best we have to offer."

The best the camp has to offer? I look over, and Alex answers the question before I even ask it out loud.

"Storm Sim Dome."

"What's in there?"

"Computers," he says as we step up to the huge building, waiting for Van to scan his fingerprint and open the door. "Turbo-fans. Storm simulators. Storm pool and plumbing."

I stare up at the dome, processing what he's just said. "Are you telling me there's real wind and rain and everything in there?" It's shiny, almost too big and bright to look at up close.

Van holds the door open. "File in." The air inside is cold and clean, and the main chamber of the dome is cavernous. It reminds me of the story Aunt Linda told me once about her family's trip to that old amusement park, Epcot Center, when she was little. It's gone now, wiped out years ago in one of the first inland hurricanes like the rest of Disney's Florida empire, but Aunt Linda said it was magical, like being inside a giant globe, the heart of the whole world.

My eyes drift down from the dome's ceiling, and I see what looks like the heart of this building—an enclosed safety-glass box housing the mainframe computer system that must control everything.

A model city surrounds the console. It looks like Oklahoma City used to look forty years ago, full of offices and shopping areas, parks and schools, homes, and barns on the outskirts, all built to scale. About half the city is in perfect condition; the rest of the buildings are as battered as the ones *outside* Placid Meadows are now.

The cement floor is still damp. Van gestures down at it. "Watch the puddles; we had a test run earlier."

I look around, wondering how it all works. The precipitation must come from the water heads mounted on the ceiling and the hoses that snake out from the walls every few meters. It even smells like a storm in here. Does that rain-ruined smell just happen, or is it pumped in with the wind, through the enormous fans that hang from the ceiling and walls?

"Why do they do all this?" I whisper to Alex. "Wouldn't computer simulations be easier?"

"They used to do that, but there were too many variables. Van says you need real buildings, real towns, to see what a real storm can do."

The last few campers file in. It's quiet, but then a motor clicks on, and the fans begin to hum quietly, almost as if they're whispering promises about what they can do.

Tomas is the first to speak up. "You gonna run this thing for us?"

Van shakes his head. "Later in the week, maybe. It doesn't mean much if you don't understand what you're seeing, but this is where our meteorology program is based. It's all exclusive, patented technology—one of a kind. Well, three of a kind, actually. There's one up at the StormSafe complex and one at the company's property in Russia. Just wanted you to have a look at it for today."

He walks us out of the dome, back into the bright light and sunshine air.

The rest of the morning is a parade of in and outs, more rooms filled with elaborate equipment. This is what I imagined Dad's

StormSafe headquarters might look like. If they provide this stuff at a camp for teenagers, what must he have at work?

After lunch, we're back in the orientation center to talk about areas of study.

This time, there's no holo-sim of Dad. Instead, a three-dimensional globe of light drops from the ceiling as classical music starts to play.

Alex leans over. "Mozart," he whispers. "They did some study that shows classical music helps to develop synapses between the hemispheres of the brain and makes us better problem solvers."

It's also Dad's favorite, but I don't mention that. Alex probably wouldn't like Mozart anymore.

Dad's voice rises over the violins. "Welcome back, Eye on Tomorrow campers. This afternoon, we'll take a look at the problems our world is facing today . . . and tomorrow. And we'll ask you to make a commitment to one of those challenges for the summer."

The globe at the center of the room spins and then explodes into a million bits of light that shoot out toward the walls, and in its place now is a spinning cloud. It's just light, just a holo-image, but somehow the air feels wetter, heavier than it did a few seconds ago. Dad's voice describes the first challenge, the one we all know about already—the storms.

"Warmer global temperatures have led to increased instances of tornadic storms, not only in the traditional storm belt, but worldwide. Through the careful planning and vigilance of the

International Climate Committee, we've managed to reverse the planetary warming trend. However, as you know, campers, it will be two more years before greenhouse gases are reduced to a level that will have a positive impact on weather patterns. Our goal at StormSafe and here at Eye on Tomorrow is to bridge the gap—to find solutions that will keep people safe until then."

It's not only the tornadoes, Dad says, but also hurricanes of greater intensity and size, tropical cyclones around the globe, droughts and heat waves, that need to be controlled. "When we master our climate," Dad's voice promises, "we'll be the masters of our planet."

He goes on to describe three more challenges: the bio-botanicals program that he promises will revolutionize the world's food supply and end hunger through an expansion of DNA-ture bioengineering and factory-grown food practices; the robotics research that will automate the world's industries and services, from motorcycles to medicine, within thirty years; and the cellular generation and human cloning center, where scholars have already begun developing successful technology to create, through DNA-based cloning, any part of the human body for transplant or other use.

When the human figure representing the last area of study fades and sinks into the floor, the lights come on and Van is back in front of us, bouncing on his sneakers. "Ready to solve the world's problems? We'll see you back here, first thing in the morning, to get started."

Chapter 6

The rest of the week flies past in a blur of computer screens, robotics, radar and satellite panels, stainless steel counters, test tubes, and greenhouses with more monitoring equipment than I could have imagined. Each day, Van leads us through a different research center on campus. Sometimes we do lab experiments and try out equipment. Van asks us questions along the way to see who might be best suited to each area of study.

I figured kids who have spent two and three summers here would be way ahead of me, but I can actually answer most of Van's questions. Especially when it comes to meteorology.

"You're doing great," Risha whispers to me as we walk between buildings.

"Thanks. I'm surprised I'm not further behind everybody who's been here before."

"You're not behind at all," Risha says, pulling open the door to the bio-botanicals building. "The program this year is way more intense than what we did last summer."

Even so, Risha knows the answer to almost every question in the bio-botanicals lab, where she spent last summer.

"Are you sure you want to switch to cloning?" I whisper.

She glances sideways at Tomas, smiles and shrugs at me, and answers another question. Her bracelets clink together whenever she raises her hand, and finally, when Van turns to explain some new kind of lower-carb sweet corn, I reach for her wrist. "What are the numbers supposed to be?"

She slips a bracelet off her hand and passes it to me. "It's binary code, the sequence of ones and zeros they used to represent processing instructions for a computer."

I run my finger along waves of numbers etched in the gold. "So what will this tell a computer to do?"

"Nothing." She wiggles the other two off her wrist. "This is just regular text." She points to the first line of numbers on one bracelet. "See this sequence?"

I read it aloud. "01011001."

"That's *y*."

"That's all one letter?"

"And then here . . ." She points to the second set of eight numbers, 01101111. ". . . is an *o*. It spells out, 'You must be the change you wish to see in the world.' It's a saying from some old Indian guy, Gandhi. My grandmother's always quoting him and trying to get me to read about him." She waves at the air with her green-and-black-striped fingernails. "She figured if she translated it into in a language I like, I might actually pay attention, so she had these made for me."

"Your grandmother sounds awesome." I try to imagine what Grandma Athena would be like if she were alive. What would she talk to me about? Risha slides the bracelets back onto her wrist as Van leads us down a hall toward the next lab.

"Is the code on your notebook a quote from the same guy?" I ask Risha.

"No . . ." She pulls me off to the side, tips her head toward Tomas, and whispers, "It's his name. In binary code."

That makes me laugh. I should have guessed. "Now I understand why you like it, even if it isn't really used anymore."

She shrugs. "Not everything has to be useful."

I think about the book of poems in my nightstand. "Don't let my dad hear you say that. You'll be tossed out of this place faster than you can blink."

She laughs and pulls me along to catch up with the boys.

On our second visit to the Storm Sim Dome, Van skips the quiz and sits us down on a row of long benches along one wall. "Instead of asking you questions here to check on your knowledge, we're going to try something else."

He pulls a box of DataSlates from under the bench and starts passing them out. "These are preloaded with the same software we have on the core system in the dome. You've all been asking me when you'll get to see the Sim Dome in action, and the answer is now. Show me what you'd do if I turned this entire dome over to you for one simulation." He hands the last DataSlate to Tomas.

"What are we doing with these?" Risha asks.

"You're formulating a theory about the effect that a given variable has on storm formation. Then I'd like you to design a simulation to test it."

Tess Beekman squints at him. "I don't get it."

Van sighs. "There's a simulation program loaded on each of these DataSlates. It will ask you for a theory. You need an if-then statement. For example, if you think that raising the temperature in the atmosphere will cause a storm to move more quickly, you select that theory. *If* the temperature is raised x degrees, *then* this will happen. Then you design a simulation. Don't worry—the software will walk you through the steps. Essentially, you'll be telling the Sim Dome what conditions to create in the atmosphere above our model town, and then you'll see what effect that has on the storms." He looks around. "At least some of you will. We're only going to run the most promising simulations in the dome." He looks back at Tess. "Understand now?"

She shrugs. "Kind of."

"Okay then. Get to it." He looks at his watch. "You have one hour." He heads for the staff computer in the corner of the room.

The DataSlate suddenly feels heavy in my hands. This isn't a quick question I can raise my hand to answer or a click-the-right-response exam. It's an actual problem with no solution in sight, and I'm supposed to come up with one.

Risha sits next to me on the bench, her fingers already flying over her DataSlate, words pouring onto her screen. I look down the row of DataSlates in laps. Everyone else is inputting text.

My heart feels like it's thumping out that frantic stream of numbers from Risha's bracelets, but I open the Sim Dome software and stare at the blank text box with "Theory" written at the top.

The only sound is the hum of fans and the tapping of fingers, reminding me that Eye on Tomorrow is in a different league. This is a place for people with theories.

I stare at the empty box and panic. I may have a head full of ideas, but none of them are my own. My parents are the scientists; I'm the kid who loves to read, who can always get a hundred on the test when the answers are supplied ahead of time. But here, we are starting from nothing.

I look down the row. The anxious boy with the brush cut types a few words. Looks at his watch. Types a few more. Rubs his finger under his lower lip. Looks at his watch again. Just being near him makes me nervous.

There must be something. Some theory I can test.

If. Then.

If. Then.

If something, then . . . what?

I close my eyes and imagine the storm from my first night here. The one that never touched Placid Meadows.

If a housing contract promises storm-free living, then the tornadoes stay away.

If a company builds a magic fence around a neighborhood, then the residents live happily ever after.

None of it makes sense. What's keeping the storms at bay? Where do they go when they turn away from the fence?

If. Then.

Where could the storms go that wouldn't hurt anyone?

Not away. But up.

Back into the sky.

If. Then.

What makes a tornado go away?

I close my eyes. The DataSlate is still cool in my hands, but the rest of me breathes in the memory of hot, humid air. An August night, five, maybe six years ago, watching a storm in the distance with Dad. It loomed, big and dark, over the Adirondacks, heading east across the lake to Vermont. We creaked back and forth on the porch swing as the thunder grew louder.

We watched that storm swell bigger, watched it uncurl a long, dark arm that wrapped around the sky and started spinning. It dropped down from the cloud, then stretched into a longer, skinnier funnel as if some potter's hands were shaping it, all the while spinning the wheel faster and faster.

"Dad, should we go downstairs?" I felt like we should. The storm was getting closer, and tree branches were starting to scratch against the porch roof in the wind.

"Soon." Dad stared at the storm, mesmerized. Then he squinted off to the west. "Or maybe not."

Another cloud was approaching, a big brother to the first, taller, with broader shoulders. When they met, it was like the younger brother flinched. The tornado lifted up from the ground and never caught its breath again. We watched, creaking back and forth as it rose slowly back up into the cloud.

Then we sat and listened to the rain.

Later, when Dad tucked me into bed, I asked where the tornado had gone. Most fathers would have made up a story for a kid my age, maybe something about God pulling on the rope, tugging it back to the heavens, away from us. A cozy-under-the-sheets, sleep-tight story. Mine gave a meteorology lesson.

"Sometimes, Jaden, a cold outflow of wind from a storm system can cause a tornado to dissipate."

"You mean go away?"

"Yes. And in this case, it was that second thunderstorm that came and wrapped up the first one in its outflow." He tucked the cool sheets around me. "Bet you can't spin around now either."

I wiggled, and giggled, and Dad kissed me on the head. "Night, WeatherGirl."

"Twenty-five minutes left." Van's voice snaps me back to now. I open my eyes and stare at the blank box on my screen.

I have an idea. It's an old one from a hot summer night that feels like a lifetime ago, but it's all I have, so I start typing.

IF a tornado-producing storm collides with a second, larger storm . . .

That's a good start. There will be data from different-size storms loaded in the simulator. I can choose two that should work.

THEN . . . Then what?

I fly through the procedural steps, and I'm thinking how to state the outcome when Van calls time, so I simply type:

PROJECTED OUTCOME: Tornado dies.

—just as he steps down the row, takes the DataSlate from my hands, and adds it to the stack teetering in his arms.

"Well, now," he says, lining them up on the counter outside the safety box that encloses the real control panel. "This is an interesting collection of theories." He picks up the first few and sets them back down without saying anything. "I can see we'll need to work on experiment design. Some of these aren't even in a format that could be entered into our dome software."

He moves on to the next DataSlate, which he reads and tucks under his arm, nodding. He goes through the rest of the slates and picks up the last one, too.

He holds those up and turns to us. "We have two theories that are developed enough—not perfect, mind you—but developed *enough* to run on the simulator. Mr. Carillo?"

Alex stands up.

"Come on into the control chamber with me. Miss Meggs? You, too. The rest of you head over to the observation area behind the glass. We'll explain each simulation on the microphone so you know what you're seeing. Let's find out if either theory holds up in the Dome."

Chapter 7

Can everyone hear me?" Van's voice booms out of the speakers, and on the other side of the room, behind the safety glass, the rest of the campers nod. He turns back to Alex and me. "Who's first?"

I look at Alex. Is his stomach churning like mine?

"I'll go first," he says. Van stands up, and Alex slides into the chair in front of the control panels. "Do you want me to explain what I wrote?"

"Of course." Van adjusts the microphone.

"My theory involves storm dissipation," Alex says. His voice echoes through the dome.

Van leans in toward the microphone, glancing back at me. "Actually, both theories do. That's why this is a particularly interesting pairing."

"Okay." Alex takes a breath. "Current theory holds that tornadoes form when the hot updraft within a supercell meets a cold rainy downdraft. So here's my idea." Alex reads from his DataSlate. His fingers have dirt and grass stains as if he came right from working on the farm this morning, but his hands aren't shaking like mine.

"*If* the cold downdraft of a tornado-forming supercell is heated with microwave energy from an orbiting satellite, *then* an essential ingredient for tornado formation will be absent, and the storm will dissipate."

He looks at Van, who nods. "Similar to the research you were doing last summer, no?"

"It is, but I've been tweaking it," Alex says. "Should I just . . . run it now?"

"Go for it. The Dome has simulated satellites built into the ceiling. Adjust the level for how much energy they'll be giving off. Choose one of the preloaded historical tornado models—any one of those should work—give it a few seconds to form, and then run your simulation. We'll see if it dissipates." He almost sounds bored, but my heart is pumping, and it's not even my turn yet.

Some of the confidence has drained out of Alex's face, but his hands are steady as he connects his DataSlate to the main system, transfers his data, and presses the button to start the Sim Dome re-creation.

The lights go down, and immediately, water vapor hisses out of ducts in the ceiling and on the upper walls. Like magic, clouds form over the model city. The synthetic fabric that makes up the tree foliage rustles and then whips in the wind generated by the fans that surround the community on all sides. When the cloud darkens and gives birth to the beginning of a swirling, charcoal-colored funnel, Van nudges Alex. "Go ahead."

Alex's finger hovers over the INTRODUCE VARIABLE button. He takes a breath and then taps it lightly.

A panel slides open on the ceiling, exposing a model satellite that lowers slowly, a foot or so. Under the clouds, the tornado stretches lower, lower, until it touches down inches from the first building—a small red barn next to a white farmhouse outside the city.

A sharp ray of light streaks down from the satellite. I can't look away from the light, the storm, the clouds, the funnel, to see how Alex is reacting, but I feel his body tensing next to me. Will this blast of energy warm the tornado away?

The tornado licks at the edges of the barn. "Come on," Alex whispers, and I tear my eyes from the storm to look at his face.

His eyes travel down the beam from the satellite, as if he could strengthen it by pure will, all the way to the heart of the cloud, where that blast of energy *should* be warming the downdraft, *should* be stopping the storm's rotation.

"Come on, come on!"

The storm explodes then, with a sharp burst of lightning, and even Van jumps in surprise. Blinding light fills the dome and seems to feed the tornado. It swells up bigger, darker. It devours the barn, the house, and then races from the farm to the first simulated neighborhood. Houses. A school. In pieces. A church steeple flies off into the vortex. The rest of the building follows. A playground. Slides. Swings. A tumbling jumble of monkey bars all sucked into the storm.

Alex's fist pounds down on the counter, and Van reaches forward to press a red button on the control panel.

The lights flicker, then come on overhead.

The rain stops pounding. Leftover drips from the ceiling plunk down onto the rubble as the clouds are sucked into the ventilation system in the walls.

When they clear, I stare out at half a town, perfect and painted with trees still standing, plastic people still posed on porches.

The other half is flattened.

Alex's jaw is tense, his fist still clenched on the counter where it landed.

"That's why we have the Sim Dome, my friend." Van puts a hand on Alex's shoulder. "Sometimes, things work on paper; they work fine in your mind, but the real deal turns out very different. That's why we don't do this all digitally anymore. Until you're dealing with real wind, meeting real buildings, you don't know what'll happen." He turns to me. "You're next, Miss Meggs. Let's see what you do with the half a city that survived your colleague's experiment."

Alex stands and steps back so I can sit down, and I feel his eyes on me as I'm opening my file. I glance over my shoulder, expecting . . . I don't know. Maybe that he'll want me to fail, too, not to show him up. But even though his eyes are still intense, frustrated, he gives me the smallest nod. Encouragement?

I make the connection and feed my data to the mainframe computer.

"Which storm's going to be your subject?" Van leans over my shoulder and taps the screen, and a list of model storms appears. I choose an NF-3 that hit Germany eight years ago. And then I'll need to introduce a larger supercell to serve as the second storm in my experiment. My hands shake so much I can barely control my finger to point to the right model. Some of the shaking is nerves—Van standing over me, Alex's eyes on me, the wall of faces behind the glass, all staring from the other side of the room—but some of it is excitement, too. Could this actually work?

"Go ahead." Van flicks his hand toward the button that will dim the lights and start the clouds building.

I swallow hard and tap the command: BEGIN SIMULATION.

Clouds swirl out of the walls and down from the ceiling, like they did with Alex's storm, and this time, I'm ready when the wind starts to whip the trees and the rain pounds down on the roofs that are left in the model city. I watch the bottom edge of the wall cloud, holding my breath, until the funnel cloud takes shape and touches down.

The ground explodes in a whirl of dust, and Van points to the words INTRODUCE VARIABLE on the screen. "Do it now."

I press the button and hold my breath.

The tornado is already on the ground as the second storm begins to form off to the left. The vapor is still gathering when the first storm hits the model town's business district. It's not as strong as Alex's tornado, so the buildings aren't flattened, but roofs tear away from shops, and debris flies.

"Come on," I whisper, and I hear the echo of Alex's hopes as I watch the new funnel finish forming, watch it darken and advance toward the first. "Come on. Go. *Go.*"

The first tornado strengthens. It tosses cars that were parked on Main Street, hurls them through store windows, and the sound of shattering sim-glass—how do they make it so loud?—crashes over the wind.

My second storm closes in on the first. "Come on," I whisper. "Knock it down. Do it."

And I hear Alex's voice, quiet behind me. "Come on, work."

For a second, the tornado stops in its path, churning up dirt, frozen in time as the two storms finally touch.

Then it goes wild.

The big brother cloud, the one that was supposed to wrap around the first storm and settle it down, does something else. It opens up its arms, sucks the first storm inside, and squeezes, until the whole thing turns into a darker, angrier, super-charged monster.

"No!" I scream. I can't help it. Because a second tornado drops down from the cloud like an angry whip. And a third. Both stronger than the first. They barrel down streets, through downtown, and the office buildings implode and feed the storm until the whole city is gone.

Van's arm blurs in front of me and presses the button to shut down the dome. Only then do I feel my face is wet with tears. I swipe at them with my sleeve.

Van smirks. "Well, scholars. We have some rebuilding to do, don't we?"

I feel a hand on my shoulder. Alex.

I brush it away, stand up, and head for the door, but Van puts up a hand to stop me. "Those were good efforts from both of you. But you've got a long road of research ahead before you can produce something that works in this world as well as that one." He nods down at the DataSlate in my hand. I'd forgotten it wasn't mine.

Mine's at home in the drawer with my poetry book. I haven't brought it back since that first day.

I set the DataSlate on the counter, but Van shakes his head. "Keep that one over the weekend. Play with some new ideas. Bring it back on Monday. I'm going to recommend you two for the meteorology team." He opens the door, and we head out into the humid air of the Dome to meet up with the others, filing out of the observation room.

"All right, campers, let's call it a day. I've seen what I need to see. On Monday, I'd like you to tell me what you'd like to study and whether you'll work alone or with a partner."

We leave the Dome and start back toward the welcome building, but there's none of the usual in-between-buildings banter. I get the feeling that even the campers who were around last summer have never seen anything in the Sim Dome quite like this.

"Whatcha doing for lunch?" Risha finally asks when we get back to our bikes.

I shrug. "I'm not too hungry. That was just so . . . intense."

"I think we need a picnic!" Risha stands up on the pedals of her bike and pulls the front wheel off the ground to spin around.

It's such a crazy idea, I laugh, which I'm sure was her whole goal. Picnics are like bike riding back home. But it figures there'd be a StormSafe picnic shelter, too. "Where do you have picnics?"

"I know a place," she says, "but I'll have to blindfold you to take you there; it's top-secret-super-classified."

I laugh again, and my stomach grumbles.

"You guys have to come, too, okay?" She makes her top secret-super-classified picnic eyes at Alex and Tomas.

"I guess." Tomas gives her the lazy smile. "As long as Alex and geek girl put their killer DataSlates away."

Risha laughs, but Alex doesn't. "I'll come," he says, and puts the DataSlate into his backpack.

I reach over my shoulder to unzip mine, and a warm hand catches my fingers.

"Got it." Alex lets go of my hand and unzips the bag so I can slip the DataSlate inside. He gives the strap a light tug, and I turn around. "Sounds like we're going to be in the met program together." He takes a deep breath. "Maybe we can talk about being partners?"

I can't help smiling a little. I wasn't crazy that day in the auditorium. It was an invitation after all.

I nod and get on my bike. "Sure. We can talk."

Chapter 8

"Your top-secret picnic location looks kind of familiar, Rish." Tomas weaves through trees to the fence, holding a cooler full of food from Risha's house out in front of him.

I scan the horizon for clouds, but the sky's all blue. My DataSlate in my backpack is quiet—no weather alerts for now—and the afternoon sun feels good after a morning of air-conditioned camp.

We climb through the gap in the fence, balance beam our way across a fallen tree stretching over the river, and follow Risha, who's run ahead through the trees, bracelets clinking on her wrist.

"Here we go." Tomas steps into a field with neatly planted rows of grain, and we head for the gazebo on the other side. Its white paint is peeling, but Risha flies up the steps and perches herself on the fence as if it's her fairy-tale castle, and she's been waiting all day for the prince to get home.

"It's beautiful." It's like I've fallen into one of the olden-days books Mom used to read to me.

"Yeah," Tomas says. He looks a little sad.

"How long have you lived around here?"

"Since I was born. It's getting hard to take care of the farm, though, with my brother gone. My dad's not sure . . ."

"You can't sell, man," Alex says. "No way."

"Yeah, I know. Dad's all talk. I don't think he'll ever leave this place." He lifts the cooler onto the picnic table.

"Jaden, sit by me!" Risha pats a spot next to her on the splintery bench.

I sit down and get a sandwich from the cooler. I'm starving, and for the first time since we left Eye on Tomorrow, I feel relaxed enough to talk about the Sim Dome. "Sure is nice to see blue sky after this morning."

"I know!" Risha takes a big bite of her sandwich and goes on talking through the lettuce. "That sim was crazy-real."

Alex sits down across from me. "Have you ever . . ." He pauses. "Never mind."

I take a bite of my DNA-ture apple and look up at Alex. "Have I ever what?"

"Well . . . have you seen the equipment your dad has at work? I mean, you probably can't talk about it if it's classified and stuff, but I wonder if it's the same."

I shake my head. "Never even been there."

"It feels like . . ." Alex unwraps his sandwich but doesn't eat. He turns it over and over in his hands, as if the bread and turkey and cheese layers hold the answer to some puzzle. "We have so much equipment at Eye on Tomorrow—and I'm sure your dad has even better stuff up there." He nods toward the StormSafe compound in the distance. The sun is reflecting off its steel and safety-glass walls, making it glow. "It feels like we should be able to figure this out."

I nod and look to the west, where the sky's clouding up. I know exactly what he means. How could we know everything we know, have everything we have, and not be able to live in a world where you can go for a walk without watching the clouds?

"I'm going to pick flowers." Risha tips her head off toward the meadow. Before she goes, she bends down by the picnic table and plucks a dandelion that's gone to seed. "Make a wish!" She blows on it, and silver stars swirl all around our heads as she runs off. Tomas picks up the bag of *nankhatai*, the Indian tea cookies Risha's grandmother made, and follows her.

Alex looks toward the clouds on the horizon. "They better not go far. This isn't Placid Meadows."

His voice has an edge.

"What's wrong with Placid Meadows?"

He shakes his head. "Nothing. I'd imagine it's great if you can afford to live there. But you must know what those places cost."

I shrug, rather than admit that I don't. I wonder if our picnic spot is part of the land Dad's trying to buy for his Phase Two.

There's a rustling in the weeds then, and a golden retriever bounds out of the brush and up the steps to our table. It puts a paw up on Alex's lap and tips its head.

"Hey, Newton." Alex scratches the dog behind an ear, then carefully untangles a burr stuck in its long reddish fur.

"Sorry," he says, looking up. "I didn't mean to make you feel crummy. It's just hard to take sometimes. But what Risha said before is right. If it weren't for your dad, I'd be right here—and only here—this summer, pulling weeds and picking worms off tomato plants and running for the storm shelter every other day instead of spending half of it in a huge science complex."

We sit for a long time, watching the clouds. Alex feeds Newton scraps of turkey from his sandwich, and I listen to Risha laughing with Tomas.

When Alex finally speaks, it's so quiet I barely hear him. "I'm frustrated, I guess. I thought I'd figured out how to stop them all together."

"The storms?"

He nods and starts picking at the weathered wood of the picnic table.

"I'm starting to think it's impossible. My dad's been working on this forever. He's got some exclusive agreement with the government for his weather manipulation research. Anyway, Mom told me they were sure they had the formulas this winter, but when they did the simulation, it failed."

"Did you see the formulas?" He leans forward.

"No. I probably wouldn't have understood them anyway. This stuff is out of our league."

"No, it's not. Last summer at Eye on Tomorrow, I had a formula drawn up, based on the same theory, and it *worked*. At least on paper."

"Did you run it through the Sim Dome?"

He sighs. "That didn't work, and I don't know why. It should have." He jerks his hand back from the table. "Ow! Splinter."

He pulls it out, and blood seeps out from under his thumbnail. He stands and shoves his hand into his pocket. "Look, I just . . . I feel like I'm out of ideas. That's why I was kind of hoping we could work together." He doesn't look at me and doesn't wait for an answer. He starts gathering sandwich wrappers and picks up the rest of my apple. "Are you going to finish this?"

I shake my head. He looks down at the DNA-ture sticker and grimaces. "Is this stuff all you ever eat?"

"It's not bad. I'm not in the mood for fruit right now."

"Oh no?" His dark eyes smile a little. "Come with me." He takes off across the field with Newton at his side.

I look over my shoulder for Risha, who's plopped down in the weeds, showing Tomas how to weave daisies together into a chain. Behind them, the clouds are growing, but they're still a long way off.

There's time before our weather alerts go off, so I catch up with Alex as he reaches the barn. It smells like old paint and hay. A twisted copper weathervane with a rooster on top leans against the side.

"That's an old one, huh?" I run my finger along the W for West.

"It was already here when my grandpa bought this place way back," Alex says. He looks up at the barn's sloped roof. "Came flying off in the wind Friday night."

"That storm we saw coming from the fence?"

He nods. "Just missed us. We were lucky. Tomas says their

neighbors two places down lost their barn and almost their whole herd of Scottish Highland cattle."

"That you, Alex?" a deep voice calls from the barn, and a man in a faded blue shirt steps out, brushing dust off his hands. His face looks like he's spent a lot of time working in the sun, and he has warm brown eyes surrounded by the kind of wrinkles you get from laughing. "You take care of the chickens yet?" he asks Alex. Then he sees me.

"Dad, this is my friend Jaden I told you about. From camp."

His father nods at me and reaches out to shake my hand. His is warm and rough with calluses. "Very nice to meet you," he says. But he doesn't smile. He looks back at Alex and raises his eyebrows. "Don't forget we have a farm to run." And heads back into the barn.

"Sorry," Alex says, turning to me. "He's . . . not thrilled with us being friends."

"Oh."

Goats or sheep bleat from inside the barn, and there's the sound of feed pouring into a trough. Alex looks at the barn door as if he can see through it. "He's really not cold like that. He's just—I made the mistake of telling him who your dad is, so . . ."

"So he figures I'm here to make another offer on your farm?" My face flushes hot, and I turn away from the barn. "I . . . I should be getting home anyway. It's—"

"Jaden, wait." He puts a hand on my shoulder. It's tentative, barely there, but it keeps me from walking away. "I want to show you something." He steps onto a low stone wall that runs along the barn. "Follow me."

I hesitate.

"Please?"

I climb up and follow him to a patch of garden on the south side of the barn. Mounds of green grow out of straw-covered soil, and ripening red spots peek out from each plant.

"You *grow* strawberries?" I've never seen strawberries growing outside, as far as I can remember. They were one of the first DNA-ture products. Dad used to bring home cartons full of fat, smooth, seedless berries. "These are so much smaller than real ones."

Alex laughs. "These *are* real ones." He squats down, gently brushes aside some leaves with one hand, reaches deep into the heart of the plant with the other, and pulls out a perfect red berry.

No. It's not perfect.

The berry is asymmetrical. One ripe, red side bulges higher than the other, and raggedy green leaves stick out the top in every direction, like some crazy puppet hat. The dimple at the base of the fruit looks a little like the one on Alex's chin.

He holds it up. "*This* is a *real* strawberry. Look."

"It looks great," I say.

"No. *Really* look." He rests one hand on my shoulder and with the other, holds the strawberry out about a foot in front of my face. "Tell me what you see." I try to ignore the warmth spreading down my arm and look, really look.

"It's red." But even as I say it, I know it's more than that. It's not red like the strawberries in Mirielle's refrigerator at the house. Not the perfect, crayon-box red, the same on every side. This one is a million shades of red, from the deep rich color of new blood to the blush that must be creeping up my cheeks. "It's a lot of different promises of red."

"What else?" He turns the strawberry slowly, but doesn't move his hand from my shoulder.

"The seeds are different colors, too." I can't compare them to the seeds on DNA-ture strawberries because they've been engineered out—people who took the "build-a-better-fruit" surveys complained they got stuck in their teeth—so they're gone now. The skin is perfectly soft and smooth. But this strawberry has tiny hairs that catch the sun and raindrop-shaped seeds spilling down the sides, around all of its uneven curves. "Gold and pink and brownish."

"Now." Alex smiles a little. "Close your eyes."

I look at him.

"Don't worry." He laughs a little and takes his hand off my shoulder. "I want you to taste this. *Really* taste it."

I close my eyes. I can still feel the warmth of his hand on my shoulder, or maybe it's the sun getting warmer.

"Ready? Open your mouth."

I do.

The soft-rough seeds brush my lips first. Then that same surface—alive, I think—settles on my tongue, along with the warmth. It feels like this berry still holds the heat of the sun inside it.

I am almost afraid to bite down, but Alex's hand rests on my shoulder again, and I am painfully self-conscious of what I must look like standing here with my mouth around a strawberry, so I take a bite.

And I taste the sun.

All of the warmth, the sweetness, this imperfect outdoor berry has collected explodes in my mouth. And eyes still closed, suddenly, I am three years old, sitting cross-legged in a garden or field—I don't know where exactly—but I am picking berries with Aunt Linda. Dropping them into a big wicker basket in the dirt between us, and my hands are stained red, and my chin is sticky with sweet red juice, and Aunt Linda is laughing in the sun.

I had forgotten what strawberries felt like until now.

I open my eyes. Alex has dropped his hand from my shoulder again, and the one that held the strawberry hangs at his side, still pinching a clump of leaves and a bit of berry with my teeth marks.

"Now are you in mood for fruit?" he asks.

I would answer, but I'm afraid it would come out a million kinds of stupid. So I nod, and bend down to pick another berry. It's rough and imperfect, and perfectly warm, in my hand.

Chapter 9

You *have* to partner with him at camp. You guys look so cute together!" Risha's cheeks are flushed as we hurry back to the fence, and I'm not sure if it's because we're rushing now that the clouds are rumbling closer or because she was having her own picnic moment with Tomas and the daisy chain.

"Aw, cut it out." I climb through the gap in the silver wires. "He did ask if I wanted to work together, though. And we're interested in the same theories of weather manipulation, so maybe . . ."

Risha strikes a professor pose, with serious eyes and hands pressed together. "We're interested in the same theories," she mimics, and laughs. "I think you're interested in more than his theories, Jaden."

When we reach the end of the dirt path, she looks up and down the street, hands on her hips. "What do you want to do? They're running *Animals of Yesterday* at the Entertainment Dome. You get to walk along a trail with a bunch of extinct wildlife—woolly mammoths and polar bears and stuff."

"No, I think I want to go home." I wonder how Mom's doing in

Costa Rica. I hope her endangered frogs don't become part of the Animals of Yesterday show anytime soon. I wish she'd get in touch.

Our DataSlate weather alerts go off, and I jump about a mile. Risha laughs.

The storm is close enough now that people outside Placid Meadows will be heading for safe rooms. Even here, the high-pitched alert makes me want to walk faster, but Risha veers off toward the park. "Relax, we're inside now. Let's hang at the playground a while."

I follow her toward the slide. "Has it been like this since you moved in?"

"Like what?" She climbs the ladder and slides down.

I wait at the bottom. "Like this . . . where you just *know* the tornadoes won't touch down here?"

Risha dusts off her shorts and heads for the monkey bars. "Yeah, I told you, it was in the contracts."

"But how can they promise that? Did the contract say *how* they do it?"

"Nope." She shrugs. "Most people moved here from places where it's gotten so bad that no one cares *why* they're safe. I mean, people ask, sure, but your dad obviously can't be giving away all his company's secrets, and really everybody's just happy to be able to go outside again, you know?" Two little kids are on the swings, daring each other to go higher, while their moms sit on a bench by the carousel talking.

"But my dad's storm dissipation project failed—that's what

Mom said. It can't be that technology. And if it's not that, then what is it? Some kind of force field around the neighborhood?" I climb up to the top of the jungle gym and sit down on one of the crossbars, dangling my feet down through the middle.

"I guess." Risha scampers up after me and hangs upside down from her knees a few bars over. "Does it matter what it is, as long as it works?" Thunder rumbles in the distance, and tree branches rustle as the wind picks up. The moms on the bench don't even miss a beat in their conversation.

"S'cuse me, lady!" One of the kids from the swing set climbs up the other side of the jungle gym and runs into our Jaden-and-Risha roadblock here at the top.

"Sorry." I lower myself to the ground, and Risha climbs down the other side.

"Let's go swing!" She takes off and is swinging six feet off the ground by the time I even get started, but pretty soon I'm flying beside her. I can't remember the last time I was on a swing outside. Our underground play centers at home have great swing sets— huge ones—but the air on your face is still indoor air. Stale and safe. Here, it's real wind, carrying the smell of the storm.

"You know," Risha says, her hair flying around her face, "if you swing back and forth a hundred times with your eyes closed and then open them at the very top, then the first boy you see from up there will be the one you marry. Think I can see Tomas from up here?"

"Doubt it." I swing forward, so high that the chain goes slack and for a second I feel like I'm hanging there, attached to nothing. Then the chain catches, and I swing back with Risha at my side. "Besides, they must be in a safe room by now. That storm's growing. Hey, how's his mom?"

Risha stops pumping her legs and just swings. "She needs to get into a treatment center, but Tomas says there's a waiting list for most of the good ones. We didn't talk about it much—and don't you dare tell Alex because he doesn't know this yet, but Tomas said they might even move."

"*Move?* What about the farm?"

Risha smiles a sad smile. "Well, they know they won't have trouble selling it." She waves her hand through the air as if that idea is a bug she can swat away. "But they've talked about other things, too, like his mom staying with his brother in New York if she can get into that clinic. I'm sure it'll be okay."

"Mama, look! Look! It's almost to the fence. Let's do the rhyme!" The two kids from the jungle gym run toward the bench, pointing to the cloud. I stop swinging and listen.

Twister, twister, go away,
Don't you bother us today.
Take your rain and winds that blow,
Turn around now, I say, GO!

They point and giggle, and make shooing motions with their hands.

I stare at them, these kids who have no memories of a place

where storms come into the neighborhood. Here, it is nothing but a game. It's like that "Ring Around the Rosy" chant Mom told me about. The rhyme was all about symptoms of the plague—rosy cheeks, sweet-smelling breath, falling down dead—and kids chanted it, laughing while they jumped rope, without ever realizing where it came from.

I look up at the monster cloud and try to imagine what it would be like never to have been afraid of it. A funnel is creeping down from it, but the storm doesn't seem to be getting any closer. It looks like the system is stalling on the other side of the fence.

Just like Dad's contracts promise.

"Better do it one more time," one of the moms says, smiling.

"I'm standing up on the bench this time," the little girl says, climbing up. "So it'll hear me better."

Twister, twister, go away,
Don't you bother us today.
Take your rain and winds that blow,
Turn around now, I say, GO!

She points fiercely toward the storm cloud, which is indeed moving away from the fence now, still churning, still blowing, but most definitely going.

"Yay!" The little girl jumps down and cheers again. "I made it go away!"

"Good job." Her mother pulls her in and kisses her above her ponytail. "Now get your jacket, and let's go make Daddy some supper."

I scuff my sneakers in the dirt under my swing and watch them leave. The mothers, the kids, the storm. All leaving.

Risha's been swinging this whole time. She jumps off and flies into the brown grass in front of me, tumbling into a somersault and laughing like the kids. "Clearly, I am the champion of the swing set," she says. "How come you stopped?"

I shake my head. "No reason. You ready to head home now?"

She shrugs. "Sure."

We make small talk on the way home, but I can't stop watching the storm as it moves away. It isn't dissipating. If anything, it looks like it's still growing.

And leaving.

As if someone steered it away, with a magic chant.

Or maybe with a bank of computers, in a home office, behind a shiny steel door?

Chapter 10

Jaden, what would you like? More oatmeal?" Mirielle is dancing around the kitchen clearing breakfast dishes and cooing to Remi, cradled in a blue and green scarf this time. She must feel like she's riding around on an ocean wave, the way Mirielle swoops and turns.

Mirielle's DataSlate reader is open next to her empty cup of tea; she must have been reading at breakfast. I'm surprised when I lean over to read the title on the screen: *Quantum Reality: The Physics of Consciousness in a Post-Romantic World*. Mirielle was one of Dad's interns in Russia; she was studying physics when they met, but she's so busy with Remi it didn't occur to me she'd still have time for science.

She sees me looking at the reader. "Would you like me to send you a copy?"

"That's okay." I look at her, spinning away with the orange juice glasses. "I didn't know you were still interested in stuff like this."

"Oh, I am interested in many things. Too busy to read about them all sometimes. Just like I'm too busy to dance anywhere but in my own kitchen these days." She tickles Remi's chin.

"Where did you used to dance?"

"In Paris, of course!" She stops spinning and smiles. "And Moscow after I moved there. I danced professionally for six years. Your father never told you?"

"No. Why'd you stop?"

"Busy with my studies at first, and then as the storms spread, there just weren't opportunities." She looks up at the kitchen lights as if she's remembering brighter lights on a stage. "And of course here in the U.S., there's only the National Ballet performed for cameras. It wouldn't be the same without a real audience." She pushes my bowl of fruit closer. "You can't be full. At least have more fruit."

"I'm fine, thanks." I poke at a strawberry with my fork and puncture two little holes in its perfectness. I can't help but think of Alex and his father, and their farm. "Do you ever get organic fruit?" I ask Mirielle.

"Oh, *mon dieu*, no!" She glances quickly at Dad's office door as if it might slide open and eat us at the very suggestion. "We eat only DNA-ture. Always. The deliveries are so convenient; I never have to go out to the market," she says as if she's in a DNA-ture advertisement. She looks at the door again, then leans in closer to me. "But your aunt Linda?" She lowers her voice. "She grows berries the old way, and vegetables, too. She gave me some raspberries when she dropped off your book. They were a bit overripe, some of them, but oh, they were so sweet!"

That makes me smile. And it makes me like Aunt Linda even more. "Can we go see her soon?"

Mirielle nods. "I think we can figure something out. Maybe later this—"

She stops at the sound of Dad's office door humming open. He's just inside the room, holding something small and round—is it a compass?—in one hand and his DataSlate in the other. He's on a video call. "No, Mom. I'm certainly not going to—" He sees us standing there and turns away, lowering his voice. All I hear after that is the word "later."

Did I hear right? He almost always called Mom by her first name, Rebekah, but sometimes he'd call her Mom if I was around. Was that Mom on the phone in Costa Rica? And if it was, why didn't he let me talk?

He steps out and presses his thumb to the fridge panel.

"Who was that?" I blurt out.

"What?" He squints at me.

"On the phone? Was that Mom in Costa Rica?"

"Oh, no. No. It was . . ." He looks at Mirielle. "Your mother. She wants you to call her later." She nods, and Dad reaches for the Bio-Wake Cola the refrigerator sent out. He's still holding the compass thing. It's made of wood and looks old.

"What's that?" I ask.

"This?" He looks down as if he'd forgotten it was in his hand. "It's an antique barometer I keep in the office. I use it as a paper-weight, picked it up while I was talking, I guess." He slips it into his pocket. "Listen, I need to head into work. I've called a meeting for noon at headquarters. We have to reevaluate the perimeter because some debris blew up against the fence. There was never any danger, but we had a few complaints."

"Was that the storm from dinnertime last night?" I take my fruit salad to the counter. "I . . . saw it turn away from Placid Meadows," I say quietly.

"Of course it turned away, and in plenty of time, too. Nothing's hit since the fence went up, and if that's not—"

"How does it work?" I'd stayed up until midnight waiting for him to come out of his office so I could ask about the storms, where they went, and what made them go. But he must have worked all night.

He takes a gulp of soda, then holds in a belch. "What do you mean? You know about my research."

"But Mom told me your project didn't work. And that was about dissipating tornadoes, anyway, wasn't it? The storm last night didn't stop rotating. It looked like it was getting bigger. If you're not destroying the storms, then what . . . what *are* you doing?"

Mirielle's DataSlate chirps on the counter. "Oh! It's my sister." She jostles Remi, who's starting to fuss a little.

"Here, I'll take her," Dad says, and carefully lifts her from the scarf. The baby wiggles a little, as if she can't quite get comfortable against Dad's bony shoulder. Dad strokes her soft fluff of hair until she settles. Then he takes a deep breath and looks at me. "You're right, Jaden. I'm not dissipating the storms." The muscles around his eyes tighten. "That was my research, and that was my intent, but as I'm sure Mom told you, after all our years of research, the simulation failed. I've been over it a thousand times. It works on paper, but not in real life."

"Have you *tried* it in real life? Maybe it does work."

He shakes his head. "We can't. What if something went wrong and we made a storm more powerful? You can't test theories with people's lives. That's why StormSafe is so far out ahead with weather modification research. We have the patent on the Sim Dome, so we can actually test our theories."

"And this one always fails when you try it as a simulation?"

He nods. "We have the very best Sim Dome money can buy up at headquarters. More advanced than yours at camp, and that's nothing to laugh at. It's failed every time." He chugs down the rest of his soda, feeds the can into the recycler, and settles into a counter chair with Remi snuggled against him. "But I had already made a promise to all these people." He nods to the hallway, where Mirielle is chatting into her DataSlate. "We *will* get it right one of these days. We will. But for the moment, the best I can do is keep my family, and a handful of other families like ours, safe another way."

"Which is?"

"An electromagnetic storm shield that we *were* able to test successfully."

"What's that do? Send the tornadoes away?"

Dad nods. "Deflects them, yes." I watch him stroking Remi's hair as she sleeps. His hands are soft, but his face is hard, eyebrows furrowed.

"So the field sends the storm . . . ?"

"Away from the most populated areas. Away from her." Dad kisses the top of Remi's head. "Away from you. Away from here, and that's the best I can do for now. At least it's something."

He says it like it's a success but still looks like someone who thinks he's a failure, and it makes me sad for him, after all his work.

"Well, it's a start anyway, right?"

He doesn't smile, but he nods.

I stand up and take a banana from the counter. "Do you think I could see StormSafe soon? Like a tour?"

"Sure. How come?"

"We're getting assignments at camp, and I may work with this other kid in weather manipulation. I . . . uh . . ." I decide to say it. "I'm interested in the dissipation technology."

"Hold on a minute then; I have something you might like to see." He disappears into his office, comes back out with his DataSlate. "Got yours?" I hand it to him, and he starts copying his file called "Effects of Microwave Radiation on Supercell Downdrafts and Vortex Formation."

"Is this your research?"

"It's the summary." The file finishes transferring. Mirielle's done talking with her sister, so Dad hands Remi over, heads for his office, and holds his thumb to the panel. "Read it," he tells me. "You'll see in the last section how the simulation failed, sent us back to square one. But maybe you'll have better luck." He steps inside, and the door slides shut.

Chapter 11

Alex is in his usual seat at camp Monday morning. He looks up from his DataSlate when I sit down next to him. "Hey."

I gasp. "What happened to you?" Even in the dim light, I can see the angry red scrape on his forehead.

"Aw, nothing." He shrugs. "It was dumb. Newton went chasing after a groundhog when you guys left. It was right as that storm turned and started heading up our way. I went after him and caught a tree branch in the head. Stupid." He touches it as if to show me it's no big deal, but he winces.

"All right, scholars!" Van jogs down the aisle holding a remote, aiming it toward the front of the room as if it's a laser gun. "Today, we face down the problems of the future." He presses a button on the remote, and Dad's holo-sim appears.

"Welcome back, campers. Today, you'll learn the concentration for your studies at Eye on Tomorrow. Please look at the screen behind me for your assignments."

A map of the campus appears on screen, with the different

buildings labeled by specialty. Then, campers' photographs start appearing next to buildings, while Dad announces who will be where. "Risha Patel, cellular generation and human cloning center." Risha's face breaks into a smile when Tomas is assigned to cloning as well.

The Beekman twins high-five one another when they both end up in robotics and artificial intelligence. The two boys they hang around with are assigned to bio-botanicals.

I already know from what Van said that I'll be in meteorology, but still, a shiver of excitement runs through me when my face appears on screen next to the Sim Dome. Alex is there, too.

Finally, the last camper's photograph appears. The brush-cut boy, whose name is Randall Harrington, is headed to cloning, and I can't help imagining an army of anxious brush-cut kids checking their watches. Then the screen goes black and it's just Dad looking out at us. "Today is the start of your life as a scientist," he says. "Make us proud. And always keep your eye on tomorrow."

Alex turns to face me when the lights come up. "So, will you work with me? Two brains are better than one."

"Depends on who the brains belong to." I smile as the door opens, and sunlight streams in. "But in this case, yeah. I think two are better."

Alex grins. "Want to start in the library? We can go over what we already know and build on that. Hopefully, Van will give us another shot at the Sim Dome soon."

"Sure." I turn to Risha. "Want to work in the library with us?"

"Not now, thanks. I'm off to the cloning lab."

"With *Tomas*?" I tease her. "I can't believe you switched from bio-botanicals just to hang out with him."

"I'm interested in *all* of it." She laughs. "So I might as well be interested *and* work with him." She gives me a shove toward the door. "Go on, weather geek. Get studying. I'll catch up with you later."

I walk with Alex across the grassy quad. "Ready to get to work?" He pulls open the library door. "Hey, Ms. Walpole." The librarian, a tall, slender woman with brown-gray dreadlocks, red-framed glasses, and dangling turquoise earrings, is twisted around a computer, apparently trying to fix something. She looks up, smiles, and waves as we step inside.

"Wow." The smell of paper books surprises me. "I thought it would be all computers."

"Over my dead body." The librarian stands there with a data cable dangling from one hand. "People ought to be able to get their information however they like best." She nods and goes back to wrestling with the computer.

"You tell 'em, Ms. Walpole." Alex laughs and heads for one of the tables. "She's awesome." He nods back over his shoulder as we sit down. "She's been here since the place started, from what I hear. She was one of the people whose property they needed to make room for the campus, but she wouldn't sell unless she got to be in charge of Eye on Tomorrow's library and education program for the little kids. Then she drafted up this list of conditions: it has to be open to the whole community—she was big on that since the town library shut down—and it has to have books in paper, too. I guess your dad agreed." Alex grins and gestures around a room full of floor-to-ceiling bookshelves, in addition to the row of computers up front. "Besides that, she brings us oatmeal raisin cookies sometimes when we're working. That's my kind of librarian."

"Me too," I say. I wonder if Ms. Walpole has paper poetry books at home, too. I bet she does. "Should we get some books?"

"There's a lot on supercell formation over in the five hundreds if you want to go look. I'll find my notes from last year."

"Okay." I head for the stacks, running my hands along the bumps of book spines as I go. A ton's been written about our topic. *Supercell, Superstorm* and *Planet Earth: The New Storm Belt* chronicle the shift from climate norms to the new weather patterns that have developed over the past fifty years, since the climate's warmed and grown so conducive to storms. *Seeds of Disaster: Foundations of Tornadogenesis* is probably the best-known text on the actual structure of tornadoes and why some supercells give rise to funnel clouds while others don't. *In the Eye of the Storm: Five Researchers on the Cutting Edge of Weather Modification* looks at the wave of scientists who worked on weather modification in the years before Dad and his colleagues.

I'm surprised to see a copy of *Playing God: The Case Against Meteorological Manipulation*; it flies in the face of everything Dad believes in, but I pull the book and add it to the teetering pile in my arms.

"You call that a few books?" Alex meets me on my way to the table, in time to keep the pile from toppling. We spread the books on the big table.

"Where should we start?" I ask.

"We're not exactly starting. I did a lot last summer." He pulls out his DataSlate. Van gave us clearance to bring them, now that we're settled in our concentrations of study. When Alex turns his on, there's a photograph of his family on the screen. There's Alex smiling at the camera in a white shirt and jeans. His mom, looking neater and less frazzled than she does when she's dropping him off. His dad, actually smiling. And a little girl hugging Newton.

"You have a little sister?"

"Julia just turned seven." He touches the DataSlate screen, and a document opens. "Here's the formula I came up with last year. It's based on some stuff from the Sim Dome computer. You know the basic premise, right? The one I tried in the dome? It's the same thing your dad is working from."

I nod. "Heat the downdraft." Dad used to talk about it all the time at dinner, back when there were still Meggs family dinners. He believed you could find the spot where a storm is beginning to rotate and stop a tornado from forming. It was like any recipe, he told me one night in between bites of chocolate cake. If you didn't have flour and cocoa and butter and all the other ingredients, you couldn't make cake. Tornadoes have ingredients, too—the rotation begins when a warmer updraft comes up against a cold, rainy downdraft. So what if you heated the air to get rid of that cold rainy downdraft? No ingredients—no tornado.

Alex turns to a sketch screen on his DataSlate, and there's a diagram like the one Dad used to draw on his napkins. He taps the center of the partially formed funnel cloud. "Right here is the spot we'd need to blast."

"Microwaves?"

"Yep. From satellites."

"Powered how?"

"Solar." He swipes the screen with his finger, and the next page appears—a sketch of a satellite with solar panels mounted on top. Yellow sketch lines representing microwave energy beam down to the bottom of the screen. "This is all in place already. They've had satellites collecting solar energy and beaming it down to storage facilities for almost ten years. It would just be a matter of amping it up and redirecting it into the heart of the storm."

"But that's what nobody can quite figure out, right? How much do you amp it up?"

"Right. Last summer, I played around with a formula for the amount of microwave energy you'd need, depending on the size and energy of the storm." He swipes to another page. "And every time I ran the numbers, it made perfect sense. But when I got time in the Sim Dome, I couldn't get it to work. It always . . . well, you saw what happened when I tried last week."

"That's what happened to my dad." I turn on my DataSlate and find the file he copied for me. "He gave me the summary."

Alex leans in, and his dark eyes scan line after line of numbers, explanations of what should have happened, but didn't.

Alex nods slowly. "Where did he do the simulation, do you know?"

"Up at StormSafe."

"Shoot." Alex sighs and tips back in his chair. "I was hoping it might have been a glitch with the Sim Dome here at Eye on Tomorrow, but if he used StormSafe equipment, that stuff's gotta be right. That means the data must be off." He stares off into a corner of the library, then nods toward my DataSlate.

"Did he use data from a real storm for the simulation?"

"I'm not sure." I skim through the document again. There's a link at the end. I click on it, and video from an online archive fills the screen. "This must be it." It's amateur storm footage from 2008, the kind people used to get when they went driving around in trucks, chasing tornadoes, back when you had to go looking for them to see one.

"Man," Alex says, breathing out. "It's a big one for back then."

Shaky video, shot through a car windshield, shows a funnel cloud forming and then touching down. It's nothing I haven't seen before, but the reaction to it—the way the guys in the car are acting—makes my stomach clench.

"We got debris! We got debris!" one of them shouts, as if he's won a new HV.

"Look at that thing!" the other one screams. "Dude, look! Can we get closer?"

They drive closer.

"Idiots," Alex whispers under his breath. But he doesn't turn away. There is something mesmerizing about watching these people sitting in the line of a tornado as if it's some kind of old-fashioned video game.

"Come on, baby," the camera guy's voice says. "Come on. Keep going." Like he's coaxing an animal out of a cave.

"Oh my God!" one of the guys yells. "Reverse! Put it in reverse!"

The tornado comes straight at them, and they're cursing and the video is shaking everywhere as they fly backward down the long stretch of road until the tornado gains on them and gains on them and they stop driving.

"Duck down! Get down!" one of them screams, and wind whips the car, pelts it with branches and dirt and rain until finally, the storm passes.

A few seconds of quiet. Then whooping, cheering. "Man, we were all over that thing! That was awesome! That was just—"

Alex presses the STOP button, and there is silence.

I realize I've been holding my breath. I breathe out and turn to him. He is shaking his head.

"It's surreal, isn't it?" he says. "That they'd put themselves in the path? That anyone could think this was entertaining?"

I stare at the frozen images, the men in their baseball caps, laughing, high-fiving each other. They must be in their twenties in this video. They're old men now. If they've survived. "They didn't know," I say. "It was fun for them. Exciting and fun. They didn't know what was about to happen with the climate, the storms."

"Stupid," Alex mutters, opening a book.

But I can't stop looking at their frozen faces amid the dust. They had no idea what was coming. Are we like that today? Is there something worse on the way that will make our storms seem like nothing at all?

"Come on," Alex says. "Let's work."

I turn the pages of the *Seeds of Disaster* book. The theories about tornado formation here are the best and latest, but there's still a big mystery about why the storms form some times and not others, when almost the exact same conditions are present.

I flip through the weather text, but in my mind, I'm turning pages in the poetry book on my nightstand, and I remember that one, "Geometry."

> *... the house expands:*
> *the windows jerk free to hover near the ceiling,*
> *the ceiling floats away with a sigh.*

I stare up at the library ceiling, gleaming golden wood with dark brown knots, and I imagine it lifting up, up over our heads and drifting off. The idea of solving a problem, feeling everything open up with possibility and with more problems to solve, too, fills me like a kite filling with wind.

Alex's shoulder brushes mine, and I jump.

"Sorry, I was looking at what you were reading." He nods down at the book. "You finding anything good?"

"Not yet. Just thinking."

"Me, too."

He lowers his head, and I watch him swiping through pages and pages of numbers, numbers that should have been the magic formula to make the winds stop blowing, to keep the weathervane on his family's barn where it belongs, to let Newton chase groundhogs in the afternoon. But the deeper his frown gets, the more I start to believe there will never be a magic formula to make everything okay.

"It's about time to call it a day, kids." Ms. Walpole steps up to our table, a stack of books in her arms. She smells like the vanilla candles my mom likes. "Did you find everything?"

"Not exactly." Alex tips back in his chair and sighs.

"Put your chair down. You'll crack your head open," she says. When his chair legs are back on the ground, she nods. "Now, what is it that you need?"

"Data," Alex and I say together, and that makes us laugh a little, even though it's been a frustrating afternoon.

"Solid tornado formation data that will work in a simulation," Alex adds. "Nothing you can help with, unfortunately."

Ms. Walpole frowns and puts down her pile of books. "The data you have isn't working?" she asks.

Alex shakes his head. "Nope. Even though it should."

"You've checked it and rechecked it?" She clicks her tongue against the roof of her mouth.

"Yep."

Ms. Walpole raises her eyebrows. "Then that's an easy one. Collect new data."

Alex lets out half a laugh. "Sure. Do you happen to know where there's a high-tech weather balloon or something we can borrow?"

She crosses her arms in front of her and looks over her glasses at us. "As a matter of fact, I do."

Chapter 12

This wasn't on our orientation tour," I say as Ms. Walpole unlocks the warehouse tucked behind the Sim Dome. It's such an unremarkable building—dull aluminum paneling, nestled among all the shiny steel and glass—that I didn't even notice when we walked past it before.

"Hmph." She presses her finger to a biometric panel alongside a garage door, and it slides open. "That's because Van Gardner's so caught up in his shiny new toys that he forgets everything else."

We step inside a room that's bigger than any airplane hangar—huge and basic.

"This place is simply to hold equipment—acres and acres of equipment that somebody thought was too old to keep using," Ms. Walpole says as we start down one of the long rows of floor-to-ceiling storage racks, and right away, I can see that people here have strange ideas about what's old.

There's a whole fleet of four-wheel-drive vehicles that look like they've been converted from gasoline to hydrogen, each one outfitted with some fancy gizmo on top. "What's sticking up from the trucks?" I ask.

"That's a mobile meso-net unit—a multipurpose measuring machine made up of steel rods and twirling computer weather sensors that record things like barometric pressure and wind speed," Ms. Walpole says.

I nod; I read about them in one of Dad's old journals. In the early days of tornado research, scientists used to drive these things close to the storms and drop off probes in the path, hoping for a direct hit. They wanted to see inside the heart of the tornado. That's how they learned a lot about storm formation, how vertical wind shear can turn an ordinary thunderstorm into something stronger.

"And they don't use these anymore?"

"Oh, they still use them. They just have better ones now." Ms. Walpole leads us around a corner and down another long row of shelves. These are loaded with computers that can't be more than a year or two old—not state of the art like the ones in the Sim Dome, but still plenty powerful.

"Hey," Alex says. "Aren't these the ones from the camp lab last summer?"

Ms. Walpole nods. "They've been replaced. They may bring these out for the Tomorrow Kids program we run during school vacations."

"Is that for younger kids?" I ask.

Alex nods. "It's open to anybody, and really, they just do fun stuff, but they're always looking for future campers. That's how I got in; two weeks after my first vacation camp, they invited my folks to get me tested. Tomas, too."

"If they'd only known what they were getting into." Ms. Walpole smiles. "How's Mrs. Hazen doing, have you heard?"

"Not that good. Tomas doesn't like to talk about it." Alex shrugs. "She needs to go to New York or somewhere for treatment."

Ms. Walpole nods. "I thought I heard him say something like that to Van this week. I hope they're not thinking of giving up the farm."

"They're not," Alex says quickly, and I bite my lip to keep from telling him what Risha said.

"Right down here," Ms. Walpole says. At the far end of the warehouse there's a tall rack filled with bins of rain gear, and one of the old National Weather Service trucks is parked behind it. In the back of the pickup is a sleek model airplane with a five- or six-foot wingspan.

Alex's eyes get huge. I step closer and see this is no toy; it's one of the original DataDrones—the indestructible, remote-operated planes that helped scientists make some of their first real breakthroughs in figuring out how tornadoes are born.

Alex runs his hand along one of the wings. "Graphene, right?"

Ms. Walpole nods. "It was the strongest substance in the world when this was developed."

And it wasn't that long ago. Five or six years, maybe? I remember Dad talking about how amazing the drones were. "They're not using it anymore?" I ask.

"This showed up a few weeks ago," Ms. Walpole says. "I guess the new ones have more efficient radar built in."

Alex reaches into the back of the truck and picks up the

remote-control device that must run the plane. It has regular remote buttons and levers with some kind of computer screen below them. "So . . ." He sounds like he's trying not to get too excited, but his eyes give him away. "This still works?"

Ms. Walpole gives a sharp nod. "I'm sure it does. Contrary to popular opinion around this place, just because something is a little older doesn't mean it's not useful." She pushes her glasses up on her nose.

Alex looks down at the control panel in his hands. "Can we . . . uh . . . borrow it?"

"Well, it's not doing anyone any good sitting in the back of a van, is it?" Behind the glasses, Ms. Walpole's green eyes have a glint of mischief in them, and I smile, imagining Dad trying to negotiate with her. "I'm certainly not going to stop you from making use of the tools you need to carry out your research. I'm here to help, after all."

"Should we check with Van or something?" I ask.

She purses her lips. "I'm not sure I would recommend that. It's often easier to be forgiven than it is to get permission in situations such as this." She pauses. "But of course, I never said that." She looks at her watch, silver and obviously antique. "I'd better get back to the library. I'm afraid I often forget to lock up when I leave a building, so you two will need to do that on your way out, all right?"

Alex grins. "You got it. And thanks."

She walks briskly back down the aisle, then turns back to us. "You'll want to leave promptly, and use the main entrance. The other staff members are all in a meeting in the auditorium for another hour. I'd best join them now."

I can't quite believe what we're about to do, so I just stand, listening to her footsteps fade all the way to the door. It thunks closed, and Alex turns to me. "Ready to borrow an airplane?"

Chapter 13

How long can you stay?" Alex leans against the bottom of the playground slide at the park near campus, frowning down at his DataSlate. A storm is forming west of us, but there's no way to tell yet if it will spawn tornadoes. Just in case, we set up the drone so it's ready to take off from the open space where kids play kickball.

"I can stay a while, I guess." Dad never mentioned a curfew, and Mirielle usually makes dinner pretty late. "So . . . if we do get a storm, the idea here is to fly the plane into it and gather data so . . ." I was so bowled over by the very idea of "borrowing" a weather drone, so nervous as we carried it silently out the Eye on Tomorrow gate and lugged it here, that I never actually processed what we're trying to do. Gather data about a storm, sure. Then what?

"Well, I figure the numbers I'm using in my project must be off. I tried the simulation with two different storms last summer and got the same results, which means maybe all the storm data in the system at camp is wrong."

"So if we have a brand new storm . . . and collect our own brand new data . . ." This kind of problem-solving is so different from the

Eye on Tomorrow entrance exam, this starting-from-scratch thinking, but I'm getting it. "Then the simulation should work?"

"Well, hopefully," Alex says. "Or if not, we'll know the data wasn't the problem and the whole theory's a bust." He sighs and looks down at the DataSlate. "Oh!" He jumps up and climbs the ladder to the top of the slide, facing west. "I think we're in business. Come up and see!"

There's not much room on the platform at the top of the slide, so we crowd together, and Alex points to the horizon. "See that rotation?"

The rotation I notice first is in my stomach, which is kind of flipping out being so close to him up here, but I force myself to focus on the clouds. "Yeah. That looks like it's going to produce a funnel cloud."

Before I've finished my sentence, he's climbing down the ladder and heading for the remote control we left by the kickball field. The storm is moving fast; the sky is darkening, and the wind is already picking up. I can't believe we're actually going to fly this thing. It feels too adult-scientist, too serious, too *real* to be happening to a couple of kids at science camp. But Alex hands me the remote.

"Hold this while I check the sensors, okay?"

My hands shake, even though Alex swears he's flown remote control planes before and this is no different. All we have to do is fly it into the storm; once we punch through the wall, the drone will be swept up into the tornado and sensors can gather data. The wireless system is set up to send information directly to my DataSlate, so we'll get readings right away. Then we'll recover the full set of data from the hard drive when the drone lands. Or crashes. I'm picturing us returning the plane to the storage building in pieces, explaining to Van or, worse, my father, what we were thinking, when Alex shouts, "Press the red button! Now!"

I press it, and the drone's engine hums to life. "I thought you were going to fly it!"

"I want to make sure the sensors are working," he says, waving over his shoulder at me as he squints down at the plane. "You'll be fine—just start it going forward and then throttle up to lift off, and I'll take over from there!"

Throttle up? The controls feel like some kids' video game in my hand, but I know this is real, with real consequences. If something happens to this plane and we have to—

"Jaden, start it! The storm's coming and if it turns away before we get there, we're not going to make it!"

I force my thumb to push the lever, and the plane jerks forward on the ground.

"Good!" Alex yells. "Good! Now speed up! Go!"

I push the lever all the way forward, and the plane bounces along, speeding up, bumping over the dusty kickball field where second base would be.

"Now throttle up! Now!" Alex shouts as he grabs the DataSlate from the grass and runs to my side.

I press the button to throttle up, and the plane rises off the ground, just missing a shrub at the edge of the park. It wavers, headed for the fence, and I can't imagine how we're going to keep it steady in the wind. "Here!" I shove the controls into Alex's hands, take my DataSlate, and call up the program that will receive the drone's data.

The page comes up blank but immediately starts filling with numbers. Columns and columns of numbers. Wind speeds. Temperatures. Barometric pressures. They're mostly the same numbers, over and over, as Alex maneuvers the plane over the fence, outside Placid Meadows and closer to the storm.

The rotation we spotted from the top of the slide is swirling faster, and already a thick, dark rope is forming, stretching down from the cloud. Alex takes his eyes off the plane to watch the storm and lets out a whoop. "We got it!" He sounds like one of those storm chasers on the video, and I wonder if we're as stupid as they were, playing with fire, with something we don't understand.

"Here we go . . . getting close now . . . Watch!" He means to watch the plane or the storm, or maybe the data, but I watch Alex, his eyes as intense as anyone's I've ever seen. He bites his lip in concentration, and the tendons in his hands tense as he clutches the remote and drives the plane full throttle—faster, faster, faster—until it surges through the gray wall of wind into the heart of the storm.

"It's in! Watch the data, Jaden! What are we getting?"

I look down at the numbers flying over the screen in my hands. Flying faster than the wind, but my eyes start to see patterns. Changes. Wind speeds rising. Temperatures rising. Barometric pressure dropping like mad. This is what it's like to be inside a storm.

"Okay, it's turning. The storm's turning. I'm going to try to keep the drone inside. Tell me what you see!" I sneak another glance at

Alex, but his eyes don't move from the handheld controls. The computer screen below the control panel shows a blinking blue dot, swirling, flying, inside the storm.

The numbers on the DataSlate hold steady. Soon, I should see . . . what? If there's a field at the edge of Placid Meadows that dissipates storms or deflects them, the numbers should start to show it weakening.

But they don't.

"I'm not sure how long before it's thrown clear. Are you getting stuff?" Alex's voice is tense with concentration. "Jaden, talk to me! We've got maybe another ten seconds. I'm losing the signal. What are you seeing?"

I can't answer. Because I can't begin to process the numbers flying past my eyes.

"I . . . It's going too fast for me to see." But that's a lie. I can see the numbers, and I know what they mean. As the storm pulls away from Placid Meadows, the wind speeds are increasing. The temperatures are getting higher. And the barometric pressure has plunged to a level I've never even seen before.

I understand, but I can't make myself say it out loud.

This storm didn't weaken when it hit the Placid Meadows perimeter. It turned away, toward someone else's home. And got stronger.

Chapter 14

The brave thing would be to ask Dad more about his failed project tonight. Ask him why he thinks his simulation went wrong, why all the number crunching wasn't enough, and what he's doing about it now. Ask him what really happens to storms when they leave Placid Meadows. And maybe that would start to answer the questions swirling in my head since Alex and I flew the drone this afternoon, since I lied to Alex. I told Alex it all went by too quickly, that my DataSlate's battery died before I could process the numbers. I told him we'd need to recover data from the hard drive to see what really happened. I couldn't tell him the truth. Not without asking my father some questions first.

But Dad's eyes are angrier than the clouds as he bursts into the kitchen, and Mirielle's delicate spinach salad just about wilts when he slams his briefcase on the table.

"Stephen, what is it?" She sets down her wineglass and rushes over to press a hand to his cheek.

He brushes it away, pops open his briefcase, pulls out his

DataSlate, and drops it onto the granite counter with a clatter. "We're losing support for Phase Two. Look!"

He turns on the DataSlate—I'm surprised the screen doesn't shatter under his glare—and jabs at it until the document appears. "This is from our investors' group. Sixty days to acquire the rest of the property we need, or we lose our funding. And I've got two hold-outs who *will not* sell."

My stomach twists. I'm pretty sure I'm working with one of the holdouts' kids. And Risha's in love with the other one.

"Can you not offer more money for the farmland?" Mirielle asks, setting a place for Dad at dinner. "It seems to me that—"

"Do you have any idea what we've offered? Ten *times* the market value of their property, but *noooo . . .* these are *family farms.* Well, they can take their worm-bitten apples and their lumpy, seedy strawberries and kiss my—"

"Stephen!" Mirielle is back in her seat at the table, but her eyes shoot lasers over the roast chicken and gravy, and Dad stops. Mirielle puts a gentle hand on Remi's head and looks my way, too. "You are scaring the children."

As much as I don't like being called a child, her words take the electricity out of Dad's anger at the farmers, and I'm thankful. No wonder Mirielle keeps Aunt Linda's berries a secret.

"Sit down." Mirielle motions to the chair next to her, and Dad sinks into it like a scarecrow that's lost its straw. She pours him a glass of Scotch.

Dad presses his hands against his eyes. "How am I going to pull this off in sixty days?"

"Isn't there somewhere else you could build? I mean, you can't very well make somebody sell land if they don't want to, right?" When Dad turns to look at me, I wish I could pull the words back, but like Risha's dandelion fluff, blown into the wind at our picnic, they're swirling all around our heads, impossible to catch.

The voice that follows his glare isn't angry; it's measured and calm, like Dad sounds in his holo-talks. "The planned expansion of Placid Meadows will allow another fifty families to live within the secure environment of a StormSafe community. This is about people's lives, Jaden—not about some silly family tradition."

"I know." I nod. But I think of Alex and the strawberries his family grows in the sun. A wad of spinach sticks in my throat. "What are you going to do?"

"I'll tell you what I'm not going to do." Dad takes a drink, then thumps his glass down, hard, on the wood table. "I am *not* losing this project."

As soon as Mirielle leaves to put Remi to bed, the storm clouds settle back in Dad's eyes, and he doesn't say another word to me. I sink into the old wooden rocking chair in the living room—perfect except that Grandma Athena's creepy photo always stares at it—and read through the files that Alex beamed to my DataSlate. I can't help keeping one eye on Dad, though, pacing back and forth from his office to the kitchen. He's in and out all night. A few times, he blusters out to the porch and stands there, muttering and looking off to the west. The last time the screen door slams, he comes back smiling.

"Jaden, you're still up?"

"I'm reading through some data my camp partner shared with me from last summer." I hesitate, afraid that talking to him at all will somehow give away what I did this afternoon at the park, who I'm working with, what I saw. "We're working together on the storm dissipation project."

Dad nods. "Good challenge, that one. You read that abstract I gave you?"

"Yeah. My partner had the same problem when he ran the simulation on his data last summer." This is where I should ask him more. Instead, I wait to see if he'll offer up details without my having to ask.

"Well, some things aren't meant to be." He yawns.

"I guess not." His office door is open, so I expect him to go back there like he usually does, to lift a tired hand to the sensor and make the steel door slide shut so he can work into the night.

But he doesn't. He stretches his arms up so high that his fingertips brush the ceiling and then heads for his bedroom. "Don't stay up too late."

I say good night.

I listen to the lock click, hear the water in the bathroom, the toilet flushing.

I hear the snap of the white noise machine turning on, the smooth, soothing whoosh that he says clears his mind of all the numbers and formulas so he can rest.

I page through Alex's files one more time, until I'm sure Dad must be asleep.

I start to stand, and the rocking chair creaks.

I freeze.

But no one's watching except Grandma Athena, trapped in her frame.

I turn away from her and head for the open office door.

Chapter 15

The room is dark.

Only the tiniest bit of kitchen light creeps in, and even with the door open, all the sounds from outside get swallowed up by this space.

I set my DataSlate on the edge of the huge mahogany desk and look out to the kitchen clock. It's midnight, and I don't know when Remi usually wakes to nurse. Will Mirielle bring her to the kitchen? Just in case, I press a button—no need for a fingerprint scan on the inside—and watch the cold steel door slide closed. The kitchen light snuffs out, but a power switch glows next to the door.

I flick it on. Overhead lights glimmer, and flat screens flicker to life on every wall.

The screen to my left shows real-time images of a row of satellites. Eight of them. I step closer. Are those solar panels attached? Underneath each image is a display panel with numbers, all gradually climbing. They are labeled in kilowatts. I reach out to touch one of the panels, and a new window emerges from the center of the screen.

It's full of constantly changing numbers. Some look like the data that whizzed past on my DataSlate while the drone was flying in the storm. Wind speeds, barometric pressure readings, and temperatures. Some look like kilowatt levels, measures of energy. Others appear to be geographic coordinates, latitude and longitude. What do they all mean?

What does any of it mean? Maybe I read the data wrong this afternoon. Maybe it's not what it looks like and I'll never have to talk to Alex about what I think I saw.

I cross the room to Dad's desk and turn on the computer.

It hums to life, flashing a blue background at me while the system loads. Over the desk is a screen showing live radar images of the region, from north of the airport, all along the river. A second big storm looks like it just missed us around the time Dad went to bed. It was close to Alex's house, from the look of this track.

I hope Newton was in for the night.

I hope they're safe.

The computer login screen appears. Dad's username, SMeggs, is already in the login box, but it's asking for a fingerprint scan or password.

I have the wrong prints, so I ignore the biometric panel and set my fingers on the keys, hoping for inspiration.

I try the obvious first. What he loves most.

stormsafe. dna-ture. I try it with the hyphen and without.

No.

Then I try mirielle. And remi. jaden.

The message flashes again: incorrect password.

I sink back in the chair. I should have known I wouldn't be able to just pop onto his computer. The desk has a single drawer, and I slide it open looking for a list or scrap of paper, even though deep down I know Dad's too smart to leave his passwords lying around. Of course he is. The only thing in the drawer is a jumble of computer and DataSlate wires, a couple of storage drives, a bottle of BioWake pills, and the barometer he had in his hand the other day.

It fills my palm when I pick it up, a perfect ring of dark, polished wood with the barometer mechanism showing through a quarter-size glass window. Around the window is a yellowed ring of barometric pressure markings and five weather patterns written in fancy old script.

Stormy.
Rain.
Change.
Fair.
Very Dry.

Why would Dad, with his walls of satellite maps and live radar screens, keep something like this around? Dad, whose motto is "Science will save us," who won't even read a paper book anymore, is hanging on to an old weather instrument that has words like *fair* instead of data? It's not even in great shape for an antique. It doesn't seem to work at all, and the wood finish is worn away at the bottom and on the sides, as if it's spent a lot of time being held in someone's hand.

I put it back in the drawer and look back at the log-in box on the computer screen.

barometer.

Incorrect password.

I try combinations of all the words that have already failed. remijaden. placidstorm. I even try Mom's name, rebekah, in case his password is left over from a long time ago. Nothing works.

And then as if the walls suddenly dissolved, I sense Grandma's eyes staring out from her photo in the living room. Grandma, who loved science as much as Dad does.

I type athena.

The desktop appears.

I pull up a search box and type in latitude and longitude coordinates from the screen across the room.

35° 24′ N 97° 36′ W

A map appears on the screen with a marker pointing to the center. I click to zoom in on the satellite image of that spot, but I already recognize enough of the streets and the bend of the river to know what I will see.

The fence. The river and the trees. The daisy and dandelion meadows, and the field with the gazebo.

The barn with the battered weathervane. And the strawberries.

The Carillo farm, where Alex's family works and lives. Why is Dad's satellite focused here?

My breathing quickens, though I still don't know what it all means. I swivel Dad's chair around—I feel too small in it, swallowed up by black leather and his smell of work, sweat, and Scotch—and face the satellite wall again.

Current output: 00:00

PowerBank: 327.9 MW

35° 24' N 97° 36' W

I stare at the numbers and wait for them to arrange themselves into something that makes sense. I wait for the windows to jerk free and hover near the ceiling, like in the poem.

They don't.

But the more I stare, the more two letters stand out.

MW. The abbreviation for megawatts. Energy.

Energy mixed with geographic coordinates.

Is someone blasting energy—microwave energy—down from the satellites?

Is this the technology that didn't work in the simulations? It didn't work in Alex's trial, and it didn't work in Dad's. The whole concept of blasting energy at a tornado to stop the rotation was deemed too risky, too dangerous for the real world. So what's going on here?

Is Dad testing it anyway? Without government approval? Do the other scientists at StormSafe even know what he's doing?

My brain is churning. I swing the chair back around to face the radar screen. The storm is getting smaller now. What happened before? Did something go wrong when Dad tried to dissipate the storms today? Did he make them bigger by accident? Is that why the numbers from the drone's data readings looked the way they did?

I look down at the computer screen and start scanning the file names. Most of them have only project numbers: RL7421, 139Q, SS451.

Meaningless. And the more I stare at the numbers, the more I want to scream. I take a deep breath and look up at the ceiling that will never float away with a sigh.

When I look back at the computer, a file called Family Photos catches my eye. I click on it and find the same collection of photos running on the Data Frame in the living room. I'm about to close the folder and go back to the numbers when I notice that one of the files in that folder isn't an image. It's text, and it's labeled AGM.

Those are Grandma's initials.

Athena Grace Meggs.

As I click to open the folder, there's a faint sound from the other side of the door. Footsteps on the kitchen floor.

I freeze.

My father's voice drifts in, muffled. "No, honey, I'm fine. Go back to bed. Couldn't sleep, so I'm going to get some work done."

My heart freezes, and my hands are shaking so much it's all I can do to close out the folder and log out.

The fingerprint sensor beeps.

The lock mechanism clicks.

The door will slide open in seconds, and no matter how wildly I look around the room, there is nowhere to hide in this sparse electronic workspace.

I race to the power switch, hit it, and the room goes dark. In the blackness, I dive under Dad's desk just before the door hums open and he turns the lights back on.

He's wearing dress shoes with his pajama bottoms. They click on the floor and echo off the walls and make my heart pound harder.

He steps right up to the desk and pauses in front of his computer. If he sits down, will he notice that his chair is warm?

The dust under here tickles my throat. I swallow a cough, eyes watering.

What am I doing? Why am I hiding from my own father in the house that's supposed to be my home?

I should come out; he'd probably laugh. But something in the click of his shoes, something in the faces I've already seen him wear this week, tells me to stay still. And quiet.

Dad doesn't sit. He walks to the satellite wall and touches the panel under the screen. He's facing away from me, and I let my eyes move around the room again. At least I got logged out of his computer. At least there's nothing to—

My heart bolts up into my throat, and I almost choke on it. Because right there, its corner hanging over the edge of Dad's desk above me, is my DataSlate.

I can't let him see it.

I take a deep breath and inch forward on the floor.

Dad turns, and I freeze. He stands still for a second—is he looking at the radar screen above the desk?—and then turns back to the satellite wall.

I stretch my arm up slowly, silently.

I can't reach it.

I slide one knee forward, then the other, and reach again. My fingers close around the edge of the DataSlate just as Dad's Data-Slate chimes.

I startle, and it falls from the edge of the desk and almost through my fingers, but I make a last mad grab and catch it.

"There you are! It's about time," Dad says quietly.

"That's a fine way to say hello, Stephen." A woman's voice. I lean out the tiniest bit, but the screen is facing away from me, so I can't see her face.

"Shh . . . hold on, let me plug in my earpiece so we don't wake the whole house."

Under the desk, I pull my DataSlate back into the shadows and try to slow my breathing while Dad talks. I can hear only his side of the conversation now.

"I know," he says into the DataSlate's camera. His shiny black shoes click back and forth, louder and fainter, over and over. When he walks away, I breathe.

"Yes, good timing." He laughs a little. "It was a monster. They won't be able to find their roof in the morning. And maybe they'll decide they don't love that farmland as much as they thought. We'll have the bulldozers here before you know it."

Dad walks away again, but I keep holding my breath. My father is *laughing* at the storm that just came through.

"Yep. Listen, I need to get some work done, but I'll see you tomorrow. . . . Love you, too. Good night."

I gasp, then hold my breath, afraid he's heard. His shoes click closer again, and I tense as he sinks into the leather office chair.

Above, there are clicks on the keyboard. I calm my breathing, but my brain feels like it's about to explode.

Love you, too? Who *was* that? He was talking like she knew all about the storm and the lawsuit. It must be someone he works with. *Love you, too.* No wonder he spends so much time at StormSafe. My heart sinks, thinking of Mirielle, so understanding while Dad's at work all the time.

"Hm." Dad's heel lifts off the floor and he starts bouncing his knee, something he's always done when he's thinking hard.

More clicks.

A sigh.

Then the chair pushes back from the desk. Shoes click all the way to the entrance, then out and through the kitchen until the door slides shut and I am alone in the office again.

I don't come out.

Not yet.

I wait with my itchy nose in the dust for what must be another ten minutes until I'm sure he won't be back until morning.

Finally, I unfold my cramped legs, climb out, and slide into the leather chair.

I log in, go straight to the AGM folder, and start reading data files.

The numbers look almost exactly like what Alex shared with me, right down to the formulas, the projected kilowatts necessary to warm a downdraft enough to stop rotation within a storm.

I read through file after file, willing my eyes to stay open.

This data should work. It all makes sense, just the way Alex explained it. The simulation should have worked, too.

I go back to the beginning and start reading again. There must be something here I'm missing. Something that will give me that understanding, that vision of how it all fits together.

But the numbers blur.

They start to spin and mix with dust and broken glass and tree limbs. I look harder. There has to be a pattern, but everything is moving so fast it's blurry.

Then the whole screen swells and darkens, and there is a monster tornado coming. I'm riding my bike, and someone is behind me—sometimes it's Risha, sometimes Alex, and sometimes Amelia from home. The voice keeps changing but it always shouts the same thing, "Go! Faster! Hurry!" But no matter how fast I try to go, how hard I push down on the pedals, they just spin effortlessly, and I go nowhere. I can see the house—not Dad's concrete block but our house back in Vermont—and I keep pedaling, pedaling, as the storm gets closer and closer. The drone flies back and forth, back and forth. Roof tiles start flying off the house. Windows shatter, and in one of the gaping empty windowpanes, I see Mom's face for a split second before the blackness swallows her up.

"NO!!"

I wake up with a jerk. My hands are sweating, despite the air-conditioning in Dad's office. And the computer clock says 4:30 AM.

How could I have let myself fall asleep? What if Dad had come back?

I take a last look at the computer screen, the folder full of swirling file names, and this time, one file stands out. Not numbers, but initials and words.

AGM-FAKEABSTRACT

Was it even here before? How could I have missed it? I shiver and click on the file.

I have read this document before. Dad put a copy on my DataSlate. It is the file that summarized his research on storm dissipation and its failure. That's what he told me.

With my heart racing, I search the folder, looking for another document, but there is nothing else labeled abstract or summary or AGM.

Nothing.

I open up each of the remaining documents. Only more data.

Now the computer clock reads 4:52. And I know that no matter how late Dad stays up, his alarm goes off at 5.

I need to get out of here.

But I can't.

I have to know.

I run a full hard-drive search.

Find: AGM

The list that scrolls down must be a hundred documents long, and it looks like all of them are in the folder I just finished reading through.

I scroll to the bottom.

All but one.

A file named AGM-AB buried five folders deep in a file called 2048 TAXES.

The digital clock reads 4:57.

I double click the file and realize I've been holding my breath.

It starts out like the other summary. I suck in words as if they're oxygen until I get to the spot in the document where it diverges from the one I've already read.

The rest of this summary is nothing like the one on my DataSlate.

The simulation did not fail.

Dad's experiment worked.

The computer clock turns to 4:58, and there is no time for questions. No time to ask why he gave me a phony summary, why he wanted the world to think he failed. I grab my DataSlate, click out the data-transfer stick, plug it into the back of Dad's drive, and drag the file over. I go back to the original folder with the data and copy that, too.

4:59.

The progress bar can't move quickly enough, and it makes me want to pound the computer. *Faster! Transfer! Go!*

The last file copies as the clock turns.

Forcing myself to keep breathing, I unplug from Dad's computer, log out, and press the button to make the steel door slide open.

Dad's alarm is beeping in the bedroom.

The SmartKitchen is brewing his coffee.

As the office door begins to slide closed behind me, I look back at the wall of satellites, the wall of radar images, of storms, and dissipation data and secrets, wondering . . . what really goes on in this room?

Chapter 16

Alex isn't at camp. When we left the park yesterday, his plan was to recover the drone and then head home. Did he find it? Has he seen the data it collected? What if that second storm hit before he made it home?

I sit through Van's morning directions with my DataSlate in my hands, half expecting him to snatch it away, even though I have permission to have it. It's off, but I can feel its weight, its danger, practically burning my hands with what I learned last night. Part of me is dying to talk to Alex about our results from the drone flight now, to show him this new data and see what he makes of it. But there's also a knot in my stomach. What if he sees something awful?

The holo-sim turns on, and Dad rises out of the floor. In today's lecture, he's talking about responsibility, integrity of data, and cooperation. My chest feels tighter with every word.

Responsibility? Integrity?

He lied. He lied about everything. Why?

I need to talk to Alex, but at the same time, I'm terrified. I've started the conversation with him in my head a thousand times, and I've thought about never telling him at all. But he needs to know that his research was solid. I want to give him that.

"Hey." I know it's Alex behind me from his whisper as he leans forward.

"You're here!" I turn in my seat to see him. "I need to—"

Even in the dim light, the sight of his face steals my words. He's hurt again. And the scrape on his temple from the other night is nothing compared to this. There's a gash across his right cheek, butterflied together with a steri-strip. Another over his left eye still bleeds under its bandage. His chin is scraped raw.

"What happened?" I whisper.

But even as the words leave my mouth, I know it was the storm I saw on the radar.

The storm that made my father smile before he went to bed.

The one he laughed about in his office with his *love-you-too* woman on the video call.

"I'm okay. And I got the drone."

"But you're not okay. Where—"

"Shhh . . . we'll talk later. Turn around now, or Van's going to get on your case," Alex whispers, so I turn back to face my father. His holo-image talks over my head, smiles at the back of the auditorium. How can he do this? How can he *laugh* at someone's farm being hit, someone's body being beaten like this? How can he have the power to stop these storms and not use it? I want to throw myself at him, pound him with my fists.

But he's untouchable.

I'd fly right through him to the floor.

"Now that you have your partners and your focus, we'll skip the lectures and go straight to morning research. This is the last day you'll see me for a while," holo-Dad says.

Unless you happen to live in my house, I think.

Dad's image disappears, and I shiver. Knowing what I know about Dad's research, what he found and isn't telling anyone, makes me wonder about camp.

The high-tech equipment. The library. The top-of-the-line computers. Why is education such a big part of his company's mission? Why spend so much money on—

"You coming?" The lights are back on, and Alex is standing halfway down the row of seats, waiting for me.

I tuck my DataSlate in my backpack as Van comes walking up the aisle. "What happened to you?" Van pauses next to Alex and raises his eyebrows. "Get in a fight with your girlfriend here?"

Alex laughs a little. "Got caught out during the storm last night."

"Be more careful, my man. We're counting on you here." Van frowns at the bandage on Alex's forehead. "Stop by the first aid station before you get to work today. Marcy'll fix you up."

"I'll come, too," I say. "I need to talk to you . . . about stuff."

Van tips his head in a question, but I don't answer. He shrugs, says "You go easy on him today," and heads out the back door.

Alex and I walk down a long hall to the first aid station, tucked into a bright room near the entrance. Every time I turn to say something, the bandages on his face feel like accusations. Dad knew how to stop the storm that did this. He chose not to.

I finally find words. "So that weather hit while you were out looking for the drone?"

Alex shakes his head. "Not really." He turns toward me and says quietly, "I got the drone, and it's fine; it's back at the house, but I haven't downloaded the data yet because that storm . . ." He shakes his head. "It came out of nowhere."

"Why weren't you in a safe room?"

"Never got the alert."

My face falls. "Was your DataSlate out of power, or—"

"There *was* no alert. You didn't get an alarm on yours last night, did you?"

I shake my head. I'd had it right in my lap, going over and over that data. The alarm that should have sounded on every data device within a ten-mile radius never went off.

"We had no clue until the wind kicked up. Thought we had time to get the chickens in, but debris started flying before I got back to the barn."

Alex pulls open the door to the first aid station, and we step inside. The room is full of sunlight, and the white walls are so bright they make me squint. A bouncy young woman in scrubs—she must be Marcy—is scrolling through records on a DataSlate. She lifts her head, takes one look at Alex, and says, "Well, I don't need to guess which one of you is my customer, do I?" She starts rummaging in a drawer full of bandages and ointment.

Alex hops onto one of the stools near the window and motions me closer. "What'd you want to talk about?"

"I . . . can talk to you later." I glance over at Marcy, who seems nice enough, but I'm not ready to tell anyone else about this. I'm not even sure I'm ready to tell Alex. But I have to.

"Here we go." Marcy swoops over Alex and eases off his old bandage. "Ooh, that's a good one. Let's clean it and get you patched up." She raises a UV wand, gives the wound a quick zap to sterilize it, and is reaching for a new bandage when the door opens.

It's Tomas. "Oh, hey, guys." He waits until Marcy looks up. "Van sent me to get him something for a headache?"

"In the meds kit right there on the counter." She starts unwrapping a bandage, but the door bangs open again, and one of the Beekman twins—I can't tell them apart—is holding her arm.

"I tripped on Ava's robot. I think I sprained something," she whines.

Marcy sighs, hands me the bandage—"Can you finish up here?"—and reaches into the freezer for an ice pack.

While she's having Tess try to move her arm in different ways, I finish unwrapping the bandage. "When you were flying the drone yesterday," I whisper, leaning in toward Alex, "I . . . I did see some of the numbers." I cover his cut gently with the clean gauze and take a deep breath. "I wasn't sure I was reading them right, but . . . I think I was."

His eyes light up. "And?"

"I'll be right back; I'm going to take her to the main office to file an accident report." Marcy hustles out of the room with Tess, and we're alone with Tomas, still shuffling through the bottles of pain reliever.

He looks over at us, then picks up one of the bottles and grins. "Better get these to Van before he gets grumpy." He leaves, and I turn back to Alex.

I have to force myself to say the words. He'll see for himself when we download the data anyway. "The storm wasn't dissipating at the fence."

"But it turned away at the perimeter."

"And kept going, remember? Whatever happened at the fence didn't weaken it, Alex. Wait until you see the numbers."

"You saw the numbers?"

I nod. "I saw enough."

He stares up at me from the stool, and I watch his eyes shift from a look of confusion to shocked understanding. "It left . . . and got stronger?"

I nod. "And then last night, my dad left his office open." I take my DataSlate from my backpack on the floor and pull up another stool next to him. "I went onto his computer and looked up his results from his dissipation research, from the simulation he did that was like yours."

"And? It failed, right? You told me that before."

"That's what I thought." I click into the folder I copied and turn the screen so he can see the full list of files. "Remember the abstract he printed up for me? The one that summarized his failed simulation?"

"Yeah."

"This is it." I point to the document.

AGM-FAKEABSTRACT

His eyebrows knit together, and the new bandage tugs at his skin. He raises a slow hand to it. "It . . . wasn't real?"

"This is the real one." I click the other document open, hand him the DataSlate, and hold my breath.

Alex reads. His eyes grow wider with every word. Finally, he shakes his head. "Why?" He turns to me, as if I'm a stranger. "Why would he hide this? This information . . ." He taps the DataSlate screen, and his voice gets louder. "This is gold. This is going to solve everything. With proof of the simulation's success, they could have gotten government clearance to do an actual storm-trial using the satellites that are already up." He's talking faster now. "I mean, I don't know if they're totally equipped to send down the right amounts of energy or if the accuracy is what it would need to be yet, given it's not the reason they were originally built, but still . . ." He shakes his head again and looks at me, angry. "What's your dad thinking?"

My mouth goes dry. "I don't know." I'm afraid to tell him more. About the wall of satellites, about the digital kilowatt readings fluctuating during last night's storm.

And I cannot bring myself to tell him the detail that haunts me, that makes my stomach hurt the most. That when the whirling cloud of dust and debris swept across the river last night, my father was happy. As happy as he had been all day.

Without warning, Alex springs up. His stool clatters against the counter and almost tips over. "We need to rerun this simulation." He waves the DataSlate at me. "We can use your dad's original numbers . . . and then try our new data from the drone, too. Let's see if there's availability this morning. It's early in the project, so most people haven't had time to get their sims set up yet."

I follow him to the door, and when he pushes it open, Tomas jumps back to avoid being smacked in the face.

"Oh!" He holds up the bottle of headache meds—"Got the wrong kind. See you guys later on"—and hurries past us back into the first aid room.

Alex walks down the hallway, out the door, and across campus so fast I can barely keep up.

Van's working on the main computer when we get to the Sim Dome. "Hey, champ," he says to Alex.

"Do you think we could run that simulation once more?" Alex blurts out, waving his DataSlate.

"Seriously, my friend?" Van folds his arms in front of him.

"I know it failed before, but I'm positive I have the numbers right now." He turns to me. "We know that—"

"That sometimes a minor input error can throw off a whole experiment," I interrupt. Was he actually going to *tell* Van that I *stole* my father's data? My eyes flash a warning at Alex before I turn back to Van. "We have two sets of numbers we want to double-check."

Van chuckles and shakes his head, but he walks to the access panel and slips in the key card that provides access to the simulation computer. "You found a kindred spirit, Alex. She's as stubborn as you are." He winks at Alex as the door slides open. "Go for it, but this is the last time I can let you run this one. It's a waste of resources."

"Okay, thanks." We step into the control room, just as Tomas arrives, hopefully with the right meds this time. We need Van in a good mood.

Alex plugs his DataSlate into the mainframe and feeds in the numbers. The same numbers my father used for the successful simulation he ran up at StormSafe. The one that worked.

The computer beeps, and a red button appears with the words BEGIN SIMULATION. Alex looks over at Van, who's huddled close to Tomas, talking. Finally, he glances up and gives us a sharp nod. Alex takes a deep breath, clicks the button, and leans back in his chair to watch.

A new button appears on the computer screen—INITIATE VARIABLE—but Alex's eyes are on the charcoal clouds forming high up in the dome to his left. They darken and swirl as they cross the river, and right before they reach the model city laid out on the grid in front of us, a funnel cloud drops down.

"Okay," Alex whispers. "Here we go." He watches, intent as the funnel widens and stretches toward the field of faux grass and synthetic trees, and just as it looks ready to touch down, he triggers the variable, presses the button that tells the computer-generated tornado that three hundred virtual kilowatts of microwave energy are blasting into its heart, heating the air in the downdraft. He's told the tornado to imagine the exact circumstances that would lead to its death.

I hold my breath and watch.

There is a spark from the vortex of the storm, and it seems to pause as if it's considering the new variable. Then the funnel cloud swells and pushes forward into the model city. It devours the library, the fire station, the school, four-five-six-seven houses, and grows fat with debris, heading for the business district.

Then the computer screen goes blank. The wind stops blowing, the clouds disappear, and the swirling-whirling-flying debris clatters to the floor. The lights in the dome flicker and go out.

When they come back on, Van and Tomas are stepping out of the observation room. Tomas leaves the dome without waving or even looking at us. "Sorry," Van radios into our cube, "I don't see the point in continuing. You're done."

Alex slides open the door, steps into the main dome, and throws his hands up in the air. "I don't understand how—"

"What you don't seem to understand is that it's time to give up on this one." Van ushers us toward the door.

"Van, wait. We have another set of numbers, different data." Alex doesn't say where the new data came from, thank God, and Van doesn't ask.

Alex starts to turn back to the control panel. "Couldn't we—"

"No," Van snaps. "At some point, you need to accept when a theory isn't working." He opens the door for us to leave, and a rush of warm air flows in. "Go back to the drawing board and consider some other ideas. You've tried the heat-the-downdraft approach, and it failed. Look into wind shear or another theory. But it's time to let this one go."

Alex's hands are clenched into fists. "But I know this should work." He looks back into the dome as if there might be someone else who will give him permission to run the other numbers. But there's just Van blocking the way.

"Has the Sim Dome been checked over since last year?" Alex asks. "Has it been recalibrated to make sure the storms react in line with the data? And the software's up to date and everything?"

Van's face relaxes into a little smile. "It stinks to be wrong, doesn't it? I wish I could tell you it wasn't you, my friend, but this Sim Dome is as up-to-date and fine-tuned as they come. It was checked over, top to bottom, and recalibrated over the weekend."

Alex sighs. "Well, couldn't the guy have made a mistake?"

"I doubt that very much." Van walks us to the door, smirking. "The guy was Dr. Meggs himself."

Chapter 17

Alex doesn't say a word as we walk across the quad. He doesn't hold open the library door.

"So now what are we going to do?" I ask Alex.

He wheels around, eyes burning. "*We?*" He looks at me hard, then lets out an incredulous little laugh. "*We* aren't going to do anything because *we* just got completely shut down. I'd say this one's in *your* court now."

"Alex, why are you mad at *me*? What's wrong?"

"What's wrong? Your father did the maintenance on the Sim Dome himself. He could calibrate that system in his sleep. Do you think for one second it's an accident our simulation didn't work?"

"Well, maybe . . . ," I begin. The thought had already crept into my brain—no, into my gut, in an awful twisting way—before we even left the observation cube. But part of me needs to believe that the dad who used to sing to me at night might still have something good inside.

Alex doesn't wait for me to finish my sentence. He plows into the library and stomps toward the table where we were working.

"I know what it looks like," I whisper, "but maybe we could talk to him about this. There might be a reason. Maybe he has, I don't know, some other information that . . ."

Alex's eyes burn the rest of my words into ashes. "Listen to you." He leans back against a bookshelf and stares at me as if I'm someone he's never met before, someone he wouldn't want to know. "This isn't a computer game." His voice trembles, and his hand shakes as he raises his arm and gestures back in the direction of the Sim Dome. "This is about people's lives. About my family. What your father is doing here is—"

"You don't *know* what he's doing."

"Yes I do, and so do you. It doesn't take a genius, Jaden. And unless you do something about it—"

"Unless *I do something about it*?"

Ms. Walpole pokes her head around the corner. "Is everything okay?"

"Fine, yeah." Alex pulls a book from the shelf and starts flipping through it.

She frowns and steps up beside us. "Shall I ask about the 'library materials' I loaned you yesterday? Or shall I presume you've returned them already?"

Alex looks up at her. "The plane is fine, but it's—"

"Mr. Carillo, the book that I loaned you is a rare volume, and I trust it will be returned in good shape when you're finished." Ms. Walpole raises her eyebrows at him and raises a finger to her lips.

I look around, but we're the only ones in the library that I can see. Is she suggesting that the place is bugged? That someone's listening in? What kind of camp *is* this?

Alex nods slowly. "The book has been very useful. Thanks. It's at my house, and I'll return it soon."

"Perfect." She walks back to her desk, picks up her book, and starts reading.

Alex goes back to flipping pages in the book he's holding, but I put out a hand to stop him. "You say you want me to *do something?* What am I supposed to do?" I whisper, and my thoughts are swirling so much I hardly care who's listening.

He looks up from the book, and says in a voice too low for anyone listening in to hear, so quiet I can barely make out the words myself, "Get yourself into the dome at his company somehow," he whispers. "Run the numbers there." His eyes are urgent, pleading. But I'm already shaking my head.

"I can't." I remember the feeling of hiding under his desk. What would he have done if he'd caught me? "It's too much of a risk. I can't."

The light in Alex's eyes clicks off. "Then you're not the person I thought you were." He looks more sad than angry as he pushes the book back onto the shelf and walks out the door.

In the morning, I sit in my usual auditorium seat and wait for a hand on my arm or a whisper in my ear. When Van finishes a quick morning update, Risha runs to meet Tomas, and I walk to the library alone.

I upload four new meteorology and climatology texts to my DataSlate and spend the next three days reading, bookmarking, and trying to get used to being a team of one.

Ms. Walpole drops a little paper bag on my table as she walks by on one of her book-shelving missions. Oatmeal raisin cookies.

"Thanks," I whisper when she comes by again.

She stops next to my chair. "Where's our boy?"

"He's . . . not happy with me," is all I can muster.

"Well, he'll get over it. Have a cookie," she says, as if it's some ordinary boy-girl thing like him having a crush on somebody else. If only. "And tell him he needs to return that rare book before people start asking questions." She raises her eyebrows at the ceiling, and I wonder again who's listening.

I keep watching the library door after she leaves, but Alex never walks through it.

He won't even look at me the rest of the week.

Saturday's too hot to go outside, so I spend the afternoon in my room, reading.

I try writing to Mom, but it bounces back again, so I call Amelia for a video-chat instead. It's good to see her face and great to hear what everyone's doing at home, but when she asks how things are going here, I don't have much to offer. I try to explain the projects at camp, but she makes a face, and I feel like I've moved away to another planet where the language isn't even the same as it is on Earth.

Sunday morning, Dad leaves for StormSafe before it's light, and when I come downstairs, Mirielle is packing the diaper bag. "Good morning!" She winks at me. "I thought we girls might go on a little adventure today."

"What kind of adventure?"

"Your aunt Linda invited us to visit." She hums a light, breezy song that seems to match the lilacs on her sleeveless blouse. I watch her tickling Remi in her bouncy chair, setting the timer to make sure Dad's dinner will be ready later, and my chest tightens.

Who was that woman on the phone? Does Mirielle have any idea what Dad's whispering to somebody else in his office late at night?

Mirielle pauses with a bottle of juice in her hand and tips her head at me. "Are you all right? I thought you'd be pleased."

I realize my whole face is clenched up, and I force myself to relax. "Yes, it's great. Thanks."

As we drive out of town, past the beat-up trailer parks, past the Corrections Department energy farm and an underground play center that's seen better days, I lower my window. The country roads are lined with big old maple and pine trees that have somehow survived the storms. The fields are strewn with wildflowers. I take a deep breath and sigh. "I know it's not as safe out here, but it feels . . . I don't know . . . fresher. Cleaner, somehow."

"It's safe enough for right now. We have two DataSlates. We'll get alerts if anything changes." Mirielle glances over at me and smiles a little. "And I know what you mean about the air. Sometimes, Remi and I go for drives when your father is at work." She glances in the rearview mirror. "Only when the weather's quiet, of course."

We drive through a long stretch of woods—even the trees smell different out here—and then out into a more open stretch where the trees are smaller, planted in rows.

"Are these fruit trees?" I ask.

"Mmm-hmm." Mirielle reaches behind her to tickle Remi's foot. "Peaches mostly. Linda grows them, too."

Around a curve, the orchards end, and finally, there's a white farmhouse. It's old, the kind you'd expect to have lots of long hallways and closets. There's a porch with big pillars and rocking chairs out front. Behind the house is an old red barn, half falling down, and a brown horse wandering around outside a stable. Next to the barn, there's a tiny farm stand that looks like someone might have nailed it together out of old barn pieces this morning. A hand-painted sign leaning against it reads:

SWEET RASPBERRIES: $12/PINT
FRESH PEACHES: $2 EACH
COMPLIMENTS: FREE

Mirielle pulls into the driveway, and I smile. This place feels like everything I remember about Aunt Linda. She comes running from the house in a flowered blouse and blue jeans and pulls me into a hug the second I'm out of the car.

"My great stars, Jaden! It's been years." She holds me back so she can look at me. "You are your mother's daughter, aren't you?"

"Most people say I look like Dad."

Aunt Linda's smile flickers like a lightbulb with a loose wire, but then it's back. "Well, I suppose you look like Jaden," she says.

The horse whinnies outside the barn, and I turn.

"That Nutmeg . . . always looking for a treat." She digs into her pocket and pulls out a few sugar cubes. "Do you want to go say hello to her before we go inside?"

"Sure."

Aunt Linda leans in to talk quietly to Remi as I clunk down the wooden porch steps and across the grass. It's hard to imagine a person as gentle and relaxed as Aunt Linda raising someone as intense as my father. But I guess part of who you are is genetics, and when I think of Grandma Athena's fiery eyes staring out from her frame, it's easy to see her spirit alive in Dad.

The sugar cubes are rough and sticky in my palm as I step up to the split-rail fence. Nutmeg ambles over, and I climb onto the first rung to pet her on the nose.

"Hold the sugar flat on your palm," Aunt Linda calls to me, "so she doesn't get your fingers."

I do, and Nutmeg's warm, snuffly lips scarf it up.

I feed her my last three cubes. She sniffs my pocket, decides I'm of no more use to her, and wanders away.

"She's beautiful," I say, joining Aunt Linda and Mirielle back on the porch.

"She's been with me a long time." Aunt Linda holds open the door to the kitchen, and we walk into a bright yellow room with a wooden chopping block in the middle and, above it, a rack of copper pots and pans. The wall over the sink has old wallpaper with tiny apples all in rows.

Aunt Linda serves up lemonade and peach pie, and we sit at the big wooden table, talking about camp and Mom's trip and Remi sitting up all by herself. When I finish my pie, I get up to look at the dishes displayed over the sink, all painted in bright colors.

"That's my wall of fame," Aunt Linda says, laughing. She pulls down a coffee mug with an old guy's face painted on it. On the other side there's a short poem called "Fire and Ice."

"Robert Frost." She nods up at the shelf. "And there's Emily Dickinson and Walt Whitman. All my favorite poets. I paint their portraits on one side and a poem on the other."

Rita Dove's not there, but the poet mugs remind me of her. "Thank you for the book."

"You are most welcome." Aunt Linda pulls me into a hug and looks at Mirielle. "Can you stay a while?"

Way in the distance, thunder rumbles, as if it's answering for Mirielle. *No, time to head home.*

Mirielle smiles but shakes her head. "We'd better go. But we'll find time for another visit soon. I'll get Remi changed, and then we'll be off." She picks up the diaper bag and carries Remi into the living room.

"Thanks for today," I tell Aunt Linda, and she has no idea how much I mean it, how much I needed some plain old family love. "I wish you lived closer."

She grins and raises her mug. "Placid Meadows is not my cup of tea, my dear. But I would love for you to visit often."

"Me too," I say, "but there's Dad . . ."

"Oh, I know. He's not too fond of me these days."

"He's not too fond of anybody. Except Mirielle and Remi some-times." I hadn't said it before, but that's how I feel. "It's kind of like he's not *my* dad anymore."

Aunt Linda puts a warm arm around my shoulders. "Oh, sweet Jaden," she says. "He loves you. But you can't count on him showing it in any of the usual ways, I'm afraid. Lord knows I loved that boy when he was growing up—still do—but he wanted his mother all those years and could never have her. Not even before she died, which is the saddest thing of all. She loved her work so much, and it was always urgent-urgent-urgent. She thought she'd have plenty of time for your dad later." She shakes her head.

In the other room, Mirielle sings to Remi, something soft in French.

"So now Dad does the same thing," I say, "to me."

Aunt Linda looks like she wants to argue, but she can't. She gives me a squeeze.

"All set?" Mirielle carries Remi back into the kitchen. "We'll be back soon, I promise." I hug Aunt Linda one more time and hope Mirielle means it.

Nutmeg is at the fence when we step off the porch, probably hoping for more sugar. "Bye, girl," I tell her, and I pat her nose. It feels like velvet in the sun, soft and warm and good.

The clouds are already closer when we pull out of the drive-way. Mirielle catches me sneaking glances out the rear window.

"Not to worry," she says. "We will be home soon. Safe and sound."

We will be, I think. But what about Aunt Linda? What about Nutmeg, who's not protected by anything other than weathered timber once she's in the barn? How long will it be before one of these storms makes a direct hit?

Chapter 18

The storm comes just as we're pulling into Placid Meadows and passes quickly. It's small, so I don't worry about Aunt Linda—this time.

With the sun blazing again, it's steaming hot, so after lunch we collapse on the couch with iced tea while Remi naps in her bouncy seat.

Mirielle turns on the entertainment window. "Oh good! There's ballet streaming from the National Arts Center." Two men and two women twirl and leap through a routine in the underground theater hundreds of miles away.

Mirielle watches the dancers. And I watch Mirielle. Her face flickers between happy and sad, and I wonder if she's remembering performances of her own, back when there were real audiences all over the world.

"Do other countries do this now, too?" I ask.

She startles as if she'd been far away. With the dancers, maybe. "Do they do what?"

"Have a national arts feed instead of live performances."

She nods sadly. "Most do. My sister in Paris says they're building a new theater there, with a safe room directly underneath. Around here, there are only tiny local dance groups. They perform in church basements mostly, community safe rooms. Your father has never wanted to go, but I'd love to see them." Her eyes drift back to the entertainment window, where one of the men is lifting the woman high over his head. In her gleaming white dress, she looks like a seagull soaring. Mirielle sighs. "They aren't professionals, of course, but it would be lovely to see real live people dancing again."

Watching Mirielle's eyes mist makes me clench my jaw. Dad was probably too busy at work, too busy with whoever he was talking to on the videophone, for some stupid ballet. "I'd go with you some time," I blurt out.

She smiles. "I'd love that. I'll see what I can find."

"Maybe Aunt Linda could come," I say. Somehow, I miss her already. I bet she'd like the dancing, too.

She nods slowly. "On some night when your father is busy." Her green eyes dart over to his office door for a second. "We will tell him we are doing some shopping, perhaps."

The doorbell rings then. "I'll get it." I step carefully around Remi in her bouncy chair and go to the door, where Risha's lifting her hand to ring again.

"Where've you been all weekend?" She pulls her BeatBuds out of her ears, steps past me into the kitchen, and paws through the fruit bowl on the counter. Her hair is tied back in a gauzy purple scarf that flows down her back. "You have to come on a bike ride with me or I'm going to die of boredom." She polishes an apple on her purple-and-red-striped T-shirt and takes a big bite.

"It's too hot."

"Jaden, pleeease? Just to the park for a while."

If I say no, Risha will want to know what's wrong, and I don't want to talk about Alex, so I call good-bye to Mirielle and get my bike.

The air is heavy as soup-steam, but it still feels good to pedal.

"Hey," I say as Risha takes a turn toward the fence. "Aren't we going to the park?"

"Change of plans." She glances back at me, eyes twinkling. She's made plans with the boys, I can tell, and my stomach twists at the thought of seeing Alex now.

"Not today, Risha." Besides, the clouds are starting to build again, and just because the first storm today was mild doesn't mean the next one will be. "You said you wanted to go to the park for a while. I'm not going outside the fence. There's weather coming."

"Not even for a little while? Tomas has hardly talked to me all week. He's been acting all weird, and I know he's worried about his mom. I just want to see him."

She keeps riding toward the fence, and I follow her, thinking I'll stay back while she goes to see the boys.

But when Risha jumps off her bike and climbs through the gap without looking back, something in me can't let her go alone with the clouds swirling. "Fine," I say. "This better be fast."

"Yay!" She's already on the other side, and I have to scramble through to catch her.

Risha winds her way toward the gazebo where we had our picnic—it's empty—and then races to the Carillos' barn and pulls open the door. Two chocolate-brown goats nuzzle each other in one stall. In another, a fat black pig is sleeping. Some chickens are wandering around, too. One wall is lined with bales of hay or straw. Another has dozens of tools—pitchforks, shovels, and axes—hanging from cast-iron hooks. "Hellooo?" Risha looks around. "Shoot," she says, turning back to me. "They probably figured we weren't coming."

I try not to look too happy. "They probably figured they should head for a safe room." The sky looks grayer and greener, more menacing than it did a few minutes ago.

"Well, boo," she says. Then she grabs my hand. "That's okay. I still want to show you something." She ducks between two vintage tractors with steering wheels for actual people who'd drive them and ride around on them. Then she bends down and tugs at a big metal ring sticking up from the floor. "Help me with this, will you?"

I wrap my hand around the cool metal, too, and pull. A creaky panel of wood lifts up from the floor—a trapdoor.

"Check this out." Risha climbs down a metal-runged ladder and fades into the dark.

I wait for her to pop up again, but she doesn't.

"Are you coming back?" I call, squatting by the swung-open door. My voice sounds echoey and cold. The skies have opened up now, and rain is pelting the roof like a mad drummer. The wind blows a flurry of wet, battered leaves through the open door, and I shiver, even though the air is still warm. "Risha, I want to go home."

She doesn't answer.

I stand up, shake out my knees, and head for the barn door. I'm about to step out into the rain when a colossal bolt of lightning cracks through the sky, close enough that the tiny hairs on the back of my neck tingle. Thunder follows half a second later—a sharp, deep crack that shakes the whole barn.

Wind rattles the windows, and outside, tree branches are starting to snap. The sky is dark. Too dark.

Don't let this happen now. Not with us out here.

There's no way I can leave now. I turn away from the pounding rain and call again, "Risha?"

Something knocks on the barn roof. Again. And then two knocks turn into frantic pounding, beating on the roof, and outside, hailstones the size of my fist pummel the dirt.

The sky explodes in light and thunder again. Vibrations shake the barn.

And then there's another sound.

A growing roar that rumbles through my body.

I run for the trapdoor.

I don't know what's down there, but I know what's coming, and I can't be in this room full of sharp metal tools when it hits.

I step onto the ladder, cling to the cool metal rungs, and lower myself, step by trembling step. Above me, where the trapdoor is flopped open, the square of light flashes with lightning. The whole foundation of the building seems to shudder, and the wind blows through the door, through gaps in the beams, with a high-pitched whine that makes me shiver.

Without stopping to think, I climb back up the ladder rungs

into the barn and tug on the handle of the trapdoor. It's solid wood, and I can barely move it, but throwing all my weight against it, I'm able to lug it up from the barn floor, ease back down onto the ladder, and let the door thump shut over my head.

I know I am on the ladder with three, maybe four rungs to climb down, but the darkness feels too thick to move through. Even with the heavy wooden door closed over my head, I can hear the wind roar.

"Risha!" I call, but her name echoes back at me off the floor.

I take a shuddery breath and blink hard, but my eyes don't adjust, so still swallowed in the dark, I start climbing down again.

The rusty metal scratches my palms. I hold on tight, concentrating on that as I lower myself one rung at a time.

Down, down, down, until I see a sliver of light off to one side. I follow it down a long hallway with cool stone walls, and the roar of the wind grows muffled. The light brightens, and finally, I get to the source, a room at the end of the long hall. I push the heavy, half-shut door until it swings open.

"You came down!" Risha is lounging on a daybed. Rock music plays from speakers mounted on the walls. She pats the seat next to her. "Isn't this so perfect?"

I step into the room, and the door swings shut behind me with a thick, wooden thud that makes me jump. *Perfect?* She's bouncing lightly on the daybed, grinning, while the storm rages outside. I can't hear it way down here, but I know it's still there.

She reaches for a bottle of water—there are cases of them, rows of canned goods and packages of all kinds of food. Might as well be comfortable if you're stuck in a tiny room, pretending everything's all right.

"Jaden, we're fine here. What's wrong?"

What's wrong? I open my mouth to answer her, but nothing comes out. This. This is wrong, I think. This world where people have to run for shelter nearly every afternoon, where most people live in fear that this storm—this one—might be the one that destroys everything. This world, where a handful of people are so used to being safe, so used to living inside StormSafe's little bubble, that they never worry at all.

"What is this?" I finally ask. "It doesn't look like a regular safe room."

"It's an old bomb shelter from the 1960s. Isn't it the best? It's just like a safe room, really—concrete walls, reinforced with steel. I think this must be what the StormSafe houses were based on." She grabs a package of chocolate sandwich cookies from the shelf above her, tears it open, and shoves a whole one in her mouth.

"Want one?" She holds the package out to me. Cookies. In the middle of a storm that looks like it could devour us whole. My stomach twists, and I shake my head.

I strain my ears for the sounds of the storm, but I can't sort anything out anymore. The fluorescent light overhead flickers. What's going on up there?

"Sure you don't want one?" she asks.

"How can you sit there eating cookies?" I blurt out.

She swallows. "We hang out here all the time. It's fine. Tomas and Alex and I kind of took this place over, so we always—"

The music stops and the lights go out, and it feels like the blackness swallows up Risha, too, because she never finishes her sentence. The roar whooshes louder, and the wind isn't low, loud static anymore. It's growling, hissing, popping over our heads.

I reach out for Risha in the blackness, where I hope her hand might be. It's cool and damp. An edge of her fingernail scratches my palm.

"Has this ever happened when you were here before?" I whisper.

"No." She squeezes my hand. "But Alex told me he rode out a storm here once. We'll be okay." But her voice is quiet. Not so confident. Not so Risha.

I don't let go of her hand.

It sounds like the storm is chewing its way through the building over our heads, spitting out mouthfuls of metal, crunching wood into splinters.

I close my eyes and open them again. It looks exactly the same. Black and terrifying and loud.

When I was little, afraid of the dark, Mom used to tell me that nothing could ever be as scary as the monsters in my imagination, that all my nightmares would vanish when she turned on the light. But this time, I already know that's not true. I am imagining a monster upstairs, and I'm afraid—so afraid—that reality will be a million times worse.

I squeeze Risha's hand and hear her ragged breath. I lean closer, and she rests her head against my shoulder, the smell of chocolate cookies on her breath mixing with something else. Sweat. Or fear.

The monster roars louder. How long can the barn hold out?

Glass shatters over our heads. Something splinters, crackle by sharp crackle by groan. Is it the support beam right above us? The barn roof? A wall? Whatever it is creaks, moans a long final moan, and then CRACKS.

Is it broken? Gone?

The wind doesn't answer; it only screams and roars.

Until finally, the sounds fade.

I don't know how long we sit. Long enough for chaos to turn to distant rumbling and then silence.

Long enough for our pounding hearts to sound like cannons in the dark.

We huddle together without moving, without speaking a word, and somewhere inside, I begin to understand what has happened. Even Risha, with all her StormSafe confidence, knows this was no everyday storm. It was bad. But we sit in the dark, still holding hands, both under the spell of the same fairy tale lie.

If you don't look, it won't hurt.

It you don't turn on the lights, you'll never see the monster.

If we stay here in the blackness, if we never go up to see what happened, then maybe it never happened at all.

But then come the sounds.

Quiet at first.

Uneven. Stopping and starting footsteps.

Creaking. Lifting. Wood-sliding-against-wood.

A voice so faint I can't tell whose it is or what it's saying. But the tone is unmistakable. The raw edge, the desperation. Someone needs help.

"Risha?" I start to pull my hand away from her, but she holds on. I wiggle my hand free and stand.

I still can't see, but I hear the daybed creak and know she's standing to follow me. I slide a hand against the cool dampness of the wall until I feel the doorframe and take a step out into the hall.

"I'm scared," Risha whispers, and admitting that is so not-Risha that a wave of cold terror races through me. What's waiting for us out there?

"Me, too." We feel our way down the still-night-black hallway, scuffing our feet all the way to the end. The toe of my sneaker bumps something that makes a dull metal clang.

The ladder.

"Ready to go up?"

I wait until I feel her closer to me, feel her shoulder brushing against mine. I take hold of a cold metal rung and start climbing.

Risha's right behind me; her hand brushes my ankle every couple of rungs.

At the top, I keep one hand clutched around a ladder rung. With the other, I reach over my head to push on the spot where the trapdoor should open.

It doesn't budge.

"Can you steady me?"

"Hold on." I feel one of Risha's arms wrap around my calves to help me stay balanced on the rung. I let go of the ladder and use both hands to push up as hard as I can, until I'm sure my face is bursting red.

There is nothing at first—as if the door's been sealed. I give it another big push, and then, a crack of light appears.

I bend my knees and push harder. Something slides off the tilting door onto the floor, and the crack grows wider, until the light opens up into a bright, narrow beam of sun. The trapdoor swings wide, thuds down on the barn floor, and there is light. Bright, blinding yellow-white light, like we've flopped open the door to heaven.

I step up another rung and see I am wrong. So wrong.

This is as far from heaven as a world can be.

The light is so bright because there is nothing between us and the sky.

The barn is gone.

Gone, except for half a wall whose skeleton teeters, creaking as if it's in pain. A splintered wooden rod sticks out from the middle of the wall—it wasn't there before—and somehow in the midst of this chaos, I am fixated on it.

I crawl up out of the hole in the floor, my knees scraping over splintered wood, and rise, shaking, to my feet.

I climb over twisted metal, boards, and beams, through wood splinters and feathers and dust—up to the wall where the wooden rod sticks straight out.

It is the pitchfork I'd seen hanging from a hook on the other wall, part of the tidy row of tools, all lined up before the storm.

I wrap my hands around the handle and pull. I hang on it with all my body weight.

It doesn't move.

I breathe, hoarse and deep, and rest my hand on a ragged beam. It feels as if it's the only thing holding me up. I hold on as if the winds might return any second and blow me away, and slowly, I turn away from this piece of wall.

Around it, beams lay scattered over one another like pickup sticks tossed by a giant.

An ax is embedded in what must have been one of the main support beams. Shreds of roofing litter the foundation like bits of paper torn to shreds.

The tractor is gone. Way down near the driveway, I make out a mass of twisted red metal wrapped around a tree.

Risha is frozen halfway up the ladder, clutching the trapdoor frame so hard I worry the metal edge will cut her hand.

"Rish?" I call. But she won't come up. She's in shock.

"Risha?"

She stares. Blinks hard. Squeezes her eyes closed. Opens them again.

I know what she is trying to do.

It doesn't work.

It's all still here.

And then the voice returns, clearer this time, but ragged and choked.

"Newton! Newton!"

I turn toward the farmhouse, or where the farmhouse would have been, and suck in my breath. The concrete safe room is all that's left, but I can breathe after I count the figures coming out of it. Alex's parents. His little sister, Julia. Tomas.

Alex climbs over the debris, and even from here, I see his tear-stained face.

"Newton! Newton, come on, boy!"

"Alex!" I call from the barn, and he whirls around as if I'm a ghost or another storm. I don't care; I start running, tripping over twisted metal tools and clambering over splintered boards until I reach him. I want to throw my arms around him.

But I don't.

"I . . . let me help you," I say.

"Where were you?"

"In that room under the barn. With Risha."

"Where is she?"

"She's okay." I turn to the barn where finally, Risha is rising up from the shelter, ladder rung by ladder rung.

When I turn back to Alex, his face is twisted in pain. "I could hear him barking," he whispers. "But we had to close the door." He turns and heads toward a high pile of debris that looks like it might have been the garage once. "Newton!"

He is flinging boards, and tears burn my eyes. If Newton is under there . . .

"Alex . . ." His father's quiet voice cuts through the clattering wood. He stands at the edge of the heap of house pieces, shakes his head, and holds out his arms. Alex collapses into them, sobbing.

"Is there anything we can do?" whispers Risha, who's made her way over to the safe room that still stands.

Alex's mom is leaning against the concrete wall, holding a first aid kit. It looks small and pathetic in her hand. She shakes her head. "Maybe . . . maybe tomorrow." She looks out over the farm, at debris that's scattered all the way out to the main road. What can we possibly do to help tomorrow? Or any day? What can anyone do?

Risha tugs my sleeve, then slides her hand down to hold mine again. Tight. "We should probably go," she says.

But I can't. I can't move from this place, watching Alex's shoulders heave under his father's arm. His dad waits until the sobs slow and finally stop. He doesn't say a word. What can he say? That everything will be all right? It won't.

"Hold on," I tell Risha. I make my way to Alex and put a hand tentatively on his back. I expect him to whirl around and push my hand away, but he doesn't. Alex's dad gives his shoulder one last squeeze and leaves us alone.

"I'm sorry," I whisper.

He doesn't answer. He stares at that one wall left of the barn with empty eyes.

The sky is so quiet now it's hard to believe what has happened. How can something vanish so quickly and leave so much brokenness behind?

"Alex, please just know that—"

"Shh!" He holds up both hands and squints his eyes shut tight, and I'm sure it's because he can't even stand the sound of my voice. But then I hear it, too.

A whimper.

"It's coming from over there!" Alex pushes past me back toward the one wall that's left of the barn. He steps over boards and twisted metal.

"Newton!"

He starts to step over another pile of rubble—did it used to be the goat pen?—but stops and collapses to the barn floor.

I run, tripping through the debris, until I reach him.

And then I stop.

Newton is splayed in the dust, panting with shallow breaths. His head is bleeding between his ears. A patch of fur is gone, and the rest is matted with blood and dust. One of his legs is twisted at a sick angle, bleeding, too. My breath catches, and my stomach twists, and I have to look away.

"Get some water," Alex's father says quietly behind me. I run back to the shelter because it's the one thing I can do instead of crumbling. I climb down the ladder, stumble down the hallway into the blackness. I crack my shin on the daybed frame, fall forward, and feel the shelf. I flail my arms around until they connect with cool smooth plastic. I take two water bottles and find my way back up into the light.

"Here." I kneel down next to Alex and unscrew the cap from one bottle. He takes it from me and pours it first over the open break in Newton's leg, then over the cut on his head. The bleeding has slowed, but Newton's breaths are coming fast and shallow.

"Shhh . . . it's okay, boy." I put a hand to Newton's shoulder and feel his heartbeat, rapid. Scared.

"We need..." Alex is choking back sobs. He squeezes his eyes shut, then opens them again. "I gotta have a bandage or ... or something."

Risha slips the scarf from her hair and hands it to him. She walks off and sits down in the grass next to Tomas, still in shock.

"Wrap it around the leg just enough to secure it," Alex's father says, leaning over us. "We'll try to get him into town to the vet. Maybe ..." But his voice trails off.

Alex wraps the scarf around Newton's leg, careful to avoid hurting him even more. He swipes at his eyes with his shirtsleeve and stands, staring over the debris of the barn. Not far from the trapdoor he finds a long piece of board and drags it back next to Newton. Together, we ease the dog onto it.

"Careful," Alex whispers. It must hurt, and I'm expecting Newton to snap at me, but he never does. He just keeps panting, looking up at Alex with big dog eyes that seem to say a million things at once. *How could you let this happen to me?* But also, *I trust you. Please help.*

"I'll get the truck," Alex's dad says quietly. Somehow, it survived the storm, parked at the edge of a field not fifty yards from the barn, as if the tornado couldn't be bothered with it. Alex's mom has already gone back to the safe room with Julia. She doesn't need to see all this.

Alex kneels next to Newton, rubbing behind his ear. His hand is caked with blood.

"I'm sorry," I whisper.

He doesn't look up.

"I am." The words are choked, but I force them out. "About Newton and the farm, and about not doing anything. This is awful, Alex, your family and Newton . . ." And Aunt Linda and Nutmeg, I think. Did this storm hit them, too?

"Alex, I was wrong. It *is* worth the risk. Stopping this is worth almost anything." Hot tears streak down my cheeks. "I'll do it. Okay? I'm going to go up there. I promise."

He turns to me and shrugs. The pickup rumbles up, and he stands to help his father lift Newton into the back.

I watch as Alex climbs in next to his dog, holding him close as the truck pulls away.

Chapter 19

It's a full week before I can make good on my promise.

A full week of watching and waiting. Of making weather small talk with Dad, chitchatting with Mirielle, and playing peek-a-boo with Remi.

A full week of camp, going through the motions without Alex.

A full week of wondering when he'll be back. Wondering if Newton is going to be okay.

Finally, on Monday morning, Dad finishes breakfast and heads to his office. Mirielle is out shopping, so there's no one to swoop in and clear the counter. I watch the door close, grab what I need, and call Risha. "I got it."

She's been amazing since the storm. I told her everything when we got back home that night, about Alex, our argument, and what I promised him I'd do. I confessed my plan to somehow get into my father's work office and access his computers. Instead of telling me how crazy I am, Risha asked about the security systems at Storm-Safe. When I told her it was probably a fingerprint scan, she smiled.

"That'll be the easy part then," she said. "You just need the right fingerprints."

And now I have them.

I meet Risha and we ride as fast as we can to camp; we get there half an hour before it starts.

Risha scans her print and ushers me into the Finger Factory, the nickname she and Tomas gave Eye on Tomorrow's cloning center.

We step into what amounts to a coatroom, with hooks on the walls and a row of lockers. Risha opens one and hands me a lab coat, hair cover, and latex gloves. "Put these on, okay? We don't want any cross contamination or it'll mess everything up."

Once we're outfitted, she scans her print again, and the door to the actual laboratory slides open. Humming with high-powered computer servers and packed with DNA extraction equipment, this is every bit as impressive as the Sim Dome.

The entire room shines with stainless steel. Every countertop gleams; most are covered with trays of test tubes in perfect lines. There are incubators—some quietly warming genetic stews, some turning in slow rotation.

Risha leads me to a workstation along the wall and nods toward a white petri dish on the counter. Something pinkish gray is floating in it. "We've been trying to grow an ear," she says. "It seems to be working, but Van says it'll be another couple weeks before we can find out if it has all the parts it'll need to hear."

"Well, good luck."

"What?" she says.

"Good luck."

"What?" She holds her hand up to her ear—her real ear—and I realize she's making a joke. I laugh a little, and it takes away some of the fear racing through me. It's not that we're not allowed to be here. Van gave Risha permission for early work sessions a while ago, and if anyone asks, she'll just say she's giving me a tour. But if anyone here found out what was in my bag—Dad's coffee mug from this morning, with his fingerprints on it—that would be another story.

"All right, let's get moving." Risha walks down the long counter to a larger, more high-tech workstation and climbs up onto a high stool.

"This is it," she says, and motions for me to take a seat next to her. In front of us is a device that looks like some combination of an electron microscope, an incubator, and a petri dish. Risha pulls clear goggles down over her eyes, picks up a pair of stainless steel forceps, and bends down over the dish, squinting. She holds her breath and pokes with steady hands at the fleshy something in the fluid.

"This turned out perfectly . . ." Slowly and smoothly, she lifts the tip of the forceps from the petri dish. Hanging from the end is a crumpled, yellowish clear membrane. "Here it is." She takes a second pair of forceps and uses it to grab the other edge so it hangs in a thin oval strip. "Got the cup?"

I pull the coffee mug from my bag and point to the clearest print.

"Perfect." Risha carefully maneuvers the tissue into place over the print and presses down on it with a gloved finger for a few seconds. She peels it back off the mug with the forceps and holds the tissue up to the light. "Beautiful." She lowers it back into the solution in the petri dish, and it floats delicately on top. "Let's give it the rest of the day for the pattern to grow. But I'd say you can stop back before you leave today to pick it up." She gestures to the dish with a flourish. "Your brand new fingerprint."

I spend the whole day in the library, half-hoping I'll look up and see Alex, but I know it's too soon. There's too much cleaning up to be done after the storm, too much debris and sadness to wade through.

Risha comes to get me at the end of the day, and we walk back to the Finger Factory while everyone else is heading for their bikes to go home.

The print is ready. I reach for it, but Risha pulls back the forceps. "Ah, ah, AH!" She shakes her head. "This isn't like a glove you can put on and take off all day. You're going to be able to wear it once for a few hours. That's it." She pulls out a shallow glass jar filled with fluid. It's shaped like the tiny container where Mom used to keep her contact lenses before she got her eyes fixed. Risha lowers the tissue into it. "Keep it in here until right before you need it."

She tightens the lid and holds it out to me but then pulls back. "Wait a second. I'm going to start another copy. It'll be easier than starting from scratch if you have a problem with this one." She takes out the tissue, presses it against some kind of glass plate, then puts it back in the jar and hands it over. "All set."

The whole bike ride home, the little jar in my pocket pokes into my hip, reminding me of the crazy thing I am about to try. I tell myself there's time; it may be days, weeks even, before Dad remembers that tour of StormSafe he promised me. There's plenty of time to think about this. Plenty of time to plan.

When I get home, the kitchen door slams closed behind me, and Dad's voice booms out, "Thank goodness!"

He rushes to the entryway, holding a BioWake Cola in one hand and bouncing Remi with the other arm. "Oh." His face falls. "You're not Mirielle."

He paces back toward the kitchen with Remi clinging to his shoulder. "She's out shopping, but she knows I need to be up at headquarters this afternoon." He taps his watch. "I'll have to take the baby with me, I suppose."

I put my backpack on the counter and take a deep breath. This is the opportunity I thought would take weeks to come. It may be my only chance. "I could come with you and help," I blurt out before I have time to think about it any more. "And maybe do that tour you promised?" My heart thuds while I wait for him to answer. The tiny jar in my pocket suddenly feels huge. How could he not see it?

"Well, that's a great idea. Thank you!" Before he even finishes the sentence, he's steering me toward the door. I grab my backpack with my DataSlate and head out to the HV.

Once Remi is strapped in her car seat, Dad pulls out of the garage and starts down the street so fast the tires actually squeal. I wonder what the big hurry is, but his brows are knit together so tightly, the line of his mouth so thin right now, that my question settles back inside me.

We're at the Placid Meadows gate when Dad's DataSlate chimes.

He presses the speaker button, and Mirielle's voice pours out in a recorded message.

"Honey, I am so, so sorry I am running late. We are about to have a storm at the mall, of all things, and I must wait until it passes." Her voice is thinner than usual, like she's scared. But I don't know if that's about the storm or about being late for Dad. "I will see you at home later."

Dad lets out a sharp sigh and veers to the side of the road.

"What are we doing?"

His face is lit by the blue glow of the DataSlate, and he either doesn't hear me or isn't answering. His eyes are trained on the screen, full of columns and numbers and symbols. Dad highlights two of the cells, types in new numbers, and pokes at the CALCU-LATE button.

A new page of numbers appears. He takes another deep breath, and I watch his eyes twitching as they move down the columns. He seems satisfied, and pokes at the APPLY button at the bottom of the screen. I catch a split-second look at the box that appears on the screen next, before Dad notices me reading over his arm and angles the screen away from me.

It was only a second, but it was long enough to read two words: "Satellites responding . . ."

Dad looks down at the DataSlate for another few seconds, then powers it down and puts the car back in drive.

"Did you . . . ?" The words are seared into my mind. *Satellites. Satellites responding.* Responding how? Responding to what? Or to whom? "Did you just . . . do something?"

"I checked on the storm path." He reaches over to turn on the music player. "Don't worry. Mirielle's fine; it took a turn to the east."

It took a turn to the east? All on its own? *Satellites responding.* Responding to commands he entered. He knows how to dissipate storms. Is that what he did? The pieces of this puzzle are popping faster and faster in my brain, like raindrops plunking into a puddle. First one, then two and three at a time, and then so many you forget the surface was ever calm at all.

I stare out the window at the retreating clouds as Dad turns into the long driveway that leads to StormSafe.

"I keep forgetting you haven't been here." He's in a better mood now. "I'll show you around a little before my meeting."

"Great," I say. But it's during his meeting that I expect to see the most. The container in my pocket presses into my hip as I shift in my seat. *Please let this work. Please let it work.*

When we round the final curve in the long driveway, I get my first glimpse of StormSafe headquarters up close.

When I look up from Placid Meadows, the buildings of this place seem to glow, and now I see why. Every wall is made of windows.

Windows like they used to have in houses when Mom and Dad were growing up. Glass ones that squeak if you lick your finger and run it down the pane, windows that smudge and streak and sparkle in the sun. Is it all safety glass?

Dad pulls into a parking space, and we get out of the HV. I balance Remi on my hip and follow Dad up a walkway lined with bright orange poppies. I don't need to check to see if they're symmetrical;

I'm sure every plant is DNA-ture. I wait while Dad presses a finger to the data panel. The door swings open, and there's a receptionist at a long chrome desk. "Hello, Nadia." Dad gives her a wave and heads for the elevator.

Nadia gives a fluttery-fingered wave and tucks a lock of black hair behind her ear. Was she the woman on Dad's DataSlate that night in his office? She doesn't say anything, so I can't compare the voices.

"Want a real quick tour?" He starts down a carpeted hallway. "We've got our conference room down here." He opens a door to a lush room with a long conference table and big leather chairs. "It's the brain center, where we have all our planning and problem-solving sessions."

I step up to the big window and see that this main office isn't all of StormSafe; there are smaller buildings around the parking lot and gardens. "What's in the other buildings?"

"More offices. Some research labs and data centers."

One of the buildings, set apart, looks less modern than the others—just a squat concrete structure, almost like an old storm shelter. There's only a steel door and one window. "What about that one?"

"Nothing exciting, just storage. Come on upstairs," he says, heading back down the hallway. "I'll show you my office."

"What about the Sim Dome?" I ask.

"That's in the basement, but it's in use right now, and I don't want to interrupt."

Dad pushes the elevator button for the eighth floor, and when the bio-scanner beeps, he presses his index finger to the panel. The elevator starts to rise.

Remi reaches for the buttons with chubby hands, too little to understand why her fingers won't get us where we need to go. It needs to be Dad's fingerprint. Or a perfect imitation.

The elevator leads directly to Dad's top-floor office and lab. It's a huge, open space, every wall made of windows with a view over the land. The mahogany desk in the center of the room is an exact copy of the one I hid under in Dad's office at home, and from his chair, he has a view of any weather system approaching.

"Not bad, huh?" Dad takes Remi from my arms and gestures toward the bank of computers. "Go ahead and have a look."

I walk over to the heart of the office—no, more like the brain. Plasma monitors taller than I am grow up out of the floor alongside each workstation. One spews out a constantly scrolling screen of computer-generated weather models. Another three are Doppler radar composites, and two more seem to be live cameras trained on the surrounding landscape. One of those shows the storm Mirielle called about, way off in the distance.

"Amazing, isn't it?" Dad says, bouncing Remi. "This place never sleeps."

"People work here all night?"

"Somebody's here around the clock, and the rest of us check in from home often. This is all tied into the wireless network so it can be controlled remotely." He motions for me to take Remi. "I have to get to that meeting."

I put Remi down on the soft rug by the couch with a couple of toys, and Dad heads for the elevator.

"Will you be long?" I call after him as the door opens. "I mean . . . I wondered if she'll need to take her nap here."

Dad shakes his head. "No, I should only be about twenty minutes." He steps into the shiny silver box, and the door closes.

"Twenty minutes," I whisper to Remi, who's chewing on her toy dolphin's tail. How could that be enough time when I don't even know what I need to do?

I arrange couch cushions around Remi to make a sort of play area, and then I head for one of the lab counters. I pull the jar from my pocket and unscrew the top slowly, as if something might jump out the minute it's open. When I lift the lid, the sharp, sour smell of preservative fluid invades my nose, but even with watering eyes, I can see it suspended in the chemical broth.

My new fingerprint.

I didn't think to bring forceps or tweezers, so I reach into the container, grasp the new tissue between the fingernails of my thumb and forefinger, and pull it out. It hangs like a wet scrap of cloud.

I take a quick glance at Remi—still playing with the dolphin, but her eyelids look heavy—and then as delicately as I possibly can, I spread the new skin over the tip of the index finger on my left hand. It's so thin and elastic that it wraps right around, and when I press the edges together, they stick.

I try bending my finger, pointing, wiggling it. The new print doesn't fall off, doesn't loosen at all. It feels like part of me. *Thank you, Risha.*

I cross the room, sink into the plush leather chair at Dad's desk, click the login button, and wait.

"Access restricted to Dr. Stephen Meggs," the screen reads. "Provide bio-verification."

I press my finger to the bio-reader and hold my breath.

The computer beeps, and Dad's desktop menu appears. I scan the icons—satellite feeds, data streams, radar from at least eight different sites in the county. Where is the latest data for his storm research?

The antique clock on the wall ticks loudly. Eight minutes have passed. Remi has fallen asleep and is drooling all over her dolphin. I need to find whatever's here and get off this thing.

The radar, satellite, and model applications seem to be the same ones running on the other computers. But in a corner of the screen, there's a folder I didn't see on any of the screens across the room.

STORMBANK

I click to open it and a box filled with dozens of sub-folders spills out on the screen. Each one is labeled with a set of numbers.

5-7-1840

6-12-1899

6-9-1953

No, not just numbers. Dates.

I scan the list.

5-27-1896

4-5-1936

3-18-1925

5-4-2007

6-17-2010

It goes on and on. Dated folder after dated folder inside the STORMBANK file. Does each folder have meteorological data for that particular date?

The clock ticks again. Ten minutes left.

There must be something here about the dissipation project. There has to be.

My eyes dart from file to file. Half the titles are simply project numbers. I can't begin to guess what Re-creation #129 means, so I keep looking, hoping that the right thing will catch my attention. I feel so certain the answer is here.

Remi murmurs in her sleep.

As I'm standing to check on her, the elevator rumbles to this floor and the door begins to slide open. I fly across the room and practically dive for the couch.

I sit next to Remi, my knees tucked up against me, heart pulsing in my throat.

My view of the elevator is blocked by the row of workstations, but I can still hear whoever it is stepping out into the reception area of the office.

"Stephen?" It's a woman's voice. Maybe the one from Dad's DataSlate that night, but I can't be sure.

I hold my breath. Should I answer? I haven't logged off the computer; the storm notes are there on the screen for anyone who approaches.

"Stephen!" The voice is sharper now, colder.

Is it the receptionist from downstairs? I can't just sit here and let her find me shaking. She'll wonder why I didn't answer.

"My dad's in a meeting right now," I call. I take a deep, shaky breath and get ready to face whoever it is when they come around the corner, but there's only quiet.

I wait, listening to my heart in my ears. Where did the woman go?

The clock on the wall ticks again, and I jerk my head to look. It's been sixteen minutes.

I need to log off that computer before Dad gets back.

I walk slowly around the bank of workstations, expecting the visitor woman to be waiting with more questions. But when I get to the elevator, there is no one. The door is closed and rumbling with a distant hum.

Whoever she was, she left without answering. Apparently, she was only interested in Dad.

The clock ticks. Dad could be back any second, but I can't walk away from this. Not now.

I go back to his desk and skim the pages on the screen. Most of it is over-my-head science, but in one file, the words I do understand jump out. They jump out and grab me by the throat, and shake.

Possibilities for Replication: In simulation exercises, researchers successfully recreated the atmospheric conditions that led to the June 17, 2010, EF4 tornado near Deer Creek, Minnesota, through the heating and cooling of particular features of supercell thunderstorms. In the Simulation Dome assessment, this resulted in the genesis of a tornado that would easily be classified NF4 or above.

In the first non-laboratory trial, certain atmospheric variables interfered, resulting in a smaller vortex forming and veering slightly off the intended track so that intervention was necessary to reroute. Still, damage was impressive, and with further development, more precision in both the scope of the storm and the track may be expected.

Damage was impressive?

I look at the date listed next to the words "first non-laboratory trial," and a throbbing pain shoots through my temple. 5-30-2050. That was our first day at camp. The day Risha and I had the picnic with Alex and Tomas. The day we watched from the jungle gym while the kids at the park "sang" the tornado away from the Placid Meadows fence.

When really, the magical storm songs were coming from this office.

My stomach churns with the poison of what I've learned. This makes it look like Dad isn't doing research to get rid of storms anymore. This research is focused on—no, that's impossible. Is it? I look back at the last paragraph, but my head hurts. Letters are swimming out of place, rearranging themselves, and I feel sick.

Bile rises in my throat, but I swallow it down and pull my DataSlate from my bag.

I don't wait for the clock to tick away my last minutes. I need this—all of it. I don't know yet what I can possibly do with it—I don't know yet what it all means or who I can possibly show—but I know I need it.

I jam my DataSlate connector into the port on Dad's computer.

"Transfer file command restricted to Stephen Meggs. Please provide bio-verification."

Come *on*, come *on*, I think, pressing my finger to the reader. After three failed reads, probably because I'm shaking too much to hold still, the computer beeps, my storage drive appears, and I'm able to drag the STORMBANK folder in to copy.

Remi stirs again.

The file transfer bar progresses slowly, and I curse under my breath because I can't make it zip to the end.

Remi's awake fussing, so I start across the room to pick her up, just as the elevator begins to hum.

No!

I fly back to the computer. Remi's crying, wiggling in my arms as I lean over the screen. The files are still copying.

Go. Go, GO.

Just a few more seconds.

But the elevator dings, and there are no more seconds. I pull the DataSlate from the port and ignore the error message that appears. Right now, it doesn't matter if any of the data actually transferred—I need to get off this thing before Dad comes. But it won't shut down.

I try the escape key.

The elevator dings again.

I yank the power cord from the back of the computer, and the screen puffs to black as the door slides open.

Dad steps out. "How are my girls doing?"

I stand up from the leather chair and bounce a little with Remi. I force my voice to sound calm. "We're fine. She's been fussy, so I thought she'd like spinning in your chair, but she wanted to grab everything." I glance at the black screen, praying it will reboot—and not return to the last screen I was on—when the power returns. "She unplugged your computer. Sorry."

"No problem." In four long steps, he's at the desk, putting the cord back where it goes.

The machine hums to life, and I hold my breath.

Dad turns back to me. "Ready to head home?"

I nod. Remi's quieting down in my arms, her head drooping onto my shoulder, and her rhythmic breathing helps my heart settle down, too. "Let me get my stuff."

I reach for my DataSlate and backpack to follow Dad to the elevator. Just before the door slides shut, I see Dad's computer monitor flash back to life on his desk. There is only a log-in screen.

No sign of the data I was never supposed to see.

No evidence at all that I logged in tonight as Stephen Meggs.

Chapter 20

Jaden, do you have plans after camp tomorrow?" Mirielle passes me the fruit salad at dinner. "I'd love for us to have a girls' afternoon— maybe some shopping?" She winks at me, and for a second, I don't know why. Then I remember "shopping" is code, and she must have found a dance performance for us to go see. I wonder if Aunt Linda is coming, too, but I can't ask now.

"Sure." I should be excited, but mostly, I'm dying to finish dinner so I can be alone and think about everything I saw on Dad's computer. I spoon out a little heap of globe-perfect blueberries and seedless strawberries. Their plastic-smooth surface feels cold on my tongue. I swallow and try not to think of berries warmed by the sun. "Shopping sounds great."

"Terrific idea." Dad's in one of his good moods. He reaches over to Remi's high chair and gives her a grape that looks like it came out of a mold in a factory. "I have a late meeting tomorrow, but I'd love to see all my girls for an early dinner. Why don't you drop by the office after your shopping, and we'll get something in the cafeteria?"

"Wonderful." Mirielle takes the grape from Remi and cuts it into quarters so she can eat it without choking.

"Perfect," I say, but my brain has left the dinner table and gone upstairs, where my DataSlate is waiting.

On the way to my room, I pass Grandma Athena's picture, and somehow her eyes seem sharper than usual. I stop and pick up the frame.

What Alex and I have been trying to do—what we're so close to figuring out—has absolutely consumed me these past weeks. If Mirielle didn't call me to the table for meals, I don't know if I'd even feel hungry. What I've been starving for is information, and the more I get, the more ravenous I am for more.

Tonight, looking into those charcoal eyes that almost pierce the glass, I understand Grandma Athena's passion for science more than ever.

I sigh and put the digital frame back on the shelf. Grandma Athena probably had a whole team of secret government scientists working with her.

Without Alex, I'm completely on my own.

I'm in pajamas, teeth brushed and lasered, and in bed, but as I'm about to power on my DataSlate, there's a knock at the door.

"Come on in." I'm expecting Mirielle with clean laundry, but when the door swings open, it's Dad.

"Hi there."

"Hi." I slide the DataSlate onto my bedside table and pull up the covers. I don't think he's been in this room since I moved in.

He sits down on the edge of my bed and picks up the poetry book. I've gotten careless about leaving it out. I hold my breath as Dad reads the title. He opens his mouth as if he's going to say something, but then closes it. He turns a few pages, and I can tell he's trying hard not to frown at it. Then he puts it down. "Sorry I've been so busy lately. I haven't even had a chance to ask how you've been doing with the move. You like Placid Meadows?"

"Sure. It's great."

He looks back at the book on my nightstand, but then reaches for my DataSlate next to it. My whole insides turn to ice. "Is your work at Eye on Tomorrow going well?"

"Yeah," I say, frantically trying to think of what I can add. What would make this sound like an ordinary father-daughter summer camp conversation? What can I say so it will never occur to him that I know what I know? "It's fantastic. The library, especially."

"Sure is. That's a top-notch facility, all around." He looks down at the DataSlate. *Don't turn it on. Don't turn it on.* "Dad, I'm really tired, okay?"

"Okay." He turns the DataSlate over in his hands and pauses, and a breath catches in my throat.

But he puts it down, the screen still empty black, and walks to the door. "Night, Jaden."

"Night."

I listen to the click of the door, his footsteps on the hardwood floor of the hallway outside my room, the groan of the spiral staircase as he heads back down to Mirielle.

And then I reach for my DataSlate. The screen lights up, and I hold my breath until the menu loads.

The files are there.

They copied before I unplugged Dad's computer.

Every last one.

I breathe out.

It is all here. The real storm dissipation simulation report. The fake one. All the data that goes with those, and the full StormBank.

I open one of the files to make sure it's intact, and out pour the details of twin tornadoes that hit Gainesville, Texas, in April of 1936. There's less information for this storm than for more recent tornadoes, but the file still paints a vivid picture.

The debris in the streets was ten feet deep.

The image swirls in my mind—whipping winds and flying windows—until I shake my head and close the file. I have to try and get to sleep.

I create a new folder, drag the files inside, and start to type a label. I can't call it "Family Photos" like Dad. That's a folder he might open if he picked up my DataSlate in one of his good-father moods. Instead, I name it "Poetry" and turn off the light.

Tomorrow at camp, I'll try to get permission to run this data through the Sim Dome. After it works and I have what we need, I'll go see Alex and tell him, and he won't look at me that awful way he looked at me before. I can't wave a magic wand and make Newton okay again, but I can give him this.

I stare at the rectangle of blue-white light the moon casts through my skylight onto the carpeted floor. I try to sleep, but funnel clouds swirl behind my closed eyes.

I turn the lamp back on and reach for the book of poems.

"Geometry" would make my head spin faster tonight, so I flip through the pages for something calmer, quieter, and I find one called "Adolescence." It is about a hot summer night, like this one, about a girl hiding with someone, her cousin, maybe, behind her grandmother's porch. And the older girl whispers secrets to her in the quiet night and firefly light, tells her how soft a boy's lips can be, like the skin of a baby.

I close the book and look up at the ceiling, where there are no fireflies, only straight rows of perfectly round, recessed lights that never flicker.

Amelia kissed a boy once. It was Nico Groves, and it was winter, not summer. She was waiting for her mom to pick her up after a dance at the StormSafe teen center, and she says one minute he was talking to her about his new air-drum kit and the next minute he kissed her right there on the sidewalk. His lips were chapped, rough, she said. She never mentioned baby's skin, but I think she liked it anyway.

I fall asleep thinking about fireflies. And strawberries with raindrop seeds.

First thing in the morning, I hop on my bike, and with the wind blowing my hair from my face, I can think clearly again. I'll go straight to

Van when I get to camp, let him know I need time in the Sim Dome. And then . . . what? I wish Mom were here. My eyes burn thinking about her, how much I miss her, how much I need her.

Maybe today will be the day she answers. With tears spilling down my cheeks, I stop my bike and pull out my DataSlate. I can't help hoping. Maybe, maybe, maybe.

But there are no video-messages. No text messages. Nothing.

I pull up her contact page and press RECORD to try one more time. "Hi, Mom," I say into the screen, and then I am sobbing. All at once, I can't hold it in anymore, and I cry and pictures flash through my head like some awful horror movie. The storm at the barn. Swirling feathers and dust. Newton whimpering in pain. And the look on Alex's face. Two weeks' worth of numbers and funnel clouds and secrets explode inside me, and I drop the DataSlate to my side, my arm hanging limp. And I cry.

I *can't* face all this by myself. But the more I think about it all, the more I realize what's happening, the more I realize I am absolutely alone.

When I'm empty from crying, I breathe in. I pick up the DataSlate—it's still recording—and I take a deep breath. "Mom." My voice breaks. "I *need* you to come home."

I stare at the red record light. I should delete this and do it over. But deep down, I know it won't matter. She'll never get it anyway; it'll be like all the rest, so I just send it. I start pedaling again, and my tears dry in the wind. They leave thin, salty trails down my cheeks.

When I pull into the Eye on Tomorrow campus, I squeeze the

brakes so hard I almost go flying with my backpack over the handlebars. Alex's mom is pulling away in the truck.

My heart jumps. Alex is here. He must be inside already.

I wave to his mother, and she gives a small, sad wave back before she drives away.

When I get to the auditorium, Alex isn't in his usual spot. He's in the back, way off to one side, a seat that has *don't-sit-by-me* written all over it.

I go to him anyway.

"Can I sit with you?"

His face is impossible to read. Empty like a cloud-gray sky. He shrugs. I take it as a yes and sit down.

I'm terrified to ask, but I force the words out. "How's Newton?"

"Not good."

My throat tightens, and I wait. *Please don't let him be dead.* "Alex?"

He looks straight ahead. "His leg's not healing right, so they have to amputate. He's having surgery this afternoon."

"Oh, Alex, I hope it goes okay." But really, nothing is okay.

I blink away tears as Van jogs down the aisle to the front. He says it's time for another holo-sim lecture, since we're at a turning point where most groups should be switching from theoretical research to practical applications.

When Dad rises out of the floor, my stomach twists.

I turn toward Alex. "I went up to StormSafe with my dad," I whisper. He doesn't respond, and his eyes are focused up front, but I keep talking over Dad's lecture on responsibility and ethics.

"I have . . . stuff from his computer. I have it here, on my DataSlate, and I was going to try and run the sim again. And then I was going to go find you and talk to you."

Alex folds his arms in front of him.

"But you're here." I turn to face front again because I'm too afraid to see his reaction to the last thing I need to say. "Maybe we could work together again?"

Before he can answer, the lights come on. Dad is gone, erased. If only it were that easy.

"All right," Van announces. "Go wherever you need to go today. I know for most of you, that's the lab, but if you have more to do in the library, that's okay, too."

"Library?" I whisper over my shoulder to Alex, hoping he'll say yes.

He doesn't say anything to me on the way out.

But Van does. "Jaden, I need a few minutes with you, okay? I've been trying to check in with all the first years for a quick conference."

Without asking, Alex lifts my backpack from my shoulders. "I'll take this to the library for you. You can meet me there when you're through."

I consider grabbing it back, but I'm so relieved he's talking to me that I just nod and watch him walk out the door.

"So," Van says, motioning me to take a seat again in the empty theater. "Things are going well?"

I nod. "Mostly, I guess."

Van smiles a little. "I know your partner was extremely frustrated when your last Sim Dome experience didn't go as he'd planned, but that's all part of the process. Have you . . . decided to go in another direction now?"

"Kind of, yeah." I consider telling him now about the new data but decide it's too risky. It will make more sense if I share it with him after we try the Sim Dome again, after I have real proof. "Can we get time in the dome soon?"

"I think so." He swipes through a few pages on his DataSlate until he gets to a weekly calendar. "Maybe Thursday? I'll check the master schedule and let you know."

"Thanks."

Van looks at my empty hands. "I was going to do a DataSlate scan. We're required to check in every couple weeks with students who carry them on campus. Don't you usually have yours with you?"

"I do. But Alex took my stuff to the library."

"No problem. I'll catch up with you later." Van stands and heads for the door. "I'm impressed with your work so far, Jaden." He holds it open for me, and the sunshine streams in from outside. It's going to be hot again. Storm weather later on.

"Thanks."

"I'm serious." He gives me a friendly cuff on the shoulder as I turn to head to the library. "If you're not StormSafe scientist material, I don't know who is."

"Hey, Jaden!" Risha races up to me on the quad after Van walks away. "Hold out your hand and close your eyes. I have a present for you."

I do what she says, and two little glass jars drop into my palm. "Same print?"

She nods. "Save them for a rainy day."

Tomas waves from the Finger Factory steps, just as Van walks up to the building. He stands close to Tomas, talking, and Tomas looks down at the steps.

"He's been hanging around Van a lot, huh?"

Risha nods. "Van's kind of taken Tomas under his wing. He says he might know somebody who can pull some strings and get his mom into a treatment center sooner." She gives me a quick hug. "I'll talk to you later, okay?" And she runs off.

Alex is back at our library table as if nothing happened. If it weren't for the healing cuts, the fading bruises on his face and arms, I might be able to pretend it didn't.

He points to a pile of books next to him. My DataSlate is on top. "I unpacked your stuff. I thought we could do a little more work on supercell formation today before we redesign the sim."

I reach for my DataSlate. "Alex, we don't need to do more research," I whisper. "I have whole folders full of—"

He puts a hand over my mouth—gentle but firm—and sweeps his eyes over toward the ceiling. *Shhh.* "Later," he whispers. "Not here."

I'm four or five pages into the supercell reading when the door opens and Van walks in from outside. "Hey, Jaden. Okay if we do that DataSlate scan now?"

"Sure." I hand it to him and get back to my notes.

"Are you kidding?" Alex hisses, staring at me from behind a thick meteorology textbook. "He's going to find those files."

"No, he won't," I whisper. "They're hidden."

"Not very well."

"How do *you* know how well they're hidden?"

"Jaden, that DataSlate's only got one storage chip and there's a search function. You can't hide anything."

"It's *fine*."

He frowns but goes back to his reading. Van is back with the DataSlate in less than half an hour. "All set, Jaden. Looking good."

"Thanks." I take it from him and set it next to the pile of books. "Any chance that Sim Dome spot worked out for us?"

He nods. "You're penciled in for Thursday, first thing at nine."

"Great," Alex says, and looks at his watch. "I know we're not done until noon, but is it okay if I leave now?" He looks up at Van. "My dog's having surgery, and I want to be there. Plus we still have a huge mess to clean up."

Van puts a hand on Alex's shoulder. "You do what you need to do, man. We're glad to see you back. Let me know if there's anything I can do to help."

Alex packs up, and they walk out together as a bank of clouds moves in from the west and swallows up the sun. My mood dims along with it. How can he leave when we didn't even get a chance to talk?

But then I remember the barn, and the house, and his family and the millions of pieces that need to be put back together.

I remember Newton.

And I feel ridiculous for thinking that Alex talking to me—no matter what it's about—would be more important.

I read through another chapter of one of the reference books, but my heart isn't in it this afternoon, so I reach for my DataSlate instead and pull up a notes page.

The Poetry file is still there, lurking in the corner of the screen, looking innocent.

The library clock ticks—twenty minutes left for today. Not enough time to start research from a new source, so instead, I decide I'll read through the entries in the StormBank file more thoroughly. Part of me—probably the same part that wants to believe in fairies and mermaids and unicorns—still hopes there's an explanation, that my father isn't what all this makes him look like.

Another part of me is afraid. Afraid that even though there are no fairies or mermaids or unicorns, there *are* human monsters. Afraid that my father might be one of them.

But maybe, maybe, maybe. Maybe there is something I'm missing, something more. Something to explain it all away.

I click on the Poetry folder.

It is completely empty.

The files are gone.

Chapter 21

The Sim Dome and reception building are blurry through my tears as I head for my bike, but I recognize the burly figure walking toward me.

Van says nothing about me crying, but his mouth twists into a little smile. "Enjoy your weekend, Jaden. Don't work too hard."

I want to scream. I want to turn around and run after him and push him to the ground.

He deleted the files! He stole them from me! I want to tear them back out of his hands, but I know they're not there. They're not anywhere I'll ever find them again.

And I can't say a word. Because I stole the files first.

Van must know that.

Soon, so will Dad, if he doesn't already.

I pedal home as hard as I can, pumping so hard my legs burn, but no matter how hard I push, I can't outpace the voices in my head.

Stupid.

How could you bring it without making a backup?

Failure.

I slam the door, hard, before I realize Mirielle's waiting for me in the kitchen. "My goodness, Jaden! It must be sweltering outside. You are all . . . eesh . . ." She makes a face and shakes her hands. "Have a drink of cold water and put on some clean clothes so we can pick up Aunt Linda and go."

The ballet.

All I want to do is close myself in my room and think about how to undo this mess, this stupid mess I made.

Instead, I am going to the ballet.

Mirielle hands me a glass of water. Excuses race through my brain like data scrolling on a storm map, and my mouth is about to choose one when I remember the other part of tonight's plan.

I'd love to see all my girls for an early dinner.

We're eating with Dad. At StormSafe.

It's crazy to think I might have another chance to get onto that computer, but I think it anyway.

I need to get that file back. Maybe I'll have a chance tonight. Unless Van has already told Dad what I did.

And *then* what? My stomach twists in fear—but fear of *what*? Am I really afraid of my own father? I shake the thought from my head and take a long drink of water.

"I'll be right down." On the way to my room, I pass Grandma Athena. I fight an urge to stop and talk with her, ask her what I should do. She might have been the only one who'd understand.

I race up the stairs, drop my backpack, and pull out the glass jars from Risha. I open my dresser drawer, shove one of the jars inside a sock and push it to the back of the drawer. I change my clothes and tuck the other jar into my pocket. I keep moving, moving, moving as if I can outrace my own thoughts by rushing around my room, but my twisting insides follow me from the closet to the dresser to the door. It's true. I'm afraid of him.

I check my DataSlate. Nothing from Mom.

Nothing at all.

I tuck it back into my bag and race down to the kitchen. "I'm ready."

The ballet is in a public school basement—a concrete cave of a room with horrible acoustics, but no one seems to mind. Mirielle's wearing a long, black dress with a jingly silver necklace that Remi keeps trying to put in her mouth, and Aunt Linda has on a gauzy white blouse and denim skirt. The best I could do was a clean pair of jeans, but people are dressed every which way, and somehow, no one in the folding-chair audience looks out of place.

The dancers aren't as smooth or as talented as the ones on TV. Their costumes aren't as elaborate, but energy pulses through their bodies, and there is something about them—some spirit or will or determination—that makes it impossible for me to look away. Their movements are fierce and gentle, all at once, and when I applaud at the end of the hour-long performance, my cheeks are wet.

"Remi needs a quick diaper change before we meet your father," Mirielle says, standing up.

Aunt Linda and I join the rest of the audience folding up chairs and leaning them against the old wooden stage. Watching the dancers was like a dream—but now that the soothing orchestra sounds have been replaced by clanging metal, I'm awake, and everything is still wrong. Has Van told Dad yet what I did?

"Wasn't that wonderful?" Aunt Linda leans a chair against the stage, starting a new row. "Just the spirit of those dancers . . ."

I toss another one against hers. "Yeah . . ."

"What's on your mind, Jaden?" Aunt Linda reaches for the chair I've just stacked upside down and flips it the right way. "Seems like you're somewhere else."

"Do you know much about Dad's work at StormSafe?" I blurt out.

She leans against the stage and pushes her hands deep into the pockets of her skirt. "Well . . . yes and no. What are you wondering?"

"Well, I . . ." I need to tell someone. And somehow, I trust her. "I was on the computer in Dad's office. . . ."

She raises her eyebrows, but I don't stop talking.

"There are files on there about the tornadoes. About controlling them."

She nods. "You know that's his area of research, right? Always has been. He's been fascinated by the idea of weather manipulation since he was a boy, back when your grandmother was studying it."

"That's what she was doing? I thought it was secret." But now that it's not, I understand a little more. Dad's password, his crazy focus on all this, makes so much more sense. "Dad's a lot like her, isn't he?"

"Very much. So much it scares me." Her mouth tightens into a grimace.

"He scares me, too." There. I said it out loud.

Aunt Linda's eyes fill with concern, and she leans close. "Jaden, did something happen?"

Yes, something did. Something *is* happening, a whole whirlwind of somethings that I can't sort out. But I shake my head. "No. Nothing really. It's just . . ." The chairs are all picked up, and most people are leaving. Mirielle's done changing Remi but is talking with one of the dancers in the hallway. I don't understand enough about what I saw in Dad's office to even start explaining, so I don't try. "It feels like StormSafe has taken over his brain or something. Like he's . . . possessed." The word sounds silly, and I expect Aunt Linda to brush it off, but she doesn't.

Instead, she pulls herself up to sit on the stage and looks out at the empty room. "Your dad had a lot to deal with at a terribly young age."

"I know. Mom told me Grandma died when he was twelve."

She shakes her head. "Your father lost his mother long before that." She looks at me. "I'm going to tell you something because . . ." She bites her lip. "Because you need to know where your dad comes from. But more than that, you need to know that I'm here if you ever need someone. Do you understand that?"

I nod. But somehow, her words make me more afraid, not less. Does she think I'm not *safe* living with Dad?

Aunt Linda looks back out at the empty room as if she's staring through time. "Athena was part of a group of elite scientists working to harness weather for military purposes. To control the winds and the rain. That job was everything she'd dreamed about when she was in school. She'd never planned to have a child so soon."

I nod. "You told me she was gone a lot."

"All the time. The project started when your dad was a few months old; your grandfather was away serving in the military, and Athena would leave your dad with me for months and months at a time. When the war in Afghanistan expanded to Iraq, she was gone more than ever. She'd come home and take him back for a little while to cuddle him and play mother. As he got older and could understand, she'd do little science experiments with him and tell him about the exciting work she was doing. Then she'd take off again. He cried every time she left."

Out in the hallway, Mirielle sways back and forth with Remi as she chats. It's hard to imagine Dad ever being small. Or crying.

"It seemed like it would never end. Even as the troops were being pulled out of Iraq, Athena kept canceling visits home, writing e-mails instead, telling us she was on the verge of a huge breakthrough."

I climb up to sit next to Aunt Linda on the stage. The old varnished wood feels warm and shiny-smooth under my hands. "What was the breakthrough?"

"I don't know. The next news we heard was that your grandfather's helicopter had crashed in the mountains between Afghanistan and Pakistan. It was awful for everyone, but most of all your dad, because Athena barely took a break for the funeral. She poured herself into her work and almost never slept from what I heard. We saw her once more, when it all fell apart."

"Was she home visiting when she had that car accident?"

"It wasn't an accident, Jaden." Aunt Linda blinks fast, and tears streak down her cheeks. "Less than a year after your grandfather died, the government declared Athena's research project a failed effort and canceled it." She shakes her head, and even though it all happened so long ago, I reach out for her hand. "She must have felt like she couldn't go on after she lost her husband and her life's work one after the other. There was a huge storm the day she came home, tornadoes dropping all over the county, but she drove through it from the airport. She had supper with us and told us the project was canceled but not to worry; she'd finish the job on her own terms. She was so calm." Aunt Linda shakes her head slowly. "But her eyes looked far away, like she was already someplace else. She gave your dad a present."

A worn wooden image flashes through my mind. Words in fancy script.

Stormy. Rain. Change.

"A barometer?"

She nods. "He carried it everywhere. He loved it."

"He still does."

Aunt Linda closes her eyes, and I wait. "And then she left. The weather was wild, but I couldn't stop her. She walked out the door and drove away. The next morning, the police found her car at the bottom of a ravine. The storms that night were . . . Pieces of her laptop computer and papers were scattered over half the county. But they never found her body."

I shiver and picture Grandma Athena's ghostly photo in the frame. I don't know how I will sit in the living room again.

"There you are! Sorry I was so long visiting," Mirielle calls from across the room, and starts walking our way.

"I thought you should know," Aunt Linda tells me quietly, as she eases herself down from the stage. "A person never really gets over something like that. And your dad . . ." She pauses. "If you ever need me, I'll be there for you."

"Ready to go?" Mirielle steps up, bouncing Remi on her hip. "Let's get some dinner."

By the time we drop off Aunt Linda at her house and drive up to StormSafe, it's quarter to five. Dad meets us at the door. "I can't stop for dinner. Sorry. Something's come up." His body language makes it clear we're not invited in.

"Don't be silly, Stephen." Mirielle switches Remi to her other hip. "What is this thing that is so important?"

Dad lifts his DataSlate up so quickly I'm afraid it'll hit Remi, but it misses. She reaches for it and laughs, but Dad doesn't even look at her. "Were you even listening when I told you about the problem with funding for Phase Two?" he says in a voice that's getting louder and tighter by the second. "It hasn't gone away."

"But surely you can take a break. You need to eat." Mirielle reaches out for Dad's arm but he yanks it back.

"What I *need* to do is get back to work. Now." He speaks to her as if she's four years old. "I will see you in the morning."

She glares at him, and for a second, I see a fire in Mirielle that I never would have guessed was there. But then she turns and heads for the HV.

I follow her and feel the weight of my DataSlate in my backpack. Heavy with everything I've lost and with what I learned tonight. What Aunt Linda told me about Grandma makes me wonder how damaged Dad might be, and what he's capable of. What I saw and heard in his office . . . I can't begin to sort it all out now. I can't even look back at the data because it's gone.

It's a quiet drive home until we turn into the Placid Meadows gate. Mirielle flashes Lou her resident card, and as the gate starts to swing open, I see movement in the brush near the main road.

"Mirielle, wait!" She's already started pulling into Placid Meadows but stops and looks over at me. "I . . . it's nice out, and I could use some air. I'm going to get out here and walk back, okay?" I pull my backpack over my shoulder.

She raises her eyebrows. "You won't be long?"

"No, and I'm not hungry yet anyway. I may go to the park or something, see if Risha's around. If that's okay."

"Of course." I watch her pull away and wait until Lou is back in his booth playing a game on his DataSlate. Then I duck back out the gate and into the trees.

"Alex?" I whisper as loud as I dare.

"Here." A hand closes on my wrist and tugs me deeper into the brush, behind a big old tree stump that's turned into a nursery for mushrooms and moss. I lean against it, and the dampness seeps through my jeans.

"What are you doing?" I ask, looking at the DataSlate in his hands. "And . . . how's Newton?"

He takes a deep breath. "He made it through the surgery okay. He's gotta stay quiet for a couple days, and then I guess he'll learn to get around on three legs." The rest of his air rushes out. He leans against the tree stump, close enough that our knees brush. "Jaden, I have to tell you something."

"What?"

Alex squeezes his eyes shut for a second, then looks straight at me. "I stole files from your DataSlate."

I grab his arm. "What?! That was *you*?"

He closes his eyes again. "When you stayed back to talk to Van this morning and I took it to the library for you? I . . . copied some files."

I stare at the DataSlate in his hands, almost afraid to hope. "You copied them onto there?"

He nods. "I know it was a crappy thing to do, but—"

"And you have them on there, *now*?"

"I felt like I *had* to, Jaden. I didn't know at first what you'd found, but I figured it was important, and I was right. This information . . . It's *exactly* what we need." His eyes plead with me to understand what he says next. "I didn't know if you'd show me or not. He is your dad, after all. But I had to do it. For *my* dad. And everybody else in my family. This is our lives, Jaden, it's—"

"But why would you erase the files from my device? Why not

leave them in case I was going to try to help, too? I *was*, you know."

His eyes cloud with confusion. "I didn't erase anything. I only copied it."

"You did so—when I turned it on after—" I interrupt my own thought: after Van borrowed it for the check, after Van said good-bye to me, smiling. It *was* him. "Never mind. It was Van."

Alex's eyes puzzle back and forth for a few seconds, and then his face falls open with understanding. "He erased your files."

I nod and shift my weight. A sharp edge of the tree stump is sticking into my hip, so I stand up and walk over to a pair of close-together cedars that didn't get cut down. "I don't know how he could have known, why he chose that day to check . . . and I can't believe I was dumb enough not to back them up. But . . ." I look at the DataSlate in his hands. "You copied everything?"

He hands it to me. "Everything."

I click on the folder, but Alex tugs my sleeve. "Not here."

"Well, I can't take it home. Not after—"

An HV turns into the gate, and I cover the DataSlate's screen with my jacket so we can't be seen.

"We need to go someplace to look at this, where we can talk about it." Alex ducks under a branch and starts heading out of the woods.

I follow him, my shoes squishing into the damp leaf litter beneath the trees. "There's campus if we can wait until tomorrow, but—"

He holds a branch out of my way and grabs my arm as I start to pass. "We *can't* wait, Jaden. *This* can't wait." Even in the shadows, intensity flashes in his eyes. "It's waited too long already."

He's right. "Then let's go now."

"To campus? It's closed for the afternoon. Everything will be locked. The outside gate, even."

I pull the jar from my pocket. "I have the right fingerprint to get in."

Alex's eyes get huge. "Your dad's?"

"Risha made it for me."

He looks at me, hard. "You're willing to do this? To risk it?"

"Yes." I am terrified, but I mean it. "My dad's gone, working on some . . . I don't know . . . but something that made him cancel dinner. He won't be home for hours, maybe not even until tomorrow. We'll have the library and the Sim Dome and whatever else we need. Come on."

This time I lift up the branch, and Alex starts to duck under, but then he stops and stands straight again, his face inches from mine in the woodsy darkness, and whispers, "Thank you."

He leans in, and his lips touch mine, gentle as the breeze, warm as summer grass.

He pulls away and ducks under the branch, a shadow walking in front of me. I put two fingers to my tingling lips and follow him out of the trees.

Chapter 22

I wave to Lou as we walk past the gate, but as soon as he looks away, we run all the way to the house. The straps of my backpack dig into my shoulders, and by the time we creep into the garage, my hair is damp with sweat.

We lift bikes from the rack, coast down the driveway, and pedal down the street. As we pass Risha's house, I squeeze the hand brakes. "Wait. Let's get Risha, okay?" Alex nods and waits for me at the bottom of the driveway.

Risha answers the doorbell two seconds after the first ring, as if she'd been waiting for us instead of eating dinner with her family.

"Jaden!" She pulls me into a hug that smells like curry, and I whisper what's happening. I tell her everything we know and step back and wait for her look of shock, but it never comes. "Whatever you need," she says, already heading to the garage for her bike. "Count me in."

We pedal the last few blocks. The breeze has died down to nothing, and the air sticks to my skin.

When we pull up to the locked front gate of Eye on Tomorrow,

I pull the jar from my pocket, wrap Dad's print around my fingertip, and press it to the biometrics panel. "I guess this counts as a rainy day, huh?" Risha looks pleased when it works on the first try. The light turns green, and the gate swings open.

"Come with me," Alex whispers, and heads straight for the library.

"Not the library, Alex. It's not—"

"Shhh. I know where we can go."

We follow the path to the library, but instead of reaching for the door, Alex veers off around the side of the building. In the back, old-fashioned fire-escape stairs lead up to the roof.

"Oh, good call. I haven't been up here since I came for my orientation tour a couple of years ago," Risha says.

She and Alex take the steps two at a time, and by the time I catch up to them at the top of the fifth flight, I'm panting. When I look up, my breath catches in my throat.

The roof is enormous and . . . amazing. A gravel pathway winds through patches of garden with lush red and pink flowers. And flowers aren't the only things growing out of the patches of green. What looks at first like some kind of sculpture garden is actually a line of old-style anemometers. They remind me of little kids' pinwheel toys, twirling and dancing in the wind, spinning like little girls in fancy dresses. I'm dizzy just watching them.

"What is all this?" I ask.

"Ms. Walpole's outdoor classroom for the community education center." He looks up at the hazy sky. "No cameras in the ceiling here."

"They run weather programs for younger kids up here," Risha says.

Alex takes my backpack and Risha's and tosses them onto a picnic table near the stairs.

"It's incredible." And beautiful, in a way I wouldn't have expected.

With the weight of my bag off my shoulders, I almost forget for a minute why we're here. I walk to the edge of the roof and look out over miles of land that used to be full of people, buzzing with lives. The roads are so quiet now it's spooky. An abandoned water tower rises up out of the dirt like a spider grown too tall to be stable, whose legs might crumble into dust any minute. The old university campus is being renovated into another energy farm. There's a scattering of patched-up homes where people are still trying to pretend this is a fine place to live, to raise a family. Will it ever be again?

"Hey, we have to get to work, but come check this out first." Alex crosses the roof to a circle of tall rectangular stones, all standing on edge and pointing at the open sky. In the center is an angled, steel rod. "It's a gnomon," he says. "Like a pointer. The whole thing is a sundial. The ancients used them—"

"—to tell time with the shadows. I know." I walk around the circle, running my hand over the rough stones. They feel so old, so yesterday, to be part of a camp with a focus on tomorrow. "Why is this here?"

"History of earth science. History of weather." Risha walks the shadow cast by the gnomon as if it's a balance beam. "Van laughs at it, but Ms. Walpole's in charge of the rooftop classroom and always says you can't just know where you're going. You need to know where you came from, too. Alex, remember that one time—"

"*Shhhh!*" He holds up his hand to quiet her, then closes his eyes, listening.

I hear it, too. Footsteps clanging on the metal fire escape stairs. I duck behind one of the stone sundial markers and hold my breath. Risha and Alex huddle behind the next one in the circle.

The thumping, clanging steps get louder—then change to the sounds of crunching gravel. Someone is on the roof.

The footsteps get louder. Closer. And pause.

I peer out from behind the marker and see a long shadow falling across the pathway. The shadow turns, and I can make out a ponytail. Van.

A DataSlate chimes and I duck back behind the stone. My stomach twists so violently I want to cry out. We left our backpacks on the picnic table. Van had to have heard that. He'll find them, find our DataSlates, and know we're here. And there's no way for us to get past him because the only entrance to the roof is that one set of—

"Yeah, what's up?" Van's voice rings out over the quiet roof. I peer out from behind the marker again, enough this time to see not only his shadow but the real Van, talking into a DataSlate. It was his. Not ours.

"I know. I'm leaving now. I was on my way out and heard noise on the library roof, so I came up to check it out. Musta been crows or something." He shoves his hand in his pocket and turns, and I pull my head back behind the stone. *Don't come over here. Don't come over here.*

His shoes crunch on the gravel again, but I can't tell if they're coming closer or going away. Another pause.

"Well, you'll be happy enough when you hear what I found out from my young friend Tomas today. Mr. Hazen's accepting our offer." Another pause. "I know. I told you he's a good kid . . . yeah . . . and he headed off a real mess letting me know about your little security breach. . . . No, he has no idea what it was really about. I just sent him to listen in on them, told him I was trying to keep his buddy out of trouble and needed his help. It's all good. And I told you I took the DataSlate and deleted it just in case. I don't think she would have understood it anyway."

I look at Alex, and the hurt in his face tells me that he's put the pieces together, too. Tomas. Waiting outside the first aid clinic while Alex and I talked. That's how Van knew I'd stolen Dad's files. And now his family is selling their farm, too.

"So here's where we are on the other thing," Van says. "I promised Tomas you'd hook his mom up with that clinic in New York as soon as they sign the contracts. I told you I'd take care of it." A pause. Then he laughs. "Okay, I'm sure the wind did some convincing, too, but hey. Done is done. And now we can move forward." More gravel crunching. Getting closer this time.

I look over at Risha. Her brown eyes are huge. And scared. Behind her, Alex has his eyes closed as if he's praying. Or maybe he can't stand to look at Van.

"Well, I don't think they'll be an issue for long." The footsteps move away again. "Yeah, I know it's gonna be a busy night. I'm on my way."

The footsteps crunch all the way back to the stairs—then pause near what must be the picnic table. Did he see our backpacks? My neck prickles with fear, but I lean out just far enough to see Van bending over near the gate, picking a stone out of his shoe. Then he starts down the stairs, and his footsteps clang away to quiet.

By the time I turn back to Risha and Alex, my neck is stiff from being twisted around so long, and Van must be long, long gone. Risha unfolds her legs and crawls to the edge of the roof to peer toward the gate.

"His HV's gone," she whispers.

Alex stares off into the clouds. On his cheek, the shiny trail of a tear ends in a smudge of dirt, where he must have wiped it away.

"Alex," I say quietly. "He couldn't have known what he was *really* telling Van about the DataSlate. Tomas must have . . ." I don't know what to say.

"Don't." He blinks fast and hard a few times, then stands up and turns away from me. "I don't want to talk about him."

"Alex, put yourself in his shoes for a minute." Risha follows him across the roof. "His mom is sick, and they need help. She needs treatment. What were they supposed to do?"

I should follow them, should say something to make it better, but I'm the one whose father has done all this. I'm the reason Tomas's

family and Alex's are under pressure to give up the life their families
have had for years. I'm the reason we're hiding up here on a roof
and—

"Jaden, come on." They're back at the picnic table, and Risha is
motioning for me. Even though guilt is churning in my stomach, I
stand up and go to them.

"Let's just do this." Alex powers up his DataSlate and blinks
hard. It's as if he's pulled a shade down over all his feelings about
Tomas. "We came here to figure this out. Let's do it."

Holding the DataSlate between us, he clicks the first folder on
the list, and numbers pour out like milk spilling from a cup.

"So what we have here is . . ." His dark eyes are focused, his jaw
clenched in concentration. I peel my eyes away from his face to
watch the stream of numbers rushing down the screen. "This is
data for . . ." He frowns and taps the folder, labeled 6-17-2010.

Inside are four documents: CONDITIONS PRECEDING,
STORM DATA, SUMMARY/RESULTS, and APPLICATIONS.
I tap on SUMMARY/RESULTS, and a document fills the screen.

An EF4 tornado touched down near Deer
Creek, Minnesota, on June 17, 2010, destroying
several houses along Otter Tail County Road 143.
One fatality was reported, and damage to trees,
farms, and vehicles was extensive.

I watch Alex read, and slowly, like stars appearing through
clouds, I see him begin to understand. "This data is unbelievable,"

he whispers. "Every detail. Atmospheric pressure, updraft activity. Everything."

He scrolls through the other folders and shakes his head. "This is crazy. It's . . . It looks like he's been *collecting* storms." He hands me the DataSlate. "Tell me what you see then."

What I see . . . makes my head spin. All the dates I had time to look at in Dad's office are here.

5-7-1840

5-27-1896

6-12-1899

3-18-1925

4-5-1936

6-9-1953

5-4-2007

There are more current folders, too. The more recent the storm, the more data fills the folder.

4-1-2019

10-10-2020

3-15-2022

9-1-2031

5-30-2050

It's like turning pages in a history book, past to present, closer and closer to today. When my eyes reach the bottom of the screen, I gasp. The final date in the list is from the day Risha and I hid in the old barn storm cellar. The day Alex's family farm blew away.

I look more closely, and other dates start to stand out, too.

10-10-2020.

That's the date of the worst storm ever to hit Paris. It was a year before city traffic was back to normal, another three before they finished rebuilding the Eiffel Tower.

4-1-2019.

Mom's talked about this one, too—the April Fool's Day storm that hit Vermont when she was in high school.

Alex reaches past me and touches the 6-17-2010 file again. "Jaden, *look*." His voice shakes with anger as he taps open the documents inside, one after another. CONDITIONS PRECEDING has a narrative of the weather conditions leading up to the storms. STORM DATA has a table of temperatures, pressure gradients, and wind speeds. Where did Dad get all this? And why? *Why?*

The APPLICATIONS folder is full of projections for how the data and other information from a storm might be used "in future research and development."

"Future research and development?" My voice shakes.

Alex pulls the DataSlate from me. He taps through, opening the dated folders. Each one holds the recipe for a perfect storm.

He points to one of the number-filled boxes. "This is *everything*. Everything you'd need to . . ."

It's too awful to be real, but he's waiting, so I whisper the words anyway.

"Everything you'd need to make it happen again." As soon as I say the words aloud, I know it's true. And that thought that's wormed its way into my brain changes everything I thought I knew about my father. "He's collected all these monster storms . . ."

Alex nods, his jaw set. "So he can bring them back."

"This doesn't make sense," Risha says slowly. "It's not like he can *make* the weather. He just sends it . . . away from here."

"And *toward* somebody else." Alex's hand goes to the scar on his forehead, and he brushes his thumb against it. "He's turning existing storms into monsters, intensifying them with this historical storm data, and then redirecting them."

"But why would he want to do that?" Risha says. "There's no point."

I wish with everything I am that I could agree with her. But I know better. So does Alex.

"No point?" Alex stands so quickly he almost knocks the DataSlate from the table. "You don't think they see a point in sending storms toward the farms?" He flings his arm toward the stairs Van climbed down a few minutes ago. "There's a point."

She doesn't want to believe it; I can tell from her face. But it's too clear to miss. The more tornadoes hit the farms, the more people have to buy DNA-ture. The more damage, the more danger, and the more reason to give up and clear the way for Phase Two of Placid Meadows.

"It's about the land," I say quietly. "Placid Meadows, Phase Two."

"It can't be," Risha says, shaking her head. "Jaden, there's no way he'd do this. It's not like your father needs the money."

"It's not about money." I think about what Aunt Linda told me about Grandma, how she ignored everything except her research. How she even forgot about being a mother. "He's obsessed. Obsessed

with getting that land, with building Phase Two of Placid Meadows."
I almost whisper the words, but I know in my bones they're true.

Risha stares at me. "Who could care so much about a project
they'd forget about *people*?"

I know the answer to her question. My father. And a long time
ago, his mother, too. But I don't say so out loud. I just shrug.

"I still can't believe . . ." Risha looks at me. She wants it to be a
mistake, almost as much as I do. "Jaden . . . your dad's spent most of
his life trying to disperse storms, hasn't he? Wasn't he figuring out
how to *stop* a tornado's rotation?"

"He *was*." I can't stop staring at the screen, can't stop my stomach from churning with truth. "It looks like he's moved on." Finally,
I tear my eyes from the columns of numbers and look up at Alex.
The words feel like I could choke on them. "The recent storms have
all been hitting the farms, haven't they?"

"Four since last month. Worst few weeks we've ever had."
He stares off to the west, where clouds are gathering again on the
horizon. "My dad kept saying, 'Somebody up there ain't happy with
us.'" He chokes out a cold laugh. "I guess he was right."

I push the heels of my hands into my closed eyes so hard that
lights dance. Explosions of yellow and blue. I hear more tapping on
the DataSlate. Risha's sigh. Finally, I open my eyes and take a shaky
breath. "We need to tell somebody."

Alex's voice is bitter. "*Who*, Jaden? Who do we need to tell? The
police your father probably has in his pocket? Or maybe we should
report him to *Van*? He's good at taking care of things. And he's been
so helpful with our work in the Sim Dome."

"That's it!" I grab Alex's DataSlate and pull my own from my backpack so I can start copying the data. "Let me get this transferred so we have a second copy, just in case. We'll go to the Sim Dome and run the command codes from this file to show what it is. It will prove what my father has been doing with the storms. We'll keep a data record of the whole thing. Nobody will have tampered with those results because no one expects us to have this." I hold up the DataSlates as the files copy. "If this is really a code to re-create the storm, then we'll have evidence."

Chapter 23

My hands shake as I plug my DataSlate into the computer port inside the clear safety glass of the Sim Dome observation box. "There. It's loading."

I'm praying this works. And at the same time, I'm trying not to think about what I'm doing to my own father—what the world will find out about him—if it does.

I'm still wearing Dad's fingerprint tissue. It's weird, like part of him is here watching us. Risha stopped me when I started to peel it off, though. She's right; we may need it again depending on what happens.

"It's all set." Alex nudges me, and I look down at the computer screen.

DATA LOADED

Below it, a green button reads: BEGIN SIMULATION.

My finger hovers above the touch pad. Will this work?

We chose the ten-ten-twenty storm; it will be the easiest to recognize. Once we see how closely it follows the real event, the triple tornadoes that converged on Paris on October 10, 2020, we'll have a better idea what we're dealing with here.

"Go on," Alex whispers. He holds up his DataSlate, its red record light flashing. "Let's see what we've got."

I tap the button, the gentlest tap. But like that old saying about a butterfly flapping its wings and triggering a storm on the other side of the world, a quiet tap is all it takes.

Alex, Risha, and I stand behind the safety glass and watch.

Storm clouds gather in the dome above us first, and the sim lights cast the familiar yellow-gray, just-before-a-storm glow.

"Rotation's starting." Alex's eyes are trained on the part of the cloud where the vapor has begun to swirl in slow, ominous circles over our heads.

The cloud grows, the funnel forms, and faux trees bend in the wind. Then a swirling, gray rope touches down.

"There's one," I whisper. It whips through a neighborhood like a moody robber, stealing some houses, leaving others untouched.

"Two." Risha points to the edge of the town, where a second funnel cloud is forming. This one starts as a loose, smoky swirl; then a tighter, more organized vortex grows up from the ground like a plant that's been nurtured and watered and fed all the right things.

I wasn't even born when the real 10-10-20 storm hit, but I've heard so much about it that seeing these twin tornadoes converge is like watching a movie I've already seen a hundred times.

Swirling dust.

Flattened buildings.

Trees flying through the air, roots first.

All of it.

Now the third tornado forms and makes a beeline for its siblings.

Within seconds, the three have merged into a wide, churning block of chaos. It starts a slow, steady course in our direction, sucking up entire houses so only their flat, chalky foundations remain.

The monster storm is almost to the edge of the Sim Dome, where I know it will be sucked back up into the ceiling.

Alex leans down over the DataSlate and starts poking at buttons.

"What are you doing?" I ask. "We have to let this one finish before you view another one."

"I'm not calling up another one." Alex doesn't look up at me; his fingers tap the touch screen furiously. "I'm entering the last command code that was listed in the folder."

"What does it do?" I ask.

"That," says Alex, tapping a few more times, "is what I want to know." He tilts the DataSlate in my direction so I can see the page he's brought up. It says SI CODE.

"S-I?" I stare at the letters, but no words form in my brain.

"S for storm?" Risha tips her head. "And I . . . I don't know."

Alex taps INTRODUCE VARIABLE and suddenly, the huge tornado turns back from the edge of the dome, almost as if it's a living thing and knows what it needs to stay alive. It grows and swirls back through the Sim Community, fueled by destruction, leveling nearly everything it missed the first time.

Finally, on the other side, the growling black cloud climbs back up into the sky.

We are all quiet, staring at what remains.

A few scattered boards. Some flat foundations. There isn't much.

There wasn't much left of the Champs-Élysées or Eiffel Tower back in 2020, either.

But that tornado had slipped back into the clouds after a single pass through the city. This one swept through twice, stronger the second time around. It had grown, intensified.

And suddenly, the letters have words to go with them.

S.I.

Storm Intensification.

Here is the evidence. My father *has* been re-creating storms.

Bringing old monsters back from the dead.

Feeding them numbers to make them stronger, bigger.

Deadlier.

"Intensity. That command intensified the storm." I shake my head as Alex bends down over the DataSlate again. "Did you hear me? You recorded, right? That simulation proves everything."

"We need more than one," Alex says, scrolling through the list of dates, whispering the storm dates one by one. Finally, he clicks on the first folder we opened—for the 2010 Minnesota storm. "Let's run this one."

He chooses a set of data, but before anything can load, a weather alert sounds its shrill, blaring tones over and over, and the warning appears on screen.

Issued: 7:09 PM, June 29
　　The National Storm Center has issued a
SEVERE TORNADO WARNING for all of Kingfisher,
Oklahoma, Lincoln, and Logan counties. A powerful
storm has been identified via radar and is making
its way east. This system has already spawned
several powerful tornadoes. Residents are advised
to take shelter in safe rooms immediately. More
information will be released as it becomes available.

Alex taps the screen to pull up the latest radar images.

"Whoa . . ." I suck in my breath and stare at the green and red blob. It's one of the most organized storm systems I've ever seen—on a screen or in real life.

I look out at the battered Sim Community and wonder whose real-life town will look like this tonight. Whose car will lift from the pavement, hurtle through the air, and wrap itself around a tree? Whose house will be ripped from its foundation and dashed to pieces? "Put a track on it."

Alex taps a button on the DataSlate to bring up the storm's projected path.

The track makes it pass north of Placid Meadows—everything

does—but then the storm's path swings east, and Alex's body tenses beside me.

"The farm," he whispers. "It's going straight for the farm." He squints at the screen, then looks up at me, his eyes bright with fear.

"It's okay, Alex. Their alert will have gone off, too," Risha says. "They're probably already in the safe room."

Alex wheels around to face her. "There *is* no alert at my house. Mom and Dad's DataSlates are still buried under the wooden beams from the porch. And the safe room . . . the safe room door hasn't even been replaced yet." He stands so fast his chair clatters over. He grabs his DataSlate, trips over the backpacks on the floor, scoops his up, and flings open the door. "I have to go warn them."

I catch his sleeve. "Wait!" My throat is dry, and the colors of the radar are still dancing in front of my eyes.

"*What?*"

I swallow hard. The storm is enormous. What if it's one of Dad's? The thought makes me want to pound my fists and scream. But more than that, it makes me want to help. I unplug my DataSlate from the system and shove it into my backpack.

"I'm coming with you."

Chapter 24

I race for our bikes leaning against the library, but Alex grabs my elbow. "No bikes. We can't take them through the gap in the fence."

"I'll come too." Risha's voice wavers in a way I've never heard before. "Just . . . let me check in with my parents so they don't freak."

"There's no time. But go. Track the storm from your house; it'll help in case we can't get a strong signal out there once it gets bad." I give her a quick, tight hug. "Keep your DataSlate on. We'll call."

I turn and run with Alex out the gate, all the way to the fence.

"When you ran that track on the storm, how fast was it moving? How long do we have?" I ask as he climbs through to the other side.

"Looked like twenty minutes, max."

By the time we reach the tree that bridges the river, my heart sounds like thunder in my ears. We have to slow down to cross.

One foot.

Then the next ahead of it.

The river is swollen and fast.

Thunder booms to the north, and in front of me, Alex teeters.

"Careful!" I grab the strap of his backpack to steady him. He reaches back to take my hand and doesn't let go, even after we've reached solid ground on the other side. We run, and he squeezes my hand as if holding on will keep the storm away.

But it doesn't.

When we reach the farm, loose bits of roofing from the last storm are flying up from the ground like ghosts out of a grave. The chickens are out of the temporary pen Alex and his dad built, clucking around in a panic. A stack of wood that used to be barn walls and hayloft floor groans in the wind and topples, and the chickens scatter in an explosion of feathers.

"Mom! Dad! Julia!" Alex calls into the trailer his uncle brought over so they'd have somewhere to sleep while they rebuilt. There's no answer. "Newton!"

"They had to have gotten the warning somehow! They must've left already!" I shout over a gust of wind that pushes me toward the remains of the house.

Alex runs to the trailer door and flings it open, still shouting. He tugs it shut, but the wind blasts it back open and rips the flimsy aluminum door from its frame. It clatters across the dust and comes to rest against an uprooted tree from the last storm.

"Alex, they're gone! I'm sure they're safe somewhere!"

But he's not listening. His eyes are focused beyond me, off to the north, and his mouth is gaping open.

I turn around in time to see the sky shape itself into a nightmare.

A wall of death-black cloud sits on the horizon. Slow-swirling charcoal fingers reach down from it. They point to the ground, hungry for dust and trees and buildings. The fingers close into thick fists, swirling, churning toward the farms.

I watch, transfixed, as the drifting clouds organize themselves into a thick funnel, spinning faster and faster, stretching closer and closer to earth until it touches, and there's an explosion of dirt and tree limbs, a second swirling circle around the tornado.

The monster barrels on toward two houses, a silo, a barn.

"No. No," I whisper, as if it might hear me and change its mind. As if anything with a soul could tear the roof off a house, hurl the walls off into fields, and keep marching on.

The tornado plows through a field, sucks up barn pieces. Nourished by splintered wood and twisted tractor metal, it grows. And I feel like I'm shrinking, about to be swallowed up. Was this the kind of storm Grandma Athena drove out into the night she died?

A flash of blue-bright-white pops at the edge of the funnel. An electrical explosion? A natural gas line?

A shower of sparks rains out one side of the surging mass of dark cloud. Pieces of roof and support beams and window frames swirl around the heart of the storm, tossed aside every so often when it's sick of playing with them.

Whose house was that?

Did they make it to a safe room?

Is the safe room still there?

"Come on!" Alex starts to run. "We have to get to shelter!"

I shout over the wind, "I thought your safe room door was—"

"Watch it!" Alex grabs my arm and yanks so hard I fall backward into the swirling dirt, just in time to miss being blindsided by a piece of barn siding that whips past in the wind. I land on my backpack, and a corner of my DataSlate jabs into my shoulder blade. I cry out, half in pain, half in fear that it's broken. But there's no time to check. Alex pulls me up, and we start running again.

"Our safe room's no good." He ducks into the trees past the clearing where the gazebo used to be. "We need to get to Tomas's place. We'll bang on the door and hope they hear."

Over our heads, trees bend and groan, grinding against one another in the wind. When they can't bend any more, a loud, deep crack splits the air, then smaller cracks as a tree falls, snapping branches in its path.

We burst out of the clearing in time to see the door ripped from the barn at Tomas's farm. It flies and bounces, top over bottom, cartwheeling across the field.

"Over here!" Alex pulls me toward the farmhouse door and bangs with both fists. "Tomas! Mr. Hazen! TOMAS!!"

Alex jiggles the lock one last time, then backs up to the driveway. "Stand back." He runs, throws his shoulder at the door. There's a sick thud of flesh and bone on a solid surface but no crack of wood splintering.

"Hold on!" I run to the barn, though the opening where the door used to be, and look wildly around. Flying branches have already smashed two windows, and wind screams through the broken glass, churning loose hay into a frenzy.

There! Still hanging on the wall is an ax, and I lunge for it, trying not to think of what the storm at Alex's barn did to the tools on the wall, how it collected them like a cache of weapons and drove them into the wood, blades first.

"Here!" I run back out and practically throw it into Alex's hands. He raises it over his head and swings.

THWACK!

The wood splinters on the first hit.

He aims lower, closer to the lock.

THWACK!

THWACK!

Beads of sweat fly from his forehead in the wind, and his breathing is fast and heavy, but he swings again—

THWACK!

—and the door makes a loud *CRACK!*

He kicks once, twice, and the third time it falls. "Go!" He pushes me ahead of him. "To the right and down!"

The safe room door is obvious—the only one plated in double-reinforced steel.

It's locked.

Alex shoves me aside and bangs until the heels of his hands start bleeding.

"They can't hear!" I scream, because the wind here is louder. "We need to go someplace else!"

"There is nowhere else!" Alex shouts.

I see the wooden board a fraction of a second before it hits the window. "Alex!"

I pull him down on top of me as it crashes through the glass.

The board flies over us and pierces the video screen in the living room.

"We have to go!" I pull him toward the door.

"The truck!" Next to the barn is a green pickup, miraculously, still unharmed, and we push back out into the wind. The whirling dust stings my eyes, and tears dry on my face as I run.

"Get in!" Alex screams, and runs to the driver's side.

I reach for the handle and fight the wind to pull open the door, but this is no shelter. Even a smaller tornado could pick it up and fling it a quarter of a mile.

I force the door closed, panting, and stare through the windshield.

My heart drops right into my stomach.

The tornado is closer, wider, swirling faster than before.

Right behind it is a second one.

Not far off to the left is a third.

All of them, NF5's, at least.

All of them heading straight for us.

Chapter 25

The truck's engine rumbles to life. "You have *keys*?" I stare. It's an old-time ignition—no fingerprint panel.

"These keys are always in the truck! Hold on!" Alex flings his backpack onto the seat between us, yanks the truck into reverse, and jerks us away from the barn. The tires spin, and we fly down the driveway onto the main road, away from the storm.

The DataSlate in my backpack pokes into my hurt shoulder, but I leave it on. Somehow, I can't let go of it right now, even to put it next to me on the seat. I reach for my seat belt, and Alex almost laughs—as if seat belts will protect us from the storm—but he puts his on, too.

"Where are we going?" I ask.

"I don't know." His jaw looked so set, his eyes burned with so much confidence driving out of there that I was sure he'd have an answer, but he's as terrified as I am, and for a moment, all that matters is easing that fear for him. I try to make my voice as light as it can possibly be with three tornadoes gunning for us in the rear-view mirror.

"Since when do fourteen-year-olds drive?"

He brakes to go around a sharp turn. "I've been driving this thing since I was eleven. Tomas and I'd sneak out and run it up and down the dirt roads while his dad was working in the barn." He almost smiles.

"Well, I guess that comes in handy when—"

He slams on the brakes so we don't hit a twisted piece of swing set that must have blown out of someone's yard. The seat belt catches me, and my shoulder stings.

"You okay?" Alex asks.

I don't answer. I'm staring at the piece of swing set, three twisted metal support bars coming off a crosspiece that still has a swing attached. The painted wooden seat is splintered, but not so much that you can't see the painted handprints that decorate it.

A big green hand. A smaller blue hand. And two tiny prints, pink and purple.

Whose handprints are these? Are they safe?

How many more swing sets and barns and houses will be swallowed up before this night is through?

Alex drives around it, and I twist in my seat to look back.

The three tornadoes are lined up, still coming our way, but something is different. It looks like they've slowed down, maybe even stopped. Will they die out before they get to Alex's farm? *Oh, please, please.* I stare out the rear window at the funnels growing more distant.

But instead of relief, I feel a chill of terror. They may have stopped, but they are growing. Churning with more intense energy. And they are coming together.

Oh, God, make them stop, make them stop. I try to pray them away, will them to be sucked back up into the sky before they do any more harm. But even as I pray, I recognize what is happening . . . three tornadoes that merge. The monster that hit Paris in 2020. A sick feeling swirls in my gut.

This is no act of God.

"Alex, look."

He puts a shaking hand over my seat and twists to stare behind him. "Ten-ten-twenty," he breathes.

Stalled for a moment, the three tornadoes dance, whirling, crunching, spinning closer together and apart, together and apart, until two of them touch, like tops spinning on a table that collide. But these tornadoes don't stop spinning; they swallow each other up, fatter, stronger, and hungrier. Even though they're not here yet, the wind is picking up.

"We have to get out of here!" Alex throws the truck into gear. "Maybe we can get back to the campus, or maybe—"

"Alex! You *know* this storm!" The truck shakes in a gust of wind, and I fling my arm back, pointing at the swelling monster behind us. "You know what it did in '20. It's going to start moving again any minute. It's going do the same thing unless somebody stops it!"

"We have to find shelter!" he screams. "We can't stop that thing! I'm taking us back to campus, or Risha's place, or—"

He turns to the left, back toward the entrance to Placid Meadows, but I reach over, grab the steering wheel, and jerk it to the right instead, toward the curve in the road that leads to StormSafe.

"What are you doing?!"

"Just go!" A thick branch flies out of the woods toward the driver's side window. Alex stomps on the accelerator, and instead of bursting through the glass, the branch clangs into the metal truck bed.

"Go!" I urge him on, and he keeps driving until we reach the first sign for StormSafe. Then he slams on the brakes. "Jaden, what are you *doing*? We need shelter, and this locked compound isn't it. We'll be trapped outside, and even if we get in, what are we supposed to do?" He pounds his hand on the steering wheel and winces. "We need to get to a safe room now! We can't stop this thing!"

"Maybe we can't!" Tears stream down my face. Tears for Tomas and his family, whose house will probably be gone within seconds once the storm starts its march forward again. Tears for Alex's parents and Julia and Newton, wherever they are. Tears for the little girls whose swing set blew into the road. Tears for this whole world, where no one can even go outside without the risk that they might be swallowed up into the sky.

And tears for myself.

Burning, shameful tears because I know the truth, that my father has waved his magic wand at this sad, hot, churning world and made it even worse.

"Maybe we *can't*! But look at it, Alex! It's going to come! We're not going to make it anywhere safe. There's no time. And when the third tornado merges—"

"Stop it! We don't *know* that's what—"

"Yes, we *do!*" I swipe at the tears in my eyes and scream over the roar of the storm. "You *know* what's going to happen! We have to find my father!"

"Your *father?*" His eyes are furious. "You think your father is going to help?"

"Listen, please. We have to . . . we can *talk* to him. Once he knows it's out . . . that people know, he'll have to—"

"Have to *what*, Jaden? *Kill* us?" he spits out.

"Stop!" I scream. "Just stop!" I choke back sobs and press my hands into my eyes to make it all vanish.

It doesn't. And all I can do, all I can hope to do, is try.

"I know you think he's a horrible human being." My voice shakes. "And right now, I do, too. But he's my *father*, Alex. My father, who used to throw me up in the air and sing me to sleep and"—I swallow hard—"and love me, the same way your dad loves you. We have to find him. He can fix this . . . he . . . he *has* to! He *will!*"

I let my head sink back into my hands, but I can still hear Alex's angry, ragged breaths. And then his voice.

"I don't believe it. Not for a second."

"But we have to at least—"

"What we have to do is get out of here!" He yanks the truck's gearshift into reverse.

"Stop!" I scream.

And he does. But he looks at me with eyes that are colder than any weather I've ever seen. "I'm leaving. *Now.*"

I squeeze my eyes shut tight for a second, then open them, throw off my seat belt, and reach for the door handle. The wind flings it open, and I hear Alex shout "No!" but the wind swallows his voice, and I jump down before I can think about it. Before I can think how stupid and dangerous it is. Before I can think about flying tree limbs or barn pieces or the three tornadoes that are about to merge into a single, churning monster and come for me.

I don't think about any of it, and I don't look back. I just run.

The wet strap from my backpack flies loose and slaps at my face over and over. I tighten it and keep running. The wind batters me back and forth across the road, like a cat playing with a half-dead mouse. If there were traffic, if there were anyone else crazy enough to be out, I'd have been run over a dozen times by now.

But I keep running. My backpack thumps against me, soaked, heavier with every step.

Horizontal rain stings my face, and my wet clothes cling. I've sucked in so much water with every desperate breath, it's a wonder I'm not drowning.

Another tree branch flies into the road a few feet in front of me, and I leap aside to keep from tripping.

My backpack strap flies loose again. I can't run with it slapping at me, and I can't keep stopping to tighten it, so I pull out my Data-Slate. As quickly as I can, I stuff it into the waistband in the back of my jeans and pull my shirt down over it. I fling the backpack off into the wind and step back onto the road, but an HV is barreling around a curve, so I leap back into the brush just in time to avoid being flattened by the only other person crazy enough to be out.

When its taillights are lost in the blur of rain, I step back out and run as fast as I can. My lungs are full of needles. My legs are burning. And my heart is breaking, wondering where Alex has gone. Whether he'll make it.

But all I can do is run.

Finally, I round the last curve, and the big steel-and-glass building looms up out of the gray.

The storm is raging, growling, roaring behind me, but I force myself to slow down as I near the entrance.

It's after hours.

The gate is closed and unmanned. But there are HVs in the lot.

I unfold my hand, cramped from being clenched in a fist so long. The bio-print is wrinkled and wet, half falling off, but I stretch it, smooth it as much as I can, and raise my finger to the bio-scan.

The gate slides open with a grinding sound, and a snapped-off pine bough goes flying through ahead of me, as if it had been waiting.

Inside, I stand dripping and panting in front of the gleaming building, unscathed by the winds howling just down the road.

Dad's office on the top floor is dark, but the lights on the ground level glow through the pounding rain. A silhouette passes across a window, and I duck behind one of the shrubs along the sidewalk. The shape passes down the long hallway toward the wood-paneled conference room at the end.

At first I can't believe there's still power in the midst of this storm, but then I remember it's StormSafe. No matter how big this storm grows when the three winding ropes merge, it will never get past the gate. Dad will make sure of that much.

Dad.

I have to find Dad.

I look back. The third tornado swirls closer to the first two. Closer—then away—as if they are dancing. But I know how this dance will end if it goes on.

I have to find Dad.

I crawl out from the bushes and hold my breath, watching the windows of the reception area. There's no activity—just quiet yellow rectangles—so I creep forward and peer inside.

Even the reception desk is empty. Are they all still in that meeting Dad was busy with earlier, when we were supposed to have dinner? And how could that have been just an hour and a half ago, when it feels like the whole world has changed?

I drop to the ground and crawl along the wall. Mud soaks through my pants, and my knees are caked with it by the time I reach what would be the end of the long hallway—the conference room.

I hold my breath and rise up enough so my eyes clear the edge of the window.

The fat leather chairs are all full except for one at the end. On one side of the table are two women I don't recognize. I don't let myself stop to stare, to wonder if one of them is the DataSlate woman whose voice I heard that night in the office. I have to find Dad. Four men face the other way, so I'm looking at the backs of their heads. The first three don't look familiar, but the last one has Van's thick ponytail.

There are papers at the empty seat. And a half-empty bottle of BioWake Cola.

Where's Dad?

I stand up, and my eyes dart from the main headquarters to the outbuildings, trying to remember what was what from our tour.

The buildings are all dark, except for the little one way down at the edge of the property where a rectangle of light glows in the lone window. Dad said it was only a storage room. Why would he be there now?

I run through rain-soaked shrubs, grass that's surrendered to the mud, until I'm crouched by the door. Even though it is made of reinforced steel, low notes of Mozart ooze out around the edges, and I know I've found him.

I reach for the door but feel a rush of fear. I pull my hand back before it touches the cool metal handle.

Who is this man behind the door?

I squeeze my eyes shut and let rain and tears wash my face clean of Alex's harsh words.

He is still my father.

I take a deep breath and hope the air filling my lungs can fill me with something stronger. Faith enough to believe.

He is still my father.

He has the same passion for science.

He still makes funny faces at babies and likes ice cream with sprinkles.

He still loves Mozart.

And I am trying to believe that he still loves me.

I raise my trembling hand to the door and turn the handle.

It's unlocked.

There is no bio-scan on this door.

No excuse not to keep going, to talk to him.

Halfway open, the door hinges let out a low groan, and I freeze, but the only sounds are Mozart and the faint clicking of quick fingers on a computer keyboard in a far corner.

I step inside and stand still as death. My heart explodes in my chest, thumping so loud in my throat and my ears, I'm surprised I can still hear the music.

The steel door swings silently shut behind me.

This room looks a lot like Dad's office, with its giant flat-screen monitors. They swirl with bright green-and-red radar images, but I can't tell if the storm is still stalled.

I try to quiet my breathing.

On the other side of the monitors, the keyboard sound grows louder, as if someone is banging on the keys. Frustrated. Or excited.

What is he doing?

Maybe—

I feel hope rising inside me. Hope that he's calling off the storms on his own. Maybe he never meant to create this nightmare. Maybe—

The tapping stops. There is a sharp huff of breath. A slamming sound, like a book being thrown onto a counter. And my heart goes wild all over again.

What was I thinking coming here?

There is still time for me to go back through the reinforced door, to go back to the reception area and wait out the storm. Time for me to play dumb and pretend I was out wandering and had to rush for shelter when I saw the tornado. Time for me to run.

But I don't. I can do this.

Dad, I'll say, *I came tonight because I know. I know everything. About your files and the storms and the farms. We need to make this right. Everything can be okay again. I need your help.*

I take a long breath and step toward the monitors.

The typing on the other side stops, and my heart stops for a second, too, but I make my feet keep moving.

The Mozart rises to a crescendo. I step around the wall of weather data.

And I freeze.

The person at the computer is not my father.

But she has the same charcoal eyes.

She speaks in a voice I've heard twice before. Once on Dad's DataSlate. And once in real life . . . in his office here at StormSafe the night I came to help with Remi.

"I thought you might show up." She stands to look at me, tucking in a sky-blue blouse that feels out of place with her dark eyes and sharp chin. Her skin is tight and pale. "Stephen said you'd never put it all together, but as usual, he was wrong." She chuckles but there's no warmth in her laugh. "Never underestimate a Meggs woman." She shakes her head, tucks a curl of gray hair behind one ear, and narrows her eyes. "You don't know who I am, do you?"

Somehow, I make my head move up and down, because I do know.

I walk by her photograph every day on my way to bed.

I know. Even though it's impossible.

"You're Grandma Athena."

Chapter 26

$\int$mart as a whip, just like they said." She cackles, sits, and spins her chair back toward the computer, and pecks at the keyboard so hard her fingers must hurt.

"Grandma Athena." I whisper the words and wonder how they could be true. But there is no mistaking the woman in front of me, no mistaking the intensity of her eyes.

"Shhh! Be quiet." Her voice is like ice. Cold. Sharp. "There's something not quite . . ." She trails off, reaches for a DataSlate, and frowns down at it. Her fingers fly, writing a message to someone, and I hear the chime that means it's sent. She calls up a radar screen, and I try to peer over her shoulder, but all I catch is a flash of green before she slams it down on the counter. "Gah! Weakening like nobody's business. Sloppy." She wheels around to face me again. "I know why you're here."

I shake my head weakly. How could this woman, this stranger, know anything about me? How could she even be alive?

She smiles, a thin, chapped line across her face, as if she's read my mind. "You look like you've seen a ghost." She whirls around in the chair again, dashes off a sequence of something on the keyboard. "Why isn't he answering?" She picks up the DataSlate, tosses it back on the desk, and stands to face me. "You thought I was dead."

"Well, yeah. They said . . . I mean, the car accident . . ."

"Brilliant, wasn't it? They knew I'd never give up. They knew I'd never rest until—"

My head is spinning. "*Who* knew you'd never rest?"

"Our *fine* and *dedicated* government leaders." She spits the words; they drip with sarcasm. "They canceled my project, the fools, but they couldn't take back what I'd already learned. I was this close." She holds up her thumb and forefingers, a hair's width apart. "This close to a breakthrough, when they cut the funding and threatened to throw me in prison if I didn't step back from my research. They didn't care that your grandfather had given his life for his country or that I was about to create a weapon so powerful that no American would have to die in battle ever again." Her eyes drift off somewhere behind me, somewhere a long time ago. "They never understood the possibilities. The power we can have."

Her eyes focus on me again. "That's why I had to die."

"You faked the car crash?"

"Oh, there was nothing fake about the crash. That car exploded at the bottom of the gorge like nothing you've ever seen."

"But you weren't in it."

"The car was rigged. Empty. I was on a plane headed for Russia. Viktor, a colleague I'd met at one of the international symposiums, assured me that his government would be happy to fund my work.

It went beautifully, and a few years ago, I sent for your father. He was overjoyed to find me alive. And he was eager to help."

She grabs the DataSlate from the desk again and looks as if she's about to throw it through the lone window. "Though he's proving to be rather worthless tonight."

"I just . . ." I shake my head, trying to loosen the nest of cobwebs sticking my thoughts together. "I can't believe you're here."

"Oh, Jaden. Never trust a death certificate unless you've seen the body for yourself." She grins, a smile so cold it makes me shiver. I take a step backward, toward the door. "But you should know that. You're a smart girl, aren't you?"

It felt like a rhetorical question, but she stares at me, waiting for an answer.

"Well, yeah, I guess."

"How smart?" Her eyes burn into me, and my throat is dry enough to catch fire.

She stands, clutching the DataSlate so tightly the tendons in her hands stick out. She takes a step toward me.

"What do you mean?" I step back. My knees wobble.

"Knock off the big eyes, Jaden. I know why you're here. You stole your father's data, ran a simulation or two with it, and figured out we're in the business of storm creation and enhancement, and not storm dissipation. Now you've come here to save the world. Am I correct?" She steps toward me again. Her eyes keep switching from brown to gray to black, like a river all churned up.

"I . . ." My DataSlate presses against my back. Can she see it under my wet shirt? My head spins with the impossibility of it all. Of her knowing what I did. Of her even being here. Alive.

Another step forward. "I knew you'd be trouble from the minute I walked in on you in your father's office. So stupid of him to leave you alone. I told him so, but he said you were too young, too green and book-smart to be any threat to the program." Another step. "He was wrong, wasn't he?"

A gust of wind rattles the window. I want to fling it open, leap out, and run. This woman, my grandmother, feels like the most dangerous person I have ever met. And yet I stand here rooted to the floor. Is it because I need answers more than safety? "How do you know all this?"

"How do you think?" She turns to the closest monitor, taps the screen once, twice, and an image of the Eye on Tomorrow quad appears. She taps again. It changes to the inside of the library, looking down on the table where Alex and I always sat. Our table, where Ms. Walpole put her finger to her lips to let us know we weren't alone. But there must have been more cameras, more microphones than she knew about.

Another tap, and the inside of the Sim Dome appears. Grandma Athena double-taps, and there is sound. The quiet hum of the fans; otherwise, the empty room is quiet. But I know what she must have heard earlier, and even thinking about it makes me feel like something's pressing on my chest, squeezing out all the air.

"You've been spying on us?" I glare at her.

"Spying?" She laughs again, a cackle that chills my blood. "It's not spying, my dear, when you install cameras in facilities that you own. Why on earth do you think we've poured so much money into Eye on Tomorrow if not to know where our brightest young minds are leading one another?"

Eye on Tomorrow. The multimillion dollar campus. The high-tech equipment. It's never been about encouraging problem solving and exceptional thinking. It's about controlling it.

I stare at the screen. The safety-glass cube where I sat, so close to Alex, working together, figuring all this out with our carefully designed scientific experiments.

Grandma Athena was the variable we never could have imagined.

"It's almost charming, really." She stands and walks to the big screen. "How you put your brainy little heads together and thought you'd found the magic formula." She taps it twice, and there's video of the Placid Meadows gate. She zooms in then, to a shadowy but perfectly clear image of Alex and me in the woods near the entrance.

Grandma Athena smiles a bitter smile as Alex steps closer to me. "Just like Romeo and Juliet, star-crossed lovers caught in a storm." She crosses her arms over her DataSlate as Alex leans into me on the video and kisses me, and at that moment, anger fills me like wind.

"No!" I scream and fly at the monitor with my hands outstretched. It barely moves half an inch.

Grandma Athena's laugh is like dry sandpaper, and I can't control myself. I lunge toward her, but her wiry body is livelier than it looks. She leaps to the side, and I stumble into the desk.

The DataSlate lets out a high warning tone in her hands. Hers is set so loud she doesn't hear mine, muffled under my clothes.

Grandma Athena stares at the screen, completely unconcerned about where I am or what I might do.

I hate her.

I hate that this stranger with my father's eyes knows me well enough to know I will not come at her again.

Instead, I peer over her shoulder at the radar alert that fills the screen, and what I see makes me want to explode.

The three tornadoes have merged into one. One churning, raging, chewing-up, spitting-out monster.

"Finally." Grandma Athena taps the DataSlate screen, hard and fast, then harder and faster when it doesn't seem to do what she wants the first time. "Why isn't it tracking? And where the devil is Stephen?"

She punches out a message, then stares at it with eyes so intense I'm surprised it doesn't burst into flames. Her fingers grow white, tightening around the DataSlate as if that will make it respond, and a whole minute ticks by.

Finally, she grunts, a sharp, irritated sound, and pulls open a desk drawer. From inside, she takes a slender metal rod, no longer than my forearm. She presses a button on the side, and the tip glows ice blue. "Do you know what this is?"

My blank stare answers, and she goes on. "A company in Russia makes them. It's a Shock Wand, capable of delivering a high-powered, deeply debilitating electrical charge. A fatal one, if it's turned up a bit. I'm going to find your father." She levels it straight at me. "You will stay here." She nods toward a painted green chair in the corner of the room. "Sit down."

I hesitate a second too long. She jerks the wand, and a sharp current of pain runs through my shoulder where the tip grazes me.

"Now!" she says. I move away from the door and sit.

She lowers the wand long enough to reach under the desk and pull out a length of thick rope—the kind you use to tie a boat to a mooring—and flits around the chair like some tiny evil bird, pulling the rope tighter and tighter, lashing me to it, pinning my arms to my sides. She leans in, tugs the rope into a tighter knot. It scratches against my rib cage, right through my shirt.

I glare at her, and for the first time, she smiles. "You know, your father showed me video files of you when he came to Russia."

She's tied me to a chair, and now she wants to reminisce? "What videos?"

"Just some footage of the two of you, reading stories, playing on the porch. But I could tell you were a spirited child. I'd wondered about you, and then I felt like I was finally able to know you a bit."

You don't know me at all, I think. But what I say is, "I wish I had known you were alive."

For a second, her face softens, and it feels like my only chance.

"Grandma, please let me go," I say. "You can't do this. You can't just—"

She slaps me across the cheek, hard and sharp. "Don't even think of telling me what I can and can't do," she whispers, her coffee-scented breath hot on my face. "I lost my husband in battle because America's weapons weren't strong enough to end the war. I have worked my whole life to change that, to build what we've created here. Nothing else matters now. Nothing."

She fumbles with a set of old-fashioned metal keys and heads for the door. I need to keep her here, keep her talking. "How come there's no bio-scan here?" I blurt out.

"Because you need fingerprints to make them work." She holds up one hand. Her fingertips are all scar tissue. "I burned them off when I moved away—too hard to disappear otherwise." She fiddles with the keys again, laughing under her breath.

She is insane. Absolutely insane.

Still . . . she's my grandmother. How could I not matter? Not at all?

My cheek still burns, but I squeeze my eyes shut. "You don't want to do this."

"Oh, I do," she says quietly.

"Grandma, *please*!"

The words seem to press a button inside her—the wrong one—and her face hardens, though her voice stays quiet. "Stay where you are, or you'll be sorry." She raises the Shock Wand to remind me how sorry. "I'll be back." She grabs her DataSlate and takes one last look at the screen on the desktop computer, still swirling with green-and-red radar images. "Here." She turns it so it's facing my chair. "You can watch the radar while you wait for me to come back."

Chapter 27

She leaves and pulls the door closed with a heavy *thunk*. I hear the *snick* of her key in the lock, and I am trapped in what must be the only room Dad's fingerprint can't open.

My legs aren't tied, so I straddle the chair and try to wiggle free. If I can get even a little slack, I might be able to get out.

But Grandma is as good at knots as she is at meteorology. The only way I can even stand is if the chair comes with me. I throw my weight forward so the back legs come up off the floor. I do it again. And again, rocking back and forth until the chair tips forward, and I'm standing with it lashed to my back.

I turn and twist, but the sharp fibers of the rope cut into my wrists, and the knots only get tighter as sweat drips into my eyes.

I let the chair clunk back to the floor and sit again, facing away from the table. If I curl my fingers in and stretch, I can feel the knot that binds my hands. I finger the rough edges of rope—is there anything here that might unravel? I tug my hands apart, but again, the ropes dig into my skin, and I feel the stickiness of blood between my wrists.

There has to be something in this awful room that can set me free. A pair of scissors. A box cutter. Anything.

I rock forward to stand again and make a slow turn with the chair on my back. There's not much here. The desk. The chair. The monitors. And a single frame on the wall, a photograph of a storm at night. Lightning blazes out in crazy jags from the bottom of a dark cloud, and the sky below it glows yellow-blue. At the bottom of the photograph in silver letters against the black silhouette of the mountains is a quote.

I believe in one thing only, the power of human will.

—*Joseph Stalin*

The photograph, the lightning, the words, are so full of my grandmother's terrifying spirit, I have to look away.

I have to *get* away. *How?*

I turn full circle, back to the desk. There's only one drawer across the top. I wiggle around until my fingers, stretched out as far as they can behind my back, close around the knob.

I pull it open and turn to look. Empty, except for a few pens and a slip of paper the size of a credit card that reads "Bio-scan override code: 4687291." This must be how Grandma gets into areas like Dad's office without a fingerprint scan. It's nothing that can help me now, not in this room with Grandma's olden-days lock, but I wiggle the paper scrap into my back pocket before I let the chair thump to the floor again.

Out of breath, I sit, helpless, and stare at the computer screen's radar swirls. My eyes burn with tears, and the colors blur together, but then I see something that nearly makes my heart stop. I blink—hard, over and over—until the tears spill out so I can see.

The storm is moving again.

No. No. No.

Let me be reading it wrong. Please. Please let me be wrong.

I throw all my weight forward, too fast this time. The chair's legs fly out from under me, and I fall. My temple cracks against the corner of the desk before I hit the floor on my side.

Lying there, my head throbbing, my arm radiating pain underneath me, all I can see is the hook of that storm. It is still growing.

I ignore the pain in my shoulder, throw all my weight forward, and roll onto my knees with the chair on my back. My forehead presses against the cold concrete floor, and I summon every bit of strength I have to push up with my legs. Up, up, until I'm standing before the desk again, facing the screen.

The storm is moving again, headed straight toward Alex's farm.

I want to scream, but instead I spin around and smash the chair into the edge of the desk. Some way, some how, I have to get loose. Without any idea what I'll do or where I'll go or how I could possibly fix this, I throw my weight at the desk again.

The chair smashes into it, over and over and over, until my wrists feel broken and I have to stop. The splintering noises I pray for never come; there's only the hard, cold thunk of solid wood on wood, over and over and over.

My DataSlate has worked its way out of my jeans. It clunks off the edge of the desk to the floor. The jolt turns it on, and the screen blinks up at me.

Dad's files.

Dad's files are here.

If this little rectangle of titanium and wires holds the power to turn this storm toward the farms, it must also hold the power to turn it back.

If I can get to the computer in Dad's office, I can try to reverse what they've done.

The lightning in Grandma's picture blurs and dances through my tears, and it makes me want to smash the photo, smash everything Grandma's ever done, onto this polished concrete floor.

Suddenly, the power of *my* will feels strong enough to shatter glass.

Glass.

I stare at the reflection of the radar in the glass that covers Grandma's storm.

This. This is what I need.

The picture hangs at eye level, so the lower edge of the frame is even with my chest. I sidestep over to it, knees bent so my shoulder is pressed against the wall. I spring upward as hard and fast as I can.

My shoulder knocks the picture up, off its hanger. It bounces off me onto the floor and shatters.

Jagged shards of glass cover the floor. They crunch under my feet as I make my way to the biggest, sharpest piece. I kick it into a far corner where there aren't so many shards, lower myself to my knees, then roll onto my side. Writhing and twisting and wiggling, I back my way into the corner until my fingers touch sharp, cool edges.

I'm facing the desk, but I try not to let my eyes fall on the radar screen as I maneuver the glass between my wrists and little by little by little, pick at the rough fibers of the rope. I can't see how much progress I'm making, and it feels like it's already been too long when there's a thump at the door, and I freeze.

My heart wants to burst out of my chest and run, but I hold my breath and wait.

There's another thud and a scraping sound—a tree branch or piece of roofing the wind has thrown against the building—and only then do I let myself look at the computer screen again.

The whole county is swallowed up in green and red, and the hook of that monster is inching closer to Alex's farm.

I can't afford to be careful anymore. Every time the glass slips, I feel the warmth of blood spilling from the cuts in my hands. But the rope is weakening; it's starting to give. I keep slicing back and forth until there's a muffled pop, and my hands—finally—are free.

Cutting the rope that binds my chest is faster with two hands, and soon the chair clatters to the floor. I grab the DataSlate with blood-smeared hands, fly to the door, and grab the handle.

Locked from the outside with Grandma's keys.

This time, I scream

I scream long and loud, and even though I know the window must be StormSafe indestructible, I slam the DataSlate onto the desk, grab the chair that held me captive, and fling it at the glass.

It shatters. Shatters into a million pieces.

The wind swoops in with a howling whistle, and for a second, I can only stare. I guess you don't need safety glass if you believe the storms will always stay away.

I grab my DataSlate, climb out the window, and run for the main building.

Chapter 28

The lights are still on, but the conference room is empty, and when I peer in the main doors, the reception desk is quiet, too. Dad's print wore off my finger long ago, so I tuck the DataSlate under my arm, pull Grandma's override card from my pocket, and look up to the sky.

Please work. Please.

I punch in the numbers and hold my breath until there's a beep and a click, and I push open the door. I run for the elevator, tap in the numbers there, and again, the beep of clearance—of course she would have access to everything.

My skin prickles as I press the button for the top floor and wait, willing it to rise faster, willing this office to be empty when I get to the top.

The DataSlate chimes in my hands and scares me so much I almost drop it. The message is short, from Risha:

Alex is here. Where are you?!?

Six words. But they are from Risha. And the tears I've been fighting for hours come back in a flood. Maybe because the cold, awful fear that something happened to Alex has melted now. Maybe because for the first time since he drove away, I feel like I am not alone.

I write back:

StormSafe HQ.

Even as I'm entering the text, I can't believe what I'm about to do. Break into my father's office. Hack into his computer. And—*please, let it work*—reverse his awful commands.

The elevator dings, and I finish:

In Dad's office—trying to retrack storm.

I tuck the DataSlate back into my pants as the door opens.

The only light comes from the wall of radar screens. They cast a green glow over the beige carpet, and shadows swirl on the walls.

I head straight for Dad's desk. The computer is logged off, but sure enough, right next to the bio-scanner is a data panel, and when I punch in the code from Grandma's card, the welcome screen appears.

ATHENA MEGGS, FULL CLEARANCE

It believes that I'm her.

A message pops up on the screen: DISABLE REMOTE ACCESS? CANCEL OR OK. I click on OK. Now everything will be up to me, and the thought makes me want to run, but I stay.

My hand trembles as I tap the screen, scrolling through folders and files, looking for the program to remotely operate the satellites.

I call up a search and type in everything I can think of: satellite, dissipation, redirection, downdraft, warming.

Nothing.

I pull up a database of the entire server and start scanning, but there must be thousands of files here. Programs with names I don't recognize. Documents full of numerical models, charts, and statistics. I'm not even halfway through the list, when my DataSlate chimes again.

It's Risha. Three words this time.

We are coming.

Another sob rises in my throat. I'm relieved and thankful and terrified, and before I can type back, I whirl around to look at the radar.

The main storm is moving slowly, giving people plenty of time to watch and be afraid and understand what nightmare is coming.

And it's spawned a slew of baby tornadoes, all over the county.

No matter how desperate I am for help, no matter how hungry I am for someone to be here with me, I can't let them do it. There is no way Risha and Alex can get here safely. None.

No! Storm is too big. Stay there.

I send the message and get an immediate auto-reply.

RECIPIENT NOT AVAILABLE

"No!" I shout, and my voice echoes in the empty office. The only answer is the hum of the computers that are my only hope.

I turn back to the screen on Dad's desk.

Be here. Be here. I scroll through the last half of the files. There must be a thousand documents and databases, and nothing that gives any clue it might be the program that whispers to satellites, tells them where to send their energy, how to turn away a storm.

What am I doing here? I bang my fist on the desk. Looking for answers in this jumble of files is like searching for a single blade of grass swirling in a storm. But I keep looking. What else can I do?

Finally, near the end of the list of folders, my eyes land on one labeled REDIRECTION and I click it open. There are fifty files, maybe more. I tap the one called SAT INPUT—it takes forever to open—and scan the screen that appears.

At the top are three satellite icons, each labeled with latitude and longitude.

With a trembling finger, I point to one of the satellites—which one? I can only guess—and tap.

The screen fills with scrolling numbers that make me want to put my head down and cry. It's some manic feed of temperatures, humidity, atmospheric pressure, cyclonic measurements, and who knows what else. What am I supposed to do with all this?

I swallow hard, reach for my DataSlate, and pull up the page with Dad's redirection codes. There must be a hundred different sequences.

I choose one.

I choose, because the only alternative is doing nothing.

Please let it work.

Please let it work.

I chant the words over and over, like some magical mantra, as I type in the code, number by letter by number. One wrong stroke, and I could make it bigger instead of turning it away.

When the last string of numbers is lined up at the bottom of the page, I hold my finger over the on-screen button.

EXECUTE SATELLITE COMMAND

I can barely breathe. *What if I've done it wrong? Who am I to even think I can do this?*

Before the voices in my head can get louder, I hold my breath and tap.

The screen flashes white, then blurs with a wild scroll of numbers, commands set into motion.

I look up at the ceiling and imagine the satellite miles overhead, stopping in its course, turning, rotating, blasting heat energy down, down, down into the cloud that gave birth to this monster.

When the numbers stop streaming, the screen reads.

COMMAND EXECUTED

Nothing more.

Did it work? I stand and run to the window, but there's no way to tell if anything's better. The wind is still blowing the rain at the building in horizontal sheets.

Stop. Stop. Stop.

A gust of wind rattles the window. It reminds me of another window, the one I threw the chair through, and I can't help wondering if Grandma Athena has come back to find it yet. If she's wondering where I escaped.

Or if she already knows.

I look up at the ceiling. No cameras, at least not that I can see. But no matter what, I'm running out of time.

I turn back to the radar image of the storm. It's actually slowed and—Is it possible? Do I dare hope?—looks like it's turning around. I tap the screen twice to put a track on the storm. The dotted line moves back across the screen.

"No!!"

Straight for Placid Meadows.

Placid Meadows, where concrete houses and storms that never cross the fence make everyone feel safe enough to ignore the warnings.

Placid Meadows, where toddlers giggle and shout nursery rhymes at the sky, even as the dark clouds swirl.

Placid Meadows, where Mirielle is probably nursing Remi on the couch right now.

Where Risha and her family and Alex are about to be—

"No!" I yell at the screen. "No! No! No!!!"

But the storm on the screen swells into something broader, stronger than it was even half an hour ago.

I leap back into the chair at Dad's computer and pull up the folder again, but all of these numbers mean nothing. Do I dare even try?

Above the humming of the computer and the beating of my heart and the rain pounding the window, I hear another sound that makes my heart freeze in my chest.

The elevator door sliding open.

I dive under the desk, shaking, and wait.

Chapter 29

Jaden! Are you here? Jaden!"

Alex's voice washes over me, and I scramble out from under the desk. "Over here!"

They are soaking wet, both of them. Risha's hair is plastered to her forehead, and Alex's face shines with rainwater or sweat, or both, as he takes in the huge room.

"How did you get in here?"

Risha holds up her finger. Her hand is shaking. "I made another print this week. Just in case."

"You guys, I tried to tell you not to come. The storm is—"

"We couldn't even see it until we were out of Placid Meadows." Risha's whole body is trembling. "Jaden, it was . . . It had to have been an NF-7 at least, it was just—"

"We're fine," Alex interrupts. "But for a minute there . . ." He shakes his head. "We thought we were okay, but then it turned, and I had to gun the truck, but we made it. I could tell it was still growing, so—" He stops when he sees the radar on the big screen. I watch him process the mix of images, the moving blobs of green and red, and

I hold my breath, waiting for him to see the path this storm is on now. He curses, and Risha rushes over to face a radar image of something too terrible for words.

She lets out a scream that shatters my heart like the glass in Grandma's picture. The scream of someone whose whole world is about to be destroyed. The scream of someone who knows she may never see her parents again.

She drops to the floor, sobbing.

I run to her, put my arms around her. Her body is hot with fear, cold with rain and air-conditioning, and she shakes harder.

"Risha, call on your DataSlate. Warn them!"

She tries twice but can't get a message through.

I jump to my feet and grab Alex's hand. "We have to stop it."

He steps up to the computer. "Where's the program to redirect? We'll have to find a track that—"

"No!"

He wheels around, bewildered. "Jaden, if we don't change this course, then—"

"Changing it won't help. We have to stop it. We have to kill this storm." I say the words out loud, even though I know they're impossible.

Alex shakes his head. "We can't. We never got to run the simulation successfully. We have no idea what the outcome would be, and we—"

"We have to try, Alex! Look!" I fling my arm toward the radar wall, where Risha is still crumpled on the floor. "We have to try. Otherwise, we're sending it *at* somebody, and even if that's not us, it's still somebody, and then we're just like—" The words get stuck in my throat. "Just like my father."

Alex closes his eyes, squeezes them tight, and I can almost see thoughts swirling behind his dark lashes. Finally, he shakes his head and opens them. "We can't take that chance. What if we end up making it worse?"

"But what if—"

"Jaden, no. There's no precedent for this. There's no research to support it. There's no—just, no!" He bends down and starts scrolling through the folders still up on Dad's screen. The dozens of data files with different codes. "Did you use one of these before?"

"Yes. And look what happened, Alex! We can't do this again. We have to—"

"Just wait!" He holds up one hand and keeps scrolling with the other. Risha has managed to pull herself together enough to stand behind us, her face red and puffy. Alex pulls her forward so she can see the screen, too. "There has to be a path here that doesn't hit any developed areas. Everybody, look. There has to be."

"Which one?" I throw my hands up. "Alex, there must be two hundred separate codes there. We can't keep trying them all until— There's no time for this!"

"Wait." Risha reaches a thin arm between us and scrolls back up through the list. Her bracelets clink together, and her eyes focus on the data scrolling past on the screen. The numbers, the patterns seem to calm her. "Which one did you run before, Jaden?"

"I don't even know. About halfway down, maybe?"

She scrolls halfway and leans in, squinting at the numbers. Then she picks up her DataSlate, calls up a map, taps at it a few times. "Yes," she whispers, and leans in to point at the computer screen again. "These numbers . . ." She runs her finger down the center part of the list. ". . . are all sequential in terms of geographic coordinates." She taps at one of them. "This must be the code you ran. It corresponds with the latitude and longitude of Placid Meadows."

"So that means . . ." I pull up a map of Logan County on the DataSlate and choose the satellite view, the one that shows all the roads and buildings. "If we can find a path without people . . ." In my mind, I draw imaginary lines from where the storm is now, trying every direction. But eventually, no matter which way it goes, the storm is going to hit someone. "It won't work. No path goes on forever."

"It doesn't have to. Hold on." Alex pulls up Dad's historical storms database. "The path just needs to be long enough for the storm's energy to run out. No tornado can last forever, and we already know what this one's got in it. It's already happened once." He calls up the 10-10-20 storm and runs his finger down the screen, stopping at a line close to the bottom. "Thirty-eight miles. We need a path that's empty for thirty-eight miles."

I look down at the map in my hands. It feels impossibly full of buildings. The path might as well be a million miles. "I can't—" The wind gusts, and the sound of rain on the roof turns harder, louder, like someone throwing stones. Hail.

"We have to hurry!" Alex brings the redirection folder back up. "I'll get this ready so when you find the coordinates, we can just do it."

Risha leans in to look at the DataSlate, so close her hair brushes against mine. "What about here?" She drags the line I've drawn a bit farther southeast, and we zoom in to see the track. It would take the storm mostly through woods near one of the energy farms, then past what looks like a few orchards from the satellite view, and close—too close—to one old farmhouse.

"That won't work." I point to the energy farm.

"They all have huge safe rooms," Alex says. "They'll get a warning."

"What about that house?" I point.

"It's not perfect, but we have to do something. That's the only building in the path," Risha argues. "It's thirty miles out. The storm will be starting to weaken, and they'll have plenty of warning time."

She starts to pull the DataSlate from me, but I hold on. "But it's still somebody's—"

"Jaden, will you look!" She lets go and points to the radar wall, where the storm on its current path is churning toward Placid Meadows. Ten minutes, maybe less, from swallowing up Risha's family. From Mirielle and Remi, who are sure they're safe inside the gates. None of them will ever see it coming.

I hand her the DataSlate, and she slides it onto the desk in front of Alex.

"Okay . . ." The computer screen reflects in his dark eyes. "What am I looking for here?"

Risha reads him the coordinates, and he scrolls down the list of command codes until he hits the one that matches. "Here?"

She double-checks it. "That's it."

He clicks it open, copies the code, and taps back to the command entry field. "Jaden, you just typed it in here before?"

"Yeah. Then run it." I look away from the screen, toward the radar, and hear his fingers tap against it.

Then quiet. Except for all of our breathing. All of our hoping.

Then the hum of the computer processing.

Risha and Alex turn to watch the radar. We hold our breath, and it feels like all of the air in the room has gone still while we wait.

The storm on the screen inches closer to Placid Meadows.

"Why isn't it turning?" Risha's voice trembles.

"It will." I take her hand, and she squeezes so hard she crushes my fingers, but I don't let go. "It should. Any second."

But it doesn't.

"It's not going to stop." She doesn't scream or cry or yell at the screen. Her voice is flat, as if she's already died with them. "It's going to hit them."

Turn, turn, turn, I think, staring at the ceiling, imagining the satellites miles above us. Why aren't they doing their job? "Wait, look!" Alex's voice brings me back to the screen, and just as the storm is about to hit the fence, it slows, like it did that day in the park, the day Risha and I listened as the moms and kids shouted their rhyme to the sky. It listened.

And it's listening now.

"Oh, thank God, thank God!" Risha's tears flow again, this time tears of thankfulness. She takes a deep breath and walks to the window. Her fingers trace raindrops down the glass.

Alex sinks back into the chair as if the storm sucked away all his energy when it turned.

I stay at the radar screen, watching the storm pick up its pace, starting a race in its new direction, ready to devour the new meal set before it.

I pick up my DataSlate and zoom in to follow its path as it moves.

The trees planted alongside Placid Meadows. When the sun comes up tomorrow, they'll be in splinters scattered over miles.

Better trees than farms, though.

I follow the path past the energy farm. Criminals or not, I hope they all get to their safe room in time.

I swipe the screen through ten, twenty, thirty miles of woods until the trees thin and arrange themselves into lines, and I know this is the orchard that the storm will level soon—in twenty minutes, maybe twenty-five.

Past the orchard and just a hair off to the east is the one house still in the path.

I zoom into the satellite view, hoping in a corner of my heart that I'll see a FOR SALE sign or already-broken windows and an empty garage to tell me no one lives there.

In another corner lives the cold, raw fear of what else I might see. Cars in the driveway. Dogs on a leash, waiting for someone to come play. Swing sets and tricycles.

I take a deep breath and zoom in as far as the satellite view allows.

And there is something I hadn't imagined even in the darkest corner of my heart.

A house with peeling white paint.

A stable and a brown mare.

A split-rail fence that I reached over with a handful of sugar cubes.

A rickety farm stand with a sign that I can't read in the satellite image, a sign I don't need to see to know that it offers sweet raspberries, fresh peaches, and compliments.

This is Aunt Linda's house.

And we have just sent a storm to swallow it up.

Chapter 30

This can't be happening. Not now. Not when it was all supposed to be over. I let out a moan.

"What?" Alex jumps from the chair, but even his shoulder brushing mine can't warm the chill that's settled on me.

"This house." I tap the screen, and it zooms in closer. The wreath Mom sent last Christmas is still on the door. A bird has built a nest in its gentle curve. "It's my great-aunt Linda's."

Aunt Linda, who fed me pie in that kitchen. Who gave me the poetry book, the one thing that's made Oklahoma feel a little like home. Who told me the truth.

Alex's face darkens. He stares at the screen, processing the information, then hands the DataSlate to me. "Call her. She may not even be home."

I nod and bring up her contact page. The call goes through, straight to Aunt Linda's video-mail, and I've never been more relieved. "Leave a message!" she says, but I don't. If she were home, she'd have answered.

"Feel better?" Alex asks, and I nod.

But then my DataSlate dings with a new message. "That's weird," I say. "I've had it on all day."

"We've probably been getting interference," Risha says, turning away from the window. "I couldn't get through before." Her eyes have relaxed some; they aren't as puffy, and her breathing is finally back to normal. "My DataSlate never connects right on storm nights."

"It's my father." Where is he? Is he on his way up here? I need to know, but I can't bring myself to open the message. Can't make myself let him into this room, even if it's only a recording. I can't help imagining him, looking right through the dark, shiny screen, seeing us here, seeing everything we've done.

But Alex is insistent. "Play it."

So I do.

Dad's face fills the screen. He's not 3-D like he is on the holo-sim at Eye on Tomorrow, but otherwise, it's just as realistic.

Only where did he record this? The shelf behind him is full of old dishes. He's definitely not here at StormSafe. And it's not our house in Placid Meadows, either.

"Jaden," Dad says from the screen in my hands. "I know where you are." He puts a hand up toward the camera in a gesture meant to keep me from freaking out, meant to keep me from throwing the DataSlate across the room and running like I want to. "I need you to stay there for now. You're not in trouble, and I—" He takes a deep breath, and instead of the usual fire in his eyes, the focused intensity, there is something else. Are they shining with *tears*? "I don't want you in danger. I can explain things to you later. It's not what it looks like." His voice breaks, and he looks down.

Alex laughs a quick, bitter laugh and walks away, but Risha stays by me and listens as Dad goes on. "But no matter what, I'm sure you're going to want to go home with Mom. She's on her way here now. So as I said, please stay where you are. Mom will be here in"— he looks at his watch—"ten to fifteen minutes, and after she and I talk, she'll be right there to pick you up."

The screen goes black.

Mom?

Mom is in town? Does that mean she was getting all my messages but couldn't respond? Did she get the last one? Does she already know what Dad has done?

And Grandma! Does Mom know Grandma Athena is alive?

Where *is* Grandma Athena now? I picture her bony fingers, curled around the Shock Wand, and I shiver.

"We can't stay here." I run to the window, where the rain should be letting up, but it's swirling harder, faster in the wind. "My grandmother might come back."

"Your grandmother?" Risha looks bewildered, and I realize I never told them. There was no time. There is no time now.

"We just—we have to go."

"Now that the storm's gone, let's go back to your house. Wouldn't that make more sense than you waiting here for them to come pick you up?"

"They're not *at* the house." It wasn't Dad and Mirielle's house in the video; there are no painted plates in Mirielle's shiny steel kitchen.

But where are they? I rewind the video-message and zoom in to see the background more clearly.

A wooden shelf.

Faded red apples on the wallpaper.

I suck in my breath. Not there. No.

Then I see the coffee mug with Emily Dickinson's face and know it's real.

Dad is at Aunt Linda's house.

And Mom is on her way. Or *was* . . . I check the time-stamp on the video. 7:22 PM. It's 7:45 now. Plenty of time for Mom to have arrived, sat down at Linda's big, wooden kitchen table with a cup of tea. Time for her to be devoured by a giant storm.

I lunge toward the radar screen. The storm is racing forward, showing no signs of weakening.

Alex points to the DataSlate in my hands. "Try calling again." His voice is so steady and calm I could scream.

I pull up Aunt Linda's contact page again.

No response.

I call up Mom's.

Nothing.

And Dad's.

Nothing.

I slam the DataSlate down on the desk and start typing blindly at the computer keyboard.

"Jaden, what are you doing?! You can't just—"

"Yes, I can!" I swipe at the tears filling my eyes, blurring my vision, and pull up the last sequence of numbers we entered, the code to turn the storm. I feed it back to the machine in reverse order. If we sent this storm to Aunt Linda's, then we can take it away, erase its path as if it never planned to flatten the white farmhouse at all. As if it never found this course toward the building with everyone I love inside.

That is the story I tell myself, and I am willing it to be true.

I finish the code, press the command button before Alex can protest again, and turn to watch the radar screen.

Like before, the storm inches forward a few more seconds before it slows and then stops, and then changes direction. And only then do I realize I was holding my breath. Aunt Linda is safe. My mother is safe. My father is . . . safe.

"Are you *insane*?!" Alex pushes me from the computer and starts entering code. "You have it coming right back at us!"

I stare at the radar image.

The storm had been so real when it was chasing us down the road, but between then and now, it's started to feel like something artificial. Something that lives in the colors of a map instead of in the real world.

My eyes trace its new path, back through the woods, along the road, around a curve, and up the driveway to the compound where we sit watching. It is headed straight for StormSafe. Straight for us.

It feels real again.

"What have you *done*?" Alex is tapping the computer screen but can't get back to the page that will let him redirect the storm.

"I had to do something!" My throat closes tight. I slump against the window and watch the clouds swirling above us. Then I whirl back to Alex. "Wait! Stop the redirection codes—what we need to do here—it's what we've needed to do all along! We have to run the dissipation code instead."

Risha shakes her head. "But that's not—"

"Not tested, I know! But it's all we have. Otherwise we can keep turning this storm around and redirecting it every two minutes, and we're going to end up with more people in danger. We have to—" I'm so certain of what I'm about to say that it surprises even me. "We have to take it out."

Chapter 31

Alex doesn't say a word. He walks to the window, presses his forehead to the glass, and closes his eyes.

Risha stares at the computer screen with big eyes, as if she expects it to make the decision all by itself.

"We have to do this." I say it again and look at my watch. For another six minutes, the storm will be swallowing up nothing but forest and fields before it gets back to the populated area. We have six minutes. "There is no. Other. Choice."

Finally, Alex turns away from the window. "It goes against everything we know. Running untested code to drive a real satellite? Testing an unproven theory on an event that's already in progress? Jaden, it's just—"

"It's our only chance! Look!" I fling a hand at the radar screen. The storm hasn't weakened; if anything, it's feeding off the chaos of being directed and redirected in a way nature never intended. "We can't keep recoding it over and over again. There's always going to be somebody in the way, and I can't—" I choke on the words, but I force them out. "I can't be responsible for this anymore."

Risha steps to my side, so we're both facing Alex. "She's right. How close were you to figuring this out?"

"More than close." Alex taps his fingers against the glass. "We . . . I'm sure we have it. But we haven't run a simulation, and—"

"We have it right, Alex. You know we do."

"I know. I'm just afraid that—" He whirls around to face me. "There's another Sim Dome here, right? We could run the code there first and then as long as—"

A gust of wind shakes the building and interrupts him before I have a chance to do it myself. There is no time.

"Where's the code?" Risha asks.

The windows shudder and rattle.

Windows. *The windows jerk free to hover near the ceiling . . .*

I call up the file and stare hard at the numbers, and somehow, they whisper back to me.

Yes. This. Yes.

Almost like a poem.

The ceiling floats away with a sigh.

This is what we need to do. It will work. It *has* to work.

I hand Risha my DataSlate and watch her dark eyes flicking up and down the rows of numbers. She gives one quick, sharp nod when they add up. "This looks perfect. I say we do it."

But Alex doesn't move from the window. I walk over to him and slowly, tentatively, put a hand on his arm.

Still gazing out at the storm, he nods. "You're right." He turns and heads for the computer, but just as I'm about to follow him, a flash of sky blue catches my eye through the rain and I stare out the window.

The rain pours down in sheets, and the wind has picked up enough to send branches whipping down from the treetops and roofing shingles flying like playing cards. The sky is even darker off to the north. The storm is coming. We need to move, to act now if we're even going to try to disperse it, but I can't take my eyes off the figure in blue, making her way through the torrents, toward the main door of the building.

"Hurry. She's coming," I whisper, even though Risha and Alex don't know who she is, and there's no time to explain. I shake my head to clear my thoughts, push off from the window, and rush to join them at the computer. Alex has already keyed in half of the long string of numbers. He hands me the DataSlate.

"Read me the next line, starting at oh-four-six-dash-two-seven-one," he says.

"Oh-four-six . . ." My eyes focus on the numbers, but in my mind, I'm picturing Grandma Athena pushing her way through the wind to the front door. Does she know the bio-scan override code by memory? She's probably in by now, probably through the door with her Shock Wand.

"Jaden!" Alex's sharp voice brings me back to the numbers. He's almost shouting now to be heard over the wind's steady, whooshing roar.

"Sorry. It was oh-four-six-dash-two-seven-one . . ."

A *thunk* against the window makes me jump. I almost drop the DataSlate but manage to fumble it in my hands and get hold of it again. "What *was* that?"

"Piece of the roof came off, it looked like." Risha takes the

DataSlate from my shaking hands and reads Alex another line of numbers. She's about to start the next line when the lights flicker and go out.

The computer's hum dies, and all we can hear is the growing roar from outside.

The windows shake.

There are more clunks and scrapes from the roof, as if pieces of it are breaking free to escape from the cruel winds.

Risha's free hand finds mine, and I hold on.

"The generator will kick in any second." Alex waits. "There has to be a generator. There must be, right?"

My heart sinks. There doesn't have to be a generator because there wasn't supposed to be a need for one. The storms were never supposed to come here.

Dad didn't count on this.

There is no generator. Only the faint glow of the DataSlate.

I let go of Risha's sweaty hand and go to the window. There, eight stories down and off into the trees, is the only other light in the compound. It is the building where I found Grandma Athena.

It must have a generator. And it has a computer.

"There's a light on down there; it's the only building with power!"

"We can't go out there!" Alex shouts.

"It's moving faster!" Risha holds up her DataSlate with a radar image. The storm is coming.

"We *have* to leave! Otherwise, we're trapped on the eighth floor of a glass building!" I scream. "Come on!"

We run, dodging desks and radar screens, past the elevators— there's no hope of them working now—and to the fire exit door that leads to the stairs.

"This way!" I tug it open. "Here!"

Behind us, there's a tremendous crash of glass on glass, and even though I can't see it, I know that one of the windows we'd been looking through is gone, shattered.

When the stairway door closes behind us, everything goes dark.

I've been clinging to Alex's hand but I let go so I can turn on my DataSlate and give us at least a little light.

Risha stumbles behind me. I feel her hands on my back, catching herself, and I grab the railing and hold on. I stumble down a few steps, but Alex reaches back to steady me, and we go down, down, down, until finally, there are no more stairs to descend.

"Ready?" I turn off the DataSlate, tuck it into the back of my jeans, and reach for the door handle.

"Wait!" Alex shouts into the darkness. "That's going to lead straight outside. Do you know where we're going?"

"The building's to the left—maybe thirty yards. We'll have to run!"

"And hold on to each other!" Risha screams.

"I've got my shoulder against the door!" Alex shouts. "On the count of three, you turn the handle, and I'll push it open, and then we need to grab on to one another and go!"

"I'm ready!" I try to ignore the noise from beyond the door, the wind that sounds ever more like that legendary freight train, ever more like a monster from mythology, ready to swallow us up. "All set?"

"Do it!" Alex shouts.

I turn the handle and we push, but nothing happens. Even when I hear Alex grunt from the effort of pushing, pushing his whole body against the door, it doesn't move except to pop open for a split second to mock us and then slam shut.

"Again! Together!" Alex cries. "One!"

The door is cold against my shoulder.

"Two!"

I think about three. Think that *if* we are successful, *if* this goes the right way, we'll fly out of here into a monster storm, and then what?

"Three!"

The door pops open like before, but this time, we are pushing, all of us, and we keep it from slamming shut. Then a swirl of wind comes, and the door that we could barely push open all together flies off its hinges as if it's nothing more than the lid of a shoe box.

And we are out.

Thrown into the wildest storm I have ever seen.

Forget freight trains. Forget Greek monsters.

It feels like the atmosphere itself has come to life, furious, ready to whip us all off the face of the earth in revenge.

Alex is shouting something at me, but I can't hear.

"What?" I scream, but it's no use. Our voices are sucked into the sky. Alex grabs my upper arm tight and pulls me away from the door. His fingers dig into my flesh so hard it hurts, and thank God for that. It feels like I'll be carried off if he ever lets go.

"This way!" I scream, but he can't hear, so I point frantically toward the outbuilding, its light flickering through the rain. I push into the wind and pull Alex along.

The closer we get, the more my stomach clenches. Is she in there?

From the second Alex and I made it out the door, I have been waiting, watching for that glimpse of sky blue. Where is she?

Alex suddenly yanks his hand away from me and pushes Risha to the side. A branch flies close to her head. But it misses her, and we press forward through the blinding rain.

I tug Alex's sleeve and point to the cold yellow light flickering through the rain. I pull Alex and Risha in that direction.

The wind blows rain into my face. I raise an arm to wipe my eyes and finally see the squat little building with its shiny steel door.

Is Grandma waiting on the other side?

There's no time to wonder, no time to worry. The solar energy panels on the next building crackle and send up a shower of sparks.

Alex reaches for the door handle, yanks it open, and pulls Risha and me inside so fast we tumble on top of him. The wind screams through the room, celebrating its newly conquered territory.

The steel door swings open and bangs shut wildly in the wind, and every time it flies open, there are great green flashes of lightning outside. Faster and faster, closer together.

The storm is coming for us.

As if it knows our plans.

And desperately wants us to fail.

But at least our voices are back. "It's over here, hurry!" I lead Alex and Risha around the radar screen to the computer desk where I first saw her. The chair I threw is still toppled on its side in a heap of broken glass. The wind's whipping through the broken window in weird whistling-glass noises. And perhaps the most eerie thing of all is the computer.

Still humming quietly against the wall.

Waiting for Grandma to come back. Where is she now?

Alex kneels down in front of it and starts pressing keys. "Here's the program. Got numbers for me?"

I pull out the DataSlate and start reading numbers, leaning over him. "Oh-four-six-dash-two-seven-one."

"Got it."

"Then five-four-zero—"

The wind shifts, and sheets of rain pour in the broken window. It stings our faces, soaks the floor and the desk.

"It's going to short out the equipment!" Risha screams. She tries to use her skinny body to shield the computer. "Hurry up!"

"FIVE-FOUR-ZERO-TWO-SEVEN!" I scream. There's a terrible scraping, crunching sound above us that can only be pieces of roof, giving up to the wind. But Alex keeps punching in numbers. I can see the strain in his eyes, the urgent effort to focus on getting this right.

The wind is blowing in the open window so hard we can barely stand.

"Then ZERO-ZERO-ONE-ZERO-FIVE— Watch out!!" I drop the DataSlate and throw my body against Risha to shove her out of the way of the radar wall, toppling in a great shattering of glass to the concrete floor.

"Jaden, what's next?!" Alex shouts.

I grab the DataSlate. Thank God it didn't break. "NINE-FOUR-THREE-ZERO-TWO!" I force myself to keep my head down, keep reading numbers, no matter what falls around me, no matter how many branches fly past my head. No matter how sure I am that we will fail. I keep going.

"SIX-FOUR—" The wall behind us explodes in a deep rumble and tears away from the rest of the structure. The wind howls in victory. The roar of the storm is louder, the lightning more frequent; it feels like we'll be hit any second. When I look up, I see why.

I stop shouting numbers because it's too late.

It's here.

"Get down!" Alex screams and tries to pull me under the heavy wooden desk, but I can only stare at the great raging whirlwind bearing down on the main building we just left.

The storm pushes forward. A violent cloud of debris swirls around its base, branches and shrubs, shingles and twisted HV parts, bits of people's lives that will never come together again.

When it reaches the main StormSafe building, it pauses.

Just for a split second.

As if whole walls of glass are a delicacy it wants to savor.

Then it plunges into the first wall. The glass crunches like falling icicles, and the shining pieces are sucked into the vortex and become part of the tornado, sharp and fast.

In twenty seconds, the building is gone.

"Get down, it's coming!" Alex pulls my arm so hard I fall to the ground beside him.

Risha drops and flattens herself next to us. "Ow!" she cries, rubbing her side. She must have landed on something. Broken glass? "You guys, look!" She bends over and pulls with all her weight on a latch screwed into one of the floorboards. "Storm shelter!" The door swings open, and we pile down a steep set of steps behind her.

It is nothing like the storm cellar at Alex's barn. No daybed. No food. But it has metal bars poured into the concrete, for holding on. And on a heavy desk in the corner, it has the one thing we need most right now.

A computer.

I race to it, wait for a home screen to load, and squeeze my eyes shut as tight as I can, as if refusing to watch will keep the tornado from jumping the last stretch of lawn, keep it from coming here where I've brought Alex and Risha.

The wind screams overhead, and I scream back. "No!!"

Because I know now what is about to happen if we cannot destroy this storm.

It is going to kill us.

Storm cellar or not. It's too big. Too strong.

It will devour us. Me, and the two people who are here with me. *Because* of me.

I squeeze my eyes shut tighter.

Please, please, please, don't let them die because of me.

When I open my eyes, the computer has booted up, and I find the file Alex was working on upstairs. "It auto-saved!" For once, it feels like someone might be on our side. "Get the last line of numbers, quick!"

Alex pages through DataSlate screens, one after another.

"Hurry up!"

The wind and rain, already impossibly loud, scream louder, and there's clunking, clanking coming from over our heads. Something—lots of somethings—being flung around like play toys, until finally, in an almighty howl of wind, the whole of the little building—everything above us, is ripped from the foundation and sucked into the sky.

I fall to the floor, grab on to one of the metal bars, and hold on. But impossibly, the wind lets up, and when I dare to peek into the screaming, high-whistling swirl above me, all I can do is stare.

The storm has lifted up; the tornado is no longer touching down, though it's close, and it is absolutely, directly on top of us.

The air feels heavy, like every last molecule of oxygen has been sucked into the sky, and this gray cloud has us encircled like a tomb.

Blue lightning flashes from the sides of the tornado. We are surrounded by a circular wall of clouds and electricity.

"We're inside," I whisper, and only then do I become aware of Alex and Risha on the ground next to me, staring into the sky, too.

"It's . . . it's beautiful," Risha says. But she is also the first to get her wits back. "But it's still moving. It could touch back down any second, and we'll have the other side to deal with. *Finish!* While we still have the computer!"

It's a miracle it still works; if the winds had raged on the ground a half-second more, it would be up there, swirling over our heads.

But it's here, and I crawl to it. There are two lines left to copy from the DataSlate. Alex reads, and I enter them with shaking, blood-stained hands.

"SEVEN-THREE-ONE," he finishes.

I stare at the columns of numbers and let my finger hover over the words EXECUTE COMMAND.

What if?

What if we are wrong?

This storm over our heads will go . . . where? And will we strengthen it along the way?

Alex's hand presses down gently on my shoulder. "It will work."

I tap the button.

Drop to my knees.

And wait.

The wind starts to blow again as the second wall of the storm moves over us.

Let it work. Please let it work.

I keep my head down and listen. I send all my hopes up into the sky.

Wind howls. Rain pelts down. The computer flies off the desk—"Look out!"—and Risha yanks Alex out of the way the instant before it explodes in a shower of sparks on the concrete floor.

We huddle close and hold on, waiting for the wind to rip us apart.

But it doesn't happen. The monster never quite comes back.

There are more distant pops from electrical explosions in blown circuits and transmitters. Branches and bits of ceiling and roofing and God knows what else bang and scrape against the one wall that remains.

But the sounds start to fade.

And we are still here.

We lift our heads and watch the storm sweep away from us, back toward Placid Meadows.

"No, no!" Risha says, and starts to lunge for the computer, in pieces on the floor now.

"No, wait." Alex's eyes are trained on the top of the storm cloud. "It's going to be okay. Watch."

And yes. The churning gray monster is tired. It slugs away from us another quarter of a mile, stirring up dust and last year's leaves.

And finally, it lifts its tail up from the ground and snakes back up into its cloud.

And is gone.

Chapter 32

There are no words to describe this sound.

The quiet after a storm has gone.

The absence of everything—birds chirping, HV motors idling, air conditioners humming.

Here in this broken shelter full of leaves and branches, shattered glass, and bits of buildings the tornado threw at us as it passed, there is almost total quiet.

Only the sound of our breathing—Alex and Risha and me, huddling together.

It feels like time should have stopped when the storm rose back into the sky, like this problem should be solved forever now that it's gone.

But I know it's not.

I know the storms will come again, on the next day when the clouds start swirling and the conditions are just right. They will come.

But right now, it's too soon to talk of next times. I am too thankful to do anything except stay here with my head on Alex's shoulder, breathing this same air with him, holding on to Risha's hand, and feeling her bracelets, cool against my wrist.

Alex is the first to speak. "Thank God we had the numbers right."

A few minutes later, Risha is the second.

"Look." She points up, out of the shelter. We uncurl ourselves like fern fronds in spring and stretch our necks up, up to the line her finger traces toward the clouds in the east.

A smudge of broken rainbow leans against the storm-bruised sky, faint color in the day's last light. I stare hard at it, willing the colors to brighten.

They don't.

I am thankful anyway. Because hope has to start somewhere. And a glimmer is better than nothing at all.

It is the sound of tires crunching over broken boards and branches that finally brings us up out of the shelter to meet Aunt Linda's blue farm truck. Mom jumps out and looks as if she can't decide whether to hug us or kill us.

"Jaden!" She flies at me and pulls me into a hug that comes dangerously close to accomplishing the latter, but I manage to push away so I don't suffocate.

"You got my messages!"

Her eyes fill with tears. "I'm sorry I didn't come home sooner. I thought you were probably getting used to everything. A new house and Mirielle and—"

"Mirielle! Remi! Are they okay? Were they with you and Dad? Or are they home at Placid Meadows? And where's Dad?"

My stomach tightens. Is he okay? Is he back in his office at Placid Meadows sending down another storm?

Mom presses her hands against her eyes and shakes her head a little. "Mirielle and Remi are fine. They're safe. So is Dad, but . . . there's . . . we have a lot to talk about, Jaden." She moves her hands and smiles a weak, exhausted smile. "And I need to say hello to your friends, too."

"This is Risha. And Alex." I wait while she shakes their hands. "Mom, where is everybody? What's going on?"

"What's going on," she says, "is that we need to get the three of you someplace safe, where we can clean up those cuts, and you can eat something." She looks at my matted hair. "And take a shower. Pile in." She opens the truck door. "We'll talk on the way back to Linda's house."

Chapter 33

Dear Dad,

I hope things are going okay for you. I wish...

I stop and stare out the window, where fat raindrops are starting to fall, pelting the red leaves on our sugar maple in the yard. A long time ago, I used to love the way September storms would make Vermont's autumn leaves shine.

Thunder rumbles, and I set the pencil down.

It feels weird writing to him like this instead of talking at my DataSlate for a video-message, but it makes sense that one of Dad's restrictions at the energy farm includes the use of any electronic communication devices.

At first when Dad turned himself in and came clean about the technology he developed with Grandma Athena, it didn't look like he'd be doing time.

After all, it was the government that opened the floodgates on weather manipulation research when it changed the laws and even paid StormSafe to redirect hurricanes in the Gulf when they were headed for populated areas. They wanted Dad's technology, so they pretty much gave him free reign, extended his patent for the Sim Dome, and didn't ask questions about how he made Placid Meadows so safe. It was the National Storm Center that funded Dad's tornado dissipation project when he came back from Russia. Weather manipulation won't be a crime until the new legislation takes effect next year.

But lying under oath has always been against the law, and Dad had testified before Congress about the failure of his dissipation research. He lied about the project he scrapped so he could go on to something bigger, technology that would let him rule the storms instead of simply sending them home to the clouds. The project Grandma Athena had always dreamed of. What she'd given up her life to do. And Dad finally got the attention he never had from her when he was a kid.

It's crazy that after all he did, all the lives he destroyed with his pet storms, that it was the lying that landed him on one of those energy farm bikes, sentenced to pedal for power in the sun for the next five years, paying back in sweat what he stole from society with his crimes.

Only he can never really pay it back. I think of Alex and Tomas whose family farms were ravaged and almost stolen away, of the countless people who lost their homes in Dad's redirected storms. Of Newton.

Thank God for Ms. Walpole, who helped Tomas's family get their farm deed back, along with a settlement so StormSafe will pay for his mother's treatment in New York, and then some. He and Alex have had a chance to talk, too. I was right; Tomas trusted Van and had no idea what he and my father were doing.

Lightning flashes, and my stomach twists, even though the only storms around tonight are small ones. I run my hand over the cover of the poetry book I brought home with me from Dad's, and I breathe in slowly. It will be a long time before my heart remembers that storms aren't all evil. That they can be ordinary rain, with thunder and lightning and a bit of wind.

I pick up the pencil again.

Set it down.

What do you write to someone who is so much like you and yet nothing like you at all? What do you say to a parent who is no one that you want to grow up to be?

And what can I say about this summer that was supposed to be our time to reconnect?

I've only been home—real home with Mom—two months, but Eye on Tomorrow already seems like forever ago. Placid Meadows, the campus, the playground . . . they all feel like memories of some high-definition dream.

That afternoon when the storm was raging, when we crouched clinging to metal bars in the storm cellar, I wanted to wake up like Dorothy from *The Wizard of Oz* and find a cold compress on my forehead because it was never real.

Just a dream.

Did Dad ever really want to know me again? Or was I there like all the others—another Eye on Tomorrow kid to watch and shape and ultimately hire to help keep secrets?

Mom unloaded the truth on the way back to Aunt Linda's house that night. When she left for Costa Rica, she hadn't known how Dad's research was evolving, how his interests had taken such a dark turn. When she finally got my message—the video-message of me crying by the side of the road—she called Mirielle, who broke into Dad's office—I still don't know how but it doesn't surprise me that she figured it out—and pieced together what was happening. That's when she learned, all at once, that her dead mother-in-law was alive and that her husband was not doing the work he said he was.

She told Mom everything. And Mom borrowed an HV, drove straight to the airport, and caught the next flight home.

Aunt Linda had picked her up at the airport, and when Dad met them at her house, Mom gave him a raging earful about the promises he'd made to her, to me, about my summer and keeping me safe.

And that's when Grandma Athena's message got through. Her face appeared on Dad's DataSlate, right there in Aunt Linda's kitchen, talking about how the storm wasn't performing as they'd planned, how she locked me in the outbuilding. I was more of a problem than he'd imagined, she said, and so the two of them would need to talk. Dad swore up and down to Mom that she never really would have hurt me. I don't think I believe it.

Dear Dad,
    I hope things are going okay for you. I wish
this summer could have been different. I really
wish...

I roll the pencil between my fingers, then snap it in half.

Thunder rumbles again, and rain pours down my window in thick rivers. Everything outside looks warped and blurry and wet.

What do I wish? I wish Eye on Tomorrow had been real, a legitimate opportunity for kids like me and Risha, Tomas and Alex, to collaborate and solve this world's problems.

I wish Dad was the father he used to be, or pretended to be anyway, the dad with the strong shoulders and rainbow sprinkles.

I wish that his corporation never existed. That he'd never gone to Russia and found Grandma Athena.

I wish I had a grandmother like Risha's, who stirred curry stews and kissed my head, instead of one who tied me to chairs.

And yet . . . I wish I'd had a chance to talk with her, really talk with her, about her life and her ideas and her choices, before she died.

I pick up a jagged pencil piece and turn it over in my hands.

It's been two months, but we haven't had a funeral yet. Mom and I will have to go make arrangements because with Dad locked up, we're the only ones who can take care of her burial.

Mom's waiting to book plane tickets. The storm was so huge it's taken them weeks to clear the debris. If Grandma had entered the main StormSafe building, or if she were right outside, she'd have been buried under a mountain of glass and steel when the tornado hit.

"Jaden?" Mom knocks at my bedroom door, then walks in with a pile of clean clothes and balances it on my dresser. "Done with the letter?"

I push the paper away. "I don't think I have anything to say."

I run my finger over the end of the pencil piece, then pick up the other one and try to fit them back together, but splintery edges stick out. Breaks are never truly clean.

"Did he really used to love me?" I try to say it as if I don't care, but my shuddery voice gives everything away.

"Yes." Her eyes are sad. "He really did and he still does, Jaden."

I almost laugh.

"Truly." Mom puts a hand on each of my cheeks so I have no choice but to look right at her. "It wasn't until that night you were in danger—you, his little girl—that he could finally see what he had done. Remember what he looked like when he called you on the videophone?"

I nod. I remember. I could never forget the first time I ever saw my father cry.

"He loves you. Nothing excuses what he's done, but he's damaged, Jaden. His thinking. Athena is—was—I can't get used to the idea of having her alive and now gone again—she was larger than life somehow. It's like . . . I don't know . . . like she had some spell cast over him."

"Yeah," I whisper. And I almost understand. I know that feeling of wanting a parent back so badly. Wanting to be celebrated and loved. It's a feeling he never really knew. Mom pushes my hair behind my ear, and all at once, I'm filled up with tears at how lucky I am that I do know.

The house videophone buzzes in the hallway, and as Mom leaves to answer it, my DataSlate dings with a video-message from Alex.

"Hey, Jaden! I gotta show you what came in the mail today."

Video-Alex holds up a fat off-white envelope, and I cheer, even though I know he can't hear me. "All *right!*" Risha and I both got similar envelopes two days ago, invitations to spend three weeks interning at the National Storm Center's new weather modification research facility this winter, and permission documents for Mom to sign. According to the paperwork, Ms. Walpole recommended all three of us, based on our "outstanding commitment to research." Everything in the NSC envelope makes me hope this is the program that Eye on Tomorrow was supposed to be.

"So I guess I'll be seeing you in a couple months!" Video-Alex winks, and the screen goes black.

I stare out the window and smile at the rain, just thin trickles down the glass now, and the clouds are thinning. It really was a small storm this time. Nothing more.

I pick up the longer of the two pencil pieces and go back to Dad's letter.

I ask him about Mirielle and Remi. They've been to visit him, Mom says, even though Mirielle isn't sure if she'll stay or take Remi back to France. I write a few lines about school, about the new schedule I'm on this fall with home connection three days a week and morning classes in person the other two. I ask how things are at the energy farm, then erase that because they're probably not great.

I'm about to sign it when Mom comes back through the door. The lines in her face are tight.

"Who was on the videophone?" I ask.

"Logan County Sheriff's office. They finished clearing all the debris from StormSafe, and Grandma . . ." Mom pauses.

They must have found the body.

Mom bites her lip. "I'm . . . not sure how to tell you this."

I stare at her for a second. Does she think I'm going to be that upset over losing a grandmother I never knew, until the night she almost killed me? "Mom, it's okay. I was there when the building went down. I know she never could have survived. Is the funeral going to be soon?"

"We'll go down for a service on Monday," Mom says. "Closed casket."

I nod, remembering the flying debris, the minefield of broken glass and twisted metal that night. "Her body was in pretty bad shape, huh?"

Mom shakes her head. "They didn't find her body."

A million thoughts swim through my head. The storm was huge; it could have picked her up and dropped her anywhere. But one thought rises to the surface—not so much a thought in words as a mental movie of Grandma Athena, standing in the outbuilding, her mouth a straight line, her hands on her hips.

Her laugh.

Never trust a death certificate.

Could she possibly have survived that monster?

My stomach twists.

Could she still be out there somewhere?

Mom goes on. "We can still have the service. But closed casket. It's not a problem."

Not a problem. I let Mom go on thinking that. She's probably right.

"When will we leave?"

"Sunday. You should call your friends. You'll have some time to see them, too." Mom leaves and closes the door behind her.

An image of Grandma's face floats through my mind, but I imagine the wind blowing it away like Risha's dandelion fluff. Like the magical numbers on her bracelet, zeros and ones, swirling through the air until the ceiling lifts away, and they arrange themselves into something that makes sense, into a world mended and whole again.

But it took decades to make this mess. It will take time for us to go back.

No. To move forward.

It'll take time and research and work. And hope. Failing and trying again and probably wanting to scream because it can't happen fast enough. It won't be impossible, but it will feel that way sometimes; I already know that. And I know I want to be part of it. I need to be.

I reach for my DataSlate to call Alex and Risha. Outside, the sun streams through a gap in the clouds. Puddles glimmer on the sidewalk, and half a rainbow arcs over the woods. This one is brighter than before.

And today feels like a good day to start.

Acknowledgments

Many thanks to all whose work, research, and support helped me to write this book, especially Dr. Howard Bluestein from the University of Oklahoma's School of Meteorology, who took time out of a stormy week in September 2010 to meet with me and answer my long list of questions, most of which began with the words, "So what if . . ." Dr. Bluestein also reviewed sections of this manuscript for scientific accuracy relating to the formation of tornadoes (even though the actual weather manipulation that happens in the book isn't possible at this time). His meteorological expertise is most appreciated, and any errors that remain are my responsibility alone.

I'm grateful to senior meteorology student Tim Marquis for the weather school and National Severe Storms Laboratory tour that provided much of the inspiration for the Eye on Tomorrow campus. The following books were also helpful: *Tornado Alley: Monster Storms of the Great Plains* by Howard B. Bluestein (Oxford University Press, 2006), *The Tornado: Nature's Ultimate Windstorm* by Thomas P. Grazulis (University of Oklahoma Press, 2003), and *Storm Warning: The Story of a Killer Tornado* by Nancy Mathis (Touchstone, 2008).

Acknowledgments

As someone who loves both science and art, I am fascinated by the idea of intersections between the two. Richard Holmes's *The Age of Wonder: How the Romantic Generation Discovered the Beauty and Terror of Science* (Pantheon, 2009) got me thinking about it in new ways.

I am grateful to poet Rita Dove for the gift of her work and for permission to include the excerpt from "Geometry" that Jaden reads in her faded paper book.

Thanks to student beta-reader Theo Gardner-Puschak for sharing his thoughts on the manuscript and to critique partners and writer friends Loree Griffin Burns, Eric Luper, Liza Martz, Ammi-Joan Paquette, Marjorie Light, Stephanie Gorin, and Linda Urban. You all make me a more thoughtful writer, and I'm grateful for your friendship.

Thanks to my agent, Jennifer Laughran, for supporting my writing, helping me weather storms, and generally being amazing; to my brilliant editor, Mary Kate Castellani, for asking just the right questions; and to Emily Easton, Beth Eller, Katie Fee, Kate Lied, Amanda Hong, Nicole Gastonguay, and the rest of the team at Walker/Bloomsbury, and to cover illustrator Vincent Chong.

A special thanks to Elizabeth Bluemle and Josie Leavitt of Flying Pig Bookstore, Marc and Sarah Galvin of The Bookstore Plus, and all the other independent booksellers who work hard for authors, books, kids, and communities every day. You rock.

Finally, thanks to Tom, Jake, and Ella. I saved you for last because the very best part of this book journey is sharing it with you.

KATE MESSNER is a former middle-school English teacher and the author of the E. B. White Read Aloud Award winner *The Brilliant Fall of Gianna Z.*, *Sugar and Ice*, *Eye of the Storm*, and *Wake Up Missing*. She lives on Lake Champlain with her husband and two kids. When she's not reading or writing, she loves hiking, kayaking, biking, and watching thunderstorms over the lake.

www.katemessner.com

@KateMessner

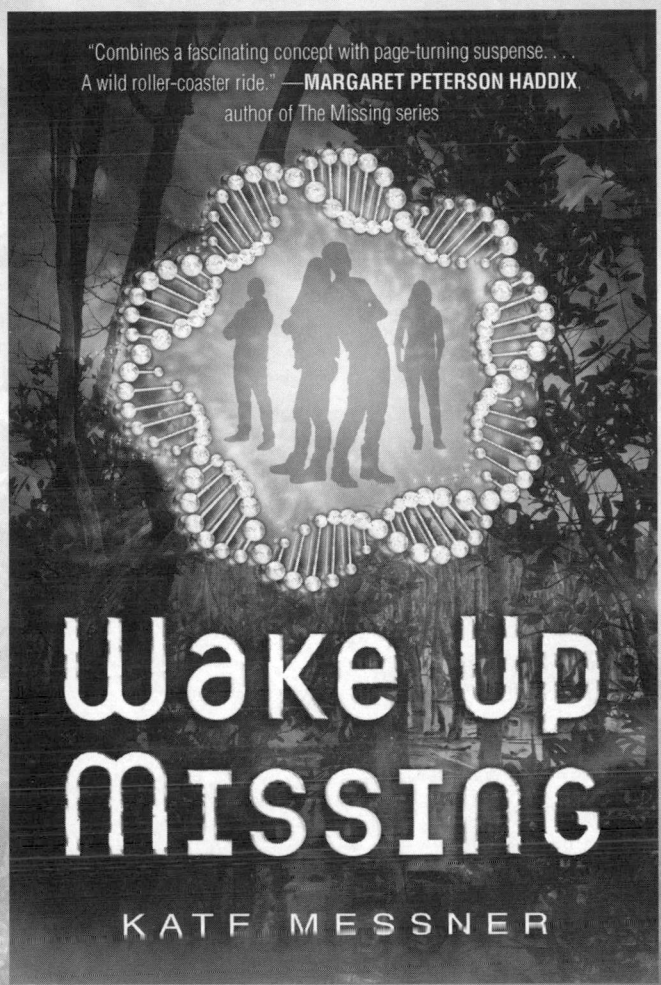

Don't miss the sweeter side of
Kate Messner!

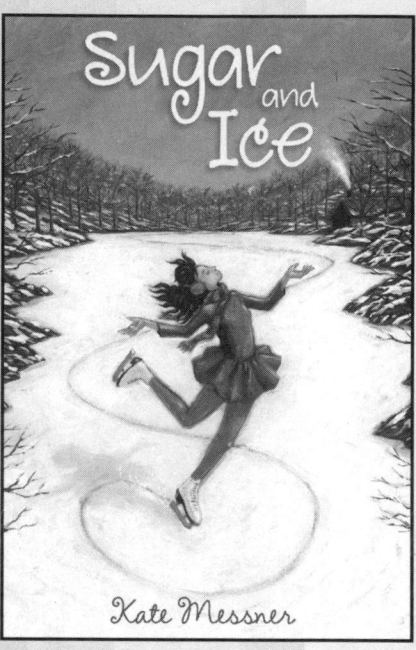

"Laced with humor and heart. . . .
An insightful and affecting read."
—*Booklist*

"A title that remains in your mind
long after you've put it down."
—**Fuse 8**

WALKER BOOKS FOR YOUNG READERS
AN IMPRINT OF BLOOMSBURY
www.bloomsbury.com
www.facebook.com/BloomsburyTeens